D0992094

Pasco County Library System

Overdue notices are a courtesy of the Library System.

Failure to receive an overdue notice does not absolve the borrower of the obligation to return the materials on time.

Quatermain

Quatermain
The Complete Adventures: 4

Finished

★

The Ivory Child

H. Rider Haggard

LEONAUR

Quatermain: the Complete Adventures: 4—
Finished & The Ivory Child
by H. Rider Haggard

Leonaur is an imprint of Oakpast Ltd

ISBN: 978-1-84677-598-7 (hardcover)
ISBN: 978-1-84677-597-0 (softcover)

http://www.leonaur.com

Publisher's Notes

Contents

Publisher's Note

Suggested reading sequence for the Allan Quatermain stories:

Finished

Dedication

Ditchingham House
Norfolk
May, 1917
My dear Roosevelt,
You are, I know, a lover of old Allan Quatermain, one who understands and appreciates the views of life and the aspirations that underlie and inform his manifold adventures.

Therefore, since such is your kind wish, in memory of certain hours wherein both of us found true refreshment and companionship amidst the terrible anxieties of the World's journey along that bloodstained road by which alone, so it is decreed, the pure Peak of Freedom must be scaled, I dedicate to you this tale telling of the events and experiences of my youth.
Your sincere friend,
H. Rider Haggard
To Colonel Theodore Roosevelt
Sagamore Hill
U.S.A.

Introduction

This book, although it can be read as a separate story, is the third of the trilogy of which *Marie* and *Child of Storm* are the first two parts. It narrates, through the mouth of Allan Quatermain, the consummation of the vengeance of the wizard Zikali, alias The Opener of Roads, or *The-Thing-that-should-never-have-been-born*, upon the royal Zulu House of which Senzangacona was the founder and Cetewayo, our enemy in the war of 1879, the last representative who ruled as a king. Although, of course, much is added for the purposes of romance, the main facts of history have been adhered to with some faithfulness.

With these the author became acquainted a full generation ago, Fortune having given him a part in the events that preceded the Zulu War. Indeed he believes that with the exception of Colonel Phillips, who, as a lieutenant, commanded the famous escort of twenty-five policemen, he is now the last survivor of the party who, under the leadership of Sir Theophilus Shepstone, or Sompseu as the natives called him from the Zambezi to the Cape, were concerned in the annexation of the Transvaal in 1877. Recently also he has been called upon as a public servant to revisit South Africa and took the opportunity to travel through Zululand, in order to refresh his knowledge of its people, their customs, their mysteries, and better to prepare himself for the writing of this book. Here he stood by the fatal Mount of Isandhlawana which, with some details of the battle, is described in these pages, among the graves of many whom once he knew, Colonels Durnford, Pulleine and others. Also he saw Ulundi's plain where the traces of war still lie thick, and talked with an old Zulu who fought in the attacking *Impi* until it crumbled away before the fire of the Martinis and shells from the heavy guns. The battle of the Wall of Sheet Iron, he called it, perhaps because of the flashing fence of bayonets.

Lastly, in a *mealie* patch, he found the spot on which the corn grows thin, where King Cetewayo breathed his last, poisoned without a doubt, as he has known for many years. It is to be seen at the *Kraal*, ominously named Jazi or, translated into English, Finished. The tragedy happened long ago, but even now the quiet-faced Zulu who told the tale, looking about him as he spoke, would not tell it all. "Yes, as a young man, I was there at the time, but I do not remember, I do not know—the *Inkoosi* Lundanda (i.e., this Chronicler, so named in past years by the Zulus) stands on the very place where the king died—His bed was on the left of the door-hole of the hut," and so forth, but no certain word as to the exact reason of this sudden and violent death or by whom it was caused. The name of that destroyer of a king is for ever hid.

In this story the actual and immediate cause of the declaration of war against the British Power is represented as the appearance of the white goddess, or spirit of the Zulus, who is, or was, called Nom-kubulwana or Inkosazana-y-Zulu, *i.e.*, the Princess of Heaven. The exact circumstances which led to this decision are not now ascertainable, though it is known that there was much difference of opinion among the Zulu *Indunas* or great captains, and like the writer, many believe that King Cetewayo was personally averse to war against his old allies, the English.

The author's friend, Mr. J. Y. Gibson, at present the representative of the Union in Zululand, writes in his admirable history: "There was a good deal of discussion amongst the assembled Zulu notables at Ul-undi, but of how counsel was swayed it is not possible now to obtain a reliable account."

The late Mr. F. B. Fynney, F.R.G.S., who also was his friend in days bygone, and, with the exception of Sir Theophilus Shepstone, who perhaps knew the Zulus and their language better than any other official of his day, speaking of this fabled goddess wrote: "I remember that just before the Zulu War Nomkubulwana appeared revealing something or other which had a great effect throughout the land."

The use made of this strange traditional Guardian Angel in the following tale is not therefore an unsupported flight of fancy, and the same may be said of many other incidents, such as the account of the reading of the proclamation annexing the Transvaal at Pretoria in 1877, which have been introduced to serve the purposes of the romance.

Mameena, who haunts its pages, in a literal as well as figurative sense, is the heroine of *Child of Storm*, a book to which she gave her own poetic title.

The Author
1916

CHAPTER 1

Allan Quatermain Meets Anscombe

You, my friend, into whose hand, if you live, I hope these scribblings of mine will pass one day, must well remember the 12th of April of the year 1877 at Pretoria. Sir Theophilus Shepstone, or Sompseu, for I prefer to call him by his native name, having investigated the affairs of the Transvaal for a couple of months or so, had made up his mind to annex that country to the British Crown. It so happened that I, Allan Quatermain, had been on a shooting and trading expedition at the back of the Lydenburg district where there was plenty of game to be killed in those times. Hearing that great events were toward I made up my mind, curiosity being one of my weaknesses, to come round by Pretoria, which after all was not very far out of my way, instead of striking straight back to Natal. As it chanced I reached the town about eleven o'clock on this very morning of the 12th of April and, trekking to the Church Square, proceeded to *outspan* there, as was usual in the Seventies. The place was full of people, English and Dutch together, and I noted that the former seemed very elated and were talking excitedly, while the latter for the most part appeared to be sullen and depressed.

Presently I saw a man I knew, a tall, dark man, a very good fellow and an excellent shot, named Robinson. By the way you knew him also, for afterwards he was an officer in the Pretoria Horse at the time of the Zulu war, the corps in which you held a commission. I called to him and asked what was up.

"A good deal, Allan," he said as he shook my hand. "Indeed we shall be lucky if all isn't up, or something like it, before the day is over. Shepstone's Proclamation annexing the Transvaal is going to be read presently."

I whistled and asked,

"How will our Boer friends take it? They don't look very pleased."

13

"That's just what no one knows, Allan. Burgers the President is squared, they say. He is to have a pension; also he thinks it the only thing to be done. Most of the Hollanders up here don't like it, but I doubt whether they will put out their hands further than they can draw them back. The question is—what will be the line of the Boers themselves? There are a lot of them about, all armed, you see, and more outside the town."

"What do you think?"

"Can't tell you. Anything may happen. They may shoot Shepstone and his staff and the twenty-five policemen, or they may just grumble and go home. Probably they have no fixed plan."

"How about the English?"

"Oh! we are all crazy with joy, but of course there is no organization and many have no arms. Also there are only a few of us."

"Well," I answered, "I came here to look for excitement, life having been dull for me of late, and it seems that I have found it. Still I bet you those Dutchmen do nothing, except protest. They are slim and know that the shooting of an unarmed mission would bring England on their heads."

"Can't say, I am sure. They like Shepstone who understands them, and the move is so bold that it takes their breath away. But as the *Kaffirs* say, when a strong wind blows a small spark will make the whole *veld* burn. It just depends upon whether the spark is there. If an Englishman and a Boer began to fight for instance, anything might happen. Goodbye, I have got a message to deliver. If things go right we might dine at the European tonight, and if they don't, goodness knows where we shall dine."

I nodded sagely and he departed. Then I went to my wagon to tell the boys not to send the oxen off to graze at present, for I feared lest they should be stolen if there were trouble, but to keep them tied to the trek-tow. After this I put on the best coat and hat I had, feeling that as an Englishman it was my duty to look decent on such an occasion, washed, brushed my hair—with me a ceremony without meaning, for it always sticks up—and slipped a loaded Smith & Wesson revolver into my inner poacher pocket. Then I started out to see the fun, and avoiding the groups of surly-looking Boers, mingled with the crowd that I saw was gathering in front of a long, low building with a broad *stoep*, which I supposed, rightly, to be one of the Government offices.

Presently I found myself standing by a tall, rather loosely-built man whose face attracted me. It was clean-shaven and much bronzed by the sun, but not in any way good-looking; the features were too irregular and the nose was a trifle too long for good looks. Still the impression it gave was pleasant and the steady blue eyes had that twinkle in them which suggests humour. He might have been thirty or thirty-five years of age, and notwithstanding his rough dress that consisted mainly of a pair of trousers held up by a belt to which hung a pistol, and a common flannel shirt, for he wore no coat, I guessed at once that he was English-born.

For a while neither of us said anything after the taciturn habit of our people even on the *veld*, and indeed I was fully occupied in listening to the truculent talk of a little party of mounted Boers behind us. I put my pipe into my mouth and began to hunt for my tobacco, taking the opportunity to show the hilt of my revolver, so that these men might see that I was armed. It was not to be found, I had left it in the wagon.

"If you smoke Boer tobacco," said the stranger, "I can help you," and I noted that the voice was as pleasant as the face, and knew at once that the owner of it was a gentleman.

"Thank you, Sir. I never smoke anything else," I answered, whereon he produced from his trousers pocket a pouch made of lion skin of unusually dark colour.

"I never saw a lion as black as this, except once beyond Buluwayo on the borders of Lobengula's country," I said by way of making conversation.

"Curious," answered the stranger, "for that's where I shot the brute a few months ago. I tried to keep the whole skin but the white ants got at it."

"Been trading up there?" I asked.

"Nothing so useful," he said. "Just idling and shooting. Came to this country because it was one of the very few I had never seen, and have only been here a year. I think I have had about enough of it, though. Can you tell me of any boats running from Durban to India? I should like to see those wild sheep in Kashmir."

I told him that I did not know for certain as I had never taken any interest in India, being an African elephant-hunter and trader, but I thought they did occasionally. Just then Robinson passed by and called to me—

"They'll be here presently, Quatermain, but Sompseu isn't coming himself."

"Does your name happen to be Allan Quatermain?" asked the stranger. "If so I have heard plenty about you up in Lobengula's country, and of your wonderful shooting."

"Yes," I replied, "but as for the shooting, natives always exaggerate."

"They never exaggerated about mine," he said with a twinkle in his eye. "Anyhow I am very glad to see you in the flesh, though in the

15

spirit you rather bored me because I heard too much of you. Whenever I made a particularly bad miss, my gun-bearer, who at some time seems to have been yours, would say, 'Ah! if only it had been the *Inkosi* Macumazahn, how different would have been the end!' My name is Anscombe, Maurice Anscombe," he added rather shyly. (Afterwards I discovered from a book of reference that he was a younger son of Lord Mountford, one of the richest peers in England.)

Then we both laughed and he said—

"Tell me, Mr. Quatermain, if you will, what those Boers are saying behind us. I am sure it is something unpleasant, but as the only Dutch I know is *'Guten Tag'* and *'Vootsack'* (good-day and get out) that takes me no forwarder."

"It ought to," I answered, "for the substance of their talk is that they object to be *vootsacked* by the British Government as represented by Sir Theophilus Shepstone. They are declaring that they won the land *with their blood* and want to keep their own flag flying over it."

"A very natural sentiment," broke in Anscombe.

"They say that they wish to shoot all damned Englishmen, especially Shepstone and his people, and that they would make a beginning now were they not afraid that the damned English Government, being angered, would send thousands of damned English *rooibatjes*, that is, red-coats, and shoot *them* out of evil revenge."

"A very natural conclusion," laughed Anscombe again, "which I should advise them to leave untested. Hush! Here comes the show."

I looked and saw a body of black coated gentlemen with one officer in the uniform of a Colonel of Engineers, advancing slowly. I remember that it reminded me of a funeral procession following the corpse of the Republic that had gone on ahead out of sight. The procession arrived upon the *stoep* opposite to us and began to sort itself out, whereon the English present raised a cheer and the Boers behind us cursed audibly. In the middle appeared an elderly gentleman with whiskers and a stoop, in whom I recognized Mr. Osborn, known by the *Kaffirs* as Malimati, the Chief of the Staff. By his side was a tall young fellow, yourself, my friend, scarcely more than a lad then, carrying papers. The rest stood to right and left in a formal line. *You* gave a printed document to Mr. Osborn who put on his glasses and began to read in a low voice which few could hear, and I noticed that his hand trembled. Presently he grew confused, lost his place, found it, lost it again and came to a full stop.

"A nervous-natured man," remarked Mr. Anscombe. "Perhaps he thinks that those gentlemen are going to shoot."

16

"That wouldn't trouble him," I answered, who knew him well. "His fears are purely mental."

That was true since I know that this same Sir Melmoth Osborn as he is now, as I have told in the book I called *Child of Storm*, swam the Tugela alone to watch the battle of Indondakasuka raging round him, and on another occasion killed two *Kaffirs* rushing at him with a right and left shot without turning a hair. It was reading this paper that paralyzed him, not any fear of what might happen.

There followed a very awkward pause such as occurs when a man breaks down in a speech. The members of the Staff looked at him and at each other, then behold! you, my friend, grabbed the paper from his hand and went on reading it in a loud clear voice.

"That young man has plenty of nerve," said Mr. Anscombe.

"Yes," I replied in a whisper. "Quite right though. Would have been a bad omen if the thing had come to a stop."

Well, there were no more breakdowns, and at last the long document was finished and the Transvaal annexed. The Britishers began to cheer but stopped to listen to the formal protest of the Boer Government, if it could be called a government when everything had collapsed and the officials were being paid in postage stamps. I can't remember whether this was read by President Burgers himself or by the officer who was called State Secretary. Anyway, it was read, after which there came an awkward pause as though people were waiting to see something happen. I looked round at the Boers who were muttering and handling their rifles uneasily. Had they found a leader I really think that some of the wilder spirits among them would have begun to shoot, but none appeared and the crisis passed.

The crowd began to disperse, the English among them cheering and throwing up their hats, the Dutch with very sullen faces. The Commissioner's staff went away as it had come, back to the building with blue gums in front of it, which afterwards became Government House, that is all except you. You started across the square alone with a bundle of printed proclamations in your hand which evidently you had been charged to leave at the various public offices.

"Let us follow him," I said to Mr. Anscombe. "He might get into trouble and want a friend."

He nodded and we strolled after you unostentatiously. Sure enough you nearly did get into trouble. In front of the first office door to which you came, stood a group of Boers, two of whom, big fellows, drew together with the evident intention of barring your way. "Mynheeren," you said, "I pray you to let me pass on the Queen's business."

17

They took no heed except to draw closer together and laugh insolently. Again you made your request and again they laughed. Then I saw you lift your leg and deliberately stamp upon the foot of one of the Boers. He drew back with an exclamation, and for a moment I believed that he or his fellow was going to do something violent. Perhaps they thought better of it, or perhaps they saw us two Englishmen behind and noticed Anscombe's pistol. At any rate you marched into the office triumphant and delivered your document.

"Neatly done," said Mr. Anscombe.

"Rash," I said, shaking my head, "very rash. Well, he's young and must be excused."

But from that moment I took a great liking to you, my friend, perhaps because I wondered whether in your place I should have been daredevil enough to act in the same way. For you see I am English, and I like to see an Englishman hold his own against odds and keep up the credit of the country. Although, of course, I sympathized with the Boers who, through their own fault, were losing their land without a blow struck. As you know well, for you were living near Majuba at the time, plenty of blows were struck afterwards, but of that business I cannot bear to write. I wonder how it will all work out after I am dead and if I shall ever learn what happens in the end.

Now I have only mentioned this business of the Annexation and the part you played in it, because it was on that occasion that I became acquainted with Anscombe. For you have nothing to do with this story which is about the destruction of the Zulus, the accomplishment of the vengeance of Zikali the wizard at the kraal named Finished, and incidentally, the love affairs of two people in which that old wizard took a hand, as I did to my sorrow. It happened that Mr. Anscombe had ridden on ahead of his wagons which could not arrive at Pretoria for a day or two, and as he found it impossible to get accommodation at the European or elsewhere, I offered to let him sleep in mine, or rather alongside in a tent I had. He accepted and soon we became very good friends. Before the day was out I discovered that he had served in a crack cavalry regiment, but resigned his commission some years before. I asked him why.

"Well," he said, "I came into a good lot of money on my mother's death and could not see a prospect of any active service. While the regiment was abroad I liked the life well enough, but at home it bored me. Too much society for my taste, and that sort of thing. Also I wanted to travel; nothing else really amuses me."

"You will soon get tired of it," I answered, "and as you are well off, marry some fine lady and settle down at home."

18

"Don't think so. I doubt if I should ever be happily married, I want too much. One doesn't pick up an earthly angel with a cast-iron constitution who adores you, which are the bare necessities of marriage, under every bush." Here I laughed. "Also," he added, the laughter going out of his eyes, "I have had enough of fine ladies and their ways."

"Marriage is better than scrapes," I remarked sententiously.

"Quite so, but one might get them both together. No, I shall never marry, although I suppose I ought as my brothers have no children."

"Won't you, my friend," thought I to myself, "when the skin grows again on your burnt fingers."

For I was sure they had been burnt, perhaps more than once. How, I never learned, for which I am rather sorry for it interests me to study burnt fingers, if they do not happen to be my own. Then we changed the subject.

Anscombe's wagons were delayed for a day or two by a broken axle or a bog hole, I forget which. So, as I had nothing particular to do until the Natal post-cart left, we spent the time in wandering about Pretoria, which did not take us long as it was but a little *dorp* in those days, and chatting with all and sundry. Also we went up to Government House as it was now called, and left cards, or rather wrote our names in a book for we had no cards, being told by one of the Staff whom we met that we should do so. An hour later a note arrived asking us both to dinner that night and telling us very nicely not to mind if we had no dress things. Of course we had to go, Anscombe rigged up in my second best clothes that did not fit him in the least, as he was a much taller man than I am, and a black satin bow that he had bought at Becket's Store together with a pair of shiny pumps.

I actually met you, my friend, for the first time that evening, and in trouble too, though you may have forgotten the incident. We had made a mistake about the time of dinner, and arriving half an hour too soon, were shown into a long room that opened on to the veranda. You were working there, being I believe a private secretary at the time, copying some despatch; I think you said that which gave an account of the Annexation. The room was lit by a paraffin lamp behind you, for it was quite dark and the window was open, or at any rate unshuttered. The gentleman who showed us in, seeing that you were very busy, took us to the far end of the room, where we stood talking in the shadow. Just then a door opened opposite to that which led to the veranda, and through it came His Excellency the Administrator, Sir Theophilus Shepstone, a stout man of medium height with a very clever, thoughtful face, as I have always thought, one of the greatest of African statesmen. He did not see us, but he caught sight of you and said testily—

"Are you mad?" To which you answered with a laugh—

"I hope not more than usual, Sir, but why?"

"Have I not told you always to let down the blinds after dark? Yet there you sit with your head against the light, about the best target for a bullet that could be imagined."

"I don't think the Boers would trouble to shoot me, Sir. If you had been here I would have drawn the blinds and shut the shutters too," you answered, laughing again.

"Go to dress or you will be late for dinner," he said still rather sternly, and you went. But when you had gone and after we had been announced to him, he smiled and added something which I will not repeat to you even now. I think it was about what you did on the Annexation day of which the story had come to him.

I mention this incident because whenever I think of Shepstone, whom I had known off and on for years in the way that a hunter knows a prominent Government official, it always recurs to my mind, embodying as it does his caution and appreciation of danger derived from long experience of the country, and the sternness he sometimes affected which could never conceal his love towards his friends. Oh! there was greatness in this man, although they did call him an "African Talleyrand." If it had not been so would every native from the Cape to the Zambezi have known and revered his name, as perhaps that of no other white man has been revered? But I must get on with my tale and leave historical discussions to others more fitted to deal with them.

We had a very pleasant dinner that night, although I was so ashamed of my clothes with smart uniforms and white ties all about me, and Anscombe kept fidgeting his feet because he was suffering agony from his new pumps which were a size too small. Everybody was in the best of spirits, for from all directions came the news that the Annexation was well received and that the danger of any trouble had passed away. Ah! if we had only known what the end of it would be!

It was on our way back to the wagon that I chanced to mention to Anscombe that there was still a herd of buffalo within a few days' trek of Lydenburg, of which I had shot two not a month before.

"Are there, by Jove!" he said. "As it happens I never got a buffalo; always I just missed them in one sense or another, and I can't leave Africa with a pair of bought horns. Let's go there and shoot some."

I shook my head and replied that I had been idling long enough and must try to make some money, news at which he seemed very disappointed.

"Look here," he said, "forgive me for mentioning it, but business is business. If you'll come you shan't be a loser."

Again I shook my head, whereat he looked more disappointed than before.

"Very well," he exclaimed, "then I must go alone. For kill a buffalo I will; that is unless the buffalo kills me, in which case my blood will be on your hands."

I don't know why, but at that moment there came into my mind a conviction that if he did go alone a buffalo or something would kill him and that then I should be sorry all my life.

"They are dangerous brutes, much worse than lions," I said.

"And yet you, who pretend to have a conscience, would expose me to their rage unprotected and alone," he replied with a twinkle in his eye which I could see even by moonlight. "Oh! Quatermain, how I have been mistaken in your character."

"Look here, Mr. Anscombe," I said, "it's no use. I cannot possibly go on a shooting expedition with you just now. Only today I have heard from Natal that my boy is not well and must undergo an operation which will lay him up for quite six weeks, and may be dangerous. So I must get down to Durban before it takes place. After that I have a contract in Matabeleland whence you have just come, to take charge of a trading store there for a year; also perhaps to try to shoot a little ivory for myself. So I am fully booked up till, let us say, October, 1878, that is for about eighteen months, by which time I daresay I shall be dead."

"Eighteen months," replied this cool young man. "That will suit me very well. I will go on to India as I intended, then home for a bit and will meet you on the 1st of October, 1878, after which we will proceed to the Lydenburg district and shoot those buffalo, or if they have departed, other buffalo. Is it a bargain?"

I stared at him, thinking that the Administrator's champagne had got into his head.

"Nonsense," I exclaimed. "Who knows where you will be in eighteen months? Why, by that time you will have forgotten all about me."

"If I am alive and well, on the 1st of October, 1878, I shall be exactly where I am now, upon this very square in Pretoria, with a wagon, or wagons, prepared for a hunting trip. But as not unnaturally you have doubts upon that point, I am prepared to pay forfeit if I fail, or even if circumstances cause you to fail."

Here he took a cheque-book from his letter-case and spread it out on the little table in the tent, on which there were ink and a pen, adding—

"Now, Mr. Quatermain, will it meet your views if I fill this up for £250?"

"No," I answered; "taking everything into consideration the sum is excessive. But if you do not mind facing the risks of my non-appearance, to say nothing of your own, you may make it £50."

"You are very moderate in your demands," he said as he handed me the cheque which I put in my pocket, reflecting that it would just pay for my son's operation.

"And you are very foolish in your offers," I replied. "Tell me, why do you make such crack-brained arrangements?"

"I don't quite know. Something in me seems to say that we *shall* make this expedition and that it will have a very important effect upon my life. Mind you, it is to be to the Lydenburg district and nowhere else. And now I am tired, so let's turn in."

Next morning we parted and went our separate ways.

CHAPTER 2

Mr. Marnham

So much for preliminaries, now for the story.

The eighteen months had gone by, bringing with them to me their share of adventure, weal and woe, with all of which at present I have no concern. Behold me arriving very hot and tired in the post-cart from Kimberley, whither I had gone to invest what I had saved out of my Matabeleland contract in a very promising speculation whereof, today, the promise remains and no more. I had been obliged to leave Kimberly in a great hurry, before I ought indeed, because of the silly bargain which I have just recorded. Of course I was sure that I should never see Mr. Anscombe again, especially as I had heard nothing of him during all this while, and had no reason to suppose that he was in Africa. Still I had taken his £50 and he *might* come. Also I have always prided myself upon keeping an appointment.

The post-cart halted with a jerk in front of the European Hotel, and I crawled, dusty and tired, from its interior, to find myself face to face with Anscombe, who was smoking a pipe upon the *stoep*!

"Hullo, Quatermain," he said in his pleasant, drawling voice, "here you are, up to time. I have been making bets with these five gentlemen," and he nodded at a group of loungers on the *stoep*, "as to whether you would or would not appear, I putting ten to one on you in drinks. Therefore you must now consume five whiskies and sodas, which will save them from consuming fifty and a subsequent appearance at the Police Court."

I laughed and said I would be their debtor to the extent of one, which was duly produced.

After it was drunk Anscombe and I had a chat. He said that he had been to India, shot, or shot at whatever game he meant to kill there, visited his relations in England and thence proceeded to keep his appointment with me in Africa. At Durban he had fitted himself out in a regal

23

way with two wagons, full teams, and some spare oxen, and trekked to Pretoria where he had arrived a few days before. Now he was ready to start for the Lydenburg district and look for those buffalo.

"But," I said, "the buffalo probably long ago departed. Also there has been a war with Sekukuni, the Basuto chief who rules all that country, which remains undecided, although I believe some kind of a peace has been patched up. This may make hunting in this neighbourhood dangerous. Why not try some other ground, to the north of the Transvaal, for instance?"

"Quatermain," he answered, "I have come all the way from England, I will not say to kill, but to try to kill buffalo in the Lydenburg district, with you if possible, if not, without you, and thither I am going. If you think it unsafe to accompany me, don't come; I will get on as best I can alone, or with some other skilled person if I can find one."

"If you put it like that I shall certainly come," I replied, "with the proviso that should the buffalo prove to be non-existent or the pursuit of them impossible, we either give up the trip, or go somewhere else, perhaps to the country at the back of Delagoa Bay."

"Agreed," he said; after which we discussed terms, he paying me my salary in advance.

On further consideration we determined, as two were quite unnecessary for a trip of the sort, to leave one of my wagons and half the cattle in charge of a very respectable man, a farmer who lived about five miles from Pretoria just over the pass near to the famous Wonderboom tree which is one of the sights of the place. Should we need this wagon it could always be sent for; or, if we found the Lydenburg hunting-ground, which he was so set upon visiting, unproductive or impossible, we could return to Pretoria over the high-*veld* and pick it up before proceeding elsewhere.

These arrangements took us a couple of days or so. On the third we started, without seeing you, my friend, or any one else that I knew, since just at that time every one seemed to be away from Pretoria. You, I remember, had by now become the Master of the High Court and were, they informed me at your office, absent on circuit.

The morning of our departure was particularly lovely and we trekked away in the best of spirits, as so often happens to people who are marching into trouble. Of our journey there is little to say as everything went smoothly, so that we arrived at the edge of the high-*veld* feeling as happy as the country which has no history is reported to do. Our road led us past the little mining settlement of Pilgrim's Rest where a number of adventurous spirits, most of them English, were engaged in washing for gold, a job at which I once took a turn near this very place without any startling success. Of the locality I need only say that the mountainous scenery is among the most beautiful, the hills are the steepest and the roads are, or were, the worst that I have ever travelled over in a wagon.

However, *going softly* as the natives say, we negotiated them without accident and, leaving Pilgrim's Rest behind us, began to descend towards the low-*veld* where I was informed a herd of buffalo could still be found, since, owing to the war with Sekukuni, no one had shot at them of late. This war had been suspended for a while, and the Land-*drost* at Pilgrim's Rest told me he thought it would be safe to hunt on the borders of that Chief's country, though he should not care to do so himself.

Game of the smaller sort began to be plentiful about here, so not more than a dozen miles from Pilgrim's Rest we outspanned early in the afternoon to try to get a blue *wildebeeste* or two, for I had seen the spoor of these creatures in a patch of soft ground, or failing them some other buck. Accordingly, leaving the wagon by a charming stream that wound and gurgled over a bed of granite, we mounted our salted horses, which were part of Anscombe's outfit, and set forth rejoicing. Riding through the scattered thorns and following the spoor where I could, within half an hour we came to a little glade. There, not fifty yards away, I caught sight of a single blue *wildebeeste* bull standing in the shadow of the trees on the further side of the glade, and pointed out the ugly beast, for it is the most grotesque of all the antelopes, to Anscombe.

"Off you get," I whispered. "It's a lovely shot, you can't miss it."

"Oh, can't I!" replied Anscombe. "Do you shoot."

I refused, so he dismounted, giving me his horse to hold, and kneeling down solemnly and slowly covered the bull. Bang went his rifle, and I saw a bough about a yard above the *wildebeeste* fall on to its back. Off it went like lightning, whereon Anscombe let drive with the left barrel of the Express, almost at hazard as it seemed to me, and by some chance hit it above the near fore-knee, breaking its leg.

"That was a good shot," he cried, jumping on to his horse.

"Excellent," I answered. "But what are you going to do?"

"Catch it. It is cruel to leave a wounded animal," and off he started.

Of course I had to follow, but the ensuing ride remains among the more painful of my hunting memories. We tore through thorn trees that scratched my face and damaged my clothes; we struck a patch of ant-bear holes, into one of which my horse fell so that my stomach bumped against its head; we slithered down granite *koppies*, and this was the worst of it, at the end of each chapter, so to speak, always caught sight of that accursed bull which I fondly hoped would have vanished into space. At length after half an hour or so of this game we reached a stretch of open, rolling ground, and there not fifty yards ahead of us was the animal still going like a hare, though how it could do so on three legs I am sure I do not know. We coursed it like greyhounds, till at last Anscombe, whose horse was the faster, came alongside of the exhausted creature, whereon it turned suddenly and charged.

Anscombe held out his rifle in his right hand and pulled the trigger, which, as he had forgotten to reload it, was a mere theatrical performance. Next second there was such a mix-up that for a while I could not distinguish which was Anscombe, which was the *wildebeeste*, and which the horse. They all seemed to be going round and round in a cloud of dust. When things settled themselves a little I discovered the horse rolling on the ground, Anscombe on his back with his hands up in an attitude of prayer and the *wildebeeste* trying to make up its mind which of them it should finish first. I settled the poor thing's doubts by shooting it through the heart, which I flatter myself was rather clever of me under the circumstances. Then I dismounted to examine Anscombe, who, I presumed, was done for. Not a bit of it. There he sat upon the ground blowing like a blacksmith's bellows and panting out—

"What a glorious gallop. I finished it very well, didn't I? You couldn't have made a better shot yourself."

"Yes," I answered, "you finished it very well as you will find out if you will take the trouble to open your rifle and count your cartridges. I may add that if we are going to hunt together I hope you will never lead me such a fool's chase again."

He rose, opened the rifle and saw that it was empty, for although he had never re-loaded he had thrown out the two cartridges which he had discharged in the glen.

"By Jingo," he said, "you must have shot it, though I could have sworn that it was I. Quatermain, has it ever struck you what a strange thing is the human imagination?"

"Drat the human imagination," I answered, wiping away the blood that was trickling into my eye from a thorn scratch. "Let's look at your horse. If it is lamed you will have to ride Imagination back to the wagon which must be six miles away, that is if we can find it before dark."

Sighing out something about a painfully practical mind, he obeyed, and when the beast was proved to be nothing more than blown and a little bruised, made remarks as to the inadvisability of dwelling on future evil events, which I reminded him had already been better summed up in the New Testament.

After this we contemplated the carcase of the *wildebeeste* which it seemed a pity to leave to rot. Just then Anscombe, who had moved a few yards to the right out of the shadow of an obstructing tree, exclaimed—

"I say, Quatermain, come here and tell me if I have been knocked silly, or if I really see a quite uncommon kind of house built in ancient Greek style set in a divine landscape."

"Temple to Diana, I expect," I remarked as I joined him on the further side of the tree.

I looked and rubbed my eyes. There, about half a mile away, situated in a bay of the sweeping hills and overlooking the measureless expanse of bush-*veld* beneath, was a remarkable house, at least for those days and that part of Africa. To begin with the situation was superb. It stood on a green and swelling mound behind which was a wooded *kloof* where ran a stream that at last precipitated itself in a waterfall over a great cliff. Then in front was that glorious view of the bush-*veld*, at which a man might look for a lifetime and not grow tired, stretching away to the Oliphant's river and melting at last into the dim line of the horizon.

The house itself also, although not large, was of a kind new to me. It was deep, but narrow fronted, and before it were four columns that carried the roof which projected so as to form a wide veranda. Moreover it seemed to be built of marble which glistened like snow in the setting sun. In short in that lonely wilderness, at any rate from this distance, it did look like the deserted shrine of some forgotten god.

"Well, I'm bothered!" I said.

"So am I," answered Anscombe, "to know the name of the Lydenburg district architect whom I should like to employ; though I suspect it is the surroundings that make the place look so beautiful. Hullo! here comes somebody, but he doesn't look like an architect; he looks like a wicked baronet disguised as a Boer."

True enough, round a clump of bush appeared an unusual looking person, mounted on a very good horse. He was tall, thin and old, at least he had a long white beard which suggested age, although his figure, so far as it could be seen beneath his rough clothes, seemed vigorous. His face was clean cut and handsome, with a rather hooked nose, and his eyes were grey, but as I saw when he came up to us, somewhat bloodshot at the corners. His general aspect was refined and benevolent, and as soon as he opened his mouth I perceived that he was a person of gentle breeding.

And yet there was something about him, something in his atmosphere, so to speak, that I did not like. Before we parted that evening I felt sure that in one way or another he was a wrong-doer, not straight; also that he had a violent temper.

He rode up to us and asked in a pleasant voice, although the manner of his question, which was put in bad Dutch, was not pleasant,

"Who gave you leave to shoot on our land?"

"I did not know that any leave was required; it is not customary in these parts," I answered politely in English. "Moreover, this buck was wounded miles away."

"Oh!" he exclaimed in the same tongue, "that makes a difference, though I expect it was still on our land, for we have a lot; it is cheap about here." Then after studying a little, he added apologetically, "You mustn't think me strange, but the fact is my daughter hates things to be killed near the house, which is why there's so much game about."

"Then pray make her our apologies," said Anscombe, "and say that it shall not happen again."

He stroked his long beard and looked at us, for by now he had dismounted, then said—

"Might I ask you gentlemen your names?"

"Certainly," I replied. "I am Allan Quatermain and my friend is the Hon. Maurice Anscombe."

He started and said—

"Of Allan Quatermain of course I have heard. The natives told me that you were trekking to those parts; and if you, sir, are one of Lord Mountford's sons, oddly enough I think I must have known your father in my youth. Indeed I served with him in the Guards."

"How very strange," said Anscombe. "He's dead now and my brother is Lord Mountford. Do you like life here better than that in the Guards? I am sure I should."

"Both of them have their advantages," he answered evasively, "of which, if, as I think, you are also a soldier, you can judge for yourself. But won't you come up to the house? My daughter Heda is away, and my partner Mr. Rodd" (as he mentioned this name I saw a blue vein, which showed above his cheek bone, swell as though under pressure of some secret emotion) "is a retiring sort of a man—indeed some might think him sulky until they came to know him. Still, we can make you comfortable and even give you a decent bottle of wine."

"No, thank you very much," I answered, "we must get back to the wagon or our servants will think that we have come to grief. Perhaps you will accept the *wildebeeste* if it is of any use to you."

"Very well," he said in a voice that suggested regret struggling with relief. To the buck he made no allusion, perhaps because he considered that it was already his own property. "Do you know your way? I believe your wagon is camped out there to the east by what we call the Granite stream. If you follow this *Kaffir* path," and he pointed to a track near by, "it will take you quite close."

"Where does the path run to?" I asked. "There are no *kraals* about, are there?"

"Oh! to the Temple, as my daughter calls our house. My partner and I are labour agents, we recruit natives for the Kimberley Mines," he said in explanation, adding, "Where do you propose to shoot?"

I told him.

"Isn't that rather a risky district?" he said. "I think that Sekukuni will soon be giving more trouble, although there is a truce between him and the English. Still he might send a regiment to raid that way."

I wondered how our friend knew so much of Sekukuni's possible intentions, but only answered that I was accustomed to deal with natives and did not fear them.

"Ah!" he said, "well, you know your own business best. But if you should get into any difficulty, make straight for this place. The Basutos will not interfere with you here."

Again I wondered why the Basutos should look upon this particular spot as sacred, but thinking it wisest to ask no questions, I only answered—

"Thank you very much. We'll bear your invitation in mind, Mr.—"

"Marnham."

"Marnham," I repeated after him. "Goodbye and many thanks for your kindness."

"One question," broke in Anscombe, "if you will not think me rude. What is the name of the architect who designed that most romantic-looking house of yours which seems to be built of marble?"

"My daughter designed it, or at least I think she copied it from some old drawing of a ruin. Also it *is* marble; there's a whole hill of the stuff not a hundred yards from the door, so it was cheaper to use than anything else. I hope you will come and see it on your way back, though it is not as fine as it appears from a distance. It would be very pleasant after all these years to talk to an English gentleman again."

Then we parted, I rather offended because he did not seem to include me in the description, he calling after us—

"Stick close to the path through the patch of big trees, for the ground is rather swampy there and it's getting dark."

Presently we came to the place he mentioned where the timber, although scattered, was quite large for South Africa, of the yellow-wood species, and interspersed wherever the ground was dry with huge *euphorbias*, of which the tall finger-like growths and sad grey colouring looked unreal and ghostlike in the waning light. Following the advice given to us, we rode in single file along the narrow path, fearing lest otherwise we should tumble into some bog hole, until we came to higher land covered with the scattered thorns of the country.

"Did that bush give you any particular impression?" asked Anscombe a minute or two later.

"Yes," I answered, "it gave me the impression that we might catch fever there. See the mist that lies over it," and turning in my saddle I pointed with the rifle in my hand to what looked like a mass of cotton wool over which, without permeating it, hung the last red glow of sunset, producing a curious and indeed rather unearthly effect. "I expect that thousands of years ago there was a lake yonder, which is why trees grow so big in the rich soil."

"You are curiously mundane, Quatermain," he answered. "I ask you of spiritual impressions and you dilate to me of geological formations and the growth of timber. You felt nothing in the spiritual line?"

"I felt nothing except a chill," I answered, for I was tired and hungry. "What the devil are you driving at?"

"Have you got that flask of Hollands about you, Quatermain?"

"Oh! those are the spirits you are referring to," I remarked with sarcasm as I handed it to him.

He took a good pull and replied—

"Not at all, except in the sense that bad spirits require good spirits to correct them, as the Bible teaches. To come to facts," he added in a changed voice, "I have never been in a place that depressed me more than that thrice accursed patch of bush."

"Why did it depress you?" I asked, studying him as well as I could in the fading light. To tell the truth I feared lest he had knocked his head when the *wildebeeste* upset him, and was suffering from delayed concussion.

"Can't tell you, Quatermain. I don't look like a criminal, do I? Well, I entered those trees feeling a fairly honest man, and I came out of them feeling like a murderer. It was as though something terrible had happened to me there; it was as though I had killed someone there. *Ugh!*" and he shivered and took another pull at the Hollands.

"What bosh!" I said. "Besides, even if it were to come true, I am sorry to say I've killed lots of men in the way of business and they don't bother me overmuch."

"Did you ever kill one to win a woman?"

"Certainly not. Why, that would be murder. How can you ask me such a thing? But I have killed several to win cattle," I reflected aloud, remembering my expedition with Saduko against the chief Bangu, and some other incidents in my career.

"I appreciate the difference, Quatermain. If you kill for cows, it is justifiable homicide; if you kill for women, it is murder."

"Yes," I replied, "that is how it seems to work out in Africa. You see, women are higher in the scale of creation than cows, therefore crimes committed for their sake are enormously greater than those committed for cows, which just makes the difference between justifiable homicide and murder."

"Good lord! what an argument," he exclaimed and relapsed into silence. Had he been accustomed to natives and their ways he would have understood the point much better than he did, though I admit it is difficult to explain.

In due course we reached the wagon without further trouble. While we were shielding our pipes after an excellent supper I asked Anscombe his impressions of Mr. Marnham.

"Queer cove, I think," he answered. "Been a gentleman, too, and still keeps the manners, which isn't strange if he is one of the Marnhams, for they are a good family. I wonder he mentioned having served with my father."

"It slipped out of him. Men who live a lot alone are apt to be surprised into saying things they regret afterwards, as I noticed he did. But why do you wonder?"

"Because as it happens, although I have only just recalled it, my father used to tell some story about a man named Marnham in his regiment. I can't remember the details, but it had to do with cards when high stakes were being played for, and with the striking of a superior officer in the quarrel that ensued, as a result of which the striker was requested to send in his papers."

"It may not have been the same man."

"Perhaps not, for I believe that more than one Marnham served in that regiment. But I remember my father saying, by way of excuse for the person concerned, that he had a most ungovernable temper. I think he added, that he left the country and took service in some army on the Continent. I should rather like to clear the thing up."

"It isn't probable that you will, for even if you should ever meet this Marnham again, I fancy you would find he held his tongue about his acquaintance with your father."

"I wonder what Miss Heda is like," went on Anscombe after a pause. "I am curious to see a girl who designs a house on the model of an ancient ruin."

"Well, you won't, for she's away somewhere. Besides we are looking for buffalo, not girls, which is a good thing as they are less dangerous."

I spoke thus decisively because I had taken a dislike to Mr. Marnham and everything to do with him, and did not wish to encourage the idea of further meetings.

"No, never, I suppose. And yet I feel as though I were certainly destined to see that accursed yellow-wood swamp again."

"Nonsense," I replied as I rose to turn in. Ah! if I had but known!

CHAPTER 3

The Hunters Hunted

While I was taking off my boots I heard a noise of jabbering in some native tongue which I took to be Sisutu, and not wishing to go to the trouble of putting them on again, called to the driver of the wagon to find out what it was. This man was a Cape Colony *Kaffir*, a Fingo I think, with a touch of Hottentot in him. He was an excellent driver, indeed I do not think I have ever seen a better, and by no means a bad shot. Among Europeans he rejoiced in the name of Footsack, a Boer Dutch term which is generally addressed to troublesome dogs and means "Get out." To tell the truth, had I been his master he would have got out, as I suspected him of drinking, and generally did not altogether trust him. Anscombe, however, was fond of him because he had shown courage in some hunting adventure in Matabeleland, I think it was at the shooting of that very dark-coloured lion whose skin had been the means of making us acquainted nearly two years before. Indeed he said that on this occasion Footsack had saved his life, though from all that I could gather I do not think this was quite the case. Also the man, who had been on many hunting trips with sportsmen, could talk Dutch well and English enough to make himself understood, and therefore was useful.

He went as I bade him, and coming back presently, told me that a party of Basutos, about thirty in number, who were returning from Kimberley, where they had been at work in the mines, under the leadership of a bastard named Karl, asked leave to camp by the wagon for the night, as they were afraid to go on to Tampel in the dark.

At first I could not make out what Tampel was, as it did not sound like a native name. Then I remembered that Mr. Marnham had spoken of his house as being called the Temple, of which, of course, Tampel was a corruption; also that he said he and his partner were labour agents.

"Why are they afraid?" I asked.

"Because, Baas, they say that they must go through a wood in a swamp, which they think is haunted by spooks, and they much afraid of spooks;" that is of ghosts.

"What spooks?" I asked.

"Don't know, Baas. They say spook of some one who has been killed."

"Rubbish," I replied. "Tell them to go and catch the spook; we don't want a lot of noisy fellows howling shanties here all night."

Then it was that Anscombe broke in in his humorous, rather drawling voice.

"How can you be so hard-hearted, Quatermain? After the supernatural terror which, as I told you, I experienced in that very place, I wouldn't condemn a kicking mule to go through it in this darkness. Let the poor devils stay; I daresay they are tired."

So I gave in, and presently saw their fires beginning to burn through the end canvas of the wagon which was unlaced because the night was hot. Also later on I woke up, about midnight I think, and heard voices talking, one of which I reflected sleepily, sounded very like that of Footsack.

Waking very early, as is my habit, I peeped out of the wagon, and through the morning mist perceived Footsack in converse with a particularly villainous-looking person. I at once concluded this must be Karl, evidently a bastard compounded of about fifteen parts of various native bloods to one of white, who, to add to his attractions, was deeply scarred with smallpox and possessed a really alarming squint. It seemed to me that Footsack handed to this man something that looked suspiciously like a bottle of *squareface* gin wrapped up in dried grass, and that the man handed back to Footsack some small object which he put in his mouth.

Now, I wondered to myself, what is there of value that one who does not eat sweets would stow away in his mouth. Gold coin perhaps, or a quid of tobacco, or a stone. Gold was too much to pay for a bottle of gin, tobacco was too little, but how about the stone? What stone? Who wanted stones? Then suddenly I remembered that these people were said to come from Kimberley, and whistled to myself. Still I did nothing, principally because the mist was still so dense that although I could see the men's faces, I could not clearly see the articles which they passed to each other about two feet lower, where it still lay very thickly, and to bring any accusation against a native which he can prove to be false is apt to destroy authority. So I held my tongue and waited my chance. It did not come at once, for before I was dressed those Basutos had departed together with their leader Karl, for now that the sun was up they no longer feared the haunted bush.

It came later, thus: We were trekking along between the thorns upon a level and easy track which enabled the driver Footsack to sit upon the *voorkisse* or driving box of the wagon, leaving the lad who is called the *voorlooper* to lead the oxen. Anscombe was riding parallel to the wagon in the hope of killing some guinea fowl for the pot (though a very poor shot with a rifle he was good with a shot-gun). I, who did not care for this small game, was seated smoking by the side of Footsack who, I noted, smelt of gin and generally showed signs of dissipation. Suddenly I said to him—

"Show me that diamond which the bastard Karl gave you this morning in payment for the bottle of your master's drink."

It was a bow drawn at a venture, but the effect of the shot was remarkable. Had I not caught it, the long bamboo whip Footsack held would have fallen to the ground, while he collapsed in his seat like a man who has received a bullet in his stomach.

"Baas," he gasped, "Baas, how did you know?"

"I knew," I replied grandly, "in the same way that I know everything. Show me the diamond."

"Baas," he said, "it was not the Baas Anscombe's gin, it was some I bought in Pilgrim's Rest."

"I have counted the bottles in the case and know very well whose gin it was," I replied ambiguously, for the reason that I had done nothing of the sort. "Show me the diamond."

Footsack fumbled about his person, his hair, his waistcoat pockets and even his *moocha*, and ultimately from somewhere produced a stone which he handed to me. I looked at it, and from the purity of colour and size, judged it to be a diamond worth £200, or possibly more. After careful examination I put it into my pocket, saying,

"This is the price of your master's gin and therefore belongs to him as much as it does to anybody. Now if you want to keep out of trouble, tell me—whence came it into the hands of that man, Karl?"

"Baas," replied Footsack, trembling all over, "how do I know? He and the rest have been working at the mines; I suppose he found it there."

"Indeed! And did he find others of the same sort?"

"I think so, Baas. At least he said that he had been buying bottles of gin with such stones all the way down from Kimberley. Karl is a great drunkard, Baas, as I am sure, who have known him for years."

35

"That is not all," I remarked, keeping my eyes fixed on him. "What else did he say?"

"He said, Baas, that he was very much afraid of returning to the Baas Marnham whom the *Kaffirs* call White-beard, with only a few stones left."

"Why was he afraid?"

"Because the Baas Whitebeard, he who dwells at Tampel, is, he says, a very angry man if he thinks himself cheated, and Karl is afraid lest he should kill him as another was killed, he whose spook haunts the wood through which those silly people feared to pass last night."

"Who was killed and who killed him?" I asked.

"Baas, I don't know," replied Footsack, collapsing into sullen silence in a way that *Kaffirs* have when suddenly they realize that they have said too much. Nor did I press the matter further, having learned enough.

What had I learned? This: that Messrs. Marnham & Rodd were illicit diamond buyers, I.D.B.'s as they are called, who had cunningly situated themselves at a great distance from the scene of operations practically beyond the reach of civilized law. Probably they were engaged also in other nefarious dealings with *Kaffirs*, such as supplying them with guns wherewith to make war upon the Whites. Sekukuni had been fighting us recently, so that there would be a very brisk market for rifles. This, too, would account for Marnham's apparent knowledge of that Chief's plans. Possibly, however, he had no knowledge and only made a pretence of it to keep us out of the country.

Later on I confided the whole story and my suspicions to Anscombe, who was much interested.

"What picturesque scoundrels!" he exclaimed, "We really ought to go back to the Temple. I have always longed to meet some real live I.D.B.'s."

"It is probable that you have done that already without knowing it. For the rest, if you wish to visit that den of iniquity, you must do so alone."

"Wouldn't whited sepulchre be a better term, especially as it seems to cover dead men's bones?" he replied in his frivolous manner.

Then I asked him what he was going to do about Footsack and the bottle of gin, which he countered by asking me what I was going to do with that diamond.

"Give it to you as Footsack's master," I said, suiting the action to the word. "I don't wish to be mixed up in doubtful transactions."

Then followed a long argument as to who was the real owner of the stone, which ended in its being hidden away be produced if called for, and in Footsack, who ought have had a round dozen, receiving a scolding from his master, coupled with the threat that if he stole more gin he would be handed over to a magistrate—when we met one.

On the following day we reached the hot, low-lying *veld* which the herd of buffalo was said to inhabit. Next morning, however, when we were making ready to begin hunting, a Basuto *Kaffir* appeared who, on being questioned, said that he was one of Sekukuni's people sent to this district to look for two lost oxen. I did not believe this story, thinking it more probable that he was a spy, but asked him whether in his hunt for oxen he had come across buffalo.

He replied that he had, a herd of thirty-two of them, counting the calves, but that they were over the Oliphant's River about five-and-twenty miles away, in a valley between some outlying hills and the rugged range of mountains, beyond which was situated Sekukuni's town. Moreover, in proof of his story he showed me spoor of the beasts heading in that direction which was quite a week old.

Now for my part, as I did not think it wise to get too near to Sekukuni, I should have given them up and gone to hunt something else. Anscombe, however, was of a different opinion and pleaded hard that we should follow them. They were the only herd within a hundred miles, he said, if indeed there were any others this side of the Lebombo Mountains. As I still demurred, he suggested, in the nicest possible manner, that if I thought the business risky, I should camp somewhere with the wagon, while he went on with Footsack to look for the buffalo. I answered that I was well used to risks, which in a sense were my trade, and that as he was more or less in my charge I was thinking of him, not of myself, who was quite prepared to follow the buffalo, not only to Sekukuni's Mountains but over them. Then fearing that he had hurt my feelings, he apologized, and offered to go elsewhere if I liked. The upshot was that we decided to trek to the Oliphant's River, camp there and explore the bush on the other side on horseback, never going so far from the wagon that we could not reach it again before nightfall.

This, then, we did, *outspanning* that evening by the hot but beautiful river which was still haunted by a few hippopotamus and many crocodiles, one of which we shot before turning in. Next morning, having breakfasted off cold guinea fowl, we mounted, crossed the river by a ford that was quite as deep as I liked, to which the *Kaffir* path led us, and, leaving Footsack with the two other boys in charge of the wagon, began to hunt for the buffalo in the rather swampy bush that stretched from the further bank to the slope of the first hills, eight or ten miles away. I did not much expect to find them, as the Basuto had said that they had gone over these hills, but either he lied or they had moved back again.

Not half a mile from the river bank, just as I was about to dismount to stalk a fine waterbuck of which I caught sight standing among some coarse grass and bushes, my eye fell upon buffalo spoor that from its appearance I knew could not be more than a few hours old. Evidently the beasts had been feeding here during the night and at dawn had moved away to sleep in the dry bush nearer the hills. Beckoning to Anscombe, who fortunately had not seen the waterbuck, at which he would certainly have fired, thereby perhaps frightening the buffalo, I showed him the spoor that we at once started to follow.

Soon it led us into other spoor, that of a whole herd of thirty or forty beasts indeed, which made our task quite easy, at least till we came to harder ground, for the animals had gone a long way. An hour or more later, when we were about seven miles from the river, I perceived ahead of us, for we were now almost at the foot of the hills, a cool and densely-wooded *kloof*.

"That is where they will be," I said. "Now come on carefully and make no noise."

We rode to the wide mouth of the *kloof* where the signs of the buffalo were numerous and fresh, dismounted and tied our horses to a thorn, so as to approach them silently on foot. We had not gone two hundred yards through the bush when suddenly about fifty paces away, standing broadside on in the shadow between two trees, I saw a splendid old bull with a tremendous pair of horns.

"Shoot," I whispered to Anscombe, "you will never get a better chance. It is the sentinel of the herd."

He knelt down, his face quite white with excitement, and covered the bull with his Express.

"Keep cool," I whispered again, "and aim behind the shoulder, half-way down."

I don't think he understood me, for at that moment off went the rifle. He hit the beast somewhere, as I heard the bullet clap, but not fatally, for it turned and lumbered off up the *kloof*, apparently unhurt, whereon he sent the second barrel after it, a clean miss this time. Then of a sudden all about us appeared buffaloes that had, I suppose, been sleeping invisible to us. These, with snorts and bellows, rushed off towards the river, for having their senses about them, they had no mind to be trapped in the *kloof*. I could only manage a shot at one of them, a large and long-horned cow which I knocked over quite dead. If I had fired again it would have been but to wound, a thing I hate. The whole business was over in a minute. We went and looked at my dead cow which I had caught through the heart.

"It's cruel to kill these things," I said, "for I don't know what use we are going to make of them, and they must love life as much as we do."

"We'll cut the horns off," said Anscombe.

"You may if you like," I answered, "but you will find it a tough job with a sheath knife."

"Yes, I think that shall be the task of the worthy Footsack tomorrow," he replied. "Meanwhile let us go and finish off my bull, as Footsack & Co. may as well bring home two pair of horns as one."

I looked at the dense bush, and knowing something of the habits of wounded buffaloes, reflected that it would be a nasty job. Still I said nothing, because if I hesitated, I knew he would want to go alone. So we started. Evidently the beast had been badly hit, for the blood spoor was easy to follow. Yet it had been able to retreat up to the end of the *kloof* that terminated in a cliff over which trickled a stream of water. Here it was not more than a hundred paces wide, and on either side of it were other precipitous cliffs. As we went from one of these a warhorn, such as the Basutos use, was blown. Although I heard it, oddly enough, I paid no attention to it at the time, being utterly intent upon the business in hand.

Following a wounded buffalo bull up a tree-clad and stony *kloof* is no game for children, as these beasts have a habit of returning on their tracks and then rushing out to gore you. So I went on with every sense alert, keeping Anscombe well behind me. As it happened our bull had either been knocked silly or inherited no guile from his parents. When he found he could go no further he stopped, waited behind a bush, and when he saw us he charged in a simple and primitive fashion. I let Anscombe fire, as I wished him to have the credit of killing it all to himself, but somehow or other he managed to miss both barrels. Then, trouble being imminent, I let drive as the beast lowered its head, and was lucky enough to break its spine (to shoot at the head of a buffalo is useless), so that it rolled over quite dead at our feet.

"You have got a magnificent pair of horns," I said, contemplating the fallen giant.

"Yes," answered Anscombe, with a twinkle of his humorous eyes, "and if it hadn't been for you I think that I should have got them in more senses than one."

As the words passed his lips some missile, from its peculiar sound

I judged it was the leg off an iron pot, hurtled past my head, fired evidently from a smoothbore gun with a large charge of bad powder. Then I remembered the war-horn and all that it meant.

"Off you go," I said, "we are ambushed by *Kaffirs*."

We were indeed, for as we tailed down that *kloof*, from the top of both cliffs above us came a continuous but luckily ill-directed fire. Lead-coated stones, pot legs and bullets whirred and whistled all round us, yet until the last, just when we were reaching the tree to which we had tied our horses, quite harmlessly. Then suddenly I saw Anscombe begin to limp. Still he managed to run on and mount, though I observed that he did not put his right foot into the stirrup.

"What's the matter?" I asked as we galloped off.

"Shot through the instep, I think," he answered with a laugh, "but it doesn't hurt a bit."

"I expect it will later," I replied. "Meanwhile, thank God it wasn't at the top of the *kloof*. They won't catch us on the horses, which they never thought of killing first."

"They are going to try though. Look behind you."

I looked and saw twenty or thirty men emerging from the mouth of the *kloof* in pursuit.

"No time to stop to get those horns," he said with a sigh.

"No," I answered, "unless you are particularly anxious to say good-bye to the world pinned over a broken ant-heap in the sun, or something pleasant of the sort."

Then we rode on in silence, I thinking what a fool I had been first to allow myself to be overruled by Anscombe and cross the river, and secondly not to have taken warning from that war-horn. We could not go very fast because of the difficult and swampy nature of the ground; also the great heat of the day told on the horses. Thus it came about that when we reached the ford we were not more than ten minutes ahead of our active pursuers, good runners every one of them, and accustomed to the country. I suppose that they had orders to kill or capture us at any cost, for instead of giving up the chase, as I hoped they would, they stuck to us in surprising fashion.

We splashed through the river, and luckily on the further bank were met by Footsack who had seen us coming and guessed that something was wrong.

"*Inspan!*" I shouted to him, "and be quick about it if you want to see tomorrow's light. The Basutos are after us."

Off he went like a shot, his face quite green with fear.

"Now," I said to Anscombe, as we let our horses take a drink for

40

which they were mad, "we have got to hold this ford until the wagon is ready, or those devils will get us after all. Dismount and I'll tie up the horses."

He did so with some difficulty, and at my suggestion, while I made the beasts fast, cut the lace of his boot which was full of blood, and soaked his wounded foot, that I had no time to examine, in the cool water. These things done, I helped him to the rear of a thorn tree which was thick enough to shield most of his body, and took my own stand behind a similar thorn at a distance of a few paces.

Presently the Basutos appeared, trotting along close together whereon Anscombe, who was seated behind the tree, fired both barrels of his Express at them at a range of about two hundred yards. It was a foolish thing to do, first because he missed them clean, for he had over-estimated the range and the bullets went above their heads, and secondly because it caused them to scatter and made them careful, whereas had they come on in a lump we could have taught them a lesson. However I said nothing, as I knew that reproaches would only make him nervous. Down went those scoundrels on to their hands and knees and, taking cover behind stones and bushes on the further bank, began to fire at us, for they were all armed with guns of one sort and another, and there was only about a hundred yards of water between us. As they effected this manoeuvre I am glad to say I was able to get two of them, while Anscombe, I think, wounded another.

After this our position grew quite warm, for as I have said the thorn trunks were not very broad, and three or four of the natives, who had probably been hunters, were by no means bad shots, though the rest of them fired wildly. Anscombe, in poking his head round the tree to shoot, had his hat knocked off by a bullet, while a slug went through the lappet of my coat. Then a worse thing happened. Either by chance or design Anscombe's horse was struck in the neck and fell struggling, whereon my beast, growing frightened, broke its *riem* and galloped to the wagon. That is where I ought to have left them at first, only I thought that we might need them to make a bolt on, or to carry Anscombe if he could not walk.

Quite a long while went by before, glancing behind me, I saw that the oxen that had been grazing at a little distance had at length arrived and were being inspanned in furious haste. The Basutos saw it also, and fearing lest we should escape, determined to try to end the business. Suddenly they leapt from their cover, and with more courage than I should have expected of them, rushed into the river, proposing to storm us, which, to speak truth, I think they would have done had I not been a fairly quick shot.

As it was, finding that they were losing too heavily from our fire, they retreated in a hurry, leaving their dead behind them, and even a wounded man who was clinging to a rock. He, poor wretch, was in mortal terror lest we should shoot him again, which I had not the heart to do, although as his leg was shattered above the knee by an Express bullet, it might have been true kindness. Again and again he called out for mercy, saying that he only attacked us because his chief, who had been warned of our coming "by the White Man," ordered him to take our guns and cattle.

"What white man?" I shouted. "Speak or I shoot."

There was no answer, for at this moment he fainted from loss of blood and vanished beneath the water. Then another Basuto, I suppose he was their captain, but do not know for he was hidden in some bushes, called out—

"Do not think that you shall escape, white men. There are many more of our people coming, and we will kill you in the night when you cannot see to shoot us."

At this moment, too, Footsack shouted that the wagon was inspanned and ready. Now I hesitated what to do. If we made for the wagon, which must be very slowly because of Anscombe's wounded foot, we had to cross seventy or eighty yards of rising ground almost devoid of cover. If, on the other hand, we stayed where we were till nightfall a shot might catch one of us, or other Basutos might arrive and rush us. There was also a third possibility, that our terrified servants might trek off and leave us in order to save their own lives, which verily I believe they would have done, not being of Zulu blood. I put the problem to Anscombe, who shook his head and looked at his foot. Then he produced a lucky penny which he carried in his pocket and said—

"Let us invoke the Fates. Heads we run like heroes; tails we stay here like heroes," and he spun the penny, while I stared at him open-mouthed and not without admiration.

Never, I thought to myself, had this primitive method of cutting a Gordian knot been resorted to in such strange and urgent circumstances.

"Heads it is!" he said coolly. "Now, my boy, do you run and I'll crawl after you. If I don't arrive, you know my people's address, and I bequeath to you all my African belongings in memory of a most pleasant trip."

"Don't play the fool," I replied sternly. "Come, put your right arm round my neck and hop on your left leg as you never hopped before."

Then we started, and really our transit was quite lively, for all those Basutos began what for them was rapid firing. I think, however, that their best shots must have fallen, for not a bullet touched us, although before we got out of their range one or two went very near.

"There," said Anscombe, as a last amazing hop brought him to the wagon rail, "there, you see how wise it is give Providence a chance sometimes."

"In the shape of a lucky penny," I grumbled as I hoisted him up.

"Certainly, for why should not Providence inhabit a penny as much as it does any other mundane thing? Oh, my dear Quatermain, have you never been taught to look to the pence and let the rest take care of itself?"

"Stop talking rubbish and look to your foot, for the wagon is starting," I replied.

Then off we went at a good round trot, for never have I seen oxen more scientifically driven than they were by Footsack and his friends on this occasion, or a greater pace got out of them. As soon as we reached a fairly level piece of ground I made Anscombe lie down on the cartel of the wagon and examined his wound as well as circumstances would allow. I found that the bullet or whatever the missile may have been, had gone through his right instep just beneath the big sinew, but so far as I could judge without injuring any bone. There was nothing to be done except rub in some carbolic ointment, which fortunately he had in his medicine chest, and bind up the wound as best I could with a clean handkerchief, after which I tied a towel, that was *not* clean, over the whole foot.

By this time evening was coming on, so we ate of such as we had with us, which we needed badly enough, without stopping the wagon. I remember that it consisted of cheese and hard biscuits. At dark we were obliged to halt a little by a stream until the moon rose, which fortunately she did very soon, as she was only just past her full. As soon as she was up we started again, and with a breathing space or two, trekked all that night, which I spent seated on the after part of the wagon and keeping a sharp look out, while, notwithstanding the roughness of the road and his hurt, Anscombe slept like a child upon the cartel inside.

I was very tired, so tired that the fear of surprise was the only thing that kept me awake, and I recall reflecting in a stupid kind of way, that it seemed always to have been my lot in life to watch thus, in one sense or another, while others slept.

The night passed somehow without anything happening, and at

dawn we halted for a while to water the oxen, which we did with buckets, and let them eat what grass they could reach from their yokes, since we did not dare to *outspan* them. Just as we were starting on again the *voortrekker*, whom I had set to watch at a little distance, ran up with his eyes bulging out of his head, and reported that he had seen a Basuto with an *assegai* hanging about in the bush, as though to keep touch with us, after which we delayed no more.

All that day we blundered on, thrashing the weary cattle that at every halt tried to lie down, and by nightfall came to the *outspan* near to the house called the Temple, where we had met the *Kaffirs* returning from the diamond fields. This journey we had accomplished in exactly half the time it had taken on the outward trip. Here we were obliged to stop, as our team must have rest and food. So we outspanned and slept that night without much fear, since I thought it most improbable that the Basutos would attempt to follow us so far, as we were now within a day's trek of Pilgrim's Rest, whither we proposed to proceed on the morrow. But that is just where I made a mistake.

CHAPTER 4

Doctor Rodd

I did get a little sleep that night, with one eye open, but before dawn I was up again seeing to the feeding of our remaining horse with some *mealies* that we carried, and other matters. The oxen we had been obliged to unyoke that they might fill themselves with grass and water, since otherwise I feared that we should never get them on to their feet again. As it was, the poor brutes were so tired that some of them could scarcely eat, and all lay down at the first opportunity.

Having awakened Footsack and the other boys that they might be ready to take advantage of the light when it came, for I was anxious to be away, I drank a nip of Hollands and water and ate a biscuit, making Anscombe do the same. Coffee would have been more acceptable, but I thought it wiser not to light a fire for fear of showing our whereabouts.

Now a faint glimmer in the east told me that the dawn was coming. Just by the wagon grew a fair-sized, green-leaved tree, and as it was quite easy to climb even by starlight, up it I went so as to get above the ground mist and take a look round before we trekked. Presently the sky grew pearly and light began to gather; then the edge of the sun appeared, throwing long level rays across the world. Everywhere the mist lay dense as cotton wool, except at one spot about a mile behind us where there was a little hill or rather a wave of the ground, over which we had trekked upon the preceding evening. The top of this rise was above mist level, and on it no trees grew because the granite came to the surface. Having discovered nothing, I called to the boys to drive up the oxen, some of which had risen and were eating again, and prepared to descend from my tree.

As I did so, out of the corner of my eye I caught sight of something that glittered far away, so far that it would only have attracted the notice of a trained hunter. Yes, something was shining on the brow of the rise of which I have spoken. I stared at it through my glasses and saw what I had feared to see. A body of natives was crossing the rise and the glitter was caused by the rays of dawn striking on their spears and gun-barrels.

I came down out of that tree like a frightened wild cat and ran to the wagon, thinking hard as I went. The Basutos were after us, meaning to attack as soon as there was sufficient light. In ten minutes or less they would be here. There was no time to *inspan* the oxen, and even if there had been, stiff and weary as the beasts were, we should be overtaken before we had gone a hundred yards on that bad road. What then was to be done? Run for it? It was impossible, Anscombe could not run. My eye fell upon the horse munching the last of his *mealies*.

"Footsack," I said as quietly as I could, "never mind about *inspanning* yet, but saddle up the horse. Be quick now."

He looked at me doubtfully, but obeyed, having seen nothing. If he had seen I knew that he would have been off. I nipped round to the end of the wagon, calling to the other two boys to let the oxen be a while and come to me.

"Now, Anscombe," I said, "hand out the rifles and cartridges. Don't stop to ask questions, but do what I tell you. They are on the rack by your side. So. Now put on your revolver and let me help you down. Man, don't forget your hat."

He obeyed quickly enough, and presently was standing on one leg by my side, looking cramped and tottery.

"The Basutos are on us," I said.

He whistled and remarked something about Chapter No. 2.

"Footsack," I called, "bring the horse here; the Baas wishes to ride a little to ease his leg."

He did so, stopping a moment to pull the second girth tight. Then we helped Anscombe into the saddle.

"Which way?" he asked.

I looked at the long slope in front of us. It was steep and bad going. Anscombe might get up it on the horse before the *Kaffirs* overtook us, but it was extremely problematical if we could do so. I might perhaps if I mounted behind him and the horse could bear us both, which was doubtful, but how about our poor servants? He saw the doubt upon my face and said in his quiet way, "You may remember that our white-bearded friend told us to make straight for his place in case of any difficulty with the Basutos. It seems to have arisen."

"I know he did," I answered, "but I cannot make up my mind which is the more dangerous, Marnham or the Basutos. I rather think that he set them on to us."

46

"It is impossible to solve problems at this hour of the morning, Quatermain, and there is no time to toss. So I vote for the Temple."

"It seems our best chance. At any rate that's your choice, so let's go."

Then I sang out to the *Kaffirs*, "The Basutos are on us. We go to Tampel for refuge. Run!"

My word! they did run. I never saw athletes make better time over the first quarter of a mile. We ran, too, or at least the horse did, I hanging on to the stirrup and Anscombe holding both the rifles beneath his arm. But the beast was tired, also blown out with that morning feed of *mealies*, so our progress was not very fast. When we were about two hundred yards from the wagon I looked back and saw the Basutos beginning to arrive. They saw us also, and uttering a sort of whistling war cry, started in pursuit.

After this we had quite an interesting time. I scrambled on to the horse behind Anscombe, whereon that intelligent animal, feeling the double weight, reduced its pace proportionately, to a slow triple, indeed, out of which it could not be persuaded to move. So I slipped off again over its tail and we went on as before. Meanwhile the Basutos, very active fellows, were coming up. By this time the yellow-wood grove in the swamp, of which I have already written, was close to us, and it became quite a question which of us would get there first (I may mention that Footsack & Co. had already attained its friendly shelter). Anscombe kicked the horse with his sound heel and I thumped it with my fist, thereby persuading it to a hand gallop.

As we reached the outlying trees of the wood the first Basuto, a lank fellow with a mouth like a rat trap, arrived and threw an *assegai* at us which passed between Anscombe's back and my nose. Then he closed and tried to stab with another *assegai*. I could do nothing, but Anscombe showed himself cleverer than I expected. Dropping the reins, he drew his pistol and managed to send a bullet through that child of nature's head, so that he went down like a stone.

"And you tell me I am a bad shot," he drawled.

"It was a fluke," I gasped, for even in these circumstances truth would prevail.

"Wait and you'll see," he replied, re-cocking the revolver.

As a matter of fact there was no need for more shooting, since at the verge of the swamp the Basutos pulled up. I do not think that the death of their companion caused them to do this, for they seemed to take no notice of him. It was as though they had reached some boundary which they knew it would not be lawful for them to pass. They simply stopped, took the dead man's *assegai* and shield from the body and walked quietly back towards the wagon, leaving him where he lay. The horse stopped also, or rather proceeded at a walk.

"There!" exclaimed Anscombe. "Did I not tell you I had a presentiment that I should kill a man in this accursed wood?"

"Yes," I said as soon as I had recovered my breath, "but you mixed up a woman with the matter and I don't see one."

"That's true," he replied, "I hope we shan't meet her later."

Then we went on as quickly as we could, which was not very fast, for I feared lest the Basutos should change their minds and follow us. As the risk of this became less our spirits rose, since if we had lost the wagon and the oxen, at least we had saved our lives, which was almost more than we could have expected in the circumstances. At last we came to that glade where we had killed the *wildebeeste* not a week before. There lay its skeleton picked clean by the great brown kites that frequent the bush-*veld*, some of which still sat about in the trees.

"Well, I suppose we must go on to Tampel," said Anscombe rather faintly, for I could see that his wound was giving him a good deal of pain.

As he spoke from round the tree whence he had first emerged, appeared Mr. Marnham, riding the same horse and wearing the same clothes. The only difference between his two entries was that the first took place in the late evening and the second in the early morning.

"So here you are again," he said cheerfully.

"Yes," I answered, "and it is strange to meet you at the same spot. Were you expecting us?"

"Not more than I expect many things," he replied with a shrewd glance at me, adding, "I always rise with the sun, and thinking that I heard a shot fired in the distance, came to see what was happening. The Basutos attacked you at daybreak, did they not?"

"They did, but how did you know that, Mr. Marnham?"

"Your servants told me. I met them running to the house looking very frightened. You are wounded, Mr. Anscombe?"

"Yes, a couple of days ago on the border of Sekukuni's country where the natives tried to murder us."

"Ah!" he replied without surprise. "I warned you the trip was dangerous, did I not? Well, come on home where my partner, Rodd, who luckily has had medical experience, will attend to you. Mr. Quatermain can tell me the story as we go."

So we went on up the long slope, I relating our adventures, to which Mr. Marnham listened without comment.

48

"I expect that the *Kaffirs* will have looted the wagon and be on the way home with your oxen by now," he said when I had finished.

"Are you not afraid that they will follow us here?" I asked.

"Oh no, Mr. Quatermain. We do business with these people, also they sometimes come to be doctored by Rodd when they are sick, so this place is sacred ground to them. They stopped hunting you when they got to the Yellow-wood swamp where our land begins, did they not?"

"Yes, but now I want to hunt them. Can you give me any help? Those oxen are tired out and footsore, so we might be able to catch them up."

He shook his head. "We have very few people here, and by the time that you could get assistance from the Camp at Barberton, if the Commandant is able and willing to give you any, which I rather doubt, they will be far away. Moreover," he added, dropping his voice, "let us come to an understanding. You are most welcome to any help or hospitality that I can offer, but if you wish to do more fighting I must ask you to go elsewhere. As I have told you, we are peaceful men who trade with these people, and do not wish to be involved in a quarrel with them, which might expose us to attack or bring us into trouble with the British Government which has annexed but not conquered their country. Do I make myself clear?"

"Perfectly. While we are with you we will do nothing, but afterwards we hold ourselves at liberty to act as we think best."

"Quite so. Meanwhile I hope that you and Mr. Anscombe will make yourselves comfortable with us for as long as you like."

In my own mind I came to the conclusion that this would be for the shortest time possible, but I only said—

"It is most kind of you to take in complete strangers thus. No, not complete," I added, looking towards Anscombe who was following on the tired horse a few paces behind, "for you knew his father, did you not?"

"His father?" he said, lifting his eyebrows. "No. Oh! I remember, I said something to that effect the other night, but it was a mistake. I mixed up two names, as one often does after a lapse of many years."

"I understand," I answered, but remembering Anscombe's story I reflected to myself that our venerable host was an excellent liar. Or more probably he meant to convey that he wished the subject of his youthful reminiscences to be taboo.

Just then we reached the house which had a pretty patch of well-kept flower-garden in front of it, surrounded by a fence covered with wire netting to keep out buck. By the gate squatted our three retainers, looking very blown and rather ashamed of themselves.

"Your master wishes to thank you for your help in a dark hour, Footsack, and I wish to congratulate you all upon the swiftness of your feet," I said in Dutch.

"Oh! Baas, the Basutos were many and their spears are sharp," he began apologetically.

"Be silent, you running dog," I said, "and go help your master to dismount."

Then we went through the gate, Anscombe leaning on my shoulder and on that of Mr. Marnham, and up the path which was bordered with fences of the monthly rose, towards the house. Really this was almost as charming to look at near at hand as it had been from far away. Of course the whole thing was crude in detail. Rough, half-shaped blocks of marble from the neighbouring quarry had been built into walls and columns. Nothing was finished, and considered bit by bit all was coarse and ugly. Yet the general effect was beautiful because it was an effect of design, the picture of an artist who did not fully understand the technicalities of painting, the work of a great writer who had as yet no proper skill in words. Never did I see a small building that struck me more. But then what experience have I of buildings, and, as Anscombe reminded me afterwards, it was but a copy of something designed when the world was young, or rather when civilization was young, and man new risen from the infinite ages of savagery, saw beauty in his dreams and tried to symbolize it in shapes of stone.

We came to the broad *stoep*, to which several rough blocks of marble served as steps. On it in a long chair made of native wood and seated with hide *rimpis*, sat or rather lolled a man in a dressing-gown who was reading a book. He raised himself as we came and the light of the sun, for the veranda faced to the east, shone full upon his face, so that I saw him well. It was that of a man of something under forty years of age, dark, powerful, and weary—not a good face, I thought. Indeed, it gave me the impression of one who had allowed the evil which exists in the nature of all of us to become his master, or had even encouraged it to do so.

In the Psalms and elsewhere we are always reading of the righteous and the unrighteous until those terms grow wearisome. It is only of late years that I have discovered, or think that I have discovered, what they mean. Our lives cannot be judged by our deeds; they must be judged by our desires or rather by our moral attitude. It is not what we do so much as what we try to do that counts in the formation of character. All fall short, all fail, but in the end those who seek to climb out of the pit, those who strive, however vainly, to fashion failure to

50

success, are, by comparison, the righteous, while those who are content to wallow in our native mire and to glut themselves with the daily bread of vice, are the unrighteous. To turn our backs thereon wilfully and without cause, is the real unforgiveable sin against the Spirit. At least that is the best definition of the problem at which I in my simplicity can arrive.

Such thoughts have often occurred to me in considering the character of Dr. Rodd and some others whom I have known; indeed the germ of them arose in my mind which, being wearied at the time and therefore somewhat vacant, was perhaps the more open to external impressions, as I looked upon the face of this stranger on the *stoep*. Moreover, as I am proud to record, I did not judge him altogether wrongly. He was a blackguard who, under other influences or with a few added grains of self-restraint and of the power of recovery, might have become a good or even a saintly man. But by some malice of Fate or some evil inheritance from an unknown past, those grains were lacking, and therefore he went not up but down the hill.

"Case for you, Rodd," called out Marnham.

"Indeed," he answered, getting to his feet and speaking in a full voice, which, like his partner's, was that of an educated Englishman. "What's the matter. Horse accident?"

Then we were introduced, and Anscombe began to explain his injury.

"Um!" said the doctor, studying him with dark eyes. "*Kaffir* bullet through the foot some days ago. Ought to be attended to at once. Also you look pretty done, so don't tire yourself with the story, which I can get from Mr. Quatermain. Come and lie down and I'll have a look at you while they are cooking breakfast."

Then he guided us to a room of which the double French windows opened on to the *stoep*, a very pretty room with two beds in it. Making Anscombe lie down on one of these he turned up his trouser, undid my rough bandage and examined the wound.

"Painful?" he asked.

"Very," answered Anscombe, "right up to the thigh."

After this he drew off the nether garments and made a further examination.

"Um," he said again, "I must syringe this out. Stay still while I get some stuff."

I followed him from the room, and when we were out of hearing on the *stoep* inquired what he thought. I did not like the look of that leg.

51

"It is very bad," he answered, "so bad that I am wondering if it wouldn't be best to remove the limb below the knee and make it a job. You can see for yourself that it is septic and the inflammation is spreading up rapidly."

"Good Heavens!" I exclaimed, "do you fear mortification?"

He nodded. "Can't say what was on that slug or bit of old iron and he hasn't had the best chance since. Mortification, or tetanus, or both, are more than possible. Is he a temperate man?"

"So far as I know," I answered, and stared at him while he thought. Then he said with decision,

"That makes a difference. To lose a foot is a serious thing; some might think almost as bad as death. I'll give him a chance, but if those symptoms do not abate in twenty-four hours, I must operate. You needn't be afraid, I was house surgeon at a London Hospital—once, and I keep my hand in. Lucky you came straight here."

Having made his preparations and washed his hands, he returned, syringed the wound with some antiseptic stuff, and dressed and bandaged the leg up to the knee. After this he gave Anscombe hot milk to drink, with two eggs broken into it, and told him to rest a while as he must not eat anything solid at present. Then he threw a blanket over him, and, signing to me to come away, let down a mat over the window.

"I put a little something into that milk," he said outside, "which will send him to sleep for a few hours. So we will leave him quiet. Now you'll want a wash."

"Where are you going to take Mr. Quatermain?" asked Marnham who was seated on the *stoep*.

"Into my room," he answered.

"Why? There's Heda's ready."

"Heda might return at any moment," replied the doctor. "Also Mr. Quatermain had better sleep in Mr. Anscombe's room. He will very likely want some one to look after him at night."

Marnham opened his mouth to speak again, then changed his mind and was silent, as a servant is silent under rebuke. The incident was quite trifling, yet it revealed to me the relative attitude of these two men. Without a doubt Rodd was the master of his partner, who did not even care to dispute with him about the matter of the use of his daughter's bedroom. They were a queer couple who, had it not been for my anxiety as to Anscombe's illness, would have interested me very much, as indeed they were destined to do.

Well, I went to tidy up in the doctor's room, and as he left me alone while I washed, had the opportunity of studying it a little. Like

52

the rest of the house it was lined with native wood which was made to serve as the backs of bookshelves and of cupboards filled with medicines and instruments. The books formed a queer collection. There were medical works, philosophical works, histories, novels, most of them French, and other volumes of a sort that I imagine are generally kept under lock and key; also some that had to do with occult matters. There was even a Bible. I opened it thoughtlessly, half in idle curiosity, to see whether it was ever used, only to replace it in haste. For at the very page that my eye fell on, I remember it was one of my favourite chapters in Isaiah, was a stamp in violet ink marked H. M.'s Prison—well, I won't say where.

I may state, however, that the clue enabled me in after years to learn an episode in this man's life which had brought about his ruin. There is no need to repeat it or to say more than that gambling and an evil use of his medical knowledge to provide the money to pay his debts, were the cause of his fall. The strange thing is that he should have kept the book which had probably been given to him by the prison chaplain. Still everybody makes mistakes sometimes. Or it may have had associations for him, and of course he had never seen this stamp upon an unread page, which happened to leap to my eye.

Now I was able to make a shrewd guess at his later career. After his trouble he had emigrated and began to practise in South Africa. Somehow his identity had been discovered; his past was dragged up against him, possibly by rivals jealous of his skill; his business went and he found it advisable to retire to the Transvaal before the Annexation, at that time the home of sundry people of broken repute. Even there he did not stop in a town, but hid himself upon the edge of savagery. Here he foregathered with another man of queer character, Marnham, and in his company entered upon some doubtful but lucrative form of trade while still indulging his love of medicine by doctoring and operating upon natives, over whom he would in this way acquire great influence. Indeed, as I discovered before the day was over, he had quite a little hospital at the back of the house in which were four or five beds occupied by *Kaffirs* and served by two male native nurses whom he had trained. Also numbers of out-patients visited him, some of whom travelled from great distances, and occasionally, but not often, he attended white people who chanced to be in the neighbourhood.

The three of us breakfasted in a really charming room from the window of which could be studied a view as beautiful as any I know. The *Kaffirs* who waited were well trained and dressed in neat linen uniforms. The cooking was good; there was real silver on the table, then a strange sight in that part of Africa, and amongst engravings and other pictures upon the walls, hung an oil portrait of a very beautiful young woman with dark hair and eyes.

"Is that your daughter, Mr. Marnham?" I asked.

"No," he replied rather shortly, "it is her mother."

Immediately afterwards he was called from the room to speak to some one, whereon the doctor said—

"A foreigner as you see, a Hungarian; the Hungarian women are very good looking and very charming."

"So I have understood," I answered, "but does this lady live here?"

"Oh, no. She is dead, or I believe that she is dead. I am not sure, because I make it a rule never to pry into people's private affairs. All I know about her is that she was a beauty whom Marnham married late in life upon the Continent when she was but eighteen. As is common in such cases he was very jealous of her, but it didn't last long, as she died, or I understand that she died, within a year of her daughter's birth. The loss affected him so much that he emigrated to South Africa with the child and began life anew. I do not think that they correspond with Hungary, and he never speaks of her even to his daughter, which suggests that she is dead."

I reflected that all these circumstances might equally well suggest several other things, but said nothing, thinking it wisest not to pursue the subject. Presently Marnham returned and informed me that a native had just brought him word that the Basutos had made off homeward with our cattle, but had left the wagon and its contents quite untouched, not even stealing the spare guns and ammunition.

"That's luck," I said, astonished, "but extremely strange. How do you explain it, Mr. Marnham?"

He shrugged his shoulders and answered—

"As every one knows, you are a much greater expert in native habits and customs than I am, Mr. Quatermain."

"There are only two things that I can think of," I said. "One is that for some reason or other they thought the wagon *tagati*, bewitched you know, and that it would bring evil on them to touch it, though this did not apply to the oxen. The other is that they supposed it, but not the oxen, to belong to some friend of their own whose property they did not wish to injure."

He looked at me sharply but said nothing, and I went on to tell them the details of the attack that had been made upon us, adding—

"The odd part of the affair is that one of those Basutos called out to us that some infernal scoundrel of a white had warned Sekukuni of our coming and that he had ordered them to take our guns and cattle. This Basuto, who was wounded and praying for mercy, was drowned before he could tell me who the white man was."

"A Boer, I expect," said Marnham quietly. "As you know they are not particularly well affected towards us English just now. Also I happen to be aware that some of them are intriguing with Sekukuni against the British through Makurupiji, his 'Mouth' or prime-minister, a very clever old scamp who likes to have two stools to sit on."

"And doubtless will end by falling between them. Well, you see, now that I think of it, the wounded *Kaffir* only said that they were ordered to take our guns and oxen, and incidentally our lives. The wagon was not mentioned."

"Quite so, Mr. Quatermain. I will send some of our boys to help your servants to bring everything it contains up here."

"Can't you lend me a team of oxen," I asked, "to drag it to the house?"

"No, we have nothing but young cattle left. Both red-water and lung-sickness have been so bad this season that all the horned stock have been swept out of the country. I doubt whether you could beg, borrow or steal a team of oxen this side of Pretoria, except from some of the Dutchmen who won't part."

"That's awkward. I hoped to be able to trek in a day or two."

"Your friend won't be able to trek for a good many days at the best," broke in the doctor, who had been listening unconcernedly, "but of course you could get away on the horse after it has rested."

"You told me you left a span of oxen at Pretoria," said Marnham. "Why not go and fetch them here, or if you don't like to leave Mr. Anscombe, send your driver and the boys."

"Thanks for the idea. I will think it over," I answered.

That morning after Footsack and the *voorlooper* had been sent with some of the servants from the Temple to fetch up the contents of the wagon, for I was too tired to accompany them, having found that Anscombe was still asleep, I determined to follow his example. Finding a long chair on the *stoep*, I sat down and slumbered in it sweetly for hours. I dreamt of all sorts of things, then through my dreams it seemed to me that I heard two voices talking, those of our Marnham and Rodd, not on the *stoep*, but at a distance from it. As a matter of fact they were talking, but so far away that in my ordinary waking state I could never have heard them. My own belief is that the senses, and I may add the semi-spiritual part of us, are much more acute when we lie half bound in the bonds of sleep, than when we are what is called wide awake. Doubtless when we are quite bound they attain the limits of their power and, I think, sail at times to the uttermost ends of being. But unhappily of their experiences we remember nothing when we awake. In half sleep it is different; then we do retain some recollection.

In this curious condition of mind it seemed to me that Rodd said to Marnham—

"Why have you brought these men here?"

"I did not bring them here," he answered. "Luck, Fate, Fortune, God or the Devil, call it what you will, brought them here, though if you had your wish, it is true they would never have come. Still, as they have come, I am glad. It is something to me, living in this hell, to get a chance of talking to English gentlemen again before I die."

"English gentlemen," remarked Rodd reflectively, "Well, Anscombe is of course, but how about that other hunter? After all, in what way is he better than the scores of other hunters and *Kaffir* traders and wanderers whom one meets in this strange land?"

"In what way indeed?" thought I to myself, in my dream.

"If you can't see, I can't explain to you. But as I happen to know, the man is of blood as good as mine—and a great deal better than yours," he added with a touch of insolence. "Moreover, he has an honest name among white and black, which is much in this country."

"Yes," replied the doctor in the same reflective voice, "I agree with you, I let him pass as a gentleman. But I repeat, Why did you bring them here when with one more word it would have been so easy—" and he stopped.

"I have told you, it was not I. What are you driving at?"

"Do you think it is exactly convenient, especially when we are under the British flag again, to have two people who, we both admit, are English gentlemen, that is, clean, clear-eyed men, considering us and our affairs for an indefinite period, just because you wish for the pleasure of their society? Would it not have been better to tell those Basutos to let them trek on to Pretoria?"

"I don't know what would have been better. I repeat, what are you driving at?

"Heda is coming home in a day or two; she might be here any time," remarked Rodd as he knocked the ashes out of his pipe.

"Yes, because you made me write and say that I wanted her. But what of that?"

"Nothing in particular, except that I am not sure that I wish her to associate with 'an English gentleman' like this Anscombe."

Marnham laughed scornfully. "Ah! I understand," he said. "Too clean and straight. Complications might ensue and the rest of it. Well, I wish to God they would, for I know the Anscombes, or used to, and I know the genus called Rodd."

"Don't be insulting; you may carry the thing too far one day, and whatever I have done I have paid for. But you've not paid—yet."

"The man is very ill. You are a skilled doctor. If you're afraid of him, why don't you kill him?" asked Marnham with bitter scorn.

"There you have me," replied Rodd. "Men may shed much, but most of them never shed their professional honour. I shall do my honest best to cure Mr. Anscombe, and I tell you that he will take some curing."

Then I woke up, and as no one was in sight, wondered whether or no I had been dreaming. The upshot of it was that I made up my mind to send Footsack to Pretoria for the oxen, not to go myself.

CHAPTER 5

A Game of Cards

I slept in Anscombe's room that night and looked after him. He was very feverish and the pain in his leg kept him awake a good deal. He told me that he could not bear Dr. Rodd and wished to get away at once. I had to explain to him that this was impossible until his spare oxen arrived which I was going to send for to Pretoria, but of other matters, including that of the dangerous state of his foot, I said nothing. I was thankful when towards two in the morning, he fell into a sound sleep and allowed me to do the same.

Before breakfast time, just as I had finished dressing myself in some of the clean things which had been brought from the wagon, Rodd came and made a thorough and business-like examination of his patient, while I awaited the result with anxiety on the *stoep*. At length he appeared and said—

"Well, I think that we shall be able to save the foot, though I can't be quite sure for another twenty-four hours. The worst symptoms have abated and his temperature is down by two degrees. Anyway he will have to stay in bed and live on light food till it is normal, after which he might lie in a long chair on the *stoep*. On no account must he attempt to stand."

I thanked him for his information heartily enough and asked him if he knew where Marnham was, as I wanted to speak to him with reference to the despatch of Footsack to fetch the oxen from Pretoria.

"Not up yet, I think," he answered. "I fancy that yesterday was one of his 'wet' nights, excitement of meeting strangers and so on."

"Wet nights?" I queried, wishing for a clearer explanation.

"Yes, he is a grand old fellow, one of the best, but like most other people he has his little weaknesses, and when the fit is on him he can put away a surprising amount of liquor. I tell you so that you should not be astonished if you notice anything, or try to argue with him

58

when he is in that state, as then his temper is apt to be—well, lively. Now I must go and give him a pint of warm milk; that is his favourite antidote, and in fact the best there is."

I thought to myself that we had struck a nice establishment in which to be tied, literally by the leg, for an indefinite period. I was not particularly flush at the time, but I know I would have paid a £100 to be out of it; before the end I should have been glad to throw in everything that I had. But mercifully that was hidden from me.

Rodd and I breakfasted together and discoursed of *Kaffir* customs, as to which he was singularly well informed. Then I accompanied him to see his native patients in the little hospital of which I have spoken. Believing the man to be a thorough scamp as I did, it was astonishing to me to note how gentle and forbearing he was to these people. Of his skill I need say nothing, as that was evident. He was going to perform an internal operation upon a burly old savage, rather a serious one I believe; at any rate it necessitated chloroform. He asked me if I would like to assist, but I declined respectfully, having no taste for such things. So I left him boiling his instruments and putting on what looked like a clean nightgown over his clothes, and returned to the *stoep*.

Here I found Marnham, whose eyes were rather bloodshot, though otherwise, except for a shaky hand, he seemed right enough. He murmured something about having overslept himself and inquired very politely, for his manners were beautiful, after Anscombe and as to whether we were quite comfortable and so forth. After this I consulted him as to the best road for our servants to travel by to Pretoria, and later on despatched them, giving Footsack various notes to ensure the delivery of the oxen to him. Also I gave him some money to pay for their keep and told him with many threats to get back with the beasts as quick as he could travel. Then I sent him and the two other boys off, not without misgivings, although he was an experienced man in his way and promised faithfully to fulfil every injunction to the letter. To me he seemed so curiously glad to go that I inquired the reason, since after a journey like ours, it would have been more natural if he had wished to rest.

"Oh! Baas," he said, "I don't think this Tampel very healthy for coloured people. I am told of some who have died here. That man Karl who gave me the diamond, I think he must have died also, at least I saw his spook last night standing over me and shaking his head, and the boys saw it too."

"Oh! be off with your talk of spooks," I said, "and come back quickly with those oxen, or I promise you that you will die and be a spook yourself."

"I will, Baas, I will!" he ejaculated and departed almost at a run, leaving me rather uncomfortable.

I believed nothing of the tale of the spook of Karl, but I saw that Footsack believed in it, and was afraid lest he might be thereby prevented from returning. I would much rather have gone myself, but it was impossible for me to leave Anscombe so ill in the hands of our strange hosts. And there was no one else whom I could send. I might perhaps have ridden to Pilgrim's Rest and tried to find a white messenger there; indeed afterwards I regretted not having done so, although it would have involved at least a day's absence at a very critical time. But the truth is I never thought of it until too late, and probably if I had, I should not have been able to discover anyone whom I could trust.

As I walked back to the house, having parted from Footsack on the top of a neighbouring ridge whence I could point out his path to him, I met Marnham riding away. He pulled up and said that he was going down to the Granite Stream to arrange about setting some one up to watch the wagon. I expressed sorrow that he should have the trouble, which should have been mine if I could have got away, whereon he answered that he was glad of the opportunity for a ride, as it was something to do.

"How do you fill in your time here," I asked carelessly, "as you don't farm?"

"Oh! by trading," he replied, and with a nod set his horse to a canter.

A queer sort of trading, thought I to myself, where there is no store. Now what exactly does he trade in, I wonder?

As it happened I was destined to find out before I was an hour older. Having given Anscombe a look and found that he was comfortable, I thought that I would inspect the quarry whence the marble came of which the house was built, as it had occurred to me that if there was plenty of it, it might be worth exploiting some time in the future. It had been pointed out to me in the midst of some thorns in a gully that ran at right angles to the main *kloof* not more than a few hundred yards from the house. Following a path over which the stones had been dragged originally, I came to the spot and discovered that a little cavity had been quarried in what seemed to me to be a positive mountain of pure white marble. I examined the place as thoroughly as I could, climbing among some bushes that grew in surface earth which had been washed down from the top, in order to do so.

At the back of these bushes there was a hole large enough for a man to creep through. I crept through with the object of ascertaining whether the marble veins continued. To my surprise I found a stout yellow-wood door within feet of the mouth of the hole. Reflecting that no doubt it was here that the quarrymen kept, or had kept tools and explosives, I gave it a push. I suppose it had been left unfastened accidentally, or that something had gone wrong with the lock; at any rate it swung open. Pursuing my researches as to the depth of the marble I advanced boldly and, the place being dark, struck a match. Evidently the marble did continue, as I could see by the glittering roof of a cavern, for such it was. But the floor attracted my attention as well as the roof, for on it were numerous cases not unlike coffins, bearing the stamp of a well-known Birmingham firm, labelled *fencing iron* and addressed to Messrs. Marnham & Rodd, Transvaal, *via* Delagoa Bay.

I knew at once what they were, having seen the like before, but if any doubt remained in my mind it was easy to solve, for as it chanced one of the cases was open and half emptied. I slipped my hand into it. As I thought it contained the ordinary *Kaffir* gun of commerce, cost delivered in Africa, say 35s.; cost delivered to native chief in cash or cattle, say £10, which, when the market is eager, allows for a decent profit. Contemplating those cases, survivors probably of a much larger stock, I understood how it came about that Sekukuni had dared to show fight against the Government. Doubtless it was hence that the guns had come which sent a bullet through Anscombe's foot and nearly polished off both of us.

Moreover, as further matches showed me, that cave contained other stores—item, kegs of gunpowder; item, casks of cheap spirit; item, bars of lead, also a box marked *bullet moulds* and another marked *percussion caps*. I think, too, there were some innocent bags full of beads and a few packages of Birmingham-made *assegai* blades. There may have been other things, but if so I did not wait to investigate them. Gathering up the ends of my matches and, in case there should be any dust in the place that would show footmarks, flapping the stone floor behind me with my pocket handkerchief, I retired and continued my investigations of that wonderful marble deposit from the bottom of the quarry, to which, having re-arranged the bushes, I descended by another route, leaping like a buck from stone to stone.

It was just as well that I did so, for a few minutes later Dr. Rodd appeared.

"Made a good job of your operation?" I asked cheerfully.

"Pretty fair, thanks," he answered, "although that *Kaffir* tried to brain the nurse-man when he was coming out of the anaesthetic. But are you interested in geology?"

"A little," I replied, "that is if there is any chance of making money out of it, which there ought to be here, as this marble looks almost as good as that of Carrara. But flint instruments are more my line, that is in an ignorant and amateur way, as I think they are in yours, for I saw some in your room. Tell me, what do you think of this. Is it a scraper?" and I produced a stone out of my pocket which I had found a week before in the bush-*veld*.

At once he forgot his suspicions, of which I could see he arrived very full indeed. This curious man, as it happened, was really fond of flint instruments, of which he knew a great deal.

"Did you find this here?" he asked.

I led him several yards further from the mouth of the cave and pointed out the exact spot where I said I had picked it up amongst some quarry debris. Then followed a most learned discussion, for it appeared that this was a flint instrument of the rarest and most valuable type, one that Noah might have used, or Job might have scraped himself with, and the question was how the dickens had it come among that quarry debris. In the end we left the problem undecided, and having presented the article to Dr. Rodd, a gift for which he thanked me with real warmth, I returned to the house filled with the glow that rewards one who has made a valuable discovery.

Of the following three days I have nothing particular to say, except that during them I was perhaps more acutely bored than ever I had been in my life before. The house was beautiful in its own fashion; the food was excellent; there was everything I could want to drink, and Rodd announced that he no longer feared the necessity of operation upon Anscombe's leg. His recovery was now a mere matter of time, and meanwhile he must not use his foot or let the blood run into it more than could be helped, which meant that he must keep himself in a recumbent position. The trouble was that I had nothing on earth do except study the characters of our hosts, which I found disagreeable and depressing. I might have gone out shooting, but nothing of the sort was allowed upon the property in obedience to the wish of Miss Heda, a mysterious young person who was always expected and never appeared, and beyond it I was afraid to travel for fear of Basutos. I might have gone to Pilgrim's Rest or Lydenburg to make report of the nefarious deeds of the said Basutos, but at best it would have taken one or two days, and possibly I should have been detained by officials who never consider any one's time except their own.

This meant that I should have been obliged to leave Anscombe alone, which I did not wish to do, so I just sat still and, as I have said, was intensely bored, hanging about the place and smoking more than was good for me.

In due course Anscombe emerged on to the *stoep*, where he lay with his leg up, and was also bored, especially after he had tried to pump old Marnham about his past in the Guards and completely failed. It was in this mood of utter dejection that we agreed to play a game of cards one evening. Not that either of us cared for cards; indeed, personally, I have always detested them because, with various-coloured counters to represent money which never passed, they had formed one of the afflictions of my youth.

It was so annoying if you won, to be handed a number of green counters and be informed that they represented so many hundreds or thousands of pounds, or *vice-versa* if you lost, for as it cost no one anything, my dear father insisted upon playing for enormous stakes. Never in any aspect of life have I cared for fooling. Anscombe also disliked cards, I think because his ancestors too had played with counters, such as some that I have seen belonging to the Cocoa-Tree Club and other gambling places of a past generation, marked as high as a thousand guineas, which counters must next morning be redeemed in hard cash, whereby his family had been not a little impoverished.

"I fancy you will find they are high-fliers," he said when the pair had left to fetch a suitable table, for the night being very hot we were going to play on the *stoep* by the light of the hanging paraffin lamp and some candles. I replied to the effect that I could not afford to lose large sums of money, especially to men who for aught I knew might then be engaged in marking the cards.

"I understand," he answered. "Don't you bother about that, old fellow. This is my affair, arranged for my special amusement. I shan't grumble if the fun costs something, for I am sure there will be fun."

"All right," I said, "only if we should happen to win money, it's yours, not mine."

To myself I reflected, however, that with these two opponents we had about as much chance of winning as a snowflake has of resisting the atmosphere of the lower regions.

Presently they returned with the table, which had a green cloth over it that hung down half-way to the ground. Also one of the native boys brought a tray with spirits, from which I judged by various signs, old Marnham, who had already drunk his share at dinner, had helped himself freely on the way. Soon we were arranged, Anscombe, who was to be my partner, opposite to me in his long chair, and the game began.

I forget what particular variant of cards it was we played, though I know it admitted of high and progressive stakes. At first, however, these were quite moderate and we won, as I suppose we were meant to do. After half an hour or so Marnham rose to help himself to brandy and water, a great deal of brandy and very little water, while I took a nip of Hollands, and Anscombe and Rodd filled their pipes.

"I think this is getting rather slow," said Rodd to Anscombe. "I vote we put a bit more on."

"As much as you like," answered Anscombe with a little drawl and twinkle of the eye, which always showed that he was amused. "Both Quatermain and I are born gamblers. Don't look angry, Quatermain, you know you are. Only if we lose you will have to take a cheque, for I have precious little cash."

"I think that will be good enough," replied the doctor quietly—"if you lose."

So the stakes were increased to an amount that made my hair stand up stiffer even than usual, and the game went on. Behold! a marvel came to pass. How it happened I do not know, unless Marnham had brought the wrong cards by mistake or had grown too fuddled to understand his partner's telegraphic signals, which I, being accustomed to observe, saw him make, not once but often, still we won! What is more, with a few set-backs, we went on winning, till presently the sums written down to our credit, for no actual cash passed, were considerable. And all the while, at the end of each bout Marnham helped himself to more brandy, while the doctor grew more mad in a suppressed-thunder kind of a way. For my part I became alarmed, especially as I perceived that Anscombe was on the verge of breaking into open merriment, and his legs being up I could not kick him under the table.

"My partner ought to go to bed. Don't you think we should stop?" I said.

"On the whole I do," replied Rodd, glowering at Marnham, who, somewhat unsteadily, was engaged in wiping drops of brandy from his long beard.

"D——d if I do," exclaimed that worthy. "When I was young and played with gentlemen they always gave losers an opportunity of revenge."

"Then," replied Anscombe with a flash of his eyes, "let us try to follow in the footsteps of the gentlemen with whom you played in your youth. I suggest that we double the stakes."

"That's right! That's the old form!" said Marnham.

The doctor half rose from his chair, then sat down again. Watching him, I concluded that he believed his partner, a seasoned vessel, was not so drunk as he pretended to be, and either in an actual or a figurative sense, had a card up his sleeve. If so, it remained there, for again we won; all the luck was with us.

"I am getting tired," drawled Anscombe. "Lemon and water are not sustaining. Shall we stop?"

"By Heaven! no," shouted Marnham, to which Anscombe replied that if it was wished, he would play another hand, but no more.

"All right," said Marnham, "but let it be for double or quits."

He spoke quite quietly and seemed suddenly to have grown sober. Now I think that Rodd made up his mind that he really was acting and that he really had that card up his sleeve. At any rate he did not object. I, however, was of a different opinion, having often seen drunken men succumb to an access of sobriety under the stress of excitement and remarked that it did not last long.

"Do you really mean that?" I said, speaking for the first time and addressing myself to the doctor. "I don't quite know what the sum involved is, but it must be large."

"Of course," he answered.

Then remembering that at the worst Anscombe stood to lose nothing, I shrugged my shoulders and held my tongue. It was Marnham's deal, and although he was somewhat in the shadow of the hanging lamp and the candles had guttered out, I distinctly saw him play some hocus-pocus with the cards, but in the circumstances made no protest. As it chanced he must have hocus-pocused them wrong, for though *his* hand was full of trumps, Rodd held nothing at all. The battle that ensued was quite exciting, but the end of it was that an ace in the hand of Anscombe, who really was quite a good player, did the business, and we won again.

In the rather awful silence that followed Anscombe remarked in his cheerful drawl—

"I'm not sure that my addition is quite right; we'll check that in the morning, but I make out that you two gentlemen owe Quatermain and myself £749 10s."

Then the doctor broke out.

"You accursed old fool," he hissed—there is no other word for it—at Marnham. "How are you going to pay all this money that you have gambled away, drunken beast that you are!"

"Easily enough, you felon," shouted Marnham. "So," and thrusting his hand into his pocket he pulled out a number of diamonds which he threw upon the table, adding, "there's what will cover it twice over, and there are more where they came from, as you know well enough, my medical jailbird."

"You dare to call me that," gasped the doctor in a voice laden with fury, so intense that it had deprived him of his reason, "you—you—murderer! Oh! why don't I kill you as I shall some day?" and lifting his glass, which was half full, he threw the contents into Marnham's face.

"That's a nice man for a prospective, son-in-law, isn't he?" exclaimed the old scamp, as, seizing the brandy decanter, he hurled it straight at Rodd's head, only missing him by an inch.

"Don't you think you had both better go to bed, gentlemen?" I inquired. "You are saying things you might regret in the morning."

Apparently they did think it, for without another word they rose and marched off in different directions to their respective rooms, which I heard both of them lock. For my part I collected the I.O.U.'s; also the diamonds which still lay upon the table, while Anscombe examined the cards.

"Marked, by Jove!" he said. "Oh! my dear Quatermain, never have I had such an amusing evening in all my life."

"Shut up, you silly idiot," I answered. "There'll be murder done over this business, and I only hope it won't be on us."

CHAPTER 6

Miss Heda

It might be thought that after all this there would have been a painful explanation on the following morning, but nothing of the sort happened. After all the greatest art is the art of ignoring things, without which the world could scarcely go on, even among the savage races. Thus on this occasion the two chief actors in the scene of the previous night pretended that they had forgotten what took place, as I believe, to a large extent truly. The fierce flame of drink in the one and of passion in the other had burnt the web of remembrance to ashes. They knew that something unpleasant had occurred and its main outlines; the rest had vanished away; perhaps because they knew also that they were not responsible for what they said and did, and therefore that what occurred had no right to a permanent niche in their memories. It was, as it were, something outside of their normal selves. At least so I conjectured, and their conduct seemed to give colour to my guess.

The doctor spoke to me of the matter first.

"I fear there was a row last night," he said; "it has happened here before over cards, and will no doubt happen again until matters clear themselves up somehow. Marnham, as you see, drinks, and when drunk is the biggest liar in the world, and I, I am sorry to say, am cursed with a violent temper. Don't judge either of us too harshly. If you were a doctor you would know that all these things come to us with our blood, and we didn't fashion our own clay, did we? Have some coffee, won't you?"

Subsequently when Rodd wasn't there, Marnham spoke also and with that fine air of courtesy which was peculiar to him.

"I owe a deep apology," he said, "to yourself and Mr. Anscombe. I do not recall much about it, but I know there was a scene last night over those cursed cards. A weakness overtakes me sometimes. I will

67

say no more, except that you, who are also a man who perhaps have felt weaknesses of one sort or another, will, I hope, make allowances for me and pay no attention to anything that I may have said or done in the presence of guests; yes, that is what pains me—in the presence of guests."

Something in his distinguished manner caused me to reflect upon every peccadillo that I had ever committed, setting it in its very worst light.

"Quite so," I answered, "quite so. Pray do not mention the matter any more, although—"These words seemed to jerk themselves out of my throat, "you did call each other by such very hard names."

"I daresay," he answered with a vacant smile, "but if so they meant nothing."

"No, I understand, just like a lovers' quarrel. But look here, you left some diamonds on the table which I took to keep the *Kaffirs* out of temptation. I will fetch them."

"Did I? Well, probably I left some I.O.U.'s also which might serve for pipe-lights. So suppose we set the one against the other. I don't know the value of either the diamonds or the pipe-lights, it may be less or more, but for God's sake don't let me see the beastly things again. There's no need, I have plenty."

"I must speak to Anscombe," I answered. "The money at stake was his, not mine."

"Speak to whom you will," he replied, and I noted that the throbbing vein upon his forehead indicated a rising temper. "But never let me see those diamonds again. Throw them into the gutter if you wish, but never let me see them again, or there will be trouble." hen he flung out of the room, leaving his breakfast almost untasted.

Reflecting that this queer old bird probably did not wish to be cross-questioned as to his possession of so many uncut diamonds, or that they were worth much less than the sum he had lost, or possibly that they were not diamonds at all but glass, I went to report the matter to Anscombe. He only laughed and said that as I had got the things I had better keep them until something happened, for we had both got it into our heads that something would happen before we had done with that establishment.

So I went to put the stones away as safely as I could. While I was doing so I heard the rumble of wheels, and came out just in time to see a Cape cart, drawn by four very good horses and driven by a Hottentot in a smart hat and a red waistband, pull up at the garden gate. Out of this cart presently emerged a neatly dressed lady, of whom all

I could see was that she was young, slender and rather tall; also, as her back was towards me, that she had a great deal of auburn hair.

"There!" said Anscombe. "I knew that something would happen. Heda has happened. Quatermain, as neither her venerated parent nor her loving fiancé, for such I gather he is, seems to be about, you had better go and give her a hand."

I obeyed with a groan, heartily wishing that Heda hadn't happened, since some sense warned me that she would only add to the present complications. At the gate, having given some instructions to a very stout young coloured woman who, I took it, was her maid, about a basket of flower roots in the cart, she turned round suddenly and we came face to face with the gate between us. For a moment we stared at each other, I reflecting that she really was very pretty with her delicately-shaped features, her fresh, healthy-looking complexion, her long dark eyelashes and her lithe and charming figure. What she reflected about me I don't know, probably nothing half so complimentary. Suddenly, however, her large greyish eyes grew troubled and a look of alarm appeared upon her face.

"Is anything wrong with my father?" she asked. "I don't see him."

"If you mean Mr. Marnham," I replied, lifting my hat, "I believe that Dr. Rodd and he—"

"Never mind about Dr. Rodd," she broke in with a contemptuous little jerk of her chin, "how is my father?"

"I imagine much as usual. He and Dr. Rodd were here a little while ago, I suppose that they have gone out" (as a matter of fact they had, but in different directions).

"Then that's all right," she said with a sigh of relief. "You see, I heard that he was very ill, which is why I have come back."

So, thought I to myself, she loves that old scamp and she—doesn't love the doctor. There will be more trouble as sure as five and two are seven. All we wanted was a woman to make the pot boil over.

Then I opened the gate and took a travelling bag from her hand with my politest bow.

"My name is Quatermain and that of my friend Anscombe. We are staying here, you know," I said rather awkwardly.

"Indeed," she answered with a delightful smile, "what a very strange place to choose to stay in."

"It is a beautiful house," I remarked.

"Not bad, although I designed it, more or less. But I was alluding to its inhabitants."

This finished me, and I am sure she felt that I could think of nothing nice to say about those inhabitants, for I heard her sigh. We walked side by side up the rose-fringed path and presently arrived at the *stoep*, where Anscombe, whose hair I had cut very nicely on the previous day, was watching us from his long chair. They looked at each other, and I saw both of them colour a little, out of mere foolishness, I suppose.

"Anscombe," I said, "this is——" and I paused, not being quite certain whether she also was called Marnham. "Heda Marnham," she interrupted.

"Yes—Miss Heda Marnham, and this is the Honourable Maurice Anscombe."

"Forgive me for not rising, Miss Marnham," said Anscombe in his pleasant voice (by the way hers was pleasant too, full and rather low, with just a suggestion of something foreign about it). "A shot through the foot prevents me at present."

"Who shot you?" she asked quickly.

"Oh! only a *Kaffir*."

"I am so sorry, I hope you will get well soon. Forgive me now, I must go to look for my father."

"She is uncommonly pretty," remarked Anscombe, "and a lady into the bargain. In reflecting on old Marnham's sins we must put it to his credit that he has produced a charming daughter."

"Too pretty and charming by half," I grunted.

"Perhaps Dr. Rodd is of the same way of thinking. Great shame that such a girl should be handed over to a medical scoundrel like Dr. Rodd. I wonder if she cares for him?"

"Just about as much as a canary cares for a tomcat. I have found that out already."

"Really, Quatermain, you are admirable. I never knew anyone who could make a better use of the briefest opportunity."

Then we were silent, waiting, not without a certain impatience, for the return of Miss Heda. She did return with surprising quickness considering that she had found time to search for her parent, to change into a clean white dress, and to pin a single hibiscus flower on to her bodice which gave just the touch of colour that was necessary to complete her costume.

"I can't find my father," she said, "but the boys say he has gone out riding. I can't find anybody. When you have been summoned from a long way off and travelled post-haste, rather to your own inconvenience, it is amusing, isn't it?"

"Wagons and carts in South Africa don't arrive like express trains, Miss Marnham," said Anscombe, "so you shouldn't be offended."

"I am not at all offended, Mr. Anscombe. Now that I know there is nothing the matter with my father I'm—But, tell me, how did you get your wound?"

So he told her with much amusing detail after his fashion. She listened quietly with a puckered up brow and only made one comment. It was,—

"I wonder what white man told those Sekukuni *Kaffirs* that you were coming."

"I don't know," he answered, "but he deserves a bullet through him somewhere above the ankle."

"Yes, though few people get what they deserve in this wicked world."

"So I have often thought. Had it been otherwise, for example, I should have been—"

"What would you have been?" she asked, considering him curiously.

"Oh! a better shot than Mr. Allan Quatermain, and as beautiful as a lady I once saw in my youth."

"Don't talk rubbish before luncheon," I remarked sternly, and we all laughed, the first wholesome laughter that I had heard at the Temple. For this young lady seemed to bring happiness and merriment with her. I remember wondering what it was of which her coming reminded me, and concluding that it was like the sight and smell of a peach orchard in full bloom stumbled on suddenly in the black desert of the burnt winter *veld*.

After this we became quite friendly. She dilated on her skill in having produced the Temple from an old engraving, which she fetched and showed to us, at no greater an expense than it would have cost to build an ordinary house.

"That is because the marble was at hand," said Anscombe.

"Quite so," she replied demurely. "Speaking in a general sense one can do many things in life—if the marble is at hand. Only most of us when we look for marble find sandstone or mud."

"Bravo!" said Anscombe, "I have generally lit upon the sandstone."

"And I on the mud," she mused.

"And I on all three, for the earth contains marble and mud and sandstone, to say nothing of gold and jewels," I broke in, being tired of silence.

But neither of them paid much attention to me. Anscombe did say, out of politeness, I suppose, that pitch and subterranean fires should be added, or some such nonsense.

Then she began to tell him of her infantile memories of Hungary, which were extremely faint; of how they came this place and lived first of all in two large *Kaffir* huts, until suddenly they began to grow rich; of her school days at Maritzburg; of the friends with whom she had been staying, and I know not what, until at last I got up and went out for a walk.

When I returned an hour or so later they were still talking, and so continued to do until Dr. Rodd arrived upon the scene. At first they did not see him, for he stood at an angle to them, but I saw him and watched his face with a great deal of interest. It, or rather its expression, was not pleasant; before now I have seen something like it on that of a wild beast which thinks that it is about to be robbed of its prey by a stronger wild beast, in short, a mixture of hate, fear and jealousy—especially jealousy. At the last I did not wonder, for these two seemed to be getting on uncommonly well.

They were, so to speak, well matched. She, of course, was the better looking of the two, a really pretty and attractive young woman indeed, but the vivacity of Anscombe's face, the twinkle of his merry blue eyes and its general refinement made up for what he lacked—regularity of feature. I think he had just told her one of his good stories which he always managed to make so humorous by a trick of pleasing and harmless exaggeration, and they were both laughing merrily. Then she caught sight of the doctor and her merriment evaporated like a drop of water on a hot shovel. Distinctly I saw her pull herself together and prepare for something.

"How do you do?" she said rapidly, rising and holding out her slim sun-browned hand. "But I need not ask, you look so well."

"How do you do, my dear," with a heavy emphasis on the *dear* he answered slowly. "But I needn't ask, for I see that you are in perfect health and spirits," and he bent forward as though to kiss her.

Somehow or other she avoided that endearment or seal of possession. I don't quite know how, as I turned my head away, not wishing to witness what I felt to be unpleasant. When I looked up again, however, I saw that she had avoided it, the scowl on his face the demureness of hers and Anscombe's evident amusement assured me of this. She was asking about her father; he answered that he also seemed quite well.

"Then why did you write to tell me that I ought to come as he was not at all well?" she inquired, with a lifting of her delicate eyebrows.

The question was never answered, for at that moment Marnham himself appeared.

"Oh! father," she said, and rushed into his arms, while he kissed her tenderly on both cheeks.

So I was not mistaken, thought I to myself, she does really love this moral wreck, and what is more, he loves her, which shows that there must be good in him. Is anyone truly bad, I wondered, or for the matter of that, truly good either? Is it not all a question of circumstance and blood?

Neither then or at any other time have I found an answer to the problem. At any rate to me there seemed something beautiful about the meeting of these two.

The influence of Miss Heda in the house was felt at once. The boys became smarter and put on clean clothes. Vases of flowers appeared in the various rooms; ours was turned out and cleaned, a disagreeable process so far as we were concerned. Moreover, at dinner both Marnham and Rodd wore dress clothes with short jackets, a circumstance that put Anscombe and myself to shame since we had none. It was curious to see how with those dress clothes, which doubtless awoke old associations within him, Marnham changed his colour like a chameleon. Really he might have been the colonel of a cavalry regiment rising to toast the Queen after he had sent round the wine, so polite and polished was his talk. Who could have identified the man with the dry old ruffian of twenty-four hours before, he who was drinking claret (and very good claret too) mixed with water and listening with a polite interest to all the details of his daughter's journey? Even the doctor looked a gentleman, which doubtless he was once upon a time, in evening dress. Moreover, some kind of truce had been arranged. He no longer called Miss Heda "My dear" or attempted any familiarities, while she on more than one occasion very distinctly called him Dr. Rodd.

So much for that night and for several others that followed. As for the days they went by pleasantly and idly. Heda walked about on her father's arm, conversed in friendly fashion with the doctor, always watching him, I noticed, as a cat watches a dog that she knows is waiting an opportunity to spring, and for the rest associated with us as much as she could. Particularly did she seem to take refuge behind my own insignificance, having, I suppose, come to the conclusion that I was a harmless person who might possibly prove useful. But all the while I felt that the storm was banking up. Indeed Marnham himself, at any rate to a great extent, played the part of the cloud-compelling Jove, for soon it became evident to me, and without doubt to Dr. Rodd also, that he was encouraging the intimacy between his daughter and Anscombe by every means in his power.

In one way and another he had fully informed himself as to Anscombe's prospects in life, which were brilliant enough. Moreover he liked the man who, as the remnant of the better perceptions of his youth told him, was one of the best class of Englishmen, and what is more, he saw that Heda liked him also, as much indeed as she disliked Rodd. He even spoke to me of the matter in a round-about kind of fashion, saying that the young woman who married Anscombe would be lucky and that the father who had him for a son-in-law might go to his grave confident of his child's happiness. I answered that I agreed with him, unless the lady's affections had already caused her to form other ties.

"Affections!" he exclaimed, dropping all pretence, "there are none involved in this accursed business, as you are quite sharp enough to have seen for yourself."

"I understood that an engagement was involved," I remarked.

"On my part, perhaps, not on hers," he answered. "Oh! can't you understand, Quatermain, that sometimes men find themselves forced into strange situations against their will?"

Remembering the very ugly name that I had heard Rodd call Marnham on the night of the card party, I reflected that I could understand well enough, but I only said—

"After all marriage is a matter that concerns a woman even more than it does her father, one, in short, of which she must be the judge."

"Quite so, Quatermain, but there are some daughters who are prepared to make great sacrifices for their fathers. Well, she will be of age ere long, if only I can stave it off till then. But how, how?" and with a groan he turned and left me.

That old gentleman's neck is in some kind of a noose, thought I to myself, and his difficulty is to prevent the rope from being drawn tight. Meanwhile this poor girl's happiness and future are at stake.

"Allan," said Anscombe to me a little later, for by now he called me by my Christian name, "I suppose you haven't heard anything about those oxen, have you?"

"No, I could scarcely expect to yet, but why do you ask?"

He smiled in his droll fashion and replied, "Because, interesting as this household is in sundry ways, I think it is about time that we, or at any rate that I, got out of it."

"Your leg isn't fit to travel yet, Anscombe, although Rodd says that all the symptoms are very satisfactory."

"Yes, but to tell you the truth I am experiencing other symptoms quite unknown to that beloved physician and so unfamiliar to myself that I attribute them to the influences of the locality. Altitude affects the heart, does it not, and this house stands high."

"Don't play off your jokes on me," I said sternly. "What do you mean?"

"I wonder if you find Miss Heda attractive, Allan, or if you are too old. I believe there comes an age when the only beauties that can move a man are those of architecture, or scenery, or properly cooked food."

"Hang it all! I am not Methuselah," I replied; "but if you mean that you are falling in love with Heda, why the deuce don't you say so, instead of wasting my time and your own?"

"Because time was given to us to waste. Properly considered it is the best use to which it can be put, or at any rate the one that does least mischief. Also because I wished to make you say it for me that I might judge from the effect of your words whether it is or is not true. I may add that I fear the former to be the case."

"Well, if you are in love with the girl you can't expect one so ancient as myself, who is quite out of touch with such follies, to teach you how to act."

"No, Allan. Unfortunately there are occasions when one must rely upon one's own wisdom, and mine, what there is of it, tells me I had better get out of this. But I can't ride even if I took the horse and you ran behind, and the oxen haven't come."

"Perhaps you could borrow Miss Marnham's cart in which to run away from her," I suggested sarcastically.

"Perhaps, though I believe it would be fatal to my foot to sit up in a cart for the next few days, and the horses seem to have been sent off somewhere. Look here, old fellow," he went on, dropping his bantering tone, "it's rather awkward to make a fool of oneself over a lady who is engaged to some one else, especially if one suspects that with a little encouragement she might begin to walk the same road. The truth is I have taken the fever pretty bad, worse than ever I did before, and if it isn't stopped soon it will become chronic."

"Oh no, Anscombe, only intermittent at the worst, and African malaria nearly always yields to a change of climate."

"How can I expect a cynic and a misogynist to understand the simple fervour of an inexperienced soul—Oh! drat it all, Quatermain, stop your acid chaff and tell me what is to be done. Really I am in a tight place."

"Very; so tight that I rejoice to think, as you were kind enough to point out, that my years protect me from anything of the sort. I have no advice to give; I think you had better ask it of the lady."

"Well, we did have a little conversation, hypothetical of course, about some friends of ours who found themselves similarly situated, and I regret to say without result."

"Indeed. I did not know you had any mutual acquaintances. What did she say and do?"

"She said nothing, only sighed and looked as though she were going to burst into tears, and all she did was to walk away. I'd have followed her if I could, but as my crutch wasn't there it was impossible. It seemed to me that suddenly I had come up against a brick wall, that there was something on her mind which she could not or would not let out."

"Yes, and if you want to know, I will tell you what it is. Rodd has got a hold over Marnham of a sort that would bring him somewhere near the gallows. As the price of his silence Marnham has promised him his daughter. The daughter knows that her father is in this man's power, though I think she does not know in what way, and being a good girl—"

"An angel you mean—do call her by her right name, especially in a place where angels are so much wanted."

"Well, an angel if you like—she has promised on her part to marry a man she loathes in order to save her parent's bacon."

"Just what I concluded, from what we heard in the row. I wonder which of that pair is the bigger blackguard. Well, Allan, that settles it. You and I are on the side of the angel. You will have to get her out of this scrape and—if she'll have me, I'll marry her; and if she won't, why it can't be helped. Now that's a fair division of labour. How are you going to do it? I haven't an idea, and if I had, I should not presume to interfere with one so much older and wiser than myself."

"I suppose that by the time you appeared in it, the game of heads I win and tails you lose had died out of the world," I replied with an indignant snort. "I think the best thing I can do will be to take the horse and look for those oxen. Meanwhile you can settle your business by the light of your native genius, and I only hope you'll finish it without murder and sudden death."

"I say, old fellow," said Anscombe earnestly, "you don't really mean to go off and leave me in this hideousness? I haven't bothered much up to the present because I was sure that you would find a way out, which would be nothing to a man of your intellect and experience. I mean it honestly, I do indeed."

"Do you? Well, I can only say that my mind is a perfect blank, but if you will stop talking I will try to think the matter over. There's Miss Heda in the garden cutting flowers. I will go to help her, which will be a very pleasant change."

And I went, leaving him to stare after me jealously.

CHAPTER 7

The Stoep

When I reached Miss Heda she was collecting half-opened monthly roses from the hedge, and not quite knowing what to say I made the appropriate quotation. At least it was appropriate to my thought, and, from her answer, to hers also.

"Yes," she said, "I am gathering them while I may," and she sighed and, as I thought, glanced towards the veranda, though of this I could not be sure because of the wide brim of the hat she was wearing.

Then we talked a little on indifferent matters, while I pricked my fingers helping to pluck the roses. She asked me if I thought that Anscombe was getting on well, and how long it would be before he could travel. I replied that Dr. Rodd could tell her better than myself, but that I hoped in about a week.

"In a week!" she said, and although she tried to speak lightly there was dismay in her voice.

"I hope you don't think it too long," I answered; "but even if he is fit to go, the oxen have not come yet, and I don't quite know when they will."

"Too long!" she exclaimed. "Too long! Oh! if you only knew what it is to me to have such guests as you are in this place," and her dark eyes filled with tears.

By now we had passed to the side of the house in search of some other flower that grew in the shade, I think it was mignonette, and were out of sight of the veranda and quite alone.

"Mr. Quatermain," she said hurriedly, "I am wondering whether to ask your advice about something, if you would give it. I have no one to consult here," she added rather piteously.

"That is for you to decide. If you wish to do so I am old enough to be your father, and will do my best to help."

We walked on to an orange grove that stood about forty yards away, ostensibly to pick some fruit, but really because we knew that there we should be out of hearing and could see any one who approached.

"Mr. Quatermain," she said presently in a low voice, "I am in great trouble, almost the greatest a woman can have. I am engaged to be married to a man whom I do not care for."

"Then why not break it off? It may be unpleasant, but it is generally best to face unpleasant things, and nothing can be so bad as marrying a man whom you do not—care for."

"Because I cannot—I dare not. I have to obey."

"How old are you, Miss Marnham?"

"I shall be of age in three months' time. You may guess that I did not intend to return here until they were over, but I was, well—trapped. He wrote to me that my father was ill and I came."

"At any rate when they are over you will not have to obey any one. It is not long to wait."

"It is an eternity. Besides this is not so much a question of obedience as of duty and of love. I love my father who, whatever his faults, has always been very kind to me."

"And I am sure he loves you. Why not go to him and tell him your trouble?"

"He knows it already, Mr. Quatermain, and hates this marriage even more than I do, if that is possible. But he is driven to it, as I am. Oh! I must tell the truth. The doctor has some hold over him. My father has done something dreadful; I don't know what and I don't want to know, but if it came out it would ruin my father, or worse, worse. I am the price of his silence. On the day of our marriage he will destroy the proofs. If I refuse to marry him, they will be produced and then—"

"It is difficult," I said.

"It is more than difficult, it is terrible. If you could see all there is in my heart, you would know how terrible."

"I think I can see, Miss Heda. Don't say any more now. Give me time to consider. In case of necessity come to me again, and be sure that I will protect you."

"But you are going in a week."

"Many things happen in a week. Sufficient to the day is its evil. At the end of the week we will come to some decision unless everything is already decided."

For the next twenty-four hours I reflected on this pretty problem as hard as ever I did on anything in all my life. Here was a young woman who must somehow be protected from a scoundrel, but who could not be protected because she herself had to protect another scoundrel—to wit, her own father. Could the thing be faced out? Impossible, for I was sure that Marnham had committed a murder, or murders, of which Rodd possessed evidence that would hang him. Could Heda be married to Anscombe at once? Yes, if both were willing, but then Marnham would still be hung. Could they elope? Possibly, but with the same result. Could I take her away and put her under the protection of the Court at Pretoria? Yes, but with the same result. I wondered what my Hottentot retainer, Hans, would have advised, he who was named Light-in-Darkness, and in his own savage way was the cleverest and most cunning man that I have met. Alas! I could not raise him from the grave to tell me, and yet I knew well what he would have answered.

"Baas," he would have said, "this is a rope which only the pale old man (*i.e.*, death) can cut. Let this doctor die or let the father die, and the maiden will be free. Surely heaven is longing for one or both of them, and if necessary, Baas, I believe that I can point out a path to heaven!"

I laughed to myself at the thought, which was one that a white man could not entertain even as a thought. And I felt that the hypothetical Hans was right, death alone could cut this knot, and the reflection made me shiver.

That night I slept uneasily and dreamed. I dreamed that once more I was in the Black Kloof in Zululand, seated in front of the huts at the end of the *kloof*. Before me squatted the old wizard, Zikali, wrapped up in his *kaross*—Zikali, the *Thing-that-should-never-have-been-born*, whom I had not seen for years. Near him were the ashes of a fire, by the help of which I knew he had been practising divination. He looked up and laughed one of his terrible laughs.

"So you are here again, Macumazahn," he said, "grown older, but still the same; here at the appointed hour. What do you come to seek from the Opener of Roads? Not Mameena as I think this time. No, no, it is she who seeks you this time, Macumazahn. She found you once, did she not? Far away to the north among a strange people who worshipped an Ivory Child, a people of whom I knew in my youth, and afterwards, for was not their prophet, Harut, a friend of mine and one of our brotherhood? She found you beneath the tusks of the elephant, Jana, whom Macumazahn the skilful could not hit. Oh! do not look astonished."

"How do you know?" I asked in my dream.

"Very simply, Macumazahn. A little yellow man named Hans has been with me and told me all the story not an hour ago, after which I sent for Mameena to learn if it were true. She will be glad to meet you, Macumazahn, she who has a hungry heart that does not forget. Oh! don't be afraid. I mean here beneath the sun, in the land beyond there will be no need for her to meet you since she will dwell ever at your side."

"Why do you lie to me, Zikali?" I seemed to ask. "How can a dead man speak to you and how can I meet a woman who is dead?"

"Seek the answer to that question in the hour of the battle when the white men, your brothers, fall beneath *assegai* as weeds fall before the hoe—or perhaps before it. But have done with Mameena, since she who never grows more old can well afford to wait. It is not of Mameena that you came to speak to me; it is of a fair white woman named Heddana you would speak, and of the man she loves, you, who will ever be mixing yourself up in affairs of others, and therefore must bear their burdens with no pay save that of honour. Hearken, for the time is short. When the storm bursts upon them bring hither the fair maiden, Heddana, and the white lord, Mauriti, and I will shelter them for your sake. Take them nowhere else. Bring them hither if they would escape trouble. I shall be glad to see you, Macumazahn, for at last I am about to smite the Zulu House of Senzangacona, my foes, with a bladder full of blood, and oh! it stains their doorposts red."

Then I woke up, feeling afraid, as one does after a nightmare, and was comforted to hear Anscombe sleeping quietly on the other side of the room.

"Mauriti. Why did Zikali call him Mauriti?" I wondered drowsily to myself. "Oh! of course his name is Maurice, and it was a Zulu corruption of a common sort as was Heddana of Heda." Then I dozed off again, and by the morning had forgotten all about my dream until it was brought back to me by subsequent events. Still it was this and nothing else that put it into my head to fly to Zululand on an emergency that was to arise ere long.

That evening Rodd was absent from dinner, and on inquiring where he might be, I was informed that he had ridden to visit a *Kaffir* headman, a patient of his who lived at a distance, and would very probably sleep at the *kraal*, returning early next day. One of the topics of conversation during dinner was as to where the exact boundary line used to run between the Transvaal and the country over which the Basuto chief, Sekukuni, claimed ownership and jurisdiction. Marnham said that it passed within a couple of miles of his house, and when we rose, the moon being very bright, offered to show me where the beacons had been placed years before by a Boer Commission. I accepted, as the night was lovely for a stroll after the hot day. Also I was half conscious

80

of another undefined purpose in my mind, which perhaps may have spread to that of Marnham. Those two young people looked very happy together there on the *stoep*, and as they must part so soon it would, I thought, be kind to give them the opportunity of a quiet chat.

So off we went to the brow of the hill on which the Temple stood, whence old Marnham pointed out to me a beacon, which I could not see in the dim, silvery bush-*veld* below, and how the line ran from it to another beacon somewhere else.

"You know the Yellow-wood swamp," he said. "It passes straight through that. That is why those Basutos who were following you pulled up upon the edge of the swamp, though as a matter of fact, according to their ideas, they had a perfect right to kill you on their side of the line which cuts through the middle."

I made some remark to the effect that I presumed that the line had in fact ceased to exist at all, as the Basuto territory had practically become British; after which we strolled back to the house. Walking quietly between the tall rose hedges and without speaking, for each of us was preoccupied with his own thoughts, suddenly we came upon a very pretty scene.

We had left Anscombe and Heda seated side by side on the *stoep*. They were still there, but much closer together. In fact his arms were round her, and they were kissing each other in a remarkably whole-hearted way. About this there could be no mistake, since the *rimpi*-strung couch on which they sat was immediately under the hanging lamp—a somewhat unfortunate situation for such endearments. But what did they think of hanging lamps or any other lights, save those of their own eyes, they who were content to kiss and murmur words of passion as though they were as much alone as Adam and Eve in Eden? What did they think either of the serpent coiled about the bole of this tree of knowledge whereof they had just plucked the ripe and maddening fruit?

By a mutual instinct Marnham and I withdrew ourselves, very gently indeed, purposing to skirt round the house and enter it from behind, or to be seized with a fit of coughing at the gate, or to do something to announce our presence at a convenient distance. When we had gone a little way we heard a crash in the bushes.

"Another of those cursed baboons robbing the garden," remarked Marnham reflectively.

"I think he is going to rob the house also," I replied, turning to point to something dark that seemed to be leaping up on to the veranda.

Next moment we heard Heda utter a little cry of alarm, and a man say in a low fierce voice—

"So I have caught you at last, have I!"

"The doctor has returned from his business rounds sooner than was expected, and I think that we had better join the party," I remarked, and made a bee line for the *stoep*, Marnham following me.

I think that I arrived just in time to prevent mischief. There, with a revolver in his hand, stood Rodd, tall and formidable, his dark face looking like that of Satan himself, a very monument of rage and jealousy. There in front of him on the couch sat Heda, grasping its edge with her fingers, her cheeks as pale as a sheet and her eyes shining. By her side was Anscombe, cool and collected as usual, I noticed, but evidently perplexed.

"If there is any shooting to be done," he was saying, "I think you had better begin with me."

His calmness seemed to exasperate Rodd, who lifted the revolver. But I too was prepared, for in that house I always went armed. There was no time to get at the man, who was perhaps fifteen feet away, and I did not want to hurt him. So I did the best I could; that is, I fired at the pistol in his hand, and the light being good, struck it near the hilt and knocked it off the barrel before the he could press the trigger, if he really meant to shoot.

"That's a good shot," remarked Anscombe who had seen me, while Rodd stared at the hilt which he still held.

"A lucky one," I answered, walking forward. "And now, Dr. Rodd, will you be so good as to tell me what you mean by flourishing a revolver, presumably loaded, in the faces of a lady and an unarmed man?"

"What the devil is that to you," he asked furiously, "and what do you mean by firing at me?"

"A great deal," I answered, "seeing that a young woman and my friend are concerned. As for firing at you, had I done so you would not be asking questions now. I fired at the pistol in your hand, but if there is more trouble next time it shall be at the holder," and I glanced at my revolver.

Seeing that I meant business he made no reply, but turned upon Marnham who had followed me.

"This is your work, you old villain," he said in a low voice that was heavy with hate. "You promised your daughter to me. She is engaged to me, and now I find her in this wanderer's arms."

"What have I to do with it?" said Marnham. "Perhaps she has changed her mind. You had better ask her."

"There is no need to ask me," interrupted Heda, who now seemed to have got her nerve again. "I *have* changed my mind. I never loved you, Dr. Rodd, and I will not marry you. I love Mr. Anscombe here, and as he has asked me to be his wife I mean to marry him."

"I see," he sneered, "you want to be a peeress one day, no doubt. Well, you never shall if I can help it. Perhaps, too, this fine gentleman of yours will not be so particularly anxious to marry you when he learns that you are the daughter of a murderer."

That word was like a bombshell bursting among us. We looked at each other as people, yet dazed with the shock, might on a battlefield when the noise of the explosion has died and the smoke cleared away, to see who is still alive. Anscombe spoke the first.

"I don't know what you mean or to what you refer," he said quietly. "But at any rate this lady who has promised to marry me is innocent, and therefore if all her ancestors had been murderers it would not in the slightest turn me from my purpose of marrying her."

She looked at him, and all the gratitude in the world shone in her frightened eyes. Marnham stepped, or rather staggered forward, the blue vein throbbing on forehead.

"He lies," he said hoarsely, tugging at his long beard. "Listen now and I will tell you the truth. Once, more than a year ago, I was drunk and in a rage. In this state I fired at a *Kaffir* to frighten him, and by some devil's chance shot him dead. That's what he calls being a murderer."

"I have another tale," said Rodd, "with which I will not trouble this company just now. Look here, Heda, either you fulfil your promise and marry me, or your father swings."

She gasped and sank together on the seat as though she had been shot. Then I took up my parable.

"Are you the man," I asked, "to accuse others of crime? Let us see. You have spent several months in an English prison (I gave the name) for a crime I won't mention."

"How do you know——" he began.

"Never mind, I do know and the prison books will show it. Further, your business is that of selling guns and ammunition to the Basutos of Sekukuni's tribe, who, although the expedition against them has been temporarily recalled, are still the Queen's enemies. Don't deny it, for I have the proofs. Further, it was you who advised Sekukuni to kill us when we went down to his country to shoot the other day, because you were afraid that we should discover whence he got his guns." (This was a bow drawn at a venture, but the arrow went home, for I saw his jaw drop.) "Further, I believe you to be an illicit diamond buyer, and I believe also that you have again been arranging with the Basutos to make an end of us, though of these last two items at present

I lack positive proof. Now, Dr. Rodd, I ask you for the second time whether you are a person to accuse others of crimes and whether, should you do so, you will be considered a credible witness when your own are brought to light?"

"If I had been guilty of any of these things, which I am not, it is obvious that my partner must have shared in all of them, except the first. So if you inform against me, you inform against him, and the father of Heda, whom your friend wishes to marry, will, according to your showing, be proved a gun-runner, a thief and a would-be murderer of his guests. I should advise you to leave that business alone, Mr. Quatermain."

The reply was bold and clever, so much so that I regarded this blackguard with a certain amount of admiration, as I answered—

"I shall take your advice if you take mine to leave another business alone, that of this young lady and her father, but not otherwise."

"Then spare your breath and do your worst; only careful, sharp as you think yourself, that your meddling does not recoil on your own head. Listen, Heda, either you make up your mind to marry me at once and arrange that this young gentleman, who as a doctor I assure you is now quite fit to travel without injury to his health, leaves this house tomorrow with the spy Quatermain—you might lend him the Cape cart to go in—or I start with the proofs to lay a charge of murder against your father. I give you till tomorrow morning to have a family council to think it over. Good-night."

"Good-night," I answered as he passed me, "and please be careful that none of us see your face again before tomorrow morning. As you may happen to have heard, my native name means Watcher-by-Night," and I looked at the revolver in my hand.

When he had vanished I remarked in as cheerful voice as I could command, that I thought it was bedtime, and as nobody stirred, added, "Don't be afraid, young lady. If you feel lonely, you must tell that stout maid of yours to sleep in your room. Also, as the night is so hot I shall take my nap on the *stoep*, there, just opposite your window. No, don't let us talk any more now. There will be plenty of time for that tomorrow."

She rose, looked at Anscombe, looked at me, looked at her father very pitifully; then with a little exclamation of despair passed into her room by the French window, where presently I heard her call the native maid and tell her that she was to sleep with her.

Marnham watched her depart. Then he too went with his head bowed and staggering a little in his walk. Next Anscombe rose and limped off into his room, I following him.

"Well, young man," I said, "you have put us all in the soup now and no mistake."

"Yes, Allan, I am afraid I have. But on the whole don't you think it rather interesting soup—so many unexpected ingredients, you see!"

"Interesting soup! Unexpected ingredients!" I repeated after him, adding, "Why not call it hell's broth at once?"

Then he became serious, dreadfully serious.

"Look here," he said, "I love Heda, and whatever her family history may be I mean to marry her and face the row at home."

"You could scarcely do less in all the circumstances, and as for rows, that young lady would soon fit herself into any place that you can give her. But the question is, how can you marry her?"

"Oh! something will happen," he replied optimistically.

"You are quite right there. Something will certainly happen, but the point is—what? Something was very near happening when I turned up on that *stoep*, so near that I think it was lucky for you, or for Miss Heda, or both, that I have learned how to handle a pistol. Now let me see your foot, and don't speak another word to me about all this business tonight. I'd rather tackle it when I am clear-headed in the morning."

Well, I examined his instep and leg very carefully and found that Rodd was right. Although it still hurt him to walk, the wound was quite healed and all inflammation had gone from the limb. Now it was only a question of time for the sinews to right themselves. While I was thus engaged he held forth on the virtues and charms of Heda, I making no comment.

"Lie down and get to sleep, if you can," I said when I had finished. "The door is locked and I am going on to the *stoep*, so you needn't be afraid of the windows. Good-night."

I went out and sat myself down in such a position that by the light of the hanging lamp, which still burned, I could make sure that no one could approach either Heda's or my room without my seeing him. For the rest, all my life I have been accustomed to night vigils, and the loaded revolver hung from my wrist by a loop of hide. Moreover, never had I felt less sleepy. There I sat hour after hour, thinking.

The substance of my thoughts does not matter, since the events that followed make them superfluous to the story. I will merely record, therefore, that towards dawn a great horror took hold of me. I did not know of what I was afraid, but I was much afraid of something. Nothing was passing in either Heda's or our room, of that I made sure by personal examination. Therefore it would seem that my terrors were

85

unnecessary, and yet they grew and grew. I felt sure that something was happening somewhere, a dread occurrence which it was beyond my power to prevent, though whether it were in this house or at the other end of Africa I did not know.

The mental depression increased and culminated. Then of a sudden it passed completely away, and as I mopped the sweat from off my brow I noticed that dawn was breaking. It was a tender and beautiful dawn, and in a dim way I took it as a good omen. Of course it was nothing but the daily resurrection of the sun, and yet it brought to me comfort and hope. The night was past with all its fears; the light had come with all its joys. From that moment I was certain that we should triumph over these difficulties and that the end of them would be peace.

So sure was I that I ventured to take a nap, knowing that the slightest movement or sound would wake me. I suppose I slept until six o'clock, when I was aroused by a footfall. I sprang up, and saw before me one of our native servants. He was trembling and his face was ashen beneath the black. Moreover he could not speak. All he did was to put his head on one side, like a dead man, and keep on pointing downwards. Then with his mouth open and starting eyes he beckoned to me to follow him.

I followed.

CHAPTER 8

Rodd's Last Card

The man led me to Marnham's room, which I had never entered before. All I could see at first, for the shutters were closed, was that the place seemed large, as bedchambers go in South Africa. When my eyes grew accustomed to the light, I made out the figure of a man seated in a chair with his head bent forward over a table that was placed at the foot of the bed almost in the centre of the room. I threw open the shutters and the morning light poured in. The man was Marnham. On the table were writing materials, also a brandy bottle with only a dreg of spirit in it. I looked for the glass and found it by his side on the floor, shattered, not merely broken.

"Drunk," I said aloud, whereon the servant, who understood me, spoke for the first time, saying in a frightened voice in Dutch—

"No, Baas, dead, half cold. I found him so just now."

I bent down and examined Marnham, also felt his face. Sure enough, he was dead, for his jaw had fallen; also his flesh was chill, and from him came a horrible smell of brandy. I thought for a moment, then bade the boy fetch Dr. Rodd and say nothing to any one else, He went, and now for the first time I noticed a large envelope addressed "Allan Quatermain, Esq." in a somewhat shaky hand. This I picked up and slipped into my pocket.

Rodd arrived half dressed.

"What's the matter now?" he growled.

I pointed to Marnham, saying—

"That is a question for you to answer."

"Oh! drunk again, I suppose," he said. Then he did as I had done, bent down and examined him. A few seconds later he stepped or reeled back, looking as frightened as a man could be, and exclaiming—

"Dead as a stone, by God! Dead these three hours or more."

"Quite so," I answered, "but what killed him?"

"How should I know?" he asked savagely. "Do you suspect me of poisoning him?"

"My mind is open," I replied; "but as you quarrelled so bitterly last night, others might."

The bolt went home; he saw his danger.

"Probably the old sot died in a fit, or of too much brandy. How can one know without a post-mortem? But that mustn't be made by me. I'm off to inform the magistrate and get hold of another doctor. Let the body remain as it is until I return."

I reflected quickly. Ought I to let him go or not? If he had any hand in this business, doubtless he intended to escape. Well, supposing this were so and he did escapee, that would be a good thing for Heda, and really it was no affair of mine to bring the fellow to justice. Moreover there was nothing to show that he was guilty; his whole manner seemed to point another way, though of course he might be acting.

"Very well," I replied, "but return as quickly as possible."

He stood for a few seconds like a man who is dazed. It occurred to me that it might have come into his mind with Marnham's death that he had lost his hold over Heda. But if so he said nothing of it, but only asked—

"Will you go instead of me?"

"On the whole I think not," I replied, "and if I did, the story I should have to tell might not tend to your advantage."

"That's true, damn you!" he exclaimed and left the room.

Ten minutes later he was galloping towards Pilgrim's Rest. Before I departed from the death chamber I examined the place carefully to see if I could find any poison or other deadly thing, but without success. One thing I did discover, however. Turning the leaf of a blotting-book that was by Marnham's elbow, I came upon a sheet of paper on which were written these words in his hand, "Greater love hath no man than this—" that was all.

Either he had forgotten the end of the quotation or changed his mind, or was unable through weakness to finish the sentence. This paper also I put in my pocket. Bolting the shutters and locking the door I returned to the *stoep*, where I was alone, for as yet no one else was stirring. Then I remembered the letter in my pocket and opened it. It ran—

Dear Mr. Quatermain,

I have remembered that those who quarrel with Dr. Rodd are apt to die soon and suddenly; at any rate life at my age is always uncertain. Therefore, as I know you to be an honest man, I am enclosing my will that it may be in safe keeping and purpose to send it to your room tomorrow morning. Perhaps when you return to Pretoria you will deposit it in the Standard Bank there, and if I am still alive, forward me the receipt. You will see that I leave everything to my daughter whom I dearly love, and that there is enough to keep the wolf from her door, besides my share in this property, if it is ever realized.

After all that has passed tonight I do not feel up to writing a long letter, so

Remain sincerely yours,

H. A. Marnham

PS.—I should like to state clearly upon paper that my earnest hope and wish are that Heda may get clear of that black-hearted, murderous, scoundrel Rodd and marry Mr. Anscombe, whom I like and who, I am sure, would make her a good husband.

Thinking to myself this did not look very like the letter of a suicide, I glanced through the will, as the testator seemed to have wished that I should do so. It was short, but properly drawn, signed, and witnessed, and bequeathed a sum of £9,000, which was on deposit at the Standard Bank, together with all his other property, real and personal, to Heda for her own sole use, free from the debts and engagements of her husband, should she marry. Also she was forbidden to spend more than £1,000 of the capital. In short the money was strictly tied up. With the will were some other papers that apparently referred to certain property in Hungary to which Heda might become entitled, but about these I did not trouble.

Replacing these documents in a safe inner pocket in the lining of my waistcoat, I went into our room and woke up Anscombe who was sleeping soundly, a fact that caused an unreasonable irritation in my mind. When at length he was thoroughly aroused I said to him—

"You are in luck's way, my friend. Marnham is dead."

"Oh! poor Heda," he exclaimed, "she loved him. It will half break her heart."

"If it breaks half of her heart," I replied, "it will mend the other half, for now her filial affection can't force her to marry Rodd, and that is where you are in luck's way."

Then I told him all the story.

"Was he murdered or did he commit suicide?" he asked when I had finished.

"I don't know, and to tell you the truth I don't want to know; nor will you if you are wise, unless knowledge is forced upon you. It is

89

enough that he is dead, and for his daughter's sake the less the circumstances of his end are examined into the better."

"Poor Heda!" he said again, "who will tell her? I can't. *You* found him, Allan."

"I expected that job would be my share of the business, Anscombe. Well, the sooner it is over the better. Now dress yourself and come on to the *stoep*."

Then I left him and next minute met Heda's fat, half-breed maid, a stupid but good sort of a woman who was called Kaatje, emerging from her mistress's room with a jug, to fetch hot water, I suppose.

"Kaatje," I said, "go back and tell the Missie Heda that I want to speak to her as soon as I can. Never mind the hot water, but stop and help her to dress."

She began to grumble a little in a good-natured way, but something in my eye stopped her and she went back into the room. Ten minutes later Heda was by my side.

"What is it, Mr. Quatermain?" she asked. "I feel sure that something dreadful has happened."

"It has, my dear," I answered, "that is, if death is dreadful. Your father died last night."

"Oh!" she said, "oh!" and sank back on to the seat.

"Bear up," I went on, "we must all die one day, and he had reached the full age of man."

"But I loved him," she moaned. "He had many faults I know, still I loved him."

"It is the lot of life, Heda, that we should lose what we love. Be thankful, therefore, that you have some one left to love."

"Yes, thank God! that's true. If it had been him—no, it's wicked to say that."

Then I told her the story, and while I was doing so, Anscombe joined us, walking by aid of his stick. Also I showed them both Marnham's letter to me and the will, but the other bit of paper I did not speak of or show.

She sat very pale and quiet and listened till I had done. Then she said—

"I should like to see him."

"Perhaps it is as well," I answered. "If you can bear it, come at once, and do you come also, Anscombe."

We went to the room, Anscombe and Heda holding each other by the hand. I unlocked the door and, entering, threw open a shutter. There sat the dead man as I had left him, only his head had fallen over a little. She gazed at him, trembling, then advanced and kissed his cold forehead, muttering,

"Goodbye, father. Oh! goodbye, father."

A thought struck me, and I asked—

"Is there any place here where your father locked up things? As I have shown you, you are his heiress, and if so it might be as well in this house that you should possess yourself of his property."

"There is a safe in the corner," she answered, "of which he always kept the key in his trouser pocket."

"Then with your leave I will open it in your presence."

Going to the dead man I searched his pocket and found in it a bunch of keys. These I withdrew and went to the safe over which a skin rug was thrown. I unlocked it easily enough. Within were two bags of gold, each marked £100; also another larger bag marked "My wife's jewellery. For Heda"; also some papers and a miniature of the lady whose portrait hung in the sitting-room; also some loose gold.

"Now who will take charge of these?" I asked. "I do not think it safe to leave them here."

"You, of course," said Anscombe, while Heda nodded.

So with a groan I consigned all these valuables to my capacious pockets. Then I locked up the empty safe, replaced the keys where I had found them on Marnham, fastened the shutter and left the room with Anscombe, waiting for a while outside till Heda joined us, sobbing a little. After this we got something to eat, insisting on Heda doing the same.

On leaving the table I saw a curious sight, namely, the patients whom Rodd was attending in the little hospital of which I have spoken, departing towards the bush-*veld*, those of them who could walk well and the attendants assisting the others. They were already some distance away, too far indeed for me to follow, as I did not wish to leave the house. The incident filled me with suspicion, and I went round to the back to make inquiries, but could find no one. As I passed the hospital door, however, I heard a voice calling in Sisutu—

"Do not leave me behind, my brothers."

I entered and saw the man on whom Rodd had operated the day of our arrival, lying in bed and quite alone. I asked him where the others had gone. At first he would not answer, but when I pretended to leave him, called out that it was back to their own country. Finally, to cut the story short, I extracted from him that they had left because they had news that the Temple was going to be attacked by Sekukuni and did not wish to be here when I and Anscombe were killed. How the news reached him he refused, or could not, say; nor did he seem to know anything of the death of Marnham. When I pressed him on the former point, he only groaned and cried for water, for he was in pain and thirsty. I asked him who had told Sekukuni's people to kill us, but he refused to speak.

"Very well," I said, "then you shall lie here alone and die of thirst," and again I turned towards the door.

At this he cried out—

"I will tell you. It was the white medicine-man who lives here; he who cut me open. He arranged it all a few days ago because he hates you. Last night he rode to tell the *impi* when to come."

"When is it to come?" I asked, holding the jug of water towards him.

"Tonight at the rising of the moon, so that it may get far away before the dawn. My people are thirsty for your blood and for that of the other white chief, because you killed so many of them by the river. The others they will not harm."

"How did you learn all this?" I asked him again, but without result, for he became incoherent and only muttered something about being left alone because the others could not carry him. So I gave him some water, after which he fell asleep, or pretended to do so, and I left him, wondering whether he was delirious, or spoke truth. As I passed the stables I saw that my own horse was there, for in this district horses are always shut up at night to keep them from catching sickness, but that the four beasts that had brought Heda from Natal in the Cape cart were gone, though it was evident that they had been kraaled here till within an hour or two. I threw my horse a bundle of forage and returned to the house by the back entrance. The kitchen was empty, but crouched by the door of Marnham's room sat the boy who had found him dead. He had been attached to his master and seemed half dazed. I asked him where the other servants were, to which he replied that they had all run away. Then I asked him where the horses were. He answered that the Baas Rodd had ordered them to be turned out before he rode off that morning. I bade him accompany me to the *stoep*, as I dared not let him out of my sight, which he did unwillingly enough.

There I found Anscombe and Heda. They were seated side by side upon the couch. Tears were running down her face and he, looking very troubled, held her by the hand. Somehow that picture of Heda has always remained fixed in my mind. Sorrow becomes some women and she was one of them. Her beautiful dark grey eyes did not grow red with weeping; the tears just welled up in them and fell like dew-drops from the heart of a flower.

She sat very upright and very still, as he did, looking straight in front of her, while a ray of sunshine, falling on her head, showed the chestnut-hued lights in her waving hair, of which she had a great abundance.

Indeed the pair of them, thus seated side by side, reminded me of an engraving I had seen somewhere of the statues of a husband and wife in an old Egyptian tomb. With just such a look did the woman of thousands of years ago sit gazing in patient hope into the darkness of the future. Death had made her sad, but it was gone by, and the little wistful smile about her lips seemed to suggest that in this darkness her sorrowful eyes already saw the stirring of the new life to be. Moreover, was not the man she loved the companion of her hopes as he had been of her woes. Such was the fanciful thought that sprang up in my mind, even in the midst of those great anxieties, like a single flower in a stony wilderness of thorns or one star on the blackness of the night.

In a moment it had gone and I was telling them of what I had learned. They listened till I had finished. Then Anscombe said slowly—

"Two of us can't hold this house against an *impi*. We must get out of it."

"Both your conclusions seem quite sound," I remarked, "that is if yonder old *Kaffir* is telling the truth. But the question is—how? We can't all three of us ride on one nag, as you are still a cripple."

"There is the Cape cart," suggested Heda.

"Yes, but the horses have been turned out, and I don't know where to look for them. Nor dare I send that boy alone, for probably he would bolt like the others. I think that you had better get on my horse and ride for it, leaving us to take our chance. I daresay the whole thing is a lie and that we shall be in no danger," I added by way of softening the suggestion.

"That I will never do," she replied with so much quiet conviction that I saw it was useless to pursue the argument.

I thought for a moment, as the position was very difficult. The boy was not to be trusted, and if I went with him I should be leaving these two alone and, in Anscombe's state, almost defenceless. Still it seemed as though I must. Just then I looked up, and there at the garden gate saw Anscombe's driver, Footsack, the man whom I had despatched to Pretoria to fetch his oxen. I noted that he looked frightened and was breathless, for his eyes started out of his head. Also his hat was gone and he bled a little from his face.

Seeing us he ran up the path and sat down as though he were tired.

"Where are the oxen?" I asked.

"Oh! Baas," he answered, "the Basutos have got them. We heard from an old black woman that Sekukuni had an *impi* out, so we waited on the top of that hill about an hour's ride away to see if it was true. Then suddenly the doctor Baas appeared riding, and I ran out and asked him if it were safe to go on. He knew me again and answered—

"'Yes, quite safe, for have I not just ridden this road without meeting so much as a black child. Go on, man; your masters will be glad to have their oxen, as they wish to trek, or will by nightfall.' Then he laughed and rode away.

"So we went on, driving the oxen. But when we came to the belt of thorns at the bottom of the hill, we found that the doctor Baas had either lied to us or he had not seen. For there suddenly the tall grass on either side of the path grew spears; yes, everywhere were spears. In a minute the two *voorloopers* were *assegaied*. As for me, I ran forward, not back, since the *Kaffirs* were behind me, across the path, Baas, driving off the oxen. They sprang at me, but I jumped this way and that way and avoided them. Then they threw assegais—see, one of them cut my cheek, but the rest missed. They had guns in their hands also, but none shot. I think they did not wish to make a noise. Only one of them shouted after me—

"'Tell Macumazahn that we are going to call on him tonight when he cannot see to shoot. We have a message for him from our brothers whom he killed at the drift of the Oliphant's River.'

"Then I ran on here without stopping, but I saw no more *Kaffirs*. That is all, Baas."

Now I did not delay to cross-examine the man or to sift the true from the false in his story, since it was clear to me that he had run into a company of Basutos, or rather been beguiled thereto by Rodd, and lost our cattle, also his companions, who were either killed as he said, or had escaped some other way.

"Listen, man," I said. "I am going to fetch some horses. Do you stay here and help the Missie to pack the cart and make the harness ready. If you disobey me or run away, then I will find you and you will never run again. Do you understand?"

He vowed that he did and went to get some water, while I explained everything to Anscombe and Heda, pointing out that all the information we could gather seemed to show that no attack was to be made upon the house before nightfall, and that therefore we had the day before us. As this was so I proposed to go to look for the horses myself, since otherwise I was sure we should never find them. Meanwhile Heda must pack and make ready the cart with the help of Footsack, Anscombe superintending everything, as he could very well do since he was now able to walk leaning on a stick.

94

Of course neither of them liked my leaving them, but in view of our necessities they raised no objection. So off I went, taking the boy with me. He did not want to go, being, as I have said, half dazed with grief or fear, or both, but when I had pointed out to him clearly that I was quite prepared to shoot him if he played tricks, he changed his mind. Having saddled my mare that was now fresh and fat, we started, the boy guiding me to a certain *kloof* at the foot of which there was a small plain of good grass where he said the horses were accustomed to graze.

Here sure enough we found two of them, and as they had been turned out with their headstalls on, were able to tie them to trees with the *riems* which were attached to the headstalls. But the others were not there, and as two horses could not drag a heavy Cape cart, I was obliged to continue the search. Oh! what a hunt those beasts gave me. Finding themselves free, for as Rodd's object was that they should stray, he had ordered the stable-boy not to kneel-halter them, after filling themselves with grass they had started off for the farm where they were bred, which, it seemed, was about fifty miles away, grazing as they went. Of course I did not know this at the time, so for several hours I rode up and down the neighbouring *kloofs*, as the ground was too hard for me to hope to follow them by their spoor.

It occurred to me to ask the boy where the horses came from, a question that he happened to be able to answer, as he had brought them home when they were bought the year before. Having learned in what direction the place lay I rode for it at an angle, or rather for the path that led to it, making the boy run alongside, holding to my stirrup leather. About three o'clock in the afternoon I struck this path, or rather track, at a point ten or twelve miles away from the Temple, and there, just mounting a rise, met the two horses quietly walking towards me. Had I been a quarter of an hour later they would have passed and vanished into a sea of thorn-*veld*. We caught them without trouble and once more headed homewards, leading them by their *riems*.

Reaching the glade where the other two were tied up, we collected them also and returned to the house, where we arrived at five o'clock. As everything seemed quiet I put my mare into the stable, slipped its bit and gave it some forage. Then I went round the house, and to my great joy found Anscombe and Heda waiting anxiously, but with nothing to report, and with them Footsack. Very hastily I swallowed some food, while Footsack inspanned the horses. In a quarter of an hour all was ready. Then suddenly, in an inconsequent female fashion, Heda developed a dislike to leaving her father unburied.

"My dear young lady," I said, "it seems that you must choose between that and our all stopping to be buried with him."

She saw the point and compromised upon paying him a visit of
farewell, which I left her to do in Anscombe's company, while I fetched
my mare. To tell the truth I felt as though I had seen enough of the
unhappy Marnham, and not for £50 would I have entered that room
again. As I passed the door of the hospital, leading my horse, I heard
the old *Kaffir* screaming within and sent the boy who was with me
to find out what was the matter with him. That was the last I saw of
either of them, or ever shall see this side of kingdom come. I wonder
what became of them?

When I got back to the front of the house I found the cart standing ready at the gate, Footsack at the head of the horses and Heda
with Anscombe at her side. It had been neatly packed during the day
by Heda with such of her and our belongings as it would hold, including our arms and ammunition. The rest, of course, we were obliged
to abandon. Also there were two baskets full of food, some bottles of
brandy and a good supply of overcoats and wraps. I told Footsack to
take the reins, as I knew him to be a good driver, and helped Anscombe to a seat at his side, while Heda and the maid Kaatje got in
behind in order to balance the vehicle. I determined to ride, at any
rate for the present.

"Which way, Baas?" asked Footsack.

"Down to the Granite Stream where the wagon stands," I answered.

"That will be through the Yellow-wood Swamp. Can't we take the
other road to Pilgrim's Rest and Lydenburg, or to Barberton?" asked
Anscombe in a vague way, and as I thought, rather nervously.

"No," I answered, "that is unless you wish to meet those Basutos
who stole the oxen and Dr. Rodd returning, if he means to return."

"Oh! let us go through the Yellow-wood," exclaimed Heda, who, I
think, would rather have met the devil than Dr. Rodd.

Ah! if I had but known that we were heading straight for that person, sooner would I have faced the Basutos twice over. But I did what
seemed wisest, thinking that he would be sure to return with another
doctor or a magistrate by the shorter and easier path which he had followed in the morning. It just shows once more how useless are all our
care and foresight, or how strong is Fate, have it which way you will.

So we started down the slope, and I, riding behind, noted poor
Heda staring at the marble house, which grew ever more beautiful as
it receded and the roughness of its building disappeared, especially at
that part of it which hid the body of her old scamp of a father whom

still she loved. We came down to the glen and once more saw the bones of the blue *wildebeeste* that we had shot—oh! years and years ago, or so it seemed. Then we struck out for the Granite Stream.

Before we reached the patch of Yellow-wood forest where I knew that the cart must travel very slowly because of the trees and the swampy nature of the ground, I pushed on ahead to reconnoitre, fearing lest there might be Basutos hidden in this cover. Riding straight through it I went as far as the deserted wagon at a sharp canter, seeing nothing and no one. Once indeed, towards the end of the wood where it was more dense, I thought that I heard a man cough and peered about me through the gloom, for here the rays of the sun, which was getting low in the heavens, scarcely penetrated. As I could perceive no one I came to the conclusion that I must have been deceived by my fancy. Or perhaps it was some baboon that coughed, though it was strange that a baboon should have come to such a low-lying spot where there was nothing for it to eat.

The place was eerie, so much so that I bethought me of tales of the ghosts whereby it was supposed to be haunted. Also, oddly enough, of Anscombe's presentiment which he had fulfilled by killing a Basuto. Look! There lay his grinning skull with some patches of hair still on it, dragged away from the rest of the bones by a hyena. I cantered on down the slope beyond the wood and through the scattered thorns to the stream on the banks of which the wagon should be. It had gone, and by the freshness of the trail, within an hour or two. A moment's reflection told me what had happened. Having stolen our oxen the Basutos drove them to the wagon, inspanned them and departed with their loot. On the whole I was glad to see this, since it suggested that they had retired towards their own country, leaving our road open.

Turning my horse I rode back again to meet the cart. As I reached the edge of the wood at the top of the slope I heard a whistle blown, a very shrill whistle, of which the sound would travel for a mile or two on that still air. Also I heard the sound of men's voices in altercation and caught words, such as—"Let go, or by Heaven—!" then a furious laugh and other words which seemed to be—"In five minutes the *Kaffirs* will be here. In ten you will be dead. Can I help it if they kill you after I have warned you to turn back?" Then a woman's scream.

Rodd's voice, Anscombe's voice and Kaatje's scream—not Heda's but Kaatje's!

Then as I rode furiously round the last patch of intervening trees the sound of a pistol shot. I was out of them now and saw everything. There was the cart on the further side of a swamp. The horses were standing still and snorting. Holding the rein of one of the leaders was Rodd, whose horse also stood close by. He was rocking on his feet and as I leapt from my mare and ran up, I saw his face. It was horrible, full of pain and devilish rage. With his disengaged hand he pointed to Anscombe sitting in the cart and grasping a pistol that still smoked.

"You've killed me," he said in a hoarse, choking voice, for he was shot through the lung, "to get her," and he waved his hand towards Heda who was peering at him between the heads of the two men. "You are a murderer, as her father was, and as David was before you. Well, I hope you won't keep her long. I hope you'll die as I do and break her false heart, you damned thief."

All of this he said in a slow voice, pausing between the words and speaking ever more thickly as the blood from his wound choked him. Then of a sudden it burst in a stream from his lips, and still pointing with an accusing finger at Anscombe, he fell backwards into the slimy pool behind him and there vanished without a struggle.

So horrible was the sight that the driver, Footsack, leapt from the cart, uttering a kind of low howl, ran to Rodd's horse, scrambled into the saddle and galloped off, striking it with his fist, where to I do not know. Anscombe put his hand before his eyes, Heda sank down on the seat in a heap, and the coloured woman, Kaatje, beat her breast and said something in Dutch about being accursed or bewitched. Luckily I kept my wits and went to the horses' heads, fearing lest they should start and drag the trap into the pool. "Wake up," I said. "That fellow has only got what he deserved, and you were quite right to shoot him."

"I am glad you think so," answered Anscombe absently. "It was so like murder. Don't you remember I told you I should kill a man in this place and about a woman?"

"I remember nothing," I answered boldly, "except that if we stop here much longer we shall have those Basutos on us. That brute was whistling to them and holding the horses till they came to kill us. Pull yourself together, take the reins and follow me."

He obeyed, being a skilful whip enough who, as he informed me afterwards, had been accustomed to drive a four-in-hand at home. Mounting my horse, which stood by, I guided the cart out of the wood and down the slope beyond, till at length we came to our old *outspan* where I proposed to turn on to the wagon track which ran to Pilgrim's Rest. I say proposed, for when I looked up it I perceived about five hundred yards away a number of armed Basutos running towards us, the red light of the sunset shining on their spears. Evidently the scout or spy to whom Rodd whistled, had called them out of their ambush which they had set for us on the Pilgrim's Rest road in order that they might catch us if we tried to escape that way.

Now there was only one thing to be done. At this spot a native track ran across the little stream and up a steepish slope beyond. On the first occasion of our *outspanning* here I had the curiosity to mount this slope, reflecting as I did so that although rough it would be quite practicable for a wagon. At the top of it I found a wide flat plain, almost high-*veld*, for the bushes were very few, across which the track ran on. On subsequent inquiry I discovered that it was one used by the Swazis and other natives when they made their raids upon the Basutos, or when bodies of them went to work in the mines.

"Follow me," I shouted and crossed the stream which was shallow between the little pools, then led the way up the stony slope. The four horses negotiated it very well and the Cape cart, being splendidly built, took no harm. At the top I looked back and saw that the Basutos were following us.

"Flog the horses!" I cried to Anscombe, and off we went at a hand gallop along the native track, the cart swaying and bumping upon the rough *veld*. The sun was setting now, in half an hour it would be quite dark.

Could we keep ahead of them for that half hour?

CHAPTER 9

Flight

The sun sank in a blaze of glory. Looking back by the light of its last rays I saw a single native silhouetted against the red sky. He was standing on a mound that we had passed a mile or more behind us, doubtless waiting for his companions whom he had outrun. So they had not given up the chase. What was to be done? Once it was completely dark we could not go on. We should lose our way; the horses would get into ant-bear holes and break their legs. Perhaps we might become bogged in some hollow, therefore we must wait till the moon rose, which would not be for a couple of hours.

Meanwhile those accursed Basutos would be following us even in the dark. This would hamper them, no doubt, but they would keep the path, with which they were probably familiar, beneath their feet, and what is more, the ground being soft with recent rain, they could feel the wheel spoor with their fingers. I looked about me. Just here another track started off in a nor'-westerly direction from that which we were following. Perhaps it ran to Lydenburg; I do not know. To our left, not more than a hundred yards or so away, the higher *veld* came to an end and sloped in an easterly direction down to bush-land below.

Should I take the westerly road which ran over a great plain? No, for then we might be seen for miles and cut off. Moreover, even if we escaped the natives, was it desirable we should plunge into civilization just now and tell all our story, as in that case we must do. Rodd's death was quite justified, but it had happened on Transvaal territory and would require a deal of explanation. Fortunately there was no witness of it, except ourselves. Yes, there was though—the driver Footsack, if he had got away, which, being mounted, would seem probable, a man who, for my part, I would not trust for a moment. It would be an ugly thing to see Anscombe in the dock charged with murder and possibly myself, with Footsack giving evidence against us before a Boer jury who might be hard on Englishmen. Also there was the body with a bullet in it.

Suddenly there came into my mind a recollection of the very vivid dream of Zikali which had visited me, and I reflected that in Zululand there would be little need to trouble about the death of Rodd. But Zululand was a long way off, and if we were to avoid the Transvaal, there was only one way of going there, namely through Swaziland. Well, among the Swazis we should be quite safe from the Basutos, since the two peoples were at fierce enmity. Moreover I knew the Swazi chiefs and king very well, having traded there, and could explain that I came to collect debts owing to me.

There was another difficulty. I had heard that the trouble between the English Government and Cetewayo, the Zulu king, was coming to a head, and that the High Commissioner, Sir Bartle Frere, talked of presenting him with an ultimatum. It would be awkward if this arrived while we were in the country, though even so, being on such friendly terms with the Zulus of all classes, I did not think that I, or any with me, would run great risks.

All these thoughts rushed through my brain while I considered what to do. At the moment it was useless to ask the opinion of the others who were but children in native matters. I and I alone must take the responsibility and act, praying that I might do so aright. Another moment and I had made up my mind.

Signing to Anscombe to follow me, I rode about a hundred yards or more down the nor'-westerly path. Then I turned sharply along a rather stony ridge of ground, the cart following me all the time, and came back across our own track, my object being of course to puzzle any *Kaffirs* who might spoor us. Now we were on the edge of the gentle slope that led down to the bush-*veld*. Over this I rode towards a deserted cattle *kraal* built of stones, in the rich soil of which grew sundry trees; doubtless one of those which had been abandoned when Mosilikatze swept all this country on his way north about the year 1838. The way to it was easy, since the surrounding stones had been collected to build the *kraal* generations before. As we passed over the edge of the slope in the gathering gloom, Heda cried—

"Look!" and pointed in the direction whence we came. Far away a sheet of flame shot upwards.

"The house is burning," she exclaimed.

"Yes," I said, "it can be nothing else;" adding to myself, "a good job too, for now there will be no *post-mortem* on old Marnham."

Who fired the place I never learnt. It may have been the Basutos, or Marnham's body-servant, or Footsack, or a spark from the kitchen fire. At any rate it blazed merrily enough notwithstanding the marble walls, as a wood-lined and thatched building of course would do. On the whole I suspected the boy, who may very well have feared lest he should be accused of having had a hand in his master's death. At least it was gone, and watching the distant flames I bethought me that with it went all Heda's past. Twenty-four hours before her father was alive, the bondservant of Rodd and a criminal. Now he was ashes and Rodd was dead, while she and the man she loved were free, with all the world before them. I wished that I could have added that they were safe. Afterwards she told me that much the same ideas passed through her own mind.

Dismounting I led the horses into the old *kraal* through the gap in the wall which once had been the gateway. It was a large *kraal* that probably in bygone days had held the cattle of some forgotten head chief whose town would have stood on the brow of the rise; so large that notwithstanding the trees I have mentioned, there was plenty of room for the cart and horses in its centre. Moreover, on such soil the grass grew so richly that after we had slipped their bits, the horses were able to fill themselves without being unharnessed. Also a little stream from a spring on the brow ran within a few yards whence, with the help of Kaatje, a strong woman, I watered them with the bucket which hung underneath the cart. Next we drank ourselves and ate some food in the darkness that was now complete. Then leaving Kaatje to stand at the head of the horses in case they should attempt any sudden movement, I climbed into the cart, and we discussed things in low whispers.

It was a curious debate in that intense gloom which, close as our faces were together, prevented us from seeing anything of each other, except once when a sudden flare of summer lightning revealed them, white and unnatural as those of ghosts. On our present dangers I did not dwell, putting them aside lightly, though I knew they were not light. But of the alternative as to whether we should try to escape to Lydenburg and civilization, or to Zululand and savagery, I felt it to be my duty to speak.

"To put it plainly," said Anscombe in his slow way when I had finished, "you mean that in the Transvaal I might be tried as a murderer and perhaps convicted, whereas if we vanish into Zululand the probability is that this would not happen."

"I mean," I whispered back, "that we might both be tried and, if

Footsack should chance to appear and give evidence, find ourselves in an awkward position. Also there is another witness—Kaatje, and for the matter of that, Heda herself. Of course her evidence would be in our favour, but to make it understood by a jury she would have to explain a great deal of which she might prefer not to speak. Further, at the best, the whole business would get into the English papers, which you and your relatives might think disagreeable, especially in view of the fact that, as I understand, you and Heda intend to marry."

"Still I think that I would rather face it out," he said in his outspoken way, "even if it should mean that I could never return to England. After all, of what have I to be afraid? I shot this scoundrel because I was obliged to do so."

"Yes, but it is of this that you may have to convince a jury who might possibly find a motive in Rodd's past, and your present, relationship to the same lady. But what has she to say?"

"I have to say," whispered Heda, "that for myself I care nothing, but that I could never bear to see all these stories about my poor father raked up. Also there is Maurice to be considered. It would be terrible if they put him in prison—or worse. Let us go to Zululand, Mr. Quatermain, and afterwards get out of Africa. Don't you agree, Maurice?"

"What does Mr. Quatermain think himself?" he answered. "He is the oldest and by far the wisest of us and I will be guided by him."

Now I considered and said—

"There is such a thing as flying from present troubles to others that may be worse, the 'ills we know not of.' Zululand is disturbed. If war broke out there we might all be killed. On the other hand we might not, and it ought to be possible for you to work up to Delagoa Bay and there get some ship home, that is if you wish to keep clear of British law. I cannot do so, as I must stay in Africa. Nor can I take the responsibility of settling what you are to do, since if things went wrong, it would be on my head. However, if you decide for the Transvaal or Natal and we escape, I must tell you that I shall go to the first magistrate we find and make a full deposition of all that has happened. It is not possible for me to live with the charge of having been concerned in the shooting of a white man hanging over me that might be brought up at any time, perhaps when no one was left in the country to give evidence on my behalf, for then, even if I were acquitted my name would always be tarnished. In Zululand, on the other hand, there are no magistrates before whom I could depose, and if this business should come out, I can always say that we went there to escape from the Basutos. Now I am going to get down to see if the horses are all right. Do you two talk the thing over and make up your minds. Whatever you agree on, I shall accept and do my best to carry through." Then, without waiting for an answer, I slipped from the cart.

Having examined the horses, who were cropping all the grass within reach of them, I crept to the wall of the *kraal* so as to be quite out of earshot. The night was now pitch dark, dark as it only knows how to be in Africa. More, a thunderstorm was coming up of which that flash of sheet lightning had been a presage. The air was electric. From the vast bush-clad valley beneath us came a wild, moaning sound caused, I suppose, by wind among the trees, though here I felt none; far away a sudden spear of lightning stabbed the sky. The brooding trouble of nature spread to my own heart. I was afraid, and not of our present dangers, though these were real enough, so real that in a few hours we might all be dead.

To dangers I was accustomed; for years they had been my daily food by day and by night, and, as I think I have said elsewhere, I am a fatalist, one who knows full well that when God wants me He will take me; that is if He can want such a poor, erring creature. Nothing that I did or left undone could postpone or hasten His summons for a moment, though of course I knew it to be my duty to fight against death and to avoid it for as long as I might, because that I should do so was a portion of His plan. For we are all part of a great pattern, and the continuance or cessation of our lives re-acts upon other lives, and therefore life is a trust.

No, it was of greater things that I felt afraid, things terrible and imminent which I could not grasp and much less understand. I understand them now, but who would have guessed that on the issue of that whispered colloquy in the cart behind me, depended the fate of a people and many thousands of lives? As I was to learn in days to come, if Anscombe and Heda had determined upon heading for the Transvaal, there would, as I believe, have been no Zulu war, which in its turn meant that there would have been no Boer Rebellion and that the mysterious course of history would have been changed.

I shook myself together and returned to the cart.

"Well," I whispered, but there was no answer. A moment later there came another flash of lightning.

"There," said Heda, "how many do you make it?"

"Ninety-eight," he answered.

"I counted ninety-nine," she said, "but anyway it was within the hundred. Mr. Quatermain, we will go to Zululand, if you please, if you will show us the way there."

"Right," I answered, "but might I ask what that has to do with your both counting a hundred?"

"Only this," she said, "we could not make up our minds. Maurice was for the Transvaal, I was for Zululand. So you see we agreed that if another flash came before we counted a hundred, we would go to Zululand, and if it didn't, to Pretoria. A very good way of settling, wasn't it?"

"Excellent!" I replied, "quite excellent for those who could think of such a thing."

As a matter of fact I don't know which of them thought of it because I never inquired. But I did remember afterwards how Anscombe had tossed with a lucky penny when it was a question whether we should or should not run for the wagon during our difficulty by the Oliphant's River; also when I asked him the reason for this strange proceeding he answered that Providence might inhabit a penny as well as anything else, and that he wished to give it—I mean Providence—a chance. How much more then, he may have argued, could it inhabit a flash of lightning which has always been considered a divine manifestation from the time of the Roman Jove, and no doubt far before him.

Forty or fifty generations ago, which is not long, our ancestors set great store by the behaviour of lightning and thunder, and doubtless the instinct is still in our blood, in the same way that all our existing superstitions about the moon come down to us from the time when our forefathers worshipped her. They did this for tens of hundreds or thousands of years, and can we expect a few coatings of the veneer that we politely call civilization, which after all is only one of our conventions that vanish in any human stress such as war, to kill out the human impulse it seems to hide? I do not know, though I have my own opinion, and probably these young people never reasoned the matter out. They just acted on an intuition as ancient as that which had attracted them to each other, namely a desire to consult the ruling fates by omens or symbols. Or perhaps Anscombe thought that as his experience with the penny had proved so successful, he would give providence another *chance*. If so it took it and no mistake. Confound it! I don't know what he thought; I only dwell on the matter because of the great results which followed this consultation of the Sibylline books of heaven.

As it happened my speculations, if I really indulged in any at that time, were suddenly extinguished by the bursting of the storm. It was of the usual character, short but very violent. Of a sudden the sky became alive with lightnings and the atmosphere with the

105

roar of winds. One flash struck a tree quite near the *kraal*, and I saw that tree seem to melt in its fiery embrace, while about where it had been, rose a column of dust from the ground beneath. The horses were so frightened that luckily they stood quite quiet, as I have often known animals to do in such circumstances. Then came the rain, a torrential rain as I, who was out in it holding the horses, became painfully aware. It thinned after a while, however, as the storm rolled away.

Suddenly in a silence between the tremendous echoes of the passing thunder I thought that I heard voices somewhere on the brow of the slope, and as the horses were now quite calm, I crept through the trees to that part of the enclosure which I judged to be nearest to them.

Voices they were sure enough, and of the Basutos who were pursuing us. What was more, they were coming down the slope. The top of the old wall reached almost to my chin. Taking off my hat I thrust my head forward between two loose stones, that I might hear the better.

The men were talking together in Sisutu. One, whom I took to be their captain, said to the others—

"That white-headed old jackal, Macumazahn, has given us the slip again. He doubled on his tracks and drove the horses down the hillside to the lower path in the valley. I could feel where the wheels went over the edge."

"It is so, Father," answered another voice, "but we shall catch him and the others at the bottom if we get there before the moon rises, since they cannot have moved far in this rain and darkness. Let me go first and guide you who know every tree and stone upon this slope where I used to herd cattle when I was a child."

"Do so," said the captain. "I can see nothing now the lightning has gone, and were it not that I have sworn to dip my spear in the blood of Macumazahn who has fooled us again, I would give up the hunt."

"I think it would be better to give it up in any case," said a third voice, "since it is known throughout the land that no luck has ever come to those who tried to trap the Watcher-by-Night. Oh! he is a leopard who springs and is gone again. How many are the throats in which his fangs have met. Leave him alone, I say, lest our fate should be that of the white doctor in the Yellow-wood Swamp, he who set us on this hunt. We have his wagon and his cattle; let us be satisfied."

"I will leave him alone when he sleeps for the last time, and not before," answered the captain, "he who shot my brother in the drift the other day. What would Sekukuni say if we let him escape to bring the Swazis on us? Moreover, we want that white maiden for a hostage in case the English should attack us again. Come, you who know the road, and lead us."

There was some disturbance as this man passed to the front. Then I heard the line move forward. Presently they were going by the wall within a foot or two of me. Indeed by ill-luck just as we were opposite to each other the captain stumbled and fell against the wall.

"There is an old cattle *kraal* here," he said. "What if those white rats have hidden in it?"

I trembled as I heard the words. If a horse should neigh or make any noise that could be heard above the hiss of the rain! I did not dare to move for fear lest I should betray myself. There I stood so close to the *Kaffirs* that I could smell them and hear the rain pattering on their bodies. Only very stealthily I drew my hunting knife with my right hand. At that moment the lightning, which I thought had quite gone by, flashed again for the last time, revealing the fat face of the Basuto captain within a foot of my own, for he was turned towards the wall on which one of his hands rested. Moreover, the blue and ghastly light revealed mine to him thrust forward between the two stones, my eyes glaring at him.

"The head of a dead man is set upon the wall!" he cried in terror. "It is the ghost of—"

He got no further, for as the last word passed his lips I drove the knife at him with all my strength deep into his throat. He fell back into the arms of his followers, and next instant I heard the sound of many feet rushing in terror down the hill. What became of him I do not know, but if he still lives, probably he agrees with his tribesman that Macumazahn—Watcher-by-Night, or his ghost "is a leopard who springs and kills and is gone again"; also, that those who try to trap him meet with no luck. I say, or his ghost—because I am sure he thought that I was a spirit of the dead; doubtless I must have looked like one with my white, rain-drowned face appearing there between the stones and made ghastly and livid by the lightning.

Well, they had gone, the whole band of them, not less than thirty or forty men, so I went also, back to the cart where I found the others very comfortable indeed beneath the rainproof tilt. Saying nothing of what had happened, of which they were as innocent as babes, I took a stiff tot of brandy, for I was chilled through by the wet, and while waiting for the moon to rise, busied myself with getting the bits back into the horses' mouths—an awkward job in the dark. At length it appeared in a clear sky, for the storm had quite departed and the rain ceased. As soon as there was light enough I took the near leader by the bridle and led the cart to the brow of the hill, which was not easy under the conditions, making Kaatje follow with my horse.

Then, as there were no signs of any Basutos, we started on again, I riding about a hundred yards ahead, keeping a sharp look-out for a possible ambush. Fortunately, however, the *veld* was bare and open, consisting of long waves of ground. One start I did get, thinking that I saw men's heads just on the crest of a wave, which turned out to be only a herd of springbuck feeding among the tussocks of grass. I was very glad to see them, since their presence assured me that no human being had recently passed that way.

All night long we trekked, following the *Kaffir* path for as long as I could see it, and after that going by my compass. I knew whereabouts the drift of the Crocodile River should be, as I had crossed it twice before in my life, and kept my eyes open for a certain tall *koppie* which stood within half a mile it on the Swazi side of the river. Ultimately to my joy I caught sight of this hill faintly outlined against the sky and headed for it. Half a mile further on I struck a wagon-track made by Boers trekking into Swazi-Land to trade or shoot. Then I knew that the drift was straight ahead of us, and called to Anscombe to flog up the weary horses.

We reached the river just before the dawn. To my horror it was very full, so full that the drift looked dangerous, for it had been swollen by the thunder-rain of the previous night. Indeed some wandering Swazis on the further bank shouted to us that we should be drowned if we tried to cross.

"Which means that the only thing to do is to stay until the water runs down," I said to Anscombe, for the two women, tired out, were asleep.

"I suppose so," he answered, "unless those Basutos—"

I looked back up the long slope down which we had come and saw no one. Then I raised myself in my stirrups and looked along another track that joined the road just here, leading from the bush-*veld*, as ours led from the high-*veld*. The sun was rising now, dispersing the mist that hung about the trees after the wet. Searching among these with my eyes, presently I perceived the light gleaming upon what I knew must be the points of spears projecting above the level of the ground vapour.

"Those devils are after us by the lower road," I said to Anscombe, adding, "I heard them pass the old cattle *kraal* last night. They followed our spoor over the edge of the hill, but in the dark lost it among the stones."

He whistled and asked what was to be done.

"That is for you to decide," I answered. "For my part I'd rather risk the river than the Basutos," and I looked at the slumbering Heda.

"Can we bolt back the way we came, Allan?"

"The horses are very spent and we might meet more Basutos," and again I looked at Heda.

"A hard choice, Allan. It is wonderful how women complicate everything in life, because they are life, I suppose." He thought a moment and went on, "Let's try the river. If we fail, it will be soon over, and it is better to drown than be speared."

"Or be kept alive by savages who hate us," I exclaimed, with my eyes still fixed upon Heda.

Then I got to business. There were hide *riems* on the bridles of the leaders. I undid these and knotted their loose ends firmly together. To them I made fast the *riem* of my own mare, slipping a loop I tied in it, over my right hand and saying—

"Now I will go first, leading the horses. Do you drive after me for all you are worth, even if they are swept off their feet. I can trust my beast to swim straight, and being a mare, I hope that the horses will follow her as they have done all night. Wake up Heda and Kaatje."

He nodded, and looking very pale, said—

"Heda my dear, I am sorry to disturb you, but we have to get over a river with a rough bottom, so you and Kaatje must hang on and sit tight. Don't be frightened, you are as safe as a church."

"God forgive him for that lie," thought I to myself as, having tightened the girths, I mounted my mare. Then gripping the *riem* I kicked the beast to a canter, Anscombe flogging up the team as we swung down the bank to the edge of the foaming torrent, on the further side of which the Swazis shouted and gesticulated to us to go back.

We were in it now, for, as I had hoped, the horses followed the mare without hesitation. For the first twenty yards or so all went well, I heading up the stream. Then suddenly I felt that the mare was swimming.

"Flog the horses and don't let them turn," I shouted to Anscombe.

Ten more yards and I glanced over my shoulder. The team was swimming also, and behind them the cart rocked and bobbed like a boat swinging in a heavy sea. There came a strain on the *riem*; the leaders were trying to turn! I pulled hard and encouraged them with my voice, while Anscombe, who drove splendidly, kept their heads as straight as he could. Mercifully they came round again and struck out for the further shore, the water-logged cart floating after them. Would it turn over? That was the question in my mind. Five seconds; ten seconds and it was still upright. Oh! it was going. No, a fierce back eddy caught it and set it straight again. My mare touched bottom and there was hope. It struggled forward, being swept down the stream all the time. Now the horses in the cart also found their footing and we were saved.

No, the wet had caused the knot of one of the *riems* to slip beneath the strain, or perhaps it broke—I don't know. Feeling the pull slacken the leaders whipped round on to the wheelers. There they all stood in a heap, their heads and part of their necks above water, while the cart floated behind them on its side. Kaatje screamed and Anscombe flogged. I leapt from my mare and struggled to the leaders, the water up to my chin. Grasping their bits I managed to keep them from turning further. But I could do no more and death came very near to us. Had it not been for some of those brave Swazis on the bank it would have found us, every one. But they plunged in, eight of them, holding each other's hands, and half-swimming, half-wading, reached us. They got the horses by the head and straightened them out, while Anscombe plied his whip. A dash forward and the wheels were on the bottom again.

Three minutes later we were safe on the further bank, which my mare had already reached, where I lay gasping on my face, ejaculating prayers of thankfulness and spitting out muddy water.

CHAPTER 10

Nombe

The Swazis, shivering, for all these people hate cold, and shaking themselves like a dog when he comes to shore, gathered round, examining me.

"Why!" said one of them, an elderly man who seemed to be their leader, "this is none other than Macumazahn, Watcher-by-Night, the old friend of all us black people. Surely the spirits of our fathers have been with us who might have risked our lives to save a Boer or a half-breed." (The Swazis, I may explain, did not like the Boers for reasons they considered sound.)

"Yes," I said, sitting up, "it is I, Macumazahn."

"Then why," asked the man, "did you, whom all know to be wise, show yourself to have suddenly become a fool?" and he pointed to the raging river.

"And why," I asked, "do you show yourself a fool by supposing that I, whom you know to be none, am a fool? Look across the water for your answer."

He looked and saw the Basutos, fifty or more of them, arriving, just too late. "Who are these?" he asked.

"They are the people of Sekukuni whom you should know well enough. They have hunted us all night, yes, and before, seeking to murder us; also they have stolen our oxen, thirty-two fine oxen which I give to your king if he can take them back. Now perhaps you understand why we dared the Crocodile River in its rage."

At the name of Sekukuni the man, who it seemed was the captain of some border guards, stiffened all over like a terrier which perceives a rat. "What!" he exclaimed, "do these dirty Basuto dogs dare to carry spears so near our country? Have they not yet learned their lesson?"

Then he rushed into the water, shaking an *assegai* he had snatched up, and shouted,

"Bide a while, you fleas from the *kaross* of Sekukuni, till I can come across and crack you between my thumb and finger. Or at the least wait until Macumazahn has time to get his rifle. No, put down those guns of yours; for every shot you fire I swear that I will cut ten Basuto throats when we come to storm your *koppies*, as we shall do ere long."

"Be silent," I said, "and let me speak."

Then I, too, called across the river, asking where was that fat captain of theirs, as I would talk with him. One of the men shouted back that he had stopped behind, very sick, because of a ghost that he had seen.

"Ah!" I answered, "a ghost who pricked him in the throat. Well, I was that ghost, and such are the things that happen to those who would harm Macumazahn and his friends. Did you not say last night that he is a leopard who leaps out in the dark, bites and is gone again?"

"Yes," the man shouted back, "and it is true, though had we known, O Macumazahn, that you were the ghost hiding in those stones, you should never have leapt again. Oh! that white medicine-man who is dead has sent us on a mad errand."

"So you will think when I come to visit you among your *koppies*. Go home and take a message from Macumazahn to Sekukuni, who believes that the English have run away from him. Tell him that they will return again and these Swazis with them, and that then he will cease to live and his town will be burnt and his tribe will no more be a tribe. Away now, more swiftly than you came, since the water by which you thought to trap us is falling, and a Swazi *impi* gathers to make an end of every one of you."

The man attempted no answer, nor did his people so much as fire on us. They turned tail and crept off like a pack of frightened jack-als—pursued by the mocking of the Swazis.

Still in a way they had the laugh of us, seeing that they gave us a terrible fright and stole our wagon and thirty-two oxen. Well, a year or two later I helped to pay them back for that fright and even recovered some of the oxen.

When they had gone the Swazis led us to a *kraal* about two miles from the river, sending on a runner with orders to make huts and food ready for us. It was just as much as we could do to reach it, for we were all utterly worn out, as were the horses. Still we did get there at last, the hot sun warming us as we went. Arrived at the *kraal* I helped Heda and Kaatje from the cart—the former could scarcely walk, poor dear—and into the guest hut which seemed clean, where food of a sort and fur *karosses* were brought to them in which to wrap them-selves while their clothes dried.

Leaving them in charge of two old women, I went to see to Anscombe, who as yet could not do much for himself, also to the *outspanning* of the horses which were put into a cattle *kraal*, where they lay down at once without attempting to eat the green forage which was given to them. After this I gave our goods into the charge of the *kraal*-head, a nice old fellow whom I had never met before, and he led Anscombe to another hut close to that where the women were. Here we drank some *maas*, that is curdled milk, ate a little mutton, though we were too fatigued to be very hungry, and stripping off our wet clothes, threw them out into the sun to dry.

"That was a close shave," said Anscombe as he wrapped up in the *kaross*.

"Very," I answered. "So close that I think you must have been started in life with an extra strong guardian angel well accustomed to native ways."

"Yes," he replied, "and, old fellow, I believe that on earth he goes by the name of Allan Quatermain."

After this I remember no more, for I went to sleep, and so remained for about twenty-four hours. This was not wonderful, seeing that for two days and nights practically I had not rested, during which time I went through much fatigue and many emotions.

When at length I did wake up, the first thing I saw was Anscombe already dressed, engaged in cleaning my clothes with a brush from his toilet case. I remember thinking how smart and incongruous that dressing-bag, made appropriately enough of crocodile hide, looked in this *Kaffir* hut with its silver-topped bottles and its ivory-handled razors.

"Time to get up, Sir. Bath ready, Sir," he said in his jolly, drawling voice, pointing to a calabash full of hot water. "Hope you slept as well as I did, Sir."

"You appear to have recovered your spirits," I remarked as I rose and began to wash myself.

"Yes, Sir, and why not? Heda is quite well, for I have seen her. These Swazis are very good people, and as Kaatje understands their language, bring us all we want. Our troubles seem to be done with. Old Marnham is dead, and doubtless cremated; Rodd is dead and, let us hope, in heaven; the Basutos have melted away, the morning is fine and warm and a whole kid is cooking for breakfast."

"I wish there were two, for I am ravenous," I remarked.

"The horses are getting rested and feeding well, though some of their legs have filled, and the trap is little the worse, for I have walked to look at them, or rather hopped, leaning on the shoulder of a very sniffy Swazi boy. Do you know, old fellow, I believe there never were any Basutos; also that the venerable Marnham and the lurid Rodd had no real existence, that they were but illusions, a prolonged nightmare—no more. Here is your shirt. I am sorry that I have not had time to wash it, but it has cooked well in the sun, which, being flannel, is almost as good."

"At any rate Heda remains," I remarked, cutting his nonsense short, "and I suppose she is not a nightmare or a delusion."

"Yes, thank God! she remains," he replied with earnestness. "Oh! Allan, I thought she must drown in that river, and if I had lost her, I think I should have gone mad. Indeed, at the moment I felt myself going mad while I dragged and flogged at those horses."

"Well, you didn't lose her, and if she had drowned, you would have drowned also. So don't talk any more about it. She is safe, and now we have got to keep her so, for you are not married yet, my boy, and there are generally more trees in a wood than one can see. Still we are alive and well, which is more than we had any right to expect, and, as you say, let us thank God for that."

Then I put on my coat and my boots which Anscombe had greased as he had no blacking, and crept from the hut.

There, only a few yards away, engaged in setting the breakfast in the shadow of another hut on a tanned hide that served for a tablecloth while Kaatje saw to the cooking close by, I found Heda, still a little pale and sorrowful but otherwise quite well and rested. Moreover, she had managed to dress herself very nicely, I suppose by help of spare clothes in the cart, and therefore looked as charming as she always did. I think that her perfect manners were one of her greatest attractions. Thus on this morning her first thought was to thank me very sweetly for all she was good enough to say I had done for her and Anscombe, thereby, as she put it, saving their lives several times over.

"My dear young lady," I answered as roughly as I could, "don't flatter yourself on that point; it was my own life of which I was thinking."

But she only smiled and, shaking her head in a fascinating way that was peculiar to her, remarked that I could not deceive her as I did the *Kaffirs*. After this the solid Kaatje brought the food and we breakfasted very heartily, or at least I did.

Now I am not going to set out all the details of our journey through Swazi-Land, for though in some ways it was interesting enough, also as comfortable as a stay among savages can be, for everywhere we were kindly received, to do so would be too long, and I must get on with my story. At the king's *kraal*, which we did not reach for some days as the absence of roads and the flooded state of the rivers, also the need of sparing our horses, caused us to travel very slowly, I met a Boer who I think was concession hunting.

He told me that things were really serious in Zululand, so serious that he thought there was a probability of immediate war between the English and the Zulus. He said also that Cetewayo, the Zulu king, had sent messengers to stir up the Basutos and other tribes against the white men, with the result that Sekukuni had already made a raid towards Pilgrim's Rest and Lydenburg.

I expressed surprise and asked innocently if he had done any harm. The Boer replied he understood that they had stolen some cattle, killed two white men, if not more, and burnt their house. He added, however, that he was not sure whether the white men had been killed by the *Kaffirs* or by other white men with whom they had quarrelled. There was a rumour to this effect, and he understood that the magistrate of Barberton had gone with some mounted police and armed natives to investigate the matter.

Then we parted, as, having got his concession to which the king Umbandine had put his mark when he was drunk on brandy that the Boer himself had brought with him as a present, he was anxious to be gone before he grew sober and revoked it. Indeed, he was in so great a hurry that he never stopped to inquire what I was doing in Swazi-Land, nor do I think he realized that I was not alone. Certainly he was quite unaware that I had been mixed up in these Basuto troubles. Still his story as to the investigation concerning the deaths of Marnham and Rodd made me uneasy, since I feared lest he should hear something on his journey and put two and two together, though as a matter of fact I don't think he ever did either of these things.

The Swazis told me much the same story as to the brewing Zulu storm. In fact an old *Induna* or councillor, whom I knew, informed me that Cetewayo had sent messengers to them, asking for their help if it should come to fighting with the white men, but that the king and councillors answered that they had always been the Queen's children (which was not strictly true, as they were never under English rule) and did not wish to "bite her feet if she should have to fight with her hands." I replied that I hoped they would always act up to these fine words, and changed the subject.

Now once more the question arose as to whether we should make for Natal or press on to Zululand. The rumour of coming war suggested that the first would be our better course, while the Boer's story as to the investigation of Rodd's death pointed the other way. Really I did not know which to do, and as usual Anscombe and Heda seemed inclined to leave the decision to me. I think that after all Natal would have gained the day had it not been for a singular circumstance, not a flash of lightning this time. Indeed, I had almost made up my mind to risk trouble and inquiry as to Rodd's death, remembering that in Natal these two young people could get married, which, being in *loco parentis*, I thought it desirable they should do as soon as possible, if only to ease me of my responsibilities. Also thence I could attend to the matter of Heda's inheritance and rid myself of her father's will that already had been somewhat damaged in the Crocodile River, though not as much as it might have been since I had taken the precaution to enclose it in Anscombe's sponge bag before we left the house.

The circumstance was this: On emerging from the cart one morning, where I slept to keep an eye upon the valuables, for it will be remembered that we had a considerable sum in gold with us, also Heda's jewels, a Swazi informed me that a messenger wished to see me. I asked what messenger and whence did he come. He replied that the messenger was a witch-doctoress named Nombe, and that she came from Zululand and said that I knew her father.

I bade the man bring her to me, wondering who on earth she could be, for it is not usual for the Zulus to send women as messengers, and from whom she came. However, I knew exactly what she would be like, some hideous old hag smelling horribly of grease and other abominations, with a worn snake skin and some human bones tied about her.

Presently she came, escorted by the Swazi who was grinning, for I think he guessed what I expected to see. I stared and rubbed my eyes, thinking that I must still be asleep, for instead of a fat old *Isanusi* there appeared a tall and graceful young woman, rather light-coloured, with deep and quiet eyes and a by no means ill-favoured face, remarkable for a fixed and somewhat mysterious smile. She was a witch-doctoress sure enough, for she wore in her hair the regulation bladders and about her neck the circlet of baboon's teeth, also round her middle a girdle from which hung little bags of medicines.

She contemplated me gravely and I contemplated her, waiting till she should choose to speak. At length, having examined me inch by inch, she saluted by raising her rounded arm and tapering hand, and remarked in a soft, full voice: "All is as the picture told. I perceive before me the lord Macumazahn."

I thought this a strange saying, seeing that I could not recollect having given my photograph to any one in Zululand.

116

"You need no magic to tell you that, doctoress," I remarked, "but where did you see my picture?"

"In the dust far away," she replied.

"And who showed it to you?"

"One who knew you, O Macumazahn, in the years before I came out of the Darkness, one named Opener of Roads, and with him another who also knew you in those years, one who has gone down to the Darkness."

Now for some occult reason I shrank from asking the name of this "one who had gone down to the Darkness," although I was sure that she was waiting for the question. So I merely remarked, without showing surprise—

"So Zikali still lives, does he? He should have been dead long ago."

"You know well that he lives, Macumazahn, for how could he die till his work was accomplished? Moreover, you will remember that he spoke to you when last moon was but just past her full—in a dream, Macumazahn. I brought that dream, although you did not see me."

"*Pish!*" I exclaimed. "Have done with your talk of dreams. Who thinks anything of dreams?"

"You do," she replied even more placidly than before, "you whom that dream has brought hither—with others."

"You lie," I said rudely. "The Basutos brought me here."

"The Watcher-by-Night is pleased to say that I lie, so doubtless I do lie," she answered, her fixed smile deepening a little. Then she folded her arms across her breast and remained silent.

"You are a messenger, O seer of pictures in the dust and bearer of the cup of dreams," I said with sarcasm. "Who sends a message by your lips for me, and what are the words of the message?"

"My Lords the Spirits spoke the message by the mouth of the master Zikali. He sends it on to you by the lips of your servant, the doctoress Nombe."

"Are you indeed a doctoress, being so young?" I asked, for somehow I wished to postpone the hearing of that message.

"O Macumazahn, I have heard the call, I have felt the pain in my back, I have drunk of the black medicine and of the white medicine, yes, for a whole year. I have been visited by the multitude of Spirits and seen the shades of those who live and of those who are dead. I have dived into the river and drawn my snake from its mud; see, its skin is about me now," and opening the mantle she wore she showed what looked like the skin of a black mamba, fastened round her slender body. "I have dwelt in the wilderness alone and listened to

117

its voices. I have sat at the feet of my master, the Opener of Roads, and looked down the road and drunk of his wisdom. Yes, I am in truth a doctoress."

"Well, after all this, you should be as wise as you are pretty."

"Once before, Macumazahn, you told a maid of my people that she was pretty and she came to no good end; though to one that was great. Therefore do not say to me that I am pretty, though I am glad that you should think so who can compare me with so many whom you have known," and she dropped her eyes, looking a little shy.

It was the first human touch I had seen about her, and I was glad to have found a weak spot in her armour. Moreover, from that moment she was always my friend.

"As you will, Nombe. Now for your message."

"My Lords the Spirits, speaking through Zikali as one who makes music speak through a pipe of reeds, say—"

"Never mind what the spirits say. Tell me what Zikali says," I interrupted.

"So be it, Macumazahn. These are the words of Zikali: 'O Watcher-by-Night, the time draws on when the Thing-who-should-never-have-been-born will be as though he never had been born, whereat he rejoices. But first there is much for him to do, and as he told you nearly three hundred moons ago, in what must be done you will have your part. Of that he will speak to you afterwards. Macumazahn, you dreamed a dream, did you not, lying asleep in the house that was built of white stone which now is black with fire? I, Zikali, sent you that dream through the arts of a child of mine who is named Nombe, she to whom I have given a Spirit to guide her feet. You did well to follow it, Macumazahn, for had you tried the other path, which would have led you back to the towns of the white men, you and those with you must have been killed, how it does not matter. Now by the mouth of Nombe I say to you, do not follow the thought that is in your mind as she speaks to you and go to Natal, since if you do so, you and those with you will come to much shame and trouble that to you would be worse than death, over the matter of the killing of a certain white doctor in a swamp where grow yellow-wood trees. For there in Natal you will be taken, all of you, and sent back to the Transvaal to be tried before a man who wears upon his head horse's hair stained white. But if you come to Zululand this shadow shall pass away from you, since great things are about to happen which will cause so small a matter to be forgot. Moreover, I Zikali, who do not lie, promise this: That however great may be their dangers here in Zululand, those half-fledged ones whom you, the old night-hawk, cover with your wings, shall in the end suffer no harm; those of whom I spoke to you in your dream, the white lord, Mauriti, and the white lady, Heddana, who stretch out their arms one to another. I wait to welcome you, here at the Black Kloof, whither my daughter Nombe will guide you. Cetewayo, the king, also will welcome you, and so will another whose name I do not utter. Now choose. I have spoken.'"

Having delivered her message Nombe stood quite still, smiling as before, and apparently indifferent as to its effect.

"How do I know that you come from Zikali?" I asked. "You may be but the bait set upon a trap."

From somewhere within her robe she produced a knife and handed it to me, remarking—

"The Master says you will remember this, and by it know that the message comes from him. He bade me add that with it was carved a certain image that once he gave to you at Panda's *kraal*, wrapped round with a woman's hair, which image you still have."

I looked at the knife and did remember it, for it was one of those of Swedish make with a wooden handle, the first that I had ever seen in Africa. I had made a present of it to Zikali when I returned to Zululand before the war between the Princes. The image, too, I still possessed. It was that of the woman called Mameena who brought about the war, and the wrapping which covered it was of the hair that once grew upon her head.

"The words are Zikali's," I said, returning her the knife, "but why do you call yourself the child of one who is too old to be a father?"

"The Master says that my great-grandmother was his daughter and that therefore I am his child. Now, Macumazahn, I go to eat with my people, for I have servants with me. Then I must speak with the Swazi king, for whom I also have a message, which I cannot do at present because he is still drunk with the white man's liquor. After that I shall be ready to return with you to Zululand."

"I never said that I was going to Zululand, Nombe."

"Yet your heart has gone there already, Macumazahn, and you must follow your heart. Does not the image which was carved with the knife you gave, hold a white heart in its hand, and although it seems to be but a bit of Umzimbeete wood, is it not alive and bewitched, which perhaps is why you could never make up your mind to burn it, Macumazahn?"

"I wish I had," I replied angrily; but having thrown this last spear, with a flash of her unholy eyes Nombe had turned and gone.

119

A clever woman and thoroughly coached, thought I. Well, Zikali was never one to suffer fools, and doubtless she is another of the pawns whom he uses on his board of policy. Oh! she, or rather he was right; my heart was in Zululand, though not in the way he thought, and I longed to see the end of that great game played by a wizard against a despot and his hosts.

So we went to Zululand because after talking it over we all came to the conclusion that this was the best thing to do, especially as there we seemed to be sure of a welcome. For later in the day Nombe repeated to Anscombe and Heda the invitation which she had delivered to me, assuring them also that in Zululand they would come to no harm.

It was curious to watch the meeting between Heda and Nombe. The doctoress appeared just as we had risen from breakfast, and Heda, turning round, came face to face with her.

"Is this your witch, Mr. Quatermain?" she asked me in her vivacious way. "Why, she is different from what I expected, quite good-looking and, yes, impressive. I am not sure that she does not frighten me a little."

"What does the *Inkosikaasi* (i.e., the chieftainess) say concerning me, Macumazahn?" asked Nombe.

"Only what I said, that you are young who she thought would be old, and pretty who she thought would be ugly."

"To grow old we must first be young, Macumazahn, and in due season all of us will become ugly, even the *Inkosikaasi*. But I thought she said also that she feared me."

"Do you know English, Nombe?"

"Nay, but I know how to read eyes, and the *Inkosikaasi* has eyes that talk. Tell her that she has no reason to fear me who would be her friend, though I think that she will bring me little luck."

It was scarcely necessary, so far as Heda was concerned, but I translated, leaving out the last sentence.

"Say to her that I am grateful who have few friends, and that I will fear her no more," said Heda.

Again I translated, whereon Nombe stretched out her hand, saying—

"Let her not scorn to take it, it is clean. It has brought no man to his death—" Here she looked at Heda meaningly. "Moreover, though she is white and I am black, I like herself am of high blood and come of a race of warriors who did nothing small, and lastly, we are of an age, and if she is beautiful, I am wise and have gifts great as her own."

Once more I interpreted for the benefit of Anscombe, for Heda understood Zulu well enough, although she had pretended not to do so, after which the two shook hands, to Anscombe's amusement and my wonder. For I felt this scene to be strained and one that hid, or presaged, something I did not comprehend.

"This is the Chief she loves?" said Nombe to me, studying Anscombe with her steady eyes after Heda had gone. "Well, he is no common man and brave, if idle; one, too, who may grow tall in the world, should he live, when he has learned to think. But, Macumazahn, if she met you both at the same time why did she not choose you?"

"Just now you said you were wise, Nombe," I replied laughing, "but now I see that, like most of your trade, you are but a vain boaster. Is there a hat upon my head that you cannot see the colour of my hair, and is it natural that youth should turn to age?"

"Sometimes if the mind is old, Macumazahn, which is why I love the Spirits only who are more ancient than the mountains, and with them Zikali their servant, who was young before the Zulus were a people, or so he says, and still year by year gathers wisdom as the bee gathers honey. *Inspan* your horses, Macumazahn, for I have done my business and am ready to start."

Chapter 11

Zikali

Ten days had gone by when once more I found myself drawing near to the mouth of the Black Kloof where dwelt Zikali the wizard. Our journey in Zululand had been tedious and uneventful. It seemed to me that we met extraordinarily few people; it was as though the place had suddenly become depopulated, and I even passed great *kraals* where there was no one to be seen. I asked Nombe what was the meaning of this, for she and three silent men she had with her were acting as our guides. Once she answered that the people had moved because of lack of food, as the season had been one of great scarcity owing to drought, and once that they had been summoned to a gathering at the king's *kraal* near Ulundi. At any rate they were not there, and the few who did appear stared at us strangely.

Moreover, I noticed that they were not allowed to speak to us. Also Heda was kept in the cart and Nombe insisted that the rear canvas curtain should be closed and a blanket fastened behind Anscombe who drove, evidently with the object that she should not be seen. Further, on the plea of weariness, from the time that we entered Zulu territory Nombe asked to be allowed to ride in the cart with Kaatje and Heda, her real reason, as I was sure, being that she might keep a watch on them. Lastly we travelled by little-frequented tracks, halting at night in out-of-the-way places, where, however, we always found food awaiting us, doubtless by arrangement.

With one man whom I had known in past days and who recognized me, I did manage to have a short talk. He asked me what I was doing in Zululand at that time. I replied that I was on a visit to Zikali, whereon he said I should be safer with him than with any one else.

Our conversation went no further, for just then one of Nombe's servants appeared and made some remark to the man of which I could not catch the meaning, whereon he promptly turned and deported, leaving me wondering and uneasy.

Evidently we were being isolated, but when I remonstrated with Nombe she only answered with her most unfathomable smile—

"O Macumazahn, you must ask Zikali of all these things. I am no one and know nothing, who only do what the Master tells me is for your good."

"I am minded to turn and depart from Zululand," I said angrily, "for in this low *veld* whither you have led us there is fever and the horses will catch sickness or be bitten by the tsetse fly and perish."

"I cannot say, Macumazahn, who only travel by the road the Master pointed out. Yet if you will be guided by me, you will not try to leave Zululand."

"You mean that I am in a trap, Nombe."

"I mean that the country is full of soldiers and that all white men have fled from it. Therefore, even if you were allowed to pass because the Zulus love you, Macumazahn, it might well happen that those with you would stay behind, sound asleep, Macumazahn, for which, like you, I should be sorry."

After this I said no more, for I knew that she meant to warn me. We had entered on this business and must see it through to its end, sweet or bitter.

As for Anscombe and Heda their happiness seemed to be complete. The novelty of the life charmed them, and of its dangers they took no thought, being content to leave me, in whom they had a blind faith, to manage everything. Moreover, Heda, who in the joy of her love was beginning to forget the sorrow of her father's death and the other tragic events through which she had just passed, took a great fancy to the young witch-doctoress who conversed with her in Zulu, a language of which, having lived so long in Natal, Heda knew much already. Indeed, when I suggested to her that to be over-trusting was not wise, she fired up and replied that she had been accustomed to natives all her life and could judge them, adding that she had every confidence in Nombe.

After this I held my tongue and said no more of my doubts. What was the use since Heda would not listen to them, and at that time Anscombe was nothing but her echo?

So this, for me, very dull journey continued, till at length, after being held up for a couple of days by a flooded river where there was nothing to do but sit and smoke, as Nombe requested me not to make a noise by shooting at the big game that abounded, we began to emerge from the bush-*veld* on to the lovely uplands in the neighbourhood of Nongoma. Leaving these on our right we headed for a place called Ceza, a natural stronghold consisting of a flat plain on the top of a mountain, which plain is surrounded by bush. It is at the foot of this stronghold that the Black Kloof lies, being one of the ravines that run up into the mountain.

So thither we came at last. It was drawing towards sunset, a tremendous and stormy sunset, as we approached the place, and lo! it looked exactly as it had done when first I saw it more than a score of years before, forbidding as the mouth of hell, vast and lonesome. There stood the columns of boulders fantastically piled one upon another; there grew the sparse trees upon its steep sides, mingled with aloes that looked like the shapes of men; there was the granite bottom swept almost clean by floods in some dim age, and the little stream that flowed along it. There, too, was the spot where once I had outspanned my wagons on the night when my servants swore that they saw the *Imikovu*, or wizard-raised spectres, floating past them on the air in the shapes of the Princes and others who were soon to fall at the battle of the Tugela. Up it we went, I riding and Nombe, who had descended from the cart that followed, walking by my side and watching me.

"You seem sad, Macumazahn," she said at length.

"Yes, Nombe, I am sad. This place makes me so."

"Is it the place, Macumazahn, or is it the thought of one whom once you met in the place, one who is dead?"

I looked at her, pretending not to understand, and she went on—

"I have the gift of vision, Macumazahn, which comes at times to those of my trade, and now and again, amongst others, I have seemed to see the spirit of a certain woman haunting this *kloof* as though she were waiting for some one."

"Indeed, and what may that woman be like?" I inquired carelessly.

"As it chances I can see her now gliding backwards in front of you just there, and therefore am able to answer your question, Macumazahn. She is tall and slender, beautifully made, and light-coloured for one of us black people. She has large eyes like a buck, and those eyes are full of fire that does not come from the sun but from within. Her face is tender yet proud, oh! so proud that she makes me afraid. She wears a cloak of grey fur, and about her neck there is a circlet of big blue beads with which her fingers play. A thought comes from her to me. These are the words of the thought: 'I have waited long in this dark place, watching by day and night till you, the Watcher-by-Night, return to meet me here. At length you have come, and in this enchanted place my hungry spirit can feed upon your spirit for a while. I thank you for coming, who now am no more lonely. Fear nothing, Macumazahn, for by a certain kiss I swear to you that till the appointed hour when you become as I am, I will be a shield upon your arm and a spear in your hand.' Such are the words of her thought, Macumazahn, but she has gone away and I hear no more. It was as though your horse rode over her and she passed through you."

Then, like one who wished to answer no questions, Nombe turned and went back to the cart, where she began to talk indifferently with Heda, for as soon as we entered the *kloof* her servants had drawn back the curtains and let fall the blanket. As for me, I groaned, for of course I knew that Zikali, who was well acquainted with the appearance of Mameena, had instructed Nombe to say all this to me in order to impress my mind for some reason of his own. Yet he had done it cleverly, for such words as those Mameena might well have uttered could her great spirit have need to walk the earth again. Was such a thing possible, I wondered? No, it was not possible, yet it was true that her atmosphere seemed to cling about this place and that my imagination, excited by memory and Nombe's suggestions, seemed to apprehend her presence.

As I reflected the horse advanced round the little bend in the ever-narrowing cliffs, and there in front of me, under the gigantic mass of overhanging rock, appeared the *kraal* of Zikali surrounded by its reed fence. The gate of the fence was open, and beyond it, on his stool in front of the large hut, sat Zikali. Even at that distance it was impossible to mistake his figure, which was like no other that I had known in the world. A broad-shouldered dwarf with a huge head, deep, sunken eyes and snowy hair that hung upon his shoulders; the whole frame and face pervaded with an air of great antiquity, and yet owing to the plumpness of the flesh and that freshness of skin which is sometimes seen in the aged, comparatively young-looking.

Such was the great wizard Zikali, known throughout the land for longer than any living man could remember as "Opener of Roads," a title that referred to his powers of spiritual vision, also as the *Thing-that-should-never-have-been-born*, a name given to him by Chaka, the first and greatest of the Zulu kings, because of his deformity.

There he sat silent, impassive, staring open-eyed at the red ball of the setting sun, looking more like some unshapely statue than a man. His silent, fierce-faced servants appeared. To me they looked like the same men whom I had seen here three and twenty years before, only grown older. Indeed, I think they were, for they greeted me by name and saluted by raising their broad spears. I dismounted and waited while Anscombe, whose foot was now quite well again, helped Heda from the cart which was led away by the servants. Anscombe, who seemed a little oppressed, remarked that this was a strange place.

"Yes," said Heda, "but it is magnificent. I like it."

Then her eye fell upon Zikali seated before the hut and she turned pale.

"Oh! what a terrible-looking man," she murmured, "if he is a man."

The maid Kaatje saw him also and uttered a little cry.

"Don't be frightened, dear," said Anscombe, "he is only an old dwarf."

"I suppose so," she exclaimed doubtfully, "but to me he is like the devil."

Nombe slid past us. She threw off the *kaross* she wore and for the first time appeared naked except for the *mucha* about her middle and her ornaments. Down she went on her hands and knees and in this humble posture crept towards Zikali. Arriving in front of him she touched the ground with her forehead, then lifting her right arm, gave the salute of *Makosi*, to which as a great wizard he was entitled, being supposed to be the home of many spirits. So far as I could see he took no notice of her. Presently she moved and squatted herself down on his right hand, while two of his attendants appeared from behind the hut and took their stand between him and its doorway, holding their spears raised. About a minute later Nombe beckoned to us to approach, and we went forward across the courtyard, I a little ahead of the others. As we drew near Zikali opened his mouth and uttered a loud and terrifying laugh. How well I remembered that laugh which I had first heard at Dingaan's *kraal* as a boy after the murder of Retief and the Boers.

"I begin to think that you are right and that this old gentleman must be the devil," said Anscombe to Heda, then lapsed into silence.

As I was determined not to speak first I took the opportunity to fill my pipe. Zikali, who was watching me, although all the while he seemed to be staring at the setting sun, made a sign. One of the servants dashed away and immediately returned, bearing a flaming brand which he proffered to me as a pipe-lighter. Then he departed again to bring three carved stools of red wood which he placed for us. I looked at mine and knew it again by the carvings. It was the same on which I had sat when first I met Zikali. At length he spoke in his deep, slow voice.

"Many years have gone by, Macumazahn, since you made use of that stool. They are cut in notches upon the leg you hold and you may count them if you will."

I examined the leg. There were the notches, twenty-two or three of them. On the other legs were more notches too numerous to reckon.

"Do not look at those, Macumazahn, for they have nothing to do with you. They tell the years since the first of the House of Senzanga-cona sat upon that stool, since Chaka sat upon it, since Dingaan and others sat upon it, one Mameena among them. Well, much has happened since it served you for a rest. You have wandered far and seen strange things and lived where others would have died because it was your lot to live, of all of which we will talk afterwards. And now when you are grey you have come back here, as the Opener of Roads told you you would do, bringing with you new companions, you who have the art of making friends even when you are old, which is one given to few men. Where are those with whom you used to company, Macumazahn? Where are Saduko and Mameena and the rest? All gone except the Thing-who-should-never-have-been-born," and again he laughed loudly.

"And who it seems has never learned when to die," I remarked, speaking for the first time.

"Just so, Macumazahn, because I cannot die until my work is finished. But thanks be to the spirits of my fathers and to my own that I live on to glut with vengeance, the end draws near at last, and as I promised you in the dead days, you shall have your share in it, Macumazahn."

He paused, then continued, still staring at the sinking sun, which made his remarks about us, whom he did not seem to see, uncanny—

"That white man with you is brave and well-born, one who loves fighting, I think, and the maiden is fair and sweet, with a high spirit. She is thinking to herself that I am an old wizard whom, if she were not afraid of me, she would ask to tell her her fortune. See, she understands and starts. Well, perhaps I will one day. Meanwhile, here is a little bit of it. She will have five children, of whom two will die and one will give her so much trouble that she will wish it had died also. But who their father will be I do not say. Nombe my child, lead away this White One and her woman to the hut that has been made ready for her, for she is weary and would rest. See, too, that she lacks for nothing which we can give her who is our guest. Let the white lord, Mauriti, accompany her to the hut and be shown that next to it in which he and Macumazahn will sleep, so that he may be sure that she is safe, and attend to the horses if he wills. There is a place to tether

127

them behind the huts, and the men who travelled with you will help him. Afterwards, when I have spoken with him, Macumazahn can join them that they may eat before they sleep."

These directions I translated to Anscombe, who went gladly enough with Heda, for I think they were both afraid of the terrible old dwarf and did not desire his company in the gathering gloom.

"The sun sinks once more, Macumazahn," he said when they were gone, "and the air grows chill. Come with me now into my hut where the fire burns, for I am aged and the cold strikes through me. Also there we can be alone."

So speaking he turned and crawled into the hut, looking like a gigantic white-headed beetle as he did so, a creature, I remembered, to which I had once compared him in the past. I followed, carrying the historic stool, and when he had seated himself on his *kaross* on the further side of the fire, took up my position opposite to him. This fire was fed with some kind of root or wood that gave a thin clear flame with little or no smoke. Over it he crouched, so closely that his great head seemed to be almost in the flame at which he stared with unblinking eyes as he had done at the sun, circumstances which added to his terrifying appearance and made me think of a certain region and its inhabitants.

"Why do you come here, Macumazahn?" he asked after studying me for a while through that window of fire.

"Because you brought me, Zikali, partly through your messenger, Nombe, and partly by means of a dream which she says you sent."

"Did I, Macumazahn? If so, I have forgotten it. Dreams are as many as gnats by the water; they bite us while we sleep, but when we wake up we forget them. Also it is foolishness to say that one man can send a dream to another."

"Then your messenger lied, Zikali, especially as she added that she brought it."

"Of course she lied, Macumazahn. Is she not my pupil whom I have trained from a child? Moreover, she lied well, it would seem, who guessed what sort of a dream you would have when you thought of turning your steps to Zululand."

"Why do you play at sticks (i.e., fence) with me, Zikali, seeing that neither of us are children?"

"O Macumazahn, that is where you are mistaken, seeing that both of us, old though we be and cunning though we think ourselves, are nothing but babes in the arms of Fate. Well, well, I will tell you the truth, since it would be foolish to try to throw dust into such eyes as yours. I knew that you were down in Sekukuni's country and I was watching you—through my spies. You have been nowhere during all these years that I was not watching you—through my spies. For instance, that Arab-looking man named Harut, whom first you met at a big *kraal* in a far country, was a spy of mine. He has visited me lately and told me much of your doings. No, don't ask me of him now who would talk to you of other matters—"

"Does Harut still live then, and has he found a new god in place of the Ivory Child?" I interrupted.

"Macumazahn, if he did not live, how could he visit and speak with me? Well, I watched you there by the Oliphant's River where you fought Sekukuni's people, and afterwards in the marble hut where you found the old white man dead in his chair and got the writings that you have in your pocket which concern the maiden Heddana; also afterwards when the white man, your friend, killed the doctor who fell into a mud hole and the Basutos stole his cattle and wagon."

"How do you know all these things, Zikali?"

"Have I not told you—through my spies. Was there not a half-breed driver called Footsack, and do not the Basutos come and go between the Black Kloof and Sekukuni's town, bearing me tidings?"

"Yes, Zikali, and so does the wind and so do the birds."

"True! O Macumazahn, I see that you are one who has watched Nature and its ways as closely as my spies watch you. So I learned these matters and knew that you were in trouble over the death of these white men, and your friends likewise, and as you were always dear to me, I sent that child Nombe to bring you to me, thinking from what I knew of you that you would be more likely to follow a woman who is both wise and good to look at, than a man who might be neither. I told her to say to you that you and the others would be safer here than in Natal at present. It seems that you hearkened and came. That is all."

"Yes, I hearkened and came. But, Zikali, that is not all, for you know well that you sent for me for your own sake, not for mine."

"O Macumazahn, who can prevent a needle from piercing cloth when it is pushed by a finger like yours? Your wits are too sharp for me, Macumazahn; your eyes read through the blanket of cunning with which I would hide my thought. You speak truly. I did send for you for my own sake as well as for yours. I sent for you because I wanted your counsel, Macumazahn, and because Cetewayo the king also wants your counsel, and I wished to see you before you saw Cetewayo. Now you have the whole truth."

"What do you want my counsel about, Zikali?"

He leaned forward till his white locks almost seemed to mingle with the thin flame, through which he glared at me with eyes that were fiercer than the fire.

"Macumazahn, you remember the story that I told you long ago, do you not?"

"Very well, Zikali. It was that you hate the House of Senzangacona which has given all its kings to Zululand. First, because you are one of the Dwandwe tribe whom the Zulus crushed and mocked at. Secondly, because Chaka the Lion named you the *Thing-that-should-never-have-been-born* and killed your wives, for which crime you brought about the death of Chaka. Thirdly, because you have matched your single wit for many years against all the power of the royal House and yet kept your life in you, notably when Panda threatened you in my presence at the trial of one who has 'gone down,' and you told him to kill you if he dared. Now you would prove that you were right by causing your cunning to triumph over the royal House."

"True, quite true, O Macumazahn. You have a good memory, Macumazahn, especially for anything that has to do with that woman who has 'gone down.' I sent her down, but how was she named, Macumazahn? I forget, I forget, whose mind being old, falls suddenly into black pits of darkness—like her who went down."

He paused and we stared at each other through the veil of fire. Then as I made no answer, he went on—

"Oh! I remember now, she was called Mameena, was she not, a name taken from the wailing of the wind? Hark! It is wailing now."

I listened; it was, and I shivered to hear it, since but a minute before the night had been quite still. Yes, the wind moaned and wailed about the rocks of the Black Kloof.

"Well, enough of her. Why trouble about the dead when there are so many to be sent to join them? Macumazahn, the hour is at hand. The fool Cetewayo has quarrelled with your people, the English, and on my counsel. He has sent and killed women, or allowed others to do so, across the river in Natal. His messengers came to me asking what he should do. I answered, 'Shall a king of the blood of Chaka fear to allow his own wicked ones to be slain because they have stepped across a strip of water, and still call himself king of the Zulus?' So those women were dragged back across the water and killed; and now the Queen's man from the Cape asks many things, great fines of cattle, the giving up of the slayers, and that an end should be made of the Zulu army, which is to lay down its spears and set to hoeing like the old women in the *kraals*."

130

"And if the king refuses, what then, Zikali?"

"Then, Macumazahn, the Queen's man will declare war on the Zulus; already he gathers his soldiers for the war."

"Will Cetewayo refuse, Zikali?"

"I do not know. His mind swings this way and that, like a pole balanced on a rock. The ends of the pole are weighted with much counsel, and it hangs so even that if a grasshopper lit on one end or the other, it would turn the scale."

"And do you wish me to be that grasshopper, Zikali?"

"Who else? That is why I brought you to Zululand."

"So you wish me to counsel Cetewayo to lie down in the bed that the English have made for him. If he seeks my advice I will do so gladly, for so I am sure he will sleep well."

"Why do you mock me, Macumazahn? I wish you to counsel Cetewayo to throw back his word into the teeth of the Queen's man and to fight the English."

"And thus bring destruction on the Zulus and death to thousands of them and of my own people, and in return gain nothing but remorse. Do you think me mad or wicked, or both, that I should do this thing?"

"Nay, Macumazahn, you would gain much. I could show you where the king's cattle are hidden. The English will never find them, and after the war you might take as many as you chose. But it would be useless, for knowing you well, I am sure that you would only hand them over to the British Government, as once you handed over the cattle of Bangu, being fashioned that way by the Great-Great, Macumazahn."

"Perhaps I might, but then what should I gain, Zikali?"

"This: you would so bring things about that, being broken by war, the Zulu power could never again menace the white men, which would be a great and good deed, Macumazahn."

"Mayhap—I am not sure. But of this I am sure, that I will not thrust my face into your nest of wasps, that the English hornets may steal the honey when they are disturbed. I leave such matters to the Queen and those who rule under her. So have done with such talk, for you do but waste your breath, Zikali."

"It is as I guessed it would be," he answered, shaking his great head. "You are too honest to prosper in the world, Macumazahn. Well, I must find other means to bring the House of Cetewayo to the end that he deserves, who has been an evil and a cruel king."

All this he said, showing neither surprise nor resentment, which convinced me of what I had suspected throughout, that never for an instant did he believe that I should fall in with his suggestions and

131

try to influence the Zulus to declare war. No, this talk of his was but a blind; there was some deeper scheme at work in his cunning old brain which he was hiding from me. Why exactly had he beguiled me to Zululand? I could not divine, and to ask him would be worse than useless, but then and there I made up my mind that I would get away from the Black Kloof early on the following morning, if that were possible.

He began to speak of other matters in a low, droning voice, like a man who converses with himself. Sad, all of them, such as the haunted death of Saduko who had betrayed his lord, the Prince Umbelazi, because of a woman, every circumstance of which seemed to be familiar to him.

I made no answer, who was waiting for an opportunity to leave the hut, and did not care to dwell on these events. He ceased and brooded for a while, then said suddenly—

"You are hungry and would eat, Macumazahn, and I who eat little would sleep, for in sleep the multitudes of Spirits visit me, bringing tidings from afar. Well, we have spoken together and of that I am glad, for who knows when the chance will come again, though I think that soon we shall meet at Ulundi, Ulundi where Fate spreads its net. What was it I had to say to you? Ah! I remember. There is one who is always in your thoughts and whom you wish to see, one too who wishes to see you. You shall, you shall in payment for the trouble you have taken in coming so far to visit a poor old Zulu doctor whom, as you told me long ago, you know to be nothing but a cheat."

He paused and, why I could not tell, I grew weak with fear of I knew not what, and bethought me of flight.

"It is cold in this hut, is it not?" he went on. "Burn up, fire, burn up!" and plunging his hand into a cat-skin bag of medicines which he wore, he drew out some powder which he threw upon the embers that instantly burst into bright flame.

"Look now, Macumazahn," he said, "look to your right."

I looked and oh Heaven! there before me with outstretched arms and infinite yearning on her face, stood Mameena, Mameena as I had last seen her after I gave her the promised kiss that she used to cover her taking of the poison. For five seconds, mayhap, she stood thus, living, wonderful, but still as death, the fierce light showing all. Then the flame died down again and she was gone.

I turned and next instant was out of the hut, pursued by the terrible laughter of Zikali.

CHAPTER 12

Trapped

Outside in the cool night air I recovered myself, sufficiently at any rate to be able to think, and saw at once that the thing was an illusion for which Zikali had prepared my mind very carefully by means of the young witch-doctoress, Nombe. He knew well enough that this remarkable woman, Mameena, had made a deep impression on me nearly a quarter of a century before, as she had done upon other men with whom she had been associated. Therefore it was probable that she would always be present to my thought, since whatever a man forgets, he remembers the women who have shown him favour, true or false, for Nature has decreed it thus.

Moreover, this was one to be remembered for herself, since she was beautiful and most attractive in her wild way. Also she had brought about a great war, causing the death of thousands, and lastly her end might fairly be called majestic. All these impressions Zikali had in-structed Nombe to revivify by her continual allusions to Mameena, and lastly by her pretence that she saw her walking in front of me. Then when I was tired and hungry, in that place which for me was so closely connected with this woman, and in his own uncanny com-pany, either by mesmerism or through the action of the drug he threw upon the fire, he had succeeded in calling up the illusion of her pres-ence to my charmed sight. All this was clear enough, what remained obscure was his object.

Possibly he had none beyond an impish desire to frighten me, which is common enough among practitioners of magic in all lands. Well, for a little while he had succeeded, although to speak truth I remained uncertain whether in a sense I was not more thrilled and re-joiced than frightened. Mameena had never been so ill to look upon, and I knew that dead or living I had nothing to fear from her who would have walked through hell fire for my sake, would have done

133

anything, except perhaps sacrifice her ambition. No, even if this were her ghost I should have been glad to see her again.

But it was not a ghost; it was only a fancy reproduced exactly as my mind had photographed her, almost as my eyes last saw her, when her kiss was still warm upon my lips.

Such were my thoughts as I stood outside that hut with the cold perspiration running down my face, for to tell the truth my nerves were upset, although without reason. So upset were they that when suddenly a silent-footed man appeared out of the darkness I jumped as high as though I had set my foot on a puff-adder, and until I recognized him by his voice as one of Nombe's servants who had accompanied us from Swazi-Land, felt quite alarmed. As a matter of fact he had only come to tell me that our meal was ready and that the other "high White Ones" were waiting for me.

He led me round the fence that encircled Zikali's dwelling-place, to two huts that stood nearly behind it, almost against the face of the rock which, overhanging in a curve, formed a kind of natural roof above them. I thought they must have been built since I visited the place, as I, who have a good memory for such things, did not remember them. Indeed, on subsequent examination I found that they were quite new, for the poles that formed their uprights were still green and the grass of the thatch was scarcely dry. It looked to me as if they had been specially constructed for our accommodation.

In one of these huts, that to the right which was allotted to Anscombe and myself, I found the others waiting for me, also the food. It was good of its sort and well cooked, and we ate it by the light of some candles that we had with us, Kaatje serving us. Yet, although a little while before I had been desperately hungry, now my appetite seemed to have left me and I made but a poor meal. Heda and Anscombe also seemed oppressed and ate sparingly. We did not talk much until Kaatje had taken away the tin plates and gone to eat her own supper by a fire that burned outside the hut. Then Heda broke out, saying that she was terrified of this place and especially of its master, the old dwarf, and felt sure that something terrible was going to happen to her. Anscombe did his best to calm her, and I also told her she had nothing to fear.

"If there is nothing to fear, Mr. Quatermain," she answered, turning on me, "why do you look so frightened yourself? By your face you might have seen a ghost."

This sudden and singularly accurate thrust, for after all I had seen something that looked very like a ghost, startled me, and before I could invent any soothing and appropriate fib, Nombe appeared, saying that she had come to lead Heda to her sleeping-place. After this further conversation was impossible since, although Nombe knew but few words of English, she was a great thought-reader and I feared to speak of anything secret in her presence. So we all went out of the hut, Nombe and I drawing back a little to the fire while the lovers said good-night to each other.

"Nombe," I said, "the *Inkosikazi* Heddana is afraid. The rocks of this *kloof* lie heavy on her heart; the face of the Opener of Roads is fearful to her and his laughter grates upon her ears. Do you understand?"

"I understand, Macumazahn, and it is as I expected. When you yourself are frightened it is natural that she, an untried maiden, should be frightened also in this home of spirits."

"It is men we fear, not spirits, now when all Zululand is boiling like a pot," I replied angrily.

"Have it as you will, Macumazahn," she said, and at that moment her quiet, searching eyes and fixed smile were hateful to me. "At least you admit that you do fear. Well, for the lady Heddana fear nothing. I sleep across the door of her hut, and while I who have learned to love her, live, I say—for her fear nothing, whatever may chance or whatever you may see or hear."

"I believe you, but, Nombe, you might die."

"Yes, I may die, but be sure of this, that when I die she will be safe, and he who loves her also. Sleep well, Macumazahn, and do not dream too much of what you heard and saw in Zikali's house."

Then before I could speak she turned and left me.

I did *not* sleep well; I slept very badly. To begin with, Maurice Anscombe, generally the most cheerful and nonchalant of mortals with a jest for every woe, was in a most depressed condition, and informed me of it several times, while I was getting ready to turn in. He said he thought the place hateful and felt as if people he could not see were looking at him (I had the same sensation but did not mention the fact to him). When I told him he was talking stuff, he only replied that he could not help it, and pointed out that it was not his general habit to be downcast in any danger, which was quite true. Now, he added, he was enjoying much the same sensations as he did when first he saw the Yellow-wood Swamp and got the idea into his head that he would kill some one there, which happened in due course.

"Do you mean that you think you are going to kill somebody else?" I asked anxiously.

"No," he answered, "I think I am going to be killed, or something

135

like it, probably by that accursed old villain of a witch-doctor, who I don't believe is altogether human."

"Others have thought that before now, Anscombe, and to be plain, I don't know that he is. He lives too much with the dead to be like other people."

"And with Satan, to whom I expect he makes sacrifices. The truth is I'm afraid of his playing some of his tricks with Heda. It is for her I fear, not for myself, Allan. Oh! why on earth did you come here?"

"Because you wished it and it seemed the safest thing to do. Look here, my boy, as usual the trouble comes through a woman. When a man's single—you know the rest. You used to be able to laugh at anything, but now that you are practically double you can't laugh any more. Well, that's the common lot of man and you've got to put up with it. Adam was pretty jolly in his garden until Eve was started, but you know what happened afterwards. The rest of his life was a compound of temptation, anxiety, family troubles, remorse, hard labour with primitive instruments, and a flaming sword behind him. If you had left your Eve alone you would have escaped all this. But you see you didn't, and as a matter of fact, nobody ever does who is worth his salt, for Nature has arranged it so."

"You appear to talk with experience, Allan," he retorted blandly. "By the way, that girl Nombe, when she isn't star-gazing or muttering incantations, is always trying to explain to Heda some tale about you and a lady called Mameena. I gather that you were introduced to her in this neighbourhood where, Nombe says, you were in the habit of kissing her in public, which sounds an odd kind of a thing to do; all of which happened before she, Nombe, was born. She adds, according to Kaatje's interpretation, that you met her again this afternoon, which, as I understand the young woman has been long dead, seems so incomprehensible that I wish you would explain."

"With reference to Heda," I said, ignoring the rest as unworthy of notice, "I think you may make your mind easy. Zikali knows that she is in my charge and I don't believe that he wants to quarrel with me. Still, as you are uncomfortable here, the best thing to do will be to get away as early as possible tomorrow morning, where to we can decide afterwards. And now I am going to sleep, so please stop arguing."

As I have already hinted, my attempts in the sleep line proved a failure, for whenever I did drop off I was pursued by bad dreams, which resulted from lying down so soon after supper. I heard the cries of desperate men in their mortal agony. I saw a rain-swollen river; its waters were red with blood. I beheld a vision of one who I knew by his dress

136

to be a Zulu king, although I could not see his face. He was flying and staggering with weariness as he fled. A great hound followed him. It lifted its head from the spoor; it was that of Zikali set upon the hound's body, Zikali who laughed instead of baying. Then one whose copper ornaments tinkled as she walked, entered beside me, whispering into my ear. "A quarter of a hundred years have gone by since we talked together in this haunted *kloof*," she seemed to whisper, "and before we talk again face to face there remain to pass of years"—

Here she ceased, though naturally I should have liked to hear the number. But that is just where dreams break down. They tell us only of what we know, or can evolve therefrom. Of what it is impossible for us to know they tell us nothing—at least as a general rule.

I woke up with a start, and feeling stifled in that hot place and aggravated by the sound of Anscombe's peaceful breathing, threw a coat about me and, removing the door-board, crept into the air. The night was still, the stars shone, and at a little distance the embers of the fire still glowed. By it was seated a figure wrapped in a *kaross*. The end of a piece of wood that the fire had eaten through fell on to the red ashes and flamed up brightly. By its light I saw that the figure was Nombe's. The eternal smile was still upon her face, the smile which suggested a knowledge of hidden things that from moment to moment amused her soul. Her lips moved as though she were talking to an invisible companion, and from time to time, like one who acts upon directions, she took a pinch of ashes and blew them, either towards Heda's hut or ours. Yes, she did this when all decent young women should have been asleep, like one who keeps some unholy, midnight assignation.

Talking with her master, Zikali, or trying to cast spells upon us, confound her! thought I to myself, and very silently crept back into the hut. Afterwards it occurred to me that she might have had another motive, namely of watching to see that none of us left the huts.

The rest of the night went by somehow. Once, listening with all my ears, I thought that I caught the sound of a number of men tramping and of some low word of command, but as I heard no more, concluded that fancy had deceived me. There I lay, puzzling over the situation till my head ached, and wondering how we were to get clear of the Black Kloof and Zikali, and out of Zululand which I gathered was no place for white people at the moment.

It seemed to me that the only thing was to make start for Dundee on the Natal border, and for the rest to trust to fortune. If we got into trouble over the death of Rodd, unpleasant as this would be, the matter must be faced out, that was all. For even if any witness appeared against us, the man had been killed in self-defence whilst trying to bring about our deaths at the hands of Basutos. I could see now that I was foolish not to have taken this line from the first, but as I think I have already explained, what weighed with me was the terror of involving these young people in a scandal which might shadow all their future lives. Also some fate inch by inch had dragged me into Zululand. Fortunately in life there are few mistakes, and even worse than mistakes that cannot be repaired, if the wish towards reparation is real and earnest. Were it otherwise not many of us would escape destruction in one form or another.

Thus I reflected until at length light flowing faintly through the smoke-hole of the hut told me that dawn was at hand. Seeing it I rose quietly, for I did not wish to wake Anscombe, dressed and left the hut. My object was to find Nombe, who I hoped would be still sitting by the fire, and send her to Zikali with a message that I wished to speak with him at once. Glancing round me in the grey dawn I saw that she was gone and that as yet no one seemed to be stirring. Hearing a horse snort at a little distance, I made my way towards the sound and in a little bay of the overhanging cliff discovered the cart and near by our beasts tied up with a plentiful supply of forage. Since so far as I could judge in that uncertain light, nothing seemed to be wrong with them except weariness, for three of them were still lying down, I walked on to the gate of the fence which surrounded Zikali's big hut, proposing to wait there until some one appeared by whom I could send my message.

I reached the gate which I tried and found to be fastened on its inner side. Then I sat down, lit my pipe and waited. It was extraordinarily lonesome in that place; at least this was the feeling that came over me. No doubt the sun was up behind the Ceza Stronghold that I have mentioned, which towered high behind me, for the sky above grew light with the red rays of its rising. But all the vast Black Kloof with its huge fantastic rocks was still plunged in gloom, whereof the shadows seemed to oppress my heart, weary as I was with my wakeful night and many anxieties. I was horribly nervous also and, as it proved, not without reason. Presently I heard rustlings on the further side of the fence as of people creeping about cautiously, and the sound of whispering. Then of a sudden the gate was thrown open and through it emerged about a dozen Zulu warriors, all of them ringed men, who instantly surrounded me, seated there upon the ground.

I looked at them and they looked at me for quite a long while, since following my usual rule, I determined not to be the first to speak. Moreover, if they meant to kill me there was no use in speaking. At length their leader, an elderly man with thin legs, a large stomach and a rather pleasant countenance, saluted politely, saying: "Good morning, O Macumazahn."

"Good morning, O Captain, whose name and business I do not know," I answered.

"The winds know the mountain on which they blow, but the mountain does not know the winds which it cannot see," he remarked with poetical courtesy; a Zulu way of saying that more people are acquainted with Tom Fool than Tom Fool is aware of.

"Perhaps, Captain; yet the mountain can feel the winds," and I might have added, smell them, for the *Kloof* was close and these *Kaffirs* had not recently bathed.

"I am named Goza and come on an errand from the king, O Macumazahn."

"Indeed, Goza, and is your errand to cut my throat?"

"Not at present, Macumazahn, that is, unless you refuse to do what the king wishes."

"And what does the king wish, Goza?"

"He wishes, Macumazahn, that you, his friend, should visit him."

"Which is just what I was on my way to do, Goza." (This was not true, but it didn't matter, for, if a lie, in the words of the schoolgirl's definition, is an abomination to the Lord, it is a very present help in time of trouble.) "After we have eaten I and my friends will accompany you to the king's *kraal* at Ulundi."

"Not so, Macumazahn. The king said nothing about your friends, of whom I do not think he has ever heard any more than we have. Moreover, if your friends are white, you will do well not to mention them, since the order is that all white people in Zululand who have not come here by the king's desire, are to be killed at once, except yourself, Macumazahn."

"Is it so, Goza? Well, as you will have understood, I am quite alone here and have no friends. Only I did not wish to travel so early."

"Of course we understand that you are quite alone and have no friends, is it not so, my brothers?"

"Yes, yes, we understand," they exclaimed in chorus, one of them adding, "and shall so report to the King."

"What kind of blankets do you like; the plain grey ones or the white ones with the blue stripes?" I asked, desiring to confirm them in this determination.

"The grey ones are warmer, Macumazahn, and do not show dirt so much," answered Goza thoughtfully.

139

"Good, I will remember when I have the chance."

"The promise of Macumazahn is known from of old to be as a tree that elephants cannot pull down and white ants will not eat," said the sententious Goza, thereby intimating his belief that some time or other they would receive those blankets. As a matter of fact the survivors of the party and the families of the others did receive them after the war, for in dealing with natives I have always made a point of trying to fulfil any promise or engagement made for value received.

"And now," went on Goza, "will the *Inkosi* be pleased to start, as we have to travel far today?"

"Impossible," I replied. "Before I leave I must eat, for who can journey upon yesterday's food? Also I must saddle my horse, collect what belongs to me, and bid farewell to my host, Zikali."

"Of meat we have plenty with us, Macumazahn, and therefore you will not hunger on the way. Your horse and everything that is yours shall be brought after you; since were you mounted on that swift beast and minded to escape, how could we catch you with our feet, and did you please to shoot us with your rifle, how could we who have only spears, save ourselves from dying? As for the Opener of Roads, his servants have told us that he means to sleep all today that he may talk with spirits in his dreams, and therefore it is useless for you to wait to bid him farewell. Moreover, the orders of the king are that we should bring you to him at once."

After this for a time there was silence, while I sat immovable revolving the situation, and the Zulus regarded me with a benignant interest. Goza took his snuff-box from his ear, shook out some into the palm of his hand and, after offering it to me in vain, inhaled it himself.

"The orders of the king are (sneeze) that we should bring you to him alive if possible, and if not (sneeze) dead. Choose which you will, Macumazahn. Perhaps you may prefer to go to Ulundi dead, which would—ah! how strong is this snuff, it makes me weep like a woman—save you the trouble of walking. But if you prefer that we should carry you, be so good, Macumazahn, first to write the words which will cause the grey blankets to be delivered to us, for we know well that even your bones would desire to keep your promise. Is it not a proverb in the land from the time of the slaying of Bangu when you gave the cattle you had earned to Saduko's wanderers?"

I listened and an idea occurred to me, as perhaps it had to Goza.

"I hear you, Goza," I said, "and I will start for Ulundi on my feet—to save *you* the trouble of carrying me. But as the times are rough and accidents may always happen; as, too, I wish to make sure that you

140

should get those blankets, and it may chance that I shall arrive there on my back, first I will write words which, if they are delivered to the witch-doctoress Nombe, will, sooner or later, turn into blankets."

"Write the words quickly, Macumazahn, and they will be delivered," said Goza.

So I drew out my pocket-book and wrote—

Dear Anscombe,

There is treachery afoot and I think that Zikali is at the bottom of it. I am being carried off to Cetewayo at Ulundi, by a party of armed Zulus who will not allow me to communicate with you, probably by Zikali's orders. You must do the best you can for Heda and yourself. Escape to Natal if you are able. Of course I will help if I get the chance, but if war is about to break out Cetewayo may kill me. I think that you can trust Nombe; also that Zikali does not wish to work you any ill unless he is obliged, though I have no doubt that he has trapped us here for some dark purpose of his own. Tell him through Nombe that if harm comes to you I will kill him if I live, and that if I die, I will settle the score with him afterwards. God save and bless you both. Keep up your courage and use your wits.
Your friend,
A. Q.

I tore out the sheet, folded, addressed it and presented it to Goza, remarking that although it seemed to be but paper, it really was fourteen blankets—if given at once to Nombe.

He nodded and handed it to one of his men, who departed in the direction of our huts. So, thought I to myself, Nombe knows all about this business, which means that it is being worked by Zikali. That is why she spoke to me as she did last night.

"It is time to start, Macumazahn, and I think you told us that you would prefer to do so on your feet," said Goza, looking suggestively at his spear.

"I am ready," I said, rising because I must. For a moment I contemplated the door in the *kraal* fence, wondering whether it would be safe to bolt through it and take refuge with Zikali. No, it was not safe, since Zikali sat there in his hut pulling the strings and probably might refuse to see me. Moreover, it was likely enough that before I could find him one of those broad spears would find my heart. There was nothing to be done except submit. Still I did call out in a loud voice—

"Farewell, Zikali. I leave you without a present against my will who am being taken by soldiers to visit the king at Ulundi. When we meet again I will talk all this matter over with you."

There was no answer, and as Goza took the opportunity to say that he disliked the noise of shouting extremely, which sometimes made him do things that he afterwards regretted, I became silent. Then we departed, I in the exact centre of that guard of Zulus, heavy-hearted and filled with fears both for myself and those I left behind me.

Down the Black Kloof we tramped, emerging on the sunlit plain beyond without meeting any one. A couple of miles further on we came to a small stream where Goza announced we would halt to eat. So we ate of cold toasted meat which one of the men produced from a basket he carried, unpalatable food but better than nothing. Just as we had finished I looked up and saw the soldier to whom my note had been given. He was leading my mare that had been saddled. On it were my large saddle-bags packed with my belongings, also my thick overcoat, mackintosh, water-bottle, and other articles down to a bag of tobacco, a spare pipe and a box of wax matches. Moreover, the man carried my double-barrelled Express rifle and a shot-gun that could be used for ball, together with two bags of cartridges. Practically nothing belonging to me had been forgotten.

I asked him who had collected the things. He replied the doctress Nombe had done so and had brought him the horse saddled to carry them. He did not know who saddled the horse as he had seen no one but Nombe to whom he had given the writing which she hid away. In answer to further questions, he said that Nombe had sent me a message. It was—

"I bid farewell to Macumazahn for a little while and wish him good fortune till we meet again. Let him not be afraid in the battle, for even if he is hurt it will not be to death, since those go with him whom he cannot see, and protect him with their shields. Say to Macumazahn that I, Nombe, remember in the morning what I said in the night and that what seems to be quite lost is oft-times found again. Wish him good fortune and tell him I am sorry that I had not time to cause his spare garments to be cleansed with water, but that I have been careful to find his little box with the white man's medicines."

I could extract nothing more from this soldier, who was either very stupid, or chose to appear so; nor indeed did I dare to put direct questions about the cart and those who travelled in it.

Soon we marched again, for Goza would not allow me to ride the horse, fearing that I should escape on it. Nor would he let me

142

carry either of the guns lest I should make use of them. All day we travelled, reaching the Nongoma heights in the late afternoon. On this beautiful spot we found a *kraal* situated where afterwards a magistracy was built when we conquered the country, whence there is one of the finest views in Zululand. There was no one in the *kraal* except two old women who appeared to be deaf and dumb for all I could get out of them. These aged dames, however, or others who were hidden, had made ready for our arrival, since a calf lay skinned and prepared for cooking, and by it big gourds filled with *Kaffir* beer and *maas* or curdled milk.

In due course we ate of these provisions, and after we had finished I gave Goza a stiff tot of brandy, of which Nombe, or perhaps Anscombe, had thoughtfully sent a bottle with my other baggage. The strong liquor made the old fellow talkative and enabled me to get a good deal of information out of him. Thus I learned that certain demands, as to which he was rather vague, had been made upon Cetewayo by the English Government, and that the King was now considering whether he should accede to them or fight. The Great Council of the nation was summoned to attend at Ulundi within a few days, when the matter would be decided. Meanwhile all the regiments were being gathered, or, as we should say, mobilized; an army, said Goza, greater than any that Chaka had ever led.

I asked him what I had to do with this business, that I, a peaceful traveller and an old friend of the Zulus, should be made prisoner and dragged off to Ulundi. He replied he did not know who was not in the council of the High Ones, but he thought that Cetewayo the king wished to see me because I was their friend, perhaps that he might send me as a messenger to the white people. I asked him how the king knew that I was in the country, to which he replied that Zikali had told him I was coming, he did not know how, whereon he, Goza, was sent at once to fetch me. I could get no more out of him.

I wondered if it would be worth while to make him quite drunk and then attempt to escape on the horse, but gave up the idea. To begin with, his men were at hand and there was not enough brandy to make them all drunk. Also even if I succeeded in winning away here in the heart of Zululand, it would not help Anscombe or Heda and I should probably be cut off and killed before I could get out of the country. So I abandoned the plan and went to sleep instead.

Next morning we left Nongoma early in the hope of reaching Ulundi that evening if the Ivuna and Black Umfolozi Rivers proved fordable. As it chanced, although they were high, we were able to cross them, I seated on the horse which two of the Zulus led. Next we tramped for miles through the terrible Bekameezi Valley, a hot and desolate place which the Zulus swear is haunted. So unhealthy is this valley, which is the home of large game, that whole *kraals* full of people who have tried to cultivate the rich land, have died in it of fever, or fled away leaving their crops unreaped. Now no man dwells there. After this we climbed a terrible mount to the high land of Mahlabatini, and having eaten, pushed on once more.

At length we sighted the great hill-encircled plain of Ulundi which may be called the cradle of the Zulu race as, politically speaking, it was destined to be its coffin. On the ridge to the west once stood the Nobamba *kraal* where dwelt Senzangacona, the father of Chaka the Lion. Nearer to the White Umfolozi was Panda's dwelling-place, Nodwengu, which once I knew so well, while on the slope of the hills of the north-east stood the town of Ulundi in which Cetewayo dwelt, bathed in the lights of sunset.

Indeed it and all the vast plain were red as though with blood, red as they were destined to be on the coming day of the last battle of the Zulus.

CHAPTER 13

Cetewayo

It was dark when at last we reached the Ulundi *kraal*, for the growing moon was obscured by clouds. Therefore I could see nothing and was only aware, by the sound of voices and the continual challenging, that we were passing through great numbers of men.

At length we were admitted at the eastern gate and I was taken to a hut where I at once flung myself down to sleep, being so weary that I could not attempt to eat. Next morning as I was finishing my breakfast in the little fenced courtyard of this guest-hut, Goza appeared and said that the king commanded me to be brought to him at once, adding that I must "speak softly" to him, as he was "very angry."

So off we went across the great cattle *kraal* where a regiment of young men, two thousand strong or so, were drilling with a fierce intensity which showed they knew that they were out for more than exercise. About the sides of the *kraal* also stood hundreds of soldiers, all of them talking and, it seemed to me, excited, for they stamped upon the ground and even jumped into the air to give point to their arguments. Suddenly some of them caught sight of me, whereon a tall, truculent fellow called out—

"What does a white man at Ulundi at such a time, when even John Dunn dare not come? Let us kill him and send his head as a present to the English general across the Tugela. That will settle this long talk about peace or war."

Others of a like mind echoed this kind proposal, with the result that presently a score or so of them made a rush at me, brandishing their sticks, since they might not carry arms in the royal *kraal*. Goza did his best to keep them off, but was swept aside like a feather, or rather knocked over, for I saw him on his back with his thin legs in the air.

"You must climb out of this pit by yourself," he began, address-

145

ing me in his pompous and figurative way. Then somebody stamped on his face, and fixing his teeth in his assailant's heel, he grew silent for a while.

The truculent blackguard, who was about six feet three high and had a mouth like a wolf's throat, arrived in front of me and, bending down, roared out—

"We are going to kill you, White Man."

I had a pistol in my pocket and could perfectly well have killed him, as I was much tempted to do. A second's reflection showed me, however, that this would be useless, and in a sense put me in the wrong, though when the matter came on for argument it would interest me no more. So I just folded my arms and, looking up at him, said—

"Why, Black Man?"

"Because your face is white," he roared.

"No," I answered, "because your heart is black and your eyes are so full of blood that you do not know Macumazahn when you see him."

"Wow!" said one, "it is Watcher-by-Night whom our fathers knew before us. Leave him alone."

"No," shouted the great fellow, "I will send him to watch where it is always night, I who keep a club for white rats," and he brandished his stick over me.

Now my temper rose. Watching my opportunity, I stretched out my right foot and hooked him round the ankle, at the same time striking up with all my force. My fist caught him beneath the chin and over he went backwards sprawling on the ground.

"Son of a dog!" I said, "if a single stick touches me, at least you shall go first," and whipping out my revolver, I pointed it at him.

He lay quiet enough, but how the matter would have ended I do not know, for passion was running high, had not Goza at this moment risen with a bleeding nose and called out—

"O Fools, would you kill the king's guest to whom the king himself has given safe-conduct. Surely you are pots full of beer, not men."

"Why not?" answered one. "This is the Place of Soldiers. The king's house is yonder. Give the old jackal a start of a length of ten assegais. If he reaches it first, he can shake hands with his friend, the king. If not we will make him into medicine."

"Yes, yes, run for it, Jackal," clamoured the others, knocking their shields with their sticks, as men do who would frighten a buck, and opening out to make a road for me.

Now while all this was going on, with some kind of sixth sense I had noted a big man whose face was shrouded by a blanket thrown over his head, who very quietly had joined these drunken rioters, and vaguely wondered who he might be.

"I will not run," I said slowly, "that I may be saved by the king. Nay, I will die here, though some of you shall die first. Go to the king, Goza, and tell him how his servants have served his guest," and I lifted my pistol, waiting till the first stick touched me to put a bullet through the bully on the ground.

"There is no need," said a deep voice that proceeded from the draped man of whom I have spoken, "for the king has come to see for himself."

Then the blanket was thrown back, revealing Cetewayo grown fat and much aged since last I saw him, but undoubtedly Cetewayo.

"*Bayete!*" roared the mob in salute, while some of those who had been most active in the tumult tried to slip away.

"Let no man stir," said Cetewayo, and they stood as though they were rooted to the ground, while I slipped my pistol back into my pocket.

"Who are you, White Man?" he asked, looking at me, "and what do you here?"

"The King should know Macumazahn," I answered, lifting my hat, "whom Dingaan knew, whom Panda knew well, and whom the King knew before he was a king."

"Yes, I know you," he answered, "although since we spoke together you have shrunk like an ox hide in the sun, and time has stained your beard white."

"And the King has grown fat like the ox on summer grass. As for what I do here, did not the King send for me by Goza, and was I not brought like a baby in a blanket."

"The last time we met," he went on, taking no heed of my words, "was yonder at Nodwengu when the witch Mameena was tried for sorcery, she who made my brother mad and brought about the great battle, in which you fought for him with the Amawombe regiment. Do you not remember how she kissed you, Macumazahn, and took poison between the kisses, and how before she grew silent she spoke evil words to me, saying that I was doomed to pull down my own House and to die as she died, words that have haunted me ever since and now haunt me most of all? I wish to speak to you concerning them, Macumazahn, for it is said in the land that this beautiful witch loved you alone and that you only knew her mind."

I made no reply, who was heartily tired of this subject of Mameena whom no one seemed able to forget.

"Well," he went on, "we will talk of that matter alone, since it is not

147

natural that you should wish to speak of your dead darlings before the world," and with a wave of the hand he put the matter aside. Then suddenly his attitude changed. His face, that had been thoughtful and almost soft, became fierce, his form seemed to swell and he grew terrible.

"What was that dog doing?" he asked of Goza, pointing to the brute whom I had knocked down and who still lay prostrate on his back, afraid to stir.

"O King," answered Goza, "he was trying to kill Macumazahn because he is a white man, although I told him that he was your guest, being brought to you by the royal command. He was trying to kill him by giving him a start of ten spears' length and making him run to the *isigodhlo* (the king's house) and beating him to death with the sticks of these men if they caught him, which, as he is old and they are young, they must have done. Only the Watcher-by-Night would not run; no, although he is so small he knocked him to the earth with his fist, and there he lies. That is all, O King."

"Rise, dog," said Cetewayo, and the man rose trembling with fear, and, being bidden, gave his name, which I forget.

"Listen, dog," went on the king in the same cold voice. "What Goza says is true, for I saw and heard it all with my eyes and ears. You would have made yourself as the king. You dared to try to kill the king's guest to whom he had given safe-conduct, and to stain the king's doorposts with his blood, thereby defiling his house and showing him to the white people as a murderer of one of them whom he had promised to protect. Macumazahn, do *you* say how he shall die, and I will have it done."

"I do not wish him to die," I answered, "I think that he and those with him were drunk. Let him go, O King."

"Aye, Macumazahn, I will let him go. See now, we are in the centre of the cattle-*kraal*, and to the eastern gate is as far as to the *isigodhlo*. Let this man have a start of ten spears' length and run to the eastern gate, as he would have made Macumazahn run to the king's house, and let his companions, those who would have hunted Macumazahn, hunt him.

"If he wins through to the gate he can go on to the Government in Natal and tell them of the cruelty of the Zulus. Only then, let those who hunted him be brought before me for trial and perhaps we shall see how *they* can run."

Now the poor wretch caught hold of my hand, begging me to intercede for him, but soldiers who had come up dragged him away and, having measured the distance allowed him, set him on a mark made upon the ground. Presently at a word off he sped like an arrow, and after him went his friends, ten or more of them. I think they caught him just by the gate doubling like a hare, or so the shouts of laughter from the watching regiment told me, for myself I would not look.

"That dog ate his own stomach," said Cetewayo grimly, thereby indicating in native fashion that the biter had been bit or the engineer hoist with his petard. "It is long since there has been a war in the land, and some of these young soldiers who have never used an *assegai* save to skin an ox or cut the head from a chicken, shout too loud and leap too high. Now they will be quieter, and while you stay here you may walk where you will in safety, Macumazahn," he added thoughtfully.

Then dismissing the matter from his mind, as we white people dismiss any trivial incident in a morning stroll, he talked for a few minutes to the commanding officer of the regiment that was drilling, who ran up to make some report to him, and walked back towards the *isigodhlo*, beckoning me to follow with Goza.

After waiting for a little while outside the gate in the surrounding fence, a body-servant ordered us to enter, which we did to find the king seated on the shady side of his big hut quite alone. At a sign I also sat myself down upon a stool that had been set for me, while Goza, whose nose was still bleeding, squatted at my side.

"Your manners are not so good as they were once, Macumazahn," said Cetewayo presently, "or perhaps you have been so long away from the royal *kraal* that you have forgotten its customs."

I stared at him, wondering what he could mean, whereon he added with a laugh—

"What is that in your pocket? Is it not a loaded pistol, and do you not remember that it is death to appear before the king armed? Now I might kill you and have no blame, although you are my guest, for who knows that you are not sent by the English Queen to shoot me?"

"I ask the King's pardon," I said humbly enough. "I did not think about the pistol. Let your servants take it away."

"Perhaps it is safer in your pocket, where I saw you place it in the cattle-*kraal*, Macumazahn, than in their hands, which do not know how to hold such things. Moreover, I know that you are not one who stabs in the dark, even when our peoples growl round each other like two dogs about to fight, and if you were, in this place your life would have to pay for mine. There is beer by your side; drink and fear nothing. Did you see the Opener of Roads, Goza, and if so, what is his answer to my message?"

"O King, I saw him," answered Goza. "The Father of the doctors, the friend and master of the Spirits, says he has heard the King's word, yes, that he heard it as it passed the King's lips, and that although he is very old, he will travel to Ulundi and be present at the Great Council of the nation which is to be summoned on the eighth day from this, that of the full moon. Yet he makes a prayer of the King. It is that a place may be prepared for him, for his people and for his servants who carry him, away from this town of Ulundi, where he may sojourn quite alone, a decree of death being pronounced against any who attempt to break in upon his privacy, either where he dwells or upon his journey. These are his very words, O King:

"'I, who am the most ancient man in Zululand, dwell with the spirits of my fathers, who will not suffer strangers to come nigh them and who, if they are offended, will bring great woes upon the land. Moreover, I have sworn that while there is a king in Zululand and I draw the breath of life, never again will I set foot in a royal *kraal*, because when last I did so at the slaying of the witch, Mameena, the king who is dead thought it well to utter threats against me, and never more will I, the Opener of Roads, be threatened by a mortal. Therefore if the King and his Council seek to drink of the water of my wisdom, it must be in the place and hour of my own choosing. If this cannot be, let me abide here in my house and let the King seek light from other doctors, since mine shall remain as a lamp to my own heart.'"

Now I saw that these words greatly disturbed Cetewayo who feared Zikali, as indeed did all the land.

"What does the old wizard mean?" he asked angrily. "He lives alone like a bat in a cave and for years has been seen of none. Yet as a bat flies forth at night, ranging far and wide in search of prey, so does his spirit seem to fly through Zululand. Everywhere I hear the same word. It is—'What says the Opener of Roads?' It is—'How can aught be done unless the Opener of Roads has declared that it shall be done, he who was here before the Black One (Chaka) was born, he who it is said was the friend of *Inkosi* Umkulu, the father of the Zulus who died before our great-grandfathers could remember; he who has all knowledge and is almost a spirit, if indeed he be not a spirit?' I ask you, Macumazahn, who are his friend, what does he mean, and why should I not kill him and be done?"

"O King," I answered, "in the days of your uncle Dingaan, when Dingaan slew the Boers who were his guests, and thus began the war between the White and the Black, I, who was a lad, heard the laughter of Zikali for the first time yonder at the *kraal* Ungungundhlovu, I who rode with Retief and escaped the slaughter, but his face I did not see. Many years later, in the days of Panda your father, I saw his face and therefore you name me his friend. Yet this friend who drew me to visit him, perhaps by your will, O King, has now caused me to be brought here to Ulundi doubtless by your will, O King, but against my own, for who wishes to come to a town where he is well-nigh slain by the first brawler he meets in the cattle *kraal*?"

"Yet you were not slain, Macumazahn, and perhaps you do not know all the story of that brawler," replied Cetewayo almost humbly, like one who begs pardon, though the rest of what I had said he ignored. "But still you are Zikali's friend, for between you and him there is a rope which enabled him to draw you to Zululand, which rope I have heard called by a woman's name. Therefore by the spirit of that woman, which still can draw you like a rope, I charge you, tell me—what does this old wizard mean, and why should I not kill him and be rid of one who haunts my heart like an evil vision of the night and, as I sometimes think, is an *umtakati*, an evil-doer, who would work ill to me and all my House, yes, and to all my people?"

"How should I know what he means, O King?" I answered with indignation, though in fact I could guess well enough. "As for killing him, cannot the King kill whom he will? Yet I remember that once I heard you father ask much the same question and of Zikali himself, saying that he was minded to find out whether or no he were mortal like other men. I remember also Zikali answered that there was a saying that when the Opener of Roads came to the end of his road, there would be no more a king of Zululand, as there was none when first he set foot upon his road. Now I have spoken, who am a white man and do not understand your sayings."

"I remember it also, Macumazahn, who was present at the time," he replied heavily. "My father feared this Zikali and his father feared him, and I have heard that the Black One himself, who feared nothing, feared him also. And I, too, fear him, so much that I dare not make up my mind upon a great matter without his counsel, lest he should bewitch me and the nation and bring us to nothing." He paused, then turning to Goza, asked, "Did the Opener of Roads tell you where he wished to dwell when he comes to visit me here at Ulundi?"

"O King," answered Goza, "yonder in the hills, not further away than an aged man can walk in the half of an hour, is a place called the Valley of Bones, because there in the days of those who went before the King, and even in the King's day, many evildoers have been led to die. Zikali would dwell in this Valley of Bones, and there and nowhere else would meet the King and the Great Council, not in the daylight but after sunset when the moon has risen."

"Why," said Cetewayo, starting, "the place is ill-omened and, they say, haunted, one that no man dares to approach after the fall of darkness for fear lest the ghosts of the dead should leap upon him gibbering."

"Such were the words of the Opener of Roads, O King," replied Goza. "There and nowhere else will he meet the King, and there he demands that three huts should be built to shelter him and his folk and stored with all things needful. If this be not granted to him, then he refuses to visit the King or to give counsel to the nation."

"So be it then," said Cetewayo. "Send messengers to the Opener of Roads, Goza, saying that what he desires shall be done. Let my command go out that under pain of death none spy upon him while he journeys hither or returns. Let the huts be built forthwith, and when it is known that he is coming, let food in plenty be placed in them and afterwards morning by morning taken to the mouth of the valley. Bid him announce his arrival and the hour he chooses for our meeting by messenger. Begone."

Goza leapt up, gave the royal salute, and retreated backwards from the presence of the king, leaving us alone. I also rose to depart, but Cetewayo motioned to me to be seated.

"Macumazahn," he said, "the Great Queen's man who has come to Natal (Sir Bartle Frere) threatens me with war because two evil-doing women were taken on the Natal side of the Tugela and brought back to Zululand and killed by Mehlokazulu, being the wives of his father, Sirayo, which was done without my knowledge. Also two white men were driven away from an island in the Tugela River by some of my soldiers."

"Is that all, O King?" I asked.

"No. The Queen's man says I kill my people without trial, which is a lie told him by the missionaries, and that girls have been killed also who refused to marry those to whom they were given and ran away with other men. Also that wizards are smelt out and slain, which happens but rarely now; all of this contrary to the promises I made to Sompseu when he came to recognize me as king upon my father's death, and some other such small matters."

"What is demanded if you would avoid war, O King?"

"Nothing less than this, Macumazahn: That the Zulu army should be abolished and the soldiers allowed to marry whom and when they please, because, says the Queen's man, he fears lest it should be used to attack the English, as though I who love the English, as those have done who went before me, desire to lay a finger on them. Also that another Queen's man should be sent to dwell here in my country, to be the eyes and ears of the English Government and have power with me

152

in the land; yes, and more demands which would destroy the Zulus as a people and make me, their king, but a petty *kraal*-head."

"And what will the King answer?" I asked.

"I know not what to answer. The fine of two thousand cattle I will pay for the killing of the women. If it may be, I wish no quarrel with the English, though gladly I would have fought the Dutch had not Sompseu stretched out his arm over their land. But how can I disband the army and make an end of the regiments that have conquered in so many wars? Macumazahn, I tell you that if I did this, in a moon I should be dead. Oh! you white people think there is but one will in Zululand, that of the king. But it is not so, for he is but a single man among ten thousand thousand, who lives to work the people's wish. If he beats them with too thick a stick, or if he brings them to shame or does what the most of them do not wish, then where is the king? Then, I say, he goes a road that was trodden by Chaka and Dingaan who were before me, yes, the red road of the *assegai*. Therefore today, I stand like a man between two falling cliffs. If I run towards the English the Zulu cliff falls upon me. If I run towards my own people, the English cliff falls upon me, and in either case I am crushed and no more seen. Tell me then, Macumazahn, you whose heart is honest, what must I do?"

So he spoke, wringing his hands, with tears starting to his eyes, and upon my word, although I never liked Cetewayo as I had liked his father, Panda, perhaps because I loved his brother, Umbelazi, whom he killed, and had known him do many cruel deeds, my heart bled for him.

"I cannot tell you, King," I answered, thinking that I must say something, "but I pray you do not make war against the queen, for she is the most mighty One in the whole earth, and though her foot, of which you see but the little toe here in Africa, seems small to you, yet if she is angered, it will stamp the Zulus flat, so that they cease to be."

"Many have told me this, Macumazahn. Yes, even Uhamu, the son of my uncle Unzibe, or, as some say, the son of his spirit, to which his mother was married after Unzibe was dead, and others throughout the land, and in truth I think it myself. But who can hold the army which shouts for war? *Ow!* the Council must decide, which, means perhaps that Zikali will decide, for now all hang upon his lips."

"Then I am sorry," I exclaimed.

He looked at me shrewdly.

"Are you? So am I. Yet his counsel must be asked, and better that it should be here in my presence than yonder secretly at the Black Kloof. I would kill him if I dared, but I dare not, who am sure—why I may not say—that the same sun will see his death and mine."

153

He waved his hand to show that the talk on this matter was ended, then added—

"Macumazahn, you are my prisoner for a while, but give me your word that you will not try to escape and you may go where you will within an hour's ride of Ulundi. I would pay you well to stop here with me, but this I know you would never do should there be trouble between us and your people. Therefore I promise you that if war breaks out I will send you safely to Natal, or perhaps sooner, as my messenger, whence doubtless you will return to fight against me. Know that I have given orders that every other white man or woman who is found in Zululand shall be killed as a spy. Even John Dunn has fled or is flying, or so I hear, John Dunn who has fed out of my hand and grown rich on my gifts. You yourself would have been killed as you came from Swazi-Land in your cart, had not command been sent to those chiefs through whose lands you passed that neither they nor their people were so much as to look at you."

Now for one intense moment I thought, as hard as ever I had done in my life. It was evident—unless he dealing very cunningly with me, which I did not believe—that Cetewayo knew nothing of Anscombe and Heda, but thought that I had come into Zululand alone. Should I or should I not tell him and beg his protection for them? If I did so he might refuse or be unable to give it to them far away in the midst of a savage population aflame with the lust of war. As the incident of the morning showed, it was as much as he could do to protect myself, although the Zulus knew me for their friend. On the other hand no one who dwelt under Zikali's blanket, to use the *Kaffir* idiom, would be touched, because he was looked on as half divine and therefore everything under it down to the rat in his thatch was sacred. Now Zikali by implication and Nombe with emphasis, had promised to safeguard these two. Surely, therefore, they would run less risk in the Black Kloof than here at Ulundi, if ever they got so far.

All this went through my brain in an instant, with the result that I made up my mind to say nothing. As the issue proved, this was a terrible mistake, but who can always judge rightly? Had I spoken out it seems to me probable that Cetewayo would have granted my prayer and ordered that these two should be escorted out of Zululand before hostilities began, although of course they might have been murdered on the way. Also, for a reason that will become evident later, it is possible that there would never have been any hostilities. All I can plead is, that I acted for the best and Fate would have it so. Another moment and the chance was gone.

The gate opened and a body-servant appeared announcing that one of the great captains with some of his officers waited to see the king. Cetewayo made a sign, whereon the servant called out something, and they entered, three or four of them, saluting loudly. Seeing me they stopped and stared, whereon Cetewayo shortly, but with much clearness, repeated to them and to an *induna* who accompanied them, what he had already said to me, namely that I was his guest, sent for by him that he might use me as a messenger if he thought fit. He added that the man who dared to speak a word against me, or even to look at me askance, should pay the price with his life, however high his station, and he commanded that the heralds should proclaim this his decree throughout Ulundi and the neighbouring *kraals*. Then he held out his hand to me in token of friendship, bidding me to "go softly" and come to see him whenever I wished, and dismissed me in charge of the *induna*, one of the captains and some soldiers.

Within five minutes of reaching my hut I heard a loud-voiced crier proclaiming the order of the king and knew that I had no more to fear.

CHAPTER 14

The Valley of Bones

The week that followed my interview with Cetewayo was indeed a miserable time for me. For myself, as I have said, I had no fear, for the king's orders were strictly obeyed. Moreover, the tale of what had happened to the brute who wished to hunt me down in the cattle-*kraal* had travelled far and wide and none sought to share his fate. My hut was inviolate and well supplied with necessary food, as was my mare, and I could wander where I liked and talk with whom I would. I could even ride to exercise the horse, though this I did very sparingly and only in the immediate neighbourhood of the town for fear of exciting suspicion or meeting Zulus whom the king's word had not reached. Indeed on these occasions I was always accompanied by a guard of swift-footed and armed soldiers sent "to protect me," or more probably to kill me if I did anything that seemed suspicious.

In the course of my rambles I met sundry natives whom I had known in the old days, some of them a long while ago. They all seemed glad to see me and were quite ready to talk of past times, but of the present they would say little or nothing, except that they were certain there would be war. Of Anscombe and Heda I could hear nothing, and indeed did not dare to make any direct inquiries concerning them, but several reliable men assured me that the last missionaries and traders having departed, there was not a white man, woman or child left in Zululand except myself. It was "all black" they said, referring to the colour of their people, as it had been before the time of Chaka. So I was forced to eat out my heart with anxiety in silence, hoping and praying that Zikali had played an honest part and sent them away safely.

Why should he not have done so, seeing that it was my presence he had desired, not theirs? They were only taken, or rather snared, because they were with me and could not be separated, or so I believed at the time.

One ray of comfort I did get. About the fifth day after my interview I saw Goza, who told me that the king's messengers were back from the Black Kloof and had brought "a word" for me from Zikali himself. The word was—

"Bid Goza say to Macumazahn that I was sorry not to see him to say goodbye, because that morning I slept heavily. Bid him say that I am glad he has seen the king, since for this purpose I sought his presence in Zululand. Bid him say that he is to fear nothing, and that if his heart is heavy about others whom he loves, he should make it light again, since the Spirits have them in their keeping as they have him, and never were they or he more safe than they are today."

Now I looked at Goza and asked if I could see this messenger. He replied, No, as he had already been despatched upon another errand. Then I asked him if the messenger had said anything else. He answered, Yes, one thing that he had forgotten, namely that the writing about blankets should now be in Natal. Then suddenly he changed the subject and asked me if I would like to accompany him to the Valley of Bones where he was ordered to inspect the huts which were being built for Zikali and his people. Of course I said I should, hoping, quite without result, that I might get something more out of him on the road.

Now this town of Cetewayo's stands, or rather stood, for it has long been burnt, on the slope of the hills to the north-east of the plains of Ulundi. Above it these hills grow steeper, and deep in the recesses of one of them is the Valley of Bones. There is nothing particularly imposing about the place; no towering cliffs or pillars of piled granite, as at the Black Kloof. It is just a vale cut out by water, bordered by steep slopes on either side, and a still steeper slope strewn with large rocks at its end. Dotted here and there on these slopes grew tall aloes that from a little distance looked like scattered men, whereof the lower leaves were shrivelled and blackened by *veld* fires. Also there were a few *euphorbias*, grey, naked-looking things that end in points like fingers on a hand, and among them some sparse thorn trees, struggling to live in an inhospitable soil.

The place has one peculiarity. Jutting into it from the hillside is a ridge or spur, sixty or seventy yards in length by perhaps twenty broad, that ends in a flat point of rock which stands about forty feet above the level of the rest of the little valley. On this ridge also grew tall aloes until near its extremity the soil ceased, or had been washed away from the water-worn core of rock.

It was, and no doubt still is, a desolate-looking spot, at any rate for most of the day when owing to the shadow of the surrounding hills, it receives but little sun. Everything about it, especially when I was there in a time of rain, seemed dank and miserable, although the flat floor of the *kloof* was clothed with a growth of tall, coarse grass, and weeds that bore an evil-smelling flower. Perhaps some sense of appropriateness had caused the Zulu kings to choose this lonesome, deathly-looking gorge as one of their execution grounds. At any rate many had been slain here, for skulls and the larger human bones, some of them black with age, lay all about among the grass, as they had been scattered by hyenas and jackals. They were particularly thick beneath and around the table-like rock that I have mentioned.

Goza told me that this was because the King's Slayers made a custom of dragging the victim along the projecting tongue to the edge of this rock and hurling him, either dead or living, to the ground beneath; or, in the case of witches; driving them over after they had been blinded.

Such was the spot that Zikali had selected to abide in during his visit to Ulundi. Certainly where privacy was an object it was well chosen, for, as Cetewayo had said and as Goza emphasized to me, it had the repute of being the most thoroughly haunted place in all Zululand, with the sole exception, perhaps, of the ridge opposite to Dingaan's old *kraal* where once I shot the vultures for my life and those of my companions. Even in the daytime people gave it a wide berth, and at night nothing would induce them to approach it, at any rate alone.

Here to one side of and near the root of the tongue of land of which I have spoken, the huts that Zikali had demanded for himself and his company were being rapidly built, close to a spring of water, by a large body of men who laboured as though they wished to be done with their task. Also about half way up the *donga*, for really it was nothing more, at a distance of perhaps five and twenty paces from its flat point whence the condemned were hurled, a circular space of ground had been cleared and levelled which was large enough to accommodate fifty or sixty men. On this space, Goza told me, the King and the Council were to sit when they came to seek light from Zikali.

In my heart I reflected that the light they were likely to get from him would be such as may be supposed to be thrown by hell fire. For be it remembered I knew what these people never seemed to understand, that Zikali was the most bitter of their enemies. To begin with, he was of Undwandwe blood, one of the people whom the great king Chaka had destroyed. Then this same Chaka had robbed him of his wives and murdered his children, in revenge for which he had plotted the slaying of Chaka, as he did that of his brothers, Umhlangana and Dingaan, the latter of whom he involved in a quarrel with the Boers. Subsequently he brought about the war between the princes Cetewayo and Umbelazi, in which I played a part.

Now I was certain that he intended to bring about another war between the English and the Zulus, knowing well that in the end the latter would be destroyed, and with them the royal House of Senzangacona which he had sworn to level with the dust. Had he not told me as much years ago, and was he one to go back upon his word? Had he not used Mameena with her beauty and ambitions as his tool, and when she was of no further service to him, given her to death, as he had used scores of others and in due season given them to death? Was I not myself perhaps one of those tools destined to be thrown into the pit of doom when my turn came, though in what way I could help his plots was more than I could see, since he knew well that I should do my best to oppose him? Oh! I had half a mind to go to Cetewayo and tell him all I knew about Zikali, even if it involved the breaking of confidences.

But stay! Even if I were believed, this far-seeing wizard held hostages for my good behaviour, and if I betrayed him what would happen to those hostages? He sent me messages saying that they were safe, suggesting that they had escaped to Natal. How was I to know that these were true? I was utterly bewildered; I could not guess why I had been beguiled into Zululand, and I dared not step either this way or that for fear lest I should fall into some pit dug by his cunning hands and, what was worse, drag down others with me.

Moreover, was this man quite human, or perhaps an emissary of Satan upon earth who had knowledge denied to other men and a certain mastery over the Powers of Ill? Again I could not say. His term of life seemed to be extraordinarily prolonged, though none knew how old exactly he might be. Also he had a wonderful knowledge of what was passing in the minds of others, and by his arts, as I had experienced only the other day, could summon up apparitions or illusions before their eyes. Further, he was aware of events which had happened at a distance and could send or read dreams, since otherwise how did Nombe know what I had dreamt at Marnham's house? Lastly he could foretell the future, as once he had done in my own case, prophesying that I should be injured by a buffalo with a split horn.

Yet all of this might be nothing more than a mixture of keen observation, clever spying, trickery and mesmerism. I could not say which it was, nor can I with certainty to this hour.

Such were the thoughts that passed through my mind as I walked back from the Vale of Bones by the side of the big-paunched Goza, whom I caught eyeing me from time to time as a curious crow eyes any object that has attracted his attention.

"Goza," I said at last, "do the Zulus really mean to fight the English?"

He turned and pointed to a spot where the hills ran down into the great plain. Here two regiments were manoeuvring. One of these held the slopes of the hill and the other was attacking them from the plain, so fiercely that at a distance their onslaught looked like that of actual warfare.

"That looks like fighting, does it not, Macumazahn?" he replied.

"Yes, Goza, yet it may be but play."

"Quite so, Macumazahn. It may be fighting or it may be but play. Am I a prophet that I should be able to say which it is? Of that there is but one man in Zululand who knows the truth. It is he for whom the new huts are being built up yonder."

"You think he really knows, Goza?"

"No, Macumazahn, I do not think, I am sure. He is the greatest of all wizards, as he was when my father held on to his mother's apron. He pulls the strings and the Great-ones of the country dance. If he wishes war, there will be war. If he wishes peace, there will be peace."

"And which does he wish, Goza?"

"I thought perhaps you could tell me that, Macumazahn, who, he says, are such an old friend of his; also why he chooses to sojourn in a dark hole among the dead instead of in the sunshine among the living, here at Ulundi."

"Well, I cannot, Goza, since the Opener of Roads does not open his heart to me but keeps his secrets to himself. For the rest, those who talk with the dead may prefer to dwell among the dead."

"Now as always you speak truth, Macumazahn," said Goza, looking at me in a way which suggested to me that he believed I spoke anything but the truth.

Indeed I am convinced he thought that I was in the council of Zikali and acquainted with his plans. Also I am sure he knew that I had not come to Zululand alone, the incident of the blankets, which I had promised to him a bribe to keep silence, showed it, and suspected that my companions were parties to some plot together with myself. And yet at the time I could not be quite sure, and therefore dared not ask anything concerning them lest thus I should reveal their existence and bring them to death.

As a matter of fact I need not have been anxious on this point, since if Goza, who I may state, was a kind of secret service officer as well as a head messenger, knew, as I think probable, he had been commanded by Zikali to hold his tongue under penalty of a curse. Perhaps the same was true of the soldiers who had come with him to take me to Ulundi. The hint of Zikali was as powerful as the word of the king, since they, like thousands of others, believed that whereas Cetewayo could kill them, Zikali, like Satan, could blast their spirits as well as their bodies. But how was I to guess all these things at that time?

During the next two days nothing happened, though I heard that there had been one if not two meetings of the Council at the King's House during which the position of affairs was discussed. Cetewayo I did not see, although twice he sent messengers to me bringing gifts of food, who were charged to inquire whether I was well and happy and if any had offered me hurt or insult. To these I answered that I was well and unmolested but not happy, who grew lonesome, being but a solitary white man among so many thousands of the Zulus.

On the third morning, that of the day of the full moon, Goza came and informed me that Zikali had arrived at the Valley of Bones before dawn. I asked him how he, who was so old and feeble, had walked so far. He answered that he had not walked, or so he understood, but had been carried in a litter, or rather in two litters, one for himself and one for his "spirit." This staggered me even where Zikali was concerned, and I inquired what on earth Goza meant.

"Macumazahn, how can I tell you who only know what I myself am told?" he exclaimed. "Such is the report that the Opener of Roads has made himself by messengers to the king. None have seen him, for he journeys only in the night. Moreover, when Zikali passes all men are blind and even women's tongues grow dumb. Perchance by 'his spirit' he means his medicine or the witch-doctoress, Nombe, whom folks say he created, since none have seen her father or her mother, or heard who begat her; or perchance his snake is hid behind the mats of the second litter, if in truth there was one."

"It may be so," I said, feeling that it was useless to pursue the matter. "Now, Goza, I would see Zikali and at once."

"That cannot be, Macumazahn, since he has given out that he will see no one, who rests after his journey, and the king has issued orders that any who attempt to approach the Valley of Bones shall die, even if they be of the royal blood. Yes, if so much as a dog dares to draw near that place, it must die. The soldiers who ring it round have killed one already, so strict are the orders, also a boy who went towards it searching for a calf, which I think a bad omen."

"Then I will send a message to him," I persisted.

"Do so," mocked Goza. "Look, yonder sails a vulture. Ask it to take your message, for nothing else will. Be not foolish, Macumazahn, but have patience, for tonight you shall see the Opener of Roads when he attends the Council of the king in the Valley of Bones. This is the order of the king—that at the rising of the moon I lead you thither, so that you may be present at the Council in case he wishes to ask you any questions about the White People or to give you any message to the Government in Natal. Therefore at sunset I will come for you. Till then, farewell. I have business that cannot wait."

"Can I see the king?" I cried.

"Not so, Macumazahn. All today he makes sacrifice to the spirits of his ancestors and must not be approached," Goza called back as he departed.

Availing myself of the permission of the king to go where I would, a little later in the day I walked out of the town towards the Valley of Bones in order to ascertain for myself whether what Goza had told me was true. So it proved, for about three hundred yards from the mouth of the valley, which at that distance looked like a black hole in the hills, I found soldiers stationed about ten paces apart in a great circle which ran right up the hillside and vanished over the crest. Strolling up to one of these, whose face I thought I knew, I asked him if he would let me pass to see my friend, the Opener of Roads.

The man, who was something of a humorist replied—

"Certainly if you wish, Macumazahn. That is to say, I will let your spirit pass, but to do this, if you come one step nearer I must first make a hole in you with my spear out of which it can fly."

I thanked him for his information and gave him some snuff, which he took gratefully, being bored by his long vigil. Then I asked him how many people the great witch-doctor had with him. He said he did not know, but he had seen a number of tall men come to the mouth of the *donga* to fetch food that had been placed there. Again I inquired if he had seen any women, whereon he replied none, Zikali being, he understood, too old to trouble himself about the other sex. Just then an officer, making his rounds, came up and looked at me so sternly that I thought it well to retreat. Evidently there was no chance of getting through that line.

On my way back I walked as near the fence of the King's House as I dared, and saw witch-doctors passing in and out in their hideous official panoply. This told me that here also Goza had spoken the truth—the king was performing magical ceremonies, which meant

162

that it would be impossible to approach him. In every direction I met with failure. The Fates were against me; it lay over me like a spell. Indeed I grew superstitious and began to think that Zikali had bewitched me, as he was said to have the power to do. Well, perhaps he had, for the mere fact of finding myself opposed by this persistent wall of difficulties and silence convinced me that there was something behind it to be learned.

I went back very dejected to my hut and talked to my mare which whinnied and rubbed its nose against me, for although it was well fed and looked after, the poor beast seemed as lonely as I was myself. No wonder, since like myself it was separated from all its kind and weary of inaction. After this I ate and smoked and finally dozed, no more, for whenever I tried to go to sleep I thought that I heard Zikali laughing at me, as mayhap he was doing yonder in his hut.

At length that wearisome day drew towards its end. The sun began to sink, a huge red ball of fire, now and again veiled by clouds, for the sky was stormy. Its fierce rays, striking upon other clouds, peopled the enormous heavens with fantastic shapes of light which were thickest over the hills wherein was the Valley of Bones. To my strained mind these clouds looked like battling armies, figures of flame warring against figures of darkness. The darkness won; no, the light broke out again and conquered it. And see, there above them both squatted a strange black presence crowned with fire. It might have been that of Zikali magnified ten thousand times, and hark! it laughed with the low reverberating voice of distant thunder.

Suddenly I felt that I was no longer alone and looking round, saw Goza at my side.

"What do you see up there, Macumazahn, that you stare so hard?" he asked, pointing at the sky with his stick.

"*Impis* fighting," I answered briefly.

"Then you must be a 'heaven–doctor,' Macumazahn, for I only see black and red clouds. Well, it is time to go to learn whether or no the *impis* will fight, for Zikali awaits us and the Council has started already. By the way, the king says that you will do well to put your pistol in your pocket in case any should seek to harm you in the dark."

"It is there. But, Goza, I pray you to protect me, since in the dark bullets fly wide, and if I began to shoot, one might hit you, Goza."

He smiled, making no answer, but I noticed that during the rest of that night he was careful to keep behind me as much as possible.

Our way led us through the town where everybody seemed to be standing about doing nothing and speaking very little. There was a curious air of expectancy upon their faces. They knew that the crisis was at hand, that their nation's fate hung upon the scales, and they watched my every look and movement as though in them they expected to read an omen. I too watched them out of the corners of my eyes, wondering whether I should escape from their savage company alive. If once the blood lust broke out among them, it seemed to me that I should have about as much chance as a chopped fox among a pack of hungry hounds.

Once out of the town we saw no one until we came to the circle of guards which I have already mentioned, who stood there like an endless line of black statues. In answer to their challenge Goza gave some complicated password in which my name occurred, whereon they opened out and let us through. Then we marched on to the mouth of the *kloof*. The place was very dark, for now the sun was down in the west and the moon in the east was cut off from us by the hills and would not be visible here for half an hour or more. Presently I saw a spot of light. It was a small fire burning near the tongue of rock which I have described.

At a distance, in front of the fire on the patch of prepared ground, squatted a number of men, between twenty and thirty of them, in a semicircle. They were wrapped up in *karosses* and blankets, and in their centre sat a large figure on a chair of wood.

"The King and the Great Council," whispered Goza.

One of them looked round and saw us. At some sign from the king he rose, and against the fire I saw that he was the Prime Minister, Umnyamana. He came to me and, with a nod of recognition, conducted me some paces to the right where a euphorbia tree grew among the rank herbage. Here I found a stool placed ready on which I sat down, Goza, who of course was not of the Council, squatting at my side in the grass.

Now I found that I was so situated that I could not well be seen from the fire, or even from the rock above it, while I, by moving my head a little, could see both quite clearly. After this as the last reflection from the sunk sun faded, the darkness increased until nothing remained visible except the fire and the massive outline of the rock behind. The silence was complete, for none of the Council spoke. They were so still that they might have been dead, so still that a beetle suddenly booming past me made me start as though it had been a bullet. The general impression was almost mesmeric. I felt as though I were going to sleep and yet my mind remained painfully awake, so that I was able to think things out.

I understood clearly that the body of men to my left had come together to decide whether there should be peace or war; that there were divisions of opinion among them; that the king was ready to follow the party which should prove itself the strongest, but that the real voice of decision would speak from behind that fire. It was the case of the Delphic Oracle over again with a priest instead of a priestess, and what a priest!

It was evident to me also that Zikali, who knew human nature, and especially savage human nature, had arranged all this with a view to scenic and indeed supernatural effect. Moreover, he had done it very well, since I knew myself that in this place and hour words and occurrences would affect me deeply at which I should have laughed in the sunlight and open plain. Already the Zulus were affected, for I could hear the teeth of some of them chattering, and Goza began to shiver at my side. He muttered that it was cold, and lied for the *donga* was extremely hot and stuffy.

At length the silver radiance of the moon spread itself on the high curtain of the dark. Then the edge of her orb appeared above the hill and an arrow of white light fell into the little valley. It struck upon and about the jutting rock, revealing a misshapen, white-headed figure squatted between its base and the fire, the figure of Zikali.

CHAPTER 15

The Great Council

None had seen or heard him come, and though doubtless he had but crept round the rock and taken his place in the darkness, there appeared to be something mysterious about this sudden appearance of Zikali. So the Zulu nobles thought at any rate, for they uttered a low *"Ow!"* of fear and wonder.

There he sat like a huge ape staring at the sky, for the firelight shone on his deep and burning eyes. The moonlight increased, but now and again it was broken by little clouds which caused strange shadows to appear about the rock. Some of these shadows looked as though veiled figures were approaching the wizard, bending over him and departing again, after giving him their message or counsel.

"His Spirits visit him," whispered Goza, but I made no answer.

This went on for quite a long time, until the full round of the moon appeared above the hill indeed, and, for the while, the clouds had cleared away. Still Zikali sat silent and I, who was acquainted with the habits of this people, knew that I was witnessing a conflict between two they considered to be respectively a spiritual and an earthly king. It is my belief that unless he were first addressed, Zikali would have sat all night without opening his lips. Possibly Cetewayo would have done the same if the impatience of public opinion had allowed him. At any was rate it was he who gave way.

"*Makosi*, master of many Spirits, on behalf of the Council and the People of the Zulus I, the King, greet you here in the place that you have chosen," said Cetewayo.

Zikali made no answer.

The silence went on as before, till at length, after a pause and some whispering, Cetewayo repeated his salutation, adding—

"Has age made you deaf, O Opener of Roads, that you cannot hear the voice of the King?"

Then at last Zikali answered in his low voice that yet seemed to fill all the *kloof*—

"Nay, Child of Senzangacona, age has not made me deaf, but my spirit in these latter days floats far from my body. It is like a bladder filled with air that a child holds by a string, and before I can speak I must draw it from the heavens to earth again. What did you say about the place that I have chosen? Well, what better place could I choose, seeing that it was here in this very Vale of Bones that I met the first king of the Zulus, Chaka the Wild Beast, who was your uncle? Why then should I not choose it to meet the last king of the Zulus?"

Now I, listening, knew at once that this saying might be understood in two ways, namely that Cetewayo was the reigning king, or that he was the last king who would ever reign. But the Council interpreted it in the latter and worse sense, for I saw a quiver of fear go through them.

"Why should I not choose it," went on Zikali, "seeing also that this place is holy to me? Here it was, O Son of Panda, that Chaka brought my children to be killed and forced me, sitting where you sit, to watch their deaths. There on the rock above me they were killed, four of them, three sons and a daughter, and the slayers—they came to an evil end, those slayers, as did Chaka—laughed and cast them down from the rock before me. Yes, and Chaka laughed, and I too laughed, for had not the king the right to kill my children and to steal their mothers, and was I not glad that they should be taken from the world and gathered to that of Spirits whence they always talk to me, yes, even now? That is why I did not hear you at first, King, because they were talking to me."

He paused, turning one ear upwards, then continued in a new and tender voice, "What is it you say to me, Noma, my dear little Noma? Oh! I hear you, I hear you."

Now he shifted himself along the ground on his haunches some paces to the right, and began to search about, groping with his long fingers. "Where, where?" he muttered. "Oh, I understand, further under the root, a jackal buried it, did it? *Pah!* how hard is this soil. Ah! I have it, but look, Noma, a stone has cut my finger. I have it, I have it," and from beneath the root of some fallen tree he drew out the skull of a child and, holding it in his right hand, softly rubbed the mould off it with his left.

"Yes, Noma, it might be yours, it is of the right size, but how can I be sure? What is it you say? The teeth? Ah! now I remember. Only the day before you were taken I pulled out that front tooth, did I not,

167

and beneath it was another that was strangely split in two. If this skull was yours, it will be there. Come to the fire, Noma, and let us look; the moonlight is faint, is it not?"

Back to the fire he shifted himself, and bending towards the blaze, made an examination.

"True, Noma, true! Here is the split tooth, white as when I saw it all those years ago. Oh! dear child of my body, dear child of my spirit, for we do not beget with the body alone, Noma, as you know better than I do today, I greet you," and pressing the skull to his lips, he kissed it, then set it down in front of him between himself and the fire with the face part pointing to the king, and burst into one of his eerie and terrible laughs.

A low moan went up from his audience, and I felt the skin of Goza, who had shrunk against me, break into a profuse sweat. Then suddenly Zikali's voice changed one more and became hard and businesslike, if I may call it so, similar to that of other professional doctors.

"You have sent for me, O King, as those who went before you have sent when great things were about to happen. What is the matter on which you would speak to me?"

"You know well, Opener of Roads," answered Cetewayo, rather shakily I thought. "The matter is one of peace or war. The English threaten me and my people and make great demands on me; amongst others that the army should be disbanded. I can set them all out if you will. If I refuse to do as they bid me, then within a few days they will invade Zululand; indeed their soldiers are already gathered at the drifts."

"It is not needful, King," answered Zikali, "since I know what all know, neither more nor less. The winds whisper the demands of the white men, the birds sing them, the hyenas howl them at night. Let us see how the matter stands. When your father died Sompseu (Sir T. Shepstone), the great white chief, came from the English Government to name you king. This he could not do according to our law, since how can a stranger name the King of the Zulus? Therefore the Council of the Nation and the doctors—I was not among them, King—moved the spirit of Chaka the Lion into the body of Sompseu and made him as Chaka was and gave him power to name you to rule over the Zulus. So it came about that to the English Queen through the spirit of Chaka you swore certain things; that slaying for witchcraft should be abolished; that no man should die without fair and open trial, and other matters."

He paused a while, then went on, "These oaths you have broken, O King, as being of the blood you are and what you are, you must do."

168

Here there was disturbance among the Council and Cetewayo half rose from his seat, then sat down again. Zikali, gazing at the sky, waited till it had died away, then went on—

"Do any question my words? If so, then let them ask of the white men whether they be true or no. Let them ask also of the spirits of those who have died for witchcraft, and of the spirits of the women who have been slain and whose bodies were laid at the cross-roads because they married the men they chose and not the soldiers to whom the king gave them."

"How can I ask the white men who are far away?" broke out Cetewayo, ignoring the rest.

"Are the white men so far away, King? It is true that I see none and hear none, yet I seem to smell one of them close at hand." Here he took up the skull which he had laid down and whispered to it. "Ah! I thank you, my child. It seems, King, that there is a white man here hidden in this *kloof*, he who is named Macumazahn, a good man and a truthful, known to many of us from of old, who can tell you what his people think, though he is not one of their *indunas*. If you question my words, ask him."

"We know what the white men think," said Cetewayo, "so there is no need to ask Macumazahn to sing us an old song. The question is—what must the Zulus do? Must they swallow their spears and, ceasing to be a nation, become servants, or must they strike with them and drive the English into the sea, and after them the Boers?"

"Tell me first, King, who dwell far away and alone, knowing little of what passes in the land of Life, what the Zulus desire to do. Before me sits the Great Council of the Nation. Let it speak."

Then one by one the members of the Council uttered their opinions in order of rank or seniority. I do not remember the names of all who were present, or what each of them said. I recall, however, that Sigananda, a very old chief—he must have been over ninety—spoke the first. He told them that he had been friend of Chaka and one of his captains, and had fought in most of his battles. That afterwards he had been a general of Dingaan's until that king killed the Boers under Retief, when he left him and finally sided with Panda in the civil war in which Dingaan was killed with the help of the Boers. That he had been present at the battle of the Tugela, though he took no actual part in the fighting, and afterwards became a councillor of Panda's and then of Cetewayo his son. It was a long and interesting historical recital covering the whole period of the Zulu monarchy which ended suddenly with these words—

"I have noted, O King and Councillors, that whenever the black vulture of the Zulus was content to attack birds of his own feather, he has conquered. But when it has met the grey eagles of the white men, which come from over the sea, he has been conquered, and my heart tells me that as it was in the past, so it shall be in the future. Chaka was a friend of the English, so was Panda, and so has Cetewayo been until this hour. I say, therefore, let not the King tear the hand which fed him because it seems weak, lest it should grow strong and clutch him by the throat and choke him."

Next spoke Undabuko, Dabulamanzi and Magwenga, brothers of the king, who all favoured war, though the two last were guarded in their speech. After these came Uhamu, the king's uncle—he who was said to be the son of a Spirit—who was strong for peace, urging that the king should submit to the demands of the English, making the best terms he could, that he "should bend like a reed before the storm, so that after the storm had swept by, he might stand up straight again, and with him all the other reeds of the people of the Zulus."

So, too, said Seketwayo, chief of the Umdhlalosi, and more whom I cannot recall, six or seven of them. But Usibebu and the *induna* Untshingwayo, who afterwards commanded at Isandhlwana, were for fighting, as were Sirayo, the husband of the two women who had been taken on English territory and killed, and Umbilini, the chief of Swazi blood whose surrender was demanded by Sir Bartle Frere and who afterwards commanded the Zulus in the battle at Ihlobane. Last of all spoke the Prime Minister, Umnyamana, who declared fiercely that if the Zulu buffalo hid itself in the swamp like a timid calf when the white bull challenged it on the hills, the spirits of Chaka and all his forefathers would thrust its head into the mud and choke it.

When all had finished Cetewayo spoke, saying—

"That is a bad council which has two voices, for to which of them must the Captain listen when the *impis* of the foe gather in front of him? Here I have sat while the moon climbs high and counted, and what do I find? That one half of you, men of wisdom and renown, say Yes, and that the other half of you, men of wisdom and renown, say No. Which then is it to be, Yes or No? Are we to fight the English, or are we to sit still?"

"That is for the king to decide," said a voice.

"See what it is to be a king," went on Cetewayo with passion. "If I declare for war and we win, shall I be greater than I am? If victory gives me more land, more subjects, more wives and more cattle, what is the use of these things to me who already have enough of all of them? And if defeat should take everything from me, even my life perhaps, then what shall I have gained? I will tell you—the curse of the Zulus upon my name from father to son for ever. They will say, 'Cetewayo, son of Panda, pulled down a House that once was great. Because of some small matter he quarrelled with the English who were always the friends of our people, and brought the Zulus to the dust.' Sintwangu, my messenger, who brought heavy words from the Queen's *induna* which we must answer with other words or with spears, says that the English soldiers in Natal are few, so few that we Zulus can swallow them like bits of meat and still be hungry. But are these all the soldiers of the English? I am not sure. You are one of that people, Macumazahn," he added, turning his massive shape towards me, "tell us now, how many soldiers has your Queen?"

"King," I answered, "I do not know for certain. But if the Zulus can muster fifty thousand spears, the Queen, if there be need, can send against them ten times fifty thousand, and if she grows angry, another ten times fifty, every one armed with a rifle that will fire five bullets a minute, and to accompany the soldiers, hundreds of cannon whereof a single shot would give Ulundi to the flames. Out of the sea they will come, shipload after shipload, white men from where the sun sets and black men from where the sun rises, so many that Zululand would not hold them."

Now at these words, which I delivered as grandly as I could, something like a groan burst from the Council, though one man cried—

"Do not listen to the white traitor, O King, who is sent here to turn our hearts to water with his lies."

"Macumazahn may lie to us," went on Cetewayo, "though in the past none in the land have ever known him to lie, but he was not sent to do so, for I brought him here. For my part I do not believe that he lies. I believe that these English are as many as the pebbles in a river bed, and that to them Natal, yes, and all the Cape is but as a single, outlying cattle *kraal*, one cattle *kraal* out of a hundred. Did not Somp-seu once tell us that they were countless, on that day when he came many years ago after the battle of the Tugela to name me to succeed my father Panda, the day when my faction, the Usutu, roared round him for hours like a river in flood, and he sat still like a rock in the centre of a river? Also I am minded of the words that Chaka said when Dingaan and Umbopa had stabbed him and he lay dying at the *kraal* Duguza, that although the dogs of his own House whom his hand fed, had eaten him up, he heard the sound of the running of the feet of a great white people that should stamp them and the Zulus flat."

171

He paused; and the silence was so intense that the crackling of Zikali's fire, which kept on burning brightly although I saw no fuel added to it, sounded quite loud. Presently it was broken, first by a dog near at hand, howling horribly at the moon, and next by the hooting of a great owl that flitted across the donga, the shadow of its wide wings falling for a moment on the king.

"Listen!" exclaimed Cetewayo, "a dog that howls! Methinks that it stands upon the roof of the House of Senzangacona. And an owl that hoots. Methinks that owl has its nest in the world of Spirits! Are these good omens, Councillors? I think not. I say that I will not decide this matter of peace or war. If there is one of my own blood here who will do so, come, let him take my place and let me go away to my own lordship of Gikazi that I had when I was a prince before the witch Mameena who played with all men and loved but one"—here everybody turned and stared towards me, yes, even Zikali whom nothing else had seemed to move, till I wished that the ground would swallow me up—"caused the war between me and my brother Umbelazi whose blood earth will not swallow nor suns dry—"

"How can that be, O King?" broke in Umnyamana the Prime Minister. "How can any of your race sit in your seat while you still live? Then indeed there would be war, war between tribe and tribe and Zulu and Zulu till none were left, and the white hyenas from Natal would come and chew our bones and with them the Boers that have passed the Vaal. See now. Why is this *Nyanga* (*i.e.* witch-doctor) here?" and he pointed to Zikali beyond the fire. "Why has the Opener of Roads been brought from the Black Kloof which he has not left for years? Is it not that he may give us counsel in our need and show us a sign that his counsel is good, whether it be for war or peace? Then when he has made divination and given the counsel and shown the sign, then, O King, do you speak the word of war or peace, and send it to the Queen by yonder white man, and by that word we, the people, will abide."

At this suggestion, which I had no doubt was made by some secret agreement between Umnyamana and Zikali, Cetewayo seemed to grasp. Perhaps this was because it postponed for a little while the dreadful moment of decision, or perhaps because he hoped that in the eyes of the nation it would shift the responsibility from his shoulders to those of the Spirits speaking through the lips of their prophet. At any rate he nodded and answered—

"It is so. Let the Opener of Roads open us a road through the forests and the swamps and the rocks of doubt, danger and fear. Let him give us a sign that it is a good road on which we may safely travel, and let him tell us whether I shall live to walk that road and what I shall meet thereon. I promise him in return the greatest fee that ever yet was paid to a doctor in Zululand."

Now Zikali lifted his big head, shook his grey locks, and opening his wide mouth as though he expected manna to fall into it from the sky, he laughed out loud.

"O-ho-ho," he laughed, "Oho-ho-ho-o, it is worth while to have lived so long when life has brought me to such an hour as this. What is it that my ears hear? That I, the Indwande dwarf, I whom Chaka named *The-Thing-that-never-should-have-been-born*, I, one of the race conquered and despised by the Zulus, am here to speak a word which the Zulus dare not utter, which the King of the Zulus dares not utter. O-ho-ho-ho! And what does the King offer to me? A fee, a great fee for the word that shall paint the Zulus red with blood or white with the slime of shame. Nay, I take no fee that is the price of blood or shame. Before I speak that word unknown—for as yet my heart has not heard it, and what the heart has not heard the lips cannot shape—I ask but one thing. It is an oath that whatever follows on the word, while there is a Zulu left living in the world, I, the Voice of the Spirits, shall be safe from hurt or from reproach, I and those of my House and those over whom I throw my blanket, be they black or be they white. That is my fee, without which I am silent."

"*Izwa!* We hear you. We swear it on behalf of the people," said every councillor in the semi-circle in front of him; yes, and the king said it also, stretching out his hand.

"Good," said Zikali, "it is an oath, it is an oath, sworn here upon the bones of the dead. Evil-doers you call them, but I say to you that many of those who sit before me have more evil in their hearts than had those dead. Well, let it be proclaimed, O King, and with it this— that ill shall it go with him who breaks the oath, with his family, with his *kraal* and all with whom he has to do.

"Now what is it you ask of me? First of all, counsel as to whether you should fight the English Queen, a matter on which you, the Great Ones, are evenly divided in opinion, as is the nation behind you. O King, *Indunas*, and Captains, who am I that I should judge of such a matter which is beyond my trade, a matter of the world above and of men's bodies, not of the world below and of men's spirits? Yet there was one who made the Zulu people out of nothing, as a potter fashions a vessel from clay, as a smith fashions an *assegai* out of the ore of the hills, yes, and tempers it with human blood.[1] Chaka the Lion, the Wild Beast, the King among Kings, the Conqueror. I knew Chaka as I knew his father, yes, and *his* father. Others still living knew him also, say you, Sigananda there for instance," and he pointed to the old chief who had spoken first. "Yes, Sigananda knew him as a boy knows a great man, as a soldier knows a general. But I knew his heart, aye, I shaped his heart, I was its thought. Had it not been for me he would never have been great. Then he wronged me"—here Zikali took up the skull which he said was that of his daughter, and stroked it—"and I left him.

"He was not wise, he should have killed one whom he had wronged, but perhaps he knew that I could not be killed; perhaps he had tried and found that he was but throwing spears at the moon which fell back on his own head. I forget. It is so long ago, and what does it matter? At least I took away from him the prop of my wisdom, and he fell—to rise no more. And so it has been with others. So it has been with others. Yet while he was great I knew his heart who lived in his heart, and therefore I ask myself, had he been sitting where the King sits today, what would Chaka have done? I will tell you. If not only the English but the Boers also and with them the Pondos, the Basutos and all the tribes of Africa had threatened him, he would have fought them—yes, and set his heel upon their necks. Therefore, although I give no counsel upon such a matter, I say to you that the counsel of Chaka is—fight—and conquer. Hearken to it or pass it by—I care not which."

He paused and a loud *"Ow"* of wonder and admiration rose from his audience. Myself I nearly joined in it, for I thought this one of the cleverest bits of statecraft that ever I had heard of or seen. The old wizard had taken no responsibility and given no answer to the demand for advice. All this he had thrust on to the shoulders of a dead man, and that man one whose name was magical to every Zulu, the king whose memory they adored, the great General who had gorged them with victory and power. Speaking as Chaka, after a long period of peace, he urged them once more to lift their spears and know the joys of triumph, thereby making themselves the greatest nation in Southern Africa. From the moment I heard this cunning appeal, I know what the end would be; all the rest was but of minor and semi-personal interest. I knew also for the first time how truly great was Zikali and wondered what he might have become had Fortune set him in different circumstances among a civilized people.

---

1. The old Zulu smiths dipped their choicest blades in the blood of men.—A. Q.

Now he was speaking again, and quickly before the impression died away.

"Such is the word of Chaka spoken by me who was his secret councillor, the Councillor who was seldom seen, and never heard. Does not Sigananda yonder know the voice which amongst all those present echoes in his ears alone?"

"I know it," cried the old chief. Then with his eyes starting almost from his head, Sigananda leapt up and raising his hand, gave the royal salute, the *Bayete*, to the spirit of Chaka, as though the dead king stood before him.

I think that most of those there thought that it did stand before him, for some of them also gave the *Bayete* and even Cetewayo raised his arm.

Sigananda squatted down again and Zikali went on.

"You have heard. This captain of the Lion knows his voice. So, that is done with. Now you ask of me something else—that I who am a doctor, the oldest of all the doctors and, it is thought—I know not—the wisest, should be able to answer. You ask of me—How shall this war prosper, if it is made—and what shall chance to the King during and after the war, and lastly you ask of me a sign. What I tell to you is true, is it not so?"

"It is true," answered the Council.

"Asking is easy," continued Zikali in a grumbling voice, "but answering is another matter. How can I answer without preparation, without the needful medicines also that I have not with me, who did not know what would be sought of me, who thought that my opinion was desired and no more? Go away now and return on the sixth night and I will tell you what I can do."

"Not so," cried the king. "We refuse to go, for the matter is immediate. Speak at once, Opener of Roads, lest it should be said in the land that after all you are but an ancient cheat, a stick that snaps in two when it is leant on."

"Ancient cheat! I remember that is what Macumazahn yonder once told me I am, though afterwards—Perhaps he was right, for who in his heart knows whether or not he be a cheat, a cheat who deceives himself and through himself others. A stick that snaps in two when it is leant on! Some have thought me so and some have thought otherwise. Well, you would have answers which I know not how to give, being without medicine and in face of those who are quite ignorant and therefore cannot lend me their thoughts, as it sometimes happens that men do when workers of evil are sought out in the common fashion. For then, as you may have guessed, it is the evil-doer who himself tells the doctor of his

175

crime, though he may not know that he is telling it. Yet there is another stone that I alone can throw, another plan that I alone can practise, and that not always. But of this I would not make use since it is terrible and might frighten you or even send you back to your huts raving so that your wives, yes, and the very dogs fled, from you."

He stopped and for the first time did something to his fire, for I saw his hands going backwards and forwards, as though he warmed them at the flames.

At length an awed voice, I think it was that of Dabulamanzi, asked—

"What is this plan, *Inyanga*? Let us hear that we may judge."

"The plan of calling one from the dead and hearkening to the voice of the dead. Is it your desire that I should draw water from this fount of wisdom, O King and Councillors?"

CHAPTER 16

War

Now men began to whisper together and Goza groaned at my side.

"Rather would I look down a live lion's throat than see the dead," he murmured. But I, who was anxious to learn how far Zikali would carry his tricks, contemptuously told him to be silent.

Presently the king called me to him and said—

"Macumazahn, you white men are reported to know all things. Tell me now, is it possible for the dead to appear?"

"I am not sure," I answered doubtfully; "some say that it is and some say that it is not possible."

"Well," said the king. "Have you ever seen one you knew in life after death?"

"No," I replied, "that is—yes. That is—I do not know. When you will tell me, King, where waking ends and sleep begins, then I will answer."

"Macumazahn," he exclaimed, "just now I announced that you were no liar, who perceive that after all you are a liar, for how can you both have seen, and not seen, the dead? Indeed I remember that you lied long ago, when you gave it out that the witch Mameena was not your lover, and afterwards showed that she was by kissing her before all men, for who kisses a woman who is not his lover, or his mother? Return, since you will not tell me the truth."

So I went back to my stool, feeling very small and yet indignant, for how was it possible to be definite about ghosts, or to explain the exact facts of the Mameena myth which clung to me like a Wait-a-bit thorn.

Then after a little consultation Cetewayo said—

"It is our desire, O Opener of Roads, that you should draw wisdom from the fount of Death, if indeed you can do so. Now let any who are afraid depart and wait for us who are not afraid, alone and in silence at the mouth of the *kloof*."

At this some of the audience rose, but after hesitating a little, sat down again. Only Goza actually took a step forward, but on my remarking that he would probably meet the dead coming up that way, collapsed, muttering something about my pistol, for the fool seemed to think I could shoot a spirit.

"If indeed I can do so," repeated Zikali in a careless fashion. "That is to be proved, is it not? Perhaps, too, it may be better for every one of you if I fail than if I succeed. Of one thing I warn you, should the dead appear stir not, and above all touch not, for he who does either of these things will, I think, never live to look upon the sun again. But first let me try an easier fashion."

Then once again he took up the skull that he said had been his daughter's, and whispered to it, only to lay it down presently.

"It will not serve," he said with a sigh and shaking his locks. "Noma tells me that she died a child, one who had no knowledge of war or matters of policy, and that in all these things of the world she still remains a child. She says that I must seek some one who thought much of them; one, too who still lives in the heart of a man who is present here, if that be possible, since from such a heart alone can the strength be drawn to enable the dead to appear and speak. Now let there be silence—Let there be silence, and woe to him that breaks it."

Silence there was indeed, and in it Zikali crouched himself down till his head almost rested on his knee, and seemed to go to sleep. He awoke again and chanted for half a minute or so in some language I could not understand. Then voices began to answer him, as it seemed to me from all over the *kloof*, also from the sky or rock above. Whether the effect was produced by ventriloquism or whether he had confederates posted at various points, I do not know.

At any rate this lord of "multitudes of spirits" seemed to be engaged in conversation with some of them. What is more, the thing was extremely well done, since each voice differed from the other; also I seemed to recognize some of them, Dingaan's for instance, and Panda's, yes, and that of Umbelazi the Handsome, the brother of the king whose death I witnessed down by the Tugela.

You will ask me what they said. I do not know. Either the words were confused or the events that followed have blotted them from my brain. All I remember is that each of them seemed to be speaking of the Zulus and their fate and to be very anxious to refer further discussion of the matter to some one else. In short they seemed to talk under protest, or that was my impression, although Goza, the only person with whom I had any subsequent debate upon the subject, appeared to have gathered one that was different, though what it was I do not recall. The only words that remained clear to me must, I thought, have come from the spirit of Chaka, or rather from Zikali or one of his myrmidons assuming that character. They were uttered in a deep full voice, spiced with mockery, and received by the wizard with *Sibonga*, or titles of praise, which I who am versed in Zulu history and idiom knew had only been given to the great king, and indeed since his death had become unlawful, not to be used. The words were—

"What, *Thing-that-should-never-have-been-born*, do you think yourself a Thing-that-should-never-die, that you still sit beneath the moon and weave witchcrafts as of old? Often have I hunted for you in the Under-world who have an account to settle with you, as you have an account to settle with me. So, so, what does it matter since we must meet at last, even if you hide yourself at the back of the furthest star? Why do you bring me up to this place where I see some whom I would forget? Yes, they build bone on bone and taking the red earth, mould it into flesh and stand before me as last I saw them newly dead. Oh! your magic is good, Spell-weaver, and your hate is deep and your vengeance is keen. No, I have nothing to tell you today, who rule a greater people than the Zulus in another land. Who are these little men who sit before you? One of them has a look of Dingaan, my brother who slew me, yes, and wears his armlet. Is he the king? Answer not, for I do not care to know. Surely yonder withered thing is Sigananda. I know his eye and the *Iziqu* on his breast. Yes, I gave it to him after the great battle with Zweede in which he killed five men. Does he remember it, I wonder? Greeting, Sigananda; old as you are you have still twenty and one years to live, and then we will talk of the battle with Zweede. Let me begone, this place burns my spirit, and in it there is a stench of mortal blood. Farewell, O Conqueror!"

These were the words that I thought I heard Chaka say, though I daresay that I dreamt them. Indeed had it been otherwise, I mean had they really been spoken by Zikali, there would surely have been more in them, something that might have served his purpose, not mere talk which had all the inconsequence of a dream. Also no one else seemed to pay any particular attention to them, though this may have been because so many voices were sounding from different places at once, for as I have said, Zikali arranged his performance very well, as well as any medium could have done on a prepared stage in London.

In a moment, as though at a signal, the voices died away. Then other things happened. To begin with I felt very faint, as though all the strength were being taken out of me. Some queer fancy got a hold of me. I don't quite know what it was, but it had to do with the

Bible story of Adam when he fell asleep and a rib was removed from him and made into a woman. I reflected that I felt as Adam must have done when he came out of his trance after this terrific operation, very weak and empty. Also, as it chanced, presently I saw Eve—or rather a woman. Looking at the fire in a kind of disembodied way, I perceived that dense smoke was rising from it, which smoke spread itself out like a fan. It thinned by degrees, and through the veil of smoke I perceived something else, namely, a woman very like one whom once I had known. There she stood, lightly clad enough, her fingers playing with the blue beads of her necklace, an inscrutable smile upon her face and her large eyes fixed on nothingness.

Oh! Heaven, I knew her, or rather thought I did at the moment, for now I am almost sure that it was Nombe dressed, or undressed, for the part. That knowledge came with reflection, but then I could have sworn, being deceived by the uncertain light, that the long dead Mameena stood before us as she had seemed to stand before me in the hut of Zikali, radiating a kind of supernatural life and beauty.

A little wind arose, shaking the dry leaves of the aloes in the *kloof*; I thought it whispered—*Hail, Mameena!* Some of the older men, too, among them a few who had seen her die, in trembling voices murmured, "It is Mameena!" whereon Zikali scowled at them and they grew silent.

As for the figure it stood there patient and unmoved, like one who has all time at its disposal, playing with the blue beads. I heard them tinkle against each other, which proves that it was human, for how could a wraith cause beads to tinkle, although it is true that Christmas-story ghosts are said to clank their chains. Her eyes roved idly and without interest over the semi-circle of terrified men before her. Then by degrees they fixed themselves upon the tree behind which I was crouching, whereon Goza sank paralyzed to the ground. She contemplated this tree for a while that seemed to me interminable; it reminded me of a setter pointing game it winded but could not see, for her whole frame grew intent and alert. She ceased playing with the beads and stretched out her slender hand towards me. Her lips moved. She spoke in a sweet, slow voice, saying—

"O Watcher-by-Night, is it thus you greet her to whom you have given strength to stand once more beneath the moon? Come hither and tell me, have you no kiss for one from whom you parted with a kiss?"

I heard. Without doubt the voice was the very voice of Mameena (so well had Nombe been instructed). Still I determined not to obey it, who would not be made a public laughing-stock for a second time in my life. Also I confess this jesting with the dead seemed to me somewhat unholy, and not on any account would I take a part in it.

All the company turned and stared at me, even Goza lifted his head and stared, but I sat still and contemplated the beauties of the night.

"If it is the spirit of Mameena, he will come," whispered Cetewayo to Umnyamana.

"Yes, yes," answered the Prime Minister, "for the rope of his love will draw him. He who has once kissed Mameena, *must* kiss her again when she asks."

Hearing this I grew furiously indignant and was about to break into explanations, when to my horror I found myself rising from that stool. I tried to cling to it, but, as it only came into the air with me, let it go.

"Hold me, Goza," I muttered, and he like a good fellow clutched me by the ankle, whereon I promptly kicked him in the mouth, at least my foot kicked him, not my will. Now I was walking towards that Shape—shadow or woman—like a man in his sleep, and as I came she stretched out her arms and smiled oh! as sweetly as an angel, though I felt quite sure that she was nothing of the sort.

Now I stood opposite to her alongside the fire of which the smoke smelt like roses at the dawn, and she seemed to bend towards me. With shame and humiliation I perceived that in another moment those arms would be about me. But somehow they never touched me; I lost sight of them in the rose-scented smoke, only the sweet, slow voice which I could have sworn was that of Mameena, murmured in my ear—well, words known to her and me alone that I had never breathed to any living being, though of course I am aware now that they must also have been known to somebody else.

"Do you doubt me any longer?" went on the murmuring. "Say, am I Nombe now? Or—or am I in truth that Mameena, whose kiss thrills your lips and soul? Hearken, Macumazahn, for the time is short. In the rout of the great battle that shall be, do not fly with the white men, but set your face towards Ulundi. One who was your friend will guard you, and whoever dies, no harm shall come to you now that the fire which burns in my heart has set all Zululand aflame. Hearken once more. Hans, the little yellow man who was named Light-in-Darkness, he who died among the Kendah people, sends you salutations and gives you praise. He bids me tell you that now of his own accord he renders to me, Mameena, the royal salute, because royal I must ever be; because also he and I who are so far apart are yet one in the love that is our life."

The smoke blew into my face, causing me to reel back. Cetewayo caught me by the arm, saying—

"Tell us, are the lips of the dead witch warm or cold?"

"I do not know," I groaned, "for I never touched her."

"How he lies! Oh! how he lies even about what our eyes saw," said Cetewayo reflectively as I blundered past him back to my seat, on which I sank half swooning. When I got my wits again the figure that pretended to be Mameena was speaking, I suppose in answer to some question of Zikali's which I had not heard. It said—

"O Lord of the Spirits, you have called me from the land of Spirits to make reply as to two matters which have not yet happened upon the earth. These replies I will give but no others, since the mortal strength that I have borrowed returns whence it came. The first matter is, if there be war between the White and Black, what will happen in that war? I see a plain ringed round with hills and on it a strange-shaped mount. I see a great battle; I see the white men go down like corn before a tempest; I see the spears of the *impis* redden; I see the white soldiers lie like leaves cut from a tree by frost. They are dead, all dead, save a handful that have fled away. I hear the ingoma of victory sung here at Ulundi. It is finished.

"The second matter is—what shall chance to the king? I see him tossed on the Black Water; I see him in a land full of houses, talking with a royal woman and her councillors. There, too, he conquers, for they offer him tribute of many gifts. I see him here, back here in Zu-luland, and hear him greeted with the royal salute. Last of all I see him dead, as men must die, and hear the voice of Zikali and the mourning of the women of his house. It is finished. Farewell, King Cetewayo, I pass to tell Panda, your father, how it fares with you. When last we parted did I not prophesy to you that we should meet again at the bottom of a gulf? Was it this gulf, think you, or another? One day you shall learn. Farewell, or fare ill, as it may happen!"

Once more the smoke spread out like a fan. When it thinned and drew together again, the Shape was gone.

Now I thought that the Zulus would be so impressed by this very queer exhibition, that they would seek no more supernatural guidance, but make up their minds for war at once. This, however, was just what they did not do. As it happened, among the assembled chiefs, was one who himself had a great repute as a witch-doctor, and therefore burned with jealousy of Zikali who appeared to be able to do things that he had never even attempted. This man leapt up and declared that all which they had seemed to hear and see was but cunning trickery, carried out after long preparation by Zikali and his confederates. The voices, he said, came from persons placed in certain spots, or sometimes were produced by Zikali himself. As for the vision, it was not that of a spirit but of a real woman, in proof of which he called attention to certain anatomical details of the figure. Finally, with much sense, he pointed out that the Council would be mad to come to any decision upon such evidence, or to give faith to prophecies, whereof the truth or falsity could only be known in the future.

Now a fierce debate broke out, the war party maintaining that the manifestations were genuine, the peace party that they were a fraud. In the end, as neither side would give way and as Zikali, when appealed to, sat silent as a stone, refusing any explanation, the king said—

"Must we sit here talking, talking, till daylight? There is but one man who can know the truth, that is Macumazahn. Let him deny it as he will, he was the lover of this Mameena while she was alive, for with my own eyes I saw him kiss her before she killed herself. It is certain, therefore, that he knows if the woman we seemed to see was Mameena or another, since there are things which a man never forgets. I propose, therefore, that we should question him and form our own judgment of his answer."

This advice, which seemed to promise a road out of a blind ally, met with instant acceptance.

"Let it be so," they cried with one voice, and in another minute I was once more conducted from behind my tree and set down upon the stool in front of the Council, with my back to the fire and Zikali, "that his eyes might not charm me."

"Now, Watcher-by-Night," said Cetewayo, "although you have lied to us in a certain matter, of this we do not think much, since it is one upon which both men and women always lie, as every judge will know. Therefore we still believe you to be an honest man, as your dealings have proved for many years. As an honest man, therefore, we beg you to give us a true answer to a plain question. Was the Shape we saw before us just now a woman or a spirit, and if a spirit, was it the ghost of Mameena, the beautiful witch who died near this place nearly the quarter of a hundred years ago, she whom you loved, or who loved you, which is just the same thing, since a man always loves a woman who loves him, or thinks that he does?"

Now after reflection I replied in these words and as conscientiously as I could—

"King and Councillors, I do not know if what we all saw was a ghost or a living person, but, as I do not believe in ghosts, or at any rate that they come back to the world on such errands, I conclude that it was a living person. Still it may have been neither, but only

183

a mere picture produced before us by the arts of Zikali. So much for the first question. Your second is—was this spirit or woman or shadow, that of her whom I remember meeting in Zululand many years ago? King and Councillors, I can only say that it was very like her. Still one handsome young woman often greatly resembles another of the same age and colouring. Further, the moon gives an uncertain light, especially when it is tempered by smoke from a fire. Lastly, memory plays strange tricks with all of us, as you will know if you try to think of the face of any one who has been dead for more than twenty years. For the rest, the voice seemed similar, the beads and ornaments seemed similar, and the figure repeated to me certain words which I thought I alone had heard come from the lips of her who is dead. Also she gave me a strange message from another who is dead, referring to a matter which I believed was known only to me and that other. Yet Zikali is very clever and may have learned these things in some way unguessed by me, and what he has learned, others may have learned also. King and Councillors, I do not think that what we saw was the spirit of Mameena. I think it a woman not unlike to her who had been taught her lesson. I have nothing more to say, and therefore I pray you not to ask me any further questions about Mameena of whose name I grow weary."

At this point Zikali seemed to wake out of his indifference, or his torpor, for he looked up and said darkly—

"It is strange that the cleverest are always those who first fall into the trap. They go along, gazing at the stars at night, and forget the pit which they themselves have dug in the morning. O-ho-ho! Oho-ho!"

Now the wrangling broke out afresh. The peace party pointed triumphantly to the fact that I, the white man who ought to know, put no faith in this apparition, which was therefore without doubt a fraud. The war party on the other hand declared that I was deceiving them for reasons of my own, one of which would be that I did not wish to see the Zulus eat up my people. So fierce grew the debate that I thought it would end in blows and perhaps in an attack on myself or Zikali who all the while sat quite careless and unmoved, staring at the moon. At length Cetewayo shouted for silence, spitting, as was his habit when angry.

"Make an end," he cried, "lest I cause some of you to grow quiet for ever," whereon the recriminations ceased. "Opener of Roads," he went on, "many of those who are present think like Macumazahn here, that you are but an old cheat, though whether or no I be one of these I will not say. They demand a sign of you that none can dispute,

184

and I demand it also before I speak the word of peace or war. Give us then that sign or begone to whence you came and show your face no more at Ulundi."

"What sign does the Council require, Son of Panda?" asked Zikali quietly. "Let them agree on one together and tell me now at once, for I who am old grow weary and would sleep. Then if it can be given I will give it; and if I cannot give it, I will get me back to my own house and show my face no more at Ulundi, who do not desire to listen again to fools who babble like contending waters round a stone and yet never stir the stone because they run two ways at once."

Now the Councillors stared at each other, for none knew what sign to ask. At length old Sigananda said—

"O King, it is well known that the Black One who went before you had a certain little *assegai* handled with the royal red wood, which drank the blood of many. It was with this *assegai* that Mopo his servant, who vanished from the land after the death of Dingaan, let out the life of the Black One at the *kraal* Duguza, but what became of it afterwards none have heard for certain. Some say that it was buried with the Black One, some that Mopo stole it. Others that Dingaan and Umhlagana burned it. Still a saying rose like a wind in the land that when that spear shall fall from heaven at the feet of the king who reigns in the place of the Black One, then the Zulus shall make their last great war and win a victory of which all the world shall hear. Now let the Opener of Roads give us this sign of the falling of the Black One's spear and I shall be content."

"Would you know the spear if it fell?" asked Cetewayo.

"I should know it, O King, who have often held it in my hand. The end of the haft is gnawed, for when he was angry the Black One used to bite it. Also a thumb's length from the blade is a black mark made with hot iron. Once the Black One made a bet with one of his captains that at a distance of ten paces he would throw the spear deeper into the body of a chief whom he wished to kill, than the captain could. The captain threw first, for I saw him with my eyes, and the spear sank to that place on the shaft where the mark is, for the Black One burned it there. Then the Black One threw and the spear went through the body of the chief who, as he died, called to him that he too should know the feel of it in his heart, as indeed he did."

I think that Cetewayo was about to assent to this suggestion, since he who desired peace believed it impossible that Zikali should suddenly cause this identical spear to fall from heaven. But Umnyamana, the Prime *Induna*, interposed hurriedly—

"It is not enough, O King. Zikali may have stolen the spear, for he was living and at the *kraal* Duguza at that time. Also he may have put about the prophecy whereof Sigananda speaks, or at least so men would say. Let him give us a greater sign than this that all may be content, so that whether we make war or peace it may be with a single mind. Now it is known that we Zulus have a guardian spirit who watches over us from the skies, she who is called Nomkubul-wana, or by some the Inkosazana-y-Zulu, the Princess of Heaven. It is known also that this Princess, who is white of skin and ruddy-haired, appears always before great things happen in our land. Thus she appeared before the Black One died. Also she appeared to a number of children before the battle of the Tugela. It is said, too, that but lately she appeared to a woman near the coast and warned her to cross the Tugela because there would be war, though this woman cannot now be found. Let the Opener of Roads call down Nomkubulwana before our eyes from heaven and we will admit, every man of us, that this is a sign which cannot be questioned."

"And if he does this thing, which I hold no doctor in the world can do, what shall it signify?" asked Cetewayo.

"O King," answered Umnyamana, "if he does so, it shall signify war and victory. If he does not do so, it shall signify peace, and we will bow our heads before the *Amalungwana basi bodwe*" (*i.e.*, "the little English," used as a term of derision).

"Do all agree?" asked Cetewayo.

"We agree," answered every man, stretching out his hand.

"Then, Opener of Roads, it stands thus: If you can call Nom-kubulwana, should there be such a spirit, to appear before our eyes, the Council will take it as a sign that the Heavens direct us to fight the English."

So spoke Cetewayo, and I noted a tone of triumph in his voice, for his heart shrank from this war, and he was certain that Zikali could do nothing of the sort. Still the opinion of the nation, or rather of the army, was so strong in favour of it that he feared lest his refusal might bring about his deposition, if not his death. From this dilemma the supernatural test suggested by the Prime Minister and approved by the Council that represented the various tribes of people, seemed to offer a path of escape. So I read the situation, as I think rightly.

Upon hearing these words for the first time that night Zikali seemed to grow disturbed.

"What do my ears hear?" he exclaimed excitedly. "Am I the *Um-kulukulu*, the Great-Great (*i.e.*, God) himself, that it should be asked of me to draw the Princess of Heaven from beyond the stars, she who comes and goes like the wind, but like the wind cannot be commanded? Do they hear that if she will not come to my beckoning, then the great Zulu people must put a yoke upon their shoulders and be as slaves? Surely the King must have been listening to the doctrines of those English teachers who wear a white ribbon tied about their necks, and tell us of a god who suffered himself to be nailed to a cross of wood, rather than make war upon his foes, one whom they call the Prince of Peace. Times have changed indeed since the days of the Black One. Yes, generals have become like women; the captains of the *impis* are set to milk the cows. Well, what have I to do with all this? What does it matter to me who am so very old that only my head remains above the level of the earth, the rest of me being buried in the grave, who am not even a Zulu to boot, but a Dwandwe, one of the despised Dwandwe whom the Zulus mocked and conquered?

"Hearken to me, Spirits of the House of Senzangacona"—here he addressed about a dozen of Cetewayo's ancestors by name, going back for many generations. "Hearken to me, O Princess of Heaven, appointed by the Great-Great to be the guardian of the Zulu race. It is asked that you should appear, should it be your wish to signify to these your children that they must stand upon their feet and resist the white men who already gather upon their borders. And should it be your wish that they should lay down their spears and go home to sleep with their wives and hoe the gardens while the white men count the cattle and set each to his work upon the roads, then that you should not appear. Do what you will, O Spirits of the House of Senzangacona, do what you will, O Princess of Heaven. What does it matter to the Thing-that-never-should-have-been-born, who soon will be as though he never had been born, whether the House of Senzangacona and the Zulu people stand or fall?

"I, the old doctor, was summoned here to give counsel. I gave counsel, but it passed over the heads of these wise ones like a shadow of which none took note. I was asked to prophesy of what would chance if war came. I called the dead from their graves; they came in voices, and one of them put on the flesh again and spoke from the lips of flesh. The white man to whom she spoke denied her who had been his love, and the wise ones said that she was a cheat, yes, a doll that I had dressed up to deceive them. This spirit that had put on flesh, told of what would chance in the war, if war there were, and what would chance to the King, but they mock at the prophecy and now they demand a sign. Come then, Nomkubulwana, and give them the sign if you will and let there be war. Or stay away and give them no sign if you will, and let there be peace. It is nought to me, nought to the *Thing-that-should-never-have-been-born*."

Thus he rambled on, as it occurred to me who watched and listened, talking against time. For I observed that while he spoke a cloud was passing over the face of the moon, and that when he ceased speaking it was quite obscured by this cloud, so that the Vale of Bones was plunged in a deep twilight that was almost darkness. Further, in a nervous kind of way, he did something more to his wizard's fire which again caused it to throw out a fan of smoke that hid him and the execution rock in front of which he sat.

The cloud floated by and the moon came out as though from an eclipse; the smoke of the fire, too, thinned by degrees. As it melted and the light grew again, I became aware that something was materializing, or had appeared on the point of the rock above us. A few seconds later, to my wonder and amazement, I perceived that this something was the spirit-like form of a white woman which stood quite still upon the very point of the rock. She was clad in some garment of gleaming white cut low upon her breast, that may have been of linen, but from the way it shone, suggested that it was of glittering feathers, egrets' for instance. Her ruddy hair was outspread, and in it, too, something glittered, like mica or jewels. Her feet and milk-hued arms were bare and poised in her right hand was a little spear.

Nor did I see alone, since a moan of fear and worship went up from the Councillors. Then they grew silent stared and stared.

Suddenly Zikali lifted his head and looked at them through the thin flame of the fire which made his eyes shine like those of a tiger or of a cornered baboon.

"At what do you gaze so hard, King and Councillors?" he asked. "I see nothing. At what then do you gaze so hard?"

"On the rock above you stands a white spirit in her glory. It is the Inkosazana herself," muttered Cetewayo.

"Has she come then?" mocked the old wizard. "Nay, surely it is but a dream, or another of my tricks; some black woman painted white that I have smuggled here in my medicine bag, or rolled up in the blanket on my back. How can I prove to you that this is not another cheat like to that of the spirit of Mameena whom the white man, her lover, did not know again? Go near to her you must not, even if you could, seeing that if by chance she should *not* be a cheat, you would die, every man of you, for woe to him whom Nomkubulwana touches. How then, how? Ah! I have it. Doubtless in his

188

pocket Macumazahn yonder hides a little gun, Macumazahn who with such a gun can cut a reed in two at thirty paces, or shave the hair from the chin of a man, as is well known in the land. Let him then take his little gun and shoot at that which you say stands upon the rock. If it be a black woman painted white, doubtless she will fall down dead, as so many have fallen from that rock. But if it be the Princess of Heaven, then the bullet will pass through her or turn aside and she will take no harm, though whether Macumazahn will take any harm is more than I can say."

Now when they heard this many remained silent, but some of the peace party began to clamour that I should be ordered to shoot at the apparition. At length Cetewayo seemed to give way to this pressure. I say seemed, because I think he wished to give way. Whether or not a spirit stood before him, he knew no more than the rest, but he did know that unless the vision were proved to be mortal he would be driven into war with the English. Therefore he took the only chance that remained to him.

"Macumazahn," he said, "I know you have your pistol on you, for only the other day you brought it into my presence, and through light and darkness you nurse it as a mother does her firstborn. Now since the Opener of Roads desires it, I command you to fire at that which seems to stand above us. If it be a mortal woman, she is a cheat and deserves to die. If it be a spirit from heaven it can take no harm. Nor can you take harm who only do that which you must."

"Woman or spirit, I will not shoot, King," I answered.

"Is it so? What! do you defy me, White Man? Do so if you will, but learn that then your bones shall whiten here in this Vale of Bones. Yes, you shall be the first of the English to go below," and turning, he whispered something to two of the Councillors.

Now I saw that I must either obey or die. For a moment my mind grew confused in face of this awful alternative. I did not believe that I saw a spirit. I believed that what stood above me was Nombe cunningly tricked out with some native pigments which at that distance and in that light made her look like a white woman. For oddly enough at that time the truth did not occur to me, perhaps because I was too surprised. Well, if it were Nombe, she deserved to be shot for playing such a trick, and what is more her death, by revealing the fraud of Zikali, would perhaps avert a great war. But then why did he make the suggestion that I should be commanded to fire at this figure? Slowly I drew out my pistol and brought it to the full cock, for it was loaded.

"I will obey, King," I said, "to save myself from being murdered. But on your head be all that may follow from this deed."

Then it was for the first time that a new idea struck me so clearly that I believe it was conveyed direct from Zikali's brain to my own. *I might shoot, but there was no need for me to hit.* After that everything grew plain.

"King," I said, "if yonder be a mortal, she is about to die. Only a spirit can escape my aim. Watch now the centre of her forehead, for there the bullet will strike!"

I lifted the pistol and appeared to cover the figure with much care. As I did so, even from that distance I thought I saw a look of terror in its eyes. Then I fired, with a little jerk of the wrist sending the ball a good yard above her head.

"She is unharmed," cried a voice. "Macumazahn missed her."

"Macumazahn does not miss," I replied loftily. "If that at which he aimed is unharmed, it is because it cannot be hit."

"O-ho-o!" laughed Zikali, "the White Man who does not know the taste of his own love's lips, says that he has fired at that which cannot be hit. Let him try again. No, let him choose another target. The Spirit is the Spirit, but he who summoned her may still be a cheat. There is another bullet in your little gun, White Man; see if it can pierce the heart of Zikali, that the King and Council may learn whether he be a true prophet, the greatest of all the prophets that ever was, or whether he be but a common cheat."

Now a sudden rage filled me against this old rascal. I remembered how he had brought Mameena to her death, when he thought that it would serve him, and since then filled the land with stories concerning her and me, which met me whatever way I turned. I remembered that for years he had plotted to bring about the destruction of the Zulus, and to further his dark ends, was now engaged in causing a fearful war which would cost the lives of thousands. I remembered that he had trapped me into Zululand and then handed me over to Cetewayo, separating me from my friends who were in my charge, and for aught I knew, giving them to death. Surely the world would be well rid of him.

"Have your will," I shouted and covered him with the pistol.

Then there came into my mind a certain saying—"Judge not that ye be not judged." Who and what was I that I should dare to arraign and pass sentence upon this man who after all had suffered many wrongs? As I was about to fire I caught sight of some bright object flashing towards the king from above, and instantaneously shifted my

190

aim and pressed the trigger. The thing, whatever it might be, flew in two. One part of it fell upon Zikali, the other part travelled on and struck Cetewayo upon the knee.

There followed a great confusion and a cry of "The king is stabbed!" I ran forward to look and saw the blade of a little *assegai* lying on the ground and on Cetewayo's knee a slight cut from which blood trickled.

"It is nothing," I said, "a scratch, no more, though had not the spear been stopped in its course it might have been otherwise."

"Yes," cried Zikali, "but what was it that caused the cut? Take this, Sigananda, and tell me what it may be," and he threw towards him a piece of red wood.

Sigananda looked at it. "It is the haft of the Black One's spear," he exclaimed, "which the bullet of Macumazahn has severed from the blade."

"Aye," said Zikali, "and the blade has drawn the blood of the Black One's child. Read me this omen, Sigananda; or ask it of her who stands above you."

Now all looked to the rock, but it was empty. The figure had vanished.

"Your word, King," said Zikali. "Is it for peace or war?"

Cetewayo looked at the *assegai*, looked at the blood trickling from his knee, looked at the faces of the councillors.

"Blood calls for blood," he moaned. "My word is—*War!*"

CHAPTER 17

Kaatje Brings News

Zikali burst into one of his peals of laughter, so unholy that it caused the blood in me to run cold.

"The King's word is *war*," he cried. "Let Nomkubulwana take that word back to heaven. Let Macumazahn take it to the white men. Let the captains cry it to the regiments and let the world grow red. The King has chosen, though mayhap, had I been he, I should have chosen otherwise; yet what am I but a hollow reed stuck in the ground up which the spirits speak to men? It is finished, and I, too, am finished for a while. Farewell, O King! Where shall we meet again, I wonder? On the earth or under it? Farewell, Macumazahn, I know where we shall meet, though you do not. O King, I return to my own place, I pray you to command that none come near me or trouble me with words, for I am spent."

"It is commanded," said Cetewayo.

As he spoke the fire went out mysteriously, and the wizard rose and hobbled off at a surprising pace round the corner of the projecting rock.

"Stay!" I called, "I would speak with you;" but although I am sure he heard me, he did not stop or look round.

I sprang up to follow him, but at some sign from Cetewayo two *indunas* barred my way.

"Did you not hear the King's command, White Man?" one of them asked coldly, and the tone of his question told me that war having been declared, I was now looked upon as a foe. I was about to answer sharply when Cetewayo himself addressed me.

"Macumazahn," he said, "you are now my enemy, like all your people, and from sunrise tomorrow morning your safe-conduct here ends, for if you are found at Ulundi two hours after that time, it will be lawful for any man to kill you. Yet as you are still my guest, I will give you an escort to the borders of the land. Moreover, you shall take a message from me to the Queen's officers and captains. It is—that I will send an answer to their demands upon the point of an *assegai*. Yet add this, that not I but the English, to whom I have always been a friend, sought this war. If Sompseu had suffered me to fight the Boers as I wished to do, it would never have come about. But he threw the Queen's blanket over the Transvaal and stood upon it, and now he declares that lands which were always the property of the Zulus, belong to the Boers. Therefore I take back all the promises which I made to him when he came hither to call me King in the Queen's name, and no more do I call him my father. As for the disbanding of my *impis*, let the English disband them if they can. I have spoken."

"And I have heard," I answered, "and will deliver your words faithfully, though I hold, King, that they come from the lips of one whom the Heavens have made mad."

At this bold speech some of the Councillors started up with threatening gestures. Cetewayo waved them back and answered quietly, "Perhaps it was the Queen of Heaven who stood on yonder rock who made me mad. Or perhaps she made me wise, as being the Spirit of our people she should surely do. That is a question which the future will decide, and if ever we should meet after it is decided, we will talk it over. Now, *hamba gachle!* (go in peace)."

"I hear the king and I will go, but first I would speak with Zikali."

"Then, White Man, you must wait till this war is finished or till you meet him in the Land of Spirits. Goza, lead Macumazahn back to his hut and set a guard about it. At the dawn a company of soldiers will be waiting with orders to take him to the border. You will go with him and answer for his safety with your life. Let him be well treated on the road as my messenger."

Then Cetewayo rose and stood while all present gave him the royal salute, after which he walked away down the *kloof*. I remained for a moment, making pretence to examine the blade of the little *assegai* that had been thrown by the figure on the rock, which I had picked from the ground. This historical piece of iron which I have no doubt is the same that Chaka always carried, wherewith, too, he is said to have killed his mother, Nandie, by the way I still possess, for I slipped it into my pocket and none tried to take it from me.

Really, however, I was wondering whether I could in any way gain access to Zikali, a problem that was settled for me by a sharp request to move on, uttered in a tone which admitted of no further argument.

Well, I trudged back to my hut in the company of Goza, who was so overcome by all the wonders he had seen that he could scarcely speak. Indeed, when I asked him what he thought of the figure that had appeared upon the rock, he replied petulantly that it was not given to him to know whence spirits came or of what stuff they were made, which showed me that he at any rate believed in its supernatural origin and that it had appeared to direct the Zulus to make war. This was all I wanted to find out, so I said nothing more, but gave up my mind to thought of my own position and difficulties.

Here I was, ordered on pain of death to depart from Ulundi at the dawn. And yet how could I obey without seeing Zikali and learning from him what had happened to Anscombe and Heda, or at any rate without communicating with him? Once more only did I break silence, offering to give Goza a gun if he would take a message from me to the great wizard. But with a shake of his big head, he answered that to do so would mean death, and guns were of no good to a dead man since, as I had shown myself that night, they had no power to shoot a spirit.

This closed the business on which I need not have troubled to enter, since an answer to all my questionings was at hand.

We reached the hut where Goza gave me over to the guard of soldiers, telling their officer that none were to be permitted to enter it save myself and that I was not to be to permitted to come out of it until he, Goza, came to fetch me a little before the dawn.

The officer asked if any one else was to be permitted to come out, a question that surprised me, though vaguely, for I was thinking of other things. Then Goza departed, remarking that he hoped I should sleep better than he would, who "felt spirits in his bones and did not wish to kiss them as I seemed to like to do." I replied facetiously, thinking of the bottle of brandy, that ere long I meant to feel them in my stomach, whereat he shook his head again with the air of one whom nothing connected with me could surprise, and vanished.

I crawled into the hut and put the board over the bee-hole-like entrance behind me. Then I began to hunt for the matches in my pocket and pricked my finger with the point of Chaka's historical *assegai*. While I was sucking it to my amazement I heard the sound of some one breathing on the further side of the hut. At first I thought of calling the guard, but on reflection found the matches and lit the candle, which stood by the blankets that served me as a bed. As soon as it burned up I looked towards the sound, and to my horror perceived the figure of a sleeping woman, which frightened me so much that I nearly dropped the candle.

To tell the truth, so obsessed was I with Zikali and his ghosts that for a few moments it occurred to me that this might be the Shape with which I had talked an hour or two before. I mean that which had seemed to resemble the long-dead lady Mameena, or rather the person made up to her likeness, come here to continue our conversation. At any rate I was sure, and rightly, that here was more of the handiwork of Zikali who wished to put me in some dreadful position for reasons of his own.

Pulling myself together I advanced upon the lady, only to find myself no wiser, since she was totally covered by a *kaross*. Now what was to be done? To escape, of which of course I had thought at once, was impossible since it meant an *assegai* in my ribs. To call to the guard for help seemed indiscreet, for who knew what those fools might say? To kick or shake her would undoubtedly be rude and, if it chanced to be the person who had played Mameena, would certainly provoke remarks that I should not care to face. There seemed to be only one resource, to sit down and wait till she woke up.

This I did for quite a long time, till at last the absurdity of the position and, I will admit, my own curiosity overcame me, especially as I was very tired and wanted to go to sleep. So advancing most gingerly, I turned down the *kaross* from over the head of the sleeping woman, much wondering whom I should see, for what man is there that a veiled woman does not interest? Indeed, does not half the interest of woman lie in the fact that her nature is veiled from man, in short a mystery which he is always seeking to solve at his peril, and I might add, never succeeds in solving?

Well, I turned down that *kaross* and next instant stepped back amazed and, to tell the truth, somewhat disappointed, for there, with her mouth open, lay no wondrous and spiritual Mameena, but the stout, earthly and most prosaic—Kaatje!

"Confound the woman!" thought I to myself. "What is she doing here?"

Then I remembered how wrong it was to give way to a sense of romantic disappointment at such a time, though as a matter of fact it is always in a moment of crisis or of strained nerves that we are most open to the insidious advances of romance. Also that there was no one on earth, or beyond it, whom I ought more greatly to have rejoiced to see. I had left Kaatje with Anscombe and Heda; therefore Kaatje could tell me what had become of them. And at this thought my heart sank—why was she here in this most inappropriate meeting-place, alone? Feeling that these were questions which must be answered

195

at once, I prodded Kaatje in the ribs with my toe until, after a good deal of prodding, she awoke, sat up and yawned, revealing an excellent set of teeth in her cavernous, quarter-cast mouth. Then perceiving a man she opened that mouth even wider, as I thought with the idea of screaming for help. But here I was first with her, for before a sound could issue I had filled it full with the corner of the *kaross*, exclaiming in Dutch as I did so—

"Idiot of a woman, do you not know the *Heer* Quatermain when you see him?"

"Oh! Baas," she answered, "I thought you were some wicked Zulu come to do me a mischief." Then she burst into tears and sobs which I could not stop for at least three minutes.

"Be quiet, you fat fool!" I cried exasperated, "and tell me, where are your mistress and the Heer Anscombe?"

"I don't know, Baas, but I hope in heaven" (Kaatje was some kind of a Christian), she replied between her sobs.

"In heaven! What do you mean?" I asked, horrified.

"I mean, Baas, that I hope they are in heaven, because when last I saw them they were both dead, and dead people must be either in heaven or hell, and heaven, they say, is better than hell."

"*Dead!* Where did you see them dead?"

"In that Black Kloof, Baas, some days after you left us and went away. The old baboon man who is called Zikali gave us leave through the witch-girl, Nombe, to go also. So the Baas Anscombe set to work to *inspan* the horses, the Missie Heda helping him, while I packed the things. When I had nearly finished Nombe came, smiling like a cat that has caught two mice, and beckoned to me to follow her. I went and saw the cart inspanned with the four horses all looking as though they were asleep, for their heads hung down. Then after she had stared at me for a long while Nombe led me past the horses into the shadow of the overhanging cliff. There I saw my mistress and the Baas Anscombe lying side by side quite dead."

"How do you know that they were dead?" I gasped. "What had killed them?"

"I know that they were dead because they *were* dead, Baas. Their mouths and eyes were open and they lay upon their backs with their arms stretched out. The witch-girl, Nombe, said some *Kaffirs* had come and strangled them and then gone away again, or so I understood who cannot speak Zulu so very well. Who the *Kaffirs* were or why they came she did not say."

"Then what did you do?" I asked.

I ran back to the hut, Baas, fearing lest I should be strangled also, and wept there till I grew hungry. When I came out of it again they were gone. Nombe showed me a place under a tree where the earth was disturbed. She said that they were buried there by order of her master, Zikali. I don't know what became of the horses or the cart."

"And what happened to you afterwards?"

"Baas, I was kept for several days, I cannot remember how many, and only allowed out within the fence round the huts. Nombe came to see me once, bringing this," and she produced a package sewn up in a skin. "She said that I was to give it to you with a message that those whom you loved were quite safe with One who is greater than any in the land, and therefore that you must not grieve for them whose troubles were over. I think it was two nights after this that four Zulus came, two men and two women, and led me away, as I thought to kill me. But they did not kill me; indeed they were very kind to me, although when I spoke to them they pretended not to understand. They took me a long journey, travelling for the most part in the dark and sleeping in the day. This evening when the sun set they brought me through a *Kaffir* town and thrust me into the hut where I am without speaking to any one. Here, being very tired, I went to sleep, and that is all."

And quite enough too, thought I to myself. Then I put her through a cross-examination, but Kaatje was a stupid woman although a good and faithful servant, and all her terrible experiences had not sharpened her intelligence. Indeed, when I pressed her she grew utterly confused, began to cry, thereby taking refuge in the last impregnable female fortification, and snivelled out that she could not bear to talk of her dear mistress any more. So I gave it up, and two minutes later she was literally snoring, being very tired, poor thing.

Now I tried to think matters out as well as this disturbance would allow, for nothing hinders thought so much as snores. But what was the use of thinking? There was her story to take or to leave, and evidently the honest creature believed what she said. Further, how could she be deceived on such a point? She swore that she had seen Anscombe and Heda dead and afterwards had seen their graves.

Moreover, there was confirmation in Nombe's message which could not well have been invented, that spoke of their being well in the charge of a "Great One," a term by which the Zulus designate God, with all their troubles finished. The reason and manner of their end were left unrevealed. Zikali might have murdered them for his own purposes, or the Zulus might have killed them in obedience to the king's order that no white people in the land were to be allowed to live. Or perhaps the Basutos from Sekukuni's country, with whom the Zulus had some understanding, had followed and done them to death; indeed the strangling sounded more Basuto than Zulu—if they were really strangled.

Almost overcome though I was, I bethought me of the package and opened it, only to find another apparent proof of their end, for it contained Heda's jewels as I had found them in the bag in the safe; also a spare gold watch belonging to Anscombe with his coat-of-arms engraved upon it. That which he wore was of silver and no doubt was buried with him, since for superstitious reasons the natives would not have touched anything on his person after death. This seemed to me to settle the matter, presumptively at any rate, since to show that robbery was not the cause of their murder, their most valuable possessions which were not upon their persons had been sent to me, their friend.

So this was the end of all my efforts to secure the safety and well-being of that most unlucky pair. I wept when I thought of it there in the darkness of the hut, for the candle had burned out, and going on to my knees, put up an earnest prayer for the welfare of their souls; also that I might be forgiven my folly in leading them into such danger. And yet I did it for the best, trying to judge wisely in the light of such experience of the world as I possessed.

Now alas! when I am old I have come to the conclusion that those things which one tries to do for the best one generally does wrong, because nearly always there is some tricky fate at hand to mar them, which in this instance was named Zikali. The fact is, I suppose, that man who thinks himself a free agent, can scarcely be thus called, at any rate so far as immediate results are concerned. But that is a dangerous doctrine about which I will say no more, for I daresay that he is engaged in weaving a great life-pattern of which he only sees the tiniest piece.

One thing comforted me a little. If these two were dead I could now leave Zululand without qualms. Of course I was obliged to leave in any case, or die, but somehow that fact would not have eased my conscience. Indeed I think that had I believed they still lived, in this way or in that I should have tried not to leave, because I should have thought it for the best to stay to help them, whereby in all human probability I should have brought about my own death without helping them at all. Well, it had fallen out otherwise and there was an end. Now I could only hope that they had gone to some place where there are no more troubles, even if, at the worst, it were a place of rest too deep for dreams.

Musing thus at last I dozed off, for I was so tired that I think I should have slept although execution awaited me at the dawn instead of another journey. I did not sleep well because of that snoring female on the other side of the hut whose presence outraged my sense of propriety and caused me to be invaded by prophetic dreams of the talk that would ensue among those scandal mongering Zulus. Yes, it was of this I dreamed, not of the great dangers that threatened me or of the terrible loss of my friends, perhaps because to many men, of whom I suppose I am one, the fear of scandal or of being the object of public notice, is more than the fear of danger or the smart of sorrow.

So the night wore away, till at length I woke to see the gleam of dawn penetrating the smoke-hole and dimly illuminating the recumbent form of Kaatje, which to me looked most unattractive. Presently I heard a discreet tapping on the door board of the hut which I at once removed, wriggling swiftly through the hole, careless in my misery as to whether I met an *assegai* the other side of it or not. Without a guard of eight soldiers was standing, and with them Goza, who asked me if I were ready to start.

"Quite," I answered, "as soon as I have saddled my horse," which by the way had been led up to the hut.

Very soon this was done, for I brought out most of my few belongings with me and the bag of jewels was in my pocket. Then it was that the officer of the guard, a thin and melancholy-looking person, said in a hollow voice, addressing himself to Goza—

"The orders are that the White Man's wife is to go with him. Where is she?"

"Where a man's wife should be, in his hut I suppose," answered Goza sleepily.

Rage filled me at the words. Seldom do I remember being so angry.

"Yes," I said, "if you mean that Half-cast whom someone has thrust upon me, she is in there. So if she is to come with us, perhaps you will get her out."

Thus adjured the melancholy-looking captain, who was named Indudu, perhaps because he or his father had longed to the Dudu regiment, crawled into the hut, whence presently emerged sounds not unlike those which once I heard when a ringhals cobra followed a hare that I had wounded into a hole, a muffled sound of struggling and terror. These ended in the sudden and violent appearance of Kaatje's fat and dishevelled form, followed by that of the snakelike Indudu.

Seeing me standing there before a bevy of armed Zulus, she promptly fell upon my neck with a cry for help, for the silly woman

199

thought she was going to be killed by them. Gripping me as an octopus grips its prey, she proceeded to faint, dragging me to my knees beneath the weight of eleven stone of solid flesh.

"Ah!" said one of the Zulus not unkindly, "she is much afraid for her husband whom she loves."

Well, I disentangled myself somehow, and seizing what I took to be a gourd of water in that dim light, poured it over her head, only to discover too late that it was not water but clotted milk. However the result was the same, for presently she sat up, made a dreadful-looking object by this liberal application of curds and whey, whereon I explained matters to her to the best of my power. The end of it was that after Indudu and Goza had wiped her down with tufts of thatch dragged from the hut and I had collected her gear with the rest of my own, we set her on the horse straddle-wise, and started, the objects of much interest among such Zulus as were already abroad.

At the gate of the town there was a delay which made me nervous, since in such a case as mine delay might always mean a death-warrant. I knew that it was quite possible Cetewayo had changed, or been persuaded to change his mind and issue a command that I should be killed as one who had seen and knew too much. Indeed this fear was my constant companion during all the long journey to the Drift of the Tugela, causing me to look askance at every man we met or who overtook us, lest he should prove to be a messenger of doom.

Nor were these doubts groundless, for as I learned in the after days, the Prime Minister, Umnyamana, and others had urged Cetewayo strongly to kill me, and what we were waiting for at the gate were his final orders on the subject. However, in this matter, as in more that I could mention, the king played the part of a man of honour, and although he seemed to hesitate for reasons of policy, never had any intention of allowing me to be harmed. On the contrary the command brought was that any one who harmed Macumazahn, the king's guest and messenger, should die with all his House.

Whilst we tarried a number of women gathered round us whose conversation I could not help overhearing. One of them said to another—

"Look at the white man, Watcher-by-Night, who can knock a fly off an ox's horn with a bullet from further away than we could see it. He it was who loved and was loved by the witch Mameena, whose beauty is still famous in the land. They say she killed herself for his sake, because she declared that she would never live to grow old and ugly, so that he turned away from her. My mother told me all about it only last night."

Then you have a liar for a mother, thought I to myself, for to contradict such a one openly would have been undignified.

"Is it so?" asked one of her friends, deeply interested. "Then the lady Mameena must have had a strange taste in men, for this one is an ugly little fellow with hair like the grey ash of stubble and a wrinkled face of the colour of a flayed skin that has lain unstretched in the sun. However, I have been told that witches always love those who look unnatural."

"Yes," said Number one, "but you see now that he is old he has to be satisfied with a different sort of wife. She is not beautiful, is she, although she has dipped her head in milk to make herself look white?"

So it went on till at length a runner arrived and whispered something to Indudu who saluted, showing me that it was a royal message, and ordered us to move. Of this I was glad, for had I stopped there much longer, I think I should have personally assaulted those gossiping female idiots.

Of our journey through Zululand there is nothing particular to say. We saw but few people, since most of the men had been called up to the army, and many of the *kraals* seemed to be deserted by the women and children who perhaps were hidden away with the cattle. Once, however, we met an *impi* about five thousand strong, that seemed to cover the hillside like a herd of game. It consisted of the Nodwengu and the Nokenke regiments, both of which afterwards fought at Isandhlwana. Some of their captains with a small guard came to see who we were, fine, fierce-looking men. They stared at me curiously, and with one of them, whom I knew, I had a little talk. He said that I was the last white man in Zululand and that I was lucky to be alive, for soon these, and he pointed to the hordes of warriors who were streaming past, would eat up the English to "the last bone." I answered that this remained to be seen, as the English were also great eaters, whereat he laughed, replying, that it was true that the white men had already taken the first bite—a very little one, from which I gathered that some small engagement had happened.

"Well, farewell, Macumazahn," he said, as he turned to go, "I hope that we shall meet in the battle, for I want to see if you can run as well as you can shoot."

This roused my temper and I answered him—

"I hope for your sake that we shall not meet, for if we do I promise that before I run I will show you what you never saw before, the gateway of the world of Spirits."

I mention this conversation because by some strange chance it happened at Isandhlwana that I killed this man, who was named Simpofu.

During all those days of trudging through hot suns and thunder-storms, for I had to give up the mare to Kaatje who was too fat to walk, or said she was, I was literally haunted by thoughts of my mur-dered friends. Heaven knows how bitterly I reproached myself for having brought them into Zululand. It seemed so terribly sad that these young people who loved each other and had so bright a future before them, should have escaped from a tragic past merely to be overwhelmed by such a fate. Again and again I questioned that lump Kaatje as to the details of their end and of all that went before and followed after the murder.

But it was quite useless; indeed, as time went on she seemed to become more nebulous on the point as though a picture were fad-ing from her mind. But as to one thing she was always quite clear, that she had seen them dead and had seen their new-made grave. This she swore "by God in Heaven," completing the oath with an outburst of tears in a way that would have carried conviction to any jury, as it did to me.

And after all, what was more likely in the circumstances? Zikali had killed them, or caused them to be killed; or possibly they were killed in spite of him in obedience to the express, or general, order of the king, if the deed was not done by the Basutos. And yet an idea occurred to me. How about the woman on the rock that the Zulus thought was their Princess of the Heavens? Obviously this must be nonsense, since no such deity existed, therefore the person must ei-ther have been a white woman or one painted up to resemble a white woman; seen from a distance in moonlight it was impossible to say which. Now, if it were a white woman, she might, from her shape and height and the colour of her hair, be Heda herself. Yet it seemed incredible that Heda, whom Kaatje had seen dead some days before, could be masquerading in such a part and make no sign of recognition to me, even when I covered her with my pistol, whereas that Nombe would play it was likely enough.

Only then Nombe must be something of a quick-change artist since but a little while before she was beyond doubt personating the dead Mameena. If it were not so I must have been suffering from illusions, for certainly I seemed to see some one who looked like Mameena, and only Zikali, and through him Nombe, had sufficient knowledge to enable her to fill that role with such success. Perhaps the whole business was an illusion, though if so Zikali's powers must be great indeed. But then how about the *assegai* that Nomkubulwana, or rather her effigy, had seemed to hold and throw, whereof the blade was at present in my saddle-bag. That at any rate was tangible and real, though of course there was nothing to prove that it had really been Chaka's famous weapon.

Another thing that tormented me was my failure to see Zikali. I felt as though I had committed a crime in leaving Zululand without doing this and hearing from his own lips—well, whatever he chose to tell me. I forget if I said that while we were waiting at the gate where those silly women talked so much nonsense about Mameena and Kaatje, that I made another effort through Goza to get into touch with the wizard, but quite without avail. Goza only answered what he said before, that if I wished to die at once I had better take ten steps towards the Valley of Bones, whence, he added parenthetically, the Opener of Roads had already departed on his homeward journey. This might or might not be true; at any rate I could find no possible way of coming face to face with him, or even of getting a message to his ear. No, I was not to blame; I had done all I could, and yet in my heart I felt guilty. But then, as cynics would, say, failure is guilt.

At length we came to the ford of the Tugela, and as fortunately the water was just low enough, bade farewell to our escort before crossing to the Natal side. My parting with Goza was quite touching, for we felt that it partook of the nature of a deathbed adieu, which indeed it did. I told him and the others that I hoped their ends be easy, and that whether they met them by bullets or by bayonet thrusts, the wounds would prove quickly mortal so that they might not linger in discomfort or pain. Recognizing my kind thought for their true welfare they thanked me for it, though with no enthusiasm. Indudu, however, filled with the spirit of repartee, or rather of *tu quoque*, said in his melancholy fashion that if he and I came face to face in war, he would be sure to remember my words and to cut me up in the best style, since he could not bear to think of me languishing on a bed of sickness without my wife Kaatje to nurse me (they knew I was touchy about Kaatje). Then we shook hands and parted. Kaatje, hung round with paraphernalia like the White Knight in *Alice Through the Looking-Glass*, clinging to a cooking-pot and weeping tears of terror, faced the foaming flood upon the mare, while I grasped its tail.

When we were as I judged out of *assegai* shot, I turned, with the water up to my armpits, and shouted some valedictory words.

"Tell your king," I said, "that he is the greatest fool in the world to fight the English, since it will bring his country to destruction and himself to disgrace and death, as at last, in the words of your proverb, 'the swimmer goes down with the stream.'"

203

Here, as it happened, I slipped off the stone on which I was standing and nearly went down with the stream myself.

Emerging with my mouth full of muddy water I waited till they had done laughing and continued—

"Tell that old rogue, Zikali, that I know he has murdered my friends and that when we meet again he and all who were in the plot shall pay for it with their lives."

Now an irritated Zulu flung an *assegai*, and as the range proved to be shorter than I thought, for it went through Kaatje's dress, causing her to scream with alarm, I ceased from eloquence, and we struggled on to the further bank, where at length we were safe.

Thus ended this unlucky trip of mine to Zululand.

CHAPTER 18

Isandhlwana

We had crossed the Tugela by what is known as the Middle Drift. A mile or so on the further side of it I was challenged by a young fellow in charge of some mounted natives, and found that I had stumbled into what was known as No. 2 Column, which consisted of a rocket battery, three battalions of the Native Contingent and some troops of mounted natives, all under the command of Colonel Durnford, R.E.

After explanations I was taken to this officer's head-quarter tent. He was a tall, nervous-looking man with a fair, handsome face and long side-whiskers. One of his arms, I remember, was supported by a sling, I think it had been injured in some *Kaffir* fighting. When I was introduced to him he was very busy, having, I understood from some one on his staff, just received orders to "operate against Matshana."

Learning that I had come from Zululand and was acquainted with the Zulus, he at once began to cross-examine me about Matshana, a chief of whom he seemed to know very little indeed. I told him what I could, which was not much, and before I could give him any information of real importance, was shown out and most hospitably entertained at luncheon, a meal of which I partook with gratitude in some garments that I had borrowed from one of the officers, while my own were set in the sun to dry. Well can I recall how much I enjoyed the first whisky and soda that I had tasted since I left "the Temple," and the good English food by which it was accompanied.

Presently I remembered Kaatje, whom I had left outside with some native women, and went to see what had happened to her. I found her finishing a hearty meal and engaged in conversation with a young gentleman who was writing in a notebook. Afterwards I discovered that he was a newspaper correspondent. What she told him and what he imagined, I do not know, but I may as well state the results at once. Within a few days there appeared in one of the Natal papers

205

and, for aught I know, all over the earth, an announcement that Mr. Allan Quatermain, a well-known hunter in Zululand, after many adventures, had escaped from that country, "together with his favourite native wife, the only survivor of his extensive domestic establishment." Then followed some wild details as to the murder of my other wives by a Zulu wizard called "Road Mender, or Sick Ass" (i.e., Opener of Roads, or Zikali), and so on.

I was furious and interviewed the editor, a mild and apologetic little man, who assured me that the despatch was printed exactly as it had been received, as though that bettered the case. After this I commenced an action for libel, but as I was absent through circumstances over which I had no control when it came on for trial, the case was dismissed. I suppose the truth was that they mixed me up with a certain well-known white man in Zululand, who had a large "domestic establishment," but however this may be, it was a long while before I heard the last of that "favourite native wife."

Later in the day I and Kaatje, who stuck to me like a burr, departed from the camp.

The rest of our journey was uneventful, except for more misunderstandings about Kaatje, one of which, wherein a clergyman was concerned, was too painful to relate. At last we reached Maritzburg, where I deposited Kaatje in a boarding-house kept by another half-cast, and with a sigh of relief betook myself to the Plough Hotel, which was a long way off her.

Subsequently she obtained a place as a cook at Howick, and for a while I saw her no more.

At Maritzburg, as in duty bound, I called upon various persons in authority and delivered Cetewayo's message, leaving out all Zikali's witchcraft which would have sounded absurd. It did not produce much impression as, hostilities having already occurred, it was superfluous. Also no one was inclined to pay attention to the words of one who was neither an official nor a military officer, but a mere hunter supposed to have brought a native wife out of Zululand.

I did, however, report the murder of Anscombe and Heda, though in such times this caused no excitement, especially as they were not known to the officials concerned with such matters. Indeed the occurrence never so much as got into the papers, any more than did the deaths of Rodd and Marnham on the borders of Sekukuni's country. When people are expecting to be massacred themselves, they do not trouble about the past killing of others far away. Lastly, I posted Marnham's will to the Pretoria bank, advising them that they had better keep it safely until some claim arose, and deposited Heda's jewels and valuables in another branch of the same bank in Maritzburg with a sealed statement as to how they came into my possession.

These things done, I found it necessary to turn myself to the eternal problem of earning my living. I am a very rich man now as I write these reminiscences here in Yorkshire—King Solomon's mines made me that—but up to the time of my journey to Kukuana Land with my friends, Curtis and Good, although plenty of money passed through my hands on one occasion and another, little of it ever seemed to stick. In this way or that it was lost or melted; also I was not born one to make the best of his opportunities in the way of acquiring wealth. Perhaps this was good for me, since if I had gained the cash early I should not have met with the experiences, and during our few transitory years, experience is of more real value than cash. It may prepare us for other things beyond, whereas the mere possession of a bank balance can prepare us for nothing in a land where gold ceases to be an object of worship as it is here. Yet wealth is our god, not knowledge or wisdom, a fact which shows that the real essence of Christianity has not yet permeated human morals. It just runs over their surface, no more, and for every eye that is turned towards the divine vision, a thousand are fixed night and day upon Mammon's glittering image.

Now I owned certain wagons and oxen, and just then the demand for these was keen. So I hired them out to the military authorities for service in the war, and incidentally myself with them. I drove what I considered a splendid bargain with an officer who wrote as many letters after his name as a Governor-General, but was really something quite humble. At least I thought it splendid until outside his tent I met a certain transport rider of my acquaintance whom I had always looked upon as a perfect fool, who told me that not half an hour before he had got twenty per cent. more for unsalted oxen and very rickety wagons. However, it did not matter much in the end as the whole outfit was lost at Isandhlwana, and owing to the lack of some formality which I had overlooked, I never recovered more than a tithe of their value. I think it was that I neglected to claim within a certain specified time.

At last my wagons were laden with ammunition and other Government goods and I trekked over awful roads to Helpmakaar, a place on the Highlands not far from Rorke's Drift where No. 3 Column was stationed. Here we were delayed awhile, I and my wagons having moved to a ford of the Buffalo, together with many others. It was during this time that I ventured to make very urgent representations to certain highly placed officers, I will not mention which, as to the necessity of laagering, that is, forming fortified camps, as soon as Zululand was entered, since from my intimate knowledge of its people I was sure that they would attack in force. These warnings of mine were received with the most perfect politeness and offers of gin to drink, which all transport riders were supposed to love, but in effect were treated with the contempt that they were held to deserve. The subject is painful and one on which I will not dwell. Why should I complain when I know that cautions from notable persons such as Sir Melmoth Osborn, and J. J. Uys, a member of one the old Dutch fighting families, met with a like fate.

By the way it was while I was waiting on the banks of the river that I came across an old friend of mine, a Zulu named Magepa, with whom I had fought at the battle of the Tugela. A few days later this man performed an extraordinary feat in saving his grandchild from death by his great swiftness in running, whereof I have preserved a note somewhere or other.

Ultimately on January 11 we received our marching orders and crossed the river by the drift, the general scheme of the campaign being that the various columns were to converge upon Ulundi. The roads, if so they can be called, were in such a fearful state that it took us ten days to cover as many miles. At length we trekked over a stony *nek* about five hundred yards in width. To the right of us was a stony eminence and to our left, its sheer brown cliffs of rock rising like the walls of some cyclopean fortress, the strange, abrupt mount of Isandhlwana, which reminded me of a huge lion crouching above the hill-encircled plain beyond. At the foot of this isolated mount, whereof the aspect somehow filled me with alarm, we camped on the night of January 21, taking no precautions against attack by way of laagering the wagons. Indeed the last thing that seemed to occur to those in command was that there would be serious fighting; men marched forward to their deaths as though they were going on a shooting-party, or to a picnic. I even saw cricketing bats and wickets occupying some of the scanty space upon the wagons.

Now I am not going to set out all the military details that preceded the massacre of Isandhlwana, for these are written in history. It is enough to say that on the night of January 21, Major Dartnell, who was in command of the Natal Mounted Police and had been sent out to reconnoitre the country beyond Isandhlwana, reported a strong force of Zulus in front of us. Thereon Lord Chelmsford, the General-in-Chief, moved out from the camp at dawn to his support, taking with him six companies of the 24th regiment, together with four guns and the mounted infantry. There were left in the camp two guns and about eight hundred white and nine hundred native troops, also some transport riders such as myself and a number of miscellaneous camp-followers. I saw him go from between the curtains of one of my wagons where I had made my bed on the top of a pile of baggage. Indeed I had already dressed myself at the time, for that night I slept very ill because I knew our danger, and my heart was heavy with fear.

About ten o'clock in the morning Colonel Durnford, whom I have mentioned already, rode up with five hundred Natal Zulus, about half of whom were mounted, and two rocket tubes which, of course, were worked by white men. This was after a patrol had reported that they had come into touch with some Zulus on the left front, who retired before them. As a matter of fact these Zulus were foraging in the *mealie* fields, since owing to the drought food was very scarce in Zululand that year and the regiments were hungry. I happened to see the meeting between Colonel Pulleine, a short, stout man who was then in command of the camp, and Colonel Durnford who, as his senior officer, took it over from him, and heard Colonel Pulleine say that his orders were "to defend the camp," but what else passed between them I do not know.

Presently Colonel Durnford saw and recognized me.

"Do you think the Zulus will attack us, Mr. Quatermain?" he said.

"I don't think so, Sir," I answered, "as it is the day of the new moon which they hold unlucky. But tomorrow it may be different."

Then he gave certain orders, dispatching Captain George Shepstone with a body of mounted natives along the ridge to the left, where presently they came in contact with the Zulus about three miles away, and making other dispositions. A little later he moved out to the front with a strong escort, followed by the rocket battery, which ultimately advanced to a small conical hill on the left front, round which it passed, never to return again.

Just before he started Colonel Durnford, seeing me still standing there, asked me if I would like to accompany him, adding that as I knew the Zulus so well I might be useful. I answered, Certainly, and called to my head driver, a man named Jan, to bring me my mare, the same that I had ridden out of Zululand, while I slipped into the wagon and, in addition to the beltful that I wore, filled all my available pockets with cartridges for my double-barrelled Express rifle.

As I mounted I gave Jan certain directions about the wagon and oxen, to which he listened, and then to my astonishment held out his hand to me, saying—

"Goodbye, Baas. You have been a kind master to me and I thank you."

"Why do you say that?" I asked.

"Because, Baas, all the *Kaffirs* declare that the great Zulu *impi* will be on to us in an hour or two and eat up every man. I can't tell how they know it, but so they swear."

"Nonsense," I answered, "it is the day of new moon when the Zulus don't fight. Still if anything of the sort should happen, you and the other boys had better slip away to Natal, since the Government must pay for the wagons and oxen."

This I said half joking, but it was a lucky jest for Jan and the rest of my servants, since they interpreted it in earnest and with the exception of one of them who went back to get a gun, got off before the Zulu horn closed round the camp, and crossed the river in safety.

Next moment I was cantering away after Colonel Durnford, whom I caught up about a quarter of a mile from the camp.

Now of course I did not see all of the terrible battle that followed and can only tell of that part of it in which I had a share. Colonel Durnford rode out about three and a half miles to the left front, I really don't quite know why, for already we were hearing firing on the top of the Nqutu Hills almost behind us, where Captain Shepstone was engaging the Zulus, or so I believe. Suddenly we met a trooper of the Natal Carabineers whose name was Whitelaw, who had been out scouting. He reported that an enormous *impi* was just ahead of us seated in an *umkumbi*, or semi-circle, as is the fashion of the Zulus before they charge. At least some of them, he said, were so seated, but others were already advancing.

Presently these appeared over the crest of the hill, ten thousand of them I should say, and amongst them I recognized the shields of the Nodwengu, the Dududu, the Nokenke and the Ingoba-*makosi* regiments. Now there was nothing to be done except retreat, for the *impi* was attacking in earnest. The General Untshingwayo, together with Undabuko, Cetewayo's brother, and the chief Usibebu who commanded the scouts, had agreed not to fight this day for the reason I have given, because it was that of the new moon, but circumstances had forced their hand and the regiments could no longer be restrained. So to the number of twenty thousand or more, say one-third of the total Zulu army, they hurled themselves upon the little English force that, owing to lack of generalship, was scattered here and there over a wide front and had no fortified base upon which to withdraw.

We fell back to a *donga* which we held for a little while, and then

210

as we saw that there we should presently be overwhelmed, withdrew gradually for another two miles or so, keeping off the Zulus by our fire. In so doing we came upon the remains of the rocket battery near the foot of the conical hill I have mentioned, which had been destroyed by some regiment that passed behind us in its rush on the camp. There lay all the soldiers dead, *assegaied* through and through, and I noticed that one young fellow who had been shot through the head, still held a rocket in his hands.

Now somewhat behind and perhaps half a mile to the right of this hill a long, shallow donga runs across the Isandhlwana plain. This we gained, and being there reinforced by about fifty of the Natal Carabineers under Captain Bradstreet, held it for a long while, keeping off the Zulus by our terrible fire which cut down scores of them every time they attempted to advance. At this spot I alone killed from twelve to fifteen of them, for if the big bullet from my Express rifle struck a man, he did not live. Messengers were sent back to the camp for more ammunition, but none arrived, Heaven knows why. My own belief is that the reserve cartridges were packed away in boxes and could not be got at. At last our supply began to run short, so there was nothing to be done except retreat upon the camp which was perhaps half a mile behind us.

Taking advantage of a pause in the Zulu advance which had lain down while waiting for reserves, Colonel Durnford ordered a retirement that was carried out very well. Up to that time we had lost only quite a few men, for the Zulu fire was wild and high and they had not been able to get at us with the *assegai*. As we rode towards the mount I observed that firing was going on in all directions, especially on the *nek* that connected it with the Nqutu range where Captain Shepstone and his mounted Basutos were wiped out while trying to hold back the Zulu right horn. The guns, too, were firing heavily and doing great execution.

After this all grew confused. Colonel Durnford gave orders to certain officers who came up to him, Captain Essex was one and Lieutenant Cochrane another. Then his force made for their wagons to get more ammunition. I kept near to the Colonel and a while later found myself with him and a large, mixed body of men a little to the right of the *nek* which we had crossed in our advance from the river. Not long afterwards there was a cry of "The Zulus are getting round us!" and looking to the left I saw them pouring in hundreds across the ridge that joins Isandhlwana Mountain to the Nqutu Range. Also they were advancing straight on to the camp.

Then the rout began. Already the native auxiliaries were slipping away and now the others followed. Of course this battle was but a small affair, yet I think that few have been more terrible, at any rate in modern times. The aspect of those plumed and shielded Zulus as they charged, shouting their war-cries and waving their spears, was awesome. They were mown down in hundreds by the Martini fire, but still they came on, and I knew that the game was up. A maddened horde of fugitives, mostly natives, began to flow past us over the *nek*, making for what was afterwards called Fugitives' Drift, nine miles away, and with them went white soldiers, some mounted, some on foot. Mingled with all these people, following them, on either side of them, rushed Zulus, stabbing as they ran. Other groups of soldiers formed themselves into rough squares, on which the savage warriors broke like water on a rock. By degrees ammunition ran out; only the bayonet remained. Still the Zulus could not break those squares. So they took another counsel. Withdrawing a few paces beyond the reach of the bayonets, they overwhelmed the soldiers by throwing assegais, then rushed in and finished them.

This was what happened to us, among whom were men of the 24th, Natal Carabineers and Mounted Police. Some had dismounted, but I sat on my horse, which stood quite still, I think from fright, and fired away so long as I had any ammunition. With my very last cartridge I killed the Captain Indudu who had been in charge of the escort that conducted me to the Tugela. He had caught sight of me and called out—

"Now, Macumazahn, I will cut you up nicely as I promised."

He got no further in his speech, for at that moment I sent an Express bullet through him and his tall, melancholy figure doubled up and collapsed.

All this while Colonel Durnford had been behaving as a British officer should do. Scorning to attempt flight, whenever I looked round I caught sight of his tall form, easy to recognize by the long fair moustaches and his arm in a sling, moving to and fro encouraging us to stand firm and die like men. Then suddenly I saw a *Kaffir*, who carried a big old smooth-bore gun, aim at him from a distance of about twenty yards, and fire. He went down, as I believe dead, and that was the end of a very gallant officer and gentleman whose military memory has in my opinion been most unjustly attacked. The real blame for that disaster does not rest upon the shoulders of either Colonel Durnford or Colonel Pulleine.

After this things grew very awful. Some fled, but the most stood and died where they were. Oddly enough during all this time I was never touched. Men fell to my right and left and in front of me; bullets and assegais whizzed past me, yet I remained quite unhurt. It was as though some Power protected me, which no doubt it did.

At length when nearly all had fallen and I had nothing left to defend myself with except my revolver, I made up my mind that it was time to go. My first impulse was to ride for the river nine miles away. Looking behind me I saw that the rough road was full of Zulus hunting down those who tried to escape. Still I thought I would try it, when suddenly there flashed across my brain the saying of whoever it was that personated Mameena in the Valley of Bones, to the effect that in the great rout of the battle I was not to join the flying but to set my face towards Ulundi and that if I did so I should be protected and no harm would come to me. I knew that all this prophecy was but a vain thing fondly imagined, although it was true that the battle and the rout had come. And yet I acted on it—why Heaven knows alone.

Setting the spurs to my horse I galloped off past Isandhlwana Mount, on the southern slopes of which a body of the 24th were still fighting their last fight, and heading for the Nqutu Range. The plain was full of Zulus, reserves running up; also to the right of me the Ulundi and Gikazi divisions were streaming forward. These, or some of them, formed the left horn of the *impi*, but owing to the un-prepared nature of the Zulu battle, for it must always be remembered that they did not mean to fight that day, their advance had been delayed until it was too late for them entirely to enclose the camp. Thus the road, if it can so be called, to Fugitives' Drift was left open for a while, and by it some effected their escape. It was this horn, or part of it, that afterwards moved on and attacked Rorke's Drift, with results disastrous to itself.

For some hundreds of yards I rode on thus recklessly, because reck-lessness seemed my only chance. Thrice I met bodies of Zulus, but on each occasion they scattered before me, calling out words that I could not catch. It was as though they were frightened of something they saw about me. Perhaps they thought that I was mad to ride thus among them. Indeed I must have looked mad, or perhaps there was something else. At any rate I believed that I was going to win right through them when an accident happened.

A bullet struck my mare somewhere in the back. I don't know where it came from, but as I saw no Zulu shoot, I think it must have been one fired by a soldier who was still fighting on the slopes of the mount. The effect of it was to make the poor beast quite ungovernable. Round she wheeled and galloped at headlong speed back towards the peak, leaping over dead and dying and breaking through the living as she went. In two minutes we were rushing up its northern flank, which seemed to be quite untenanted, towards the sheer brown cliff which rose above it, for the fighting was in progress on the other side. Suddenly at the foot of this cliff the mare stopped, shivered and sank down dead, probably from internal bleeding.

I looked about me desperately. To attempt the plain on foot meant death. What then was I to do? Glancing at the cliff I saw that there was a gully in it worn by thousands of years of rainfall, in which grew scanty bushes. Into this I ran, and finding it practicable though difficult, began to climb upwards, quite unnoticed by the Zulus who were all employed upon the further side. The end of it was that I reached the very crest of the mount, a patch of bare, brown rock, except at one spot on its southern front where there was a little hollow in which at this rainy season of the year herbage and ferns grew in the accumulated soil, also a few stunted, aloe-like plants.

Into this patch I crept, having first slaked my thirst from a little pool of rain water that lay in a cup-like depression of the rock, which tasted more delicious than any nectar, and seemed to give me new life. Then covering myself as well as I could with grasses and dried leaves from the aloe plants, I lay still.

Now I was right on the brink of the cliff and had the best view of the Isandhlwana plain and the surrounding country that can be imagined. From my lofty eyrie some hundreds of feet in the air, I could see everything that happened beneath. Thus I witnessed the destruction of the last of the soldiers on the slopes below. They made a gallant end, so gallant that I was proud to be of the same blood with them. One fine young fellow escaped up the peak and reached a plateau about fifty feet beneath me. He was followed by a number of Zulus, but took refuge in a little cave whence he shot three or four of them; then his cartridges were exhausted and I heard the savages speaking in praise of him—dead. I think he was the last to die on the field of Isandhlwana.

The looting of the camp began; it was a terrible scene. The oxen and those of the horses that could be caught were driven away, except certain of the former which were harnessed to the guns and some of the wagons and, as I afterwards learned, taken to Ulundi in proof of victory. Then the slain were stripped and Kaffirs appeared wearing the red coats of the soldiers and carrying their rifles. The stores were broken into and all the spirits drunk. Even the medical drugs were swallowed by these ignorant men, with the result that I saw some of them reeling about in agony and others fall down and go to sleep.

An hour or two later an officer who came from the direction in which the General had marched, cantered right into the camp where the tents were still standing and even the flag was flying. I longed to be able to warn him, but could not. He rode up to the headquarters marquee, whence suddenly issued a Zulu waving a great spear. I saw the officer pull up his horse, remain for a moment as though indecisive, then turn and gallop madly away, quite unharmed, though one or two assegais were thrown and many shots fired at him. After this considerable movements of the Zulus went on, of which the net result was, that they evacuated the place.

Now I hoped that I might escape, but it was not to be, since on every side numbers of them crept up Isandhlwana Mountain and hid behind rocks or among the tall grasses, evidently for purposes of observation. Moreover some captains arrived on the little plateau where was the cave in which the soldier had been killed, and camped there. At least at sundown they unrolled their mats and ate, though they lighted no fire.

The darkness fell and in it escape for me from that guarded place was impossible, since I could not see where to set my feet and one false step on the steep rock would have meant my death. From the direction of Rorke's Drift I could hear continuous firing; evidently some great fight was going on there, I wondered vaguely—with what result. A little later also I heard the distant tramp of horses and the roll of gun wheels. The captains below heard it too and said one to another that it was the English soldiers returning, who had marched out of the camp at dawn. They debated one with another whether it would be possible to collect a force to fall upon them, but abandoned the idea because the regiments who had fought that day were now at a distance and too tired, and the others had rushed forward with orders to attack the white men on and beyond the river.

So they lay still and listened, and I too lay still and listened, for on that cloudy, moonless night I could see nothing. I heard smothered words of command. I heard the force halt because it could not travel further in the gloom. Then they lay down, the living among the dead, wondering doubtless if they themselves would not soon be dead, as of course must have happened had the Zulu generalship been better, for if even five thousand men had been available to attack at dawn not one of them could have escaped. But Providence ordained it otherwise. Some were taken and the others left.

About an hour before daylight I heard them stirring again, and when its first gleams came all of them had vanished over the *nek* of slaughter, with what thoughts in their hearts, I wondered, and to what fate. The captains on the plateau beneath had gone also, and so had the circle of guards upon the slopes of the mount, for I saw these depart through the grey mist. As the light gathered, however, I observed bodies of men collecting on the *nek*, or rather on both *neks*, which made it impossible for me to do what I had hoped, and run to overtake the English troops. From these I was utterly cut off. Nor could I remain longer without food on my point of rock, especially as I was sure that soon some Zulus would climb there to use it as an outlook post. So while I was still more or less hidden by the mist and morning shadows, I climbed down it by the same road that I had climbed up, and thus reached the plain. Not a living man, white or black, was to be seen, only the dead, only the dead. I was the last Englishman to stand upon the plain of Isandhlwana for weeks or rather months to come.

Of all my experiences this was, I think, the strangest, after that night of hell, to find myself alone upon this field of death, staring everywhere at the distorted faces which on the previous morn I had seen so full of life. Yet my physical needs asserted themselves. I was very hungry, who for twenty-four hours had eaten nothing, faint with hunger indeed. I passed a provision wagon that had been looted by the Zulus. Tins of bully beef lay about, also, among a wreck of broken glass, some bottles of Bass's beer which had escaped their notice. I found an *assegai*, cleaned it in the ground which it needed, and opening one of the tins, lay down in a tuft of grass by a dead man, or rather between him and some Zulus whom he had killed, and devoured its contents. Also I knocked the tops off a couple of the beer bottles and drank my fill. While I was doing this a large rough dog with a silver-mounted collar on its neck, I think of the sort that is called an Airedale terrier, came up to me whining. At first I thought it was an hyena, but discovering my mistake, threw it some bits of meat which it ate greedily. Doubtless it had belonged to some dead officer, though there was no name on the collar. The poor beast, which I named Lost, at once attached itself to me, and here I may say that I kept it till its death, which occurred of jaundice at Durban not long before I started on my journey to King Solomon's Mines. No man ever had a more faithful friend and companion.

When I had eaten and drunk I looked about me, wondering what I should do. Fifty yards away I saw a stout Basuto pony still saddled and bridled, although the saddle was twisted out of its proper position, which was cropping the grass as well as it could with the bit in its mouth. Advancing gently I caught it without trouble, and led it back to the plundered wagon. Evidently from the marks upon the saddlery it had belonged to Captain Shepstone's force of mounted natives.

Here I filled the large saddlebags made of buckskin with tins of beef, a couple more bottles of beer and a packet of *tandstickor* matches which I was fortunate enough to find. Also I took the Martini rifle from a dead soldier, together with a score or so of cartridges that remained in his belt, for apparently he must have been killed rather early in the fight.

Thus equipped I mounted the pony and once more bethought me of escaping to Natal. A look towards the *nek* cured me of that idea, for coming over it I saw the plumed heads of a whole horde of warriors. Doubtless these were returning from the unsuccessful attack on Rorke's Drift, though of that I knew nothing at the time. So whistling to the dog I bore to the left for the Nqutu Hills, riding as fast as the rough ground would allow, and in half an hour was out of sight of that accursed plain.

One more thing too I did. On its confines I came across a group of dead Zulus who appeared to have been killed by a shell. Dismounting I took the headdress of one of them and put it on, for I forgot to say that I had lost my hat. It was made of a band of otter-skin from which rose large tufts of the black feathers of the finch which the natives call *sakabula*. Also I tied his kilt of white oxtails about my middle, precautions to which I have little doubt I owe my life, since from a distance they made me look like a *Kaffir* mounted on a captured pony.

Then I started on again, whither I knew not.

CHAPTER 19

Allan Awakes

Now I have no intention of setting down all the details of that dreadful journey through Zululand, even if I could recall them, which, for a reason to be stated, I cannot do. I remember that at first I thought of proceeding to Ulundi with some wild idea of throwing myself on the mercy of Cetewayo under pretence that I brought him a message from Natal. Within a couple of hours, however, from the top of a hill I saw ahead of me an *impi* and with it captured wagons, which was evidently heading for the king's *kraal*. So as I knew what kind of a greeting these warriors would give me, I bore away in another direction with the hope of reaching the border by a circuitous route. In this too I had no luck, since presently I caught sight of outposts stationed upon rocks, which doubtless belonged to another *impi* or regiment. Indeed one soldier, thinking from my dress that I also was a Zulu, called to me for news from about half a mile away, in that peculiar carrying voice which *Kaffirs* can command. I shouted back something about victory and that the white men were wiped out, then put an end to the conversation by vanishing into a patch of dense bush.

It is a fact that after this I have only the dimmest recollection of what happened. I remember off-saddling at night on several occasions. I remember being very hungry because all the food was eaten and the dog, Lost, catching a bush buck fawn, some of which I partially cooked on a fire of dead wood, and devoured. Next I remember—I suppose this was a day or two later—riding at night in a thunderstorm and a particularly brilliant flash of lightning which revealed scenery that seemed to be familiar to me, after which came a shock and total unconsciousness.

At length my mind returned to me. It was reborn very slowly and with horrible convulsions, out of the womb of death and terror. I saw blood flowing round me in rivers, I heard the cries of triumph and

218

of agony. I saw myself standing, the sole survivor, on a grey field of death, and the utter loneliness of it ate into my soul, so that with all its strength it prayed that it might be numbered in this harvest. But oh! it was so strong, that soul which could not, would not die or fly away. So strong, that then, for the first time, I understood its immortality and that it could *never* die. This everlasting thing still clung for a while to the body of its humiliation, the mass of clay and nerves and appetites which it was doomed to animate, and yet knew its own separateness and eternal individuality. Striving to be free of earth, still it seemed to walk the earth, a spirit and a shadow, aware of the hatefulness of that to which it was chained, as we might imagine some lovely butterfly to be that is fated by nature to suck its strength from carrion, and remains unable to soar away into the clean air of heaven.

Something touched my hand and I reflected dreamily that if I had been still alive, for in a way I believed that I was dead, I should have thought it was a dog's tongue. With a great effort I lifted my arm, opened my eyes and looked at the hand against the light, for there was light, to see it was so thin that this light shone through between the bones. Then I let it fall again, and lo! it rested on the head of a dog which went on licking it.

A dog! What dog? Now I remembered; one that I had found on the field of Isandhlwana. Then I must be still alive. The thought made me cry, for I could feel the tears run down my cheeks, not with joy but with sorrow. I did not wish to go on living. Life was too full of struggle and of bloodshed and bereavement and fear and all horrible things. I was prepared to exchange my part in it just for rest, for the blessing of deep, unending sleep in which no more dreams could come, no more cups of joy could be held to thirsting lips, only to be snatched away.

I heard something shuffling towards me at which the dog growled, then seemed to slink away as though it were afraid. I opened my eyes again, looked, and closed them once more in terror, for what I saw suggested that perhaps I was dead after all and had reached that hell which a certain class of earnest Christian promises to us as the reward of the failings that Nature and those who begat us have handed on to us as a birth doom. It was something unnatural, grey-headed, terrific—doubtless a devil come to torment me in the inquisition vaults of Hades. Yet I had known the like when I was alive. How had it been called? I remembered, *The-thing-that-never-should-have-been-born*. Hark! It was speaking in that full deep voice which was unlike to any other.

"Greeting, Macumazahn," it said. "I see that you have come back from among the dead with whom you have been dwelling for a moon and more. It is not wise of you, Macumazahn, yet I am glad who have matched my skill against Death and won, for now you will have much to tell me about his kingdom."

So it was Zikali—Zikali who had butchered my friends.

"Away from me, murderer!" I said faintly, "and let me die, or kill me as you did the others."

He laughed, but very softly, not in his usual terrific fashion, repeating the word "murderer" two or three times. Then with his great hand he lifted my head gently as a woman might, saying—

"Look before you, Macumazahn."

I looked and saw that I was in some kind of a cave. Outside the sun was setting and against its brightness I perceived two figures, a white man and a white woman who were walking hand in hand and gazing into each other's eyes. They were Anscombe and Heda passing the mouth of the cave.

"Behold the murdered, O Macumazahn, dealer of hard words."

"It is only a trick," I murmured. "Kaatje saw them dead and buried."

"Yes, yes, I forgot. The fat fool-woman saw them dead and buried. Well, sometimes the dead come to life again and for good purpose, as you should know, Macumazahn, who followed the counsel of a certain Mameena and wandered here instead of rushing onto the Zulu spears."

I tried to think the thing out and could not, so only asked—

"How did I come? What happened to me?"

"I think the sun smote you first who had no covering on your head and the lightning smote you afterwards. Yet all the while that reason had left you, One led your horse and after the Heavens had tried to kill you and failed, perhaps because my magic was too strong for them, One sent that beast which you found, yes, sent it here to lead us to where you lay. There you were discovered and brought hither. Now sleep lest you should go further than even I can fetch you back again."

He held his hands above my head, seeming to grow in stature till his white hair touched the roof of the cave, and in an instant I fancied that I was falling away, deep, deep into a gulf of nothingness.

There followed another period of dreaming, in which dreams I seemed to meet all sorts of people, dead and living, especially Lady Ragnall, a friend of mine with whom I had been concerned in a very strange adventure among the Kendah people and with whom in days to come I was destined to be concerned again, although of course I knew nothing of this, in a still stranger adventure of what I may call a spiritual order, which I may or may not try to reduce to writing. It seemed to me that I was constantly dining with her *tete-a-tete* and that she told me all sorts of queer things between the courses. Doubtless these illusions occurred when I was fed.

At length I woke up again, feeling much stronger, and saw the dog, Lost, watching me with its great tender eyes—oh! they talk of the eyes of women, but are they ever as beautiful as those of a loving dog? It lay by my low bed-stead, a rough affair fashioned of poles and strung with *rimpis* or strings of raw hide, and by it, stroking its head, sat the witch-doctoress, Nombe. I remember how pleasing she looked, a perfect type of the eternal feminine with her graceful, rounded shape and her continual, mysterious smile which suggested so much more than any mortal woman has to give.

"Good-day to you, Macumazahn," she said in her gentle voice, "you have gone through much since last we met on the night before Goza took you away to Ulundi."

Now remembering all, I was filled with indignation against this little humbug. "The last time we met, Nombe," I said, "was when you played the part of a woman who is dead in the Vale of Bones by the king's *kraal*."

She regarded me with a kindly commiseration, and answered, shaking her head—

"You have been very ill, Macumazahn, and your spirit still tricks you. I played the part of no woman in any valley by the king's *kraal*, nor were my eyes rejoiced with the sight of you there or elsewhere till they brought you to this place, so changed that I should scarcely have known you."

"You little liar!" I said rudely.

"Do the white people always name those liars who tell them true things they cannot understand?" she inquired with a sweet innocence. Then without waiting for an answer, she patted my hand as though I were a fretful child and gave me some soup in a gourd, saying, "Drink it, it is good. The lady Heddana made it herself in the white man's fashion."

I drank the soup, which was very good, and as I handed back the gourd, answered—

"Kaatje has told me that the lady Heddana is dead. Can the dead make soup?"

She considered the point while she threw some bits of meat out of the bottom of the gourd to the dog, Lost, then replied—

"I do not know, Macumazahn, or indeed whether the dead eat as we do. Next time my Spirit visits me I will make inquiry and tell you

221

the answer. But I do know that it is very strange that you, who always turn your back upon the truth, are so ready to accept falsehoods. Why should you believe that the lady Heddana is dead just because Kaatje told you so, when I who am still alive had sworn to you that I would protect her with my life? Nay, speak no more now. Tomorrow if you are well enough you shall see and judge for yourself."

She drew up the *kaross* over me, again patted my hand in her motherly fashion and departed, still smiling, after which I went to sleep again, so dreamlessly that I think there was some native soporific in that soup.

On the following day two of Zikali's servants who did the rougher work of my sick room, if I may so call it, arrived and said that they were going to carry me out of the cave for a while, if that were my will. I who longed to breathe the fresh air again, said that it was very much my will, whereon they grasped the rough bedstead which I have described by either end and very carefully bore me down the cave and through its narrow entrance, where they set the bedstead in the shadow of the overhanging rock without. When I had recovered a little, for even that short journey tired me, I looked about me and perceived that as I had expected, I was in the Black Kloof, for there in front of me were the very huts which we had occupied on our arrival from Swazi-Land.

I lay a while drawing in the sweet air which to me was like a draught of nectar, and wondering whether I were not still in a dream. For instance, I wondered if I had truly seen the figures of Anscombe and Heda pass the mouth of the cave, on that day when I awoke, or if these were but another of Zikali's illusions imprinted on my weak-ened mind by his will power. For of what he and Nombe told me I believed nothing. Thus marvelling I fell into a doze and in my doze heard whisperings. I opened my eyes and lo! there before me stood Anscombe and Heda. It was she who spoke the first, for I was tongue-tied; I could not open my lips.

"Dear Mr. Quatermain, dear Mr. Quatermain!" she murmured in her sweet voice, then paused.

Now at last words came to me. "I thought you were both dead," I said. "Tell me, are you really alive?"

She bent down and kissed my brow, while Anscombe took my hand.

"Now you know," she answered. "We are both of us alive and well."

"Thank God!" I exclaimed. "Kaatje swore that she saw you dead and buried."

"One sees strange things in the Black Kloof," replied Anscombe speaking for the first time, "and much has happened to us since we were parted, to which you are not strong enough to listen now. When you are better, then we will tell you all. So grow well as soon as you can."

After this I think I fainted, for when I came to myself again I was back in the cave.

Another ten days or so went by before I could even leave my bed, for my recovery was very slow. Indeed for weeks I could scarcely walk at all, and six whole months passed before I really got my strength again and became as I used to be. During those days I often saw Anscombe and Heda, but only for a few minutes at a time. Also occasionally Zikali would visit me, speaking a little, generally about past history, or something of the sort, but never of the war, and go away. At length one day he said to me—

"Macumazahn, now I am sure you are going to live, a matter as to which I was doubtful, even after you seemed to recover. For, Macumazahn, you have endured three shocks, of which today I am not afraid to talk to you. First there was that of the battle of Isandhlwana where you were the last white man left alive."

"How do you know that, Zikali?" I asked.

"It does not matter. I do know. Did you not ride through the Zulus who parted this way and that before you, shouting what you could not understand? One of them you may remember even saluted with his spear."

"I did, Zikali. Tell me, why did they behave thus, and what did they shout?"

"I shall not tell you, Macumazahn. Think over it for the rest of your life and conclude what you choose; it will not be so wonderful as the truth. At least they did so, as a certain doll I dressed up yonder in the Vale of Bones told you they would, she whose advice you followed in riding towards Ulundi instead of back to the river where you would have met your death, like so many others of the white people."

"Who was that doll, Zikali?"

"Nay, ask me not. Perhaps it was Nombe, perhaps another. I have forgotten. I am very old and my memory begins to play me strange tricks. Still I recollect that she was a good doll, so like a dead woman called Mameena that I could scarcely have known them apart. Ah! that was a great game I played in the Vale of Bones, was it not, Macumazahn?"

"Yes, Zikali, yet I do not understand why it was played."

"Being so young you still have the impatience of youth, Macumazahn, although your hair grows white. Wait a while and you will understand all. Well, you lay that night on the topmost rock of Isandhlwana, and there you saw and heard strange things. You heard the rest of the white soldiers come and lie down to rest among their dead brothers, and depart again unharmed. Oh! what fools are these Zulu generals nowadays. They send out an *impi* to attack men behind walls, spears against rifles, and are defeated. Had they kept that *impi* to fall on the rest of the English when they walked into the trap, not a man of your people would have been left alive. Would that have happened in the time of Chaka?"

"I think not, Zikali. Still I am glad that it did happen."

"I think not too, Macumazahn, but small men, small wit. Also like you I am glad that it did not happen, since it is the Zulus I hate, not the English who have now learned a lesson and will not be caught again. Oh! many a captain in Zululand is today flat as a pricked bladder, and even their victory, as they call it, cost them dear. For, mind you, Macumazahn, for every white man they killed two of them died. So, so! In the morning you left the hill—do not look astonished, Macumazahn. Perhaps those captains on the rock beneath you let you go for their own purposes, or because they were commanded, for though weak I can still lift a stone or two, Macumazahn, and afterwards told me all about it. Then you found yourself alone among the dead, like the last man in the world, Macumazahn, and that dog at your side, also a horse came to you. Perhaps I sent them, perhaps it was a chance. Who knows? Not I myself, for as I have said, my memory has grown so bad. That was your first shock, Macumazahn, the shock of standing alone among the dead like the last man in the world. You felt it, did you not?"

"As I hope I shall never feel anything again. It nearly drove me mad," I answered.

"Very nearly indeed, though I have felt worse things and only laughed, as I would tell you, had I the time. Well, then the sun struck you, for at this season of the year it is very hot in those valleys for a white man with no covering to his head, and you went quite mad, though fortunately the dog and the horse remained as Heaven had made them. That was the second shock. Then the storm burst and the lightning fell. It ran down the rifle that you still carried, Macumazahn. I will show it to you and you will see that its stock is shattered. Perhaps I turned the flash aside, for I am a great thunder-herd, or perhaps it was One mightier than I. That was the third shock, Macumazahn. Then you were found, still living—how, the white man, your friend, will tell you. But you should cherish that dog of yours, Macumazahn, for many a man might have served you worse. And being strong, though small, or perhaps because you still have work left to do in the world before you leave it for a while, you have lived through all these things and will in time recover, though not yet."

"I hope so, Zikali, though on the whole I am not sure that I wish to recover."

"Yes, you do, Macumazahn, because the religion of you white men makes you fear death and what may come after it. You think of what you call your sins and are afraid lest you should be tortured because of them, not understanding that the spirit must be judged not by what the flesh has done but by what the spirit desired to do, by *will* not by *deed*, Macumazahn. The evil man is he who wishes to do evil, not he who wishes to do good and falls now and again into evil. Oh! I have hearkened to your white teachers and I know, I know."

"Then by your own standard you are evil, Zikali, since you wished to bring about war, and not in vain."

"Oho! Macumazahn, you think that, do you, who cannot understand that what seems to be evil is often good. I wished to bring about war and brought it about, and maybe what bred the wish was all that I have suffered in the past. But say you, who have seen what the Zulu Power means, who have seen men, women and children killed by the thousand to feed that Power, and who have seen, too, what the English Power means, is it evil that I should wish to destroy the House of the Zulu kings that the English House may take its place and that in a time to come the Black people may be free?"

"You are clever, Zikali, but it is of your own wrongs that you think. How about that skull which you kissed in the Vale of Bones?"

"Mayhap, Macumazahn, but my wrongs are the wrongs of a nation, therefore I think of the nation, and at least I do not fear death like you white men. Now hearken. Presently your friends will tell you a story. The lady Heddana will tell you how I made use of her for a certain purpose, for which purpose indeed I drew the three of you into Zululand, because without her I could not have brought about this war into which Cetewayo did not wish to enter. When you have heard that story, do not judge me too hardly, Macumazahn, who had a great end to gain."

"Yet whatever the story may be, I do judge you hardly, Zikali, who tormented me with a false tale, causing the woman Kaatje to lie to me and swear that she saw these two dead before her—how I know not."

"She did not lie to you, Macumazahn. Has not such a one as I the power to make a fat fool think that she saw what she did not see? As to how! How did I make you think in yonder hut of mine that you saw what you did not see—perhaps."

"But why did you mock me in this fashion, Zikali?"

"Truly, Macumazahn, you are blind as a bat in sunlight. When your friends have told you the story, you will understand why. Yet I admit to you that things went wrong. You should have heard that tale *before* Cetewayo brought you to the Vale of Bones. But the fool-woman delayed and blundered, and when she reached Ulundi the gates were shut against her as a spy, and not opened till too late, so that you only found her when you returned from the Council. I knew this, and that was why I dared to bid you fire at that which stood upon the rock. Had you heard Kaatje's tale you might have aimed straight, as also you would have certainly shot straight at me, out of revenge for the deaths of those you loved, Macumazahn, though whether you could have killed me before all the game is played is another matter. As it was, I was sure that you would not pierce the heart of one who *might* be a certain white woman, sure also that you would not pierce my heart whose death *might* bring about her death and that of another."

"You are very subtle, Zikali," I said in astonishment.

"So you hold because I am very simple, who understand the spirit of man—and some other things. For the rest, had you not believed that these two were dead, you would never have left Zululand. You would have tried to escape to get to them and have been killed. Is it not so?"

"Yes, I think I should have tried, Zikali. But why did you keep them prisoner?"

"For the same reason that I still keep them—and you—to hold them back a while from the world of ghosts. Had I sent them away after that night of the declaration of war, they would have been killed before they had gone an hour's journey. Oh! I am not so bad as you think, Macumazahn, and I never break my word. Now I have done."

"How goes the war?" I asked as he shuffled to his feet.

"As it must go, very ill for the Zulus. They have driven back the white men who gather strength from over the Black Water and will come on presently and wipe them out. Umnyamana would have had Cetewayo invade Natal and sweep it clean, as of course he should have done. But I sent him word that if he did so Nomkubulwana, yes, she and no other, had told me that all the spirits would be against him, and he hearkened. When next you think me wicked, remember that, Macumazahn. Now it is but a matter of time, and here you must bide till all is finished. That will be good for you who need rest, though the other two find it wearisome. Still for them it is good also to watch the fruit ripen on their tree of love. It will be the sweeter when they eat it, Macumazahn, and teach them how to live together. *Oho! Oho-ho!*" and he shambled off.

CHAPTER 20

Heda's Tale

That evening when I was lying on my bed outside the cave, I heard the tale of Anscombe and Heda. Up to a certain point he told it, then she went on with the story.

"On the morning after our arrival at this place, Allan," said Anscombe, "I woke up to find you gone from the hut. As you did not come back I concluded that you were with Zikali, and walked about looking for you. Then food was brought to us and Heda and I breakfasted together, after which we went to where we heard the horses neighing and found that yours was gone. Returning, much frightened, we met Nombe, who gave me your note which explained everything, and we inquired of her why this had been done and what was to become of us. She smiled and answered that we had better ask the first question of the king and the second of her master Zikali, and in the meanwhile be at peace since we were quite safe.

"I tried to see Zikali but could not. Then I went to *inspan* the horses with the idea of following you, only to find that they were gone. Indeed I have not seen them from that day to this. Next we thought of starting on foot, for we were quite desperate. But Nombe intervened and told us that if we ventured out of the Black Kloof we should be killed. In short we were prisoners.

"This went on for some days, during which we were well treated but could not succeed in seeing Zikali. At length one morning he sent for us and we were taken to the enclosure in front of his hut, Kaatje coming with us as interpreter. For a while he sat still, looking very grim and terrible. Then he said—

"'White Chief and Lady, you think ill of me because Macumazahn has gone and you are kept prisoners here, and before all is done you will think worse. Yet I counsel you to trust me since everything that happens is for your good.'

227

"At this point Heda, who, as you know, talked Zulu fairly well, though not so well as she does now, broke in, and said some very angry things to him."

"Yes," interrupted Heda. "I told him that he was a liar and I believed that he had murdered you and meant to murder us."

"He listened stonily," continued Anscombe, "and answered, 'I perceive, Lady Heddana, that you understand enough of our tongue to enable me to talk to you; therefore I will send away this half-breed woman, since what I have to say is secret.'

"Then he called servants by clapping his hands and ordered them to remove Kaatje, which was done.

"'Now, Lady Heddana,' he said, speaking very slowly so that Heda might interpret to me and repeating his words whenever she did not understand, 'I have a proposal to make to you. For my own ends it is necessary that you should play a part and appear before the king and the Council as the goddess of this land who is called the Chieftainess of Heaven, which goddess is always seen as a white woman. Therefore you must travel with me to Ulundi and there do those things which I shall tell you.'

"'And if I refuse to play this trick,' said Heda, 'what then?'

"'Then, Lady Heddana, this white lord whom you love and who is to be your husband will—die—and after he is dead you must still do what I desire of you, or—die also.'

"'Would he come with me to Ulundi?' asked Heda.

"'Not so, Lady. He would stay here under guard, but quite safe, and you will be brought back to him, safe. Choose now, with death on the one hand and safety on the other. I would sleep a little. Talk the matter over in your own tongue and when it is settled awaken me again,' and he shut his eyes and appeared to go to sleep.

"So we discussed the situation, if you can call it discussion when we were both nearly mad. Heda wished to go. I begged her to let me be killed rather than trust herself into the hands of this old villain. She pointed out that even if I were killed, which she admitted might not happen, she would still be in his hands whence she could only escape by her own death, whereas if she went there was a chance that we might both continue to live, and that after all death was easy to find. So in the end I gave way and we woke up Zikali and told him so.

"He seemed pleased and spoke to us gently, saying, 'I was sure that wisdom dwelt behind those bright eyes of yours, Lady, and again I promise you that neither you nor the lord your lover shall come to any harm. Also that in payment I and my child, Nombe, will protect you even with our lives, and further, that I will bring back your friend, Macumazahn, to you, though not yet. Now go and be happy together. Nombe will tell the lady Heddana when she is to start. Of all this say nothing on your peril to the woman Kaatje, since if you do, it will be necessary that she should be made silent. Indeed, lest she should learn something, tomorrow I shall send her on to await you at Ulundi, therefore be not surprised if you see her go, and take no heed of aught she may say in going. Nombe, my child, will fill her place as servant to the lady Heddana and sleep with her at night that she may not be lonely or afraid.'

"Then he clapped his hands again and servants came and conducted us back to the huts. And now, Allan, Heda will go on with the story."

"Well, Mr. Quatermain," she said, "nothing more happened that day which we spent with bursting hearts. Kaatje did not question us as to what the witch-doctor had said after she was sent away. Indeed I noticed that she was growing very stupid and drowsy, like a person who has been drugged, as I daresay she was, and would insist upon beginning to pack up the things in a foolish kind of way, muttering something about our trekking on the following day. The night passed as usual, Kaatje sleeping very heavily by my side and snoring so much" (here I groaned sympathetically) "that I could get little rest. On the next morning after breakfast as the huts were very hot, Nombe suggested that we should sit under the shadow of the overhanging rock, just where we are now. Accordingly we went, and being tired out with all our troubles and bad nights, I fell into a doze, and so, I think, did Maurice, Nombe sitting near to us and singing all the while, a very queer kind of song.

"Presently, through my doze as it were, I saw Kaatje approaching. Nombe went to meet her, still singing, and taking her hand, led her to the cart, where they seemed to talk to the horses, which surprised me as there were no horses. Then she brought her round the cart and pointed to us, still singing. Now Kaatje began to weep and throw her hands about, while Nombe patted her on the shoulder. I tried to speak to her but could not. My tongue was tied, why I don't know, but I suppose because I was really asleep, and Maurice also was asleep and did not wake at all."

"Yes," said Anscombe, "I remember nothing of all this business."

"After a while Kaatje went away, still weeping, and then I fell asleep in earnest and did not wake until the sun was going down, when I roused Maurice and we both went back to the hut, where I found that Nombe had cooked our evening meal. I looked for Kaatje, but could not find her. Also in searching through my things I missed the bag of jewels. I called to Nombe and asked where Kaatje was, whereon she smiled and said that she had gone away, taking the bag with her. This pained me, for I had always found Kaatje quite honest—"

"Which she is," I remarked, "for those jewels are now in a bank at Maritzburg."

Heda nodded and went on, "I am glad to hear it; indeed, remembering what Zikali had said, I never really suspected her of being a thief, but thought it was all part of some plan. After this things went on as before, except that Nombe took Kaatje's place and was with me day and night. Of Kaatje's disappearance she would say nothing. Zikali we did not see.

"On the third evening after the vanishing of Kaatje, Nombe came and said that I must make ready for a journey, and while she spoke men arrived with a litter that had grass mats hung round it. Nombe brought out my long cape and put it over me, also a kind of veil of white stuff which she threw over my head, so as to hide my face. I think it was made out of one of our travelling mosquito nets. Then she said I must say goodbye to Maurice for a while. There was a scene as you may imagine. He grew angry and said that he would come with me, whereon armed men appeared, six of them, and pushed him away with the handles of their spears. In another minute I was lifted into the litter which Nombe entered with me, and so we were parted, wondering if we should ever see each other more. At the mouth of the *kloof* I saw another litter surrounded by a number of Zulus, which Nombe said contained Zikali.

"We travelled all that night and two succeeding nights, resting during the day in deserted *kraals* that appeared to have been made ready for us. It was a strange journey, for although the armed men flitted about us, neither they nor the bearers ever spoke, nor did I see Zikali, or indeed any one else. Only Nombe comforted me from time to time, telling me there was nothing to fear. Towards dawn on the third night we travelled over some hills and I was put into a new hut and told that my journey was done as we had reached a place near Ulundi.

"I slept most of the following day, but after I had eaten towards evening, Zikali crept into the hut, just as a great toad might do, and squatted down in front of me.

"'Lady,' he said, 'listen. Tonight, perhaps one hour after sundown, perhaps two, perhaps three, Nombe will lead you, dressed in a certain fashion, from this hut. See now, outside of it there is a tongue of rock up which you may climb unnoted by the little path that runs between those big stones. Look,' and he showed me the place through the door-hole. 'The path ends on a flat boulder at the end of the rock. There you will take your stand, holding in your right hand a little *assegai* which will be given to you. Nombe will not accompany you to the rock, but she will crouch between the stones at the head of the path and perhaps from time to time whisper to you what to do. Thus when she tells you, you must throw the little spear into the air, so that it falls among a number of men gathered in debate who will be seated about twenty paces from the rock. For the rest you are to stand quite still, saying nothing and showing no alarm whatever you may hear or see. Among the men before you may be your friend, Macumazahn, but you must not appear to recognize him, and if he speaks to you, you must make no answer. Even if he should seem to shoot at you, do not be afraid. Do you understand? If so, repeat what I have told you.' I obeyed him and asked what would happen if I did not do these things, or some of them.

"He answered, 'You will be killed, Nombe will be killed, the Lord Mauriti your lover will be killed, and your friend Macumazahn will be killed. Perhaps even I shall be killed and we will talk the matter over in the land of ghosts.'

"On hearing this I said I would do my best to carry out his orders, and after making me repeat them once more, he went away. Later, Nombe dressed me up as you saw me, Mr. Quatermain, put some glittering powder into my hair and touched me beneath the eyes with a dark kind of pigment. Also she gave me the little spear and made me practise standing quite still with it raised in my right hand, telling me that when I heard her say the word 'Throw,' I was to cast it into the air. Then the moon rose and we heard men talking at a distance. At last some one came to the hut and whispered to Nombe, who led me out to the little path between the rocks.

"This must have been nearly two hours after I heard the men begin to talk——"

"Excuse me," I interrupted, "but where was Nombe all those two hours?"

"With me. She never left my side, Mr. Quatermain, and while I was on the rock she was crouched within three paces of me between two big stones at the mouth of the path."

"Indeed," I replied faintly, "this is very interesting. Please continue—but one word, how was Nombe dressed? Did she wear a necklace of blue beads?"

"Just as she always is, or rather less so, for she had nothing on except her *moocha*, and certainly no blue beads. But why do you ask?"

"From curiosity merely. I mean, I will tell you afterwards, pray go on."

"Well, I stepped forward on to the rock and at first saw nothing, because at that moment the moon was hid by a cloud; indeed Nombe had waited for the cloud to pass over its face, before she thrust me forward. Also some smoke from a fire below was rising straight in front of me. Presently the cloud passed, the smoke thinned, and I saw the circle of those savage men seated beneath, and in their centre a great chief wearing a leopard's skin cloak who I guessed was the king. You I did not see, Mr. Quatermain, because you were behind a tree, yet I felt that you were there, a friend among all those foes. I stood still, as I had been taught to do, and heard the murmur of astonishment and caught the gleam of the moonlight from the white feathers that were sewn upon my robe.

"Then I heard also the voice of Zikali speaking from beneath. He called on you to come out to shoot at me, and the man whom I took to be the king, ordered you to obey. You appeared from behind the tree, and I was certain from the look upon your face that at that distance you did not know who I was in my strange and glittering raiment. You lifted the pistol and I was terribly afraid, for I had seen you shoot with it before on the veranda of the Temple and knew well that you do not miss. Very nearly I screamed out to you, but remembered and was silent, thinking that after all it did not much matter if I died, except for the sake of Maurice here. Also by now I guessed that I was being used to deceive those men before me into some terrible act, and that if I died, at least they would be undeceived.

"I thought that an age passed between the time you pointed the pistol and I saw the flash for which I was waiting."

"You need not have waited, Heda," I interposed, "for if I had really aimed at you you would never have seen that flash, at least so it is said. I too guessed enough to shoot above you, although at the time I did not know that it was you on the rock; indeed I thought it was Nombe painted up."

"Yes, I heard the bullet sing over me. Then I heard the voice of Zikali challenging you to shoot him, and to tell the truth, hoped that you would do so. Just before you fired for the second time, Nombe whispered to me—'Throw' and I threw the little red-handled spear into the air. Then as the pistol went off Nombe whispered—'Come.' I slipped away down the path and back with her into the hut, where she kissed me and said that I had done well indeed, after which she took off my strange robe and helped me to put on my own dress.

232

"That is all I know, except that some hours later I was awakened from sleep and put into the litter where I went to sleep again, for what I had gone through tired me very much. I need not trouble you with the rest, for we journeyed here in the same way that we had journeyed to Ulundi—by night. I did not see Zikali, but in answer to my questions, Nombe told me that the Zulus had declared war against the English. What part in the business I had played, she would not tell me, and I do not know to this hour, but I am sure that it was a great one.

"So we came back to the Black Kloof, where I found Maurice quite well, and now he had better go on with the tale, for if I begin to tell you of our meeting I shall become foolish."

"There isn't much more to tell," said Anscombe, "except about yourself. While Heda was away I was kept a prisoner and watched day and night by Zikali's people who would not let me stir a yard, but otherwise treated me kindly. Then one day at sunrise, or shortly after it, Heda re-appeared and told me all this story, for the end of which, as you may imagine, I thanked God.

"After that we just lived on here, happily enough since we were together, until one day Nombe told us that there had been a great battle in which the Zulus had wiped out the English, killing hundreds and hundreds of them, although for every soldier that they killed, they had lost two. Of course this made us very sad, especially as we were afraid you might be with our troops. We asked Nombe if you were present at the battle. She answered that she would inquire of her Spirit and went through some very strange performances with ashes and knuckle bones, after which she announced that you had been in the battle but were alive and coming this way with a dog that had silver on it. We laughed at her, saying that she could not possibly know anything of the sort, also that dogs as a rule did not carry silver. Whereon she only smiled and said—'Wait.'

"I think it was three days later that one night towards dawn I was awakened by hearing a dog barking outside my hut, as though it wished to call attention to its presence. It barked so persistently and in a way so unlike a *Kaffir* dog, that at length about dawn I went out of the hut to see what was the matter. There, standing a few yards away surrounded by some of Zikali's people, I saw Lost and knew at once that it was an English Airedale, for I have had several of the breed. It looked very tired and frightened, and while I was wondering whence on earth it could have come, I noticed that it had a silver-mounted collar and remembered Nombe and her talk about you and a dog that carried silver on it. From that moment, Allan, I was certain that you

233

were somewhere near, especially as the beast ran up to me—it would take no notice of the *Kaffirs*—and kept looking towards the mouth of the *kloof*, as though it wished me to follow it. Just then Nombe arrived, and on seeing the dog looked at me oddly.

"'I have a message for you from my master, Mauriti,' she said to me through Heda, who by now had arrived upon the scene, having also been aroused by Lost's barking. 'It is that if you wish to take a walk with a strange dog you can do so, and bring back anything you may find.'"

"The end of it was that after we had fed Lost with milk and meat, I and six of Zikali's men started down the *kloof*, Lost going ahead of us and now and again running back and whining. At the mouth of the *kloof* it led us over a hill and down into a bush-*veld* valley where the thorns grew very thick. When we had gone along the valley for about two miles, one of the *Kaffirs* saw a Basuto pony still saddled, and caught it. The dog went on past the pony to a tree that had been shattered by lightning, and there within a few yards of the tree we found you lying senseless, Allan, or, as I thought at first, dead, and by your side a Martini rifle of which the stock also seemed to have been broken by lightning.

"Well, we put you on a shield and carried you here, meeting no one, and that is all the story, Allan."

He stopped and we stared at each other. Then I called Lost and patted its head, and the dear beast licked my hand as though it understood that it was being thanked.

"A strange tale," I said, "but God Almighty has put much wisdom into His creatures of which we know nothing. Let us thank Him," and in our hearts we did.

Thus was I rescued from death by the intelligence and fidelity of a four-footed creature. Doubtless in my semi-conscious state that resulted from shock, weariness and sun-stroke, I had all the while headed sub-consciously and without any definite object for the Black Kloof. When I was within a few miles of it I was stunned by the lightning which ran down the rifle to the ground, though not actually struck. Then the dog, which had escaped, played its part, wandering about the country to find help for me, and so I was saved.

Now of the long months that followed I have little to tell. They were not unhappy in their way, for week by week I felt myself growing stronger, though very slowly. There was a path, steep, difficult and secret, which could be gained through one of the caves in the precipice, not that in which I slept. This path ran up a water-cut *kloof* through a patch of thorns to a flat tableland that was part of the Ceza stronghold. By it, when I had gained sufficient strength, sometimes we used to climb to the plateau, and there take exercise. It was an agreeable change from the stifling atmosphere of the Black Kloof. The days were very dull, for we were as much out of the world as though we had been marooned on a desert island. Still from time to time we heard of the progress of the war through Nombe, for Zikali I saw but seldom.

She told of disasters to the English, of the death of a great young Chief who was deserted by his companions and died fighting bravely—afterwards I discovered that this was the Prince Imperial of France—of the advance of our armies, of defeats inflicted upon Cetewayo's *impis*, and finally of the destruction of the Zulus on the battle-field of Ulundi, where they hurled themselves by thousands upon the British square, to be swept away by case-shot and the hail of bullets. This battle, by the way, the Zulus call, not Ulundi or Nodwengu, for it was fought in front of Panda's old *kraal* of that name, but Ocwecweni, which means—"the fight of the sheet-iron fortress." I suppose they give it this name because the hedge of bayonets, flashing in the sunlight, reminded them of sheet-iron. Or it may be because these proved as impenetrable as would have done walls of iron. At any rate they dashed their naked bodies against the storm of lead and fell in heaps, only about a dozen of our men being killed, as the little graveyard in the centre of the square entrenchment, about which still lie the empty cartridge cases, records today.

There, then, on that plain perished the Zulu kingdom which was built up by Chaka.

Now it was after this event that I saw Zikali and begged him to let us go. I found him triumphant and yet strangely disturbed and, as I thought, more apprehensive than I had ever seen him.

"So, Zikali," I said, "if what I hear is true, you have had your way and destroyed the Zulu people. Now you should be happy."

"Is man ever happy, Macumazahn, when he has gained that which he sought for years? The two out there sigh and are sad because they cannot be married after their own white fashion, though what there is to keep them apart I do not know. Well, in time they will be married, only to find that they are not so happy as they thought they would be. Oh! a day will come when they will talk to each other and say—'Those moons which we spent waiting together in the Black Kloof were the true moons of sweetness, for then we had something to gain; now we have gained all—and what is it?'

"So it is with me, Macumazahn. Since the Zulus under Chaka killed out my people, the Ndwandwe, year by year I have plotted and waited to see them wedded to the *assegai*. Now it has come about. You white men have stamped them flat upon the plain of Ulundi; they are no more a nation. And yet I am not happy, for after all it was the House of Senzangacona and not the people of the Zulus, that harmed me and mine, and Cetewayo still lives. While the queen bee remains there may be a hive again. While an ember still glows in the dead ashes, the forest may yet be fired. Perhaps when Cetewayo is dead, then I shall be happy. Only his death and mine are set by Fate as close together as two sister grains of corn upon the cob."

I turned the subject, again asking his leave to depart to Natal or to join the English army.

"You cannot go yet," he answered sternly, "so trouble me no more. The land is full of wandering bands of Zulus who would kill you and your blood would be on my head. Moreover, if they saw a white woman who had sheltered with me, might they not guess something? To dress a doll for the part of the Inkosazana-y-Zulu is the greatest crime in the world, Macumazahn, and what would happen to the Opener of Roads and all his House if it were even breathed that he had dressed that doll and thus brought about the war which ruined them? When Cetewayo is killed and the dead are buried and peace falls upon the land, the peace of death, then you shall go, Macuma-zahn, and not before."

"At least, Zikali, send a message to the captains of the English army and tell them that we are here."

"Send a message to the hyenas and tell them where the carcase is; send a message to the hunters and tell them where the buck Zikali crouches on its form! Hearken, Macumazahn, if you do this, or even urge me again to do it, neither you nor your friends shall ever leave the Black Kloof. I have spoken."

Then understanding that the case was hopeless, I left him and he glowered after me, for fear had made him cruel. He had won the long game and success had turned to ashes in his mouth. Or rather, he had not won—yet—since his war was against the House of Senzangacona from which he and his tribe had suffered cruel wrong. To pull it down he must pull down the Zulu nation; it was like burning a city to destroy a compro-mising letter. He had burnt the city, but the letter still remained intact and might be produced in evidence against him. In other words Cetewayo yet lived. Therefore his vengeance remained quite unslaked and his danger was as great, or perhaps greater than it had ever been before. For was he not the prophet who by producing the Princess of Heaven, the traditional goddess of the Zulus, before the eyes of the king and Council, had caused them to decide for war? And supposing it were so much as breathed that this spirit which they seemed to see, had been but a trick and a fraud, what then? He would be tortured to death if his dupes had time, or torn limb from limb if they had not, that is if he could die like other men—a matter as to which personally I had no doubts.

Shortly after I left Zikali Heda and I ate our evening meal together. Anscombe, as it chanced, had gone by the secret path to the tableland of which I have spoken, where he amused himself, as of course we were not allowed to fire a gun, by catching partridges, with the help of an ingenious system of grass nets which he had invented. There were springs on this tableland that formed little pools of water, at which the partridges, also occasionally guinea fowl and bush pheasants, came to drink at sunrise and sunset. Here it was that he set his nets and retired to work them at those hours by means of strings that he pulled from hiding-places. So Heda and I were alone.

I told her of my ill success with Zikali, at which she was much disappointed. Then by an afterthought I suggested that perhaps she might try to do something in the way of getting a message through to the English camp at Ulundi, or elsewhere, by help of the witch-doctoress, Nombe, adding that I would speak to her myself had I not observed that I seemed to be out of favour with her of late. Heda shook her head and answered that she thought it would be useless to try, also too dangerous. Remembering Zikali's threat, on reflection I agreed with her.

"Tell me, Mr. Quatermain," she added, "is it possible for one woman to be in love with another?"

I stared at her and replied that I did not understand what she meant, since women, so far as I had observed them, were generally in love either with a man or with themselves, perhaps more often with the latter than the former. Rather a cheap joke I admit, with just enough truth in it to make it acceptable—in the Black Kloof.

"So I thought," she answered, "but really Nombe behaves in a most peculiar way. As you know she took a fancy to me from the beginning, perhaps because she had never had any other woman with whom to associate, having, so far as I can make out, been brought up here among men from a child. Indeed, her story is that she was one of twins and therefore as the younger, was exposed to die according to the Zulu superstition. Zikali, however, or a servant of his who knew what was happening, rescued and reared her, so practically I am the only female with whom she has ever been intimate. At any rate her affection for me has grown and grown until, although it seems ungrateful to say so, it has become something of a nuisance. She has told me again and again that she would die to protect me, and that if by chance anything happened to me, she would kill herself and follow me into another world. She is continually making divinations about my future, and as these, in which she entirely believes, always show me as living without her, she is much distressed and at times bursts into tears."

"Hysteria! It is very common among the Zulu women, and especially those of them who practise magic arts," I answered.

"Perhaps, but as it results in the most intense jealousy, Nombe's hysteria is awkward. For instance, she is horribly jealous of Maurice."

"The instincts of a chaperone developed early," I suggested again.

"That won't quite do, Mr. Quatermain," answered Heda with a laugh, "since she is even more jealous of you. With reference to Maurice, she explains frankly that if we marry she might, as she puts it, 'continue to sit outside the hut,' but that in your case you live 'in my head,' where she cannot come between you and me."

"Mad," I remarked, "quite mad. Still madness has to be dealt with in this world like other things, and Nombe, being an abnormal person, may suffer from abnormal ideas. It just amounts to this; she has conceived a passionate devotion to you, at which I am sure neither Maurice nor I can wonder."

"Are those the kind of compliments you used to pay in your youth, Mr. Quatermain? I expect so, and now that you are old you cannot stop them. Well, I thank you all the same, because perhaps you mean what you say. But what is to be done about Nombe? Hush! here she comes. I will leave you to reason with her, if you get the chance," and she departed in a hurry.

Nombe arrived, and something in her aspect told me that I was going to get the chance. Her eternal smile was almost gone and her dark, beautiful eyes flashed ominously. Still she began by asking in a mild voice whether the lady Heddana had eaten her supper with appetite. It will be observed that she was not interested in my appetite or whether enough was left for Anscombe when he returned. I replied that so far as I noted she had consumed about half a partridge, with other things.

"I am glad," said Nombe, "since I was not here to attend upon her, having been summoned to speak with the Master."

Then she sat down and looked at me like a thunder storm.

"I nursed you when you were so ill, Macumazahn," she began, "but now I learn that for the milk with which I fed you, you would force me to drink bitter water that will poison me."

I replied I was well aware that without her nursing I should long ago have been dead, which was what caused me to love her like my own daughter. But would she kindly explain? This she did at once.

"You have been plotting to take away from me the lady Heddana who to me is as mother and sister and child. It is useless to lie to me, for the Master has told me all; moreover, I knew it for myself, both through my Spirit and because I had watched you."

"I have no intention of lying to you, Nombe, about this or any other matter, though I think that sometimes in the past you have lied to me. Tell me, do you expect the *Inkosi* Mauriti, the lady Heddana and myself to pass the rest of our lives in the Black Kloof, when they wish to get married and go across the Black Water to where their home will be, and I wish to attend to my affairs?"

"I do not know what I expect, Macumazahn, but I do know that never while I live will I be parted from the lady Heddana. At last I have found some one to love, and you and the other would steal her away from me."

I studied her for a while, then asked—

"Why do you not marry, Nombe, and have a husband, and children to love?"

"Marry?" she replied. "I am married to my Spirit which does not dwell beneath the sun, and my children are not of earth; moreover, all men are hateful to me," and her eyes added, "especially you."

"That is a calf with a dog's head," I replied in the words of the native proverb, meaning that she said what was not natural. "Well, Nombe, if you are so fond of the lady Heddana, you had better arrange with her and the *Inkosi* Mauriti to go away with them."

"You know well I cannot, Macumazahn. I am tied to my Master by ropes that are stronger than iron, and if I attempted to break them my Spirit would wither and I should wither with it."

"Dear me! what a dreadful business. That is what comes of taking to magic. Well, Nombe, I am afraid I have nothing to suggest, nor, to tell you the truth, can I see what I have to do with the matter."

Then she sprang up in a rage, saying—

"I understand that not only will you give me no help, but that you also mock at me, Macumazahn. Moreover, as it is with you, so it is with Mauriti, who pretends to love my lady so much, though I love her more with my little finger than he does with all his body and what he calls his soul. Yes, he too mocks at me. Now if you were both dead," she added with sudden venom, "my lady would not wish to go away. Be careful lest a spell should fall upon you, Macumazahn," and without more words she turned and went.

At first I was inclined to laugh; the whole thing seemed so absurd. On reflection, however, I perceived that in reality it was very serious to people situated as we were. This woman was a savage; more, a mystic savage of considerable powers of mind—a formidable combination. Also there were no restraints upon her, since public opinion had as little authority in the Black Kloof as the Queen's Writ. Lastly, it was not unknown for women to conceive these violent affections which, if thwarted, filled them with something like madness. Thus I remembered a very terrible occurrence of my youth which resulted in the death of one who was most dear to me. I will not dwell on it, but this, too, was the work of a passionate creature, woman I can scarcely call her, who thought she was being robbed of one whom she adored.

The end of it was that I did not enjoy my pipe that night, though luckily Anscombe returned after a successful evening's netting, about which he was so full of talk that there was no need for me to say much. So I put off any discussion of the problem until the morrow.

CHAPTER 21

The King Visits Zikali

Next morning, as a result of my cogitations, I went to see Zikali. I was admitted after a good deal of trouble and delay, for although his retinue was limited and, with the exception of Nombe, entirely male, this old prophet kept a kind of semi-state and was about as difficult to approach as a European monarch. I found him crouching over a fire in his hut, since at this season of the year even in that hot place the air was chilly until midday.

"What is it, Macumazahn?" he asked. "As to your going away, have patience. I learn that he who was King of the Zulus is in full flight, with the white men tracking him like a wounded buck. When the buck is caught and killed, then you can go."

"It is about Nombe," I answered, and told him all the story, which did not seem to surprise him at all.

"Now see, Macumazahn," he said, taking some snuff, "how hard it is to dam up the stream of nature. This child, Nombe, is of my blood, one whom I saved from death in a strange way, not because she was of my blood but that I might make an experiment with her. Women, as you who are wise and have seen much will know, are in truth superior to men, though, because they are weaker in body, men have the upper hand of them and think themselves their masters, a state they are forced to accept because they must live and cannot defend themselves. Yet their brains are keener, as an *assegai* is keener than a hoe; they are more in touch with the hidden things that shape out fate for people and for nations; they are more faithful and more patient, and by instinct if not by reason, more far-seeing, or at least the best of them are so, and by their best, like men, they should be judged. Yet this is the hole in their shield. When they love they become the slaves of love, and for love's sake all else is brought to naught, and for this reason they cannot be trusted. With men, as you know, this is otherwise. They, too, love, by Nature's law, but always behind there is something greater than love, although often they do not understand what that may be. To be powerful, therefore, a woman must be one who does not love too much. If she cannot love at all, then she is hated and has no power, but she must not love too much.

"Once I thought that I had found such a woman; she was named Mameena, whom all men worshipped and who played with all men, as I played with her. But what was the end of it? Just as things were going very well she learned to love too much some man of strange notions, who would have thwarted me and brought everything to nothing, and therefore I had to kill her, for which I was sorry."

Here he paused to take some more snuff, watching me over the spoon as he drew it up his great nostrils, but as I said nothing, went on—

"Now after Mameena was dead I bethought me that I would rear up a woman who could still love but should never love a man and therefore never become mad or foolish, because I believed that it was only man who in taking her heart from woman, would take her wits also. This child, Nombe, came to my hand, and as I thought, so I did. Never mind how I did it, by medicine perhaps, by magic perhaps, by watering her pride and making it grow tall perhaps, or by all three. At least it was done, and this I know of Nombe, she will never care for any man except as a woman may care for a brother.

"But now see what happens. She, the wise, the instructed, the man-despiser, meets a woman of another race who is sweet and good, and learns to love her, not as maids and mothers love, but as one loves the Spirit that she worships. Yes, yes, to her she is a goddess to be worshipped, one whom she desires to serve with all her heart and strength, to bow down before, making offerings, and at the end to follow into death. So it comes about that this Nombe, whose mind I thought to make as the wings of a bird floating on the air while it searches for its prey, has become even madder than other women. It is a disappointment to me, Macumazahn."

"It may be a disappointment to you, Zikali, and all that you say is very interesting. But to us it is a danger. Tell me, will you command Nombe to cease from her folly?"

"Will I forbid the mist to rise, or the wind to blow, or the lightning to strike? As she is, she is. Her heart is filled with black jealousy of Mauriti and of you, as a butcher's gourd is filled with blood, for she is not one who desires that her goddess should have other worshippers; she would keep her for herself alone."

"Then in this way or in that the gourd must be emptied, Zikali, lest we should be forced to drink from it and that black blood should poison us."

"How, unless it be broken, Macumazahn? If Heddana departs and leaves her, she will go mad, and accompany her she cannot, for her Spirit dwells here," and he tapped his own breast. "It would pull her back again and she would become a great trouble to me, for then that Spirit of hers would not suffer me to sleep, with its continual startings in search of what it had lost, and its returnings empty-handed. Well, have no fear, for at the worst the bowl can be broken and the blood poured upon the earth, as I have broken finer bowls than this before; had I all the bits of them they would make a heap so high, Macumazahn!" and he held out his hand on a level with his head, a gesture that made my back creep. "I will tell her this and it may keep her quiet for a while. Of poison you need not be afraid, since unlike mine, her Spirit hates it. Poison is not one of its weapons as it is with mine. But of spells, beware, for her Spirit has some which are very powerful."

Now I jumped up, filled with indignation, saying—

"I do not believe in Nombe's spells, and in any case how am I to guard against them?"

"If you do not believe there is no need to guard, and if you do believe, then it is for you to find out how to guard, Macumazahn. Oh! I could tell you the story of a white teacher who did not believe and would not guard—but never mind, never mind. Goodbye, Macumazahn, I will speak with Nombe. Ask her for a lock of her hair to wear upon your heart after she has enchanted it. The charm is good against spells. O-ho—Oho-o! What fools we are, white and black together! That is what Cetewayo is thinking today."

After this Nombe became much more agreeable. That is to say she was very polite, her smile was more fixed and her eyes more unfathomable than ever. Evidently Zikali had spoken to her and she had listened. Yet to tell the truth my distrust of this handsome young woman grew deeper day by day. I recognized that there was a great gulf between her and the normal, that she was a creature fashioned by Zikali who had trained her as a gardener trains a tree, nay, who had done more, who had grafted some foreign growth of exotic and unnatural spiritualism on to her primitive nature. The nature remained the same, but the graft or grafts bore strange flowers and fruit, unholy flowers and poisonous fruit. Therefore she was not to blame—sometimes I wonder whether in this curious world, could one see their past and their future, anybody is to blame for anything—but this did not make her the less dangerous.

243

Some talks I had with her only increased my apprehensions, for I found that in a way she had no conscience. Life, she told me, was but a dream, and all its laws as evolved by man were but illusions. The real life was elsewhere. There was the distant lake on which the flower of our true existence floated. Without this unseen lake of supernatural water the flower could not float; indeed there would be no flower. Moreover, the flower did not matter; sometimes it would have this shape and colour, sometimes that. It was but a thing destined to grow and bloom and rot, and during its day to be ugly or to be beautiful, to smell sweet or ill, as it might chance, and ultimately to be absorbed back into the general water of Life.

I pointed out to her that all flowers had roots which grew in soil. Looking at an orchid-like plant that crept along the bough of a tree, she answered that this was not true as some grew upon air. But however this might be, the soil, or the moisture in the air, was distilled from thousands of other flower lives that had flourished in their day and been forgotten. It did not matter when they died or how many other flowers they choked that they might live. Yet each flower had its own spirit which always had been and always would be.

I asked her of the end and the object of that spirit. She answered darkly that she did not know and if she did, would not say, but that these were very dreadful.

Such were some of her vague and figurative assertions which I only record to indicate their uncomfortable and indeed but half human nature. I forgot to add that she declared that every flower or life had a twin flower or life, which in each successive growth it was bound to find and bloom beside, or wither to the root and spring again and that ultimately these two would become one, and as one flourish eternally. Of all of which I understood and understand little, except that she had grasped the elements of some truth which she could not express in clear and definite language.

One day I was seated in Zikali's hut whither by permission I had come to ask the latest news, when suddenly Nombe appeared and crouched down before him.

"Who gave you leave to enter here, and what is your business?" he asked angrily.

"Home of Spirits," she replied in a humble voice, "be not angry with your servant. Necessity gave me leave, and my business is to tell you that strangers approach."

"Who are they that dare to enter the Black Kloof unannounced?"

"Cetewayo the King is one of them, the others I do not know, but

244

they are many, armed all of them. They approach your gate; before a man can count two hundred they will be here."

"Where are the white chief and the lady Heddana?" asked Zikali.

"By good fortune they have gone by the secret path to the table-land and will not be back till sunset. They wished to be alone, so I did not accompany them, and Macumazahn here said that he was too weary to do so." (This was true. Also like Nombe I thought that they wished to be alone.)

"Good. Go, tell the king that I knew of his coming and am await-ing him. Bid my servants kill the ox which is in the *kraal*, the fat ox that they thought is sick and therefore fit food for a sick king," he added bitterly.

She glided away like a startled snake. Then Zikali turned to me and said swiftly—

"Macumazahn, you are in great danger. If you are found here you will be killed, and so will the others whom I will send to warn not to return till this king has gone away. Go at once to join them. No, it is too late, I hear the Zulus come. Take that *kaross*, cover yourself with it and lie among the baskets and beer pots here near the entrance of the hut in the deepest of the shadows, so that if any enter, perchance you will not be found. I too am in danger who shall be held to account for all that has happened. Perhaps they will kill me, if I can be killed. If so, get away with the others as best you can. Nombe will tell you where your horses are hidden. In that case let Heddana take Nombe with her, for when I am dead she will go, and shake her off in Natal if she trou-bles her. Whatever chances, remember, Macumazahn, that I have done my best to keep my word to you and to protect you and your friends. Now I go to look on this pricked bladder who was once a king."

He scrambled from the hut with slow, toad-like motions, while I with motions that were anything but slow, grabbed the grey cat-skin *kaross* and ensconced myself among the beer pots and mats in such a position that my head, over which I set a three-legged carved stool of Zikali's own cutting, was but a few inches to the left of the door-hole and therefore in the deepest of the shadows. Thence by stretching out my neck a little, I could see through the hole, also hear all that passed outside. Unless a deliberate search of the hut should be made I was fairly safe from observation, even if it were entered by strangers. One fear I had, however, it was lest the dog Lost should get into the place and smell me out. I had left him tied to the centre pole in my own hut, because he hated Zikali and always growled at him. But suppose he gnawed through the cord, or any one let him loose!

Scarcely had Zikali seated himself in his accustomed place before the hut, than the gate of the outer fence opened and approaching through it I saw forty or fifty fierce and way-worn men. In front of them, riding on a tired horse that was led by a servant, was Cetewayo himself. He was assisted to dismount, or rather threw his great bulk into the arms that were waiting to receive him.

Then after some words with his following and with one of Zikali's people, followed by three or four *indunas* and leaning on the arm of Umnyamana, the Prime Minister, he entered the enclosure, the rest remaining without. Zikali, who sat as though asleep, suddenly appeared to wake up and perceive him. Struggling to his feet he lifted his right arm and gave the royal salute of *Bayete*, and with it titles of praise, such as "Black One!" "Elephant!" "Earth-Shaker!" "Conqueror!" "Eater-up of the White men!" "Child of the Wild Beast (Chaka) whose teeth are sharper than the wild beast's ever were!" and so on, until Cetewayo, growing impatient, cried out—

"Be silent, wizard. Is this a time for fine words? Do you not know my case that you offend my ears with them? Give us food to eat if you have it, after which I would speak with you alone. Be swift also; here I may not stay for long, since the white dogs are at my heels."

"I knew that you were coming, O King, to honour my poor house with a visit," said Zikali slowly, "and therefore the ox is already killed and the meat will soon be on the fire. Meanwhile drink a sup of beer, and rest."

He clapped his hands, whereon Nombe and some servants appeared with pots of beer, of which, after Zikali had tasted it to show that it was not poisoned, the king and his people drank thirstily. Then it was taken to those outside.

"What is this that my ears hear?" asked Zikali when Nombe and the others had gone, "that the White Dogs are on the spoor of the Black Bull?"

Cetewayo nodded heavily, and answered—

"My *impis* were broken to pieces on the plain of Ulundi; the cowards ran from the bullets as children run from bees. My *kraals* are burnt and I, the King, with but a faithful remnant fly for my life. The prophecy of the Black One has come true. The people of the Zulus are stamped flat beneath the feet of the great White People."

"I remember that prophecy, O King. Mopo told it to me within an hour of the death of the Black One when he gave me the little red-handled *assegai* that he snatched from the Black One's hand to do the deed. It makes me almost young again to think of it, although

246

even then I was old," replied Zikali in a dreamy voice like one who speaks to himself.

Hearing him from under my *kaross* I bethought me that he had really grown old at last, who for the moment evidently forgot the part which this very *assegai* had played a few months before in the Vale of Bones. Well, even the greatest masters make such slips at times when their minds are full of other things. But if Zikali forgot, Cetewayo and his councillors remembered, as I could see by the look of quick intelligence that flashed from face to face.

"So! Mopo the murderer, he who vanished from the land after the death of my uncle Dingaan, gave you the little red *assegai*, did he, Opener of Roads! And but a few months ago that *assegai*, which old Siganamda knew again, thrown by the hand of the Inkosazana-y-Zulu, drew blood from my body after the white man, Macumazahn, had severed its shaft with his bullet. Now tell me, Opener of Roads, how did it pass from your keeping into that of the spirit Nomkubulwana?"

At this question I distinctly saw a shiver shake the frame of Zikali who realized too late the terrible mistake he had made. Yet as only the great can do, he retrieved and even triumphed over his error.

"Oho-ho!" he laughed, "who am I that I can tell how such things happen? Do you not know, O King, that the Spirits leave what they will and take what they will, whether it be but a blade of grass, or the life of a man"—here he looked at Cetewayo—"or even of a people? Sometimes they take the shadow and sometimes the substance, since spirit or matter, all is theirs. As for the little *assegai*, I lost it years ago. I remember that the last time I saw it was in the hands of a woman named Mameena to whom I showed it as a strange and bloody thing. After her death I found that it was gone, so doubtless she took it with her to the Under-world and there gave it to the Queen Nomkubulwana, with whom you may remember this Mameena returned from that Under-world yonder in the Bones."

"It may be so," said Cetewayo sullenly, "yet it was no spirit iron that cut my thigh, but what do I know of the ways of Spirits? Wizard, I would speak with you in your hut alone where no ear can hear us."

"My hut is the King's," answered Zikali, "yet let the King remember that those Spirits of which he does not know the ways, can always hear, yes, even the thoughts of men, and on them do judgment."

"Fear not," said Cetewayo, "amongst many other things I remember this also."

Then Zikali turned and crept into the hut, whispering as he passed me—

"Lie silent for your life." And Cetewayo having bidden his retinue to depart outside the fence and await him there, followed after him.

They sat them down on either side of the smouldering fire and stared at each other through the thin smoke there in the gloom of the hut. By turning my head that the foot of the king had brushed as he passed, I could watch them both. Cetewayo spoke the first in a hoarse, slow voice, saying—

"Wizard, I am in danger of my life and I have come to you who know all the secrets of this land, that you may tell me in what place I may hide where the white men cannot find me. It must be told into my ear alone, since I dare not trust the matter to any other, at any rate until I must. They are traitors every man of them, yes, even those who seem to be most faithful. The fallen man has no friends, least of all if he chances to be a king. Only the dead will keep his counsel. Tell me of the place I need."

"Dingaan, who was before you, once asked this same thing of me, O King, when he was flying from Panda your father, and the Boers. I gave him advice that he did not take, but sought a refuge of his own upon a certain Ghost-mountain. What happened to him there that Mopo, of whom you spoke a while ago, can tell you if he still lives."

"Surely you are an ill-omened night-bird who thus croak to me continually of the death of kings," broke in Cetewayo with suppressed rage. Then calming himself with an effort added, "Tell me now, where shall I hide?"

"Would you know, King? Then hearken. On the south slope of the Ingome Range west of the Ibululwana River, on the outskirts of the great forest, there is a *kloof* whereof the entrance, which only one man can pass at a time, is covered by a thicket of thorns and marked by a black rock shaped like a great toad with an open mouth, or, as some say, like myself, *The-Thing-that-should-never-have-been-born*. Near to this rock dwells an old woman, blind of one eye and lacking a hand, which the Black One cut off shortly before his death, because when he killed her father, she saw the future and prophesied a like death to him, although then she was but a child. This woman is of our company, being a witch-doctoress. I will send a Spirit to her, if you so will it, to warn her to watch for you and your company, O King, and show you the mouth of the *kloof*, where are some old huts and water. There you will never be found unless you are betrayed."

"Who can betray me when none know whither I am going?" asked Cetewayo. "Send the Spirit, send it at once, that this one-armed witch may make ready."

"What is the hurry, King, seeing that the forest is far away? Yet be it as you will. Keep silence now, lest evil should befall you."

Then of a sudden Zikali seemed to go off into one of his trances. His form grew rigid, his eyes closed, his face became fixed as though in death, and foam appeared upon his lips. He was a dreadful sight to look on, there in the gloomy hut.

Cetewayo watched him and shivered. Then he opened his blanket and I perceived that fastened about him by a loop of hide in such a fashion that it could be drawn out in a moment, was the blade of a broad *assegai*, the shaft of which was shortened to about six inches. His hand grasped this shaft, and I understood that he was contemplating the murder of Zikali. Then it seemed to me that he changed his mind and that his lips shaped the words—"Not yet," though whether he really spoke them I do not know. At least he withdrew his hand and closed the blanket.

Slowly Zikali opened his eyes, staring at the roof of the hut, whence came a curious sound as of squeaking bats. He looked like a dead man coming to life again. For a few moments he turned up his ear as though he listened to the squealing, then said—

"It is well. The Spirit that I summoned has visited her of our company who is named One-hand and returned with the answer. Did you not hear it speaking in the thatch, O King?"

"I heard something, Wizard," answered Cetewayo in an awed voice. "I thought it was a bat."

"A bat it is, O King, one with wide wings and swift. This bat says that my sister, One-hand, will meet you on the third day from now at this hour on the further side of the ford of the Ibululwana, where three milk-trees grow together on a knoll. She will be sitting under the centre milk-tree and will wait for two hours, no more, to show you the secret entrance to the *kloof*."

"The road is rough and long, I shall have to hurry when worn out with travelling," said Cetewayo.

"That is so, O King. Therefore my counsel is that you begin the journey as soon as possible, especially as I seem to hear the baying of the white dogs not far away."

"By Chaka's head! I will not," growled Cetewayo, "who thought to sleep here in peace this night."

"As the King wills. All that I have is the King's. Only then One-hand will not be waiting and some other place of hiding must be found, since this is known to me only and to her; also that Spirit which I sent will make no second journey, nor can I travel to show it to the King."

"Yes, Wizard, it is known to you and to myself. Methinks it would be better were it known to me alone. I have a spoonful of snuff to share (*i.e.*, a bone to pick) with you, Wizard. It would seem that you set my feet and those of the Zulu people upon a false road, yonder in the Vale of Bones, causing me to declare war upon the white men and thereby bringing us all to ruin."

"Mayhap my memory grows bad, O King, for I do not remember that I did these things. I remember that the spirit of a certain Mameena whom I called up from the dead, prophesied victory to the King, which victory has been his. Also it prophesied other victories to the King in a far land across the water, which victories doubtless shall be his in due season; for myself I gave no 'counsel to the King or to his *indunas* and generals.'"

"You lie, Wizard," exclaimed Cetewayo hoarsely. "Did you not summon the shape of the Princess of Heaven to be the sign of war, and did she not hold in her hand that *assegai* of the Black One which you have told me was in your keeping? How did it pass from your keeping into the hand of a spirit?"

"As to that matter I have spoken, O King. For the rest, is Nomkubulwana my servant to come and go at my bidding?"

"I think so," said Cetewayo coldly. "I think also that you who know the place where I purpose to hide, would do well to forget it. Surely you have lived too long, O Opener of Roads, and done enough evil to the House of Senzangacona, which you ever hated."

So he spoke, and once more I saw his hand steal towards the spearhead which was hidden beneath the blanket that he wore.

Zikali saw it also and laughed. "Oho!" he laughed, "forgetting all my warnings, and that the day of my death will be his own, the King thinks to kill me because I am old and feeble and alone and unarmed. He thinks to kill me as the Black One thought, as Dingaan thought, as even Panda thought, yet I live on to this day. Well, I bear no malice since it is natural that the King should wish to kill one who knows the secret of where he would hide himself for his own life's sake. That spearhead which the King is fingering is sharp, so sharp that my bare breast cannot turn its edge. I must find me a shield! I must find me a shield! Fire, you are not yet dead. Awake, make smoke to be my shield!" and he waved his long, monkey-like arms over the embers, from which instantly there sprang up a reek of thin white smoke that appeared to take a vague and indefinite shape which suggested the shadow of a man; for to me it seemed a nebulous and wavering shadow, no more.

"What are you staring at, O King?" went on Zikali in a fierce and thrilling voice. "Who is it that you see? Who has the fire sent to be my shield? Ghosts are so thick here that I do not know. I cannot tell one of them from the other. Who is it? Who, who of all that you have slain and who therefore are your foes?"

"Umbelazi, my brother," groaned Cetewayo. "My brother Umbelazi stands before me with spear raised; he whom I brought to his death at the battle of the Tugela. His eyes flame upon me, his spear is raised to strike. He speaks words I cannot understand. Protect me, O Wizard! Lord of Spirits, protect me from the spirit of Umbelazi."

Zikali laughed wildly and continued to wave his arms above the fire from which smoke poured ever more densely, till the hut was full of it.

When it cleared away again Cetewayo was gone!

"Saw you ever the like of that?" said Zikali, addressing the *kaross* under which I was sweltering. "Tell me, Macumazahn."

"Yes," I answered, thrusting out my head as a tortoise does, "when in this very hut you seemed to produce the shape, also out of smoke, I think, of one whom I used to know. Say, how do you do it, Zikali?"

"Do it. Who knows? Perchance I do nothing. Perchance I think and you fools see, no more. Or perchance the spirits of the dead who are so near to us, come at my call and take themselves bodies out of the charmed smoke of my fire. You white men are wise, answer your own question, Macumazahn. At least that smoke or that ghost saved me from a spear thrust in the heart, wherewith Cetewayo was minded to pay me for showing him a hiding-place which he desired should be secret to himself alone. Well, well, I can pay as well as Cetewayo and my count is longer. Now lie you still, Macumazahn, for I go out to watch. He will not bide long in this place which he deems haunted and ill-omened. He will be gone ere sunset, that is within an hour, and sleep elsewhere."

Then he crept from the hut and presently, though I could see nothing, for now the gate of the fence was shut, I heard voices debating and finally that of Cetewayo say angrily—

"Have done! It is my will. You can eat your food outside of this place which is bewitched; the girl will show us where are the huts of which the wizard speaks."

A few minutes later Zikali crept back into the hut, laughing to himself. "All is safe," he said, "and you can come out of your hole, old jackal. He who calls himself a king is gone, taking with him those whom he thinks faithful, most of whom are but waiting a chance to betray him. What did I say, a king? Nay, in all Africa there is no slave

251

so humble or so wretched as this broken man. Oh! feather by feather I have plucked my fowl and by and by I shall cut his throat. You will be there, Macumazahn, you will be there."

"I trust not," I answered as I mopped my brow. "We have been near enough to throat-cutting this afternoon to last me a long while. Where has the king gone?"

"Not far, Macumazahn. I have sent Nombe to guide him to the huts in the little dip five spear throws to the right of the mouth of the *kloof* where live the old herdsman and his people who guard my cattle. He and all the rest are away with the cattle that are hidden in the Ceza Forest out of reach of the white men, so the huts are empty. Oh! now I read what you are thinking. I do not mean that he should be taken there. It is too near my house and the king still has friends."

"Why did you send Nombe?" I asked.

"Because he would have no other guide, who does not trust my men. He means to keep her with him for some days and then let her go, and thus she will be out of mischief. Meanwhile you and your friends can depart untroubled by her fancies, and join the white men who are near. Tomorrow you shall start."

"That is good," I said with a sigh of relief. Then an idea struck me and I added, "I suppose no harm will come to Nombe, who might be thought to know too much?"

"I hope not," he replied indifferently, "but that is a matter for her Spirit to decide. Now go, Macumazahn, for I am weary."

I also was weary after my prolonged seclusion under that very hot skin rug. For be it remembered I was not yet strong again, and although this was not the real reason why I had stopped behind when the others went to the plateau, I still grew easily tired. My real reason was that of Nombe—that I thought they preferred to be alone. I looked about me and saw with relief that Cetewayo and every man of his retinue were really gone. They had not even waited to eat the ox that had been killed for them, but had carried off the meat with other provisions to their sleeping-place outside the *kloof*. Having made sure of this I went to my hut and loosed Lost that fortunately enough had been unable to gnaw through the thick buffalo-hide *riem* with which I had fastened him to the pole.

He greeted me with rapture as though we had been parted for years. Had he belonged to Ulysses himself he could not have been more joyful. When one is despondent and lonesome, how grateful is the whole-hearted welcome of a dog which, we are sometimes tempted to think, is the only creature that really cares for us in the world. Every other living thing has side interests of its own, but that of a dog is centred in its master, though it is true that it also dreams affectionately of dinner and rabbits.

Then with Lost at my feet I sat outside the hut smoking and wait-ing for the return of Anscombe and Heda. Presently I caught sight of them in the gloaming. Their arms were around one another, and in some remarkable way they had managed to dispose their heads, forgetting that the sky was still light behind them, in such fashion that it was difficult to tell one from the other. I reflected that it was a good thing that at last we were escaping from this confounded *kloof* and country for one where they could marry and make an end, and became afflicted with a sneezing fit.

Heda asked where Nombe was and why supper was not ready, for Nombe played the part of cook and parlour maid combined. I told her something of what had happened, whereon Heda, who did not appreciate its importance in the least, remarked that she, Nombe, might as well have put on the pot before she went and done sundry other things which I forget. Ultimately we got something to eat and turned in, Heda grumbling a little because she must sleep alone, for she had grown used to the company of the ever-watchful Nombe, who made her bed across the door-hole of the hut.

Anscombe was soon lost in dreams, if he did dream, but I could not sleep well that night. I was fearful of I knew not what, and so, I think, was Lost, for he fidgeted and kept poking me with his nose. At last, I think it must have been about two hours after midnight, he began to growl. I could hear nothing, although my ears are sharp, but as he went on growling I crept to the door-hole and drew aside the board. Lost slipped out and vanished, while I waited, listening. Presently I thought I heard a soft foot-fall and a whisper, also that I saw the shape of a woman which reminded me of Nombe, shown faintly by the starlight. It vanished in a moment and Lost returned wagging his tail, as he might well have done if it were Nombe who was attached to the dog. As nothing further happened I went back to bed, reflecting that I was probably mistaken, since Nombe had been sent away for some days by Zikali and would scarcely dare to return at once, even if she could do so.

Shortly before daylight Lost began to growl again in a subdued and thunderous fashion. This time I got up and dressed myself more or less. Then I went out. The dawn was just breaking and by its light I saw a strange scene. About fifty yards away in the narrow *nek* that ran over some boulders to the site of our huts, stood what seemed to be the

253

goddess Nomkubulwana as I had seen her on the point of rock in the Vale of Bones. She wore the same radiant dress and in the dim glow had all the appearance of a white woman. I stood amazed, thinking that I dreamt, when from round the bend emerged a number of Zulus, creeping forward stealthily with raised spears.

They caught sight of the supernatural figure which barred their road, halted and whispered to each other. Then they turned to fly, but before they went one of them, as it seemed to me through sheer terror, hurled his *assegai* at the figure which remained still and unmoved.

In thirty seconds they were gone; in sixty their footsteps had died away. Then the figure wheeled slowly round and by the strengthening light I perceived that a spear transfixed its breast.

As it sank to the ground I ran up to it. It was Nombe with her face and arms whitened and her life-blood running down the glittering feather robe.

CHAPTER 22

The Madness of Nombe

The dog reached Nombe first and began to lick her face, its tongue removing patches of the white which had not had time to dry. She was lying, her back supported by one of the boulders. With her left hand she patted the dog's head feebly and with her right drew out the *assegai* from her body, letting it fall upon the ground. Recognizing me she smiled in her usual mysterious fashion and said—

"All is well, Macumazahn, all is very well. I have deserved to die and I do not die in vain."

"Don't talk, let me see your wound," I exclaimed.

She opened her robe and pointed; it was quite a small gash beneath the breast from which blood ebbed slowly.

"Let it be, Macumazahn," she said. "I am bleeding inside and it is mortal. But I shall not die yet. Listen to me while I have my mind. Yesterday when Mauriti and Heddana went up to the plain I wished to go with them because I had news that Zulus were wandering everywhere and thought that I might be able to protect my mistress from danger. Mauriti spoke to me roughly, telling me that I was not wanted. Of that I thought little, for to such words I am accustomed from him; moreover, they are to be forgiven to a man in love. But it did not end there, for my lady Heddana also pierced me with her tongue, which hurt more than this spear thrust does, Macumazahn, for I could see that her speech had been prepared and that she took this chance to throw it at me. She said that I did not know where I should sit; that I was a thorn beneath her nail, and that whenever she wished to talk with Mauriti, or with you, Macumazahn, I was ever there with my ear open like the mouth of a gourd. She commanded me in future to come only when I was called; all of which things I am sure Mauriti had taught her, who in herself is too gentle even to think them—unless you taught her, Macumazahn."

255

I shook my head and she went on—

"No, it was not you who also are too gentle, and having suffered yourself, can feel for those who suffer, which Mauriti who has never suffered cannot do. Still, you too thought me a trouble, one that sticks in the flesh like a hooked thorn, or a tick from the grass, and cannot be unfastened. You spoke to the Master about it and he spoke to me."

This time I nodded in assent.

"I do not blame you, Macumazahn; indeed now I see that you were wise, for what right has a poor black doctoress to seek the love, or even to look upon the face of the great white lady whom for a little while Fate has caused to walk upon the same path with her? But yesterday I forgot that, Macumazahn, for you see we are all of us, not one self, but many selves, and each self has its times of rule. Nombe alive and well was one woman, Nombe dying is another, and doubtless Nombe dead will be a third, unless, as she prays, she should sleep for ever.

"Macumazahn, those words of Heddana's were to me what gall is to sweet milk. My blood clotted and my heart turned sour. It was not against her that I was angry, because that can never happen, but against Mauriti and against you. My Spirit whispered in my ear. It said, 'If Mauriti and Macumazahn were dead the lady Heddana would be left alone in a strange land. Then she would learn to rest upon you as upon a stick, and learn to love the stick on which she rested, though it be so rough and homely.' But how can I kill them, I asked of my Spirit, and myself escape death?

"'Poison is forbidden to you by the pact between us,' answered my Spirit, 'yet I will show you a way, who am bound to serve you in all things good or ill.'

"Then we nodded to each other in my breast, Macumazahn, and I waited for what should happen who knew that my Spirit would not lie. Yes, I waited for a chance to kill you both, forgetting, as the wicked forget in their madness, that even if I were not found out, soon or late Heddana would guess the truth and then, even if she had learned to love me a thousand times more than she ever could, would come to hate me as a mother hates a snake that has slain her child. Or even if she never learned or guessed in life, after death she would learn and hunt me and spit on me from world to world as a traitoress and a murderer, one who has sinned past pardon."

Here she seemed to grow faint and I turned to seek for help. But she caught hold of my coat and said—

"Hear me out, Macumazahn, or I will run after you till I fall and die."

256

So thinking it best, I stayed and she went on—

"My Spirit, which must be an evil one since Zikali gave it me when I was made a doctoress, dealt truly with me, for presently the king and his people came. Moreover, my Spirit brought it about that the king would have no other guide but me to lead him to the *kraal* where he slept last night, and I went as though unwillingly. At the *kraal* the king sent for me and questioned me in a dark hut, pretending to be alone, but I who am a doctoress knew that two other men were in that hut, taking note of all my words. He asked me of the Inkosazana-y-Zulu who appeared in the Vale of Bones and of the little *assegai* she held in her hand, and of the magic of the Opener of Roads, and many other things. I said that I knew nothing of the Inkosazana, but that without doubt my Master was a great magician. He did not believe me. He threatened that I should be tortured very horribly and was about to call his servants to torment me till I told the truth. Then my Spirit spoke in my heart saying, 'Now the door is open to you, as I promised. Tell the king of the two white men whom the Master hides, and he will send to kill them, leaving the lady Heddana and you alone together.' So I pretended to be afraid and told him, whereon he laughed and answered—

"'For your sake I am glad, girl, that you have spoken the truth; besides it is useless to torture a witch, since then the spirit in her only vomits lies.'

"Next he called aloud and a man came, who it was I could not see in the dark. The king commanded him to take me to one of the other huts and tie me up there to the roof-pole. The man obeyed, but he did not tie me up; he only blocked the hut with the door-board, and sat with me there in the dark alone.

"Now I grew cunning and began to talk with him, spreading a net of sweet words, as the fowler spreads a net for cranes from which he would tear the crests. Soon by his talk I found out that the king and his people knew more than I guessed. Macumazahn, they had seen the cart which still stands under the overhanging rock by the mouth of the cave. I asked him if that were all, pretending that the cart belonged to my Master, to whom it had been brought from the field of Isandhlwana, that he might be drawn about in it, who was too weak to walk.

"The man said that if I would kiss him he would tell me everything. I bade him tell me first, swearing that then I would kiss him. Yes, Macumazahn, I, whom no man's lips have ever touched, fell as low as this. So he grew foolish and told me. He told me that they

257

had also seen a *kappje* such as white women wear, hanging on the hut fence, and I remembered that after washing the headdress of my mistress I had set it there to dry in the sun. He told me also that the King suspected that she who wore that *kappje* was she who had played the part of the Inkosazana in the Vale of Bones. I asked him what the king would do about the matter, at the same time denying that there was any white woman in the Black Kloof. He said that at dawn the king would send and kill these foreign rats, whom the Opener of Roads kept in the thatch of his hut. Now he drew near and asked his pay. I gave it to him—with a knife-point, Macumazahn. Oh! that was a good thrust. He never spoke again. Then I slipped away, for all the others were asleep, and was here a little after midnight."

"I thought I saw you, Nombe," I said, "but was not sure, so I did nothing."

She smiled and answered—

"Ah! I was afraid that the Watcher-by-Night would be watching by night; also the dog ran up to me, but he knew me and I sent him back again. Now while I was coming home, thoughts entered my heart. I saw, as one sees by a lightning flash, all that I had done. The king and his people were not sure that the Master was hiding white folk here and would never have sent back to kill them on the chance. I had made them sure, as indeed, being mad, I meant to do. Moreover, in throwing spears at the kites I had killed my own dove, since it was on the false Inkosazana who had caused them to declare war and brought the land to ruin, that they wished to be avenged, and perchance on him who taught her her part, not on one or two wandering white men. I saw that when Cetewayo's people came, and there were many more of them outside, several hundreds I think, they would shave the whole head and burn the whole tree. Every one in the *kloof* would be killed.

"How could I undo the knot that I had tied and stamp out the fire that I had lit? That was the question. I bethought me of coming to you, but without arms how could you help? I bethought me of going to the Master, but I was ashamed. Also, what could he do with but a few servants, for the most of his people are away with the cattle? He is too weak to climb the steep path to the plain above, nor was there time to gather folk to carry him. Lastly, even if there were time which there was not, and we went thither they track us out and kill us. For the rest I did not care, nor for myself, but that the lady Heddana should be butchered who was more to me than a hundred lives, and through my treachery—ah! for that I cared.

"I called on my Spirit to help me, but it would not come. My Spirit was dead in me because now I would do good and not ill. Yet another Spirit came, that of one Mameena whom once you knew. She came angrily, like a storm, and I shrank before her. She said, 'Vile witch, you have plotted to murder Macumazahn, and for that you shall answer to me before another sun has set over this earth of yours. Now you seek a way of escape from your own wickedness. Well, it can be had, but at a price.'

"'What price, O Lady of Death?' I asked.

"'The price of your own life, Witch.'

"I laughed into that ghost face of hers and said—

"'Is this all? Be swift and show me the way, O Lady of Death, and afterwards we will balance our account.'

"Then she whispered into the ear of my heart and was gone. I ran on, for the dawn was near. I whitened myself with lime, I put on the glittering cloak and powdered my hair with the sparkling earth. I took a little stick in my hand since I could find no spear and had no time to search, and just as day began to break, I crept out and stood in the bend of the path. The slayers came, twelve or so of them, but behind were many more. They saw the Inkosazana-y-Zulu barring their way and were much afraid. They fled, but out of his fright one of them threw a spear which went home, as I knew it would. He watched to see if I should fall, but I would not fall. Then he fled faster than the rest, knowing himself accursed who had lifted steel against the Queen of Heaven, and oh! I am glad, I am glad!"

She ceased, exhausted, yet with a great exultation in her beautiful eyes; indeed at that moment she looked a most triumphant creature. I stared at her, thrilled through and through. She had been wicked, no doubt, but how splendid was her end; and, thank Heaven! she was troubled with no thought of what might befall her after that end, although I was sure she believed that she would live again to face Mameena.

I knew not what to do. I did not like to leave her, especially as no earthly power could help her case, since slowly but quite surely she was bleeding to death from an internal wound. By now the sun was up and Zikali's people were about. One of them appeared suddenly and saw, then with a howl of terror turned to fly away.

"Fool! Fool!" I cried, "go summon the lady Heddana and the *Inko-si* Mauriti. Bid them come swiftly if they would see the doctoress Nombe before she dies."

The man leapt off like a buck, and within a few minutes I saw Heda and Anscombe running towards us, half dressed, and went to meet them.

"What is it?" she gasped.

"I have only time to tell you this," I answered. "Nombe is dying. She gave her life to save you, how I will explain afterwards. The *assegai* that pierced her was meant for your heart. Go, thank her, and bid her farewell. Anscombe, stop back with me."

We stood still and watched from a little distance. Heda knelt down and put her arms about Nombe. They whispered together into each other's ears. Then they kissed.

It was at this moment that Zikali appeared, leaning on two of his servants. By some occult art or instinct he seemed to know all that had happened, and oh! he looked terrible. He crouched down in front of the dying woman and, toad-like, spat his venom at her.

"You lost your Spirit, did you?" he said. "Well, it came back to me laden with the black honey of your treachery, to me, its home, as a bee comes to its hive. It has told me everything, and well for you, Witch, it is that you are dying. But think not that you shall escape me there in the world below, for thither I will follow you. Curses on you, traitress, who would have betrayed me and brought all my plans to naught. *Ow!* in a day to come I will pay you back a full harvest for this seed of shame that you have sown."

She opened her eyes and looked at him, then answered quite softly—"I think your chain is broken, O Zikali, no more my master. I think that love has cut your chain in two and I fear you never more. Keep the spirit you lent to me; it is yours, but the rest of me is my own, and in the house of my heart another comes to dwell."

Then once more she stretched out her arms towards Heda and murmuring, "Sister, forget me not, Sister, who will await you for a thousand years," she passed away.

It was a good ending to a bad business, and I confess I felt glad when it was finished. Only afterwards I regretted very much that I had not found an opportunity to ask her whether or no she had masqueraded as Mameena in the Valley of Bones. Now it is too late.

We buried poor Nombe decently in her own little hut where she used to practise her incantations. Zikali and his people wished apparently to throw her to the vultures for some secret reason that had to do with their superstitions. But Heda, who, now that Nombe was dead, developed a great affection for her not unmixed with a certain amount of compunction for which really she had no cause, withstood him to his face and insisted upon a decent interment. So she was laid to earth still plastered with the white pigment and wrapped in the bloodstained feather robe. I may add that on the following morning one of Zikali's servants informed me solemnly that because of this she had been seen during the night riding up and down the rocks on a baboon as Zulu *umtagati* are supposed to do. I have small doubt that as soon as we were gone they dug her up again and threw her to the vultures and the jackals according to their first intention.

On this day we at length escaped from the Black Kloof, and in our own cart, for during the night our horses arrived mysteriously from somewhere, in good condition though rather wild. I went to say goodbye to Zikali, who said little, except that we should meet once more after many moons. Anscombe and Heda he would not see at all, but only sent them a message, to the effect that he hoped they would think kindly of him through the long years to come, since he had kept his promise and preserved them safe through many dangers. I might have answered that he had first of all put them into the dangers, but considered it wise to hold my tongue. I think, however, that he guessed my thought, if one can talk of guessing in connection with Zikali, for he said that they had no reason to thank him, since if he had served their turn they had served his, adding—

"It will be strange in the times to be for the lady Heddana to re-member that it was she and no other who crumpled up the Zulus like a frostbitten winter reed, since had she not appeared upon the rock in the Valley of Bones, there would have been no war."

"She did not do this, you did it, Zikali," I said, "making her your tool through love and fear."

"Nay, Macumazahn, I did not do it; it was done by what you call God and I call Fate in whose hand I am the tool. Well, say to the lady Heddana that in payment I will hold back the ghost of Nombe from haunting her, if I can. Say also that if I had not brought her and her lover to Zululand they would have been killed."

So we went from that hateful *kloof* which I have never seen since and hope I shall never see again, two of Zikali's men escorting us until we got into touch with white people. To these we said as little as possible. I think they believed that we were only premature tourists who had made a dash into Zululand to visit some of the battlefields. Indeed none of us ever reported our strange adventures, and after my experience with Kaatje we were particularly careful to say nothing in the hearing of any gentleman connected with the Press. But as a matter of fact there were so many people moving about and such a continual coming and going of soldiers and their belongings, that after we had managed to buy some decent clothes, which we did at the little town of Newcastle, nobody paid any attention to us.

On our way to Maritzburg one amusing thing did happen. We met Kaatje! It was about sunset that we were driving up a steep hill not far from Howick. At least I was driving, but Anscombe and Heda were walking about a hundred yards ahead of the cart, when suddenly Kaatje appeared over a rise and came face to face with them while taking an evening stroll, or as I concluded afterwards, making some journey. She saw, she stared, she uttered one wild yell, and suddenly bundled over the edge of the road. Never would I have believed that such a fat woman could have run so fast. In a minute she was down the slope and had vanished into a dense *kloof* where, as night was closing in and we were very tired, it was impossible for us to follow her. Nor did subsequent inquiry in Howick tell us where she was living or whence she came, for some months before she had left the place she had taken there as a cook.

Such was the end of Kaatje so far as we were concerned. Doubtless to her dying day she remained, or will remain, a firm believer in ghosts.

Anscombe and Heda were married at Maritzburg as soon as the necessary formalities had been completed. I could not attend the ceremony, which was a disappointment to me and I hope to them, but unfortunately I had a return of my illness and was laid up for a week. Perhaps this was owing to the hot sun that struck me on the neck one afternoon coming down the Town Hill where I was obliged to hang on to the rear of the cart because the brakes had given out. However I was able to send Heda a wedding gift in the shape of her jewels and money that I recovered from the bank, which she had never expected to see again; also to arrange everything about her property.

They went down to Durban for their honeymoon and, some convenient opportunity arising, sailed thence for England. I received an affectionate letter from them both, which I still treasure, thanking me very much for all I had done for them, that after all was little enough. Also Anscombe enclosed a blank cheque, begging me to fill it in for whatever sum I considered he was indebted to me on the balance of account. I thought this very kind of him and a great mark of confidence, but the cheque remained blank.

I never saw either of them again, and though I believe that they are both living, for the most part abroad—in Hungary I think—I do not suppose that I ever shall. When I came to England some years later after King Solomon's mines had made me rich, I wrote Anscombe a letter. He never answered it, which hurt me at the time. Afterwards I remembered that in their fine position it was very natural that they should not wish to renew acquaintance with an individual who had so intimate a knowledge of certain incidents that they probably regarded as hateful, such as the deaths of Marnham and Dr. Rodd, and all the surrounding circumstances. If so, I daresay that they were wise, but of course it may have been only carelessness. It is so easy for busy and fashionable folk not to answer a rather troublesome letter, or to forget to put that answer in the post. Or, indeed, the letter may never have reached them—such things often go astray, especially when people live abroad. At any rate, perhaps through my own fault, we have drifted apart. I daresay they believe that I am dead, or not to be found somewhere in Africa. However, I always think of them with affection, for Anscombe was one of the best travelling companions I ever had, and his wife a most charming girl, and wonder whether Zikali's prophecy about their children will come true. Good luck go with them!

As it chances, since then I passed the place where the Temple stood, though at a little distance. I had the curiosity, however, at some inconvenience, to ride round and examine the spot. I suppose that Heda had sold the property, for a back-*veld* Boer, who was absent at the time, had turned what used to be Rodd's hospital into his house. Close by, grim and gaunt, stood the burnt-out marble walls of the Temple. The veranda was still roofed over, and standing on the spot whence I had shot the pistol out of Rodd's hand, I was filled with many memories.

I could trace the whole plan of the building and visited that part of it which had been Marnham's room. The iron safe that stood in the corner had been taken away, but the legs of the bedstead remained. Also not far from it, over grown with running plants, was a little heap which I took to be the ashes of his desk, for bits of burnt wood protruded. I grubbed among them with my foot and riding crop and presently came across the remains of a charred human skull. Then I departed in a hurry.

My way took me through the Yellow-wood grove, past the horns of the blue *wildebeeste* which still lay there, past that mud-hole also into which Rodd had fallen dead. Here, however, I made no more search, who had seen enough of bones. To this day I do not know whether he still lies beneath the slimy ooze, or was removed and buried.

Also I saw the site of our wagon camp where the Basutos attacked us. But I will have done with these reminiscences which induce melancholy, though really there is no reason why they should.

Tout lasse, tout casse, tout passe—everything wears out, everything crumbles, everything vanishes—in the words of the French proverb that my friend Sir Henry Curtis is so fond of quoting, that at last I wrote it down in my pocket-book, only to remember afterwards that when I was a boy I had heard it from the lips of an old scamp of a Frenchman, of the name of Leblanc, who once gave me and another lessons in the Gallic tongue. But of him I have already written in *Marie*, which is the first chapter in the Book of the fall of the Zulus. That headed *Child of Storm* is the second. These pages form the third and last.

Ah! indeed, *tout lasse, tout casse, tout passe!*

CHAPTER 23

The Kraal Jazi

Now I shall pass over all the Zulu record of the next four years, since after all it has nothing to do with my tale and I do not pretend to be writing a history.

Sir Garnet Wolseley set up his Kilkenny cat Government in Zululand, or the Home Government did it for him, I do not know which. In place of one king, thirteen chiefs were erected who got to work to cut the throats of each other and of the people.

As I expected would be the case, Zikali informed the military authorities of the secret hiding-place in the Ingome Forest where he suggested to Cetewayo that he should refuge. The ex-king was duly captured there and taken first to the Cape and then to England, where, after the disgrace of poor Sir Bartle Frere, an agitation had been set on foot on his behalf. Here he saw the Queen and her ministers, once more conquering, as it had been prophesied that he would by her who wore the shape of Mameena at the memorable scene in the Valley of Bones when I was present. Often I have thought of him dressed in a black coat and seated in that villa in Melbury Road in the suburb of London which I understand is populated by artists. A strange contrast truly to the savage prince receiving the salute of triumph after the Battle of the Tugela in which he won the kingship, or to the royal monarch to whose presence I had been summoned at Ulundi. However, he was brought back to Zululand again by a British man-of-war, re-installed to a limited chieftainship by Sir Theophilus Shepstone, and freed from the strangling embrace of the black coat.

Then of course there was more fighting, as every one knew would happen, except the British Colonial Office; indeed all Zululand ran with blood. For in England Cetewayo and his rights, or wrongs, had, like the Boers and their rights, or wrongs, become a matter of Party politics to which everything else must give way. Often I wonder whether Party politics will not in the end prove the ruin of the British Empire. Well, thank Heaven, I shall not live to learn.

So Cetewayo came back and fought and was defeated by those who once had been his subjects. Now for the last scene, that is all with which I need concern myself.

At the beginning of February, 1884, business took me to Zululand; it had to do with a deal in cattle and blankets. As I was returning towards the Tugela who should I meet but friend Goza, he who had escorted me from the Black Kloof to Ulundi before the outbreak of war, and who afterwards escorted me and that unutterable nuisance, Kaatje, out of the country. At first I thought that we came together by accident, or perhaps that he had journeyed a little way to thank me for the blankets which I had sent to him, remembering my ancient promise, but afterwards I changed my opinion on this point.

Well, we talked over many matters, the war, the disasters that had befallen Zululand, and so forth. Especially did we talk of that night in the Valley of Bones and the things we had seen there side by side. I asked him if the people still believed in the Inkosazana-y-Zulu who then appeared in the moonlight on the rock. He answered that some did and some did not. For his part, he added, looking at me fixedly, he did not, since it was rumoured that Zikali had dressed up a white woman to play the part of the Spirit. Yet he could not be sure of the matter, since it was also said that when some of Cetewayo's people went to kill this white woman in the Black Kloof, Nomkubulwana, the Princess of Heaven herself, rose before them and frightened them away.

I remarked that this was very strange, and then quite casually asked him whom Zikali had dressed up to play the part of the dead Mameena upon that same occasion, since this was a point upon which I always thirsted for definite intelligence. He stared at me and replied that I ought to be able to answer my own question, since I had been much nearer to her who looked like Mameena than any one else, so near indeed that all present distinctly saw her kiss me, as it was well known she had liked to do while still alive. I replied indignantly that they saw wrong and repeated my question. Then he answered straight out—

"O Macumazahn, we Zulus believe that what we saw on that night was not Nombe or another dressed up, but the spirit of the witch Mameena itself. We believe it because we could see the light of Zikali's fire through her, not always, but sometimes; also because all that she said has come true, though everything is not yet finished."

I could get no more out of him about the matter, for when I tried to speak of it again, he turned the subject, telling me of his wonderful escapes during the war. Presently he rose to go and said casually—

"Surely I grow old in these times of trouble, Macumazahn, for thoughts slip through my head like water through the fingers. Almost I had forgotten what I wished to say to you. The other day I met Zikali, the Opener of Roads. He told me that you were in Zululand and that I should meet you—he did not say where, only that when I did meet you, I was to give you a message. This was the message—that when on your way to Natal you came to the *kraal* Jazi, you would find him there; also another whom you used to know, and must be sure not to go away without seeing him, since that was about to happen in which you must take your part."

"Zikali!" I exclaimed. "I have heard nothing of him since the war. I thought that by now he was certainly dead."

"Oh! no, Macumazahn, he is certainly not dead, but just the same as ever. Indeed it is believed that he and no other has kept all this broth of trouble on the boil, some say for Cetewayo's sake, and some say because he wishes to destroy Cetewayo. But what do I know of such matters who only desire to live in peace under whatever chief the English Queen sends to us, as she has a right to do having conquered us in war? When you meet the Opener of Roads at the *kraal* Jazi, ask him, Macumazahn."

"Where the devil is the *kraal* Jazi?" I inquired with irritation. "I never heard of such a place."

"Nor did I, therefore I cannot tell you, Macumazahn. For aught I can say it may be down beneath where dead men go. But wherever it is there certainly you will meet the Opener of Roads. Now farewell, Macumazahn. If it should chance that we never look into each other's eyes again, I am sure you will think of me sometimes, as I shall of you, and of all that we have seen together, especially on that night in the Vale of Bones when the ghost of the witch Mameena prophesied to us and kissed you before us all. She must have been very beautiful, Macumazahn, as indeed I have heard from those who remember her, and I don't wonder that you loved her so much. Still for my part I had rather be kissed by a living woman than by one who is dead, though doubtless it is best to be kissed by none at all. Again, farewell, and be sure to tell the Opener of Roads that I gave you his message, lest he should lay some evil charm upon me, who have seen enough evil of late."

Thus talking Goza departed. I never saw him again, and do not know if he is dead or alive. Well, he was a kindly old fellow, if no hero.

I had almost forgotten the incident of this meeting when a while later I found myself in the neighbourhood of the beautiful but semi-tropical place called Eshowe, which since those days has become the official home of the British Resident in Zululand. Indeed, although the house was not then finished, if it had been begun, Sir Melmoth Osborn already had an office there. I wished to see him in order to give him some rather important information, but when I reached a *kraal* of about fifty huts some five hundred yards from the site of the present Residency, my wagon stuck fast in the boggy ground. While I was trying to get it out a quiet-faced Zulu, whose name, I remember, was Umnikwa, informed me that Malimati, that is Sir Melmoth Osborn's native name, was somewhere at a little distance from Eshowe, too far away for me to get to him that night. I answered, Very well, I would sleep where I was, and asked the name of the *kraal*.

He replied, Jazi, at which I started, but only said that it was a strange name, seeing that it meant "Finished," or "Finished with joy." Umnikwa answered, Yes, but that it had been so called because the chief Umfokaki, or The Stranger, who married a sister of the king, was killed at this *kraal* by his brother, Gundane, or the Bat. I remarked that it was an ill-omened kind of name, to which the man replied, Yes, and likely to become more so, since the King Cetewayo who had been sheltering there "beneath the armpit" of Malimati, the white lord, for some months, lay in it dying. I asked him of what he was dying, and he replied that he did not know, but that doubtless the father of the witch-doctors, named Zikali, the Opener of Roads, would be able to tell me, as he was attending on Cetewayo.

"He has sent me to bid you to come at once, O Macumazahn," he added casually, "having had news that you were arriving here."

Showing no surprise, I answered that I would come, although goodness knows I was surprised enough, and leaving my servants to get my wagon out of the bog, I walked into the *kraal* with the messenger. He took me to a large hut placed within a fence about the gate of which some women were gathered, who all looked very anxious and disturbed. Among them I saw Dabuko the king's brother, whom I knew slightly. He greeted me and told me that Cetewayo was at the point of death within the hut, but like Umnikwa, professed ignorance of the cause of his illness.

For a long while, over an hour I should think, I sat there outside the hut, or walked to and fro. Until darkness came I could occupy myself with contemplating the scenery of the encircling hills, which is among the most beautiful in Zululand with its swelling contours and rich colouring. But after it had set in only my thoughts remained, and these I found depressing.

At length I made up my mind that I would go away, for after all what had I to do with this business of the death of Cetewayo, if in truth he was dying? I wished to see no more of Cetewayo of whom all my recollections were terrific or sorrowful. I rose to depart, when suddenly a woman emerged from the hut. I could not see who she was or even what she was like, because of the gloom; also for the reason that she had the corner of her blanket thrown over her face as though she wished to keep it hidden. For a moment she stopped opposite to me and said—

"The king who is sick desires to see you, Macumazahn." Then she pointed to the door-hole of the hut and vanished, shutting the gate of the fence behind her. Curiosity overcame me and I crawled into the hut, pushing aside the door-board in order to do so and setting it up again when I was through.

Inside burned a single candle fixed in the neck of a bottle, faintly illuminating that big and gloomy place. By its feeble light I saw a low bedstead on the left of the entrance and lying on it a man half covered by a blanket in whom I recognized Cetewayo. His face was shrunken and distorted with pain, and his great bulk seemed less, but still without doubt it was Cetewayo.

"Greeting, Macumazahn," he said feebly, "you find me in evil case, but I heard that you were here and thought that I should like to see you before I die, because I know that you are honest and will report my words faithfully. I wish you to tell the white men that my heart never really was against them; they have always been the friends of my heart, but others forced me down a road I did not wish to travel, of which now I have come to the end."

"What is the matter with you, King?" I asked.

"I do not know, Macumazahn, but I have been sick for some days. The Opener of Roads who came to doctor me, because my wives believed those white medicine-men wished me dead, says that I have been poisoned and must die. If you had been here at first you might perhaps have given me some medicine. But now it is too late," he added with a groan.

"Who then poisoned you, King?"

"I cannot tell you, Macumazahn. Perhaps my enemies, perhaps my brothers, perhaps my wives. All wish to have done with me, and the Great One, who is no longer wanted, is soon dead. Be thankful, Macumazahn, that you never were a king, for sad is the lot of kings."

"Where, then, is the Opener of Roads?" I asked.

"He was here a little while ago. Perhaps he has gone out to take the King's head" (i.e., to announce his death) "to Malimati and the white men," he answered in a faint voice.

Just then I heard a shuffling noise proceeding from that part of the hut where the shadow was deepest, and looking, saw an emaciated arm projected into the circle of the light. It was followed by another arm, then by a vast head covered with long white hair that trailed upon the ground, then by a big, misshapen body, so wasted that it looked like a skeleton covered with corrugated black skin. Slowly, like a chameleon climbing a bough, the thing crept forward, and I knew it for Zikali. He reached the side of the bed and squatted down in his toad-like fashion, then, again like a chameleon, without moving his head turned his deep and glowing eyes towards me.

"Hail, O Macumazahn," he said in his low voice. "Did I not promise you long ago that you should be with me at the last, and are you not with me and another?"

"It seems so, Zikali," I answered. "But why do you not send for the white doctors to cure the king?"

"All the doctors, white and black, in the whole world cannot cure him, Macumazahn. The Spirits call him and he dies. At his call I came fast and far, but even I cannot cure him—although because of him I myself must die."

"Why?" I asked.

"Look at me, Macumazahn, and say if I am one who should travel. Well, all come to their end at last, even the *Thing-that-should-never-have-been-born*."

Cetewayo lifted his head and looked at him, then said heavily—

"Perchance it would have been better for our House if that end had been sooner. Now that I lie dying many sayings concerning you come into my mind that I had forgotten. Moreover, Opener of Roads, I never sent for you, whoever may have done so, and it was not until after you came here that the great pain seized me. How did it happen," he went on with gathering force, "that the white men caught me in the secret place where you told me I should hide? Who pointed out that hidden hole to the white men? But what does it matter now?"

"Nothing at all, O Son of Panda," answered Zikali, "even less than it matters how I escaped the spear-head hidden in your robe, yonder in my hut in the Black Kloof where, had it not been for a certain spirit that stood between you and me, you would have murdered me. Tell me, Son of Panda, during these last three days have you thought at all of your brother Umbelazi, and of certain other brethren of yours whom you killed at the battle of the Tugela, when the white man here led the charge of the Amawombe against your regiments and ate up three of them?"

Cetewayo groaned but said nothing. I think he had become too faint to speak.

"Listen, Son of Panda," went on Zikali in an intense and hissing voice. "Many, many years ago, before Senzangacona, your grandfather, saw the light—who knows how long before—a man was born of high blood in the Dwandwe tribe, which man was a dwarf. Chaka the Black One conquered the Dwandwe, but this man of high blood was spared because he was a dwarf, an abortion, to whom Chaka gave the name of the 'Thing-that-never-should-have-been-born,' keeping him about him to be a mock in times of peace and safety, and because he was wise and learned in magic, to be a counsellor in times of trouble. Moreover, Chaka killed this man's wives and children for his sport, save one whom he kept to be his 'sister.'

"Therefore for the sake of his people and his butchered wives and children, this wizard swore an oath of vengeance against Chaka and all his House. Working beneath the ground like a rat, he undermined the throne of Chaka and brought him to his death by the spears of his brethren and of Mopo his servant, whom Chaka had wronged. Still working in the dark like a rat, he caused Dingaan, who stabbed Chaka, to murder the Boer Retief and his people, and thus called down upon his head the vengeance of the Whites, and afterwards brought Dingaan to his death. Then Panda, your father, arose, and his life this 'Thing-that-never-should-have-been-born' spared because once Panda had done him a kindness. Only through the witch Mameena he brought sorrow on him, causing war to arise between his children, one of whom was named Cetewayo.

"Then this Cetewayo ruled, first with his father Panda and afterwards in his place, and trouble arose between him and the English. Son of Panda, you will remember that this Cetewayo was in doubt whether to fight the English and demanded a sign of the Thing-that-never-should-have-been-born. He gave the sign, causing the Inkosazana-y-Zulu, the Princess of Heaven, to appear before him and thereby lifting the spear of War. Son of Panda, you know how that war went, how this Cetewayo was defeated and came to the 'Thing-that-never-should-have-been-born' like a hunted hyena, to learn of a hole where he might hide. You know, too, how he strove to murder the poor old doctor who showed him such a hole; how he was taken prisoner and sent across the water and afterwards set up again in the land that had learned to hate him, to bring its children to death by thousands. And you know how at last he took refuge beneath the wing of the white chief, here in the *kraal* Jazi, and lived, spat upon, an outcast, until at length he fell sick, as such men are apt to do, and the Thing-that-never-should-have-been-born was sent for to doctor him. And you know also how he lies dying, within him an agony as though he had swallowed a red hot spear, and before him a great blackness peopled by the ghosts of those whom he has slain, and of his forefathers whose House he has pulled down and burned."

Zikali ceased, and thrusting his hideous head to within an inch or two of that of the dying man, he glowered at him with his fierce and fiery eyes. Then he began to whisper into the king's ear, who quivered at his words, as the victim quivers beneath the torturer's looks.

At that moment the end of the candle fell into the bottle which was of clear white glass, and there burned for a little while dully before it went out. Never shall I forget the scene illumined by its blue and ghastly light. The dying man lying on the low couch, rocking his head to and fro; the wizard bending over him like some grey vampire bat sucking the life-blood from his helpless throat. The terror in the eyes of the one, the insatiable hate in the eyes of the other. Oh! it was awful!

"Macumazahn," gasped Cetewayo in a rattling whisper, "help me, Macumazahn. I say that I am poisoned by this Zikali, who hates me. Oh! drive away the ghosts! Drive them away!"

I looked at him and at his tormentor squatted by him like a mocking fiend, and as I looked the candle went out.

Then my nerve broke, the cold sweat poured from my face and I fled from the hut as a man might from a scene in hell, followed by the low mocking laugh of Zikali.

Outside the women and others were gathered in the gloom. I told them to go to the king, who was dying, and blundered up the slope to search for some white man. No one was to be found, but a *Kaffir* messenger by the office told me that Malimati was still away and had been sent for. So I returned to my wagon and lay down in it exhausted, for what more could I do?

It was a rough night. Thunder muttered and rain fell in driving gusts. I dozed off, only to be awakened by a sound of wailing. Then I knew that the king was dead, for this was the *Isililo*, the cry of mourning. I wondered whether the murderers—for that he was poisoned I had no doubt—were among those who wailed.

Towards dawn the storm rolled off and the night grew serene and clear, for a waning moon was shining in the sky. The heat of that stiffing place oppressed me; my blood seemed to be afire. I knew that there was a stream in a gorge about half a mile away, for it had been pointed out to me. I longed for a swim in cool water, who, to tell truth, had found none for some days, and bethought me that I would bathe in this stream before I trekked from that hateful spot, for to me it had become hateful. Calling my driver, who was awake and talking with the *voorloopers*, for they knew what was passing at the *kraal* and were alarmed, I told them to get the oxen ready to start as I would be back presently. Then I set off for the stream and, after a longish walk, scrambled down a steep ravine to its banks, following a path made by *Kaffir* women going to draw water. Arrived there at last I found that it was in flood and rising rapidly, at least so I judged from the sound, for in that deep, tree-hung place the light was too faint to allow me to see anything. So I sat down waiting for the dawn and wishing that I had not come because of the mosquitoes.

At length it broke and the mists lifted, showing that the spot was one of great beauty. Opposite to me was a waterfall twenty or thirty feet high, over which the torrent rushed into a black pool below. Everywhere grew tall ferns and beyond these graceful trees, from whose leaves hung raindrops. In the centre of the stream on the edge of the fall was a rock not a dozen feet away from me, round which the water foamed. Something was squatted on this rock, at first I could not see what because of the mist, but thought that it was a grey-headed baboon, or some other animal, and regretted that I had not brought a gun with me. Presently I became aware that it must be a man, for, in a chanting voice, it began to speak or pray in Zulu, and hidden behind a flowering bush, I could hear the words. They were to this effect—

"O my Spirit, here where thou foundest me when I was young, hundreds of years ago" (he said hundreds, but I suppose he meant tens), "I come back to thee. In this pool I dived and beneath the waters found thee, my Snake, and thou didst wind thyself about my body and about my heart" (here I understood that the speaker was alluding to his initiation as a witch-doctor which generally includes, or used to include, the finding of a snake in a river that coils itself about the neophyte). "About my body and in my heart thou hast dwelt from that sun to this, giving me wisdom and good and evil counsel, and that which thou hast counselled, I have done. Now I return thee whence thou camest, there to await me in the new birth.

"O Spirits of my fathers, toiling through many years I have avenged

273

you on the House of Senzangacona, and never again will there be a king of the Zulus, for the last of them lies dead by my hand. O my murdered wives and my children, I have offered up to you a mighty sacrifice, a sacrifice of thousands upon thousands.

"O Umkulu-kulu, Great One of the heavens, who sentest me to earth, I have done thy work upon the earth and bring back to thee thy harvest of the seed that thou hast sown, a blood-red harvest, O Umkulu-kulu. Be still, be still, my Snake, the sun arises, and soon, soon shalt thou rest in the water that wast thine from the beginning of the world!"

The voice ceased, and presently a spear of light piercing the mists, lit upon the speaker. It was Zikali and about him was wound a great yellow-bellied snake, of which the black head with flickering tongue waved above his head and seemed from time to time to lick him on the brow. (I suppose it had come to him from the water, for its skin glittered as though with wet.) He stood up on tottering feet, staring at the red eye of the rising sun, then crying, *"Finished, finished with joy!"* with a loud and dreadful laughter, he plunged into the foaming pool beneath.

Such was the end of Zikali the wizard, Opener of Roads, the *Thing-that-should-never-have-been-born,* and such was the vengeance that he worked upon the great House of Senzangacona, bringing it to naught and with it the nation of the Zulus.

The Ivory Child

CHAPTER 1

Allan Gives a Shooting Lesson

Now I, Allan Quatermain, come to the story of what was, perhaps, one of the strangest of all the adventures which have befallen me in the course of a life that so far can scarcely be called tame or humdrum.

Amongst many other things it tells of the war against the Black Kendah people and the dead of Jana, their elephant god. Often since then I have wondered if this creature was or was not anything more than a mere gigantic beast of the forest. It seems improbable, even impossible, but the reader of future days may judge of this matter for himself.

Also he can form his opinion as to the religion of the White Kendah and their pretensions to a certain degree of magical skill. Of this magic I will make only one remark: If it existed at all, it was by no means infallible. To take a single instance, Harût and Marût were convinced by divination that I, and I only, could kill Jana, which was why they invited me to Kendahland. Yet in the end it was Hans who killed him. Jana nearly killed me!

Now to my tale.

* * * * * * * *

In another history, called *The Holy Flower*, I have told how I came to England with a young gentleman of the name of Scroope, partly to see him safely home after a hunting accident, and partly to try to dispose of a unique orchid for a friend of mine called Brother John by the white people, and Dogeetah by the natives, who was popularly supposed to be mad, but, in fact, was very sane indeed. So sane was he that he pursued what seemed to be an absolutely desperate quest for over twenty years, until, with some humble assistance on my part, he brought it to a curiously successful issue. But all this tale is told in "The Holy Flower," and I only allude to it here, that is at present, to explain how I came to be in England.

While in this country I stayed for a few days with Scroope, or, rather, with his fiancée and her people, at a fine house in Essex. (I called it Essex to avoid the place being identified, but really it was one of the neighbouring counties.) During my visit I was taken to see a much finer place, a splendid old castle with brick gateway towers, that had been wonderfully well restored and turned into a most luxurious modern dwelling. Let us call it Ragnall, the seat of a baron of that name.

I had heard a good deal about Lord Ragnall, who, according to all accounts, seemed a kind of Admirable Crichton. He was said to be wonderfully handsome, a great scholar—he had taken a double first at college; a great athlete—he had been captain of the Oxford boat at the University race; a very promising speaker who had already made his mark in the House of Lords; a sportsman who had shot tigers and other large game in India; a poet who had published a successful volume of verse under a pseudonym; a good solider until he left the Service; and lastly, a man of enormous wealth, owning, in addition to his estates, several coal mines and an entire town in the north of England.

"Dear me!" I said when the list was finished, "he seems to have been born with a whole case of gold spoons in his mouth. I hope one of them will not choke him," adding: "Perhaps he will be unlucky in love."

"That's just where he is most lucky of all," answered the young lady to whom I was talking—it was Scroope's fiancée, Miss Manners—"for he is engaged to a lady that, I am told, is the loveliest, sweetest, cleverest girl in all England, and they absolutely adore each other."

"Dear me!" I repeated. "I wonder what Fate *has* got up its sleeve for Lord Ragnall and his perfect lady-love?"

I was doomed to find out one day.

So it came about that when, on the following morning, I was asked if I would like to see the wonders of Ragnall Castle, I answered "Yes." Really, however, I wanted to have a look at Lord Ragnall himself, if possible, for the account of his many perfections had impressed the imagination of a poor colonist like myself, who had never found an opportunity of setting his eyes upon a kind of human angel. Human devils I had met in plenty, but never a single angel—at least, of the male sex. Also there was always the possibility that I might get a glimpse of the still more angelic lady to whom he was engaged, whose name, I understood, was the Hon. Miss Holmes. So I said that nothing would please me more than to see this castle.

Thither we drove accordingly through the fine, frosty air, for the month was December. On reaching the castle, Mr. Scroope was told that Lord Ragnall, whom he knew well, was out shooting somewhere in the park, but that, of course, he could show his friend over the place. So we went in, the three of us, for Miss Manners, to whom Scroope was to be married very shortly, had driven us over in her pony carriage. The porter at the gateway towers took us to the main door of the castle and handed us over to another man, whom he addressed as Mr. Savage, whispering to me that he was his lordship's personal attendant.

I remember the name, because it seemed to me that I had never seen anyone who looked much less savage. In truth, his appearance was that of a duke in disguise, as I imagine dukes to be, for I never set eyes on one. His dress—he wore a black morning cut-away coat—was faultless. His manners were exquisite, polite to the verge of irony, but with a hint of haughty pride in the background. He was handsome also, with a fine nose and a hawk-like eye, while a touch of baldness added to the general effect. His age may have been anything between thirty-five and forty, and the way he deprived me of my hat and stick, to which I strove to cling, showed, I thought, resolution of character. Probably, I reflected to myself, he considers me an unusual sort of person who might damage the pictures and other objects of art with the stick, and not seeing his way how to ask me to give it up without suggesting suspicion, has hit upon the expedient of taking my hat also.

In after days Mr. Samuel Savage informed me that I was quite right in this surmise. He said he thought that, judging from my somewhat unconventional appearance, I might be one of the dangerous class of whom he had been reading in the papers, namely, a *hanarchist*. I write the word as he pronounced it, for here comes the curious thing. This man, so flawless, so well instructed in some respects, had a fault which gave everything away. His *h*'s were uncertain. Three of them would come quite right, but the fourth, let us say, would be conspicuous either by its utter absence or by its unwanted appearance. He could speak, when describing the Ragnall pictures, in rotund and flowing periods that would scarcely have disgraced the pen of Gibbon. Then suddenly that *h* would appear or disappear, and the illusion was over. It was like a sudden shock of cold water down the back. I never discovered the origin of his family; it was a matter of which he did not speak, perhaps because he was vague about it himself; but if an earl of Norman blood had married a handsome Cockney kitchen maid of native ability, I can quite imagine that Samuel Savage might have been a child of the union. For the rest he was a good man and a faithful one, for whom I have a high respect.

On this occasion he conducted us round the castle, or, rather, its more public rooms, showing us many treasures and, I should think, at least two hundred pictures by eminent and departed artists, which gave him an opportunity of exhibiting a peculiar, if somewhat erratic, knowledge of history. To tell the truth, I began to wish that it were a little less full in detail, since on a December day those large apartments felt uncommonly cold. Scroope and Miss Manners seemed to keep warm, perhaps with the inward fires of mutual admiration, but as I had no one to admire except Mr. Savage, a temperature of about 35 degrees produced its natural effect upon me.

At length we took a short cut from the large to the little gallery through a warmed and comfortable room, which I understood was Lord Ragnall's study. Halting for a moment by one of the fires, I observed a picture on the wall, over which a curtain was drawn, and asked Mr. Savage what it might be.

"That, sir," he replied with a kind of haughty reserve, "is the portrait of her future ladyship, which his lordship keeps for his private heye."

Miss Manners sniggered, and I said:

"Oh, thank you. What an ill-omened kind of thing to do!"

Then, observing through an open door the hall in which my hat had been taken from me, I lingered and as the others vanished in the little gallery, slipped into it, recovered my belongings, and passed out to the garden, purposing to walk there till I was warm again and Scroope reappeared. While I marched up and down a terrace, on which, I remember, several very cold-looking peacocks were seated, like conscientious birds that knew it was their duty to be ornamental, however low the temperature, I heard some shots fired, apparently in a clump of ilex oaks which grew about five hundred yards away, and reflected to myself that they seemed to be those of a small rifle, not of a shotgun.

My curiosity being excited as to what was to be an almost professional matter, I walked towards the grove, making a circuit through a shrubbery. At length I found myself near to the edge of a glade, and perceived, standing behind the shelter of a magnificent ilex, two men. One of these was a young keeper, and the other, from his appearance, I felt sure must be Lord Ragnall himself. Certainly he was a splendid-looking man, very tall, very broad, very handsome, with a peaked beard, a kind and charming face, and large dark eyes. He wore a cloak upon his shoulders, which was thrown back from over a velvet coat, and, except for the light double-barrelled rifle in his hand, looked exactly like a picture by Van Dyck which Mr. Savage had just informed me was that of one of his lordship's ancestors of the time of Charles I.

Standing behind another oak, I observed that he was trying to shoot wood-pigeons as they descended to feed upon the acorns, for which the hard weather had made them greedy. From time to time these beautiful blue birds appeared and hovered a moment before they settled, whereon the sportsman fired and—they flew away. *Bang! Bang!* went the double-barrelled rifle, and off fled the pigeon.

"Damn!" said the sportsman in a pleasant, laughing voice; "that's the twelfth I have missed, Charles."

"You hit his tail, my lord. I saw a feather come out. But, my lord, as I told you, there ain't no man living what can kill pigeons on the wing with a bullet, even when they seem to sit still in the air."

"I have heard of one, Charles. Mr. Scroope has a friend from Africa staying with him who, he swears, could knock over four out of six."

"Then, my lord, Mr. Scroope has a friend what lies," replied Charles as he handed him the second rifle.

This was too much for me. I stepped forward, raising my hat politely, and said:

"Sir, forgive me for interrupting you, but you are not shooting at those wood-pigeons in the right way. Although they seem to hover just before they settle, they are dropping much faster than you think. Your keeper was mistaken when he said that you knocked a feather out of the tail of that last bird at which you fired two barrels. In both cases you shot at least a foot above it, and what fell was a leaf from the ilex tree."

There was a moment's silence, which was broken by Charles, who ejaculated in a thick voice:

"Well, of all the cheek!"

Lord Ragnall, however, for it was he, looked first angry and then amused.

"Sir," he said, "I thank you for your advice, which no doubt is excellent, for it is certainly true that I have missed every pigeon which I tried to shoot with these confounded little rifles. But if you could demonstrate in practice what you so kindly set out in precept, the value of your counsel would be enhanced."

Thus he spoke, mimicking, I have no doubt (for he had a sense of humour), the manner of my address, which nervousness had made somewhat pompous.

"Give me the rifle," I answered, taking off my greatcoat.

He handed it me with a bow.

"Mind what you are about," growled Charles. "That there thing is full cocked and 'air-triggered.'"

I withered, or, rather, tried to wither him with a glance, but this unbelieving keeper only stared back at me with insolence in his round and bird-like eyes. Never before had I felt quite so angry with a menial. Then a horrible doubt struck me. Supposing I should miss! I knew very little of the manner of flight of English wood-pigeons, which are not difficult to miss with a bullet, and nothing at all of these particular rifles, though a glance at them showed me that they were exquisite weapons of their sort and by a great maker. If I muffed the thing now, how should I bear the scorn of Charles and the polite amusement of his noble master? Almost I prayed that no more pigeons would put in an appearance, and thus that the issue of my supposed skill might be left in doubt.

But this was not to be. These birds came from far in ones or twos to search for their favourite food, and the fact that others had been scared away did not cause them to cease from coming. Presently I heard Charles mutter:

"Now, then, look out, guv'nor. Here's your chance of teaching his lordship how to do it, though he does happen to be the best shot in these counties."

While he spoke two pigeons appeared, one a little behind the other, coming down very straight. As they reached the opening in the ilex grove they hovered, preparing to alight, for of us they could see nothing, one at a distance of about fifty and the other of, say, seventy yards away. I took the nearest, got on to it, allowing for the drop and the angle, and touched the trigger of the rifle, which fell to my shoulder very sweetly. The bullet struck that pigeon on the crop, out of which fell a shower of acorns that it had been eating, as it sank to the ground stone dead. Number two pigeon, realizing danger, began to mount upwards almost straight. I fired the second barrel, and by good luck shot its head off. Then I snatched the other rifle, which Charles had been loading automatically, from his outstretched hand, for at that moment I saw two more pigeons coming. At the first I risked a difficult shot and hit it far back, knocking out its tail, but bringing it, still fluttering, to the ground. The other, too, I covered, but when I touched the trigger there was a click, no more.

This was my opportunity of coming even with Charles, and I availed myself of it.

"Young man," I said, while he gaped at me open-mouthed, "you should learn to be careful with rifles, which are dangerous weapons. If you give one to a shooter that is not loaded, it shows that you are capable of anything."

Then I turned, and addressing Lord Ragnall, added:

"I must apologize for that third shot of mine, which was infamous, for I committed a similar fault to that against which I warned you, sir, and did not fire far enough ahead. However, it may serve to show your attendant the difference between the tail of a pigeon and an oak leaf," and I pointed to one of the feathers of the poor bird, which was still drifting to the ground.

"Well, if this here snipe of a chap ain't the devil in boots!" exclaimed Charles to himself.

But his master cut him short with a look, then lifted his hat to me and said:

"Sir, the practice much surpasses the precept, which is unusual. I congratulate you upon a skill that almost partakes of the marvellous, unless, indeed, chance———"And he stopped.

"It is natural that you should think so," I replied; "but if more pigeons come, and Mr. Charles will make sure that he loads the rifle, I hope to undeceive you."

At this moment, however, a loud shout from Scroope, who was looking for me, reinforced by a shrill cry uttered by Miss Manners, banished every pigeon within half a mile, a fact of which I was not sorry, since who knows whether I should have it all, or any, of the next three birds?

"I think my friends are calling me, so I will bid you good morning," I said awkwardly.

"One moment, sir," he exclaimed. "Might I first ask you your name? Mine is Ragnall—Lord Ragnall."

"And mine is Allan Quatermain," I said.

"Oh!" he answered, "that explains matters. Charles, this is Mr. Scroope's friend, the gentleman that you said—exaggerated. I think you had better apologize."

But Charles was gone, to pick up the pigeons, I suppose.

At this moment Scroope and the young lady appeared, having heard our voices, and a general explanation ensued.

"Mr. Quatermain has been giving me a lesson in shooting pigeons on the wing with a small-bore rifle," said Lord Ragnall, pointing to the dead birds that still lay upon the ground.

"He is competent to do that," said Scroope.

"Painfully competent," replied his lordship. "If you don't believe me, ask the under-keeper."

"It is the only thing I can do," I explained modestly. "Rifle-shooting is my trade, and I have made a habit of practising at birds on the wing with ball. I have no doubt that with a shot-gun your lordship would leave me nowhere, for that is a game at which I have had little practice, except when shooting for the pot in Africa."

"Yes," interrupted Scroope, "you wouldn't have any chance at that, Allan, against one of the finest shots in England."

"I'm not so sure," said Lord Ragnall, laughing pleasantly. "I have an idea that Mr. Quatermain is full of surprises. However, with his leave, we'll see. If you have a day to spare, Mr. Quatermain, we are going to shoot through the home coverts tomorrow, which haven't been touched till now, and I hope you will join us."

"It is most kind of you, but that is impossible," I answered with firmness. "I have no gun here."

"Oh, never mind that, Mr. Quatermain. I have a pair of breech-loaders"—these were new things at that date—"which have been sent down to me to try. I am going to return them, because they are much too short in the stock for me. I think they would just suit you, and you are quite welcome to the use of them."

Again I excused myself, guessing that the discomfited Charles would put all sorts of stories about concerning me, and not wishing to look foolish before a party of grand strangers, no doubt chosen for their skill at this particular form of sport.

"Well, Allan," exclaimed Scroope, who always had a talent for saying the wrong thing, "you are quite right not to go into a competition with Lord Ragnall over high pheasants."

I flushed, for there was some truth in his blundering remark, whereon Lord Ragnall said with ready tact:

"I asked Mr. Quatermain to shoot, not to a shooting match, Scroope, and I hope he'll come."

This left me no option, and with a sinking heart I had to accept.

"Sorry I can't ask you too, Scroope," said his lordship, when details had been arranged, "but we can only manage seven guns at this shoot. But will you and Miss Manners come to dine and sleep tomorrow evening? I should like to introduce your future wife to my future wife," he added, colouring a little.

Miss Manners being devoured with curiosity as to the wonderful Miss Holmes, of whom she had heard so much but never actually seen, accepted at once, before her lover could get out a word, whereon Scroope volunteered to bring me over in the morning and load for me. Being possessed by a terror that I should be handed over to the care of the unsympathetic Charles, I replied that I should be very grateful, and so the thing was settled.

On our way home we passed through a country town, of which

I forget the name, and the sight of a gunsmith's shop there reminded me that I had no cartridges. So I stopped to order some, as, fortunately, Lord Ragnall had mentioned that the guns he was going to lend me were twelve-bores. The tradesman asked me how many cartridges I wanted, and when I replied "a hundred," stared at me and said:

"If, as I understood, sir, you are going to the big winter shoot at Ragnall tomorrow, you had better make it three hundred and fifty at least. I shall be there to watch, like lots of others, and I expect to see nearly two hundred fired by each gun at the last Lake stand."

"Very well," I answered, fearing to show more ignorance by further discussion. "I will call for the cartridges on my way tomorrow morning. Please load them with three drachms of powder."

"Yes, sir, and an ounce and an eighth of No. 5 shot, sir? That's what all the gentlemen use."

"No," I answered, "No. 3; please be sure as to that. Good evening."

The gunsmith stared at me, and as I left the shop I heard him remark to his assistant:

"That African gent must think he's going out to shoot ostriches with buck shot. I expect he ain't no good, whatever they may say about him."

CHAPTER 2

Allan Makes a Bet

On the following morning Scroope and I arrived at Castle Ragnall at or about a quarter to ten. On our way we stopped to pick up my three hundred and fifty cartridges. I had to pay something over three solid sovereigns for them, as in those days such things were dear, which showed me that I was not going to get my lesson in English pheasant shooting for nothing. The gunsmith, however, to whom Scroope gave a lift in his cart to the castle, impressed upon me that they were dirt cheap, since he and his assistant had sat up most of the night loading them with my special No. 3 shot.

As I climbed out of the vehicle a splendid-looking and portly person, arrayed in a velvet coat and a scarlet waistcoat, approached with the air of an emperor, followed by an individual in whom I recognized Charles, carrying a gun under each arm.

"That's the head-keeper," whispered Scroope; "mind you treat him respectfully."

Much alarmed, I took off my hat and waited.

"Do I speak to Mr. Allan Quatermain?" said his majesty in a deep and rumbling voice, surveying me the while with a cold and disapproving eye. I intimated that he did.

"Then, sir," he went on, pausing a little at the "sir," as though he suspected me of being no more than an African colleague of his own, "I have been ordered by his lordship to bring you these guns, and I hope, sir, that you will be careful of them, as they are here on sale or return. Charles, explain the working of them there guns to this foreign gentleman, and in doing so keep the muzzles up *or* down. They ain't loaded, it's true, but the example is always useful."

"Thank you, Mr. Keeper," I replied, growing somewhat nettled, "but I think that I am already acquainted with most that there is to learn about guns."

"I am glad to hear it, sir," said his majesty with evident disbelief. "Charles, I understand that Squire Scroope is going to load for the gentleman, which I hope he knows how to do with safety. His lordship's orders are that you accompany them and carry the cartridges. And, Charles, you will please keep count of the number fired and what is killed dead, not reckoning runners. I'm sick of them stories of runners."

These directions were given in a portentous stage aside which we were not supposed to hear. They caused Scroope to snigger and Charles to grin, but in me they raised a feeling of indignation.

I took one of the guns and looked at it. It was a costly and beautifully made weapon of the period, with an under-lever action.

"There's nothing wrong with the gun, sir," rumbled Red Waistcoat. "If you hold it straight it will do the rest. But keep the muzzle up, sir, keep it up, for I know what the bore is without studying the same with my eye. Also perhaps you won't take it amiss if I tell you that here at Ragnall we hates a low pheasant. I mention it because the last gentleman who came from foreign parts—he was French, he was—shot nothing all day but one hen bird sitting just on the top of the brush, two beaters, his lordship's hat, and a starling."

At this point Scroope broke into a roar of idiotic laughter. Charles, from whom Fortune decreed that I was not to escape, after all, turned his back and doubled up as though seized with sudden pain in the stomach, and I grew absolutely furious.

"Confound it, Mr. Keeper," I explained, "what do you mean by lecturing me? Attend to your business, and I'll attend to mine."

At this moment who should appear from behind the angle of some building—we were talking in the stable yard, near the gun-room—but Lord Ragnall himself. I could see that he had overheard the conversation, for he looked angry.

"Jenkins," he said, addressing the keeper, "do what Mr. Quatermain has said and attend to your own business. Perhaps you are not aware that he has shot more lions, elephants, and other big game than you have cats. But, however that may be, it is not your place to try to instruct him or any of my guests. Now go and see to the beaters."

"Beg pardon, my lord," ejaculated Jenkins, his face, that was as florid as his waistcoat, turning quite pale; "no offence meant, my lord, but elephants and lions don't fly, my lord, and those accustomed to such ground varmin are apt to shoot low, my lord. Beaters all ready at the Hunt Copse, my lord."

Thus speaking he backed himself out of sight. Lord Ragnall watched him go, then said with a laugh:

"I apologize to you, Mr. Quatermain. That silly old fool was part of my inheritance, so to speak; and the joke of it is that he is himself the worst and most dangerous shot I ever saw. However, on the other hand, he is the best rearer of pheasants in the county, so I put up with him. Come in, now, won't you? Charles will look after your guns and cartridges."

So Scroope and I were taken through a side entrance into the big hall and there introduced to the other members of the shooting party, most of whom were staying at the castle. They were famous shots. Indeed, I had read of the prowess of some of them in *The Field*, a paper that I always took in Africa, although often enough, when I was on my distant expeditions, I did not see a copy of it for a year at a time.

To my astonishment I found that I knew one of these gentlemen. We had not, it is true, met for a dozen years; but I seldom forget a face, and I was sure that I could not be mistaken in this instance. That mean appearance, those small, shifty grey eyes, that red, pointed nose could belong to nobody except Van Koop, so famous in his day in South Africa in connexion with certain gigantic and most successful frauds that the law seemed quite unable to touch, of which frauds I had been one of the many victims to the extent of £250, a large sum for me.

The last time we met there had been a stormy scene between us, which ended in my declaring in my wrath that if I came across him on the *veld* I should shoot him at sight. Perhaps that was one of the reasons why Mr. van Koop vanished from South Africa, for I may add that he was a cur of the first water. I believe that he had only just entered the room, having driven over from wherever he lived at some distance from Ragnall. At any rate, he knew nothing of my presence at this shoot. Had he known I am quite sure that he would have been absent. He turned, and seeing me, ejaculated: "Allan Quatermain, by heaven!" beneath his breath, but in such a tone of astonishment that it attracted the attention of Lord Ragnall, who was standing near.

"Yes, Mr. van Koop," I answered in a cheerful voice, "Allan Quatermain, no other, and I hope you are as glad to see me as I am to see you."

"I think there is some mistake," said Lord Ragnall, staring at us. "This is Sir Junius Fortescue, who used to be Mr. Fortescue."

"Indeed," I replied. "I don't know that I ever remember his being called by that particular name, but I do know that we are old—friends."

Lord Ragnall moved away as though he did not wish to continue the conversation, which no one else had overheard, and Van Koop sidled up to me.

"Mr. Quatermain," he said in a low voice, "circumstances have changed with me since last we met."

"So I gather," I replied; "but mine have remained much the same, and if it is convenient to you to repay me that £250 you owe me, with interest, I shall be much obliged. If not, I think I have a good story to tell about you."

"Oh, Mr. Quatermain," he answered with a sort of smile which made me feel inclined to kick him, "you know I dispute that debt."

"Do you?" I exclaimed. "Well, perhaps you will dispute the story also. But the question is, will you be believed when I give the proofs?"

"Ever heard of the Statute of Limitations, Mr. Quatermain?" he asked with a sneer.

"Not where character is concerned," I replied stoutly. "Now, what are you going to do?"

He reflected for a moment, and answered:

"Look here, Mr. Quatermain, you were always a bit of a sportsman, and I'll make you an offer. If I kill more birds than you do today, you shall promise to hold your tongue about my affairs in South Africa; and if you kill more than I do, you shall still hold your tongue, but I will pay you that £250 and interest for six years."

I also reflected for a moment, knowing that the man had something up his sleeve. Of course, I could refuse and make a scandal. But that was not in my line, and would not bring me nearer my £250, which, if I chanced to win, might find its way back to me.

"All right, done!" I said.

"What is your bet, Sir Junius?" asked Lord Ragnall, who was approaching again.

"It is rather a long story," he answered, "but, to put it shortly, years ago, when I was travelling in Africa, Mr. Quatermain and I had a dispute as to a sum of £5 which he thought I owed him, and to save argument about a trifle we have agreed that I should shoot against him for it today."

"Indeed," said Lord Ragnall rather seriously, for I could see that he did not believe Van Koop's statement as to the amount of the bet; perhaps he had heard more than we thought. "To be frank, Sir Junius, I don't much care for betting—for that's what it comes to—here. Also I think Mr. Quatermain said yesterday that he had never shot pheasants in England, so the match seems scarcely fair. However, you gentlemen know your own business best. Only I must tell you both that if money is concerned, I shall have to set someone whose decision will be final to count your birds and report the number to me."

"Agreed," said Van Koop, or, rather, Sir Junius; but I answered nothing, for, to tell the truth, already I felt ashamed of the whole affair.

As it happened, Lord Ragnall and I walked together ahead of the others, to the first covert, which was half a mile or more away.

"You have met Sir Junius before?" he said to me interrogatively.

"I have met Mr. van Koop before," I answered, "about twelve years since, shortly after which he vanished from South Africa, where he was a well-known and very successful—speculator."

"To reappear here. Ten years ago he bought a large property in this neighbourhood. Three years ago he became a baronet."

"How did a man like Van Koop become a baronet?" I inquired.

"By purchase, I believe."

"By purchase! Are honours in England purchased?"

"You are delightfully innocent, Mr. Quatermain, as a hunter from Africa should be," said Lord Ragnall, laughing. "Your friend——"

"Excuse me, Lord Ragnall, I am a very humble person, not so elevated, indeed, as that gamekeeper of yours; therefore I should not venture to call Sir Junius, late Mr. van Koop, my friend, at least in earnest."

He laughed again.

"Well, the individual with whom you make bets subscribed largely to the funds of his party. I am telling you what I know to be true, though the amount I do not know. It has been variously stated to be from fifteen to fifty thousand pounds, and, perhaps by coincidence, subsequently was somehow created a baronet."

I stared at him.

"That's all the story," he went on. "I don't like the man myself, but he is a wonderful pheasant shot, which passes him everywhere. Shooting has become a kind of fetish in these parts, Mr. Quatermain. For instance, it is a tradition on this estate that we must kill more pheasants than on any other in the country, and therefore I have to ask the best guns, who are not always the best fellows. It annoys me, but it seems that I must do what was done before me."

"Under those circumstances I should be inclined to give up the thing altogether, Lord Ragnall. Sport as sport is good, but when it becomes a business it grows hateful. I know, who have had to follow it as a trade for many years."

"That's an idea," he replied reflectively. "Meanwhile, I do hope that you will win back your—£5 from Sir Junius. He is so vain that I would gladly give £50 to see you do so."

"There is little chance of that," I said, "for, as I told you, I have never shot pheasants before. Still, I'll try, as you wish it."

"That's right. And look here, Mr. Quatermain, shoot well forward of them. You see, I am venturing to advise you now, as you advised me yesterday. Shot does not travel so fast as ball, and the pheasant is a bird that is generally going much quicker than you think. Now, here we are. Charles will show you your stand. Good luck to you."

Ten minutes later the game began outside of a long covert, all the seven guns being posted within sight of each other. So occupied was I in watching the preliminaries, which were quite new to me, that I allowed first a hare and then a hen pheasant to depart without firing at them, which hen pheasant, by the way, curved round and was beautifully killed by Van Koop, who stood two guns off upon my right.

"Look here, Allan," said Scroope, "if you are going to beat your African friend you had better wake up, for you won't do it by admiring the scenery or that squirrel on a tree."

So I woke up. Just at that moment there was a cry of "cock forward." I thought it meant a cock pheasant, and was astonished when I saw a beautiful brown bird with a long beak flitting towards me through the tops of the oak trees.

"Am I to shoot at that?" I asked.

"Of course. It is a woodcock," answered Scroope.

By this time the brown bird was rocking past me within ten yards. I fired and killed it, for where it had been appeared nothing but a cloud of feathers. It was a quick and clever shot, or so I thought. But when Charles stepped out and picked from the ground only a beak and a head, a titter of laughter went down the whole line of guns and loaders.

"I say, old chap," said Scroope, "if you will use No. 3 shot, let your birds get a little farther off you."

The incident upset me so much that immediately afterwards I missed three easy pheasants in succession, while Van Koop added two to his bag.

Scroope shook his head and Charles groaned audibly. Now that I was not in competition with his master he had become suddenly anxious that I should win, for in some mysterious way the news of that bet had spread, and my adversary was not popular amongst the keeper class.

"Here you come again," said Scroope, pointing to an advancing pheasant.

It was an extraordinarily high pheasant, flushed, I think, outside the covert by a stop, so high that, as it travelled down the line, although three guns fired at it, including Van Koop, none of them seemed to touch it. Then I fired, and remembering Lord Ragnall's advice, far in front. Its flight changed. Still it travelled through the air, but with the momentum of a stone to fall fifty yards to my right, dead.

291

"That's better!" said Scroope, while Charles grinned all over his round face, muttering:

"Wiped his eye that time."

This shot seemed to give me confidence, and I improved considerably, though, oddly enough, I found that it was the high and difficult pheasants which I killed and the easy ones that I was apt to muff. But Van Koop, who was certainly a finished artist, killed both.

At the next stand Lord Ragnall, who had been observing my somewhat indifferent performance, asked me to stand back with him behind the other guns.

"I see the tall ones are your line, Mr. Quatermain," he said, "and you will get some here."

On this occasion we were placed in a dip between two long coverts which lay about three hundred yards apart. That which was being beaten proved full of pheasants, and the shooting of those picked guns was really a thing to see. I did quite well here, nearly, but not altogether, as well as Lord Ragnall himself, though that is saying a great deal, for he was a lovely shot.

"Bravo!" he said at the end of the beat. "I believe you have got a chance of winning your £5, after all."

When, however, at luncheon, more than an hour later, I found that I was thirty pheasants behind my adversary, I shook my head, and so did everybody else. On the whole, that luncheon, of which we partook in a keeper's house, was a very pleasant meal, though Van Koop talked so continuously and in such a boastful strain that I saw it irritated our host and some of the other gentlemen, who were very pleasant people. At last he began to patronize me, asking me how I had been getting on with my "elephant-potting" of late years.

I replied, "Fairly well."

"Then you should tell our friends some of your famous stories, which I promise I won't contradict," he said, adding: "You see, they are different from us, and have no experience of big-game shooting."

"I did not know that you had any, either, Sir Junius," I answered, nettled. "Indeed, I thought I remembered your telling me in Africa that the only big game you had ever shot was an ox sick with the redwater. Anyway, shooting is a business with me, not an amusement, as it is to you, and I do not talk shop."

At this he collapsed amid some laughter, after which Scroope, the most loyal of friends, began to repeat exploits of mine till my ears tingled, and I rose and went outside to look at the weather.

It had changed very much during luncheon. The fair promise of the morning had departed, the sky was overcast, and a wind, blowing in strong gusts, was rising rapidly, driving before it occasional scurries of snow.

"My word," said Lord Ragnall, who had joined me, "the Lake covert—that's our great stand here, you know—will take some shooting this afternoon. We ought to kill seven hundred pheasants in it with this team, but I doubt if we shall get five. Now, Mr. Quatermain, I am going to stand Sir Junius Fortescue and you back in the covert, where you will have the best of it, as a lot of pheasants will never face the lake against this wind. What is more, I am coming with you, if I may, as six guns are enough for this beat, and I don't mean to shoot any more today."

"I fear that you will be disappointed," I said nervously.

"Oh, no, I sha'n't," he answered. "I tell you frankly that if only you could have a season's practice, in my opinion you would make the best pheasant shot of the lot of us. At present you don't quite understand the ways of the birds, that's all; also those guns are strange to you. Have a glass of cherry brandy; it will steady your nerves."

I drank the cherry brandy, and presently off we went. The covert we were going to shoot, into which we had been driving pheasants all the morning, must have been nearly a mile long. At the top end it was broad, narrowing at the bottom to a width of about two hundred yards. Here it ran into a horse-shoe shaped piece of water that was about fifty yards in breadth. Four of the guns were placed round the bow of this water, but on its farther side, in such a position that the pheasants should stream over them to yet another covert behind at the top of a slope, Van Koop and I, however, were ordered to take our places, he to the right and I to the left, about seventy yards up the tongue in little glades in the woodland, having the lake to our right and our left respectively. I noticed with dismay that we were so set that the guns below us on its farther side could note all that we did or did not do; also that a little band of watchers, among whom I recognized my friend the gunsmith, were gathered in a place where, without interfering with us, they could see the sport. On our way to the boat, however, which was to row us across the water, an incident happened that put me in very good spirits and earned some applause.

I was walking with Lord Ragnall, Scroope and Charles, about sixty yards clear of a belt of tall trees, when from far away on the other side of the trees came a cry of "Partridges over!" in the hoarse voice of the red-waistcoated Jenkins, who was engaged in superintending the driving in of some low scrub before he joined his army at the top of the covert.

"Look out, Mr. Quatermain, they are coming this way," said Lord Ragnall, while Charles thrust a loaded gun into my hand.

Another moment and they appeared over the tree-tops, a big covey of them in a long, straggling line, travelling at I know not what speed, for a fierce gust from the rising gale had caught them. I fired at the first bird, which fell at my feet. I fired again, and another fell behind me. I snatched up the second gun and killed a third as it passed over me high up. Then, wheeling round, I covered the last retreating bird, and lo! it too fell, a very long shot indeed.

"By George!" said Scroope, "I never saw that done before," while Ragnall stared and Charles whistled.

But now I will tell the truth and expose all my weakness. The second bird was not the one I aimed at. I was behind it and caught that which followed. And in my vanity I did not own up, at least not till that evening.

The four dead partridges—there was not a runner among them—having been collected amidst many congratulations, we went on and were punted across the lake to the covert. As we entered the boat I observed that, in addition to the great bags, Charles was carrying a box of cartridges under his arm, and asked him where he got it from.

He replied, from Mr. Popham—that was the gunsmith's name—who had brought it with him in case I should not have enough. I made no remark, but as I knew I had quite half of my cartridges left out of the three hundred and fifty that I had bought, I wondered to myself what kind of a shoot this was going to be.

Well, we took up our stands, and while we were doing so, suddenly the wind increased to a tearing gale, which seemed to me to blow from all points of the compass in turn. Rooks flying homewards, and pigeons disturbed by the beaters were swept over us like drifting leaves; wild duck, of which I got one, went by like arrows; the great bare oaks tossed their boughs and groaned; while not far off a fir tree was blown down, falling with a splash into the water.

"It's a wild afternoon," said Lord Ragnall, and as he spoke Van Koop came from his stand, looking rather scared, and suggested that the shoot should be given up.

Lord Ragnall asked me what I wished to do. I replied that I would rather go on, but that I was in his hands.

"I think we are fairly safe in these open places, Sir Junius," he said; "and as the pheasants have been so much disturbed already, it does not much matter if they are blown about a bit. But if you are of another opinion, perhaps you had better get out of it and stand with the others over the lake. I'll send for my guns and take your place."

On hearing this Van Koop changed his mind and said that he would go on.

So the beat began. At first the wind blew from behind us, and pheasants in increasing numbers passed over our heads, most of them rather low, to the guns on the farther side of the water, who, skilled though they were, did not make very good work with them. We had been instructed not to fire at birds going forward, so I let these be. Van Koop, however, did not interpret the order in the same spirit, for he loosed at several, killing one or two and missing others.

"That fellow is no sportsman," I heard Lord Ragnall remark. "I suppose it is the bet."

Then he sent Charles to ask him to desist.

Shortly after this the gale worked round to the north and settled there, blowing with ever-increasing violence. The pheasants, however, still flew forward in the shelter of the trees, for they were making for the covert on the hill, where they had been bred. But when they got into the open and felt the full force of the wind, quite four out of six of them turned and came back at a most fearful pace, many so high as to be almost out of shot.

For the next three-quarters of an hour or more—as I think I have explained, the beat was a very long one—I had such covert shooting as I suppose I shall never see again. High above those shrieking trees, or over the lake to my left, flashed the wind-driven pheasants in an endless procession. Oddly enough, I found that this wild work suited me, for as time went on and the pheasants grew more and more impossible, I shot better and better. One after another down they came far behind me with a crash in the brushwood or a splash in the lake, till the guns grew almost too hot to hold. There were so many of them that I discovered I could pick my shots; also that nine out of ten were caught by the wind and curved at a certain angle, and that the time to fire was just before they took the curve. The excitement was great and the sport splendid, as anyone will testify who has shot December pheasants breaking back over the covert and in a tearing gale. Van Koop also was doing very well, but the guns in front got comparatively little shooting. They were forced to stand there, poor fellows, and watch our performance from afar.

As the thing drew towards an end the birds came thicker and thicker, and I shot, as I have said, better and better. This may be judged from the fact that, notwithstanding their height and tremendous pace, I killed my last thirty pheasants with thirty-five cartridges. The final bird of all, a splendid cock, appeared by himself out of nothingness

295

when we thought that all was done. I think it must have been flushed from the covert on the hill, or been turned back just as it reached it by the resistless strength of the storm. Over it came, so high above us that it looked quite small in the dark snow-scud.

"Too far—no use!" said Lord Ragnall, as I lifted the gun.

Still, I fired, holding I know not how much in front, and lo! that pheasant died in mid air, falling with a mighty splash near the bank of the lake, but at a great distance behind us. The shot was so remarkable that everyone who saw it, including most of the beaters, who had passed us by now, uttered a cheer, and the red-waistcoated old Jenkins, who had stopped by us, remarked: "Well, bust me if that bain't a master one!"

Scroope made me angry by slapping me so hard upon the back that it hurt, and nearly caused me to let off the other barrel of the gun. Charles seemed to become one great grin, and Lord Ragnall, with a brief congratulatory "Never enjoyed a shoot so much in my life," called to the men who were posted behind us to pick up all the dead pheasants, being careful to keep mine apart from those of Sir Junius Fortescue.

"You should have a hundred and forty-three at this stand," he said, "allowing for every possible runner. Charles and I make the same total."

I remarked that I did not think there were many runners, as the No. 3 shot had served me very well, and getting into the boat was rowed to the other side, where I received more congratulations. Then, as all further shooting was out of the question because of the weather, we walked back to the castle to tea.

As I emptied my cup Lord Ragnall, who had left the room, returned and asked us to come and see the game. So we went, to find it laid out in endless lines upon the snow-powdered grass in the quadrangle of the castle, arranged in one main and two separate lots.

"Those are yours and Sir Junius's," said Scroope. "I wonder which of you has won. I'll put a sovereign on you, old fellow."

"Then you're a donkey for your pains," I answered, feeling vexed, for at that moment I had forgotten all about the bet.

I do not remember how many pheasants were killed altogether, but the total was much smaller than had been hoped for, because of the gale.

"Jenkins," said Lord Ragnall presently to Red Waistcoat, "how many have you to the credit of Sir Junius Fortescue?"

"Two hundred and seventy-seven, my lord, twelve hares, two woodcocks, and three pigeons."

"And how many to that of Mr. Quatermain?" adding: "I must remind you both, gentlemen, that the birds have been picked as carefully

296

as possible and kept unmixed, and therefore that the figures given by Jenkins must be considered as final."

"Quite so," I answered, but Van Koop said nothing. Then, while we all waited anxiously, came the amazing answer:

"Two hundred and seventy-seven pheasants, my lord, same number as those of Sir Junius, Bart., fifteen hares, three pigeons, four partridges, one duck, and a beak—I mean a woodcock."

"Then it seems you have won your £5, Mr. Quatermain, upon which I congratulate you," said Lord Ragnall.

"Stop a minute," broke in Van Koop. "The bet was as to pheasants; the other things don't count."

"I think the term used was 'birds,'" I remarked. "But to be frank, when I made it I was thinking of pheasants, as no doubt Sir Junius was also. Therefore, if the counting is correct, there is a dead heat and the wager falls through."

"I am sure we all appreciate the view you take of the matter," said Lord Ragnall, "for it might be argued another way. In these circumstances Sir Junius keeps his £5 in his pocket. It is unlucky for you, Quatermain," he added, dropping the "mister," "that the last high pheasant you shot can't be found. It fell into the lake, you remember, and, I suppose, swam ashore and ran."

"Yes," I replied, "especially as I could have sworn that it was quite dead."

"So could I, Quatermain; but the fact remains that it isn't there."

"If we had all the pheasants that we think fall dead our bags would be much bigger than they are," remarked Van Koop, with a look of great relief upon his face, adding in his horrid, patronizing way: "Still, you shot uncommonly well, Quatermain. I'd no idea you would run me so close."

I felt inclined to answer, but didn't. Only Lord Ragnall said:

"Mr. Quatermain shot more than well. His performance in the Lake covert was the most brilliant that I have ever seen. When you went in there together, Sir Junius, you were thirty ahead of him, and you fired seventeen more cartridges at the stand."

Then, just as we turned to go, something happened. The round-eyed Charles ran puffing into the quadrangle, followed by another man with a dog, who had been specially set to pick my birds, and carrying in his hand a much-bedraggled cock pheasant without a tail.

"I've got him, my lord," he gasped, for he had run very fast; "the little gent's—I mean that which he killed in the clouds with the last shot he fired. It had gone right down into the mud and stuck there. Tom and me fished him up with a pole."

Lord Ragnall took the bird and looked at it. It was almost cold, but evidently freshly killed, for the limbs were quite flexible.

"That turns the scale in favour of Mr. Quatermain," he said, "so, Sir Junius, you had better pay your money and congratulate him, as I do."

"I protest," exclaimed Van Koop, looking very angry and meaner than usual. "How am I to know that this was Mr. Quatermain's pheasant? The sum involved is more than £5 and I feel it is my duty to protest."

"Because my men say so, Sir Junius; moreover, seeing the height from which the bird fell, their story is obviously true."

Then he examined the pheasant further, pointing out that it appeared to have only one wound—a shot through the throat almost exactly at the root of the beak, of which shot there was no mark of exit. "What sized shot were you using, Sir Junius?" he asked.

"No. 4 at the last stand."

"And you were using No. 3, Mr. Quatermain. Now, was any other gun using No. 3?"

All shook their heads.

"Jenkins, open that bird's head. I think the shot that killed it will be found in the brain."

Jenkins obeyed, using a penknife cleverly enough. Pressed against the bone of the skull he found the shot.

"No. 3 it is, sure enough, my lord," he said.

"You will agree that settles the matter, Sir Junius," said Lord Ragnall. "And now, as a bet has been made here it had better be paid."

"I have not enough money on me," said Van Koop sulkily.

"I think your banker is mine," said Lord Ragnall quietly, "so you can write a cheque in the house. Come in, all of you, it is cold in this wind."

So we went into the smoking-room, and Lord Ragnall, who, I could see, was annoyed, instantly fetched a blank cheque from his study and handed it to Van Koop in rather a pointed manner.

He took it, and turning to me, said:

"I remember the capital sum, but how much is the interest? Sorry to trouble you, but I am not very good at figures."

"Then you must have changed a good deal during the last twelve years, Sir Junius," I could not help saying. "Still, never mind the interest, I shall be quite satisfied with the principal."

So he filled up the cheque for £250 and threw it down on the table before me, saying something about its being a bother to mix up business with pleasure.

I took the draft, saw that it was correct though rather illegible, and proceeded to dry it by waving it in the air. As I did so it came into my mind that I would not touch the money of this successful scamp, won back from him in such a way.

Yielding to a perhaps foolish impulse, I said:

"Lord Ragnall, this cheque is for a debt which years ago I wrote off as lost. At luncheon today you were talking of a Cottage Hospital for which you are trying to get up an endowment fund in this neighbourhood, and in answer to a question from you Sir Junius Fortescue said that he had not as yet made any subscription to its fund. Will you allow me to hand you Sir Junius's subscription—to be entered in his name, if you please?" And I passed him the cheque, which was drawn to myself or bearer.

He looked at the amount, and seeing that it was not £5, but £250, flushed, then asked:

"What do you say to this act of generosity on the part of Mr. Quatermain, Sir Junius?"

There was no answer, because Sir Junius had gone. I never saw him again, for years ago the poor man died quite disgraced. His passion for semi-fraudulent speculations reasserted itself, and he became a bankrupt in conditions which caused him to leave the country for America, where he was killed in a railway accident while travelling as an immigrant. I have heard, however, that he was not asked to shoot at Ragnall any more.

The cheque was passed to the credit of the Cottage Hospital, but not, as I had requested, as a subscription from Sir Junius Fortescue. A couple of years later, indeed, I learned that this sum of money was used to build a little room in that institution to accommodate sick children, which room was named the Allan Quatermain ward.

Now, I have told this story of that December shoot because it was the beginning of my long and close friendship with Ragnall.

When he found that Van Koop had gone away without saying good-bye, Lord Ragnall made no remark. Only he took my hand and shook it.

I have only to add that, although, except for the element of competition which entered into it, I enjoyed this day's shooting very much indeed, when I came to count up its cost I felt glad that I had not been asked to any more such entertainments. Here it is, taken from an old note-book:

Cartridges, including those not used and given to Charles	£4	0	0
Game License	£3	0	0

Tip to Red Waistcoat (keeper)	£2	0	0
Tip to Charles	£0	10	0
Tip to man who helped Charles to find pheasant	£0	5	0
Tip to man who collected pheasants behind me	£0	10	0
	£10	5	0

Truly pheasant shooting in England is, or was, a sport for the rich!

CHAPTER 3

Miss Holmes

Two and a half hours passed by, most of which time I spent lying down to rest and get rid of a headache caused by the continual, rapid firing and the roar of the gale, or both; also in rubbing my shoulder with ointment, for it was sore from the recoil of the guns. Then Scroope appeared, as, being unable to find my way about the long passages of that great old castle, I had asked him to do, and we descended together to the large drawing-room.

It was a splendid apartment, only used upon state occasions, lighted, I should think, with at least two or three hundred wax candles, which threw a soft glow over the panelled and pictured walls, the priceless antique furniture, and the bejewelled ladies who were gathered there. To my mind there never was and never will be any artificial light to equal that of wax candles in sufficient quantity. The company was large; I think thirty sat down to dinner that night, which was given to introduce Lord Ragnall's future wife to the neighbourhood, whereof she was destined to be the leader.

Miss Manners, who was looking very happy and charming in her jewels and fine clothes, joined us at once, and informed Scroope that "she" was just coming; the maid in the cloakroom had told her so.

"Is she?" replied Scroope indifferently. "Well, so long as you have come I don't care about anyone else."

Then he told her she was looking beautiful, and stared at her with such affection that I fell back a step or two and contemplated a picture of Judith vigorously engaged in cutting off the head of Holofernes.

Presently the large door at the end of the room was thrown open and the immaculate Savage, who was acting as a kind of master of the ceremonies, announced in well-bred but penetrating tones, "Lady Longden and the Honourable Miss Holmes." I stared, like everybody else, but for a while her ladyship filled my eye. She was an ample and,

301

to my mind, rather awful-looking person, clad in black satin—she was a widow—and very large diamonds. Her hair was white, her nose was hooked, her dark eyes were penetrating, and she had a bad cold in her head. That was all I found time to notice about her, for suddenly her daughter came into my line of vision.

Truly she was a lovely girl, or rather, young woman, for she must have been two or three-and-twenty. Not very tall, her proportions were rounded and exquisite, and her movements as graceful as those of a doe. Altogether she was doe-like, especially in the fineness of her lines and her large and liquid eyes. She was a dark beauty, with rich brown, waving hair, a clear olive complexion, a perfectly shaped mouth and very red lips. To me she looked more Italian or Spanish than Anglo-Saxon, and I believe that, as a matter of fact, she had some southern blood in her on her father's side. She wore a dress of soft rose colour, and her only ornaments were a string of pearls and a single red camellia. I could see but one blemish, if it were a blemish, in her perfect person, and that was a curious white mark upon her breast, which in its shape exactly resembled the crescent moon.

The face, however, impressed me with other than its physical qualities. It was bright, intelligent, sympathetic and, just now, happy. But I thought it more, I thought it mystical. Something that her mother said to her, probably about her dress, caused her smile to vanish for a moment, and then, from beneath it as it were, appeared this shadow of innate mysticism. In a second it was gone and she was laughing again; but I, who am accustomed to observe, had caught it, perhaps alone of all that company. Moreover, it reminded me of something.

What was it? Ah! I knew. A look that sometimes I had seen upon the face of a certain Zulu lady named Mameena, especially at the moment of her wonderful and tragic death. The thought made me shiver a little; I could not tell why, for certainly, I reflected, this high-placed and fortunate English girl had nothing in common with that fate-driven Child of Storm, whose dark and imperial spirit dwelt in the woman called Mameena. They were as far apart as Zululand is from Essex. Yet it was quite sure that both of them had touch with hidden things.

Lord Ragnall, looking more like a splendid Van Dyck than ever in his evening dress, stepped forward to greet his fiancée and her mother with a courtly bow, and I turned again to continue my contemplation of the stalwart Judith and the very ugly head of Holofernes. Presently I was aware of a soft voice—a very rich and thrilling voice—asking quite close to me:

"Which is he? Oh! you need not answer, dear. I know him from the description."

"Yes," replied Lord Ragnall to Miss Holmes—for it was she—"you are quite right. I will introduce you to him presently. But, love, whom do you wish to take you in to dinner? I can't—your mother, you know; and as there are no titles here tonight, you may make your choice. Would you like old Dr. Jeffreys, the clergyman?"

"No," she replied, with quiet firmness, "I know him; he took me in once before. I wish Mr. Allan Quatermain to take me in. He is interesting, and I want to hear about Africa."

"Very well," he answered, "and he *is* more interesting than all the rest put together. But, Luna, why are you always thinking and talking about Africa? One might imagine that you were going to live there."

"So I may one day," she answered dreamily. "Who knows where one has lived, or where one will live!" And again I saw that mystic look come into her face.

I heard no more of that conversation, which it is improbable that anyone whose ears had not been sharpened by a lifetime of listening in great silences would have caught at all. To tell the truth, I made myself scarce, slipping off to the other end of the big room in the hope of evading the kind intentions of Miss Holmes. I have a great dislike of being put out of my place, and I felt that among all these local celebrities it was not fitting that I should be selected to take in the future bride on an occasion of this sort. But it was of no use, for presently Lord Ragnall hunted me up, bringing the young lady with him.

"Let me introduce you to Miss Holmes, Quatermain," he said. "She is anxious that you should take her in to dinner, if you will be so kind. She is very interested in—in——"

"Africa," I suggested.

"In Mr. Quatermain, who, I am told, is one of the greatest hunters in Africa," she corrected me, with a dazzling smile.

I bowed, not knowing what to say. Lord Ragnall laughed and vanished, leaving us together. Dinner was announced. Presently we were wending in the centre of a long and glittering procession across the central hall to the banqueting chamber, a splendid room with a roof like a church that was said to have been built in the times of the Plantagenets. Here Mr. Savage, who evidently had been looking out for her future ladyship, conducted us to our places, which were upon the left of Lord Ragnall, who sat at the head of the broad table with Lady Longden on his right. Then the old clergyman, Dr. Jeffreys, a pompous and rather frowsy ecclesiastic, said grace, for grace was still in fashion at such feasts in those days, asking Heaven to make us truly thankful for the dinner we were about to consume.

Certainly there was a great deal to be thankful for in the eating and drinking line, but of all I remember little, except a general vision of silver dishes, champagne, splendour, and things I did not want to eat being constantly handed to me. What I do remember is Miss Holmes, and nothing but Miss Holmes; the charm of her conversation, the light of her beautiful eyes, the fragrance of her hair, her most flattering interest in my unworthy self. To tell the truth, we got on "like fire in the winter grass," as the Zulus say, and when that dinner was over the grass was still burning.

I don't think that Lord Ragnall quite liked it, but fortunately Lady Longden was a talkative person. First she conversed about her cold in the head, sneezing at intervals, poor soul, and being reduced to send for another handkerchief after the entrées. Then she got off upon business matters; to judge from the look of boredom on her host's face, I think it must have been of settlements. Three times did I hear him refer her to the lawyers—without avail. Lastly, when he thought he had escaped, she embarked upon a quite vigorous argument with Dr. Jeffreys about church matters—I gathered that she was *low* and he was *high*—in which she insisted upon his lordship acting as referee.

"Do try and keep your attention fixed, George," I heard her say severely. "To allow it to wander when high spiritual affairs are under discussion (sneeze) is scarcely reverent. Could you tell the man to shut that door? The draught is dreadful. It is quite impossible for you to agree with both of us, as you say you do, seeing that metaphorically Dr. Jeffreys is at one pole and I am at the other." (Sneeze.)

"Then I wish I were at the Tropic of Cancer," I heard him mutter with a groan.

In vain; he had to keep his "attention fixed" on this point for the next three-quarters of an hour. So as Miss Manners was at the other side of me, and Scroope, unhampered by the presence of any prospective mother-in-law, was at the other side of her, for all practical purposes Miss Holmes and I were left alone.

She began by saying:

"I hear you beat Sir Junius Fortescue out shooting today, and won a lot of money from him which you gave to the Cottage Hospital. I don't like shooting, and I don't like betting; and it's strange, because you don't look like a man who bets. But I detest Sir Junius Fortescue, and that is a bond of union between us."

"I never said I detested him."

"No, but I am sure you do. Your face changed when I mentioned his name."

"As it happens, you are right. But, Miss Holmes, I should like you to understand that you were also right when you said I did not look like a betting man." And I told her some of the story of Van Koop and the £250.

"Ah!" she said, when I had finished, "I always felt sure he was a horror. And my mother wanted me, just because he pretended to be low church—but that's a secret."

Then I congratulated her upon her approaching marriage, saying what a joyful thing it was now and again to see everything going in real, happy, storybook fashion: beauty, male and female, united by love, high rank, wealth, troops of friends, health of body, a lovely and an ancient home in a settled land where dangers do not come—at present—respect and affection of crowds of dependants, the prospect of a high and useful career of a sort whereof the door is shut to most people, everything in short that human beings who are not actually royalty could desire or deserve. Indeed after my second glass of champagne I grew quite eloquent on these and kindred points, being moved thereto by memories of the misery that is in the world which formed so great a contrast to the lot of this striking and brilliant pair.

She listened to me attentively and answered:

"Thank you for your kind thoughts and wishes. But does it not strike you, Mr. Quatermain, that there is something ill-omened in such talk? I believe that it does; that as you finished speaking it occurred to you that after all the future is as much veiled from all of us as—as the picture which hangs behind its curtain of rose-coloured silk in Lord Ragnall's study is from you."

"How did you know that?" I asked sharply in a low voice. For by the strangest of coincidences, as I concluded my somewhat old-fashioned little speech of compliments, this very reflection had entered my mind, and with it the memory of the veiled picture which Mr. Savage had pointed out to me on the previous morning.

"I can't say, Mr. Quatermain, but I did know it. You were thinking of the picture, were you not?"

"And if I was," I said, avoiding a direct reply, "what of it? Though it is hidden from everybody else, he has only to draw the curtain and see—you."

"Supposing he should draw the curtain one day and see nothing, Mr. Quatermain?"

"Then the picture would have been stolen, that is all, and he would have to search for it till he found it again, which doubtless sooner or later he would do."

"Yes, sooner or later. But where? Perhaps you have lost a picture or two in your time, Mr. Quatermain, and are better able to answer the question than I am."

There was silence for a few moments, for this talk of lost pictures brought back memories which choked me.

Then she began to speak again, low, quickly, and with suppressed passion, but acting wonderfully all the while. Knowing that eyes were on her, her gestures and the expression of her face were such as might have been those of any young lady of fashion who was talking of everyday affairs, such as dancing, or flowers, or jewels. She smiled and even laughed occasionally. She played with the golden salt-cellar in front of her and, upsetting a little of the salt, threw it over her left shoulder, appearing to ask me if I were a victim of that ancient habit, and so on.

But all the while she was talking deeply of deep things, such as I should never have thought would pass her mind. This was the substance of what she said, for I cannot set it all down verbatim; after so many years my memory fails me.

"I am not like other women. Something moves me to tell you so, something very real and powerful which pushes me as a strong man might. It is odd, because I have never spoken to anyone else like that, not to my mother for instance, or even to Lord Ragnall. They would neither of them understand, although they would misunderstand differently. My mother would think I ought to see a doctor—and if you knew that doctor! He," and she nodded towards Lord Ragnall, "would think that my engagement had upset me, or that I had grown rather more religious than I ought to be at my age, and been reflecting too much—well, on the end of all things. From a child I have understood that I am a mystery set in the midst of many other mysteries. It all came to me one night when I was about nine years old. I seemed to see the past and the future, although I could grasp neither. Such a long, long past and such an infinite future. I don't know what I saw, and still see sometimes. It comes in a flash, and is in a flash forgotten. My mind cannot hold it. It is too big for my mind; you might as well try to pack Dr. Jeffreys there into this wineglass. Only two facts remain written on my heart. The first is that there is trouble ahead of me, curious and unusual trouble; and the second, that permanently, continually, I, or a part of me, have something to do with Africa, a country of which I know nothing except from a few very dull books. Also, by the way—this is a new thought—that I have a great deal to do with *you*. That is why I am so interested in Africa and you. Tell me about Africa and yourself now, while we have the chance." And she ended rather abruptly, adding in a louder voice, "You have lived there all your life, have you not, Mr. Quatermain?"

"I rather think your mother would be right—about the doctor, I mean," I said.

"You *say* that, but you don't *believe* it. Oh! you are very transparent, Mr. Quatermain—at least, to me."

So, hurriedly enough, for these subjects seemed to be uncomfortable, even dangerous in a sense, I began to talk of the first thing about Africa that I remembered—namely, of the legend of the Holy Flower that was guarded by a huge ape, of which I had heard from a white man who was supposed to be rather mad, who went by the name of Brother John. Also I told her that there was something in it, as I had with me a specimen of the flower.

"Oh! show it me," she said.

I replied that I feared I could not, as it was locked away in a safe in London, whither I was returning on the morrow. I promised, however, to send her a life-sized water-colour drawing of which I had caused several to be made. She asked me if I were going to look for this flower, and I said that I hoped so if I could make the necessary arrangements. Next she asked me if there chanced to be any other African quests upon which I had set my mind. I replied that there were several. For instance, I had heard vaguely through Brother John, and indirectly from one or two other sources, of the existence of a certain tribe in East Central Africa—Arabs or semi-Arabs—who were reported to worship a child that always remained a child. This child, I took it, was a dwarf; but as I was interested in native religious customs which were infinite in their variety, I should much like to find out the truth of the matter.

"Talking of Arabs," she broke in, "I will tell you a curious story. Once when I was a little girl, eight or nine years of age—it was just before that kind of awakening of which I have spoken to you—I was playing in Kensington Gardens, for we lived in London at the time, in the charge of my nurse-governess. She was talking to some young man who she said was her cousin, and told me to run about with my hoop and not to bother. I drove the hoop across the grass to some elm trees. From behind one of the trees came out two tall men dressed in white robes and turbans, who looked to me like scriptural characters in a picture-book. One was an elderly man with flashing, black eyes, hooked nose, and a long grey beard. The other was much younger, but I do not remember him so well. They were both brown in colour, but otherwise almost like white men; not Negroes by any means. My hoop hit the elder man, and I stood still, not knowing what to say. He bowed politely and picked it up, but did not offer to return it to me. They talked together rapidly, and one of them pointed to the moon-shaped birthmark which you see I have upon my neck, for it was hot weather, and I was wearing a low-cut frock. It was because of this mark that my father named me Luna. The elder of the two said in broken English:

"'What is your name, pretty little girl?'

"I told him it was Luna Holmes. Then he drew from his robe a box made of scented wood, and, opening it, took out some sweetmeat which looked as if it had been frozen, and gave me a piece that, being very fond of sweet, I put into my mouth. Next, he bowled the hoop along the ground into the shadow of the trees—it was evening time and beginning to grow dark—saying, 'Run, catch it, little girl!'

"I began to run, but something in the taste of that sweet caused me to drop it from my lips. Then all grew misty, and the next thing I remember was finding myself in the arms of the younger Eastern, with the nurse and her 'cousin,' a stalwart person like a soldier, standing in front of us.

"'Little girl go ill,' said the elder Arab. 'We seek policeman.'

"'You drop that child,' answered the 'cousin,' doubling his fists. Then I grew faint again, and when I came to myself the two white-robed men had gone. All the way home my governess scolded me for accepting sweets from strangers, saying that if my parents came to know of it, I should be whipped and sent to bed. Of course, I begged her not to tell them, and at last she consented. Do you know, I think you are the first to whom I have ever mentioned the matter, of which I am sure the governess never breathed a word, though after that, whenever we walked in the gardens, her 'cousin' always came to look after us. In the end I think she married him."

"You believe the sweet was drugged?" I asked.

She nodded. "There was something very strange in it. It was a night or two after I had tasted it that I had what just now I called my awakening, and began to think about Africa."

"Have you ever seen these men again, Miss Holmes?"

"No, never."

At this moment I heard Lady Longden say, in a severe voice:

"My dear Luna, I am sorry to interrupt your absorbing conversation, but we are all waiting for you."

So they were, for to my horror I saw that everyone was standing up except ourselves.

Miss Holmes departed in a hurry, while Scroope whispered in my ear with a snigger:

"I say, Allan, if you carry on like that with his young lady, his lordship will be growing jealous of you."

"Don't be a fool," I said sharply. But there was something in his remark, for as Lord Ragnall passed on his way to the other end of the table, he said in a low voice and with rather a forced smile:

"Well, Quatermain, I hope your dinner has not been as dull as mine, although your appetite seemed so poor."

Then I reflected that I could not remember having eaten a thing since the first entrée. So overcome was I that, rejecting all Scroope's attempts at conversation, I sat silent, drinking port and filling up with dates, until not long afterwards we went into the drawing-room, where I sat down as far from Miss Holmes as possible, and looked at a book of views of Jerusalem.

While I was thus engaged, Lord Ragnall, pitying my lonely condition, or being instigated thereto by Miss Holmes, I know not which, came up and began to chat with me about African big-game shooting. Also he asked me what was my permanent address in that country. I told him Durban, and in my turn asked why he wanted to know.

"Because Miss Holmes seems quite crazy about the place, and I expect I shall be dragged out there one day," he replied, quite gloomily. It was a prophetic remark.

At this moment our conversation was interrupted by Lady Longden, who came to bid her future son-in-law goodnight. She said that she must go to bed, and put her feet in mustard and water as her cold was so bad, which left me wondering whether she meant to carry out this operation in bed. I recommended her to take quinine, a suggestion she acknowledged rather inconsequently by remarking in somewhat icy tones that she supposed I sat up to all hours of the night in Africa. I replied that frequently I did, waiting for the sun to rise next day, for that member of the British aristocracy irritated me.

Thus we parted, and I never saw her again. She died many years ago, poor soul, and I suppose is now freezing her former acquaintances in the Shades, for I cannot imagine that she ever had a friend. They talk a great deal about the influences of heredity nowadays, but I don't believe very much in them myself. Who, for instance, could conceive that persons so utterly different in every way as Lady Longden and her daughter, Miss Holmes, could be mother and child? Our bodies, no doubt, we do inherit from our ancestors, but not our individualities. These come from far away.

A good many of the guests went at the same time, having long distances to drive on that cold frosty night, although it was only just ten o'clock. For as was usual at that period even in fashionable houses, we had dined at seven.

CHAPTER 4

Harût and Marût

After Lord Ragnall had seen his guests to the door in the old-fashioned manner, he returned and asked me if I played cards, or whether I preferred music. I was assuring him that I hated the sight of a card when Mr. Savage appeared in his silent way and respectfully inquired of his lordship whether any gentleman was staying in the house whose Christian name was *Here-come-a-zany*. Lord Ragnall looked at him with a searching eye as though he suspected him of being drunk, and then asked what he meant by such a ridiculous question.

"I mean, my lord," replied Mr. Savage with a touch of offence in his tone, "that two foreign individuals in white clothes have arrived at the castle, stating that they wish to speak at once with a *Mr. Here-come-a-zany* who is staying here. I told them to go away as the butler said he could make nothing of their talk, but they only sat down in the snow and said they would wait for *Here-come-a-zany*."

"Then you had better put them in the old guardroom, lock them up with something to eat, and send the stable-boy for the policeman, who is a zany if ever anybody was. I expect they are after the pheasants."

"Stop a bit," I said, for an idea had occurred to me. "The message may be meant for me, though I can't conceive who sent it. My native name is Macumazana, which possibly Mr. Savage has not caught quite correctly. Shall I go to see these men?"

"I wouldn't do that in this cold, Quatermain," Lord Ragnall answered. "Did they say what they are, Savage?"

"I made out that they were conjurers, my lord. At least when I told them to go away one of them said, 'You will go first, gentleman.' Then, my lord, I heard a hissing sound in my coat-tail pocket and, putting my hand into it, I found a large snake which dropped on the ground and vanished. It quite paralysed me, my lord, and while I stood there wondering whether I was bitten, a mouse jumped out of the kitchen maid's hair. She had been laughing at their dress, my lord, but *now* she's screaming in hysterics."

The solemn aspect of Mr. Savage as he narrated these unholy marvels was such that, like the kitchen maid, we both burst into ill-timed merriment. Attracted by our laughter, Miss Holmes, Miss Manners, with whom she was talking, and some of the other guests, approached and asked what was the matter.

"Savage here declares that there are two conjurers in the kitchen premises, who have been producing snakes out of his pocket and mice from the hair of one of the maids, and who want to see Mr. Quatermain," Lord Ragnall answered.

"Conjurers! Oh, do have them in, George," exclaimed Miss Holmes; while Miss Manners and the others, who were getting a little tired of promiscuous conversation, echoed her request.

"By all means," he answered, "though we have enough mice here without their bringing any more. Savage, go and tell your two friends that *Mr. Here-come-a-zany* is waiting for them in the drawing-room, and that the company would like to see some of their tricks."

Savage bowed and departed, like a hero to execution, for by his pallor I could see that he was in a great fright. When he had gone we set to work and cleared a space in the middle of the room, in front of which we arranged chairs for the company to sit on.

"No doubt they are Indian jugglers," said Lord Ragnall, "and will want a place to grow their mango-tree, as I remember seeing them do in Kashmir."

As he spoke the door opened and Mr. Savage appeared through it, walking much faster than was his wont. I noted also that he gripped the pockets of his swallow-tail coat firmly in his hand.

"Mr. Hare-root and Mr. Mare-root," he announced.

"Hare-root and Mare-root!" repeated Lord Ragnall.

"Harût and Marût, I expect," I said. "I think I have read somewhere that they were great magicians, whose names these conjurers have taken." (Since then I have discovered that they are mentioned in the Koran as masters of the Black Art.)

A moment later two men followed him through the doorway. The first was a tall, Eastern-looking person with a grave countenance, a long, white beard, a hooked nose, and flashing, hawk-like eyes. The second was shorter and rather stout, also much younger. He had a genial, smiling face, small, beady-black eyes, and was clean-shaven. They were very light in colour; indeed I have seen Italians who are much darker; and there was about their whole aspect a certain air of power.

Instantly I remembered the story that Miss Holmes had told me at dinner and looked at her covertly, to see that she had turned quite pale and was trembling a little. I do not think that anyone else noticed this, however, as all were staring at the strangers. Moreover she recovered herself in a moment, and, catching my eye, laid her finger on her lips in token of silence.

The men were clothed in thick, fur-lined cloaks, which they took off and, folding them neatly, laid upon the floor, standing revealed in robes of a beautiful whiteness and in large plain turbans, also white.

"High-class Somali Arabs," thought I to myself, noting the while that as they arranged the robes they were taking in every one of us with their quick eyes. One of them shut the door, leaving Savage on this side of it as though they meant him to be present. Then they walked towards us, each of them carrying an ornamental basket made apparently of split reeds, that contained doubtless their conjuring out-fit and probably the snake which Savage had found in his pocket. To my surprise they came straight to me, and, having set down the baskets, lifted their hands above their heads, as a person about to dive might do, and bowed till the points of their fingers touched the floor. Next they spoke, not in Arabic as I had expected that they would, but in Bantu, which of course I understood perfectly well.

"I, Harût, head priest and doctor of the White Kendah People, greet you, O Macumazana," said the elder man.

"I, Marût, a priest and doctor of the People of the White Kendah, greet you, O Watcher-by-night, whom we have travelled far to find," said the younger man. Then together,

"We both greet you, O Lord, who seem small but are great, O Chief with a troubled past and with a mighty future, O Beloved of Mameena who has 'gone down' but still speaks from beneath, Mameena who was and is of our company."

At this point it was my turn to shiver and become pale, as any may guess who may have chanced to read the history of Mameena, and the turn of Miss Holmes to watch *me* with animated interest.

"O Slayer of evil men and beasts!" they went on, in their rich-voiced, monotonous chant, "who, as our magic tells us, are destined to deliver our land from the terrible scourge, we greet you, we bow before you, we acknowledge you as our lord and brother, to whom we vow safety among us and in the desert, to whom we promise a great reward."

Again they bowed, once, twice, thrice; then stood silent before me with folded arms.

313

"What on earth are they saying?" asked Scroope. "I could catch a few words"—he knew a little kitchen Zulu—"but not much."

I told him briefly while the others listened.

"What does Mameena mean?" asked Miss Holmes, with a horrible acuteness. "Is it a woman's name?"

Hearing her, Harût and Marût bowed as though doing reverence to that name. I am sorry to say that at this point I grew confused, though really there was no reason why I should, and muttered something about a native girl who had made trouble in her day.

Miss Holmes and the other ladies looked at me with amused disbelief, and to my dismay the venerable Harût turned to Miss Holmes, and with his inevitable bow, said in broken English:

"Mameena very beautiful woman, perhaps more beautiful than you, lady. Mameena love the white lord Macumazana. She love him while she live, she love him now she dead. She tell me so again just now. You ask white lord tell you pretty story of how he kiss her before she kill herself."

Needless to say all this very misleading information was received by the audience with an attention that I can but call rapt, and in a kind of holy silence which was broken only by a sudden burst of sniggering on the part of Scroope. I favoured him with my fiercest frown. Then I fell upon that venerable villain Harût, and belaboured him in Bantu, while the audience listened as intently as though they understood.

I asked him what he meant by coming here to asperse my character. I asked him who the deuce he was. I asked him how he came to know anything about Mameena, and finally I told him that soon or late I would be even with him, and paused exhausted.

He stood there looking for all the world like a statue of the patriarch Job as I imagine him, and when I had done, replied without moving a muscle and in English:

"O Lord, Zikali, Zulu wizard, friend of mine! All great wizard friend just like all elephant and all snake. Zikali make me know Mameena, and she tell me story and send you much love, and say she wait for you always." (More sniggers from Scroope, and still intenser interest evinced by Miss Holmes and others.) "If you like, I show you Mameena 'fore I go." (Murmurs from Miss Holmes and Miss Manners of "Oh, *please* do!") "But that very little business, for what one long-ago lady out of so many?"

Then suddenly he broke into Bantu, and added: "A jest is a jest, Macumazana, though often there is meaning in a jest, and you shall see Mameena if you will. I come here to ask you to do my people

314

a service for which you shall not lack reward. We, the White Kendah, the People of the Child, are at war with the Black Kendah, our subjects who outnumber us. The Black Kendah have an evil spirit for a god, which spirit from the beginning has dwelt in the largest elephant in all the world, a beast that none can kill, but which kills many and bewitches more. While that elephant, which is named Jana, lives we, the People of the Child, go in terror, for day by day it destroys us. We have learned—how it does not matter—that you alone can kill that elephant. If you will come and kill it, we will show you the place where all the elephants go to die, and you shall take their ivory, many wagon-loads, and grow rich. Soon you are going on a journey that has to do with a flower, and you will visit peoples named the Mazitu and the Pongo who live on an island in a lake. Far beyond the Pongo and across the desert dwell my people, the Kendah, in a secret land. When you wish to visit us, as you will do, journey to the north of that lake where the Pongo dwell, and stay there on the edge of the desert shooting till we come. Now mock me if you will, but do not forget, for these things shall befall in their season, though that time be far. If we meet no more for a while, still do not forget. When you have need of gold or of the ivory that is gold, then journey to the north of the lake where the Pongo dwell, and call on the names of Harût and Marût."

"And call on the names of Harût and Marût," repeated the younger man, who hitherto appeared to take no interest in our talk.

Next, before I could answer, before I could think the thing out indeed, for all this breath from savage and mystical Africa blowing on me suddenly here in an Essex drawing-room, seemed to overwhelm me, the ineffable Harût proceeded in his English conjurer's patter:

"Rich ladies and gentlemen want see trick by poor old wizard from centre Africa. Well, we show them, but please 'member no magic, all quite simple trick. Teach it you if you pay. Please not look too hard, no want you learn how it done. What you like see? Tree grow out of nothing, eh? Good! Please lend me that plate—what you call him—china."

Then the performance began. The tree grew admirably upon the china plate under the cover of an antimacassar. A number of bits of stick danced together on the said plate, apparently without being touched. At a whistle from Marût a second snake crawled out of the pocket of the horrified Mr. Savage, who stood observing these proceedings at a respectful distance, erected itself on its tail upon the plate and took fire till it was consumed to ashes, and so forth.

The show was very good, but to tell the truth I did not take much notice of it, for I had seen similar things before and was engaged in thoughts much excited by what Harût had said to me. At length the pair paused amidst the clapping of the audience, and Marût began to pack up the properties as though all were done. Then Harût observed casually:

"The Lord Macumazana think this poor business and he right. Very poor business, any conjurer do better. All common trick"—here his eye fell upon Mr. Savage who was wriggling uneasily in the background. "What matter with that gentleman? Brother Marût, go see."

Brother Marût went and freed Mr. Savage from two more snakes which seemed to have taken possession of various parts of his garments. Also, amidst shouts of laughter, from a large dead rat which he appeared to draw from his well-oiled hair.

"Ah!" said Harût, as his confederate returned with these prizes, leaving Savage collapsed in a chair, "snake love that gentleman much. He earn great money in Africa. Well, he keep rat in hair; hungry snake always want rat. But as I say, this poor business. Now you like to see some better, eh? Mameena, eh?"

"No," I replied firmly, whereat everyone laughed.

"Elephant Jana we want you kill, eh? Just as he look this minute."

"Yes," I said, "very much indeed, only how will you show it me?"

"That quite easy, Macumazana. You just smoke little Kendah 'bacco and see many things, if you have gift, as I *think* you got, and as I almost *sure* that lady got," and he pointed to Miss Holmes. "Sometimes they things people want see, and sometimes they things people not want see."

"*Dakka*," I said contemptuously, alluding to the Indian hemp on which natives make themselves drunk throughout great districts of Africa.

"Oh! no, not *dakka*, that common stuff; this 'bacco much better than *dakka*, only grow in Kendahland. You think all nonsense? Well, you see. Give me match please."

Then while we watched he placed some tobacco, at least it looked like tobacco, in a little wooden bowl that he also produced from his basket. Next he said something to his companion, Marût, who drew a flute from his robe made out of a thick reed, and began to play on it a wild and melancholy music, the sound of which seemed to affect my backbone as standing on a great height often does. Presently too Harût broke into a low song whereof I could not understand a word, that rose and fell with the music of the flute. Now he struck a match, which seemed incongruous in the midst of this semi-magical ceremony, and taking a pinch of the tobacco, lit it and dropped it

316

among the rest. A pale, blue smoke arose from the bowl and with it a very sweet odour not unlike that of the tuberoses gardeners grow in hot-houses, but more searching.

"Now you breath smoke, Macumazana," he said, "and tell us what you see. Oh! no fear, that not hurt you. Just like cigarette. Look," and he inhaled some of the vapour and blew it out through his nostrils, after which his face seemed to change to me, though what the change was I could not define.

I hesitated till Scroope said:

"Come, Allan, don't shirk this Central African adventure. I'll try if you like."

"No," said Harût brusquely, "*you* no good."

Then curiosity and perhaps the fear of being laughed at overcame me. I took the bowl and held it under my nose, while Harût threw over my head the antimacassar which he had used in the mango trick, to keep in the fumes I suppose.

At first these fumes were unpleasant, but just as I was about to drop the bowl they seemed to become agreeable and to penetrate to the inmost recesses of my being. The general affect of them was not un-like that of the laughing gas which dentists give, with this difference, that whereas the gas produces insensibility, these fumes seemed to set the mind on fire and to burn away all limitations of time and distance. Things shifted before me. It was as though I were no longer in that room but travelling with inconceivable rapidity.

Suddenly I appeared to stop before a curtain of mist. The mist rolled up in front of me and I saw a wild and wonderful scene. There lay a lake surrounded by dense African forest. The sky above was still red with the last lights of sunset and in it floated the full moon. On the eastern side of the lake was a great open space where nothing seemed to grow and all about this space were the skeletons of hundreds of dead elephants. There they lay, some of them almost covered with grey mosses hanging to their bones, through which their yellow tusks projected as though they had been dead for centuries; others with the rotting hide still on them. I knew that I was looking on a cemetery of elephants, the place where these great beasts went to die, as I have since been told the extinct moas did in New Zealand. All my life as a hunter had I heard rumours of these cemeteries, but never before did I see such a spot even in a dream.

See! There was one dying now, a huge gaunt bull that looked as though it were several hundred years old. It stood there swaying to and fro. Then it lifted its trunk, I suppose to trumpet, though of course

I could hear nothing, and slowly sank upon its knees and so remained in the last relaxation of death.

Almost in the centre of this cemetery was a little mound of water-washed rock that had endured when the rest of the stony plain was denuded in past epochs. Suddenly upon that rock appeared the shape of the most gigantic elephant that ever I beheld in all my long experience. It had one enormous tusk, but the other was deformed and broken off short. Its sides were scarred as though with fighting and its eyes shone red and wickedly. Held in its trunk was the body of a woman whose hair hung down upon one side and whose feet hung down upon the other. Clasped in her arms was a child that seemed to be still living.

The rogue, as a brute of this sort is called, for evidently such it was, dropped the corpse to the ground and stood a while, flapping its ears. Then it felt for and picked up the child with its trunk, swung it to and fro and finally tossed it high into the air, hurling it far away. After this it walked to the elephant that I had just seen die, and charged the carcass, knocking it over. Then having lifted its trunk as though to trumpet in triumph, it shambled off towards the forest and vanished.

The curtain of mist fell again and in it, dimly, I thought I saw—well, never mind who or what I saw. Then I awoke.

"Well, did you see anything?" asked a chorus of voices.

I told them what I had seen, leaving out the last part.

"I say, old fellow," said Scroope, "you must have been pretty clever to get all that in, for your eyes weren't shut for more than ten seconds."

"Then I wonder what you would say if I repeated everything," I answered, for I still felt dreamy and not quite myself.

"You see elephant Jana?" asked Harût. "He kill woman and child, eh? Well, he do that every night. Well, that why people of White Kendah want you to kill *him* and take all that ivory which they no dare touch because it in holy place and Black Kendah not let them. So he live still. That what we wish know. Thank you much, Macumazana. You very good look through-distance man. Just what I think. Kendah 'bacco smoke work very well in you. Now, beautiful lady," he added turning to Miss Holmes, "you like look too? Better look. Who knows what you see?"

Miss Holmes hesitated a moment, studying me with an inquiring eye. But I made no sign, being in truth very curious to hear *her* experience.

"Yes," she said.

"I would prefer, Luna, that you left this business alone," remarked Lord Ragnall uneasily. "I think it is time that you ladies went to bed."

"Here is a match," said Miss Holmes to Harût who was engaged in putting more tobacco into the bowl, the suspicion of a smile upon his grave and statuesque countenance. Harût received the match with a low bow and fired the stuff as before. Then he handed the bowl, from which once again the blue smoke curled upwards, to Miss Holmes, and gently and gracefully let the antimacassar fall over it and her head, which it draped as a wedding veil might do. A few seconds later she threw off the antimacassar and cast the bowl, in which the fire was now out, on to the floor. Then she stood up with wide eyes, looking wondrous lovely and, notwithstanding her lack of height, majestic.

"I have been in another world," she said in a low voice as though she spoke to the air, "I have travelled a great way. I found myself in a small place made of stone. It was dark in the place, the fire in that bowl lit it up. There was nothing there except a beautiful statue of a naked baby which seemed to be carved in yellow ivory, and a chair made of ebony inlaid with ivory and seated with string. I stood in front of the statue of the Ivory Child. It seemed to come to life and smile at me. Round its neck was a string of red stones. It took them from its neck and set them upon mine. Then it pointed to the chair, and I sat down in the chair. That was all."

Harût followed her words with an interest that I could see was intense, although he attempted to hide it. Then he asked me to translate them, which I did.

As their full sense came home to him, although his face remained impassive, I saw his dark eyes shine with the light of triumph. Moreover I heard him whisper to Marût words that seemed to mean,

"The Sacred Child accepts the Guardian. The Spirit of the White Kendah finds a voice again."

Then as though involuntarily, but with the utmost reverence, both of them bowed deeply towards Miss Holmes.

A babble of conversation broke out.

"What a ridiculous dream," I heard Lord Ragnall say in a vexed voice. "An ivory child that seemed to come to life and to give you a necklace. Whoever heard such nonsense?"

"Whoever heard such nonsense?" repeated Miss Holmes after him, as though in polite acquiescence, but speaking as an automaton might speak.

"I say," interrupted Scroope, addressing Miss Manners, "this is a drawing-room entertainment and a half, isn't it, dear?"

"I don't know," answered Miss Manners, doubtfully, "it is rather too queer for my taste. Tricks are all very well, but when it comes to magic and visions I get frightened."

"Well, I suppose the show is over," said Lord Ragnall. "Quatermain, would you mind asking your conjurer friends what I owe them?"

Here Harût, who had understood, paused from packing up his properties and answered,

"Nothing, O great Lord, nothing. It is we owe you much. Here we learn what we want know long time. I mean if elephant Jana still kill people of Kendah. Kendah 'bacco no speak to us. Only speak to new spirit. You got great gift, lady, and you too, Macumazana. You not like smoke more Kendah 'bacco and look into past, eh? Better look! Very full, past, learn much there about all us; learn how things begin. Make you understand lot what seem odd today. No! Well, one day you look p'raps, 'cause past pull hard and call loud, only no one hear what it say. Goodnight, O great Lord. Goodnight, O beautiful lady. Goodnight, O Macumazana, till we meet again when you come kill elephant Jana. Blessing of the Heaven-Child, who give rain, who protect all danger, who give food, who give health, on you all."

Then making many obeisances they walked backwards to the door where they put on their long cloaks.

At a sign from Lord Ragnall I accompanied them, an office which, fearing more snakes, Mr. Savage was very glad to resign to me. Presently we stood outside the house amidst the moaning trees, and very cold it was there.

"What does all this mean, O men of Africa?" I asked.

"Answer the question yourself when you stand face to face with the great elephant Jana that has in it an evil spirit, O Macumazana," replied Harût. "Nay, listen. We are far from our home and we sought tidings through those who could give it to us, and we have won those tidings, that is all. We are worshippers of the Heavenly Child that is eternal youth and all good things, but of late the Child has lacked a tongue. Yet tonight it spoke again. Seek to know no more, you who in due season will know all things."

"Seek to know no more," echoed Marût, "who already, perhaps, know too much, lest harm should come to you, Macumazana."

"Where are you going to sleep tonight?" I asked.

"We do not sleep here," answered Harût, "we walk to the great city and thence find our way to Africa, where we shall meet you again. You know that we are no liars, common readers of thought and makers of tricks, for did not Dogeetah, the wandering white man, speak to you of the people of whom he had heard who worshipped the Child of

Heaven? Go in, Macumazana, ere you take harm in this horrible cold, and take with you this as a marriage gift from the Child of Heaven whom she met tonight, to the beautiful lady stamped with the sign of the young moon who is about to marry the great lord she loves."

Then he thrust a little linen-wrapped parcel into my hand and with his companion vanished into the darkness.

I returned to the drawing-room where the others were still discussing the remarkable performance of the two native conjurers.

"They have gone," I said in answer to Lord Ragnall, "to walk to London as they said. But they have sent a wedding-present to Miss Holmes," and I showed the parcel.

"Open it, Quatermain," he said again.

"No, George," interrupted Miss Holmes, laughing, for by now she seemed to have quite recovered herself, "I like to open my own presents."

He shrugged his shoulders and I handed her the parcel, which was neatly sewn up. Somebody produced scissors and the stitches were cut. Within the linen was a necklace of beautiful red stones, oval-shaped like amber beads and of the size of a robin's egg. They were roughly polished and threaded on what I recognized at once to be hair from an elephant's tail. From certain indications I judged these stones, which might have been spinels or carbuncles, or even rubies, to be very ancient. Possibly they had once hung round the neck of some lady in old Egypt. Indeed a beautiful little statuette, also of red stone, which was suspended from the centre of the necklace, suggested that this was so, for it may well have been a likeness of one of the great gods of the Egyptians, the infant Horus, the son of Isis.

"That is the necklace I saw which the Ivory Child gave me in my dream," said Miss Holmes quietly.

Then with much deliberation she clasped it round her throat.

CHAPTER 5

The Plot

The sequel to the events of this evening may be told very briefly and of it the reader can form his own judgment. I narrate it as it happened.

That night I did not sleep at all well. It may have been because of the excitement of the great shoot in which I found myself in competition with another man whom I disliked and who had defrauded me in the past, to say nothing of its physical strain in cold and heavy weather. Or it may have been that my imagination was stirred by the arrival of that strange pair, Harût and Marût, apparently in search of myself, seven thousand miles away from any place where they can have known aught of an insignificant individual with a purely local repute. Or it may have been that the pictures which they showed me when under the influence of the fumes of their *tobacco*—or of their hypnotism—took an undue possession of my brain.

Or lastly, the strange coincidence that the beautiful betrothed of my host should have related to me a tale of her childhood of which she declared she had never spoken before, and that within an hour the two principal actors in that tale should have appeared before my eyes and hers (for I may state that from the beginning I had no doubt that they were the same men), moved me and filled me with quite natural foreboding. Or all these things together may have tended to a concomitant effect. At any rate the issue was that I could not sleep.

For hour after hour I lay thinking and in an irritated way listening for the chimes of the Ragnall stable-clock which once had adorned the tower of the church and struck the quarters with a damnable reiteration. I concluded that Messrs. Harût and Marût were a couple of common Arab rogues such as I had seen performing at the African ports. Then a quarter struck and I concluded that the elephants' cemetery which I beheld in the smoke undoubtedly existed and that I meant to collar those thousands of pounds' worth of ivory before

I died. Then after another quarter I concluded that there was no elephants' cemetery—although by the way my old friend, Dogeetah or Brother John, had mentioned such a thing to me—but that probably there was a tribe, as he had also mentioned, called the Kendah, who worshipped a baby, or rather its effigy.

Well now, as had already occurred to me, the old Egyptians, of whom I was always fond of reading when I got a chance, also worshipped a child, Horus the Saviour. And that child had a mother called Isis symbolized in the crescent moon, the great Nature goddess, the mistress of mysteries to whose cult ten thousand priests were sworn—do not Herodotus and others, especially Apuleius, tell us all about her? And by a queer coincidence Miss Holmes had the mark of a crescent moon upon her breast. And when she was a child those two men, or others very like them, had pointed out that mark to each other. And I had seen them staring hard at it that night. And in her vapour-invoked dream the Heavenly Child, *alias* Horus, or the double of Horus, the *Ka*, I think the Egyptians called it, had awakened at the sight of her and kissed her and given her the necklace of the goddess, and—all the rest. What did it mean?

I went to sleep at last wondering what on earth it *could* mean, till presently that confounded clock woke me up again and I must go through the whole business once more.

By degrees, this was towards dawn, I became aware that all hope of rest had vanished from me utterly; that I was most painfully awake, and what is more, oppressed by a curious fear to the effect that something was going to happen to Miss Holmes. So vivid did this fear become that at length I arose, lit a candle and dressed myself. As it happened I knew where Miss Holmes slept. Her room, which I had seen her enter, was on the same corridor as mine though at the other end of it near the head of a stair that ran I knew not whither. In my portmanteau that had been sent over from Miss Manners's house, amongst other things was a small double-barrelled pistol which from long habit I always carried with me loaded, except for the caps that were in a little leather case with some spare ammunition attached to the pistol belt. I took it out, capped it and thrust it into my pocket. Then I slipped from the room and stood behind a tall clock in the corridor, watching Miss Holmes's door and reflecting what a fool I should look if anyone chanced to find me.

Half an hour or so later by the light of the setting moon which struggled through a window, I saw the door open and Miss Holmes emerge in a kind of dressing-gown and still wearing the necklace which Harût and Marût had given her. Of this I was sure for the light gleamed upon the red stones.

323

Also it shone upon her face and showed me without doubt that she was walking in her sleep.

Gliding as silently as a ghost she crossed the corridor and vanished. I followed and saw that she had descended an ancient, twisting stairway which I had noted in the castle wall. I went after her, my stockinged feet making no noise, feeling my way carefully in the darkness of the stair, for I did not dare to strike a match. Beneath me I heard a noise as of someone fumbling with bolts. Then a door creaked on its hinges and there was some light. When I reached the doorway I caught sight of the figure of Miss Holmes flitting across a hollow garden that was laid out in the bottom of the castle moat which had been drained. The garden, as I had observed when we walked through it on the previous day on our way to the first covert that we shot, was bordered by a shrubbery through which ran paths that led to the back drive of the castle.

Across the garden glided the figure of Miss Holmes and after it went I, crouching and taking cover behind every bush as though I were stalking big game, which indeed I was. She entered the shrubbery, moving much more swiftly now, for as she went she seemed to gather speed, like a stone which is rolled down a hill. It was as though whatever might be attracting her, for I felt sure that she was being drawn by something, acted more strongly upon her sleeping will as she drew nearer to it. For a while I lost sight of her in the shadow of the tall trees. Then suddenly I saw her again, standing quite still in an opening caused by the blowing down in the gale of one of the avenue of elms that bordered the back drive. But now she was no longer alone, for advancing towards her were two cloaked figures in whom I recognized Harût and Marût.

There she stood with outstretched arms, and towards her, stealthily as lions stalking a buck, came Harût and Marût. Moreover, between the naked boughs of the fallen elm I caught sight of what looked like the outline of a closed carriage standing upon the drive. Also I heard a horse stamp upon the frosty ground. Round the edge of the little glade I ran, keeping in the dark shadow, as I went cocking the pistol that was in my pocket. Then suddenly I darted out and stood between Harût and Marût and Miss Holmes.

Not a word passed between us. I think that all three of us subconsciously were anxious not to awake the sleeping woman, knowing that if we did so there would be a terrible scene. Only after motioning to me to stand aside, of course in vain, Harût and Marût drew from their robes curved and cruel-looking knives and bowed, for even now their politeness did not forsake them. I bowed back and when I straightened myself those enterprising Easterns found that I was covering the heart of Harût with my pistol. Then with that perception which is part of the mental outfit of the great, they saw that the game was up since I could have shot them both before a knife touched me.

"You have won this time, O Watcher-by-Night," whispered Harût softly, "but another time you will lose. That beautiful lady belongs to us and the People of the White Kendah, for she is marked with the holy mark of the young moon. The call of the Child of Heaven is heard in her heart, and will bring her home to the Child as it has brought her to us tonight. Now lead her hence still sleeping, O brave and clever one, so well named Watcher-by-Night."

Then they were gone and presently I heard the sound of horses being driven rapidly along the drive.

For a moment I hesitated as to whether I would or would not run in and shoot those horses. Two considerations stayed me. The first was that if I did so my pistol would be empty, or even if I shot one horse and retained a barrel loaded, with it I could only kill a single man, leaving myself defenceless against the knife of the other. The second consideration was that now as before I did not wish to wake up Miss Holmes.

I crept to her and not knowing what else to do, took hold of one of her outstretched hands. She turned and came with me at once as though she knew me, remaining all the while fast asleep. Thus we went back to the house, through the still open door, up the stairway straight to her own room, on the threshold of which I loosed her hand. The room was dark and I could see nothing, but I listened until I heard a sound as of a person throwing herself upon the bed and drawing up the blankets. Then knowing that she was safe for a while, I shut the door, which opened outwards as doors of ancient make sometimes do, and set against it a little table that stood in the passage.

Next, after reflecting for a minute, the circumstances being awkward in many ways, I went to my room and lit a candle. Obviously it was my duty to inform Lord Ragnall of what had happened and that as soon as possible. But I had no idea in what part of that huge building his sleeping place might be, nor, for patent reasons, was it desirable that I should disturb the house and so create talk. In this dilemma I remembered that Lord Ragnall's confidential servant, Mr. Savage, when he conducted me to my room on the previous night, which he made a point of doing perhaps because he wished to talk over the matter of the snakes that had found their way into his pockets, had shown me a bell in it which he said rang outside his door. He called it an *emergency bell.* I remarked idly that it was improbable that I should have any occasion for its use.

"Who knows, sir?" said Mr. Savage prophetically. "There are folk who say that this old castle is haunted, which after what I have seen tonight I can well believe. If you should chance to meet a ghost looking, let us say, like those black villains, Harum and Scarum, or whatever they call themselves—well, sir, two's better company than one."

I considered that bell but was loath to ring it for the reasons I have given. Then I went outside the room and looked. As I had hoped might be the case, there ran the wire on the face of the wall connected along its length by other wires with the various rooms it passed.

I set to work and followed that wire. It was not an easy job; indeed once or twice it reminded me of that story of the old Greek hero who found his way through a labyrinth by means of a silken thread. I forget whether it were a bull or a lady he was looking for, but with care and perseverance he found one or the other, or it may have been both.

Down staircases and various passages I went with my eye glued upon the wire, which occasionally got mixed up with other wires, till at length it led me through a swing door covered with red baize into what appeared to be a modern annexe to the castle. Here at last it terminated on the spring of an alarming-looking and deep-throated bell that hung immediately over a certain door.

On this door I knocked, hoping that it might be that of Mr. Savage and praying earnestly that it did not enclose the chaste resting-place of the cook or any other female. Too late, I mean after I had knocked, it occurred to me that if so my position would be painful to a degree. However in this particular Fortune stood my friend, which does not always happen to the virtuous. For presently I heard a voice which I recognized as that of Mr. Savage, asking, not without a certain quaver in its tone, "Who the devil is that?"

"Me," I replied, being flustered.

"'Me' won't do," said the voice. "'Me' might be Harum or it might be Scarum, or it might be someone worse. Who's 'Me'?"

"Allan Quatermain, you idiot," I whispered through the keyhole.

"Anna who? Well, never mind. Go away, Hanna. I'll talk to you in the morning."

Then I kicked the door, and at length, very cautiously, Mr. Savage opened it.

"Good heavens, sir," he said, "what are you doing here, sir? Dressed too, at this hour, and with the handle of a pistol sticking out of your pocket—or is it—the head of a snake?" and he jumped back, a strange and stately figure in a long white nightshirt which apparently he wore over his underclothing.

I entered the room and shut the door, whereon he politely handed me a chair, remarking,

"Is it ghosts, sir, or are you ill, or is it Harum and Scarum, of whom I have been thinking all night? Very cold too, sir, being afraid to pull up the bedclothes for fear lest there might be more reptiles in them." He pointed to his dress-coat hanging on the back of another chair with both the pockets turned inside out, adding tragically, "To think, sir, that this new coat has been a nest of snakes, which I have hated like poison from a child, and me almost a teetotaller!"

"Yes," I said impatiently, "it's Harum and Scarum as you call them. Take me to Lord Ragnall's bedroom at once."

"Ah! sir, burgling, I suppose, or mayhap worse," he exclaimed as he threw on some miscellaneous garments and seized a life-preserver which hung upon a hook. "Now I'm ready, only I hope they have left their snakes behind. I never could bear the sight of a snake, and they seem to know it—the brutes."

In due course we reached Lord Ragnall's room, which Mr. Savage entered, and in answer to a stifled inquiry exclaimed,

"Mr. Allan Quatermain to see you, my lord."

"What is it, Quatermain?" he asked, sitting up in bed and yawning. "Have you had a nightmare?"

"Yes," I answered, and Savage having left us and shut the door, I told him everything as it is written down.

"Great heavens!" he exclaimed when I had finished. "If it had not been for you and your intuition and courage——"

"Never mind me," I interrupted. "The question is—what should be done now? Are you going to try to arrest these men, or will you—hold your tongue and merely cause them to be watched?"

"Really I don't know. Even if we can catch them the whole story would sound so strange in a law-court, and all sorts of things might be suggested."

"Yes, Lord Ragnall, it would sound so strange that I beg you will come at once to see the evidences of what I tell you, before rain or snow obliterates them, bringing another witness with you. Lady Longden, perhaps."

"Lady Longden! Why one might as well write to *The Times*. I have it! There's Savage. He is faithful and can be silent."

So Savage was called in and, while Lord Ragnall dressed himself hurriedly, told the outline of his story under pain of instant dismissal if he breathed a word. Really to watch his face was as good as a play. So astonished was he that all he could ejaculate was—

"The black-hearted villains! Well, they ain't friendly with snakes for nothing."

Then having made sure that Miss Holmes was still in her room, we went down the twisting stair and through the side doorway, locking the door after us. By now the dawn was breaking and there was enough light to enable me in certain places where the snow that fell after the gale remained, to show Lord Ragnall and Savage the impress of the little bedroom slippers which Miss Holmes wore, and of my stockinged feet following after.

In the plantation things were still easier, for every detail of the movements of the four of us could be traced. Moreover, on the back drive was the spoor of the horses and the marks of the wheels of the carriage that had been brought for the purposes of the abduction. Also my great good fortune, for this seemed to prove my theory, we found a parcel wrapped in native linen that appeared to have fallen out of the carriage when Harût and Marût made their hurried escape, as one of the wheels had gone over it. It contained an Eastern woman's dress and veil, intended, I suppose, to be used in disguising Miss Holmes, who thence-forward would have appeared to be the wife or daughter of one of the abductors.

Savage discovered this parcel, which he lifted only to drop it with a yell, for underneath it lay a torpid snake, doubtless one of those that had been used in the performance.

Of these discoveries and many other details, on our return to the house, Lord Ragnall made full notes in a pocket-book, that when completed were signed by all three of us.

There is not much more to tell, that is of this part of the story. The matter was put into the hands of detectives who discovered that the Easterns had driven to London, where all traces of the carriage which conveyed them was lost. They, however, embarked upon a steamer called the *Antelope*, together with two native women, who probably had been provided to look after Miss Holmes, and sailed that very afternoon for Egypt. Thither, of course, it was useless to follow them in those days, even if it had been advisable to do so.

* * * * * * * *

To return to Miss Holmes. She came down to breakfast looking very charming but rather pale. Again I sat next to her and took some opportunity to ask her how she had rested that night.

She replied, very well and yet very ill, since, although she never remembered sleeping more soundly in her life, she had experienced all sorts of queer dreams of which she could remember nothing at all, a circumstance that annoyed her much, as she was sure that they were most interesting. Then she added,

"Do you know, Mr. Quatermain, I found a lot of mud on my dressing-gown this morning, and my bedroom slippers were also a mass of mud and wet through. How do you account for that? It is just as though I had been walking about outside in my sleep, which is absurd, as I never did such a thing in my life."

Not feeling equal to the invention of any convincing explanation of these phenomena, I upset the marmalade pot on to the table in such a way that some of it fell upon her dress, and then covered my retreat with profuse apologies. Understanding my dilemma, for he had heard something of this talk, Lord Ragnall came to my aid with a startling statement of which I forget the purport, and thus that crisis passed.

Shortly after breakfast Scroope announced to Miss Manners that her carriage was waiting, and we departed. Before I went, as it chanced, I had a few private words with my host, with Miss Holmes, and with the magnificent Mr. Savage. To the last, by the way, I offered a tip which he refused, saying that after all we had gone through together he could not allow "money to come between us," by which he meant, to pass from my pocket to his. Lord Ragnall asked me for both my English and my African addresses, which he noted in his pocket-book. Then he said,

"Really, Quatermain, I feel as though I had known you for years instead of three days; if you will allow me I will add that I should like to know a great deal more of you." (He was destined to do so, poor fellow, though neither of us knew it at the time.) "If ever you come to England again I hope you will make this house your headquarters."

"And if ever you come to South Africa, Lord Ragnall, I hope you will make my four-roomed shanty on the Berea at Durban your head-quarters. You will get a hearty welcome there and something to eat, but little more."

"There is nothing I should like better, Quatermain. Circumstances have put me in a certain position in this country, still to tell you the truth there is a great deal about the life of which I grow very tired. But you see I am going to be married, and that I fear means an end of travelling, since naturally my wife will wish to take her place in society and the rest."

"Of course," I replied, "for it is not every young lady who has the luck to become an English peeress with all the *etceteras*, is it? Still I am not so sure but that Miss Holmes will take to travelling some day, although I *am* sure that she would do better to stay at home."

He looked at me curiously, then asked,

"You don't think there is anything really serious in all this business, do you?"

"I don't know what to think," I answered, "except that you will do well to keep a good eye upon your wife. What those Easterns tried to do last night and, I think, years ago, they may try again soon, or years hence, for evidently they are patient and determined men with much to win. Also it is a curious coincidence that she should have that mark upon her which appeals so strongly to Messrs. Harût and Marût, and, to be brief, she is in some ways different from most young women. As she said to me herself last night, Lord Ragnall, we are surrounded by mysteries; mysteries of blood, of inherited spirit, of this world generally in which it is probable that we all descended from quite a few common ancestors. And beyond these are other mysteries of the measureless universe to which we belong, that may already be exercising their strong and secret influences upon us, as perhaps, did we know it, they have done for millions of years in the Infinite whence we came and whither we go."

I suppose I spoke somewhat solemnly, for he said,

"Do you know you frighten me a little, though I don't quite understand what you mean." Then we parted.

With Miss Holmes my conversation was shorter. She remarked,

"It has been a great pleasure to me to meet you. I do not remember anybody with whom I have found myself in so much sympathy—except one of course. It is strange to think that when we meet again I shall be a married woman."

"I do not suppose we shall ever meet again, Miss Holmes. Your life is here, mine is in the wildest places of a wild land far away."

"Oh! yes, we shall," she answered. "I learned this and lots of other things when I held my head in that smoke last night."

Then we also parted.

Lastly Mr. Savage arrived with my coat. "Goodbye, Mr. Quatermain," he said. "If I forget everything else I shall never forget you and those villains, Harum and Scarum and their snakes. I hope it won't be my lot ever to clap eyes on them again, Mr. Quatermain, and yet somehow I don't feel so sure of that."

"Nor do I," I replied, with a kind of inspiration, after which followed the episode of the rejected tip.

CHAPTER 6

The *Bona Fide* Gold Mine

Fully two years had gone by since I bade farewell to Lord Ragnall and Miss Holmes, and when the curtain draws up again behold me seated on the *stoep* of my little house at Durban, plunged in reflection and very sad indeed. Why I was sad I will explain presently.

In that interval of time I had heard once or twice about Lord Ragnall. Thus I received from Scroope a letter telling of his lordship's marriage with Miss Holmes, which, it appeared, had been a very fine affair indeed, quite one of the events of the London season. Two Royalties attended the ceremony, a duke was the best man, and the presents according to all accounts were superb and of great value, including a priceless pearl necklace given by the bridegroom to the bride. A cutting from a society paper which Scroope enclosed dwelt at length upon the splendid appearance of the bridegroom and the sweet loveliness of the bride. Also it described her dress in language which was Greek to me. One sentence, however, interested me intensely. It ran:

> The bride occasioned some comment by wearing only one ornament, although the Ragnall family diamonds, which have not seen the light for many years, are known to be some of the finest in the country. It was a necklace of what appeared to be large but rather roughly polished rubies, to which hung a small effigy of an Egyptian god also fashioned from a ruby. It must be added that although of an unusual nature on such an occasion this jewel suited her dark beauty well. Lady Ragnall's selection of it, however, from the many she possesses was the cause of much speculation. When asked by a friend why she had chosen it, she is reported to have said that it was to bring her good fortune.

Now why did she wear the barbaric marriage gift of Harût and Marût in preference to all the other gems at her disposal, I wondered. The thing was so strange as to be almost uncanny.

The second piece of information concerning this pair reached me through the medium of an old *Times* newspaper which I received over a year later. It was to the effect that a son and heir had been born to Lord Ragnall and that both mother and child were doing well.

So there's the end to a very curious little story, thought I to myself.

* * * * * * * *

Well, during those two years many things befell me. First of all, in company with my old friend Sir Stephen Somers, I made the expedition to Pongoland in search of the wonderful orchid which he desired to add to his collection. I have already written of that journey and our extraordinary adventures, and need therefore allude to it no more here, except to say that during the course of it I was sorely tempted to travel to the territory north of the lake in which the Pongos dwelt. Much did I desire to see whether Messrs. Harût and Marût would in truth appear to conduct me to the land where the wonderful elephant which was supposed to be animated by an evil spirit was waiting to be killed by my rifle. However, I resisted the impulse, as indeed our circumstances obliged me to do. In the end we returned safely to Durban, and here I came to the conclusion that never again would I risk my life on such mad expeditions.

Owing to circumstances which I have detailed elsewhere I was now in possession of a considerable sum of cash, and this I determined to lay out in such a fashion as to make me independent of hunting and trading in the wilder regions of Africa. As usual when money is forthcoming, an opportunity soon presented itself in the shape of a gold mine which had been discovered on the borders of Zululand, one of the first that was ever found in those districts. A Jew trader named Jacob brought it to my notice and offered me a half share if I would put up the capital necessary to work the mine. I made a journey of inspection and convinced myself that it was indeed a wonderful proposition. I need not enter into the particulars nor, to tell the truth, have I any desire to do so, for the subject is still painful to me, further than to say that this Jew and some friends of his panned out visible gold before my eyes and then revealed to me the magnificent quartz reef from which, as they demonstrated, it had been washed in the bygone ages of the world. The news of our discovery spread like wildfire, and as, whatever else I might be, everyone knew that I was honest, in the end a small company was formed with Allan Quatermain, Esq., as the chairman of the Bona Fide Gold Mine, Limited.

Oh! that company! Often to this day I dream of it when I have indigestion.

Our capital was small, £10,000, of which the Jew, who was well named Jacob, and his friends, took half (for nothing of course) as the purchase price of their rights. I thought the proportion large and said so, especially after I had ascertained that these rights had cost them exactly three dozen of square-face gin, a broken-down wagon, four cows past the bearing age and £5 in cash. However, when it was pointed out to me that by their peculiar knowledge and genius they had located and provided the value of a property of enormous potential worth, moreover that this sum was to be paid to them in scrip which would only be realizable when success was assured and not in money, after a night of anxious consideration I gave way.

Personally, before I consented to accept the chairmanship, which carried with it a salary of £100 a year (which I never got), I bought and paid for in cash, shares to the value of £1,000 sterling. I remember that Jacob and his friends seemed surprised at this act of mine, as they had offered to give me five hundred of their shares for nothing "in consideration of the guarantee of my name." These I refused, saying that I would not ask others to invest in a venture in which I had no actual money stake; whereon they accepted my decision, not without enthusiasm. In the end the balance of £4,000 was subscribed and we got to work. Work is a good name for it so far as I was concerned, for never in all my days have I gone through so harrowing a time.

We began by washing a certain patch of gravel and obtained results which seemed really astonishing. So remarkable were they that on publication the shares rose to 10s. premium. Jacob and Co. took advantage of this opportunity to sell quite half of their bonus holding to eager applicants, explaining to me that they did so not for personal profit, which they scorned, but "to broaden the basis of the undertaking by admitting fresh blood."

It was shortly after this boom that the gravel surrounding the rich patch became very gravelly indeed, and it was determined that we should buy a small battery and begin to crush the quartz from which the gold was supposed to flow in a Pactolian stream. We negotiated for that battery through a Cape Town firm of engineers—but why follow the melancholy business in all its details? The shares began to decrease in value. They shrank to their original price of £1, then to 15s., then

333

to 10s. Jacob, he was managing director, explained to me that it was necessary to "support the market," as he was already doing to an enormous extent, and that I as chairman ought to take a "lead in this good work" in order to show my faith in the concern.

I took a lead to the extent of another £500, which was all that I could afford. I admit that it was a shock to such trust in human nature as remained to me when I discovered subsequently that the 1,000 shares which I bought for my £500 had really been the property of Jacob, although they appeared to be sold to me in various other names.

The crisis came at last, for before that battery was delivered our available funds were exhausted, and no one would subscribe another halfpenny. Debentures, it is true, had been issued and taken up to the extent of about £1,000 out of the £5,000 offered, though who bought them remained at the time a mystery to me. Ultimately a meeting was called to consider the question of liquidating the company, and at this meeting, after three sleepless nights, I occupied the chair.

When I entered the room, to my amazement I found that of the five directors only one was present besides myself, an honest old retired sea captain who had bought and paid for 300 shares. Jacob and the two friends who represented his interests had, it appeared, taken ship that morning for Cape Town, whither they were summoned to attend various relatives who had been seized with illness.

It was a stormy meeting at first. I explained the position to the best of my ability, and when I had finished was assailed with a number of questions which I could not answer to the satisfaction of myself or of anybody else. Then a gentleman, the owner of ten shares, who had evidently been drinking, suggested in plain language that I had cheated the shareholders by issuing false reports.

I jumped up in a fury and, although he was twice my size, asked him to come and argue the question outside, whereon he promptly went away. This incident excited a laugh, and then the whole truth came out. A man with coloured blood in him stood up and told a story which was subsequently proved to be true. Jacob had employed him to *salt* the mine by mixing a heavy sprinkling of gold in the gravel we had first washed (which the coloured man swore he did in innocence), and subsequently had defrauded him of his wages. That was all. I sank back in my chair overcome. Then some good fellow in the audience, who had lost money himself in the affair and whom I scarcely knew, got up and made a noble speech which went far to restore my belief in human nature.

He said in effect that it was well known that I, Allan Quatermain, after working like a horse in the interests of the shareholders, had practically ruined myself over this enterprise, and that the real thief was Jacob, who had made tracks for the Cape, taking with him a large cash profit resulting from the sale of shares. Finally he concluded by calling for "three cheers for our honest friend and fellow sufferer, Mr. Allan Quatermain."

Strange to say the audience gave them very heartily indeed. I thanked them with tears in my eyes, saying that I was glad to leave the room as poor as I had ever been, but with a reputation which my conscience as well as their kindness assured me was quite unblemished.

Thus the winding-up resolution was passed and that meeting came to an end. After shaking hands with my deliverer from a most unpleasant situation, I walked homewards with the lightest heart in the world. My money was gone, it was true; also my over-confidence in others had led me to make a fool of myself by accepting as fact, on what I believed to be the evidence of my eyes, that which I had not sufficient expert knowledge to verify. But my honour was saved, and as I have again and again seen in the course of life, money is nothing when compared with honour, a remark which Shakespeare made long ago, though like many other truths this is one of which a full appreciation can only be gained by personal experience.

Not very far from the place where our meeting had been held I passed a side street then in embryo, for it had only one or two houses situated in their gardens and a rather large and muddy *sluit* of water running down one side at the edge of the footpath. Save for two people this street was empty, but that pair attracted my attention. They were a white man, in whom I recognized the stout and half-intoxicated individual who had accused me of cheating the company and then departed, and a withered old Hottentot who at that distance, nearly a hundred yards away, much reminded me of a certain Hans.

This Hans, I must explain, was originally a servant of my father, who was a missionary in the Cape Colony, and had been my companion in many adventures. Thus in my youth he and I alone escaped when Dingaan murdered Retief and his party of Boers, and he had been one of my party in our quest for the wonderful orchid, the record of which I have written down in *The Holy Flower*.

Hans had his weak points, among which must be counted his love of liquor, but he was a gallant and resourceful old fellow as indeed he had amply proved upon that orchid-seeking expedition. Moreover he loved me with a love passing the love of women. Now, having acquired some money in a way I need not stop to describe—for is it not written elsewhere?—he was settled as a kind of little chief on a farm not very far from Durban, where he lived in great honour because of the fame of his deeds.

The white man and Hans, if Hans it was, were engaged in violent altercation whereof snatches floated to me on the breeze, spoken in the Dutch tongue.

"You dirty little Hottentot!" shouted the white man, waving a stick, "I'll cut the liver out of you. What do you mean by nosing about after me like a jackal?" And he struck at Hans, who jumped aside.

"Son of a fat white sow," screamed Hans in answer (for the moment I heard his voice I knew that it was Hans), "did you dare to call the Baas a thief? Yes, a thief, O Rooter in the mud, O Feeder on filth and worms, O Hog of the gutter—the Baas, the clipping of whose nail is worth more than you and all your family, he whose honour is as clear as the sunlight and whose heart is cleaner than the white sand of the sea."

"Yes, I did," roared the white man; "for he got my money in the gold mine."

"Then, hog, why did you run away. Why did you not wait to tell him so outside that house?"

"I'll teach you about running away, you little yellow dog," replied the other, catching Hans a cut across the ribs.

"Oh! you want to see me run, do you?" said Hans, skipping back a few yards with wonderful agility. "Then look!"

Thus speaking he lowered his head and charged like a buffalo. Fair in the middle he caught that white man, causing him to double up, fly backwards and land with a most resounding splash in the deepest part of the muddy *sluit*. Here I may remark that, as his shins are the weakest, a Hottentot's head is by far the hardest and most dangerous part of him. Indeed it seems to partake of the nature of a cannon ball, for, without more than temporary disturbance to its possessor, I have seen a half-loaded wagon go over one of them on a muddy road.

Having delivered this home thrust Hans bolted round a corner and disappeared, while I waited trembling to see what happened to his adversary. To my relief nearly a minute later he crept out of the *sluit* covered with mud and dripping with water and hobbled off slowly down the street, his head so near his feet that he looked as though he had been folded in two, and his hands pressed upon what I believe is medically known as the diaphragm. Then I also went upon my way roaring with laughter. Often I have heard Hottentots called the lowest of mankind, but, reflected I, they can at any rate be good friends to those who treat them well—a fact of which I was to have further proof ere long.

By the time I reached my house and had filled my pipe and sat myself down in the dilapidated cane chair on the veranda, that natural reaction set in which so often follows rejoicing at the escape from a great danger. It was true that no one believed I had cheated them over that thrice-accursed gold mine, but how about other matters?

I mused upon the Bible narrative of Jacob and Esau with a new and very poignant sympathy for Esau. I wondered what would become of my Jacob. Jacob, I mean the original, prospered exceedingly as a result of his deal in porridge, and, as thought I, probably would his artful descendant who so appropriately bore his name. As a matter of fact I do not know what became of him, but bearing his talents in mind I think it probable that, like Van Koop, under some other patronymic he has now been rewarded with a title by the British Government. At any rate I had eaten the porridge in the shape of worthless but dearly purchased shares, after labouring hard at the chase of the golden calf, while brother Jacob had got my inheritance, or rather my money. Probably he was now counting it over in sovereigns upon the ship and sniggering as he thought of the shareholders' meeting with me in the chair. Well, he was a thief and would run his road to whatever end is appointed for thieves, so why should I bother my head more about him? As I had kept my honour—let him take my savings.

But I had a son to support, and now what was I to do with scarcely three hundred pounds, a good stock of guns and this little Durban property left to me in the world? Commerce in all its shapes I renounced once and for ever. It was too high—or too low—for me; so it would seem that there remained to me only my old business of professional hunting. Once again I must seek those adventures which I had forsworn when my evil star shone so brightly over a gold mine. What was it to be? Elephants, I supposed, since these are the only creatures worth killing from a money point of view. But most of my old haunts had been more or less shot out. The competition of younger professionals, of wandering *backveld* Boers and even of poaching natives who had obtained guns, was growing severe. If I went at all I should have to travel farther afield.

Whilst I meditated thus, turning over the comparative advantages or disadvantages of various possible hunting grounds in my mind, my attention was caught by a kind of cough that seemed to proceed from the farther side of a large gardenia bush. It was not a human cough, but rather resembled that made by a certain small buck at night, probably to signal to its mate, which of course it could not be

337

as there were no buck within several miles. Yet I knew it came from a human throat, for had I not heard it before in many an hour of difficulty and danger?

"Draw near, Hans," I said in Dutch, and instantly out of a clump of aloes that grew in front of the pomegranate hedge, crept the withered shape of the old Hottentot, as a big yellow snake might do. Why he should choose this method of advance instead of that offered by the garden path I did not know, but it was quite in accordance with his secretive nature, inherited from a hundred generations of ancestors who spent their lives avoiding the observation of murderous foes.

He squatted down in front of me, staring in a vacant way at the fierce ball of the westering sun without blinking an eyelid, just as a vulture does.

"You look to me as though you had been fighting, Hans," I said. "The crown of your hat is knocked out; you are splashed with mud and there is the mark of a stick upon your left side."

"Yes, Baas. You are right as usual, Baas. I had a quarrel with a man about sixpence that he owed me, and knocked him over with my head, forgetting to take my hat off first. Therefore it is spoiled, for which I am sorry, as it was quite a new hat, not two years old. The Baas gave it me. He bought it in a store at Utrecht when we were coming back from Pongoland."

"Why do you lie to me?" I asked "You have been fighting a white man and for more than sixpence. You knocked him into a *sluit* and the mud splashed up over you."

"Yes, Baas, that is so. Your spirit speaks truly to you of the matter. Yet it wanders a little from the path, since I fought the white man for less than sixpence. I fought him for love, which is nothing at all."

"Then you are even a bigger fool than I took you for, Hans. What do you want now?"

"I want to borrow a pound, Baas. The white man will take me before the magistrate, and I shall be fined a pound, or fourteen days in the *trunk* (*i.e.* jail). It is true that the white man struck me first, but the magistrate will not believe the word of a poor old Hottentot against his, and I have no witness. He will say, 'Hans, you were drunk again. Hans, you are a liar and deserve to be flogged, which you will be next time. Pay a pound and ten shillings more, which is the price of good white justice, or go to the *trunk* for fourteen days and make baskets there for the great Queen to use.' Baas, I have the price of the justice which is ten shillings, but I want to borrow the pound for the fine."

"Hans, I think that just now you are better able to lend me a pound than I am to lend one to you. My bag is empty, Hans."

"Is it so, Baas? Well, it does not matter. If necessary I can make baskets for the great white Queen to put her food in, for fourteen days, or mats on which she will wipe her feet. The *trunk* is not such a bad place, Baas. It gives time to think of the white man's justice and to thank the Great One in the Sky, because the little sins one did not do have been found out and punished, while the big sins one did do, such as—well, never mind, Baas—have not been found out at all. Your reverend father, the Predikant, always taught me to have a thankful heart, Baas, and when I remember that I have only been in the *trunk* for three months altogether who, if all were known, ought to have been there for years, I remember his words, Baas."

"Why should you go to the *trunk* at all, Hans, when you are rich and can pay a fine, even if it were a hundred pounds?"

"A month or two ago it is true I was rich, Baas, but now I am poor. I have nothing left except ten shillings."

"Hans," I said severely, "you have been gambling again; you have been drinking again. You have sold your property and your cattle to pay your gambling debts and to buy square-face gin."

"Yes, Baas, and for no good it seems; though it is not true that I have been drinking. I sold the land and the cattle for £650, Baas, and with the money I bought other things."

"What did you buy?" I said.

He fumbled first in one pocket of his coat and then in the other, and ultimately produced a crumpled and dirty-looking piece of paper that resembled a bank-note. I took and examined this document and next minute nearly fainted. It certified that Hans was the proprietor of I know not how many debentures or shares, I forget which they were, in the Bona Fide Gold Mine, Limited, that same company of which I was the unlucky chairman, in consideration for which he had paid a sum of over six hundred and fifty pounds.

"Hans," I said feebly, "from whom did you buy this?"

"From the baas with the hooked nose, Baas. He who was named Jacob, after the great man in the Bible of whom your father, the Predikant, used to tell us, that one who was so slim and dressed himself up in a goatskin and gave his brother mealie porridge when he was hungry, after he had come in from shooting buck, Baas, and got his farm and cattle, Baas, and then went to Heaven up a ladder, Baas."

"And who told you to buy them, Hans?"

"Sammy, Baas, he who was your cook when we went to Pon-

339

goland, he who hid in the mealie-pit when the slavers burned Beza Town and came out half cooked like a fowl from the oven. The Baas Jacob stopped at Sammy's hotel, Baas, and told him that unless he bought bits of paper like this, of which he had plenty, you would be brought before the magistrate and sent to the *trunk*, Baas. So Sammy bought some, Baas, but not many for he had only a little money, and the Baas Jacob paid him for all he ate and drank with other bits of paper. Then Sammy came to me and showed me what it was my duty to do, reminding me that your reverend father, the Predikant, had left you in my charge till one of us dies, whether you were well or ill and whether you got better or got worse—just like a white wife, Baas. So I sold the farm and the cattle to a friend of the Baas Jacob's, at a very low price, Baas, and that is all the story."

I heard and, to tell the honest truth, almost I wept, since the thought of the sacrifice which this poor old Hottentot had made for my sake on the instigation of a rogue utterly overwhelmed me.

"Hans," I asked recovering myself, "tell me what was that new name which the Zulu captain Mavovo gave you before he died, I mean after you had fired Beza Town and caught Hassan and his slavers in their own trap?"

Hans, who had suddenly found something that interested him extremely out at sea, perhaps because he did not wish to witness my grief, turned round slowly and answered:

"Mavovo named me Light-in-Darkness, and by that name the *Kafirs* know me now, Baas, though some of them call me Lord-of-the-Fire."

"Then Mavovo named you well, for indeed, Hans, you shine like a light in the darkness of my heart. I whom you think wise am but a fool, Hans, who has been tricked by a *vernuker*, a common cheat, and he has tricked you and Sammy as well. But as he has shown me that man can be very vile, you have shown me that he can be very noble; and, setting the one against the other, my spirit that was in the dust rises up once more like a withered flower after rain. Light-in-Darkness, although if I had ten thousand pounds I could never pay you back—since what you have given me is more than all the gold in the world and all the land and all the cattle—yet with honour and with love I will try to pay you," and I held out my hand to him.

He took it and pressed it against his wrinkled old forehead, then answered:

"Talk no more of that, Baas, for it makes me sad, who am so happy. How often have you forgiven me when I have done wrong? How often have you not flogged me when I should have been flogged for being

340

drunk and other things—yes, even when once I stole some of your powder and sold it to buy square-face gin, though it is true I knew it was bad powder, not fit for you to use? Did I thank you then overmuch? Why therefore should you thank me who have done but a little thing, not really to help you but because, as you know, I love gambling, and was told that this bit of paper would soon be worth much more than I gave for it. If it had proved so, should I have given you that money? No, I should have kept it myself and bought a bigger farm and more cattle."

"Hans," I said sternly, "if you lie so hard, you will certainly go to hell, as the Predikant, my father, often told you."

"Not if I lie for you, Baas, or if I do it doesn't matter, except that then we should be separated by the big *kloof* written of in the Book, especially as there I should meet the Baas Jacob, as I very much want to do for a reason of my own."

Not wishing to pursue this somewhat unchristian line of thought, I inquired of him why he felt happy.

"Oh! Baas," he answered with a twinkle in his little black eyes, "can't you guess why? Now you have very little money left and I have none at all. Therefore it is plain that we must go somewhere to earn money, and I am glad of that, Baas, for I am tired of sitting on that farm out there and growing mealies and milking cows, especially as I am too old to marry, Baas, as you are tired of looking for gold where there isn't any and singing sad songs in that house of meeting yonder like you did this afternoon. Oh! the Great Father in the skies knew what He was about when He sent the Baas Jacob our way. He beat us for our good, Baas, as He does always if we could only understand."

I reflected to myself that I had not often heard the doctrine of the Church better or more concisely put, but I only said:

"That is true, Hans, and I thank you for the lesson, the second you have taught me today. But where are we to go to, Hans? Remember, it must be elephants."

He suggested some places; indeed he seemed to have come provided with a list of them, and I sat silent making no comment. At length he finished and squatted there before me, chewing a bit of tobacco I had given him, and looking up at me interrogatively with his head on one side, for all the world like a dilapidated and inquisitive bird.

"Hans," I said, "do you remember a story I told you when you came to see me a year or more ago, about a tribe called the Kendah in whose country there is said to be a great cemetery of elephants which travel there to die from all the land about? A country that lies somewhere to the north-east of the lake island on which the Pongo used to dwell?"

"Yes, Baas."

"And you said, I think, that you had never heard of such a people."

"No, Baas, I never said anything at all. I have heard a good deal about them."

"Then why did you not tell me so before, you little idiot?" I asked indignantly.

"What was the good, Baas? You were hunting gold then, not ivory. Why should I make you unhappy, and waste my own breath by talking about beautiful things which were far beyond the reach of either of us, far as that sky?"

"Don't ask fool's questions but tell me what you know, Hans. Tell me at once."

"This, Baas: When we were up at Beza Town after we came back from killing the gorilla-god, and the Baas Stephen your friend lay sick, and there was nothing else to do, I talked with everyone I could find worth talking to, and they were not many, Baas. But there was one very old woman who was not of the Mazitu race and whose husband and children were all dead, but whom the people in the town looked up to and feared because she was wise and made medicines out of herbs, and told fortunes. I used to go to see her. She was quite blind, Baas, and fond of talking with me—which shows how wise she was. I told her all about the Pongo gorilla-god, of which already she knew something. When I had done she said that he was as nothing compared with a certain god that she had seen in her youth, seven tens of years ago, when she became marriageable. I asked her for that story, and she spoke it thus:

"Far away to the north and east live a people called the Kendah, who are ruled over by a sultan. They are a very great people and inhabit a most fertile country. But all round their country the land is desolate and manless, peopled only by game, for the reason that they will suffer none to dwell there. That is why nobody knows anything about them: he that comes across the wilderness into that land is killed and never returns to tell of it.

"She told me also that she was born of this people, but fled because their sultan wished to place her in his house of women, which she did not desire. For a long while she wandered southwards, living on roots and berries, till she came to desert land and at last, worn out, lay down to die. Then she was found by some of the Mazitu who were on an expedition seeking ostrich feathers for war-plumes. They gave her food and, seeing that she was fair, brought her back to their country, where one of them married her. But of her own land she uttered only lying words to them because she feared that if she told the truth the gods who guard its secrets would be avenged on her, though now when she was near to death she dreaded them no more, since even the Kendah gods cannot swim through the waters of death. That is all she said about her journey because she had forgotten the rest."

"Bother her journey, Hans. What did she say about her god and the Kendah people?"

"This, Baas: that the Kendah have not one god but two, and not one ruler but two. They have a good god who is a child-fetish" (here I started) "that speaks through the mouth of an oracle who is always a woman. If that woman dies the god does not speak until they find another woman bearing certain marks which show that she holds the spirit of the god. Before the woman dies she always tells the priests in what land they are to look for her who is to come after her; but sometimes they cannot find her and then trouble falls because 'the Child has lost its tongue,' and the people become the prey of the other god that never dies."

"And what is that god, Hans?"

"That god, Baas, is an elephant" (here I started again), "a very bad elephant to which human sacrifice is offered. I think, Baas, that it is the devil wearing the shape of an elephant, at least that is what she said. Now the sultan is a worshipper of the god that dwells in the elephant Jana" (here I positively whistled) "and so are most of the people, indeed all those among them who are black. For once far away in the beginning the Kendah were two peoples, but the lighter-coloured people who worshipped the Child came down from the north and conquered the black people, bringing the Child with them, or so I understood her, Baas, thousands and thousands of years ago when the world was young. Since then they have flowed on side by side like two streams in the same channel, never mixing, for each keeps its own colour. Only, she said, that stream which comes from the north grows weaker and that from the south more strong."

"Then why does not the strong swallow up the weak?"

"Because the weak are still the pure and the wise, Baas, or so the old *vrouw* declared. Because they worship the good while the others worship the devil, and as your father the Predikant used to say, Good is the cock which always wins the fight at the last, Baas. Yes, when he seems to be dead he gets up again and kicks the devil in the stomach and stands on him and crows, Baas. Also these northern folk are mighty magicians. Through their Child-fetish they give rain and fat seasons and keep away sickness, whereas Jana gives only evil gifts that have to do with cruelty and war and so forth. Lastly, the priests who rule through the Child have the secrets of wealth and ancient knowledge, whereas the sultan and his followers have only the might of the spear. This was the song which the old woman sang to me, Baas."

"Why did you not tell me of these matters when we were at Beza Town and I could have talked with her myself, Hans?"

"For two reasons, Baas. The first was that I feared, if I told you, you would wish to go on to find these people, whereas I was tired of travelling and wanted to come to Natal to rest. The second was that on the night when the old woman finished telling me her story, she was taken sick and died, and therefore it would have been no use to bring you to see her. So I saved it up in my head until it was wanted. Moreover, Baas, all the Mazitu declared that old woman to be the greatest of liars."

"She was not altogether a liar, Hans. Hear what I have learned," and I told him of the magic of Harût and Marût and of the picture that I had seemed to see of the elephant Jana and of the prayer that Harût and Marût had made to me, to all of which he listened quite stolidly. It is not easy to astonish a Hottentot's brain, which often draws no accurate dividing-line between the possible and what the modern world holds to be impossible.

"Yes, Baas," he said when I had finished, "then it seems that the old woman was not such a liar after all. Baas, when shall we start after that hoard of dead ivory, and which way will you go? By Kilwa or through Zululand? It should be settled soon because of the seasons."

After this we talked together for a long while, for with pockets as empty as mine were then, the problem seemed difficult, if not insoluble.

CHAPTER 7

Lord Ragnall's Story

That night Hans slept at my house, or rather outside of it in the garden, or upon the *stoep*, saying that he feared arrest if he went to the town, because of his quarrel with the white man. As it happened, however, the other party concerned never stirred further in the business, probably because he was too drunk to remember who had knocked him into the *sluit* or whether he had gravitated thither by accident.

On the following morning we renewed our discussion, debating in detail every possible method of reaching the Kendah people by help of such means as we could command. Like that of the previous night it proved somewhat abortive. Obviously such a long and hazardous expedition ought to be properly financed and—where was the money? At length I came to the conclusion that if we went at all it would be best, in the circumstances, for Hans and myself to start alone with a Scotch cart drawn by oxen and driven by a couple of Zulu hunters, which we could lade with ammunition and a few necessaries.

Thus lightly equipped we might work through Zululand and thence northward to Beza Town, the capital of the Mazitu, where we were sure of a welcome. After that we must take our chance. It was probable that we should never reach the district where these Kendah were supposed to dwell, but at least I might be able to kill some elephants in the wild country beyond Zululand.

While we were talking I heard the gun fired which announced the arrival of the English mail, and stepping to the end of the garden, saw the steamer lying at anchor outside the bar. Then I went indoors to write a few business letters which, since I had become immersed in the affairs of that unlucky gold mine, had grown to be almost a daily task with me. I had got through several with many groanings, for none were agreeable in their tenor, when Hans poked his head through the window in a silent kind of a way as a big snake might do, and said: "Baas, I think there are two *baases* out on the road there who are looking for you. Very fine *baases* whom I don't know."

"Shareholders in the Bona Fide Gold Mine," thought I to myself, then added as I prepared to leave through the back door: "If they come here tell them I am not at home. Tell them I left early this morning for the Congo River to look for the sources of the Nile."

"Yes, Baas," said Hans, collapsing on to the *stoep*.

I went out through the back door, sorrowing that I, Allan Quatermain, should have reached a rung in the ladder of life whence I shrank from looking any stranger in the face, for fear of what he might have to say to me. Then suddenly my pride asserted itself. After all what was there of which I should be ashamed? I would face these irate shareholders as I had faced the others yesterday.

I walked round the little house to the front garden which was planted with orange trees, and up to a big moonflower bush, I believe *datura* is its right name, that grew near the pomegranate hedge which separated my domain from the road. There a conversation was in progress, if so it may be called.

"*Ikona*" (that is: "I don't know"), "*Inkoosi*" (i.e. "Chief"), said some *Kafir* in a stupid drawl.

Thereon a voice that instantly struck me as familiar, answered:

"We want to know where the great hunter lives."

"*Ikona*," said the *Kafir*.

"Can't you remember his native name?" asked another voice which was also familiar to me, for I never forget voices though I am unable to place them at once.

"The great hunter, Here-come-a-zany," said the first voice triumphantly, and instantly there flashed back upon my mind a vision of the splendid drawing-room at Ragnall Castle and of an imposing major-domo introducing into it two white-robed, Arab-looking men.

"Mr. Savage, by the Heavens!" I muttered. "What in the name of goodness is he doing here?"

"There," said the second voice, "your black friend has bolted, and no wonder, for who can be called by such a name? If you had done what I told you, Savage, and hired a white guide, it would have saved us a lot of trouble. Why will you always think that you know better than anyone else?"

"Seemed an unnecessary expense, my lord, considering we are travelling incog., my lord."

"How long shall we travel 'incog.' if you persist in calling me my lord at the top of your voice, Savage? There is a house beyond those trees; go in and ask where——"

By this time I had reached the gate which I opened, remarking quietly,

"How do you do, Lord Ragnall? How do you do, Mr. Savage? I thought that I recognized your voices on the road and came to see if I was right. Please walk in; that is, if it is I whom you wish to visit."

As I spoke I studied them both, and observed that while Savage looked much the same, although slightly out of place in these strange surroundings, the time that had passed since we met had changed Lord Ragnall a good deal. He was still a magnificent-looking man, one of those whom no one that had seen him would ever forget, but now his handsome face was stamped with some new seal of suffering. I felt at once that he had become acquainted with grief. The shadow in his dark eyes and a certain worn expression about the mouth told me that this was so.

"Yes, Quatermain," he said as he took my hand, "it is you whom I have travelled seven thousand miles to visit, and I thank God that I have been so fortunate as to find you. I feared lest you might be dead, or perhaps far away in the centre of Africa where I should never be able to track you down."

"A week later perhaps you would not have found me, Lord Ragnall," I answered, "but as it happens misfortune has kept me here."

"And misfortune has brought me here, Quatermain."

Then before I had time to answer Savage came up and we went into the house.

"You are just in time for lunch," I said, "and as luck will have it there is a good rock cod and a leg of *oribé* buck for you to eat. Boy, set two more places."

"One more place, if you please, sir," said Savage. "I should prefer to take my food afterwards."

"You will have to get over that in Africa," I muttered. Still I let him have his way, with the result that presently the strange sight was seen of the magnificent English major-domo standing behind my chair in the little room and handing round the square-face as though it were champagne. It was a spectacle that excited the greatest interest in my primitive establishment and caused Hans with some native hangers-on to gather at the window. However, Lord Ragnall took it as a matter of course and I thought it better not to interfere.

When we had finished we went on to the *stoep* to smoke, leaving

Savage to eat his dinner, and I asked Lord Ragnall where his luggage was. He replied that he had left it at the Customs. "Then," I said, "I will send a native with Savage to arrange about getting it up here. If you do not mind my rough accommodation there is a room for you, and your man can pitch a tent in the garden."

After some demur he accepted with gratitude, and a little later Savage and the native were sent off with a note to a man who hired out a mule-cart.

"Now," I said when the gate had shut behind them, "will you tell me why you have come to Africa?"

"Disaster," he replied. "Disaster of the worst sort."

"Is your wife dead, Lord Ragnall?"

"I do not know. I almost hope that she is. At any rate she is lost to me."

An idea leapt to my mind to the effect that she might have run away with somebody else, a thing which often happens in the world. But fortunately I kept it to myself and only said,

"She was nearly lost once before, was she not?"

"Yes, when you saved her. Oh! if only you had been with us, Quatermain, this would never have happened. Listen: About eighteen months ago she had a son, a very beautiful child. She recovered well from the business and we were as happy as two mortals could be, for we loved each other, Quatermain, and God has blessed us in every way; we were so happy that I remember her telling me that our great good fortune made her feel afraid. One day last September when I was out shooting, she drove in a little pony cart we had, with the nurse, and the child but no man, to call on Mrs. Scroope who also had been recently confined. She often went out thus, for the pony was an old animal and quiet as a sheep.

"By some cursed trick of fate it chanced that when they were passing through the little town which you may remember near Ragnall, they met a travelling menagerie that was going to some new encampment. At the head of the procession marched a large bull elephant, which I discovered afterwards was an ill-tempered brute that had already killed a man and should never have been allowed upon the roads. The sight of the pony cart, or perhaps a red cloak which my wife was wearing, as she always liked bright colours, for some unknown reason seems to have infuriated this beast, which trumpeted. The pony becoming frightened wheeled round and overturned the cart right in front of the animal, but apparently without hurting anybody. Then"—here he paused a moment and with an effort continued—"that devil in beast's shape cocked its ears, stretched out its long trunk, dragged the baby from the nurse's arms, whirled it round and threw it high into the air, to fall crushed upon the kerb. It sniffed at the body of the child, feeling it over with the tip of its trunk, as though to make sure that it was dead. Next, once more it trumpeted triumphantly, and without attempting to harm my wife or anybody else, walked quietly past the broken cart and continued its journey, until outside the town it was made fast and shot."

"What an awful story!" I said with a gasp.

"Yes, but there is worse to follow. My poor wife went off her head, with the shock I suppose, for no physical injury could be found upon her. She did not suffer in health or become violent, quite the reverse indeed for her gentleness increased. She just went off her head. For hours at a time she would sit silent and smiling, playing with the stones of that red necklace which those conjurers gave her, or rather counting them, as a nun might do with the beads of her rosary. At times, however, she would talk, but always to the baby, as though it lay before her or she were nursing it. Oh! Quatermain, it was pitiful, pitiful!

"I did everything I could. She was seen by three of the greatest brain-doctors in England, but none of them was able to help. The only hope they gave was that the fit might pass off as suddenly as it had come. They said too that a thorough change of scene would perhaps be beneficial, and suggested Egypt; that was in October. I did not take much to the idea, I don't know why, and personally should not have acceded to it had it not been for a curious circumstance. The last consultation took place in the big drawing-room at Ragnall. When it was over my wife remained with her mother at one end of the room while I and the doctors talked together at the other, as I thought quite out of her earshot. Presently, however, she called to me, saying in a perfectly clear and natural voice:

"'Yes, George, I will go to Egypt. I should like to go to Egypt.' Then she went on playing with the necklace and talking to the imaginary child.

"Again on the following morning as I came into her room to kiss her, she exclaimed,

"'When do we start for Egypt? Let it be soon.'

"With these sayings the doctors were very pleased, declaring that they showed signs of a returning interest in life and begging me not to thwart her wish.

"So I gave way and in the end we went to Egypt together with Lady Longden, who insisted upon accompanying us although she is a wretched sailor. At Cairo a large *dahabeeyah* that I had hired in advance, manned by an excellent crew and a guard of four soldiers, was awaiting us. In it we started up the Nile. For a month or more all went well; also to my delight my wife seemed now and again to show signs of returning intelligence. Thus she took some interest in the sculptures on the walls of the temples, about which she had been very fond of reading when in health. I remember that only a few days before the—the catastrophe, she pointed out one of them to me, it was of Isis and the infant Horus, saying, 'Look, George, the holy Mother and the holy Child,' and then bowed to it reverently as she might have done to an altar. At length after passing the First Cataract and the Island of Philae we came to the temple of Abu Simbel, opposite to which our boat was moored. On the following morning we explored the temple at daybreak and saw the sun strike upon the four statues which sit at its farther end, spending the rest of that day studying the colossal figures of Rameses that are carved upon its face and watching some cavalcades of Arabs mounted upon camels travelling along the banks of the Nile.

"My wife was unusually quiet that afternoon. For hour after hour she sat still upon the deck, gazing first at the mouth of the rock-hewn temple and the mighty figures which guard it and then at the surrounding desert. Only once did I hear her speak and then she said, 'Beautiful, beautiful! Now I am at home.' We dined and as there was no moon, went to bed rather early after listening to the Sudanese singers as they sang one of their weird shanties.

"My wife and her mother slept together in the state cabin of the *dahabeeyah*, which was at the stern of the boat. My cabin, a small one, was on one side of this, and that of the trained nurse on the other. The crew and the guard were forward of the saloon. A gangway was fixed from the side to the shore and over it a sentry stood, or was supposed to stand. During the night a *Khamsin* wind began to blow, though lightly as was to be expected at this season of the year. I did not hear it for, as a matter of fact, I slept very soundly, as it appears did everyone else upon the *dahabeeyah*, including the sentry as I suspect.

"The first thing I remember was the appearance of Lady Longden just at daybreak at the doorway of my cabin and the frightened sound of her voice asking if Luna, that is my wife, was with me. Then it transpired that she had left her cabin clad in a fur cloak, evidently some time before, as the bed in which she had been lying was quite cold. Quatermain, we searched everywhere; we searched for four days, but from that hour to this no trace whatever of her has been found."

"Have you any theory?" I asked.

"Yes, or at least all the experts whom we consulted have a theory. It is that she slipped down the saloon in the dark, gained the deck and thence fell or threw herself into the Nile, which of course would have carried her body away. As you may have heard, the Nile is full of bodies. I myself saw two of them during that journey. The Egyptian police and others were so convinced that this was what had happened that, notwithstanding the reward of a thousand pounds which I offered for any valuable information, they could scarcely be persuaded to continue the search."

"You said that a wind was blowing and I understand that the shores are sandy, so I suppose that all footprints would have been filled in?"

He nodded and I went on. "What is your own belief? Do you think she was drowned?"

He countered my query with another of:

"What do *you* think?"

"I? Oh! although I have no right to say so, I don't think at all. I am quite sure that she was *not* drowned; that she is living at this moment."

"Where?"

"As to that you had better inquire of our friends, Harût and Marût," I answered dryly.

"What have you to go on, Quatermain? There is no clue."

"On the contrary I hold that there are a good many clues. The whole English part of the story in which we were concerned, and the threats those mysterious persons uttered are the first and greatest of these clues. The second is the fact that your hiring of the *dahabeeyah* regardless of expense was known a long time before your arrival in Egypt, for I suppose you did so in your own name, which is not exactly that of Smith or Brown. The third is your wife's sleepwalking propensities, which would have made it quite easy for her to be drawn ashore under some kind of mesmeric influence. The fourth is that you had seen Arabs mounted on camels upon the banks of the Nile. The fifth is the heavy sleep you say held everybody on board that particular night, which suggests to me that your food may have been drugged. The sixth is the apathy displayed by those employed in the search, which suggests to me that some person or persons in authority may have been bribed, as is common in the East, or perhaps frightened with threats of bewitchment. The seventh is that a night was chosen when a wind blew which would obliterate all spoor whether of men or of swiftly travelling camels. These are enough to begin with, though doubtless if I had time to think I could find others. You must remember too that although the journey would be long, this country of the Kendah can doubtless be reached from the Sudan by those who know the road, as well as from southern or eastern Africa."

"Then you think that my wife has been kidnapped by those villains, Harût and Marût?"

"Of course, though villains is a strong term to apply to them. They might be quite honest men according to their peculiar lights, as indeed I expect they are. Remember that they serve a god or a fetish, or rather, as they believe, a god *in* a fetish, who to them doubtless is a very terrible master, especially when, as I understand, that god is threatened by a rival god."

"Why do you say that, Quatermain?"

By way of answer I repeated to him the story which Hans said he had heard from the old woman at Beza, the town of the Mazitu. Lord Ragnall listened with the deepest interest, then said in an agitated voice:

"That is a very strange tale, but has it struck you, Quatermain, that if your suppositions are correct, one of the most terrible circumstances connected with my case is that our child should have chanced to come to its dreadful death through the wickedness of an elephant?"

"That curious coincidence has struck me most forcibly, Lord Ragnall. At the same time I do not see how it can be set down as more than a coincidence, since the elephant which slaughtered your child was certainly not that called Jana. To suppose because there is a war between an elephant-god and a child-god somewhere in the heart of Africa, that therefore another elephant can be so influenced that it kills a child in England, is to my mind out of all reason."

That is what I said to him, as I did not wish to introduce a new horror into an affair that was already horrible enough. But, recollecting that these priests, Harût and Marût, believed the mother of this murdered infant to be none other than the oracle of their worship (though how this chanced passed my comprehension), and therefore the great enemy of the evil elephant-god, I confess that at heart I felt afraid. If any powers of magic, black or white or both, were mixed up with the matter as my experiences in England seemed to suggest, who could say what might be their exact limits? As, however, it has been demonstrated again and again by the learned that no such thing as African magic exists, this line of thought appeared to be too foolish to follow. So passing it by I asked Lord Ragnall to continue.

"For over a month," he went on, "I stopped in Egypt waiting till emissaries who had been sent to the chiefs of various tribes in the Sudan and elsewhere, returned with the news that nothing whatsoever had been seen of a white woman travelling in the company of natives, nor had they heard of any such woman being sold as a slave. Also through the Khedive, on whom I was able to bring influence to bear by help of the British Government, I caused many harems in Egypt to be visited, entirely without result. After this, leaving the inquiry in the hands of the British Consul and a firm of French lawyers, although in truth all hope had gone, I returned to England whither I had already sent Lady Longden, broken-hearted, for it occurred to me as possible that my wife might have drifted or been taken thither. But here, too, there was no trace of her or of anybody who could possibly answer to her description. So at last I came to the conclusion that her bones must lie somewhere at the bottom of the Nile, and gave way to despair."

"Always a foolish thing to do," I remarked.

"You will say so indeed when you hear the end, Quatermain. My bereavement and the sleeplessness which it caused prayed upon me so much, for now that the child was dead my wife was everything to me, that, I will tell you the truth, my brain became affected and like Job I cursed God in my heart and determined to die. Indeed I should have died by my own hand, had it not been for Savage. I had procured the laudanum and loaded the pistol with which I proposed to shoot myself immediately after it was swallowed so that there might be no mistake. One night only a couple of months or so ago, Quatermain, I sat in my study at Ragnall, with the doors locked as I thought, writing a few final letters before I did the deed. The last of them was just finished about twelve when hearing a noise, I looked up and saw Savage standing before me. I asked him angrily how he came there (I suppose he must have had another key to one of the other doors) and what he wanted. Ignoring the first part of the question he replied:

"'My lord, I have been thinking over our trouble'—he was with us in Egypt—'I have been thinking so much that it has got a hold of my sleep. Tonight as you said you did not want me any more and I was tired, I went to bed early and had a dream. I dreamed that we were once more in the shrubbery, as happened some years ago, and that the little African gent who shot like a book, was showing us the traces of those two black men, just as he did when they tried to steal her ladyship. Then in my dream I seemed to go back to bed and that beastly snake which we found lying under the parcel in the road seemed to follow me. When I had got to sleep again, all in the dream, there it was standing on its tail at the end of the bed, hissing till it woke me. Then it spoke in good English and not in African as might have been expected.

"'Savage,'" it said, "get up and dress yourself and go at once and tell his lordship to travel to Natal and find Mr. Allan Quatermain" (you may remember that was the African gentleman's name, my lord, which, with so many coming and going in this great house, I had quite forgotten, until I had the dream). "Find Mr. Allan Quatermain," that slimy reptile went on, opening and shutting its mouth for all the world like a Christian making a speech, "for he will have something to tell him as to that which has made a hole in his heart that is now filled with the seven devils. Be quick, Savage, and don't stop to put on your shirt or your tie"—I have not, my lord, as you may see. "He is shut up in the study, but you know how to get into it. If he will not listen to you let him look round the study and he will see something which will tell him that this is a true dream."

"'Then the snake vanished, seeming to wriggle down the left bottom bed-post, and I woke up in a cold sweat, my lord, and did what it had told me.'

"Those were his very words, Quatermain, for I wrote them down afterwards while they were fresh in my memory, and you see here they are in my pocket-book.

"Well, I answered him, rather brusquely I am afraid, for a crazed man who is about to leave the world under such circumstances does not show at his best when disturbed almost in the very act, to the edge of which long agony has brought him. I told him that all his dream of snakes seemed ridiculous, which obviously it was, and was about to send him away, when it occurred to me that the suggestion it conveyed that I should put myself in communication with you was not ridiculous in view of the part you had already played in the story."

"Very far from ridiculous," I interpolated.

"To tell the truth," went on Lord Ragnall, "I had already thought of doing the same thing, but somehow beneath the pressure of my imminent grief the idea was squeezed out of my mind, perhaps because you were so far away and I did not know if I could find you even if I tried. Pausing for a moment before I dismissed Savage, I rose from the desk at which I was writing and began to walk up and down the room thinking what I would do. I am not certain if you saw it when you were at Ragnall, but it is a large room, fifty feet long or so though not very broad. It has two fireplaces, in both of which fires were burning on this night, and it was lit by four standing lamps besides that upon my desk. Now between these fireplaces, in a kind of niche in the wall, and a little in the shadow because none of the lamps was exactly opposite to it, hung a portrait of my wife which I had caused to be painted by a fashionable artist when first we became engaged."

"I remember it," I said. "Or rather, I remember its existence. I did not see it because a curtain hung over the picture, which Savage told me you did not wish to be looked at by anybody but yourself. At the time I remarked to him, or rather to myself, that to veil the likeness of a living woman in such a way seemed to me rather an ill-omened thing to do, though why I should have thought it so I do not quite know."

"You are quite right, Quatermain. I had that foolish fancy, a lover's freak, I suppose. When we married the curtain was removed although the brass rod on which it hung was left by some oversight. On my return to England after my loss, however, I found that I could not bear to look upon this lifeless likeness of one who had been taken from me so cruelly, and I caused it to be replaced. I did more. In order that it might not be disturbed by some dusting housemaid, I myself made it fast with three or four tin-tacks which I remember I drove through the velvet stuff into the panelling, using a fire iron as a hammer. At the time I thought it a good job although by accident I struck the nail of the third finger of my left hand so hard that it came off. Look, it has not quite finished growing again," and he showed the finger on which the new nail was still in process of formation.

"Well, as I walked up and down the room some impulse caused me to look towards the picture. To my astonishment I saw that it was no longer veiled, although to the best of my belief the curtain had been drawn over it as lately as that afternoon; indeed I could have sworn that this was so. I called to Savage to bring the lamp that stood upon my table, and by its light made an examination. The curtain was drawn back, very tidily, being fastened in its place clear of the little alcove by means of a thin brass chain. Also along one edge of it, that which I had nailed to the panelling, the tin-tacks were still in their places; that is, three of them were, the fourth I found afterwards upon the floor.

"'She looks beautiful, doesn't she, my lord,' said Savage, 'and please God so we shall still find her somewhere in the world.'

"I did not answer him, or even remark upon the withdrawal of the curtain, as to which indeed I never made an inquiry. I suppose that it was done by some zealous servant while I was pretending to eat my dinner—there were one or two new ones in the house whose names and appearance I did not know. What impressed itself upon my mind was that the face which I had never expected to see again on the earth, even in a picture, was once more given to my eyes, it mattered not how. This, in my excited state, for laudanum waiting to be swallowed and a pistol at full cock for firing do not induce calmness in a man already almost mad, at any rate until they have fulfilled their offices, did in truth appear to me to be something of the nature of a sign such as that spoken of in Savage's idiotic dream, which I was to find if 'I looked round the study.'

"'Savage,' I said, 'I don't think much of your dreams about snakes that talk to you, but I do think that it might be well to see Mr. Quatermain. Today is Sunday and I believe that the African mail sails on Friday. Go to town early tomorrow and book passages.'

"Also I told him to see various gunsmiths and bid them send down a selection of rifles and other weapons for me to choose from, as I did not know whither we might wander in Africa, and to make further necessary arrangements. All of these things he did, and—here we are."

"Yes," I answered reflectively, "here you are. What is more, here is your luggage of which there seems to be enough for a regiment," and I pointed to a Scotch cart piled up with baggage and followed by a long line of *Kafirs* carrying sundry packages upon their heads that, marshalled by Savage, had halted at my gate.

CHAPTER 8

The Start

That evening when the baggage had been disposed of and locked up in my little stable and arrangements were made for the delivery of some cases containing tinned foods, etc., which had proved too heavy for the Scotch cart, Lord Ragnall and I continued our conversation. First, however, we unpacked the guns and checked the ammunition, of which there was a large supply, with more to follow.

A beautiful battery they were of all sorts from elephant guns down, the most costly and best finished that money could buy at the time. It made me shiver to think what the bill for them must have been, while their appearance when they were put together and stood in a long line against the wall of my sitting-room, moved old Hans to a kind of ecstasy. For a long while he contemplated them, patting the stocks one after the other and giving to each a name as though they were all alive, then exclaimed:

"With such weapons as these the Baas could kill the devil himself. Still, let the Baas bring *Intombi* with him"—a favourite old rifle of mine and a mere toy in size, that had however done me good service in the past, as those who have read what I have written in *Marie* and *The Holy Flower* may remember. "For, Baas, after all, the wife of one's youth often proves more to be trusted than the fine young ones a man buys in his age. Also one knows all her faults, but who can say how many there may be hidden up in new women however beautifully they are tattooed?" and he pointed to the elaborate engraving upon the guns.

I translated this speech to Lord Ragnall. It made him laugh, at which I was glad for up till then I had not seen him even smile. I should add that in addition to these sporting weapons there were no fewer than fifty military rifles of the best make, they were large-bore Sniders that had just then been put upon the market, and with them, packed in tin cases, a great quantity of ammunition. Although the

357

regulations were not so strict then as they are now, I met with a great deal of difficulty in getting all this armament through the Customs. Lord Ragnall however had letters from the Colonial Office to such authorities as ruled in Natal, and on our giving a joint undertaking that they were for defensive purposes only in unexplored territory and not for sale, they were allowed through. Fortunate did it prove for us in after days that this matter was arranged.

That night before we went to bed I narrated to Lord Ragnall all the history of our search for the Holy Flower, which he seemed to find very entertaining. Also I told him of my adventures, to me far more terrible, as chairman of the Bona Fide Gold Mine and of their melancholy end.

"The lesson of which is," he remarked when I had finished, "that because a man is master of one trade, it does not follow that he is master of another. You are, I should judge, one of the finest shots in the world, you are also a great hunter and explorer. But when it comes to companies, Quatermain———! Still," he went on, "I ought to be grateful to that Bona Fide Gold Mine, since I gather that had it not been for it and for your rascally friend, Mr. Jacob, I should not have found you here."

"No," I answered, "it is probable that you would not, as by this time I might have been far in the interior where a man cannot be traced and letters do not reach him."

Then he made a few pointed inquiries about the affairs of the mine, noting my answers down in his pocket-book. I thought this odd but concluded that he wished to verify my statements before entering into a close companionship with me, since for aught he knew I might be the largest liar in the world and a swindler to boot. So I said nothing, even when I heard through a roundabout channel on the morrow that he had sought an interview with the late secretary of the defunct company.

A few days later, for I may as well finish with this matter at once, the astonishing object of these inquiries was made clear to me. One morning I found upon my table a whole pile of correspondence, at the sight of which I groaned, feeling sure that it must come from duns and be connected with that infernal mine. Curiosity and a desire to face the worst, however, led me to open the first letter which as it happened proved to be from that very shareholder who had proposed a vote of confidence in me at the winding-up meeting. By the time that it was finished my eyes were swimming and really I felt quite faint. It ran:

Honoured Sir,—I knew that I was putting my money on the right horse when I said the other day that you were one of the straightest that ever ran. Well, I have got the cheque sent me by the lawyer on your account, being payment in full for every farthing I invested in the Bona Fide Gold Mine, and I can only say that it is uncommonly useful, for that business had pretty well cleaned me out. God bless you, Mr. Quatermain.

I opened another letter, and another, and another. They were all to the same effect. Bewildered I went on to the *stoep*, where I found Hans with an epistle in his hand which he requested me to be good enough to read. I read it. It was from a well-known firm of local lawyers and said:

On behalf of Allan Quatermain, Esq., we beg to enclose a draft for the sum of £650, being the value of the interest in the Bona Fide Gold Company, Limited (in liquidation), which stands in your name on the books of the company. Please sign enclosed receipt and return same to us.

Yes, and there was the draft for £650 sterling!

I explained the matter to Hans, or rather I translated the document, adding:

"You see you have got your money back again. But Hans, I never sent it; I don't know where it comes from."

"Is it money, Baas?" asked Hans, surveying the draft with suspicion. "It looks very much like the other bit of paper for which I paid money."

Again I explained, reiterating that I knew nothing of the transaction.

"Well, Baas," he said, "if you did not send it someone did—perhaps your father the reverend Predikant, who sees that you are in trouble and wishes to wash your name white again. Meanwhile, Baas, please put that bit of paper in your pocket-book and keep it for me, for otherwise I might be tempted to buy square-face with it."

"No," I answered, "you can now buy your land back, or some other land, and there will be no need for you to come with me to the country of the Kendah."

Hans thought a moment and then very deliberately began to tear up the draft; indeed I was only just in time to save it from destruction.

"If the Baas is going to turn me off because of this paper," he said, "I will make it small and eat it."

"You silly old fool," I said as I possessed myself of the cheque.

Then the conversation was interrupted, for who should appear but Sammy, my old cook, who began in his pompous language:

"The perfect rectitude of your conduct, Mr. Quatermain, moves me to the deepest gratitude, though indeed I wish that I had put something into the food of the knave Jacob who beguiled us all, that would have caused him internal pangs of a severe if not of a dangerous order. My holding in the gold mine was not extensive, but the unpaid bill of the said Jacob and his friends——"

Here I cut him short and fled, since I saw yet another shareholder galloping to the gate, and behind him two more in a spider. First I took refuge in my room, my idea being to put away that pile of letters. In so doing I observed that there was one still unopened. Half mechanically I took it from the envelope and glanced at its contents. They were word for word identical with those of that addressed to "Mr. Hans, Hottentot," only my name was at the bottom of it instead of that of Hans and the cheque was for £1,500, the amount I had paid for the shares I held in the venture.

Feeling as though my brain were in a melting-pot, I departed from the house into a patch of native bush that in those days still grew upon the slope of the hill behind. Here I sat myself down, as I had often done before when there was a knotty point to be considered, aimlessly watching a lovely emerald cuckoo flashing, a jewel of light, from tree to tree, while I turned all this fairy-godmother business over in my mind.

Of course it soon became clear to me. Lord Ragnall in this case was the little old lady with the wand, the touch of which could convert worthless share certificates into bank-notes of their face value. I remembered now that his wealth was said to be phenomenal and after all the cash capital of the company was quite small. But the question was—could I accept his bounty?

I returned to the house where the first person whom I met was Lord Ragnall himself, just arrived from some interview about the fifty Snider rifles, which were still in bond. I told him solemnly that I wished to speak to him, whereon he remarked in a cheerful voice,

"Advance, friend, and all's well!"

I don't know that I need set out the details of the interview. He waited till I had got through my halting speech of mingled gratitude and expostulation, then remarked:

"My friend, if you will allow me to call you so, it is quite true that I have done this because I wished to do it. But it is equally true that to me it is a small thing—to be frank, scarcely a month's income; what I have saved travelling on that ship to Natal would pay for it all. Also I have weighed my own interest in the matter, for I am anxious that you should start upon this hazardous journey of ours up country with a mind absolutely free from self-reproach or any money care, for thus you will be able to do me better service. Therefore I beg that you will say no more of the episode. I have only one thing to add, namely that I have myself bought up at par value a few of the debentures. The price of them will pay the lawyers and the liquidation fees; moreover they give me a status as a shareholder which will enable me to sue Mr. Jacob for his fraud, to which business I have already issued instructions. For please understand that I have not paid off any shares still standing in his name or in those of his friends."

Here I may add that nothing ever came of this action, for the lawyers found themselves unable to serve any writ upon that elusive person, Mr. Jacob, who by then had probably adopted the name of some other patriarch.

"Please put it all down as a rich man's whim," he concluded.

"I can't call that a whim which has returned £1,500 odd to my pocket that I had lost upon a gamble, Lord Ragnall."

"Do you remember, Quatermain, how you won £250 upon a gamble at my place and what you did with it, which sum probably represented to you twenty or fifty times what it would to me? Also if that argument does not appeal to you, may I remark that I do not expect you to give me your services as a professional hunter and guide for nothing."

"Ah!" I answered, fixing on this point and ignoring the rest, "now we come to business. If I may look upon this amount as salary, a very handsome salary by the way, paid in advance, you taking the risks of my dying or becoming incapacitated before it is earned, I will say no more of the matter. If not I must refuse to accept what is an unearned gift."

"I confess, Quatermain, that I did not regard it in that light, though I might have been willing to call it a retaining fee. However, do not let us wrangle about money any more. We can always settle our accounts when the bill is added up, if ever we reach so far. Now let us come to more important details."

So we fell to discussing the scheme, route and details of our proposed journey. Expenditure being practically no object, there were several plans open to us. We might sail up the coast and go by Kilwa, as I had done on the search for the Holy Flower, or we might retrace the line of our retreat from the Mazitu country which ran through Zululand. Again, we might advance by whatever road we selected with a small army of drilled and disciplined retainers, trusting to force to break a way through to the Kendah. Or we might go practically unaccompanied, relying on our native wit and good fortune to attain our ends. Each of these alternatives had so much to recommend it and yet presented so many difficulties, that after long hours of discussion, for this talk was renewed again and again, I found it quite impossible to decide upon any one of them, especially as in the end Lord Ragnall always left the choice with its heavy responsibilities to me.

At length in despair I opened the window and whistled twice on a certain low note. A minute later Hans shuffled in, shaking the wet off the new corduroy clothes which he had bought upon the strength of his return to affluence, for it was raining outside, and squatted himself down upon the floor at a little distance. In the shadow of the table which cut off the light from the hanging lamp he looked, I remember, exactly like an enormous and antique toad. I threw him a piece of tobacco which he thrust into his corn-cob pipe and lit with a match.

"The Baas called me," he said when it was drawing to his satisfaction, "what does Baas want of Hans?"

"Light in darkness!" I replied, playing on his native name, and proceeded to set out the whole case to him.

He listened without a word, then asked for a small glass of gin, which I gave him doubtfully. Having swallowed this at a gulp as though it were water, he delivered himself briefly to this effect:

"I think the Baas will do well not to go to Kilwa, since it means waiting for a ship, or hiring one; also there may be more slave-traders there by now who will bear him no love because of a lesson he taught them a while ago. On the other hand the road through Zululand is open, though it be long, and there the name of Macumazana is one well known. I think also that the Baas would do well not to take too many men, who make marching slow, only a wagon or two and some drivers which might be sent back when they can go no farther. From Zululand messengers can be dispatched to the Mazitu, who love you, and Bausi or whoever is king there today will order bearers to meet us on the road, until which time we can hire other bearers in Zululand. The old woman at Beza Town told me, moreover, as you will remember, that the Kendah are a very great people who live by themselves and will allow none to enter their land, which is bordered by deserts. Therefore no force that you could take with you and feed upon a road without water would be strong enough to knock down their gates like an elephant, and it seems better that you should try to creep through them like a wise snake, although they appear to be shut in your face. Perhaps also they will not be shut since did you not say that two of their great doctors promised to meet you and guide you through them?"

"Yes," I interrupted, "I dare say it will be easier to get in than to get out of Kendahland."

"Last of all, Baas, if you take many men armed with guns, the black part of the Kendah people of whom I told you will perhaps think you come to make war, whatever the white Kendah may say, and kill us all, whereas if we be but a few perchance they will let us pass in peace. I think that is all, Baas. Let the Baas and the Lord Igeza forgive me if my words are foolish."

Here I should explain that Igeza was the name which the natives had given to Lord Ragnall because of his appearance. The word means a handsome person in the Zulu tongue. Savage they called Bena, I don't know why. *Bena* in Zulu means to push out the breast and it may be that the name was a round-about allusion to the proud appearance of the dignified Savage, or possibly it had some other recondite signification. At any rate Lord Ragnall, Hans and myself knew the splendid Savage thenceforward by the homely appellation of Beans. His master said it suited him very well because he was so green.

"The advice seems wise, Hans. Go now. No, no more gin," I answered. As a matter of fact careful consideration convinced us it was so wise that we acted on it down to the last detail.

* * * * * * * *

So it came about that one fine afternoon about a fortnight later, for hurry as we would our preparations took a little time, we trekked for Zululand over the sandy roads that ran from the outskirts of Durban. Our baggage and stores were stowed in two half-tented wagons, very good wagons since everything we had with us was the best that money could buy, the after-part of which served us as sleeping-places at night. Hans sat on the *voor-kisse* or driving-seat of one of the wagons; Lord Ragnall, Savage and I were mounted upon *salted* horses, that is, horses which had recovered from and were therefore supposed to be proof against the dreadful sickness, valuable and docile animals which were trained to shooting.

At our start a little contretemps occurred. To my amazement I saw Savage, who insisted upon continuing to wear his funereal upper servant's cut-away coat, engaged with grim determination in mounting his steed from the wrong side. He got into the saddle somehow, but there was worse to follow. The horse, astonished at such treatment, bolted a little way, Savage sawing at its mouth. Lord Ragnall and I cantered after it past the wagons, fearing disaster. All of a sudden it swerved violently and Savage flew into the air, landing heavily in a sitting posture.

"Poor Beans!" ejaculated Lord Ragnall as we sped forward. "I expect there is an end of his journeyings."

To our surprise, however, we saw him leap from the ground with the most marvellous agility and begin to dance about slapping at his posterior parts and shouting,

"Take it off! Kill it!"

A few seconds later we discovered the reason. The horse had shied at a sleeping puff adder which was curled up in the sand of that little frequented road, and on this puff adder Savage had descended with so much force, for he weighed thirteen stone, that the creature was squashed quite flat and never stirred again. This, however, he did not notice in his agitation, being convinced indeed that it was hanging to him behind like a bulldog.

"Snakes! my lord," he exclaimed, when at last after careful search we demonstrated to him that the adder had died before it could come into action.

"I hate 'em, my lord, and they haunts" (he said 'aunts) "me. If ever I get out of this I'll go and live in Ireland, my lord, where they say there ain't none. But it isn't likely that I shall," he added mournfully, "for the omen is horrid."

"On the contrary," I answered, "it is splendid, for you have killed the snake and not the snake you. 'The dog it was that died,' Savage."

After this the *Kafirs* gave Savage a second very long name which meant "He-who-sits-down-on-snakes-and-makes-them-flat." Having remounted him on his horse, which was standing patiently a few yards away, at length we got off. I lingered a minute behind the others to give some directions to my old Griqua gardener, Jack, who snivelled at parting with me, and to take a last look at my little home. Alack! I feared it might be the last indeed, knowing as I did that this was a dangerous enterprise upon which I found myself embarked, I who had vowed that I would be done with danger.

With a lump in my throat I turned from the contemplation of that peaceful dwelling and happy garden in which each tree and plant was dear to me, and waving a good-bye to Jack, cantered on to where Ragnall was waiting for me.

"I am afraid this is rather a sad hour for you, who are leaving your little boy and your home," he said gently, "to face unknown perils."

"Not so sad as others I have passed," I answered, "and perils are my daily bread in every sense of the word. Moreover, whatever it is for me it is for you also."

"No, Quatermain. For me it is an hour of hope; a faint hope, I admit, but the only one left, for the letters I got last night from Egypt and England report that no clue whatsoever has been found, and indeed that the search for any has been abandoned. Yes, I follow the last star left in my sky and if it sets I hope that I may set also, at any rate to this world. Therefore I am happier than I have been for months, thanks to you," and he stretched out his hand, which I shook.

It was a token of friendship and mutual confidence which I am glad to say nothing that happened afterwards ever disturbed for a moment.

CHAPTER 9

The Meeting in the Desert

Now I do not propose to describe all our journey to Kendahland, or at any rate the first part thereof. It was interesting enough in its way and we met with a few hunting adventures, also some others. But there is so much to tell of what happened to us after we reached the place that I have not the time, even if I had the inclination to set all these matters down. Let it be sufficient, then, to say that although owing to political events the country happened to be rather disturbed at the time, we trekked through Zululand without any great difficulty. For here my name was a power in the land and all parties united to help me. Thence, too, I managed to dispatch three messengers, half-bred border men, lean fellows and swift of foot, forward to the king of the Mazitu, as Hans had suggested that I should do, advising him that his old friends, Macumazana, Watcher-by-Night, and the yellow man who was named Light-in-Darkness and Lord-of-the-Fire, were about to visit him again.

As I knew we could not take the wagons beyond a certain point where there was a river called the Luba, unfordable by anything on wheels, I requested him, moreover, to send a hundred bearers with whatever escort might be necessary, to meet us on the banks of that river at a spot which was known to both of us. These words the messengers promised to deliver for a fee of five head of cattle apiece, to be paid on their return, or to their families if they died on the road, which cattle we purchased and left in charge of a chief, who was their kinsman. As it happened two of the poor fellows did die, one of them of cold in a swamp through which they took a short cut, and the other at the teeth of a hungry lion. The third, however, won through and delivered the message.

After resting for a fortnight in the northern parts of Zululand, to give time to our way-worn oxen to get some flesh on their bones in

366

the warm *bushveld* where grass was plentiful even in the dry season, we trekked forward by a route known to Hans and myself. Indeed it was the same which we had followed on our journey from Mazituland after our expedition in search for the Holy Flower.

We took with us a small army of Zulu bearers. This, although they were difficult to feed in a country where no corn could be bought, proved fortunate in the end, since so many of our cattle died from tsetse bite that we were obliged to abandon one of the wagons, which meant that the goods it contained must be carried by men. At length we reached the banks of the river, and camped there one night by three tall peaks of rock which the natives called the Three Doctors, where I had instructed the messengers to tell the Mazitu to meet us. For four days we remained here, since rains in the interior had made the river quite impassable. Every morning I climbed the tallest of the Doctors and with my glasses looked over its broad yellow flood, searching the wide, bush-clad land beyond in the hope of discovering the Mazitu advancing to meet us. Not a man was to be seen, however, and on the fourth evening, as the river had now become fordable, we determined that we would cross on the morrow, leaving the remaining wagon, which it was impossible to drag over its rocky bottom, to be taken back to Natal by our drivers.

Here a difficulty arose. No promise of reward would induce any of our Zulu bearers even to wet their feet in the waters of this River Luba, which for some reason that I could not extract from them they declared to be *tagati*, that is, bewitched, to people of their blood. When I pointed out that three Zulus had already undertaken to cross it, they answered that those men were half-breeds, so that for them it was only half bewitched, but they thought that even so one or more of them would pay the penalty of death for this rash crime.

It chanced that this happened, for, as I have said, two of the poor fellows did die, though not, I think, owing to the magical properties of the waters of the Luba. This is how African superstitions are kept alive. Sooner or later some saying of the sort fulfils itself and then the instance is remembered and handed down for generations, while other instances in which nothing out of the common has occurred are not heeded, or are forgotten.

This decision on the part of those stupid Zulus put us in an awkward fix, since it was impossible for us to carry over all our baggage and ammunition without help. Therefore glad was I when before dawn on the fifth morning the nocturnal Hans crept into the wagon, in the after part of which Ragnall and I were sleeping, and informed us that he heard men's voices on the farther side of the river, though how he could hear anything above that roar of water passed my comprehension.

At the first break of dawn again we climbed the tallest of the "Doctor" rocks and stared into the mist. At length it rolled away and there on the farther side of the river I saw quite a hundred men who by their dress and spears I knew to be Mazitu. They saw me also and raising a cheer, dashed into the water, groups of them holding each other round the middle to prevent their being swept away. Thereupon our silly Zulus seized their spears and formed up upon the bank. I slid down the steep side of the Great Doctor and ran forward, calling out that these were friends who came.

"Friends or foes," answered their captain sullenly, "it is a pity that we should walk so far and not have a fight with those Mazitu dogs."

Well, I drove them off to a distance, not knowing what might happen if the two peoples met, and then went down to the bank. By now the Mazitu were near, and to my delight at the head of them I perceived no other than my old friend, their chief general, Babemba, a one-eyed man with whom Hans and I had shared many adventures. Through the water he plunged with great bounds and reaching the shore, greeted me literally with rapture.

"O Macumazana," he said, "little did I hope that ever again I should look upon your face. Welcome to you, a thousand welcomes, and to you too, Light-in-Darkness, Lord-of-the-Fire, Cunning-one whose wit saved us in the battle of the Gate. But where is Dogeetah, where is Wazeela, and where are the mother and the child of the Flower?"

"Far away across the Black Water, Babemba," I answered. "But here are two others in place of them," and I introduced him to Ragnall and Savage by their native names of Igeza and Bena.

He contemplated them for a moment, then said:

"This," pointing to Ragnall, "is a great lord, but this," pointing to Savage, who was much the better dressed of the two, "is a cock of the ash-pit arrayed in an eagle's feathers," a remark I did not translate, but one which caused Hans to snigger vacuously.

While we breakfasted on food prepared by the cock of the ash-pit, who amongst many other merits had that of being an excellent cook, I heard all the news. Bausi the king was dead but had been succeeded by one of his sons, also named Bausi, whom I remembered. Beza Town had been rebuilt after the great fire that destroyed the slavers, and much more strongly fortified than before. Of the slavers themselves nothing more had been seen, or of the Pongo either, though the Mazitu declared that their ghosts, or those of their victims, still haunted the island in the lake. That was all, except the ill tidings as to two of our messengers which the third, who had returned with the Mazitu, reported to us.

After breakfast I addressed and sent away our Zulus, each with a handsome present from the trade goods, giving into their charge the remaining wagon and our servants, none of whom, somewhat to my relief, wished to accompany us farther. They sang their song of good-bye, saluted and departed over the rise, still looking hungrily behind them at the Mazitu, and we were very pleased to see the last of them without bloodshed or trouble.

When we had watched the white tilt of the wagon vanish, we set to work to get ourselves and our goods across the river. This we accomplished safely, for the Mazitu worked for us like friends and not as do hired men. On the farther bank, however, it took us two full days so to divide up the loads that the bearers could carry them without being overladen.

At length all was arranged and we started. Of the month's trek that followed there is nothing to tell, except that we completed it without notable accidents and at last reached the new Beza Town, which much resembled the old, where we were accorded a great public reception. Bausi II himself headed the procession which met us outside the south gate on that very mound which we had occupied in the great fight, where the bones of the gallant Mavovo and my other hunters lay buried. Almost did it seem to me as though I could hear their deep voices joining in the shouts of welcome.

That night, while the Mazitu feasted in our honour, we held an *indaba* in the big new guest house with Bausi II, a pleasant-faced young man, and old Babemba. The king asked us how long we meant to stay at Beza Town, intimating his hope that the visit would be prolonged. I replied, but a few days, as we were travelling far to the north to find a people called the Kendah whom we wished to see, and hoped that he would give us bearers to carry our goods as far as the confines of their country. At the name of Kendah a look of astonishment appeared upon their faces and Babemba said:

"Has madness seized you, Macumazana, that you would attempt this thing? Oh surely you must be mad."

"You thought us mad, Babemba, when we crossed the lake to Rica Town, yet we came back safely."

"True, Macumazana, but compared to the Kendah the Pongo were but as the smallest star before the face of the sun."

369

"What do you know of them then?" I asked. "But stay—before you answer, I will speak what I know," and I repeated what I had learned from Hans, who confirmed my words, and from Harût and Marût, leaving out, however, any mention of their dealings with Lady Ragnall.

"It is all true," said Babemba when I had finished, "for that old woman of whom Light-in-the-Darkness speaks, was one of the wives of my uncle and I knew her well. Hearken! These Kendah are a terrible nation and countless in number and of all the people the fiercest. Their king is called Simba, which means *lion*. He who rules is always called Simba, and has been so called for hundreds of years. He is of the Black Kendah whose god is the elephant Jana, but as Light-in-Darkness has said, there are also the White Kendah who are Arab men, the priests and traders of the people. The Kendah will allow no stranger within their doors; if one comes they kill him by torment, or blind him and turn him out into the desert which surrounds their country, there to die. These things the old woman who married my uncle told me, as she told them to Light-in-Darkness, also I have heard them from others, and what she did not tell me, that the White Kendah are great breeders of the beasts called camels which they sell to the Arabs of the north. Go not near them, for if you pass the desert the Black Kendah will kill you; and if you escape these, then their king, Simba, will kill you; and if you escape him, then their god Jana will kill you; and if you escape him, then their white priests will kill you with their magic. Oh! long before you look upon the faces of those priests you will be dead many times over."

"Then why did they ask me to visit them, Babemba?"

"I know not, Macumazana, but perhaps because they wished to make an offering of you to the god Jana, whom no spear can harm; no, nor even your bullets that pierce a tree."

"I am willing to make trial of that matter," I answered confidently, "and any way we must go to see these things for ourselves."

"Yes," echoed Ragnall, "we must certainly go," while even Savage, for I had been translating to them all this while, nodded his head although he looked as though he would much rather stay behind.

"Ask him if there are any snakes there, sir," he said, and foolishly enough I put the question to give me time to think of other things.

"Yes, O Bena. Yes, O Cock of the Ash-pit," replied Babemba. "My uncle's Kendar wife told me that one of the guardians of the shrine of the White Kendah is such a snake as was never seen elsewhere in the world."

"Then say to him, sir," said Savage, when I had translated almost automatically, "that shrine ain't a church where *I* shall go to say my prayers."

Alas! poor Savage little knew the future and its gifts.

Then we came to the question of bearers. The end of it was that after some hesitation Bausi II, because of his great affection for us, promised to provide us with these upon our solemnly undertaking to dismiss them at the borders of the desert, "so that they might escape our doom," as he remarked cheerfully.

Four days later we started, accompanied by about one hundred and twenty picked men under the command of old Babemba himself, who, he explained, wished to be the last to see us alive in the world. This was depressing, but other circumstances connected with our start were calculated to weigh even more upon my spirit. Thus the night before we left Hans arrived and asked me to "write a paper" for him. I inquired what he wanted me to put in the paper. He replied that as he was going to his death and had property, namely the £650 that had been left in a bank to his credit, he desired to make a "white man's will" to be left in the charge of Babemba. The only provision of the said will was that I was to inherit his property, if I lived. If I died, which, he added, "of course you must, Baas, like the rest of us," it was to be devoted to furnishing poor black people in hospital with something comforting to drink instead of the "cow's water" that was given to them there. Needless to say I turned him out at once, and that testamentary deposition remained unrecorded. Indeed it was unnecessary, since, as I reminded him, on my advice he had already made a will before we left Durban, a circumstance that he had quite forgotten.

The second event, which occurred about an hour before our departure, was, that hearing a mighty wailing in the market-place where once Hans and I had been tied to stakes to be shot to death with arrows, I went out to see what was the matter. At the gateway I was greeted by the sight of about a hundred old women plastered all over with ashes, engaged in howling their loudest in a melancholy unison. Behind these stood the entire population of Beza Town, who chanted a kind of chorus.

"What the devil are they doing?" I asked of Hans.

"Singing our death-song, Baas," he replied stolidly, "as they say that where we are going no one will take the trouble to do so, and it is not right that great lords should die and the heavens above remain uninformed that they are coming."

"That's cheerful," I remarked, and wheeling round, asked Ragnall straight out if he wished to persevere in this business, for to tell the truth my nerve was shaken.

"I must," he answered simply, "but there is no reason why you and Hans should, or Savage either for the matter of that."

371

"Oh! I'm going where you go," I said, "and where I go Hans will go. Savage must speak for himself."

This he did and to the same effect, being a very honest and faithful man. It was the more to his credit since, as he informed me in private, he did not enjoy African adventure and often dreamed at nights of his comfortable room at Ragnall whence he superintended the social activities of that great establishment.

So we departed and marched for the matter of a month or more through every kind of country. After we had passed the head of the great lake wherein lay the island, if it really was an island, where the Pongo used to dwell (one clear morning through my glasses I discerned the mountain top that marked the former residence of the Mother of the Flower, and by contrast it made me feel quite homesick), we struck up north, following a route known to Babemba and our guides. After this we steered by the stars through a land with very few inhabitants, timid and nondescript folk who dwelt in scattered villages and scarcely understood the art of cultivating the soil, even in its most primitive form.

A hundred miles or so farther on these villages ceased and thenceforward we only encountered some nomads, little bushmen who lived on game which they shot with poisoned arrows. Once they attacked us and killed two of the Mazitu with those horrid arrows, against the venom of which no remedy that we had in our medicine chest proved of any avail. On this occasion Savage exhibited his courage if not his discretion, for rushing out of our thorn fence, after missing a bushmen with both barrels at a distance of five yards—he was, I think, the worst shot I ever saw—he seized the little viper with his hands and dragged him back to camp. How Savage escaped with his life I do not know, for one poisoned arrow went through his hat and stuck in his hair and another just grazed his leg without drawing blood.

This valorous deed was of great service to us, since we were able through Hans, who knew something of the bushmen's language, to explain to our prisoner that if we were shot at again he would be hung. This information he contrived to shout, or rather to squeak and grunt, to his amiable tribe, of which it appeared he was a kind of chief, with the result that we were no more molested. Later, when we were clear of the bushmen country, we let him depart, which he did with great rapidity.

By degrees the land grew more and more barren and utterly devoid of inhabitants, till at last it merged into desert. At the edge of this desert which rolled away without apparent limit we came, however, to a kind of oasis where there was a strong and beautiful spring of water that formed a stream which soon lost itself in the surrounding sand. As we could go no farther, for even if we had wished to do so, and were able to find water there, the Mazitu refused to accompany us into the desert, not knowing what else to do, we camped in the oasis and waited.

As it happened, the place was a kind of hunter's paradise, since every kind of game, large and small, came to the water to drink at night, and in the daytime browsed upon the saltish grass that at this season of the year grew plentifully upon the edge of the wilderness.

Amongst other creatures there were elephants in plenty that travelled hither out of the bushlands we had passed, or sometimes emerged from the desert itself, suggesting that beyond this waste there lay fertile country. So numerous were these great beasts indeed that for my part I hoped earnestly that it would prove impossible for us to continue our journey, since I saw that in a few months I could collect an enormous amount of ivory, enough to make me comparatively rich, if only I were able to get it away. As it was we only killed a few of them, ten in all to be accurate, that we might send back the tusks as presents to Bausi II. To slaughter the poor animals uselessly was cruel, especially as being unaccustomed to the sight of man, they were as easy to approach as cows. Even Savage slew one—by carefully aiming at another five paces to its left.

For the rest we lived on the fat of the land and, as meat was necessary to us, had as much sport as we could desire among the various antelope.

For fourteen days or so this went on, till at length we grew thoroughly tired of the business, as did the Mazitu, who were so gorged with flesh that they began to desire vegetable food. Twice we rode as far into the desert as we dared, for our horses remained to us and had grown fresh again after the rest, but only to return without information. The place was just a vast wilderness strewn with brown stones beautifully polished by the wind-driven sand of ages, and quite devoid of water.

After our second trip, on which we suffered severely from thirst, we held a consultation. Old Babemba said that he could keep his men no longer, even for us, as they insisted upon returning home, and inquired what we meant to do and why we sat here "like a stone." I answered that we were waiting for some of the Kendah who had bid me to shoot game hereabouts until they arrived to be our guides. He remarked that the Kendah to the best of his belief lived in a country that was still hundreds of miles away and that, as they did not know of our presence, any communication across the desert being impossible, our proceedings seemed to be foolish.

373

I retorted that I was not quite so sure of this, since the Kendah seemed to have remarkable ways of acquiring information.

"Then, Macumazana, I fear that you will have to wait by yourselves until you discover which of us is right," he said stolidly.

Turning to Ragnall, I asked him what he would do, pointing out that to journey into the desert meant death, especially as we did not know whither we were going, and that to return alone, without the stores which we must abandon, through the country of the bushmen to Mazituland, would also be a risky proceeding. However, it was for him to decide.

Now he grew much perturbed. Taking me apart again he dwelt earnestly upon his secret reasons for wishing to visit these Kendah, with which of course I was already acquainted, as indeed was Savage.

"I desire to stay here," he ended.

"Which means that we must all stay, Ragnall, since Savage will not desert you. Nor will Hans desert me although he thinks us mad. He points out that I came to seek ivory and here about is ivory in plenty for the trouble of taking."

"I might remain alone, Quatermain——" he began, but I looked at him in such a way that he never finished the sentence.

Ultimately we came to a compromise. Babemba, on behalf of the Mazitu, agreed to wait three more days. If nothing happened during that period we on our part agreed to return with them to a stretch of well-watered bush about fifty miles behind us, which we knew swarmed with elephants, that by now were growing shy of approaching our oasis where there was so much noise and shooting. There we would kill as much ivory as we could carry, an operation in which they were willing to assist for the fun of it, and then go back with them to Mazituland.

The three days went by and with every hour that passed my spirits rose, as did those of Savage and Hans, while Lord Ragnall became more and more depressed. The third afternoon was devoted to a jubilant packing of loads, for in accordance with the terms of our bargain we were to start backwards on our spoor at dawn upon the morrow. Most happily did I lay myself down to sleep in my little bough shelter that night, feeling that at last I was rid of an uncommonly awkward adventure. If I thought that we could do any good by staying on, it would have been another matter. But as I was certain that there was no earthly chance of our finding among the Kendah—if ever we reached them—the lady who had tumbled in the Nile in Egypt, well, I was glad that providence had been so good as to make it impossible for us to commit suicide by thirst in a desert, or otherwise. For, notwith-standing my former reasonings to the contrary, I was now convinced that this was what had happened to poor Ragnall's wife.

That, however, was just what providence had not done. In the middle of the night, to be precise, at exactly two in the morning, I was awakened by Hans, who slept at the back of my shanty, into which he had crept through a hole in the faggots, exclaiming in a frightened voice,

"Open your eyes and look, Baas. There are two *spooks* waiting to see you outside, Baas."

Very cautiously I lifted myself a little and stared out into the moon-light. There, seated about five paces from the open end of the hut were the *spooks* sure enough, two white-robed figures squatting silent and immovable on the ground. At first I was frightened. Then I bethought me of thieves and felt for my Colt pistol under the rug that served me as a pillow. As I got hold of the handle, however, a deep voice said:

"Is it your custom, O Macumazana, Watcher-by-Night, to receive guests with bullets?"

Now thought I to myself, who is there in the world who could see a man catch hold of the handle of a pistol in the recesses of a dark place and under a blanket at night, except the owner of that voice which I seemed to remember hearing in a certain drawing-room in England?

"Yes, Harût," I answered with an unconcerned yawn, "when the guests come in such a doubtful fashion and in the middle of the night. But as you are here at last, will you be so good as to tell us why you have kept us waiting all this time? Is that your way of fulfilling an engagement?"

"O Lord Macumazana," answered Harût, for of course it was he, in quite a perturbed tone, "I offer to you our humble apologies. The truth is that when we heard of your arrival at Beza Town we started, or tried to start, from hundreds of miles away to keep our tryst with you here as we promised we would do. But we are mortal, Macumazana, and accidents intervened. Thus, when we had ascertained the weight of your baggage, camels had to be collected to carry it, which were grazing at a distance. Also it was necessary to send forward to dig out a certain well in the desert where they must drink. Hence the delay. Still, you will admit that we have arrived in time, five, or at any rate four hours before the rising of that sun which was to light you on your homeward way."

"Yes, you have, O Prophets, or O Liars, whichever you may be," I exclaimed with pardonable exasperation, for really their knowledge of my private affairs, however obtained, was enough to anger a saint. "So as you are here at last, come in and have a drink, for whether you are men or devils, you must be cold out there in the damp."

In they came accordingly, and, not being Mohammedans, partook of a tot of square-face from a bottle which I kept locked in a box to put Hans beyond the reach of temptation.

"To your health, Harût and Marût," I said, drinking a little out of the pannikin and giving the rest to Hans, who gulped the fiery liquor down with a smack of his lips. For I will admit that I joined in this unholy midnight potation to gain time for thought and to steady my nerve.

"To your health, O Lord Macumazana," the pair answered as they swallowed their tots, which I had made pretty stiff, and set down their pannikins in front of them with as much reverence as though these had been holy vessels.

"Now," I said, throwing a blanket over my shoulders, for the air was chilly, "now let us talk," and taking the lantern which Hans had thoughtfully lighted, I held it up and contemplated them.

There they were, Harût and Marût without doubt, to all appearance totally unchanged since some years before I had seen them at Ragnall in England. "What are you doing here?" I asked in a kind of fiery indignation inspired by my intense curiosity. "How did you get out of England after you had tried to steal away the lady to whom you sent the necklace? What did you do with that lady after you had beguiled her from the boat at Abu-Simbel? In the name of your Holy Child, or of Shaitan of the Mohammedans, or of Set of the Egyptians, answer me, lest I should make an end of both of you, which I can do here without any questions being asked," and I whipped out my pistol.

"Pardon us," said Harût with a grave smile, "but if you were to do as you say, Lord Macumazana, many questions would be asked which *you* might find it hard to answer. So be pleased to put that death-dealer back into its place, and to tell us before we reply to you, what you know of Set of the Egyptians."

"As much or as little as you do," I replied.

Both bowed as though this information were of the most satisfactory order. Then Harût went on: "In reply to your requests, O Macumazana, we left England by a steamboat and in due course after long journeyings we reached our own country. We do not understand your allusions to a place called Abu-Simbel on the Nile, whence, never having been there, we have taken no lady. Indeed, we never meant to take that lady to whom we sent a necklace in England. We only meant to ask certain questions of her, as she had the gift of vision, when you appeared and interrupted us. What should we want with white ladies, who have already far too many of our own?"

"I don't know," I replied, "but I do know that you are the biggest liars I ever met."

At these words, which some might have thought insulting, Harût and Marût bowed again as though to acknowledge a great compliment. Then Harût said:

"Let us leave the question of ladies and come to matters that have to do with men. You are here as we told you that you would be at a time when you did not believe us, and we here to meet *you*, as we told you that we would be. How we knew that you were coming and how we came do not matter at all. Believe what you will. Are you ready to start with us, O Lord Macumazana, that you may bring to its death the wicked elephant Jana which ravages our land, and receive the great reward of ivory? If so, your camel waits."

"One camel cannot carry four men," I answered, avoiding the question.

"In courage and skill you are more than many men, O Macumazana, yet in body you are but one and not four."

"If you think that I am going with you alone, you are much mistaken, Harût and Marût," I exclaimed. "Here with me is my servant without whom I do not stir," and I pointed to Hans, whom they contemplated gravely. "Also there is the Lord Ragnall, who in this land is named Igeza, and his servant who here is named Bena, the man out of whom you drew snakes in the room in England. They also must accompany us."

At this news the impassive countenances of Harût and Marût showed, I thought, some signs of disturbance. They muttered together in an unknown tongue. Then Harût said:

"Our secret land is open to you alone, O Macumazana, for one purpose only—to kill the elephant Jana, for which deed we promise you a great reward. We do not wish to see the others there."

"Then you can kill your own elephant, Harût and Marût, for not one step do I go with you. Why should I when there is as much ivory here as I want, to be had for the shooting?"

"How if we take you, O Macumazana?"

"How if I kill you both, O Harût and Marût? Fools, here are many brave men at my command, and if you or any with you want fighting it shall be given you in plenty. Hans, bid the Mazitu stand to their arms and summon Igeza and Bena."

"Stay, Lord," said Harût, "and put down that weapon," for once more I had produced the pistol. "We would not begin our fellowship by shedding blood, though we are safer from you than you think. Your companions shall accompany you to the land of the Kendah, but let them know that they do so at their own risk. Learn that it is revealed to us that if they go in there some of them will pass out again as spirits but not as men."

"Do you mean that you will murder them?"

"No. We mean that yonder are some stronger than us or any men, who will take their lives in sacrifice. Not yours, Macumazana, for that, it is decreed, is safe, but those of two of the others, which two we do not know."

"Indeed, Harût and Marût, and how am I to be sure that any of us are safe, or that you do not but trick us to your country, there to kill us with treachery and steal our goods?"

"Because we swear it by the oath that may not be broken; we swear it by the Heavenly Child," both of them exclaimed solemnly, speaking with one voice and bowing till their foreheads almost touched the ground.

I shrugged my shoulders and laughed a little.

"You do not believe us," went on Harût, "who have not heard what happens to those who break this oath. Come now and see something. Within five paces of your hut is a tall ant-heap upon which doubtless you have been accustomed to stand and overlook the desert." (This was true, but how did they guess it, I wondered.) "Go climb that ant-heap once more."

Perhaps it was rash, but my curiosity led me to accept this invitation. Out I went, followed by Hans with a loaded double-barrelled rifle, and scrambled up the ant-heap which, as it was twenty feet high and there were no trees just here, commanded a very fine view of the desert beyond.

"Look to the north," said Harût from its foot.

I looked, and there in the bright moonlight five or six hundred yards away, ranged rank by rank upon a slope of sand and along the crest of the ridge beyond, I saw quite two hundred kneeling camels, and by each camel a tall, white-robed figure who held in his hand a long lance to the shaft of which, not far beneath the blade, was attached a little flag. For a while I stared to make sure that I was not the victim of an illusion or a mirage. Then when I had satisfied myself that these were indeed men and camels I descended from the ant-heap.

"You will admit, Macumazana," said Harût politely, "that if we had meant you any ill, with such a force it would have been easy for us to take a sleeping camp at night. But these men come here to be your escort, not to kill or enslave you or yours. And, Macumazana, we have sworn to you the oath that may not be broken. Now we go to our people. In the morning, after you have eaten, we will return again unarmed and alone."

Then like shadows they slipped away.

CHAPTER 10

Charge!

Ten minutes later the truth was known and every man in the camp was up and armed. At first there were some signs of panic, but these with the help of Babemba we managed to control, setting the men to make the best preparations for defence that circumstances would allow, and thus occupying their minds. For from the first we saw that, except for the three of us who had horses, escape was impossible. That great camel corps could catch us within a mile.

Leaving old Babemba in charge of his soldiers, we three white men and Hans held a council at which I repeated every word that had passed between Harût and Marût and myself, including their absolute denial of their having had anything to do with the disappearance of Lady Ragnall on the Nile.

"Now," I asked, "what is to be done? My fate is sealed, since for purposes of their own, of which probably we know nothing, these people intend to take me with them to their country, as indeed they are justified in doing, since I have been fool enough to keep a kind of assignation with them here. But they don't want anybody else. Therefore there is nothing to prevent you Ragnall, and you Savage, and you Hans, from returning with the Mazitu."

"Oh! Baas," said Hans, who could understand English well enough although he seldom spoke it, "why are you always bothering me with such *praatjes?*"—(that is, chatter). "Whatever you do I will do, and I don't care what you do, except for your own sake, Baas. If I am going to die, let me die; it doesn't at all matter how, since I must go soon and make report to your reverend father, the Predikant. And now, Baas, I have been awake all night, for I heard those camels coming a long while before the two spook men appeared, and as I have never heard camels before, could not make out what they were, for they don't walk like giraffes. So I am going to sleep, Baas, there in the sun. When you

380

have settled things, you can wake me up and give me your orders," and he suited the action to the word, for when I glanced at him again he was, or appeared to be, slumbering, just like a dog at its master's feet.

I looked at Ragnall in interrogation.

"I am going on," he said briefly.

"Despite the denial of these men of any complicity in your wife's fate?" I asked. "If their words are true, what have you to gain by this journey, Ragnall?"

"An interesting experience while it lasts; that is all. Like Hans there, if what they say *is* true, my future is a matter of complete indifference to me. But I do not believe a word of what they say. Something tells me that they know a great deal which they do not choose to repeat— about my wife I mean. That is why they are so anxious that I should not accompany you."

"You must judge for yourself," I answered doubtfully, "and I hope to Heaven that you are judging right. Now, Savage, what have you decided? Remember before you reply that these uncanny fellows declare that if we four go, two of us will never return. It seems impossible that they can read the future, still, without doubt, they *are* most uncanny."

"Sir," said Savage, "I will take my chance. Before I left England his lordship made a provision for my old mother and my widowed sister and her children, and I have none other dependent upon me. Moreover, I won't return alone with those Mazitu to become a barbarian, for how could I find my way back to the coast without anyone to guide me? So I'll go on and leave the rest to God."

"Which is just what we have all got to do," I remarked. "Well, as that is settled, let us send for Babemba and tell him."

This we did accordingly. The old fellow received the news with more resignation than I had anticipated. Fixing his one eye upon me, he said:

"Macumazana, these words are what I expected from you. Had any other man spoken them I should have declared that he was quite mad. But I remember that I said this when you determined to visit the Pongo, and that you came back from their country safe and sound, having done wonderful things there, and that it was the Pongo who suffered, not you. So I believe it will be again, so far as you are concerned, Macumazana, for I think that some devil goes with you who looks after his own. For the others I do not know. They must settle the matter with their own devils, or with those of the Kendah people. Now farewell, Macumazana, for it comes to me that we shall meet no more. Well, that happens to all at last, and it is good to have known you who are so great in your own way. Often I shall think of you as you will think of me, and hope that in a country beyond that of the Kendah I may hear from your lips all that has befallen you on this and other journeys. Now I go to withdraw my men before these white-robed Arabs come on their strange beasts to seize you, lest they should take us also and there should be a fight in which we, being the fewer, must die. The loads are all in order ready to be laden on their strange beasts. If they declare that the horses cannot cross the desert, leave them loose and we will catch them and take them home with us, and since they are male and female, breed young ones from them which shall be yours when you send for them, or Bausi the king's if you never send. Nay, I want no more presents who have the gun and the powder and the bullets you gave me, and the tusks of ivory for Bausi the king, and what is best of all, the memory of you and of your courage and wisdom. May these and the gods you worship befriend you. From yonder hill we will watch till we see that you have gone. Farewell," and waiting for no answer, he departed with the tears running from his solitary eye.

Ten minutes later the Mazitu bearers had also saluted us and gone, leaving us seated in that deserted camp surrounded by our baggage, and so far as I was concerned, feeling most lonely. Another ten minutes went by which we occupied in packing our personal belongings. Then Hans, who was now washing out the coffee kettle at a little distance, looked up and said:

"Here come the spook-men, Baas, the whole regiment of them." We ran and looked. It was true. Marshalled in orderly squadrons, the camels with their riders were sweeping towards us, and a fine sight the beasts made with their swaying necks and long, lurching gait. About fifty yards away they halted just where the stream from our spring entered the desert, and there proceeded to water the camels, twenty of them at a time. Two men, however, in whom I recognized Harût and Marût, walked forward and presently were standing before us, bowing obsequiously.

"Good morning, Lord," said Harût to Ragnall in his broken English. "So you come with Macumazana to call at our poor house, as we call at your fine one in England. You think we got the beautiful lady you marry, she we give old necklace. That is not so. No white lady ever in Kendahland. We hear story from Macumazana and believe that lady drowned in Nile, for you 'member she walk much in her sleep. We very sorry for you, but gods know their business. They leave when they will leave, and take when they will take. You find her again some day more beautiful still and with her soul come back."

Here I looked at him sharply. I had told him nothing about Lady Ragnall having lost her wits. How then did he know of the matter? Still I thought it best to hold my peace. I think that Harût saw he had made some mistake, for leaving the subject of Lady Ragnall, he went on:

"You very welcome, O Lord, but it right tell you this most dangerous journey, since elephant Jana not like strangers, and," he continued slowly, "think no elephant like your blood, and all elephants brothers. What one hate rest hate everywhere in world. See it in your face that you already suffer great hurt from elephant, you or someone near you. Also some of Kendah very fierce people and love fighting, and p'raps there war in the land while you there, and in war people get killed."

"Very good, my friend," said Ragnall, "I am prepared to take my chance of these things. Either we all go to your country together, as Macumazana has explained to you, or none of us go."

"We understand. That is our bargain and we no break word," replied Harût. Then he turned his benevolent gaze upon Savage, and said: "So you come too, Mr. Bena. That your name here, eh? Well, you learn lot things in Kendahland, about snakes and all rest."

Here the jovial-looking Marût whispered something into the ear of his companion, smiling all over his face and showing his white teeth as he did so. "Oh!" went on Harût, "my brother tells me you meet one snake already, down in country called Natal, but sit on him so hard, that he grow quite flat and no bite."

"Who told him that?" gasped Savage.

"Oh! forget. Think Macumazana. No? Then p'raps you tell him in sleep, for people talk much in sleep, you know, and some other people got good ears and hear long way. Or p'raps little joke Harût. You 'member, he first-rate conjurer. P'raps he send that snake. No trouble if know how. Well, we show you much better snake Kendahland. But you no sit on *him*, Mr. Bena."

To me, I know not why, there was something horrible in all this jocosity, something that gave me the creeps as always does the sight of a cat playing with a mouse. I felt even then that it foreshadowed terrible things. How *could* these men know the details of occurrences at which they were not present and of which no one had told them? Did that strange "tobacco" of theirs really give them some clairvoyant power, I wondered, or had they other secret methods of obtaining news? I glanced at poor Savage and perceived that he too felt as I did, for he had turned quite pale beneath his tan. Even Hans was affected, for he whispered to me in Dutch: "These are not men; these are devils, Baas, and this journey of ours is one into hell."

Only Ragnall sat stern, silent, and apparently quite unmoved. Indeed there was something almost sphinx-like about the set and expression of his handsome face. Moreover, I felt sure that Harût and Marût recognized the man's strength and determination and that he was one with whom they must reckon seriously. Beneath all their smiles and courtesies I could read this knowledge in their eyes; also that it was causing them grave anxiety. It was as though they knew that here was one against whom their power had no avail, whose fate was the master of their fate. In a sense Harût admitted this to me, for suddenly he looked up and said in a changed voice and in Bantu:

"You are a good reader of hearts, O Macumazana, almost as good as I am. But remember that there is One Who writes upon the book of the heart, Who is the Lord of us who do but read, and that what He writes, that will befall, strive as we may, for in His hands is the future."

"Quite so," I replied coolly, "and that is why I am going with you to Kendahland and fear you not at all."

"So it is and so let it be," he answered. "And now, Lords, are you ready to start? For long is the road and who knows what awaits us ere we see its end?"

"Yes," I replied, "long is the road of life and who knows what awaits us ere we see its end—and after?"

* * * * * * * *

Three hours later I halted the splendid white riding-camel upon which I was mounted, and looked back from the crest of a wave of the desert. There far behind us on the horizon, by the help of my glasses, I could make out the site of the camp we had left and even the tall ant-hill whence I had gazed in the moonlight at our mysterious escort which seemed to have sprung from the desert as though by magic.

This was the manner of our march: A mile or so ahead of us went a picket of eight or ten men mounted on the swiftest beasts, doubtless to give warning of any danger. Next, three or four hundred yards away, followed a body of about fifty Kendah, travelling in a double line, and behind these the baggage men, mounted like everyone else, and leading behind them strings of camels laden with water, provisions, tents of skin and all our goods, including the fifty rifles and the ammunition that Ragnall had brought from England. Then came we three white men and Hans, each of us riding as swift and fine a camel as Africa can breed. On our right at a distance of about half a mile, and also on our left, travelled other bodies of the Kendah of the same numerical strength as that ahead, while the rear was brought up by the remainder of the company who drove a number of spare camels.

Thus we journeyed in the centre of a square whence any escape would have been impossible, for I forgot to say that our keepers Harût and Marût rode exactly behind us, at such a distance that we could call to them if we wished.

At first I found this method of travelling very tiring, as does everyone who is quite unaccustomed to camel-back. Indeed the swing and the jolt of the swift creature beneath me seemed to wrench my bones asunder to such an extent that at the beginning I had once or twice to be lifted from the saddle when, after hours of torture, at length we camped for the night. Poor Savage suffered even more than I did, for the motion reduced him to a kind of jelly. Ragnall, however, who I think had ridden camels before, felt little inconvenience, and the same may be said of Hans, who rode in all sorts of positions, sometimes sideways like a lady, and at others kneeling on the saddle like a monkey on a barrel-organ. Also, being very light and tough as *rimpis*, the swaying motion did not seem to affect him.

By degrees all these troubles left us to such an extent that I could cover my fifty miles a day, more or less, without even feeling tired. Indeed I grew to like the life in that pure and sparkling desert air, perhaps because it was so restful. Day after day we journeyed on across the endless, sandy plain, watching the sun rise, watching it grow high, watching it sink again. Night after night we ate our simple food with appetite and slept beneath the glittering stars till the new dawn broke in glory from the bosom of the immeasurable East.

We spoke but little during all this time. It was as though the silence of the wilderness had got hold of us and sealed our lips. Or perhaps each of us was occupied with his own thoughts. At any rate I know that for my part I seemed to live in a kind of dreamland, thinking of the past, reflecting much upon the innumerable problems of this passing show called life, but not paying much heed to the future. What did the future matter to me, who did not know whether I should have a share of it even for another month, or week, or day, surrounded as I was by the shadow of death? No, I troubled little as to any earthly future, although I admit that in this oasis of calm I reflected upon that state where past, present and future will all be one; also that those reflections, which were in their essence a kind of unshaped prayer, brought much calm to my spirit.

With the regiment of escort we had practically no communication;

I think that they had been forbidden to talk to us. They were a very silent set of men, finely-made, capable persons, of an Arab type, light rather than dark in colour, who seemed for the most part to communicate with each other by signs or in low-muttered words. Evidently they looked upon Harût and Marût with great veneration, for any order which either of these brethren gave, if they were brethren, was obeyed without dispute or delay. Thus, when I happened to mention that I had lost a pocket-knife at one of our camping-places two days' journey back, three of them, much against my wish, were ordered to return to look for it, and did so, making no question. Eight days later they rejoined us much exhausted and having lost a camel, but with the knife, which they handed to me with a low bow; and I confess that I felt ashamed to take the thing.

Nor did we exchange many further confidences with Harût and Marût. Up to the time of our arrival at the boundaries of the Kendah country, our only talk with them was of the incidents of travel, of where we should camp, of how far it might be to the next water, for water-holes or old wells existed in this desert, of such birds as we saw, and so forth. As to other and more important matters a kind of truce seemed to prevail. Still, I observed that they were always studying us, and especially Lord Ragnall, who rode on day after day, self-absorbed and staring straight in front of him as though he looked at something we could not see.

Thus we covered hundreds of miles, not less than five hundred at the least, reckoning our progress at only thirty miles a day, including stoppages. For occasionally we stopped at the water-holes or small oases, where the camels drank and rested. Indeed, these were so conveniently arranged that I came to the conclusion that once there must have been some established route running across these wastelands to the south, of which the traditional knowledge remained with the Kendah people. If so, it had not been used for generations, for save those of one or two that had died on the outward march, we saw no skeletons of camels or other beasts, or indeed any sign of man. The place was an absolute wilderness where nothing lived except a few small mammals at the oases and the birds that passed over it in the air on their way to more fertile regions. Of these, by the way, I saw many that are known both to Europe and Africa, especially ducks and cranes; also storks that, for aught I can say, may have come from far-off, homely Holland.

At last the character of the country began to change. Grass appeared on its lower-lying stretches, then bushes, then occasional trees and among the trees a few buck. Halting the caravan I crept out and shot two of these buck with a right and left, a feat that caused our grave escort to stare in a fashion which showed me that they had never seen anything of the sort done before.

That night, while we were eating the venison with relish, since it was the first fresh meat that we had tasted for many a day, I observed that the disposition of our camp was different from its common form. Thus it was smaller and placed on an eminence. Also the camels were not allowed to graze where they would as usual, but were kept within a limited area while their riders were arranged in groups outside of them. Further, the stores were piled near our tents, in the centre, with guards set over them. I asked Harût and Marût, who were sharing our meal, the reason of these alterations.

"It is because we are on the borders of the Kendah country," answered old Harût. "Four days' more march will bring us there, Macumazana."

"Then why should you take precautions against your own people? Surely they will welcome you."

"With spears perhaps. Macumazana, learn that the Kendah are not one but two people. As you may have heard before, we are the White Kendah, but there are also Black Kendah who outnumber us many times over, though in the beginning we from the north conquered them, or so says our history. The White Kendah have their own territory; but as there is no other road, to reach it we must pass through that of the Black Kendah, where it is always possible that we may be attacked, especially as we bring strangers into the land."

"How is it then that the Black Kendah allow you to live at all, Harût, if they are so much the more numerous?"

"Because of fear, Macumazana. They fear our wisdom and the decrees of the Heavenly Child spoken through the mouth of its oracle, which, if it is offended, can bring a curse upon them. Still, if they find us outside our borders they may kill us, if they can, as we may kill them if we find them within our borders."

"Indeed, Harût. Then it looks to me as though there were a war breeding between you."

"A war is breeding, Macumazana, the last great war in which either the White Kendah or the Black Kendah must perish. Or perhaps both will die together. Maybe that is the real reason why we have asked you to be our guest, Macumazana," and with their usual courteous bows, both of them rose and departed before I could reply.

"You see how it stands," I said to Ragnall. "We have been brought here to fight for our friends, Harût, Marût and Co., against their rebellious subjects, or rather the king who reigns jointly with them."

"It looks like it," he replied quietly, "but doubtless we shall find out the truth in time and meanwhile speculation is no good. Do you go to bed, Quatermain, I will watch till midnight and then wake you."

That night passed in safety. Next day we marched before the dawn, passing through country that grew continually better watered and more fertile, though it was still open plain but sloping upwards ever more steeply. On this plain I saw herds of antelopes and what in the distance looked like cattle, but no human being. Before evening we camped where there was good water and plenty of food for the camels.

While the camp was being set Harût came and invited us to follow him to the outposts, whence he said we should see a view. We walked with him, a matter of not more than a quarter of a mile to the head of that rise up which we had been travelling all day, and thence perceived one of the most glorious prospects on which my eyes have fallen in all great Africa. From where we stood the land sloped steeply for a matter of ten or fifteen miles, till finally the fall ended in a vast plain like to the bottom of a gigantic saucer, that I presume in some far time of the world's history was once an enormous lake. A river ran east and west across this plain and into it fell tributaries. Far beyond this river the contours of the country rose again till, many, many miles away, there appeared a solitary hill, tumulus-shaped, which seemed to be covered with bush.

Beyond and surrounding this hill was more plain which with the aid of my powerful glasses was, we could see, bordered at last by a range of great mountains, looking like a blue line pencilled across the northern distance. To the east and west the plain seemed to be illimitable. Obviously its soil was of a most fertile character and supported numbers of inhabitants, for everywhere we could see their kraals or villages. Much of it to the west, however, was covered with dense forest with, to all appearance, a clearing in its midst.

"Behold the land of the Kendah," said Harût. "On this side of the River Tava live the Black Kendah, on the farther side, the White Kendah."

"And what is that hill?"

"That is the Holy Mount, the Home of the Heavenly Child, where no man may set foot"—here he looked at us meaningly—"save the priests of the Child."

"What happens to him if he does?" I asked.

"He dies, my Lord Macumazana."

"Then it is guarded, Harût?"

"It is guarded, not with mortal weapons, Macumazana, but by the spirits that watch over the Child."

388

As he would say no more on this interesting matter, I asked him as to the numbers of the Kendah people, to which he replied that the Black Kendah might number twenty thousand men of arm-bearing age, but the White Kendah not more than two thousand.

"Then no wonder you want spirits to guard your Heavenly Child," I remarked, "since the Black Kendah are your foes and with you warriors are few."

At this moment our conversation was interrupted by the arrival of a picket on a camel, who reported something to Harût which appeared to disturb him. I asked him what was the matter.

"That is the matter," he said, pointing to a man mounted on a rough pony who just then appeared from behind some bushes about half a mile away, galloping down the slope towards the plain. "He is one of the scouts of Simba, King of the Black Kendah, and he goes to Simba's town in yonder forest to make report of our arrival. Return to camp, Macumazana, and eat, for we must march with the rising of the moon."

As soon as the moon rose we marched accordingly, although the camels, many of which were much worn with the long journey, scarcely had been given time to fill themselves and none to rest. All night we marched down the long slope, only halting for half an hour before daylight to eat something and rearrange the loads on the baggage beasts, which now, I noticed, were guarded with extra care. When we were starting again Marût came to us and remarked with his usual smile, on behalf of his brother Harût, who was otherwise engaged, that it might be well if we had our guns ready, since we were entering the land of the elephant Jana and "who knew but that we might meet him?"

"Or his worshippers on two legs," I suggested, to which his only reply was a nod.

So we got our repeating rifles, some of the first that were ever made, serviceable but rather complicated weapons that fired five cartridges. Hans, however, with my permission, armed himself with the little Purdey piece that was named *Intombi*, the singe-barrelled, muzzle-loading gun which had done me so much service in earlier days, and even on my last journey to Pongoland. He said that he was accustomed to it and did not understand these new-fangled breechloaders, also that it was *lucky*. I consented as I did not think that it made much difference with what kind of rifle Hans was provided. As a marksman he had this peculiarity: up to a hundred yards or so he was an excellent shot, but beyond that distance no good at all.

A quarter of an hour later, as the dawn was breaking, we passed through a kind of *nek* of rough stones bordering the flat land, and emerged into a compact body on to the edge of the grassy plain. Here the word was given to halt for a reason that became clear to me so soon as I was out of the rocks. For there, marching rapidly, not half a mile away, were some five hundred white-robed men. A large proportion of these were mounted, the best being foot-soldiers, of whom more were running up every minute, appearing out of bush that grew upon the hill-side, apparently to dispute our passage. These people, who were black-faced with fuzzy hair upon which they wore no head-dress, all seemed to be armed with spears.

Presently from out of the mass of them two horsemen dashed forward, one of whom bore a white flag in token that they came to parley. Our advance guard allowed them to pass and they galloped on, dodging in and out between the camels with wonderful skill till at length they came to where we were with Harût and Marût, and pulling up their horses so sharply that the animals almost sat down on their haunches, saluted by raising their spears. They were very fine-looking fellows, perfectly black in colour with a negroid cast of countenance and long frizzled hair which hung down on to their shoulders. Their clothing was light, consisting of hide riding breeches that resembled bathing drawers, sandals, and an arrangement of triple chains which seemed to be made of some silvery metal that hung from their necks across the breast and back. Their arms consisted of a long lance similar to that carried by the White Kendah, and a straight, cross-handled sword suspended from a belt. This, as I ascertained afterwards, was the regulation cavalry equipment among these people. The footmen carried a shorter spear, a round leather shield, two throwing javelins or *assegais*, and a curved knife with a horn handle.

"Greeting, Prophets of the Child!" cried one of them. "We are messengers from the god Jana who speaks through the mouth of Simba the King."

"Say on, worshippers of the devil Jana. What word has Simba the King for us?" answered Harût.

"The word of war, Prophet. What do you beyond your southern boundary of the Tava river in the territory of the Black Kendah, that was sealed to them by pact after the battle of a hundred years ago? Is not all the land to the north as far as the mountains and beyond the mountains enough for you? Simba the King let you go out, hoping that the desert would swallow you, but return you shall not."

"That we shall know presently," replied Harût in a suave voice. "It depends upon whether the Heavenly Child or the devil Jana is the more powerful in the land. Still, as we would avoid bloodshed if

390

we may, we desire to explain to you, messengers of King Simba, that we are here upon a peaceful errand. It was necessary that we should convey the white lords to make an offering to the Child, and this was the only road by which we could lead them to the Holy Mount, since they come from the south. Through the forests and the swamps that lie to the east and west camels cannot travel."

"And what is the offering that the white men would make to the Child, Prophet? Oh! we know well, for like you we have our magic. The offering that they must make is the blood of Jana our god, which you have brought them here to kill with their strange weapons, as though any weapon could prevail against Jana the god. Now, give to us these white men that we may offer them to the god, and perchance Simba the King will let you go through."

"Why?" asked Harût, "seeing that you declare that the white men cannot harm Jana, to whom indeed they wish no harm. To surrender them to you that they may be torn to pieces by the devil Jana would be to break the law of hospitality, for they are our guests. Now return to Simba the King, and say to Simba that if he lifts a spear against us the threefold curse of the Child shall fall upon him and upon you his people: The curse of Heaven by storm or by drought. The curse of famine. The curse of war. I the prophet have spoken. Depart."

Watching, I could see that this ultimatum delivered by Harût in a most impressive voice, and seconded as it was by the sudden and simultaneous lifting of the spears of all our escort that were within hearing, produced a considerable effect upon the messengers. Their faces grew afraid and they shrank a little. Evidently the "threefold curse of the Child" suggested calamities which they dreaded. Making no answer, they wheeled their horses about and galloped back to the force that was gathering below as swiftly as they had come.

"We must fight, my Lord Macumazana," said Harût, "and if we would live, conquer, as I know that we shall do."

Then he issued some orders, of which the result was that the caravan adopted a wedge-shaped formation like to that of a great flock of wildfowl on the wing. Harût stationed himself almost at the apex of the triangle. I with Hans and Marût were about the centre of the line, while Ragnall and Savage were placed opposite to us in the right line, the whole width of the wedge being between us. The baggage camels and their leaders occupied the middle space between the lines and were followed by a small rear-guard.

At first we white men were inclined to protest at this separation, but when Marût explained to us that its object was to give confidence

391

to the two divisions of the force and also to minimize the risk of destruction or capture of all three of us, of course we had nothing more to say. So we just shook hands, and with as much assurance as we could command wished each other well through the job.

Then we parted, poor Savage looking very limp indeed, for this was his first experience of war. Ragnall, however, who came of an old fighting stock, seemed to be happy as a king. I who had known so many battles, was the reverse of happy, for inconveniently enough there flashed into my mind at this juncture the dying words of the Zulu captain and seer, Mavovo, which foretold that I too should fall far away in war; and I wondered whether this were the occasion that had been present to his foreseeing mind.

Only Hans seemed quite unconcerned. Indeed I noted that he took the opportunity of the halt to fill and light his large corn-cob pipe, a bit of bravado in the face of Providence for which I could have kicked him had he not been perched in his usual monkey fashion on the top of a very tall camel. The act, however, excited the admiration of the Kendah, for I heard one of them call to the others:

"Look! He is not a monkey after all, but a man—more of a man than his master."

The arrangements were soon made. Within a quarter of an hour of the departure of the messengers Harût, after bowing thrice towards the Holy Mountain, rose in his stirrups and shaking a long spear above his head, shouted a single word:

"*Charge!*"

CHAPTER 11

Allan is Captured

The ride that followed was really quite exhilarating. The camels, notwithstanding their long journey, seemed to have caught some of the enthusiasm of the war-horse as described in the Book of Job; indeed I had no idea that they could travel at such a rate. On we swung down the slope, keeping excellent order, the forest of tall spears shining and the little lancer-like pennons fluttering on the breeze in a very gallant way. In silence we went save for the thudding of the hoofs of the camels and an occasional squeal of anger as some rider drove his lance handle into their ribs. Not until we actually joined battle did a single man open his lips. Then, it is true, there went up one simultaneous and mighty roar of:

"The Child! Death to Jana! The Child! The Child!"

But this happened a few minutes later.

As we drew near the enemy I saw that they had massed their footmen in a dense body, six or eight lines thick. There they stood to receive the impact of our charge, or rather they did not all stand, for the first two ranks were kneeling with long spears stretched out in front of them. I imagine that their appearance must have greatly resembled that of the Greek phalanx, or that of the Swiss prepared to receive cavalry in the Middle Ages. On either side of this formidable body, which by now must have numbered four or five hundred men, and at a distance perhaps of a quarter of a mile from them, were gathered the horsemen of the Black Kendah, divided into two bodies of nearly equal strength, say about a hundred horse in each body.

As we approached, our triangle curved a little, no doubt under the direction of Harût. A minute or so later I saw the reason. It was that we might strike the foot-soldiers not full in front but at an angle. It was an admirable manoeuvre, for when presently we did strike, we caught them swiftly on the flank and crumpled them up. My word!

393

we went through those fellows like a knife through butter; they had as much chance against the rush of our camels as a brown-paper screen has against a typhoon. Over they rolled in heaps while the White Kendah spitted them with their lances.

"The Child is top dog! My money on the Child," reflected I in irreverent ecstasy. But that exultation was premature, for those Black Kendah were by no means all dead. Presently I saw that scores of them had appeared among the camels, which they were engaged in stabbing, or trying to stab, in the stomach with their spears. Also I had forgotten the horsemen. As our charge slackened owing to the complication in front, these arrived on our flanks like two thunderbolts. We faced about and did our best to meet the onslaught, of which the net result was that both our left and right lines were pierced through about fifty yards behind the baggage camels. Luckily for us the very impetuosity of the Black Kendah rush deprived it of most of the fruits of victory, since the two squadrons, being unable to check their horses, ended by charging into each other and becoming mixed in inextricable confusion. Then, I do not know who gave the order, we wheeled our camels in and fell upon them, a struggling, stationary mass, with the result that many of them were speared, or overthrown and trampled.

"I have said we, but that is not quite correct, at any rate so far as Marût, Hans, I and about fifteen camelmen were concerned. How it happened I could not tell in that dust and confusion, but we were cut off from the main body and presently found ourselves fighting desperately in a group at which Black Kendah horsemen were charging again and again. We made the best stand we could. By degrees the bewildered camels sank under the repeated spear-thrusts of the enemy, all except one, oddly enough that ridden by Hans, which by some strange chance was never touched. The rest of us were thrown or tumbled off the camels and continued the fight from behind their struggling bodies."

That is where I came in. Up to this time I had not fired a single shot, partly because I do not like missing, which it is so easy to do from the back of a swaying camel, and still more for the reason that I had not the slightest desire to kill any of these savage men unless I was obliged to do so in self-defence. Now, however, the thing was different, as I was fighting for my life. Leaning against my camel, which was dying and beating its head upon the ground, groaning horribly the while, I emptied the five cartridges of the repeater into those Black Kendah, pausing between each shot to take aim, with the result that presently five riderless horses were galloping loose about the *veld*.

The effect was electrical, since our attackers had never seen anything of the kind before. For a while they all drew off, which gave me time to reload. Then they came on again and I repeated the process. For a second time they retreated and after consultation which lasted for a minute or more, made a third attack. Once more I saluted them to the best of my ability, though on this occasion only three men and a horse fell. The fifth shot was a clean miss because they came on in such a scattered formation that I had to turn from side to side to fire.

Now at last the game was up, for the simple reason that I had no more cartridges save two in my double-barrelled pistol. It may be asked why. The answer is, want of foresight. Too many cartridges in one's pocket are apt to chafe on camel-back and so is a belt full of them. In those days also the engagements were few in which a man fired over fifteen. I had forty or fifty more in a bag, which bag Savage with his usual politeness had taken and hung upon his saddle without saying a word to me. At the beginning of the action I found this out, but could not then get them from him as he was separated from me. Hans, always careless in small matters, was really to blame as he ought to have seen that I had the cartridges, or at any rate to have carried them himself. In short, it was one of those accidents that will happen. There is nothing more to be said.

After a still longer consultation our enemies advanced on us for the fourth time, but very slowly. Meanwhile I had been taking stock of the position. The camel corps, or what was left of it, oblivious of our plight which the dust of conflict had hidden from them, was travelling on to the north, more or less victorious. That is to say, it had cut its way through the Black Kendah and was escaping unpursued, huddled up in a mob with the baggage animals safe in its centre. The Black Kendah themselves were engaged in killing our wounded and suc-couring their own; also in collecting the bodies of the dead. In short, quite unintentionally, we were deserted. Probably, if anybody thought about us at all in the turmoil of desperate battle, they concluded that we were among the slain. Marût came up to me, unhurt, still smiling and waving a bloody spear.

"Lord Macumazana," he said, "the end is at hand. The Child has saved the others, or most of them, but us it has abandoned. Now what will you do? Kill yourself, or if that does not please you, suffer me to kill you? Or shoot on until you must surrender?"

"I have nothing to shoot with any more," I answered. "But if we surrender, what will happen to us?"

"We shall be taken to Simba's town and there sacrificed to the devil Jana—I have not time to tell you how. Therefore I propose to kill myself."

"Then I think you are foolish, Marût, since once we are dead, we are dead; but while we are alive it is always possible that we may escape from Jana. If the worst comes to the worst I have a pistol with two bullets in it, one for you and one for me."

"The wisdom of the Child is in you," he replied. "I shall surrender with you, Macumazana, and take my chance."

Then he turned and explained things to his followers, who spoke together for a moment. In the end these took a strange and, to my mind, a very heroic decision. Waiting till the attacking Kendah were quite close to us, with the exception of three men, who either because they lacked courage or for some other reason, stayed with us, they advanced humbly as though to make submission. A number of the Black Kendah dismounted and ran up, I suppose to take them prisoners. The men waited till these were all round them. Then with a yell of "The Child!" they sprang forward, taking the enemy unawares and fighting like demons, inflicted great loss upon them before they fell themselves covered with wounds.

"Brave men indeed!" said Marût approvingly. "Well, now they are all at peace with the Child, where doubtless we shall find them ere long."

I nodded but answered nothing. To tell the truth, I was too much engaged in nursing the remains of my own courage to enter into conversation about that of other people.

This fierce and cunning stratagem of desperate men which had cost their enemies so dear, seemed to infuriate the Black Kendah.

At us came the whole mob of them—we were but six now—roaring "Jana! Jana!" and led by a grey-beard who, to judge from the number of silver chains upon his breast and his other trappings, seemed to be a great man among them. When they were about fifty yards away and I was preparing for the worst, a shot rang out from above and behind me. At the same instant Greybeard threw his arms wide and letting fall the spear he held, pitched from his horse, evidently stone dead. I glanced back and saw Hans, the corn-cob pipe still in his mouth and the little rifle, *Intombi*, still at his shoulder. He had fired from the back of the camel, I think for the first time that day, and whether by chance or through good marksmanship, I do not know, had killed this man.

His sudden and unexpected end seemed to fill the Black Kendah with grief and dismay. Halting in their charge they gathered round him, while a fierce-looking middle-aged man, also adorned with much barbaric finery, dismounted to examine him.

"That is Simba the King," said Marût, "and the slain one is his uncle, Goru, the great general who brought him up from a babe."

"Then I wish I had another cartridge left for the nephew," I began and stopped, for Hans was speaking to me.

"Good-bye, Baas," he said, "I must go, for I cannot load *Intombi* on the back of this beast. If you meet your reverend father the Predikant before I do, tell him to make a nice place ready for me among the fires."

Then before I could get out an answer, Hans dragged his camel round; as I have said, it was quite uninjured. Urging it to a shambling gallop with blows of the rifle stock, he departed at a great rate, not towards the home of the Child but up the hill into a brake of giant grass mingled with thorn trees that grew quite close at hand. Here with startling suddenness both he and the camel vanished away.

If the Black Kendah saw him go, of which I am doubtful, for they all seemed to be lost in consultation round their king and the dead general, Goru, they made no attempt to follow him. Another possibility is that they thought he was trying to lead them into some snare or ambush.

I do not know what they thought because I never heard them mention Hans or the matter of his disappearance, if indeed they ever realized that there was such a person. Curiously enough in the case of men who had just shown themselves so brave, this last accident of the decease of Goru coming on the top of all their other casualties, seemed to take the courage out of them. It was as though they had come to the conclusion that we with our guns were something more than mortal.

For several minutes they debated in evident hesitation. At last from out of their array rode a single man, in whom I recognized one of the envoys who had met us in the morning, carrying in his hand a white flag as he had done before. Thereon I laid down my rifle in token that I would not fire at him, which indeed I could not do having nothing to fire. Seeing this he came to within a few yards and halting, addressed Marût.

"O second Prophet of the Child," he said, "these are the words of Simba the King: Your god has been too strong for us today, though in a day to come it may be otherwise. I thought I had you in a pit; that you were the bucks and I the hunter. But, though with loss, you have escaped out of the pit," and the speaker glanced towards our retreating force which was now but a cloud of dust in the far distance, "while I the hunter have been gored by your horns," and again he glanced at the dead that were scattered about the plain. "The noblest of the buck, the white bull of the herd," and he looked at me, who in any other circumstances would have felt complimented, "and you, O Prophet Marût, and one or two others, besides those that I have slain, are however still in the pit and your horn is a magic horn," here he pointed to my rifle, "which pierces from afar and kills dead all by whom it is touched."

"So I caught those gentry well in the middle," thought I to myself, "and with soft-nosed bullets!"

"Therefore I, Simba the King, make you an offer. Yield yourselves and I swear that no spear shall be driven through your hearts and no knife come near your throats. You shall only be taken to my town and there be fed on the best and kept as prisoners, till once more there is peace between the Black Kendah and the White. If you refuse, then I will ring you round and perhaps in the dark rush on you and kill you all. Or perhaps I will watch you from day to day till you, who have no water, die of thirst in the heat of the sun. These are my words to which nothing may be added and from which nothing shall be taken away."

Having finished this speech he rode back a few yards out of earshot, and waited.

"What will you answer, Lord Macumazana?" asked Marût.

I replied by another question. "Is there any chance of our being rescued by your people?"

He shook his head. "None. What we have seen today is but a small part of the army of the Black Kendah, one regiment of foot and one of horse, that are always ready. By tomorrow thousands will be gathered, many more than we can hope to deal with in the open and still less in their strongholds, also Harût will believe that we are dead. Unless the Child saves us we shall be left to our fate."

"Then it seems that we are indeed in a pit, as that black brute of a king puts it, Marût, and if he does what he says and rushes us at sundown, everyone of us will be killed. Also I am thirsty already and there is nothing to drink. But will this king keep his word? There are other ways of dying besides by steel."

"I think that he will keep his word, but as that messenger said, he will not add to his word. Choose now, for see, they are beginning to hedge us round."

"What do you say, men?" I asked of the three who had remained with us.

"We say, Lord, that we are in the hands of the Child, though we wish now that we had died with our brothers," answered their spokesman fatalistically.

So after Marût and I had consulted together for a little as to the form of his reply, he beckoned to the messenger and said:

"We accept the offer of Simba, although it would be easy for this lord to kill him now where he stands, namely, to yield ourselves as prisoners on his oath that no harm shall come to us. For know that if harm does come, the vengeance will be terrible. Now in proof of his good faith, let Simba draw near and drink the cup of peace with us, for we thirst."

"Not so," said the messenger, "for then that white lord might kill him with his tube. Give me the tube and Simba shall come."

"Take it," I said magnanimously, handing him the rifle, which he received in a very gingerly fashion. After all, I reflected, there is nothing much more useless than a rifle without ammunition.

Off he went holding the weapon at arm's length, and presently Simba himself, accompanied by some of his men, one of whom carried a skin of water and another a large cup hollowed from an elephant's tusk, rode up to us. This Simba was a fine and rather terrifying person with a large moustache and a chin shaved except for a little tuft of hair which he wore at its point like an Italian. His eyes were big and dark, frank-looking, yet now and again with sinister expression in the corners of them. He was not nearly so black as most of his followers; probably in bygone generations his blood had been crossed with that of the White Kendah. He wore his hair long without any head-dress, held in place by a band of gold which I suppose represented a crown. On his forehead was a large white scar, probably received in some battle. Such was his appearance.

He looked at me with great curiosity, and I have often wondered since what kind of an impression I produced upon him. My hat had fallen off, or I had knocked it off when I fired my last cartridge into his people, and forgotten to replace it, and my intractable hair, which was longer than usual, had not been recently brushed. My worn Norfolk jacket was dyed with blood from a wounded or dying man who had tumbled against me in the scrimmage when the cavalry charged us, and my right leg and boot were stained in a similar fashion from having rubbed against my camel where a spear had entered it. Altogether I must have appeared a most disreputable object.

Some indication of his opinion was given, however, in a remark, which of course I pretended not to understand, that I overheard him make to one of his officers:

"Truly," he said, "we must not always look to the strong for strength. And yet this little white porcupine is strength itself, for see how much damage he has wrought us. Also consider his eyes that appear to pierce everything. Jana himself might fear those eyes. Well, time that grinds the rocks will tell us all."

All of this I caught perfectly, my ears being very sharp, although he thought that he spoke out of my hearing, for after spending a month in their company I understood the Kendah dialect of Bantu very well.

Having delivered himself thus he rode nearer and said:

"You, Prophet Marût, my enemy, have heard the terms of me, Simba the King, and have accepted them. Therefore discuss them no more. What I have promised I will keep. What I have given I give, neither greater nor less by the weight of a hair."

"So be it, O King," answered Marût with his usual smile, which nothing ever seemed to disturb. "Only remember that if those terms are broken either in the letter or in the spirit, especially the spirit" (that is the best rendering I can give of his word), "the manifold curses of the Child will fall upon you and yours. Yes, though you kill us all by treachery, still those curses will fall."

"May Jana take the Child and all who worship it," exclaimed the king with evident irritation.

"In the end, O King, Jana will take the Child and its followers—or the Child will take Jana and his followers. Which of these things must happen is known to the Child alone, and perchance to its prophets. Meanwhile, for every one of those of the Child I think that three of the followers of Jana, or more, lie dead upon this field. Also the caravan is now out of your reach with two of the white lords and many of such tubes which deal death, like that which we have surrendered to you. Therefore because we are helpless, do not think that the Child is helpless. Jana must have been asleep, O King, or you would have set your trap better."

I thought that this coolly insolent speech would have produced some outburst, but in fact it seemed to have an opposite effect. Making no reply to it, Simba said almost humbly:

"I come to drink the cup of peace with you and the white lord, O Prophet. Afterwards we can talk. Give me water, slave."

Then a man filled the great ivory cup with water from the skin he carried. Simba took it and having sprinkled a little upon the ground, I suppose as an offering, drank from the cup, doubtless to show that it was not poisoned. Watching carefully, I made sure that he swallowed what he drank by studying the motions of his throat. Then he handed the cup with a bow to Marût, who with a still deeper bow passed it to me. Being absolutely parched I absorbed about a pint of it, and feeling a new man, passed the horn to Marût, who swallowed the rest. Then it was filled again for our three White Kendah, the King first tasting the water as before, after which Marût and I had a second pull.

When at length our thirst was satisfied, horses were brought to us, serviceable and docile little beasts with sheepskins for saddles and loops of hide for stirrups. On these we mounted and for the next three hours rode across the plain, surrounded by a strong escort and with an armed Black Kendah running on each side of our horses and holding in his hand a thong attached to the ring of the bridle, no doubt to prevent any attempt to escape.

Our road ran past but not through some villages whence we saw many women and children staring at us, and through beautiful crops of mealies and other sorts of grain that in this country were now just ripening. The luxuriant appearance of these crops suggested that the rains must have been plentiful and the season all that could be desired. From some of the villages by the track arose a miserable sound of wailing. Evidently their inhabitants had already heard that certain of their men had fallen in that morning's fight.

At the end of the third hour we began to enter the great forest which I had seen when first we looked down on Kendahland. It was filled with splendid trees, most of them quite strange to me, but perhaps because of the denseness of their overshadowing crowns there was comparatively no undergrowth. The general effect of the place was very gloomy, since little light could pass through the interlacing foliage of the tops of those mighty trees.

Towards evening we came to a clearing in this forest, it may have been four or five miles in diameter, but whether it was natural or artificial I am not sure. I think, however, that it was probably the former for two reasons: the hollow nature of the ground, which lay a good many feet lower than the surrounding forest, and the wonderful fertility of the soil, which suggested that it had once been deposited upon an old lake bottom. Never did I see such crops as those that grew upon that clearing; they were magnificent.

Wending our way along the road that ran through the tall corn, for here every inch was cultivated, we came suddenly upon the capital of the Black Kendah, which was known as Simba Town. It was a large place, somewhat different from any other African settlement with which I am acquainted, inasmuch as it was not only stockaded but completely surrounded by a broad artificial moat filled with water from a stream that ran through the centre of the town, over which moat there were four timber bridges placed at the cardinal points of the compass. These bridges were strong enough to bear horses or stock, but so made that in the event of attack they could be destroyed in a few minutes.

Riding through the eastern gate, a stout timber structure on the farther side of the corresponding bridge, where the king was received with salutes by an armed guard, we entered one of the main streets of the town which ran from north to south and from east to west. It was broad and on either side of it were the dwellings of the inhabitants set close together because the space within the stockade was limited. These were not huts but square buildings of mud with flat roofs of some kind of cement. Evidently they were built upon the model of Oriental and North African houses of which some debased tradition remained with these people. Thus a stairway or ladder ran from the interior to the roof of each house, whereon its inhabitants were accustomed, as I discovered afterwards, to sleep during a good part of the year, also to eat in the cool of the day. Many of them were gathered there now to watch us pass, men, women, and children, all except the little ones decently clothed in long garments of various colours, the women for the most part in white and the men in a kind of bluish linen.

I saw at once that they had already heard of the fight and of the considerable losses which their people had sustained, for their reception of us prisoners was most unfriendly. Indeed the men shook their fists at us, the women screamed out curses, while the children stuck out their tongues in token of derision or defiance. Most of these demonstrations, however, were directed at Marût and his followers, who only smiled indifferently. At me they stared in wonder not unmixed with fear.

A quarter of a mile or so from the gate we came to an inner enclosure, that answered to the South African cattle kraal, surrounded by a dry ditch and a timber palisade outside of which was planted a green fence of some shrub with long white thorns. Here we passed through more gates, to find ourselves in an oval space, perhaps five acres in extent. Evidently this served as a market ground, but all around it were open sheds where hundreds of horses were stabled. No cattle seemed to be kept there, except a few that with sheep and goats were driven in every day for slaughter purposes at a shambles at the north end, from the great stock kraals built beyond the forest to the south, where they were safe from possible raiding by the White Kendah.

A tall reed fence cut off the southern end of this marketplace, outside of which we were ordered to dismount. Passing through yet another gate we found within the fence a large hut or house built on the

402

same model as the others in the town, which Marût whispered to me was that of the king. Behind it were smaller houses in which lived his queen and women, good-looking females, who advanced to meet him with obsequious bows. To the right and left were two more buildings of about equal size, one of which was occupied by the royal guard and the other was the guest-house whither we were conducted.

It proved to be a comfortable dwelling about thirty feet square but containing only one room, with various huts behind it that served for cooking and other purposes. In one of these the three camelmen were placed. Immediately on our arrival food was brought to us, a lamb or kid roasted whole upon a wooden platter, and some green mealie-cobs boiled upon another platter; also water to drink and wash with in earthenware jars of sun-dried clay.

I ate heartily, for I was starving. Then, as it was useless to attempt precautions against murder, without any talk to my fellow prisoner, for which we were both too tired, I threw myself down on a mattress stuffed with corn husks in a corner of the hut, drew a skin rug over me and, having commended myself to the protection of the Power above, fell fast asleep.

CHAPTER 12

The First Curse

The next thing I remember was feeling upon my face the sunlight that poured through a window-place which was protected by immovable wooden bars. For a while I lay still, reflecting as memory returned to me upon all the events of the previous day and upon my present unhappy position. Here I was a prisoner in the hands of a horde of fierce savages who had every reason to hate me, for though this was done in self-defence, had I not killed a number of their people against whom personally I had no quarrel? It was true that their king had promised me safety, but what reliance could be put upon the word of such a man? Unless something occurred to save me, without doubt my days were numbered. In this way or in that I should be murdered, which served me right for ever entering upon such a business.

The only satisfactory point in the story was that, for the present at any rate, Ragnall and Savage had escaped, though doubtless sooner or later fate would overtake them also. I was sure that they had escaped, since two of the camelmen with us had informed Marût that they saw them swept away surrounded by our people and quite unharmed. Now they would be grieving over my death, since none survived who could tell them of our capture, unless the Black Kendah chose to do so, which was not likely. I wondered what course they would take when Ragnall found that his quest was vain, as of course must happen. Try to get out of the country, I suppose, as I prayed they might succeed in doing, though this was most improbable.

Then there was Hans. He of course would attempt to retrace our road across the desert, if he had got clear away. Having a good camel, a rifle and some ammunition, it was just possible that he might win through, as he never forgot a path which he had once travelled, though probably in a week's time a few bones upon the desert would be all that remained of him. Well, as he had suggested, perhaps we should soon be talking the event over in some far sphere with my father—and others. Poor old Hans!

I opened my eyes and looked about me. The first thing I noticed was that my double-barrelled pistol, which I had placed at full cock beside me before I went to sleep, was gone, also my large clasp-knife. This discovery did not tend to raise my spirits, since I was now quite weaponless. Then I observed Marût seated on the floor of the hut staring straight in front of him, and noted that at length even he had ceased to smile, but that his lips were moving as though he were engaged in prayer or meditation.

"Marût," I said, "someone has been in this place while we were asleep and stolen my pistol and knife."

"Yes, Lord," he answered, "and my knife also. I saw them come in the middle of the night, two men who walked softly as cats, and searched everything."

"Then why did you not wake me?"

"What would have been the use, Lord? If we had caught hold of the men, they would have called out and we should have been murdered at once. It was best to let them take the things, which after all are of no good to us here."

"The pistol might have been of some good," I replied significantly.

"Yes," he said, nodding, "but at the worst death is easy to find."

"Do you think, Marût, that we could manage to let Harût and the others know our plight? That smoke which I breathed in England, for instance, seemed to show me far-off things—if we could get any of it."

"The smoke was nothing, Lord, but some harmless burning powder which clouded your mind for a minute, and enabled you to see the thoughts that were in *our* minds. *We* drew the pictures at which you looked. Also here there is none."

"Oh!" I said, "the old trick of suggestion; just what I imagined. Then there's an end of that, and as the others will think that we are dead and we cannot communicate with them, we have no hope except in ourselves."

"Or the Child," suggested Marût gently.

"Look here!" I said with irritation. "After you have just told me that your smoke vision was a mere conjurer's trick, how do you expect me to believe in your blessed Child? Who is the Child? What is the Child, and—this is more important—what can it do? As your throat is going to be cut shortly you may as well tell me the truth."

"Lord Macumazana, I will. Who and what the Child is I cannot

405

say because I do not know. But it has been our god for thousands of years, and we believe that our remote forefathers brought it with them when they were driven out of Egypt at some time unknown. We have writings concerning it done up in little rolls, but as we cannot read them they are of no use to us. It has an hereditary priesthood, of which Harût my uncle, for he is my uncle, is the head. We believe that the Child is God, or rather a symbol in which God dwells, and that it can save us in this world and the next, for we hold that man is an immortal spirit. We believe also that through its Oracle—a priestess who is called Guardian of the Child—it can declare the future and bring blessings or curses upon men, especially upon our enemies. When the Oracle dies we are helpless since the Child has no 'mouth' and our enemies prevail against us. This happened a long while ago, and the last Oracle having declared before her death that her successor was to be found in England, my uncle and I travelled thither disguised as conjurers and made search for many years. We thought that we had found the new Oracle in the lady who married the Lord Igeza, because of that mark of the new moon upon her neck. After our return to Africa, however, for as I have spoken of this matter I may as well tell you all," here he stared me full in the eyes and spoke in a clear metallic voice which somehow no longer convinced me, "we found that we had made a mistake, for the real Oracle, a mere girl, was discovered among our own people, and has now been for two years installed in her office. Without doubt the last Guardian of the Child was wandering in her mind when she told us that story before her death as to a woman in England, a country of which she had heard through Arabs. That is all."

"Thank you," I replied, feeling that it would be useless to show any suspicion of his story. "Now will you be so good as to tell me who and what is the god, or the elephant Jana, whom you have brought me here to kill? Is the elephant a god, or is the god an elephant? In either case what has it to do with the Child?"

"Lord, Jana among us Kendah represents the evil in the world, as the Child represents the good. Jana is he whom the Mohammedans call Shaitan and the Christians call Satan, and our forefathers, the old Egyptians, called Set."

"Ah!" thought I to myself, "now we have got it. Horus the Divine Child, and Set the evil monster, with whom it strives everlastingly."

"Always," went on Marût, "there has been war between the Child and Jana, that is, between Good and Evil, and we know that in the end one of them must conquer the other."

406

"The whole world has known that from the beginning," I interrupted. "But who and what is this Jana?"

"Among the Black Kendah, Lord, Jana is an elephant, or at any rate his symbol is an elephant, a very terrible beast to which sacrifices are made, that kills all who do not worship him if he chances to meet them. He lives farther on in the forest yonder, and the Black Kendah make use of him in war, for the devil in him obeys their priests."

"Indeed, and is this elephant always the same?"

"I cannot tell you, but for many generations it has been the same, for it is known by its size and by the fact that one of its tusks is twisted downwards."

"Well," I remarked, "all this proves nothing, since elephants certainly live for at least two hundred years, and perhaps much longer. Also, after they become 'rogues' they acquire every kind of wicked and unnatural habit, as to which I could tell you lots of stories. Have you seen this elephant?"

"No, Macumazana," he answered with a shiver. "If I had seen it should I have been alive today? Yet I fear I am fated to see it ere long, not alone," and again he shivered, looking at me in a very suggestive manner.

At this moment our conversation was interrupted by the arrival of two Black Kendahs who brought us our breakfast of porridge and a boiled fowl, and stood there while we ate it. For my part I was not sorry, as I had learned all I wanted to know of the theological opinions and practice of the land, and had come to the conclusion that the terrible devil-god of the Black Kendah was merely a rogue elephant of unusual size and ferocity, which under other circumstances it would have given me the greatest pleasure to try to shoot.

When we had finished eating, that is soon, for neither of our appetites was good that morning, we walked out of the house into the surrounding compound and visited the camelmen in their hut. Here we found them squatted on the ground looking very depressed indeed. When I asked them what was the matter they replied, "Nothing," except that they were men about to die and life was pleasant. Also they had wives and children whom they would never see again.

Having tried to cheer them up to the best of my ability, which I fear I did without conviction, for in my heart I agreed with their view of the case, we returned to the guest-house and mounted the stair which led to the flat roof. Hence we saw that some curious ceremony was in progress in the centre of the market-place. At that distance we could not make out the details, for I forgot to say that my glasses had

407

been stolen with the pistol and knife, probably because they were supposed to be lethal weapons or instruments of magic.

A rough altar had been erected, on which a fire burned. Behind it
the king, Simba, was seated on a stool with various councillors about
him. In front of the altar was a stout wooden table, on which lay what
looked like the body of a goat or a sheep. A fantastically dressed man,
assisted by other men, appeared to be engaged in inspecting the inside
of this animal with, we gathered, unsatisfactory results, for presently
he raised his arms and uttered a loud wail. Then the creature's viscera
were removed from it and thrown upon the fire, while the rest of the
carcass was carried off.

I asked Marût what he thought they were doing. He replied de-
jectedly:

"Consulting their Oracle; perhaps as to whether we should live or
die, Macumazana."

Just then the priest in the strange, feathered attire approached the
king, carrying some small object in his hand. I wondered what it
could be, till the sound of a report reached my ears and I saw the man
begin to jump round upon one leg, holding the other with both his
hands at the knee and howling loudly.

"Ah!" I said, "that pistol was full cocked, and the bullet got him in
the foot."

Simba shouted out something, whereon a man picked up the pistol
and threw it into the fire, round which the others gathered to watch
it burn.

"You wait," I said to Marût, and as I spoke the words the inevitable
happened.

Off went the other barrel of the pistol, which hopped out of the
fire with the recoil like a living thing. But as it happened one of the
assistant priests was standing in front of the mouth of that barrel, and
he also hopped once, but never again, for the heavy bullet struck him
somewhere in the body and killed him. Now there was consternation.
Everyone ran away, leaving the dead man lying on the ground. Simba
led the rout and the head-priest brought up the rear, skipping along
upon one leg.

Having observed these events, which filled me with an unholy joy,
we descended into the house again as there was nothing more to see,
also because it occurred to me that our presence on the roof, watching their discomfiture, might irritate these savages. About ten minutes
later the gate of the fence round the guest-house was thrown open, and
through it came four men carrying on a stretcher the body of the priest

whom the bullet had killed, which they laid down in front of our door. Then followed the king with an armed guard, and after him the be-feathered diviner with his foot bound up, who supported himself upon the shoulders of two of his colleagues. This man, I now perceived, wore a hideous mask, from which projected two tusks in imitation of those of an elephant. Also there were others, as many as the space would hold.

The king called to us to come out of the house, which, having no choice, we did. One glance at him showed me that the man was frantic with fear, or rage, or both.

"Look upon your work, magicians!" he said in a terrible voice, pointing first to the dead priest, then to the diviner's wounded foot.

"It is no work of ours, King Simba," answered Marût. "It is your own work. You stole the magic weapon of the white lord and made it angry, so that it has revenged itself upon you."

"It is true," said Simba, "that the tube has killed one of those who took it away from you and wounded the other" (here was luck indeed). "But it was you who ordered it to do so, magicians. Now, hark! Yesterday I promised you safety, that no spear should pierce your hearts and no knife come near your throats, and drank the cup of peace with you. But you have broken the pact, working us more harm, and therefore it no longer holds, since there are many other ways in which men can die. Listen again! This is my decree. By your magic you have taken away the life of one of my servants and hurt another of my servants, destroying the middle toe of his left foot. If within three days you do not give back the life to him who seems to be dead, and give back the toe to him who seems to be hurt, as you well can do, then you shall join those whom you have slain in the land of death, how I will not tell you."

Now when I heard this amazing sentence I gasped within myself, but thinking it better to keep up my rôle of understanding nothing of their talk, I preserved an immovable countenance and left Marût to answer. This, to his credit be it recorded, he did with his customary pleasant smile.

"O King," he said, "who can bring the dead back to life? Not even the Child itself, at any rate in this world, for there is no way."

"Then, Prophet of the Child, you had better find a way, or, I repeat, I send you to join them," he shouted, rolling his eyes.

"What did my brother, the great Prophet, promise to you but yes-terday, O King, if you harmed us?" asked Marût. "Was it not that the three great curses should fall upon your people? Learn now that if so much as one of us is murdered by you, these things shall swiftly come to pass. I, Marût, who am also a Prophet of the Child, have said it."

Now Simba seemed to go quite mad, so mad that I thought all was over. He waved his spear and danced about in front of us, till the silver chains clanked upon his breast. He vituperated the Child and its worshippers, who, he declared, had worked evil on the Black Kendah for generations. He appealed to his god Jana to avenge these evils, "to pierce the Child with his tusks, to tear it with his trunk, and to trample it with his feet," all of which the wounded diviner ably seconded through his horrid mask.

There we stood before him, I leaning against the wall of the house with an air of studied nonchalance mingled with mild interest, at least that is what I meant to do, and Marût smiling sweetly and staring at the heavens. Whilst I was wondering what exact portion of my frame was destined to become acquainted with that spear, of a sudden Simba gave it up. Turning to his followers, he bade them dig a hole in the corner of our little enclosure and set the dead man in it, "with his head out so that he may breathe," an order which they promptly executed.

Then he issued a command that we should be well fed and tended, and remarking that if the departed was not alive and healthy on the third morning from that day, we should hear from him again, he and his company stalked off, except those men who were occupied with the interment.

Soon this was finished also. There sat the deceased buried to the neck with his face looking towards the house, a most disagreeable sight. Presently, however, matters were improved in this respect by one of the sextons fetching a large earthenware pot and several smaller pots full of food and water. The latter they set round the head, I suppose for the sustenance of the body beneath, and then placed the big vessel inverted over all, "to keep the sun off our sleeping brother," as I heard one say to the other.

This pot looked innocent enough when all was done, like one of those that gardeners in England put over forced rhubarb, no more. And yet, such is the strength of the imagination, I think that on the whole I should have preferred the object underneath naked and unadorned. For instance, I have forgotten to say that the heads of those of the White Kendah who had fallen in the fight had been set up on poles in front of Simba's house. They were unpleasant to contemplate, but to my mind not so unpleasant as that pot.

As a matter of fact, this precaution against injury from the sun to the late diviner proved unnecessary, since by some strange chance from that moment the sun ceased to shine. Quite suddenly clouds arose which gradually covered the whole sky and the weather began

410

to turn very cold, unprecedentedly so, Marût informed me, for the time of year, which, it will be remembered, in this country was the season just before harvest. Obviously the Black Kendah thought so also, since from our seats on the roof, whither we had retreated to be as far as possible from the pot, we saw them gathered in the market-place, staring at the sky and talking to each other.

The day passed without any further event, except the arrival of our meals, for which we had no great appetite. The night came, earlier than usual because of the clouds, and we fell asleep, or rather into a series of dozes. Once I thought that I heard someone stirring in the huts behind us, but as it was followed by silence I took no more notice. At length the light broke very slowly, for now the clouds were denser than ever. Shivering with the cold, Marût and I made a visit to the camel-drivers, who were not allowed to enter our house. On going into their hut we saw to our horror that only two of them remained, seated stonily upon the floor. We asked where the third was. They replied they did not know. In the middle of the night, they said, men had crept in, who seized, bound and gagged him, then dragged him away. As there was nothing to be said or done, we returned to breakfast filled with horrid fears.

Nothing happened that day except that some priests arrived, lifted the earthenware pot, examined their departed colleague, who by now had become an unencouraging spectacle, removed old dishes of food, arranged more about him, and went off. Also the clouds grew thicker and thicker, and the air more and more chilly, till, had we been in any northern latitude, I should have said that snow was pending. From our perch on the roof-top I observed the population of Simba Town discussing the weather with ever-increasing eagerness; also that the people who were going out to work in the fields wore mats over their shoulders.

Once more darkness came, and this night, notwithstanding the cold, we spent wrapped in rugs, on the roof of the house. It had occurred to us that kidnapping would be less easy there, as we could make some sort of a fight at the head of the stairway, or, if the worst came to the worst, dive from the parapet and break our necks. We kept watch turn and turn about. During my watch about midnight I heard a noise going on in the hut behind us; scuffling and a stifled cry which turned my blood cold. About an hour later a fire was lighted in the centre of the market-place where the sheep had been sacrificed, and by the flare of it I could see people moving. But what they did I could not see, which was perhaps as well.

411

Next morning only one of the camelmen was left. This remaining man was now almost crazy with fear, and could give no clear account of what had happened to his companion.

The poor fellow implored us to take him away to our house, as he feared to be left alone with "the black devils." We tried to do so, but armed guards appeared mysteriously and thrust him back into his own hut.

This day was an exact repetition of the others. The same inspection of the deceased and renewal of his food; the same cold, clouded sky, the same agitated conferences in the market-place.

For the third time darkness fell upon us in that horrible place. Once more we took refuge on the roof, but this night neither of us slept. We were too cold, too physically miserable, and too filled with mental apprehensions. All nature seemed to be big with impending disaster. The sky appeared to be sinking down upon the earth. The moon was hidden, yet a faint and lurid light shone now in one quarter of the horizon, now in another. There was no wind, but the air moaned audibly. It was as though the end of the world were near as, I reflected, probably might be the case so far as we were concerned. Never, perhaps, have I felt so spiritually terrified as I was during the dreadful inaction of that night. Even if I had known that I was going to be executed at dawn, I think that by comparison I should have been light-hearted. But the worst part of the business was that I knew nothing. I was like a man forced to walk through dense darkness among precipices, quite unable to guess when my journey would end in space, but enduring all the agonies of death at every step.

About midnight again we heard that scuffle and stifled cry in the hut behind us.

"He's gone," I whispered to Marût, wiping the cold sweat from my brow.

"Yes," answered Marût, "and very soon we shall follow him, Macumazana."

I wished that his face were visible so that I could see if he still smiled when he uttered those words.

An hour or so later the usual fire appeared in the marketplace, round which the usual figures flitted dimly. The sight of them fascinated me, although I did not want to look, fearing what I might see. Luckily, however, we were too far off to discern anything at night.

While these unholy ceremonies were in progress the climax came, that is so far as the weather was concerned. Of a sudden a great gale sprang up, a gale of icy wind such as in Southern Africa sometimes precedes a thunderstorm. It blew for half an hour or more, then lulled. Now lightning flashed across the heavens, and by the glare of it we perceived that all the population of Simba Town seemed to be gathered in the market-place. At least there were some thousands of them, talking, gesticulating, pointing at the sky.

A few minutes later there came a great crash of thunder, of which it was impossible to locate the sound, for it rolled from everywhere. Then suddenly something hard struck the roof by my side and rebounded, to be followed next moment by a blow upon my shoulder which nearly knocked me flat, although I was well protected by the skin rugs.

"Down the stair!" I called. "They are stoning us," and suited the action to the word.

Ten seconds later we were both in the room, crouched in its farther corner, for the stones or whatever they were seemed to be following us. I struck a match, of which fortunately I had some, together with my pipe and a good pocketful of tobacco—my only solace in those days—and, as it burned up, saw first that blood was running down Marût's face, and secondly, that these stones were great lumps of ice, some of them weighing several ounces, which hopped about the floor like live things.

"Hailstorm!" remarked Marût with his accustomed smile.

"Hell storm!" I replied, "for whoever saw hail like that before?"

Then the match burnt out and conversation came to an end for the reason that we could no longer hear each other speak. The hail came down with a perpetual, rattling roar, that in its sum was one of the most terrible sounds to which I ever listened. And yet above it I thought that I could catch another, still more terrible, the wail of hundreds of people in agony. After the first few minutes I began to be afraid that the roof would be battered in, or that the walls would crumble beneath this perpetual fire of the musketry of heaven. But the cement was good and the place well built.

So it came about that the house stood the tempest, which had it been roofed with tiles or galvanized iron I am sure it would never have done, since the lumps of ice must have shattered one and pierced the other like paper. Indeed I have seen this happen in a bad hailstorm in Natal which killed my best horse. But even that hail was as snowflakes compared to this.

I suppose that this natural phenomenon continued for about twenty minutes, not more, during ten of which it was at its worst. Then by degrees it ceased, the sky cleared and the moon shone out beautifully. We climbed to the roof again and looked. It was several inches deep in jagged ice, while the market-place and all the country round appeared in the bright moonlight to be buried beneath a veil of snow.

Very rapidly, as the normal temperature of that warm land reasserted itself, this snow or rather hail melted, causing a flood of water which, where there was any fall, began to rush away with a gurgling sound. Also we heard other sounds, such as that from the galloping hoofs of many of the horses which had broken loose from their wrecked stables at the north end of the market-place, where in great number they had been killed by the falling roofs or had kicked each other to death, and a wild universal wail that rose from every quarter of the big town, in which quantities of the worst-built houses had collapsed. Further, lying here and there about the market-place we could see scores of dark shapes that we knew to be those of men, women and children, whom those sharp missiles hurled from heaven had caught before they could escape and slain or wounded almost to death. For it will be remembered that perhaps not fewer than two thousand people were gathered on this market-place, attending the horrid midnight sacrifice and discussing the unnatural weather when the storm burst upon them suddenly as an avalanche.

"The Child is small, yet its strength is great. Behold the first curse!" said Marût solemnly.

I stared at him, but as he chose to believe that a very unusual hailstorm was a visitation from heaven I did not think it worth while arguing the point. Only I wondered if he really did believe this. Then I remembered that such an event was said to have afflicted the old Egyptians in the hour of their pride because they would not "let the people go." Well, these blackguardedly Black Kendah were certainly worse than the Egyptians can ever have been; also they would not let *us* go. It was not wonderful therefore that Marût should be the victim of fantasies on the matter.

Not until the following morning did we come to understand the full extent of the calamity which had overtaken the Black Kendah. I think I have said that their crops this year were magnificent and just ripening to harvest. From our roof on previous days we could see a great area of them stretching to the edge of the forest. When the sun rose that morning this area had vanished, and the ground was covered with a carpet of green pulp. Also the forest itself appeared suddenly to have experienced the full effects of a northern winter. Not a leaf was left upon the trees, which stood their pointing their naked boughs to heaven.

No one who had not seen it could imagine the devastating fury of that storm. For example, the head of the diviner who was buried in the court-yard awaiting resurrection through our magic was, it may be recalled, covered with a stout earthenware pot. Now that pot had shattered into shards and the head beneath was nothing but bits of broken bone which it would have been impossible for the very best magic to reconstruct to the likeness of a human being.

Calamity indeed stalked naked through the land.

CHAPTER 13

Jana

No breakfast was brought to us that morning, probably for the reason that there was none to bring. This did not matter, however, seeing that plenty of food accumulated from supper and other meals stood in a corner of the house practically untouched. So we ate what we could and then paid our usual visit to the hut in which the camelmen had been confined. I say had been, for now it was quite empty, the last poor fellow having vanished away like his companions.

The sight of this vacuum filled me with a kind of fury.

"They have all been murdered!" I said to Marût.

"No," he replied with gentle accuracy. "They have been sacrificed to Jana. What we have seen on the market-place at night was the rite of their sacrifice. Now it will be our turn, Lord Macumazana."

"Well," I exclaimed, "I hope these devils are satisfied with Jana's answer to their accursed offerings, and if they try their fiendish pranks on us——"

"Doubtless there will be another answer. But, Lord, the question is, will that help us?"

Dumb with impotent rage I returned to the house, where presently the remains of the reed gate opened. Through it appeared Simba the King, the diviner with the injured foot walking upon crutches, and others of whom the most were more or less wounded, presumably by the hailstones. Then it was that in my wrath I put off the pretence of not understanding their language and went for them before they could utter a single word.

"Where are our servants, you murderers?" I asked, shaking my fist at them. "Have you sacrificed them to your devil-god? If so, behold the fruits of sacrifice!" and I swept my arm towards the country beyond. "Where are your crops?" I went on. "Tell me on what you will live this winter?" (At these words they quailed. In their imagination

416

already they saw famine stalking towards them.) "Why do you keep us here? Is it that you wait for a worse thing to befall you? Why do you visit us here now?" and I paused, gasping with indignation.

"We came to look whether you had brought back to life that doctor whom you killed with your magic, white man," answered the king heavily.

I stepped to the corner of the court-yard and, drawing aside a mat that I had thrown there, showed them what lay beneath.

"Look then," I said, "and be sure that if you do not let us go, as yonder thing is, so shall all of you be before another moon has been born and died. Such is the life we shall give to evil men like you."

Now they grew positively terrified.

"Lord," said Simba, for the first time addressing me by a title of respect, "your magic is too strong for us. Great misfortune has fallen upon our land. Hundreds of people are dead, killed by the ice-stones that you have called down. Our harvest is ruined, and there is but little corn left in the storepits now when we looked to gather the new grain. Messengers come in from the outlying land telling us that nearly all the sheep and goats and very many of the cattle are slain. Soon we shall starve."

"As you deserve to starve," I answered. "Now—will you let us go?"

Simba stared at me doubtfully, then began to whisper into the ear of the lamed diviner. I could not catch what they said, so I watched their faces. That of the diviner whose head I was glad to see had been cut by a hailstone so that both ends of him were now injured, told me a good deal. His mask had been ugly, but now that it was off the countenance beneath was far uglier. Of a negroid type, pendulous-lipped, sensuous and loose-eyed, he was indeed a hideous fellow, yet very cunning and cruel-looking, as men of his class are apt to be. Humbled as he was for the moment, I felt sure that he was still plotting evil against us, somewhat against the will of his master. The issue showed that I was right. At length Simba spoke, saying:

"We had intended, Lord, to keep you and the priest of the Child here as hostages against mischief that might be worked on us by the followers of the Child, who have always been our bitter enemies and done us much undeserved wrong, although on our part we have faithfully kept the pact concluded in the days of our grandfathers. It seems, however, that fate, or your magic, is too strong for us, and therefore I have determined to let you go. Tonight at sundown we will set you on the road which leads to the ford of the River Tava, which divides our territory from that of the White Kendah, and you may depart where you will, since our wish is that never again may we see your ill-omened faces."

At this intelligence my heart leapt in joy that was altogether premature. But, preserving my indignant air, I exclaimed:

"Tonight! Why tonight? Why not at once? It is hard for us to cross unknown rivers in the dark."

"The water is low, Lord, and the ford easy. Moreover, if you started now you would reach it in the dark; whereas if you start at sundown, you will reach it in the morning. Lastly, we cannot conduct you hence until we have buried our dead."

Then, without giving me time to answer, he turned and left the place, followed by the others. Only at the gateway the diviner wheeled round on his crutches and glared at us both, muttering something with his thick lips; probably it was curses.

"At any rate they are going to set us free," I said to Marût, not without exultation, when they had all vanished.

"Yes, Lord," he replied, "but *where* are they going to set us free? The demon Jana lives in the forests and the swamps by the banks of the Tava River, and it is said that he ravages at night."

I did not pursue the subject, but reflected to myself cheerfully that this mystic rogue-elephant was a long way off and might be circumvented, whereas that altar of sacrifice was extremely near and very difficult to avoid.

Never did a thief with a rich booty in view, or a wooer having an assignation with his lady, wait for sundown more eagerly than I did that day. Hour after hour I sat upon the house-top, watching the Black Kendah carrying off the dead killed by the hailstones and generally trying to repair the damage done by the terrific tempest. Watching the sun also as it climbed down the cloudless sky, and literally counting the minutes till it should reach the horizon, although I knew well that it would have been wiser after such a night to prepare for our journey by lying down to sleep.

At length the great orb began to sink in majesty behind the tattered western forest, and, punctual to the minute, Simba, with a mounted escort of some twenty men and two led horses, appeared at our gate. As our preparations, which consisted only of Marût stuffing such food as was available into the breast of his robe, were already made, we walked out of that accursed guest-house and, at a sign from the king, mounted the horses. Riding across the empty market-place and past the spot where the rough stone altar still stood with charred bones protruding from the ashes of its extinguished fire—were they those of our friends the camel-drivers? I wondered—we entered the north street of the town.

Here, standing at the doors of their houses, were many of the inhabitants who had gathered to watch us pass. Never did I see hate more savage than was written on those faces as they shook their fists at us and muttered curses not loud but deep.

No wonder! for they were all ruined, poor folk, with nothing to look forward to but starvation until long months hence the harvest came again for those who would live to gather it. Also they were convinced that we, the white magician and the prophet of their enemy the Child, had brought this disaster on them. Had it not been for the escort I believe they would have fallen on us and torn us to pieces. Considering them I understood for the first time how disagreeable real unpopularity *can be*. But when I saw the actual condition of the fruitful gardens without in the waning daylight, I confess that I was moved to some sympathy with their owners. It was appalling. Not a handful of grain was there left to gather, for the corn had been not only "laid" but literally cut to ribbons by the hail.

After running for some miles through the cultivated land the road entered the forest. Here it was dark as pitch, so dark that I wondered how our guides found their way. In that blackness dreadful apprehensions seized me, for I became convinced that we had been brought here to be murdered. Every minute I expected to feel a knife-thrust in my back. I thought of digging my heels into the horse's sides and trying to gallop off anywhere, but abandoned the idea, first because I could not desert Marût, of whom I had lost touch in the gloom, and secondly because I was hemmed in by the escort. For the same reason I did not try to slip from the horse and glide away into the forest. There was nothing to be done save to go on and await the end.

It came at last some hours later. We were out of the forest now, and there was the moon rising, past her full but still very bright. Her light showed me that we were on a wild moorland, swampy, with scattered trees growing here and there, across which what seemed to be a game track ran down hill. That was all I could make out. Here the escort halted, and Simba the King said in a sullen voice:

"Dismount and go your ways, evil spirits, for we travel no farther across this place which is haunted. Follow the track and it will lead you to a lake. Pass the lake and by morning you will come to the river beyond which lies the country of your friends. May its waters swallow you if you reach them. For learn, there is one who watches on this road whom few care to meet."

As he finished speaking men sprang at us and, pulling us from the horses, thrust us out of their company. Then they turned and in another minute were lost in the darkness, leaving us alone.

"What now, friend Marût?" I asked.

"Now, Lord, all we can do is to go forward, for if we stay here Simba and his people will return and kill us at the daylight. One of them said so to me."

"Then, 'come on, Macduff,'" I exclaimed, stepping out briskly, and though he had never read Shakespeare, Marût understood and followed.

"What did Simba mean about 'one on the road whom few care to meet'?" I asked over my shoulder when we had done half a mile or so.

"I think he meant the elephant Jana," replied Marût with a groan.

"Then I hope Jana isn't at home. Cheer up, Marût. The chances are that we shall never meet a single elephant in this big place."

"Yet many elephants have been here, Lord," and he pointed to the ground. "It is said that they come to die by the waters of the lake and this is one of the roads they follow on their death journey, a road that no other living thing dare travel."

"Oh!" I exclaimed. "Then after all that was a true dream I had in the house in England."

"Yes, Lord, because my brother Harût once lost his way out hunting when he was young and saw what his mind showed you in the dream, and what we shall see presently, if we live to come so far."

I made no reply, both because what he said was either true or false, which I should ascertain presently, and because I was engaged in searching the ground with my eyes. He was right; many elephants had travelled this path—one quite recently. I, a hunter of those brutes, could not be deceived on this point. Once or twice also I thought that I caught sight of the outline of some tall creature moving silently through the scattered thorns a couple of hundred yards or so to our right. It might have been an elephant or a giraffe, or perhaps nothing but a shadow, so I said nothing. As I heard no noise I was inclined to believe the latter explanation. In any case, what was the good of speaking? Unarmed and solitary amidst unknown dangers, our position was desperate, and as Marût's nerve was already giving out, to emphasize its horrors to him would be mere foolishness.

On we trudged for another two hours, during which time the only living thing that I saw was a large owl which sailed round our heads as though to look at us, and then flew away ahead.

This owl, Marût informed me, was one of "Jana's spies" that kept him advised of all that was passing in his territory. I muttered "Bosh" and tramped on. Still I was glad that we saw no more of the owl, for in certain circumstances such dark fears are catching.

We reached the top of a rise, and there beneath us lay the most desolate scene that ever I have seen. At least it would have been the most desolate if I did not chance to have looked on it before, in the drawing-room of Ragnall Castle! There was no doubt about it. Below was the black, melancholy lake, a large sheet of water surrounded by reeds. Around, but at a considerable distance, appeared the tropical forest. To the east of the lake stretched a stony plain. At the time I could make out no more because of the uncertain light and the distance, for we had still over a mile to go before we reached the edge of the lake.

The aspect of the place filled me with tremblings, both because of its utter uncanniness and because of the inexplicable truth that I had seen it before. Most people will have experienced this kind of moral shock when on going to some new land they recognize a locality as being quite familiar to them in all its details. Or it may be the rooms of a house hitherto unvisited by them. Or it may be a conversation of which, when it begins, they already foreknow the sequence and the end, because in some dim state, when or how who can say, they have taken part in that talk with those same speakers. If this be so even in cheerful surroundings and among our friends or acquaintances, it is easy to imagine how much greater was the shock to me, a traveller on such a journey and in such a night.

I shrank from approaching the shores of this lake, remembering that as yet all the vision was not unrolled. I looked about me. If we went to the left we should either strike the water, or if we followed its edge, still bearing to the left, must ultimately reach the forest, where probably we should be lost. I looked to the right. The ground was strewn with boulders, among which grew thorns and rank grass, impracticable for men on foot at night. I looked behind me, meditating retreat, and there, some hundreds of yards away behind low, scrubby mimosas mixed with aloe-like plants, I saw something brown toss up and disappear again that might very well have been the trunk of an elephant. Then, animated by the courage of despair and a desire to know the worst, I began to descend the elephant track towards the lake almost at a run.

Ten minutes or so more brought us to the eastern head of the lake, where the reeds whispered in the breath of the night wind like things alive. As I expected, it proved to be a bare, open space where

421

nothing seemed to grow. Yes, and all about me were the decaying remains of elephants, hundreds of them, some with their bones covered in moss, that may have lain here for generations, and others more newly dead. They were all old beasts as I could tell by the tusks, whether male or female. Indeed about me within a radius of a quarter of a mile lay enough ivory to make a man very rich for life, since although discoloured, much of it seemed to have kept quite sound, like human teeth in a mummy case. The sight gave me a new zest for life. If only I could manage to survive and carry off that ivory! I would. In this way or in that I swore that I would! Who could possibly die with so much ivory to be had for the taking? Not that old hunter, Allan Quatermain.

Then I forgot about the ivory, for there in front of me, just where it should be, just as I had seen it in the dream-picture, was the bull elephant dying, a thin and ancient brute that had lived its long life to the last hour. It searched about as though to find a convenient resting-place, and when this was discovered, stood over it, swaying to and fro for a full minute. Then it lifted its trunk and trumpeted shrilly thrice, singing its swan-song, after which it sank slowly to its knees, its trunk outstretched and the points of its worn tusks resting on the ground. Evidently it was dead.

I let my eyes travel on, and behold! about fifty yards beyond the dead bull was a mound of hard rock. I watched it with gasping expectation and—yes, on the top of the mound something slowly materialized. Although I knew what it must be well enough, for a while I could not see quite clearly because there were certain little clouds about and one of them had floated over the face of the moon. It passed, and before me, perhaps a hundred and forty paces away, outlined clearly against the sky, I perceived the devilish elephant of my vision.

Oh! what a brute was that! In bulk and height it appeared to be half as big again as any of its tribe which I had known in all my life's experience. It was enormous, unearthly; a survivor perhaps of some ancient species that lived before the Flood, or at least a very giant of its kind. Its grey-black sides were scarred as though with fighting. One of its huge tusks, much worn at the end, for evidently it was very old, gleamed white in the moonlight. The other was broken off about halfway down its length. When perfect it had been malformed, for it curved downwards and not upwards, also rather out to the right.

There stood this mammoth, this leviathan, this *monstrum horrendum, informe, ingens*, as I remember my old father used to call a certain gigantic and misshapen bull that we had on the Station, flapping a pair of ears that looked like the sides of a *Kafir* hut, and waving a trunk as big as a weaver's beam—whatever a weaver's beam may be—an appalling and a petrifying sight.

I squatted behind the skeleton of an elephant which happened to be handy and well covered with moss and ferns and watched the beast, fascinated, wishing that I had a large-bore rifle in my hand. What became of Marût I do not exactly know, but I think that he lay down on the ground.

During the minute or so that followed I reflected a good deal, as we do in times of emergency, often after a useless sort of a fashion. For instance, I wondered why the brute appeared thus upon yonder mound, and the thought suggested itself to me that it was summoned thither from some neighbouring lair by the trumpet call of the dying elephant. It occurred to me even that it was a kind of king of the elephants, to which they felt bound to report themselves, as it were, in the hour of their decease. Certainly what followed gave some credence to my fantastical notion which, if there were anything in it, might account for this great graveyard at that particular spot.

After standing for a while in the attitude that I have described, testing the air with its trunk, Jana, for I will call him so, lumbered down the mound and advanced straight to where the elephant that I had thought to be dead was kneeling. As a matter of fact it was not quite dead, for when Jana arrived it lifted its trunk and curled it round that of Jana as though in affectionate greeting, then let it fall to the ground again. Thereon Jana did what I had seen it do in my dream or vision at Ragnall, namely, attacked it, knocking it over on to its side, where it lay motionless; quite dead this time.

Now I remembered that the vision was not accurate after all, since in it I had seen Jana destroy a woman and a child, who on the present occasion were wanting. Since then I have thought that this was because Harût, clairvoyantly or telepathically, had conveyed to me, as indeed Marût declared, a scene which he had witnessed similar to that which I was witnessing, but not identical in its incidents. Thus it happened, perhaps, that while the act of the woman and the child was omitted, in our case there was another act of the play to follow of which I had received no inkling in my Ragnall experience. Indeed, if I had received it, I should not have been there that night, for no inducement on earth would have brought me to Kendahland.

This was the act. Jana, having prodded his dead brother to his satisfaction, whether from viciousness or to put it out of pain, I cannot say, stood over the carcass in an attitude of grief or pious meditation. At this time, I should mention, the wind, which had been rustling the hail-stripped reeds at the lake border, had died away almost, but not completely; that is to say, only a very faint gust blew now and again, which, with a hunter's instinct, I observed with satisfaction drew *from* the direction of Jana towards ourselves. This I knew, because it struck on my forehead, which was wet with perspiration, and cooled the skin.

Presently, however, by a cursed spite of fate, one of these gusts—a very little one—came from some quarter behind us, for I felt it in my back hair, that was as damp as the rest of me. Just then I was glancing to my right, where it seemed to me that out of the corner of my eye I had caught sight of something passing among the stones at a distance of a hundred yards or so, possibly the shadow of a cloud or another elephant. At the time I did not ascertain which it was, since a faint rattle from Jana's trunk reconcentrated all my faculties on him in a painfully vivid fashion.

I looked to see that all the contemplation had departed from his attitude, now as alert as that of a fox-terrier which imagines he has seen a rat. His vast ears were cocked, his huge bulk trembled, his enormous trunk sniffed the air.

"Great Heavens!" thought I to myself, "he has winded us!" Then I took such consolation as I could from the fact that the next gust once more struck upon my forehead, for I hoped he would conclude that he had made a mistake.

Not a bit of it! Jana as far too old a bird—or beast—to make any mistake. He grunted, got himself going like a luggage train, and with great deliberation walked towards us, smelling at the ground, smelling at the air, smelling to the right, to the left, and even towards heaven above, as though he expected that thence might fall upon him vengeance for his many sins. A dozen times as he came did I cover him with an imaginary rifle, marking the exact spots where I might have hoped to send a bullet to his vitals, in a kind of automatic fashion, for all my real brain was contemplating my own approaching end.

I wondered how it would happen. Would he drive that great tusk through me, would he throw me into the air, or would he kneel upon my poor little body, and avenge the deaths of his kin that had fallen at my hands? Marût was speaking in a rattling whisper:

"His priests have told Jana to kill us; we are about to die," he said. "Before I die I want to say that the lady, the wife of the lord——"

"Silence!" I hissed. "He will hear you," for at that instant I took not the slightest interest in any lady on the earth. Fiercely I glared at

Marût and noted even then how pitiful was his countenance. There was no smile there now. All its jovial roundness had vanished. It had sunk in; it was blue and ghastly with large, protruding eyes, like to that of a man who had been three days dead.

I was right—Jana *had* heard. Low as the whisper was, through that intense silence it had penetrated to his almost preternatural senses. Forward he came at a run for twenty paces or more with his trunk held straight out in front of him. Then he halted again, perhaps the length of a cricket pitch away, and smelt as before.

The sight was too much for Marût. He sprang up and ran for his life towards the lake, purposing, I suppose, to take refuge in the water. Oh! how he ran. After him went Jana like a railway engine—express this time—trumpeting as he charged. Marût reached the lake, which was quite close, about ten yards ahead, and plunging into it with a bound, began to swim.

Now, I thought, he may get away if the crocodiles don't have him, for that devil will scarcely take to the water. But this was just where I made a mistake, for with a mighty splash in went Jana too. Also he was the better swimmer. Marût soon saw this and swung round to the shore, by which manoeuvre he gained a little as he could turn quicker than Jana.

Back they came, Jana just behind Marût, striking at him with his great trunk. They landed, Marût flew a few yards ahead doubling in and out among the rocks like a hare and, to my horror, making for where I lay, whether by accident or in a mad hope of obtaining protection, I do not know.

It may be asked why I had not taken the opportunity to run also in the opposite direction. There are several answers. The first was that there seemed to be nowhere to run; the second, that I felt sure, if I did run, I should trip up over the skeletons of those elephants or the stones; the third, that I did not think of it at once; the fourth, that Jana had not yet seen me, and I had no craving to introduce myself to him personally; and the fifth and greatest, that I was so paralysed with fear that I did not feel as though I could lift myself from the ground. Everything about me seemed to be dead, except my powers of observation, which were painfully alive.

Of a sudden Marût gave up. Less than a stone's throw from me he wheeled round and, facing Jana, hurled at him some fearful and concentrated curse, of which all that I could distinguish were the words: "The Child!"

Oddly enough it seemed to have an effect upon the furious rogue, which halted in its rush and, putting its four feet together, slid a few

425

paces nearer and stood still. It was just as though the beast had understood the words and were considering them. If so, their effect was to rouse him to perfect madness. He screamed terribly; he lashed his sides with his trunk; his red and wicked eyes rolled; foam flew from the cavern of his open mouth; he danced upon his great feet, a sort of hideous Scottish reel. Then he charged!

I shut my eyes for a moment. When I opened them again it was to see poor Marût higher in the air than ever he flew before. I thought that he would never come down, but he did at last with an awesome thud. Jana went to him and very gently, now that he was dead, picked him up in his trunk. I prayed that he might carry him away to some hiding-place and leave me in peace. But not so. With slow and stately strides, rocking the deceased Marût up and down in his trunk, as a nurse might rock a baby, he marched on to the very stone where I lay, behind which I suppose he had seen or smelt me all the time.

For quite a long while, it seemed more than a century, he stood over me, studying me as though I interested him very much, the water of the lake trickling in a refreshing stream from his great ears on to my back. Had it not been for that water I think I should have fainted, but as it was I did the next best thing—pretended to be dead. Perhaps this monster would scorn to touch a dead man. Watching out of the corner of my eye, I saw him lift one vast paw that was the size of an arm-chair and hold it over me.

Now good-bye to the world, thought I. Then the foot descended as a steam-hammer does, but also as a steam-hammer sometimes does when used to crack nuts, stopped as it touched my back, and presently came to earth again alongside of me, perhaps because Jana thought the foothold dangerous. At any rate, he took another and better way. Depositing the remains of Marût with the most tender care beside me, as though the nurse were putting the child to bed, he unwound his yards of trunk and began to feel me all over with its tip, commencing at the back of my neck. Oh! the sensation of that clammy, wriggling tip upon my spinal column!

Down it went till it reached the seat of my trousers. There it pinched, presumably to ascertain whether or no I were malingering, a most agonizing pinch like to that of a pair of blacksmith's tongs. So sharp was it that, although I did not stir, who was aware that the slightest movement meant death, it tore a piece out of the stout cloth of my breeches, to say nothing of a portion of the skin beneath. This seemed to astonish the beast, for it lifted the tip of its trunk and shifted its head, as though to examine the fragment by the light of the moon.

Now indeed all was over, for when it saw blood upon that cloth——! I put up one short, piteous prayer to Heaven to save me from this terrible end, and lo, it was answered!

For just as Jana, the results of the inspection being unsatisfactory, was cocking his ears and making ready to slay me, there rang out the short, sharp report of a rifle fired within a few yards. Glancing up at the instant, I saw blood spurt from the monster's left eye, where evidently the bullet had found a home.

He felt at his eye with his trunk; then, uttering a scream of pain, wheeled round and rushed away.

CHAPTER 14

The Chase

I suppose that I swooned for a minute or two. At any rate I remember a long and very curious dream, such a dream as is evolved
by a patient under laughing gas, that is very clear and vivid at the
time but immediately afterwards slips from the mind's grasp as
water does from the clenched hand. It was something to the effect
that all those hundreds of skeleton elephants rose and marshalled
themselves before me, making obeisance to me by bending their
bony knees, because, as I quite understood, I was the only human
being that had ever escaped from Jana. Moreover, on the foremost
elephant's skull Hans was perched like a mahout, giving words
of command, to their serried ranks and explaining to them that
it would be very convenient if they would carry their tusks, for
which they had no further use, and pile them in a certain place—I
forget where—that must be near a good road to facilitate their
subsequent transport to a land where they would be made into
billiard balls and the backs of ladies' hair-brushes. Next, through
the figments of that retreating dream, I heard the undoubted voice
of Hans himself, which of course I knew to be absurd as Hans was
lost and doubtless dead, saying:

"If you are alive, Baas, please wake up soon, as I have finished reloading *Intombi*, and it is time to be going. I think I hit Jana in the eye,
but so big a beast will soon get over so little a thing as that and look for
us, and the bullet from *Intombi* is too small to kill him, Baas, especially
as it is not likely that either of us could hit him in the other eye."

Now I sat up and stared. Yes, there was Hans himself looking just
the same as usual, only perhaps rather dirtier, engaged in setting a cap
on to the nipple of the little rifle *Intombi*.

"Hans," I said in a hollow voice, "why the devil are you here?"

"To save you from the devil, of course, Baas," he replied aptly.

Then, resting the gun against the stone, the old fellow knelt down by my side and, throwing his arms around me, began to blubber over me, exclaiming:

"Just in time, Baas! Only just in time, for as usual Hans made a mess of things and judged badly—I'll tell you afterwards. Still, just in time, thanks be to your reverend father, the Predikant. Oh! if he had delayed me for one more minute you would have been as flat as my nose, Baas. Now come quickly. I've got the camel tied up there, and he can carry two, being fat and strong after four days' rest with plenty to eat. This place is haunted, Baas, and that king of the devils, Jana, will be back after us presently, as soon as he has wiped the blood out of his eye."

I didn't make any remark, having no taste for conversation just then, but only looked at poor Marût, who lay by me as though he was sleeping.

"Oh, Baas," said Hans, "there is no need to trouble about him, for his neck is broken and he's quite dead. Also it is as well," he added cheerfully. "For, as your reverend father doubtless remembered, the camel could never carry three. Moreover, if he stops here, perhaps Jana will come back to play with him instead of following us."

Poor Marût! This was his requiem as sung by Hans.

With a last glance at the unhappy man to whom I had grown attached in a way during our time of joint captivity and trial, I took the arm of the old Hottentot, or rather leant upon his shoulder, for at first I felt too weak to walk by myself, and picked my path with him through the stones and skeletons of elephants across the plateau eastwards, that is, away from the lake. About two hundred yards from the scene of our tragedy was a mound of rock similar to that on which Jana had appeared, but much smaller, behind which we found the camel, kneeling as a well-trained beast of the sort should do and tethered to a stone.

As we went, in brief but sufficient language Hans told me his story. It seemed that after he had shot the Kendah general it came into his cunning, foreseeing mind that he might be of more use to me free than as a companion in captivity, or that if I were killed he might in that case live to bring vengeance on my slayers. So he broke away, as has been described, and hid till nightfall on the hill-side. Then by the light of the moon he tracked us, avoiding the villages, and ultimately found a place of shelter in a kind of cave in the forest near to Simba Town, where no people lived. Here he fed the camel at night, concealing it at dawn in the cave. The days he spent up a tall tree, whence he could watch all that went on in the town beneath, living meanwhile on some food which he carried in a bag tied to the saddle, helped out by green mealies which he stole from a neighbouring field.

Thus he saw most of what passed in the town, including the desolation wrought by the fearful tempest of hail, which, being in their cave, both he and the camel escaped without harm. On the next evening from his post of outlook up the tree, where he had now some difficulty in hiding himself because the hail had stripped off all its leaves, he saw Marût and myself brought from the guest-house and taken away by the escort. Descending and running to the cave, he saddled the camel and started in pursuit, plunging into the forest and hiding there when he perceived that the escort were leaving us.

Here he waited until they had gone by on their return journey. So close did they pass to him that he could overhear their talk, which told him they expected, or rather were sure, that we should be destroyed by the elephant Jana, their devil god, to whom the camelmen had been already sacrificed. After they had departed he remounted and followed us. Here I asked him why he had not overtaken us before we came to the cemetery of elephants, as I presumed he might have done, since he stated that he was close in our rear. This indeed was the case, for it was the head of the camel I saw behind the thorn trees when I looked back, and not the trunk of an elephant as I had supposed.

At the time he would give me no direct answer, except that he grew muddled as he had already suggested, and thought it best to keep in the background and see what happened. Long afterwards, however, he admitted to me that he acted on a presentiment.

"It seemed to me, Baas," he said, "that your reverend father was telling me that I should do best to let you two go on and not show myself, since if I did so we should all three be killed, as one of us must walk whom the other two could not desert. Whereas if I left you as you were, one of you would be killed and the other escape, and that the one to be killed would not be *you*, Baas. All of which came about as the Spirit spoke in my head, for Marût was killed, who did not matter, and—you know the rest, Baas."

To return to Hans' story. He saw us march down to the borders of the lake, and, keeping to our right, took cover behind the knoll of rock, whence he watched also all that followed. When Jana advanced to attack us Hans crept forward in the hope, a very wild one, of crippling him with the little Purdey rifle. Indeed, he was about to fire at the hind leg when Marût made his run for life and plunged into the lake. Then he crawled on to lead me away to the camel, but when he was within a few yards the chase returned our way and Marût was killed.

From that moment he waited for an opportunity to shoot Jana in the only spot where so soft a bullet would, as he knew, have the faintest chance of injuring him vitally—namely, in the eye—for he was sure that its penetration would not be sufficient to reach the vitals through that thick hide and the mass of flesh behind. With an infinite and wonderful patience he waited, knowing that my life or death hung in the balance. While Jana held his foot over me, while he felt me with his trunk, still Hans waited, balancing the arguments for and against firing upon the scales of experience in his clever old mind, and in the end coming to a right and wise conclusion.

At length his chance came, the brute exposed his eye, and by the light of the clear moon Hans, always a very good shot at a distance when it was not necessary to allow for trajectory and wind, let drive and *hit*. The bullet did not get to the brain as he had hoped; it had not strength for that, but it destroyed this left eye and gave Jana such pain that for a while he forgot all about me and everything else except escape.

Such was the Hottentot's tale as I picked it up from his laconic, colourless, Dutch *patois* sentences, then and afterwards; a very wonderful tale I thought. But for him, his fidelity and his bushman's cunning, where should I have found myself before that moon set?

****

We mounted the camel after I had paused a minute to take a pull from a flask of brandy which remained in the saddlebags. Although he loved strong drink so well Hans had saved it untouched on the mere chance that it might some time be of service to me, his master. The monkey-like Hottentot sat in front and directed the camel, while I accommodated myself as best I could on the sheepskins behind. Luckily they were thick and soft, for Jana's pinch was not exactly that of a lover.

Off we went, picking our way carefully till we reached the elephant track beyond the mound where Jana had appeared, which, in the light of faith, we hoped would lead us to the River Tava. Here we made better progress, but still could not go very fast because of the holes made by the feet of Jana and his company. Soon we had left the cemetery behind us, and lost sight of the lake which I devoutly trusted I might never see again.

Now the track ran upwards from the hollow to a ridge two or three miles away. We reached the crest of this ridge without accident, except that on our road we met another aged elephant, a cow with very poor tusks, travelling to its last resting place, or so I suppose. I don't know which was the more frightened, the sick cow or the camel, for camels hate elephants as horses hate camels until they get used to them. The cow bolted to the right as quickly as it could, which was not very fast, and the camel bolted to the left with such convulsive bounds that we were nearly thrown off its back. However, being an equable brute, it soon recovered its balance, and we got back to the track beyond the cow.

From the top of the rise we saw that before us lay a sandy plain lightly clothed in grass, and, to our joy, about ten miles away at the foot of a very gentle slope, the moonlight gleamed upon the waters of a broad river. It was not easy to make out, but it was there, we were both sure it was there; we could not mistake the wavering, silver flash. On we went for another quarter of a mile, when something caused me to turn round on the sheepskin and look back.

Oh Heavens! At the very top of the rise, clearly outlined against the sky, stood Jana himself with his trunk lifted. Next instant he trumpeted, a furious, rattling challenge of rage and defiance.

"*Allemagte!* Baas," said Hans, "the old devil is coming to look for his lost eye, and has seen us with that which remains. He has been travelling on our spoor."

"Forward!" I answered, bringing my heels into the camel's ribs.

Then the race began. The camel was a very good camel, one of the real running breed; also, as Hans said, it was comparatively fresh, and may, moreover, have been aware that it was near to the plains where it had been bred. Lastly, the going was now excellent, soft to its spongy feet but not too deep in sand, nor were there any rocks over which it could fall. It went off like the wind, making nothing of our united weights which did not come to more than two hundred pounds, or a half of what it could carry with ease, being perhaps urged to its top speed by the knowledge that the elephant was behind. For mile after mile we rushed down the plain. But we did not go alone, for Jana came after us like a cruiser after a gunboat. Moreover, swiftly as we travelled, he travelled just a little swifter, gaining say a few yards in every hundred. For the last mile before we came to the river bank, half an hour later perhaps, though it seemed to be a week, he was not more than fifty paces to our rear. I glanced back at him, and in the light of the moon, which was growing low, he bore a strange resemblance to a mud cottage with broken chimneys (which were his ears flapping on each side of him), and the yard pump projecting from the upper window.

"We shall beat him now, Hans," I said looking at the broad river which was now close at hand.

"Yes, Baas," answered Hans doubtfully and in jerks. "This is very good camel, Baas. He runs so fast that I have no inside left, I suppose because he smells his wife over that river, to say nothing of death behind him. But, Baas, I am not sure; that devil Jana is still faster than the camel, and he wants to settle for his lost eye, which makes him lively. Also I see stones ahead, which are bad for camels. Then there is the river, and I don't know if camels can swim, but Jana can as Marût learned. Do you think, Baas, that you could manage to sting him up with a bullet in his knee or that great trunk of his, just to give him something to think about besides ourselves?"

Thus he prattled on, I believe to occupy my mind and his own, till at length, growing impatient, I replied:

"Be silent, donkey. Can I shoot an elephant backwards over my shoulder with a rifle meant for springbuck? Hit the camel! Hit it hard!"

Alas! Hans was right! There *were* stones at the verge of the river, which doubtless it had washed out in periods of past flood, and presently we were among them. Now a camel, so good on sand that is its native heath, is a worthless brute among stones, over which it slips and flounders. But to Jana these appeared to offer little or no obstacle. At any rate he came over them almost if not quite as fast as before. By the time that we reached the brink of the water he was not more than ten yards behind. I could even see the blood running down from the socket of his ruined eye.

Moreover, at the sight of the foaming but shallow torrent, the camel, a creature unaccustomed to water, pulled up in a mulish kind of way and for a moment refused to stir. Luckily at this instant Jana let off one of his archangel kind of trumpetings which started our beast again, since it was more afraid of elephants than it was of water.

In we went and were presently floundering among the loose stones at the bottom of the river, which was nowhere over four feet deep, with Jana splashing after us not more than five yards behind. I twisted myself round and fired at him with the rifle. Whether I hit him or no I could not say, but he stopped for a few seconds, perhaps because he remembered the effect of a similar explosion upon his eye, which gave us a trifling start. Then he came on again in his steam-engine fashion.

When we were about in the middle of the river the inevitable happened. The camel fell, pitching us over its head into the stream. Still clinging to the rifle I picked myself up and began half to swim half to wade towards the farther shore, catching hold of Hans with my free hand. In a moment Jana was on to that camel. He gored it with his tusks, he trampled it with his feet, he got it round the neck with his trunk, dragging nearly the whole bulk of it out of the water. Then he set to work to pound it down into the mud and stones at the bottom of the river with such a persistent thoroughness, that he gave us time to reach the other bank and climb up a stout tree which grew there, a sloping, flat-topped kind of tree that was fortunately easy to ascend, at least for a man. Here we sat gasping, perhaps about thirty feet above the ground level, and waited.

Presently Jana, having finished with the camel, followed us, and without any difficulty located us in that tree. He walked all round it considering the situation. Then he wound his huge trunk about the bole of the tree and, putting out his strength, tried to pull it over. It was an anxious moment, but this particular child of the forest had not grown there for some hundreds of years, withstanding all the shocks of wind, weather and water, in order to be laid low by an elephant, however enormous. It shook a little—no more. Abandoning this attempt as futile, Jana next began to try to dig it up by driving his tusk under its roots. Here, too, he failed because they grew among stones which evidently jarred him.

Ceasing from these agricultural efforts with a deep rumble of rage, he adopted yet a third expedient. Rearing his huge bulk into the air he brought down his forefeet with all the tremendous weight of his great body behind them on to the sloping trunk of the tree just below where the branches sprang, perhaps twelve or thirteen feet above the ground. The shock was so heavy that for a moment I thought the tree would be uprooted or snapped in two. Thank Heaven! it held, but the vibration was such that Hans and I were nearly shaken out of the upper branches, like autumn apples from a bough. Indeed, I think I should have gone had not the monkey-like Hans, who had toes to cling with as well as fingers, gripped me by the collar.

Thrice did Jana repeat this manoeuvre, and at the third onslaught I saw to my horror that the roots were loosening. I heard some of them snap, and a crack appeared in the ground not far from the bole. Fortunately Jana never noted these symptoms, for abandoning a plan which he considered unavailing, he stood for a while swaying his trunk and lost in gentle thought.

"Hans," I whispered, "load the rifle quick! I can get him in the spine or the other eye."

"Wet powder won't go off, Baas," groaned Hans. "The water got to it in the river."

"No," I answered, "and it is all your fault for making me shoot at him when I could take no aim."

"It would have been just the same, Baas, for the rifle went under water also when we fell from the camel, and the cap would have been damp, and perhaps the powder too. Also the shot made Jana stop for a moment."

This was true, but it was maddening to be obliged to sit there with an empty gun, when if I had but one charge, or even my pistol, I was sure that I could have blinded or crippled this satanic pachyderm.

A few minutes later Jana played his last card. Coming quite close to the trunk of the tree he reared himself up as before, but this time stretched out his forelegs so that these and his body were supported on the broad bole. Then he elongated his trunk and with it began to break off boughs which grew between us and him.

"I don't think he can reach us," I said doubtfully to Hans, "that is, unless he brings a stone to stand on."

"Oh! Baas, pray be silent," answered Hans, "or he will understand and fetch one."

Although the idea seemed absurd, on the whole I thought it well to take the hint, for who knew how much this experienced beast did or did not understand? Then, as we could go no higher, we wriggled as far as we dared along our boughs and waited.

Presently Jana, having finished his clearing operations, began to lengthen his trunk to its full measure. Literally, it seemed to expand like a telescope or an India rubber ring. Out it came, foot after foot, till its snapping tip was waving within a few inches of us, just short of my foot and Han's head, or rather felt hat. One final stretch and he reached the hat, which he removed with a flourish and thrust into the red cavern of his mouth. As it appeared no more I suppose he ate it. This loss of his hat moved Hans to fury. Hurling horrible curses at Jana he drew his butcher's knife and made ready.

Once more the sinuous brown trunk elongated itself. Evidently Jana had got a better hold with his hind legs this time, or perhaps had actually wriggled himself a few inches up the tree. At any rate I saw to my dismay that there was every prospect of my making a second acquaintance with that snapping tip. The end of the trunk was lying along my bough like a huge brown snake and creeping up, up, up.

"He'll get us," I muttered.

Hans said nothing but leaned forward a little, holding on with his left hand. Next instant in the light of the rising sun I saw a knife flash, saw also that the point of it had been driven through the lower lip of Jana's trunk, pinning it to the bough like a butterfly to a board.

435

My word! what a commotion ensued! Up the trunk came a scream which nearly blew me away. Then Jana, with a wriggling motion, tried to unnail himself as gently as possible, for it was clear that the knife point hurt him, but could not do so because Hans still held the handle and had driven the blade deep into the wood. Lastly he dragged himself downwards with such energy that something had to go, that something being the skin and muscle of the lower lip, which was cut clean through, leaving the knife erect in the bough.

Over he went backwards, a most imperial cropper. Then he picked himself up, thrust the tip of his trunk into his mouth, sucked it as one does a cut finger, and finally, roaring in defeated rage, fled into the river, which he waded, and back upon his tracks towards his own home. Yes, off he went, Hans screaming curses and demands that he should restore his hat to him, and very seldom in all my life have I seen a sight that I thought more beautiful than that of his whisking tail.

"Now, Baas," chuckled Hans, "the old devil has got a sore nose as well as a sore eye by which to remember us. And, Baas, I think we had better be going before he has time to think and comes back with a long stick to knock us out of this tree."

So we went, in double-quick time I can assure you, or at any rate as fast as my stiff limbs and general condition would allow. Fortunately we had now no doubt as to our direction, since standing up through the mists of dawn with the sunbeams resting on its forest-clad crest, we could clearly see the strange, tumulus-shaped hill which the White Kendah called the Holy Mount, the Home of the Child. It appeared to be about twenty miles away, but in reality was a good deal farther, for when we had walked for several hours it seemed almost as distant as ever.

In truth that was a dreadful trudge. Not only was I exhausted with all the terrors I had passed and our long midnight flight, but the wound where Jana had pinched out a portion of my frame, inflamed by the riding, had now grown stiff and intolerably sore, so that every step gave me pain which sometimes culminated in agony. Moreover, it was no use giving in, foodless as we were, for Marût had carried the provisions, and with the chance of Jana returning to look us up. So I stuck to it and said nothing.

For the first ten miles the country seemed uninhabited; doubtless it was too near the borders of the Black Kendah to be popular as a place of residence. After this we saw herds of cattle and a few camels, apparently untended; perhaps their guards were hidden away in the long grass. Then we came to some fields of mealies that were, I noticed, quite untouched by the hailstorm, which, it would seem, had confined its attentions to the land of the Black Kendah. Of these we ate thankfully enough. A little farther on we perceived huts perched on an inaccessible place in a *kloof*. Also their inhabitants perceived us, for they ran away as though in a great fright.

Still we did not try to approach the huts, not knowing how we should be received. After my sojourn in Simba Town I had become possessed of a love of life in the open.

For another two hours I limped forward with pain and grief—by now I was leaning on Hans' shoulder—up an endless, uncultivated rise clothed with *euphorbias* and fern-like *cycads*. At length we reached its top and found ourselves within a rifle shot of a fenced native village. I suppose that its inhabitants had been warned of our coming by runners from the huts I have mentioned. At any rate the moment we appeared the men, to the number of thirty or more, poured out of the south gate armed with spears and other weapons and proceeded to ring us round and behave in a very threatening manner. I noticed at once that, although most of them were comparatively light in colour, some of these men partook of the negro characteristics of the Black Kendah from whom we had escaped, to such an extent indeed that this blood was clearly predominant in them. Still, it was also clear that they were deadly foes of this people, for when I shouted out to them that we were the friends of Harût and those who worshipped the Child, they yelled back that we were liars. No friends of the Child, they said, came from the country of the Black Kendah, who worshipped the devil Jana. I tried to explain that least of all men in the world did we worship Jana, who had been hunting us for hours, but they would not listen.

"You are spies of Simba's, the smell of Jana is upon you" (this may have been true enough), they yelled, adding: "We will kill you, white-faced goat. We will kill you, little yellow monkey, for none who are not enemies come here from the land of the Black Kendah."

"Kill us then," I answered, "and bring the curse of the Child upon you. Bring famine, bring hail, bring war!"

These words were, I think, well chosen; at any rate they induced a pause in their murderous intentions. For a while they hesitated, all talking together at once. At last the advocates of violence appeared to get the upper hand, and once more a number of the men began to dance about us, waving their spears and crying out that we must die who came from the Black Kendah.

I sat down upon the ground, for I was so exhausted that at the time I did not greatly care whether I died or lived, while Hans drew his knife and stood over me, cursing them as he had cursed at Jana. By slow degrees they drew nearer and nearer. I watched them with a kind of idle curiosity, believing that the moment when they came within actual spear-thrust would be our last, but, as I have said, not greatly caring because of my mental and physical exhaustion.

I had already closed my eyes that I might not see the flash of the falling steel, when an exclamation from Hans caused me to open them again. Following the line of the knife with which he pointed, I perceived a troop of men on camels emerging from the gates of the village at full speed. In front of these, his white garments fluttering on the wind, rode a bearded and dignified person in whom I recognized Harût, Harût himself, waving a spear and shouting as he came. Our assailants heard and saw him also, then flung down their weapons as though in dismay either at his appearance or his words, which I could not catch. Harût guided his rushing camel straight at the man who I presume was their leader, and struck at him with his spear, as though in fury, wounding him in the shoulder and causing him to fall to the ground. As he struck he called out:

"Dog! Would you harm the guests of the Child?"

Then I heard no more because I fainted away.

CHAPTER 15

The Dweller in the Cave

After this it seemed to me that I dreamed a long and very troubled dream concerning all sorts of curious things which I cannot remember. At last I opened my eyes and observed that I lay on a low bed raised about three inches above the floor, in an Eastern-looking room, large and cool. It had window-places in it but no windows, only grass mats hung upon a rod which, I noted inconsequently, worked on a rough, wooden hinge, or rather pin, that enabled the curtain to be turned back against the wall.

Through one of these window-places I saw at a little distance the slope of the forest-covered hill, which reminded me of something to do with a child—for the life of me I could not remember what. As I lay wondering over the matter I heard a shuffling step which I recognized, and, turning, saw Hans twiddling a new hat made of straw in his fingers.

"Hans," I said, "where did you get that new hat?"

"They gave it me here, Baas," he answered. "The Baas will remember that the devil Jana ate the other."

Then I did remember more or less, while Hans continued to twiddle the hat. I begged him to put it on his head because it fidgeted me, and then inquired where we were.

"In the Town of the Child, Baas, where they carried you after you had seemed to die down yonder. A very nice town, where there is plenty to eat, though, having been asleep for three days, you have had nothing except a little milk and soup, which was poured down your throat with a spoon whenever you seemed to half wake up for a while."

"I was tired and wanted a long rest, Hans, and now I feel hungry. Tell me, are the lord and Bena here also, or were they killed after all?"

"Yes, Baas, they are safe enough, and so are all our goods. They

439

were both with Harût when he saved us down by the village yonder, but you went to sleep and did not see them. They have been nursing you ever since, Baas."

Just then Savage himself entered, carrying some soup upon a wooden tray and looking almost as smart as he used to do at Ragnall Castle.

"Good day, sir," he said in his best professional manner. "Very glad to see you back with us, sir, and getting well, I trust, especially after we had given you and Mr. Hans up as dead."

I thanked him and drank the soup, asking him to cook me something more substantial as I was starving, which he departed to do. Then I sent Hans to find Lord Ragnall, who it appeared was out walking in the town. No sooner had they gone than Harût entered looking more dignified than ever and, bowing gravely, seated himself upon the mat in the Eastern fashion.

"Some strong spirit must go with you, Lord Macumazana," he said, "that you should live today, after we were sure that you had been slain."

"That's where you made a mistake. Your magic was not of much service to you there, friend Harût."

"Yet my magic, as you call it, though I have none, was of some service after all, Macumazana. As it chanced I had no opportunity of breathing in the wisdom of the Child for two days from the hour of our arrival here, because I was hurt on the knee in the fight and so weary that I could not travel up the mountain and seek light from the eyes of the Child. On the third day, however, I went and the Oracle told me all. Then I descended swiftly, gathered men and reached those fools in time to keep you from harm. They have paid for what they did, Lord."

"I am sorry, Harût, for they knew no better; and, Harût, although I saved myself, or rather Hans saved me, we have left your brother behind, and with him the others."

"I know. Jana was too strong for them; you and your servant alone could prevail against him."

"Not so, Harût. He prevailed against us; all we could do was to injure his eye and the tip of his trunk and escape from him."

"Which is more than any others have done for many generations, Lord. But doubtless as the beginning was, so shall the end be. Jana, I think, is near his death and through you."

"I don't know," I repeated. "Who and what is Jana?"

"Have I not told you that he is an evil spirit who inhabits the body of a huge elephant?"

"Yes, and so did Marût; but I think that he is just a huge elephant with a very bad temper of his own. Still, whatever he is, he will take some killing, and I don't want to meet him again by that horrible lake."

"Then you will meet him elsewhere, Lord. For if you do not go to look for Jana, Jana will come to look for you who have hurt him so sorely. Remember that henceforth, wherever you go in all this land, it may happen that you will meet Jana."

"Do you mean to say that the brute comes into the territory of the White Kendah?"

"Yes, Macumazana, at times he comes, or a spirit wearing his shape comes; I know not which. What I do know is that twice in my life I myself have seen him upon the Holy Mount, though how he came or how he went none can tell."

"Why was he wandering there, Harût?"

"Who can say, Lord? Tell me why evil wanders through the world and I will answer your question. Only I repeat—let those who have harmed Jana beware of Jana."

"And let Jana beware of me if I can meet him with a decent gun in my hand, for I have a score to settle with the beast. Now, Harût, there is another matter. Just before he was killed Marût, your brother, began to tell me something about the wife of the Lord Ragnall. I had no time to listen to the end of his words, though I thought he said that she was upon yonder Holy Mount. Did I hear aright?"

Instantly Harût's face became like that of a stone idol, impenetrable, impassive.

"Either you misunderstood, Lord," he answered, "or my brother raved in his fear. Wherever she may be, that beautiful lady is not upon the Holy Mount, unless there is another Holy Mount in the Land of Death. Moreover, Lord, as we are speaking of this matter, let me tell you the forest upon that Mount must be trodden by none save the priest of the Child. If others set foot there they die, for it is watched by a guardian more terrible even than Jana, nor is he the only one. Ask me nothing of that guardian, for I will not answer, and, above all, if you or your comrades value life, let them not seek to look upon him."

Understanding that it was quite useless to pursue this subject farther at the moment, I turned to another, remarking that the hailstorm which had smitten the country of the Black Kendah was the worst that I had ever experienced.

"Yes," answered Harût, "so I have learned. That was the first of the curses which the Child, through my mouth, promised to Simba and his people if they molested us upon our road. The second, you will remember, was famine, which for them is near at hand, seeing that they have little corn in store and none left to gather, and that most of their cattle are dead of the hail."

"If they have no corn while, as I noted, you have plenty which the storm spared, will not they, who are many in number but near to starving, attack you and take your corn, Harût?"

"Certainly they will do so, Lord, and then will fall the third curse, the curse of war. All this was foreseen long ago, Macumazana, and you are here to help us in that war. Among your goods you have many guns and much powder and lead. You shall teach our people how to use those guns, that with them we may destroy the Black Kendah."

"I think not," I replied quietly. "I came here to kill a certain elephant, and to receive payment for my service in ivory, not to fight the Black Kendah, of whom I have already seen enough. Moreover, the guns are not my property but that of the Lord Ragnall, who perhaps will ask his own price for the use of them."

"And the Lord Ragnall, who came here against our will, is, as it chances, our property and we may ask your own price for his life. Now, farewell for a while, since you, who are still sick and weak, have talked enough. Only before I go, as your friend and that of those with you, I will add one word. If you would continue to look upon the sun, let none of you try to set foot in the forest upon the Holy Mount. Wander where you will upon its southern slopes, but strive not to pass the wall of rock which rings the forest round." Then he rose, bowed gravely and departed, leaving me full of reflections.

Shortly afterwards Savage and Hans returned, bringing me some meat which the former had cooked in an admirable fashion. I ate of it heartily, and just as they were carrying off the remains of the meal Ragnall himself arrived. Our greeting was very warm, as might be expected in the case of two comrades who never thought to speak to each other again on this side of the grave. As I had supposed, he was certain that Hans and I had been cut off and killed by the Black Kendah, as, after we were missed, some of the camelmen asserted that they had actually seen us fall. So he went on, or rather was carried on by the rush of the camels, grieving, since, it being impossible to attempt to recover our bodies or even to return, that was the only thing to do, and in due course reached the Town of the Child without further accident. Here they rested and mourned for us, till some days later Harût suddenly announced that we still lived, though how he knew this they could not ascertain. Then they sallied out and found us, as has been told, in great danger from the ignorant villagers who, until we appeared, had not even heard of our existence.

I asked what they had done and what information they had obtained since their arrival at this place. His answer was: Nothing and none worth mentioning. The town appeared to be a small one of not much over two thousand inhabitants, all of whom were engaged in agricultural pursuits and in camel-breeding. The herds of camels, however, they gathered, for the most part were kept at outlying settlements on the farther side of the cone-shaped mountain. As they were unable to talk the language the only person from whom they could gain knowledge was Harût, who spoke to them in his broken English and told them much what he had told me, namely that the upper mountain was a sacred place that might only be visited by the priests, since any uninitiated person who set foot there came to a bad end. They had not seen any of these priests in the town, where no form of worship appeared to be practised, but they had observed men driving small numbers of sheep or goats up the flanks of the mountain towards the forest.

Of what went on upon this mountain and who lived there they remained in complete ignorance. It was a case of stalemate. Harût would not tell them anything nor could they learn anything for themselves. He added in a depressed way that the whole business seemed very hopeless, and that he had begun to doubt whether there was any tidings of his lost wife to be gained among the Kendah, White or Black.

Now I repeated to him Marût's dying words, of which most unhappily I had never heard the end. These seemed to give him new life since they showed that tidings there was of some sort, if only it could be extracted. But how might this be done? How, how?

* * * * * * * *

For a whole week things went on thus. During this time I recovered my strength completely, except in one particular which reduced me to helplessness. The place on my thigh where Jana had pinched out a bit of the skin healed up well enough, but the inflammation struck inwards to the nerve of my left leg, where once I had been injured by a lion, with the result that whenever I tried to move I was tortured by pains of a sciatic nature. So I was obliged to lie still and to content myself with being carried on the bed into a little garden which surrounded the mud-built and white-washed house that had been allotted to us as a dwelling-place.

There I lay hour after hour, staring at the Holy Mount which

443

began to spring from the plain within a few hundred yards of the scattered township. For a mile or so its slopes were bare except for grass on which sheep and goats were grazed, and a few scattered trees. Studying the place through glasses I observed that these slopes were crowned by a vertical precipice of what looked like lava rock, which seemed to surround the whole mountain and must have been quite a hundred feet high. Beyond this precipice, which to all appearance was of an unclimbable nature, began a dense forest of large trees, cedars I thought, clothing it to the very top, that is so far as I could see.

One day when I was considering the place, Harût entered the garden suddenly and caught me in the act.

"The House of the god is beautiful," he said, "is it not?"

"Very," I answered, "and of a strange formation. But how do those who dwell on it climb that precipice?"

"It cannot be climbed," he answered, "but there is a road which I am about to travel who go to worship the Child. Yet I have told you, Macumazana, that any strangers who seek to walk that road find death. If they do not believe me, let them try," he added meaningly.

Then, after many inquiries about my health, he informed me that news had reached him to the effect that the Black Kendah were mad at the loss of their crops which the hail had destroyed and because of the near prospect of starvation.

"Then soon they will be wishing to reap yours with spears," I said.

"That is so. Therefore, my Lord Macumazana, get well quickly that you may be able to scare away these crows with guns, for in fourteen days the harvest should begin upon our uplands. Farewell and have no fears, for during my absence my people will feed and watch you and on the third night I shall return again."

After Harût's departure a deep depression fell upon all of us. Even Hans was depressed, while Savage became like a man under sentence of execution at a near but uncertain date. I tried to cheer him up and asked him what was the matter.

"I don't know, Mr. Quatermain," he answered, "but the fact is this is a 'ateful and un'oly 'ole" (in his agitation he quite lost grip of his *h*'s, which was always weak), "and I am sure that it is the last I shall ever see, except one."

"Well, Savage," I said jokingly, "at any rate there don't seem to be any snakes here."

"No, Mr. Quatermain. That is, I haven't met any, but they crawl about me all night, and whenever I see that prophet man he talks of them to me. Yes, he talks of them and nothing else with a sort of cold

444

look in his eyes that makes my back creep. I wish it was over, I do, who shall never see old England again," and he went away, I think to hide his very painful and evident emotion.

That evening Hans returned from an expedition on which I had sent him with instructions to try to get round the mountain and report what was on its other side. It had been a complete failure, as after he had gone a few miles men appeared who ordered him back. They were so threatening in their demeanour that had it not been for the little rifle, *Intombi*, which he carried under pretence of shooting buck, a weapon that they regarded with great awe, they would, he thought, have killed him. He added that he had been quite unsuccessful in his efforts to collect any news of value from man, woman or child, all of whom, although very polite, appeared to have orders to tell him nothing, concluding with the remark that he considered the White Kendah bigger devils than the Black Kendah, inasmuch as they were more clever.

* * * * * * * *

Shortly after this abortive attempt we debated our position with earnestness and came to a certain conclusion, of which I will speak in its place.

If I remember right it was on this same night of our debate, after Harût's return from the mountain, that the first incident of interest happened. There were two rooms in our house divided by a partition which ran almost up to the roof. In the left-hand room slept Ragnall and Savage, and in that to the right Hans and I. Just at the breaking of dawn I was awakened by hearing some agitated conversation between Savage and his master. A minute later they both entered my sleeping place, and I saw in the faint light that Ragnall looked very disturbed and Savage very frightened.

"What's the matter?" I asked.

"We have seen my wife," answered Ragnall.

I stared at him and he went on:

"Savage woke me by saying that there was someone in the room. I sat up and looked and, as I live, Quatermain, standing gazing at me in such a position that the light of dawn from the window-place fell upon her, was my wife."

"How was she dressed?" I asked at once.

"In a kind of white robe cut rather low, with her hair loose hanging to her waist, but carefully combed and held outspread by what appeared to be a bent piece of ivory about a foot and a half long, to which it was fastened by a thread of gold."

"Is that all?"

"No. Upon her breast was that necklace of red stones with the little image hanging from its centre which those rascals gave her and she always wore."

"Anything more?"

"Yes. In her arms she carried what looked like a veiled child. It was so still that I think it must have been dead."

"Well. What happened?"

"I was so overcome I could not speak, and she stood gazing at me with wide-opened eyes, looking more beautiful than I can tell you. She never stirred, and her lips never moved—that I will swear. And yet both of us heard her say, very low but quite clearly: 'The mountain, George! Don't desert me. Seek me on the mountain, my dear, my husband.'"

"Well, what next?"

"I sprang up and she was gone. That's all."

"Now tell me what *you* saw and heard, Savage."

"What his lordship saw and heard, Mr. Quatermain, neither more nor less. Except that I was awake, having had one of my bad dreams about snakes, and saw her come through the door."

"Through the door! Was it open then?"

"No, sir, it was shut and bolted. She just came through it as if it wasn't there. Then I called to his lordship after she had been looking at him for half a minute or so, for I couldn't speak at first. There's one more thing, or rather two. On her head was a little cap that looked as though it had been made from the skin of a bird, with a gold snake rising up in front, which snake was the first thing I caught sight of, as of course it would be, sir. Also the dress she wore was so thin that through it I could see her shape and the sandals on her feet, which were fastened at the instep with studs of gold."

"I saw no feather cap or snake," said Ragnall.

"Then that's the oddest part of the whole business," I remarked. "Go back to your room, both of you, and if you see anything more, call me. I want to think things over."

They went, in a bewildered sort of fashion, and I called Hans and spoke with him in a whisper, repeating to him the little that he had not understood of our talk, for as I have said, although he never spoke it, Hans knew a great deal of English.

"Now, Hans," I said to him, "what is the use of you? You are no better than a fraud. You pretend to be the best watchdog in Africa, and yet a woman comes into this house under your nose and in the grey of the morning, and you do not see her. Where is your reputation, Hans?"

The old fellow grew almost speechless with indignation, then he spluttered his answer:

"It was not a woman, Baas, but a spook. Who am I that I should be expected to catch *spooks* as though they were thieves or rats? As it happens I was wide awake half an hour before the dawn and lay with my eyes fixed upon that door, which I bolted myself last night. It never opened, Baas; moreover, since this talk began I have been to look at it. During the night a spider has made its web from door-post to door-post, and that web is unbroken. If you do not believe me, come and see for yourself. Yet they say the woman came through the doorway and therefore through the spider's web. Oh! Baas, what is the use of wasting thought upon the ways of *spooks* which, like the wind, come and go as they will, especially in this haunted land from which, as we have all agreed, we should do well to get away."

I went and examined the door for myself, for by now my sciatica, or whatever it may have been, was so much better that I could walk a little. What Hans said was true. There was the spider's web with the spider sitting in the middle. Also some of the threads of the web were fixed from post to post, so that it was impossible that the door could have been opened or, if opened, that anyone could have passed through the doorway without breaking them. Therefore, unless the woman came through one of the little window-places, which was almost incredible as they were high above the ground, or dropped from the smoke-hole in the roof, or had been shut into the place when the door was closed on the previous night, I could not see how she had arrived there. And if any one of these incredible suppositions was correct, then how did she get out again with two men watching her?

There were only two solutions to the problem—namely, that the whole occurrence was hallucination, or that, in fact, Ragnall and Savage had seen something unnatural and uncanny. If the latter were correct I only wished that I had shared the experience, as I have always longed to see a ghost. A real, indisputable ghost would be a great support to our doubting minds, that is if we *knew* its owner to be dead.

But—this was another thought—if by any chance Lady Ragnall were still alive and a prisoner upon that mountain, what they had seen was no ghost, but a shadow or *simulacrum* of a living person projected consciously or unconsciously by that person for some unknown purpose. What could the purpose be? As it chanced the answer was not difficult, and to it the words she was reported to have uttered gave a cue. Only a few hours ago, just before we turned in indeed, as I have said, we had been discussing matters. What I have not said is that in the end we arrived at the conclusion that our quest here was wild and useless and that we should do well to try to escape from the place before we became involved in a war of extermination between two branches of an obscure tribe, one of which was quite and the other semi-savage.

Indeed, although Ragnall still hung back a little, it had been arranged that I should try to purchase camels in exchange for guns, unless I could get them for nothing which might be less suspicious, and that we should attempt such an escape under cover of an expedition to kill the elephant Jana.

Supposing such a vision to be possible, then might it not have come, or been sent to deter us from this plan? It would seem so.

Thus reflecting I went to sleep worn out with useless wonderment, and did not wake again till breakfast time. That morning, when we were alone together, Ragnall said to me:

"I have been thinking over what happened, or seemed to happen last night. I am not at all a superstitious man, or one given to vain imaginings, but I am sure that Savage and I really did see and hear the spirit or the shadow of my wife. Her body it could not have been as you will admit, though how she could utter, or seem to utter, audible speech without one is more than I can tell. Also I am sure that she is captive upon yonder mountain and came to call me to rescue her. Under these circumstances I feel that it is my duty, as well as my desire, to give up any idea of leaving the country and try to find out the truth."

"And how will you do that," I asked, "seeing that no one will tell us anything?"

"By going to see for myself."

"It is impossible, Ragnall. I am too lame at present to walk half a mile, much less to climb precipices."

"I know, and that is one of the reasons why I did not suggest that you should accompany me. The other is that there is no object in all of us risking our lives. I wished to face the thing alone, but that good fellow Savage says that he will go where I go, leaving you and Hans here to make further attempts if we do not return. Our plan is to slip out of the town during the night, wearing white dresses like the Kendah, of which I have bought some for tobacco, and make the best of our way up the slope by starlight that is very bright now. When dawn comes we will try to find the road through that precipice, or over it, and for the rest trust to Providence."

Dismayed at this intelligence, I did all I could to dissuade him from such a mad venture, but quite without avail, for never did I know a more determined or more fearless man than Lord Ragnall. He had made up his mind and there was an end of the matter. Afterwards I talked with Savage, pointing out to him all the perils involved in the attempt, but likewise without avail. He was more depressed than usual, apparently on the ground that "having seen the ghost of her ladyship" he was sure he had not long to live. Still, he declared that where his master went he would go, as he preferred to die with him rather than alone.

So I was obliged to give in and with a melancholy heart to do what I could to help in the simple preparations for this crazy undertaking, realizing all the while that the only real help must come from above, since in such a case man was powerless. I should add that after consultation, Ragnall gave up the idea of adopting a Kendah disguise which was certain to be discovered, also of starting at night when the town was guarded.

That very afternoon they went, going out of the town quite openly on the pretext of shooting partridges and small buck on the lower slopes of the mountain, where both were numerous, as Harût had informed us we were quite at liberty to do. The farewell was somewhat sad, especially with Savage, who gave me a letter he had written for his old mother in England, requesting me to post it if ever again I came to a civilized land.

I did my best to put a better spirit in him but without avail. He only wrung my hand warmly, said that it was a pleasure to have known such a "real gentleman" as myself, and expressed a hope that I might get out of this hell and live to a green old age amongst Christians. Then he wiped away a tear with the cuff of his coat, touched his hat in the orthodox fashion and departed. Their outfit, I should add, was very simple: some food in bags, a flask of spirits, two double-barrelled guns that would shoot either shot or ball, a bull's-eye lantern, matches and their pistols.

Hans walked with them a little way and, leaving them outside the town, returned.

"Why do you look so gloomy, Hans?" I asked.

"Because, Baas," he answered, twiddling his hat, "I had grown to be fond of the white man, Bena, who was always very kind to me and did not treat me like dirt as low-born whites are apt to do. Also he cooked well, and now I shall have to do that work which I do not like."

"What do you mean, Hans? The man isn't dead, is he?"

"No, Baas, but soon he will be, for the shadow of death is in his eyes."

"Then how about Lord Ragnall?"

"I saw no shadow in his eyes; I think that he will live, Baas."

I tried to get some explanation of these dark sayings out of the Hottentot, but he would add nothing to his words.

All the following night I lay awake filled with heavy fears which deepened as the hours went on. Just before dawn we heard a knocking on our door and Ragnall's voice whispering to us to open. Hans did so while I lit a candle, of which we had a good supply. As it burned up Ragnall entered, and from his face I saw at once that something terrible had happened. He went to the jar where we kept our water and drank three pannikinfuls, one after the other. Then without waiting to be asked, he said:

"Savage is dead," and paused a while as though some awful recollection overcame him. "Listen," he went on presently. "We worked up the hill-side without firing, although we saw plenty of partridges and one buck, till just as twilight was closing in, we came to the cliff face. Here we perceived a track that ran to the mouth of a narrow cave or tunnel in the lava rock of the precipice, which looked quite unclimbable. While we were wondering what to do, eight or ten white-robed men appeared out of the shadows and seized us before we could make any resistance. After talking together for a little they took away our guns and pistols, with which some of them disappeared. Then their leader, with many bows, indicated that we were at liberty to proceed by pointing first to the mouth of the cave, and next to the top of the precipice, saying something about *ingane*, which I believe means a little child, does it not?"

I nodded, and he went on:

"After this they all departed down the hill, smiling in a fashion that disturbed me. We stood for a while irresolute, until it became quite dark. I asked Savage what he thought we had better do, expecting that he would say 'Return to the town.' To my surprise, he answered:

"'Go on, of course, my lord. Don't let those brutes say that we white men daren't walk a step without our guns. Indeed, in any case I mean to go on, even if your lordship won't.'

"Whilst he spoke he took a bull's-eye lantern from his food bag, which had not been interfered with by the Kendah, and lit it. I stared at him amazed, for the man seemed to be animated by some tremendous purpose. Or rather it was as though a force from without had got hold of his will and were pushing him on to an unknown end. Indeed his next words showed that this was so, for he exclaimed:

"'There is something drawing me into that cave, my lord. It may be death; I think it is death, but whatever it be, go I must. Perhaps you would do well to stop outside till I have seen.'

"I stepped forward to catch hold of the man, who I thought had gone mad, as perhaps was the case. Before I could lay my hands on him he had run rapidly to the mouth of the cave. Of course I followed, but when I reached its entrance the star of light thrown forward by the bull's-eye lantern showed me that he was already about eight yards down the tunnel. Then I heard a terrible hissing noise and Savage exclaiming: 'Oh! my God!' twice over. As he spoke the lantern fell from his hand, but did not go out, because, as you know, it is made to burn in any position. I leapt forward and picked it from the ground, and while I was doing so became aware that Savage was running still farther into the depths of the cave. I lifted the lantern above my head and looked.

"This was what I saw: About ten paces from me was Savage with his arms outstretched and dancing—yes, dancing—first to the right and then to the left, with a kind of horrible grace and to the tune of a hideous hissing music. I held the lantern higher and perceived that beyond him, lifted eight or nine feet into the air, nearly to the roof of the tunnel in fact, was the head of the hugest snake of which I have ever heard. It was as broad as the bottom of a wheelbarrow—were it cut off I think it would fill a large wheelbarrow—while the neck upon which it was supported was quite as thick as my middle, and the undulating body behind it, which stretched far away into the darkness, was the size of an eighteen-gallon cask and glittered green and grey, lined and splashed with silver and with gold.

"It hissed and swayed its great head to the right, holding Savage with cold eyes that yet seemed to be on fire, whereon he danced to the right. It hissed again and swayed its head to the left, whereon he danced to the left. Then suddenly it reared its head right to the top of the cave and so remained for a few seconds, whereon Savage stood still, bending a little forward, as though he were bowing to the reptile. Next instant, like a flash it struck, for I saw its white fangs bury themselves in the back of Savage, who with a kind of sigh fell forward on to his face. Then there was a convulsion of those shining folds, followed by a sound as of bones being ground up in a steam-driven mortar.

"I staggered against the wall of the cave and shut my eyes for a moment, for I felt faint. When I opened them again it was to see something flat, misshapen, elongated like a reflection in a spoon, something that had been Savage lying on the floor, and stretched out over it the huge serpent studying me with its steely eyes. Then I ran; I am not ashamed to say I ran out of that horrible hole and far into the night."

451

"Small blame to you," I said, adding: "Hans, give me some square-face neat." For I felt as queer as though I also had been in that cave with its guardian.

"There is very little more to tell," went on Ragnall after I had drunk the Hollands. "I lost my way on the mountain-side and wandered for many hours, till at last I blundered up against one of the outermost houses of the town, after which things were easy. Perhaps I should add that wherever I went on my way down the mountain it seemed to me that I heard people laughing at me in an unnatural kind of voice. That's all."

After this we sat silent for a long while, till at length Hans said in his unmoved tone:

"The light has come, Baas. Shall I blow out the candle, which it is a pity to waste? Also, does the Baas wish me to cook the breakfast, now that the snake devil is making his off Bena, as I hope to make mine off him before all is done. Snakes are very good to eat, Baas, if you know how to dress them in the Hottentot way."

CHAPTER 16

Hans Steals the Keys

A few hours later some of the White Kendah arrived at the house and very politely delivered to us Ragnall's and poor Savage's guns and pistols, which they said they had found lying in the grass on the mountain-side, and with them the bull's-eye lantern that Ragnall had thrown away in his flight; all of which articles I accepted without comment. That evening also Harût called and, after salutations, asked where Bena was as he did not see him. Then my indignation broke out:

"Oh! white-bearded father of liars," I said, "you know well that he is in the belly of the serpent which lives in the cave of the mountain."

"What, Lord!" exclaimed Harût addressing Ragnall in his peculiar English, "have you been for walk up to hole in hill? Suppose Bena want see big snake. He always very fond of snake, you know, and they very fond of him. You 'member how they come out of his pocket in your house in England? Well, he know all about snake now."

"You villain!" exclaimed Ragnall, "you murderer! I have a mind to kill you where you are."

"Why you choke me, Lord, because snake choke your man? Poor snake, he only want dinner. If you go where lion live, lion kill you. If you go where snake live, snake kill you. I tell you not to. You take no notice. Now I tell you all—go if you wish, no one stop you. Perhaps you kill snake, who knows? Only you no take gun there, please. That not allowed. When you tired of this town, go see snake. Only, 'member that not right way to House of Child. There another way which you never find."

"Look here," said Ragnall, "what is the use of all this foolery? You know very well why we are in your devilish country. It is because I believe you have stolen my wife to make her the priestess of your evil religion whatever it may be, and I want her back."

"All this great mistake," replied Harût blandly. "We no steal beautiful

453

lady you marry because we find she not right priestess. Also Macumazana here not to look for lady but to kill elephant Jana and get pay in ivory like good business man. You, Lord, come with him as friend though we no ask you, that all. Then you try find temple of our god and snake which watch door kill your servant. Why we not kill *you*, eh?"

"Because you are afraid to," answered Ragnall boldly. "Kill me if you can and take the consequences. I am ready."

Harût studied him not without admiration.

"You very brave man," he said, "and we no wish kill you and p'raps after all everything come right in end. Only Child know about that. Also you help us fight Black Kendah by and by. So, Lord, you quite safe unless you big fool and go call on snake in cave. He very hungry snake and soon want more dinner. You hear, Light-in-Darkness, Lord-of-the-Fire," he added suddenly turning on Hans who was squatted near by twiddling his hat with a face that for absolute impassiveness resembled a deal board. "You hear, he very hungry snake, and you make nice tea for him."

Hans rolled his little yellow eyes without even turning his head until they rested on the stately countenance of Harût, and answered in Bantu:

"I hear, Liar-with-the-White-Beard, but what have I to do with this matter? Jana is my enemy who would have killed Macumazana, my master, not your dirty snake. What is the good of this snake of yours? If it were any good, why does it not kill Jana whom you hate? And if it is no good, why do you not take a stick and knock it on the head? If you are afraid I will do so for you if you pay me. That for your snake," and very energetically he spat upon the floor.

"All right," said Harût, still speaking in English, "you go kill snake. Go when you like, no one say no. Then we give you new name. Then we call you Lord-of-the-Snake."

As Hans, who now was engaged in lighting his corn-cob pipe, did not deign to answer these remarks, Harût turned to me and said:

"Lord Macumazana, your leg still bad, eh? Well, I bring you some ointment what make it quite well; it holy ointment come from the Child. We want you get well quick."

Then suddenly he broke into Bantu. "My Lord, war draws near. The Black Kendah are gathering all their strength to attack us and we must have your aid. I go down to the River Tava to see to certain matters, as to the reaping of the outlying crops and other things. Within a week I will be back; then we must talk again, for by that time, if you will use the ointment that I have given you, you will be as well as ever you were in your life. Rub it on your leg, and mix a piece as large as a mealie grain in water and swallow it at night. It is not poison, see," and taking the cover off a little earthenware pot which he produced he scooped from it with his finger some of the contents, which looked like lard, put it on his tongue and swallowed it.

Then he rose and departed with his usual bows.

Here I may state that I used Harût's prescription with the most excellent results. That night I took a dose in water, very nasty it was, and rubbed my leg with the stuff, to find that next morning all pain had left me and that, except for some local weakness, I was practically quite well. I kept the rest of the salve for years, and it proved a perfect specific in cases of sciatica and rheumatism. Now, alas! it is all used and no recipe is available from which it can be made up again.

The next few days passed uneventfully. As soon as I could walk I began to go about the town, which was nothing but a scattered village much resembling those to be seen on the eastern coasts of Africa. Nearly all the men seemed to be away, making preparations for the harvest, I suppose, and as the women shut themselves up in their houses after the Oriental fashion, though the few that I saw about were unveiled and rather good-looking, I did not gather any intelligence worth noting.

To tell the truth I cannot remember being in a more uninteresting place than this little town with its extremely uncommunicative population which, it seemed to me, lived under a shadow of fear that prevented all gaiety. Even the children, of whom there were not many, crept about in a depressed fashion and talked in a low voice. I never saw any of them playing games or heard them shouting and laughing, as young people do in most parts of the world. For the rest we were very well looked after. Plenty of food was provided for us and every thought taken for our comfort. Thus a strong and quiet pony was brought for me to ride because of my lameness. I had only to go out of the house and call and it arrived from somewhere, all ready saddled and bridled, in charge of a lad who appeared to be dumb. At any rate when I spoke to him he would not answer.

Mounted on this pony I took one or two rides along the southern slopes of the mountain on the old pretext of shooting for the pot. Hans accompanied me on these occasions, but was, I noted, very silent and thoughtful, as though he were hunting something up and down his tortuous intelligence. Once we got quite near to the mouth of the cave or tunnel where poor Savage had met his horrid end. As we stood studying it a white-robed man whose head was shaved, which made me think he must be a priest, came up and asked me mockingly why we did not go through the tunnel and see what lay beyond, adding, almost in the words of Harût himself, that none would attempt to interfere with us as the road was open to any who could travel it. By way of answer I only smiled and put him a few questions about a very beautiful breed of goats with long silky hair, some of which he seemed to be engaged in herding. He replied that these goats were sacred, being the food of "one who dwelt in the Mountain who only ate when the moon changed."

When I inquired who this person was he said with his unpleasant smile that I had better go through the tunnel and see for myself, an invitation which I did not accept.

That evening Harût appeared unexpectedly, looking very grave and troubled. He was in a great hurry and only stayed long enough to congratulate me upon the excellent effects of his ointment, since "no man could fight Jana on one leg."

I asked him when the fight with Jana was to come off. He replied:

"Lord, I go up to the Mountain to attend the Feast of the First-fruits, which is held at sunrise on the day of the new moon. After the offering the Oracle will speak and we shall learn when there will be war with Jana, and perchance other things."

"May we not attend this feast, Harût, who are weary of doing nothing here?"

"Certainly," he answered with his grave bow. "That is, if you come unarmed; for to appear before the Child with arms is death. You know the road; it runs through yonder cave and the forest beyond the cave. Take it when you will, Lord."

"Then if we can pass the cave we shall be welcome at the feast?"

"You will be very welcome. None shall hurt you there, going or returning. I swear it by the Child. Oh! Macumazana," he added, smiling a little, "why do you talk folly, who know well that one lives in yonder cave whom none may look upon and love, as Bena learned not long ago? You are thinking that perhaps you might kill this Dweller in the cave with your weapons. Put away that dream, seeing that henceforth those who watch you have orders to see that none of you leave this house carrying so much as a knife. Indeed, unless you promise me that this shall be so you will not be suffered to set foot outside its garden until I return again. Now do you promise?"

I thought a while and, drawing the two others aside out of hearing, asked them their opinion.

Ragnall was at first unwilling to give any such promise, but Hans said: "Baas, it is better to go free and unhurt without guns and knives than to become a prisoner once, as you were among the Black Kendah. Often there is but a short step between the prison and the grave."

Both Ragnall and I acknowledged the force of this argument and in the end we gave the promise, speaking one by one.

"It is enough," said Harût; "moreover, know, Lord, that among us White Kendah he who breaks an oath is put across the River Tava unarmed to make report thereof to Jana, Father of Lies. Now farewell. If we do not meet at the Feast of the First-fruits on the day of the new moon, whither once more I invite you, we can talk together here after I have heard the voice of the Oracle."

Then he mounted a camel which awaited him outside the gate and departed with an escort of twelve men, also riding camels.

"There is some other road up that mountain, Quatermain," said Ragnall. "A camel could sooner pass through the eye of a needle than through that dreadful cave, even if it were empty."

"Probably," I answered, "but as we don't know where it is and I dare say it lies miles from here, we need not trouble our heads on the matter. The cave is *our* only road, which means that there is *no* road."

That evening at supper we discovered that Hans was missing; also that he had got possession of my keys and broken into a box containing liquor, for there it stood open in the cooking-hut with the keys in the lock.

"He has gone on the drink," I said to Ragnall, "and upon my soul I don't wonder at it; for sixpence I would follow his example."

Then we went to bed. Next morning we breakfasted rather late, since when one has nothing to do there is no object in getting up early. As I was preparing to go to the cook-house to boil some eggs, to our astonishment Hans appeared with a kettle of coffee.

"Hans," I said, "you are a thief."

"Yes, Baas," answered Hans.

"You have been at the gin box and taking that poison."

"Yes, Baas, I have been taking poison. Also I took a walk and all is right now. The Baas must not be angry, for it is very dull doing nothing here. Will the Baases eat porridge as well as eggs?"

As it was no use scolding him I said that we would. Moreover, there was something about his manner which made me suspicious, for really he did not look like a person who has just been very drunk.

After we had finished breakfast he came and squatted down before me. Having lit his pipe he asked suddenly:

"Would the Baases like to walk through that cave tonight? If so, there will be no trouble."

"What do you mean?" I asked, suspecting that he was still drunk.

"I mean, Baas, that the Dweller-in-the-cave is fast asleep."

"How do you know that, Hans?"

"Because I am the nurse who put him to sleep, Baas, though he kicked and cried a great deal. He is asleep; he will wake no more. Baas, I have killed the Father of Serpents."

"Hans," I said, "now I am sure that you are still drunk, although you do not show it outside."

"Hans," added Ragnall, to whom I had translated as much of this as he did not understand, "it is too early in the day to tell good stories. How could you possibly have killed that serpent without a gun—for you took none with you—or with it either for that matter?"

"Will the Baases come and take a walk through the cave?" asked Hans with a snigger.

"Not till I am quite sure that you are sober," I replied; then, re-membering certain other events in this worthy's career, added; "Hans, if you do not tell us the story at once I will beat you."

"There isn't much story, Baas," replied Hans between long sucks at his pipe, which had nearly gone out, "because the thing was so easy. The Baas is very clever and so is the Lord Baas, why then can they never see the stones that lie under their noses? It is because their eyes are always fixed upon the mountains between this world and the next. But the poor Hottentot, who looks at the ground to be sure that he does not stumble, ah! he sees the stones. Now, Baas, did you not hear that man in a night shirt with his head shaved say that those goats were food for One who dwelt in the mountain?"

"I did. What of it, Hans?"

"Who would be the One who dwelt in the mountain except the Father of Snakes in the cave, Baas? Ah, now for the first time you see the stone that lay at your feet all the while. And, Baas, did not the bald man add that this One in the mountain was only fed at new and full moon, and is not tomorrow the day of new moon, and therefore would he not be very hungry on the day before new moon, that is, last night?"

"No doubt, Hans; but how can you kill a snake by feeding it?"

"Oh! Baas, you may eat things that make you ill, and so can a snake. Now you will guess the rest, so I had better go to wash the dishes."

"Whether I guess or do not guess," I replied sagely, the latter being the right hypothesis, "the dishes can wait, Hans, since the Lord there has not guessed; so continue."

"Very well, Baas. In one of those boxes are some pounds of stuff which, when mixed with water, is used for preserving skins and skulls."

458

"You mean the arsenic crystals," I said with a flash of inspiration.

"I don't know what you call them, Baas. At first I thought they were hard sugar and stole some once, when the real sugar was left behind, to put into the coffee—without telling the Baas, because it was my fault that the sugar was left behind."

"Great Heavens!" I ejaculated, "then why aren't we all dead?"

"Because at the last moment, Baas, I thought I would make sure, so I put some of the hard sugar into hot milk and, when it had melted, I gave it to that yellow dog which once bit me in the leg, the one that came from Beza Town, Baas, that I told you had run away. He was a very greedy dog, Baas, and drank up the milk at once. Then he gave a howl, twisted about, foamed at the mouth and died and I buried him at once. After that I threw some more of the large sugar mixed with mealies to the fowls that we brought with us for cooking. Two cocks and a hen swallowed them by mistake for the corn. Presently they fell on their backs, kicked a little and died. Some of the Mazitu, who were great thieves, stole those dead fowls, Baas. After this, Baas, I thought it best not to use that sugar in the coffee, and later on Bena told me that it was deadly poison. Well, Baas, it came into my mind that if I could make that great snake swallow enough of this poison, he, too, might die.

"So I stole your keys, as I often do, Baas, when I want anything, because you leave them lying about everywhere, and to deceive you first opened one of the boxes that are full of square-face and brandy and left it open, for I wished you to think that I had just gone to get drunk like anybody else. Then I opened another box and got out two one-pound tins of the sugar which kills dogs and fowls. Half a pound of it I melted in boiling water with some real sugar to make the stuff sweet, and put it into a bottle. The rest I tied with string in twelve little packets in the soft paper which is in one of the boxes, and put them in my pocket. Then I went up the hill, Baas, to the place where I saw those goats are kraaled at night behind a reed fence. As I had hoped, no one was watching them because there are no tigers so near this town, and man does not steal the goats that are sacred. I went into the kraal and found a fat young ewe which had a kid. I dragged it out and, taking it behind some stones, I made its leg fast with a bit of cord and poured this stuff out of the bottle all over its skin, rubbing it in well. Then I tied the twelve packets of hard poison-sugar everywhere about its body, making them very fast deep in the long hair so that they could not tumble or rub off.

459

"After this I untied the goat, led it near to the mouth of the cave and held it there for a time while it kept on bleating for its kid. Next I took it almost up to the cave, wondering how I should drive it in, for I did not wish to enter there myself, Baas. As it happened I need not have troubled about that. When the goat was within five yards of the cave, it stopped bleating, stood still and shivered. Then it began to go forward with little jumps, as though it did not want to go, yet must do so. Also, Baas, I felt as though *I* wished to go with it. So I lay down and put my heels against a rock, leaving go of the goat.

"For now, Baas, I did not care where that goat went so long as I could keep out of the hole where dwelt the Father of Serpents that had eaten Bena. But it was all right, Baas; the goat knew what it had to do and did it, jumping straight into the cave. As it entered it turned its head and looked at me. I could see its eyes in the starlight, and, Baas, they were dreadful. I think it knew what was coming and did not like it at all. And yet it had to walk on because it could not help it. Just like a man going to the devil, Baas!

"Holding on to the stone I peered after it, for I had heard something stirring in the cave making a soft noise like a white lady's dress upon the floor. There in the blackness I saw two little sparks of fire, which were the eyes of the serpent, Baas. Then I heard a sound of hissing like four big kettles boiling all at once, and a little bleat from the goat. After this there was a noise as of men wrestling, followed by another noise as of bones breaking, and lastly, yet another sucking noise as of a pump that won't draw up the water. Then everything grew nice and quiet and I went some way off, sat down a little to one side of the cave, and waited to see if anything happened.

"It must have been nearly an hour later that something did begin to happen, Baas. It was as though sacks filled with chaff were being beaten against stone walls there in the cave. Ah! thought I to myself, your stomach is beginning to ache, Eater-up-of-Bena, and, as that goat had little horns on its head—to which I tied two of the bags of the poison, Baas—and, like all snakes, no doubt you have spikes in your throat pointing downwards, you won't be able to get it up again. Then—I expect this was after the poison-sugar had begun to melt nicely in the serpent's stomach, Baas—there was a noise as though a whole company of girls were dancing a war-dance in the cave to a music of hisses.

"And then—oh! then, Baas, of a sudden that Father of Serpents came out. I tell you, Baas, that when I saw him in the bright starlight my hair stood up upon my head, for never has there been such another snake in the whole world. Those that live in trees and eat bucks in Zululand, of whose skins men make waistcoats and slippers, are but babies compared to this one. He came out, yard after yard of him. He wriggled about, he stood upon his tail with his head where the top of a tree might be, he made himself into a ring, he bit at stones and at his own stomach, while I hid behind my rock praying to your reverend father that he might not see me. Then at last he rushed away down the hill, faster than any horse could gallop.

"Now I hoped that he had gone for good and thought of going myself. Still I feared to do so lest I should meet him somewhere, so I made up my mind to wait till daylight. It was as well, Baas, for about half an hour later he came back again. Only now he could not jump, he could only crawl. Never in my life did I see a snake look so sick, Baas. Into the cave he went and lay there hissing. By degrees the hissing grew very faint, till at length they died away altogether. I waited another half-hour, Baas, and then I grew so curious that I thought that I would go to look in the cave.

"I lit the little lantern I had with me and, holding it in one hand and my stick in the other, I crept into the hole. Before I had crawled ten paces I saw something white stretched along the ground. It was the belly of the great snake, Baas, which lay upon its back quite dead.

"I know that it was dead, for I lit three wax matches, setting them to burn upon its tail and it never stirred, as any live snake will do when it feels fire. Then I came home, Baas, feeling very proud because I had outwitted that great-grandfather of all snakes who killed Bena my friend, and had made the way clear for us to walk through the cave.

"That is all the story, Baas. Now I must go to wash those dishes," and without waiting for any comment off he went, leaving us marvelling at his wit, resource and courage.

"What next?" I asked presently.

"Nothing till tonight," answered Ragnall with determination, "when I am going to look at the snake which the noble Hans has killed and whatever lies beyond the cave, as you will remember Harût invited us to do unmolested, if we could."

"Do you think Harût will keep his word, Ragnall?"

"On the whole, yes, and if he doesn't I don't care. Anything is better than sitting here in this suspense."

"I agree as to Harût, because we are too valuable to be killed just now, if for no other reason; also as to the suspense, which is unendurable. Therefore I will walk with you to look at that snake, Ragnall, and so no doubt will Hans. The exercise will do my leg good."

"Do you think it wise?" he asked doubtfully; "in your case, I mean."

"I think it most unwise that we should separate any more. We had better stand or fall altogether; further, we do not seem to have any luck apart."

CHAPTER 17

The Sanctuary and the Oath

That evening shortly after sundown the three of us started boldly from our house wearing over our clothes the Kendah dresses which Ragnall had bought, and carrying nothing save sticks in our hands, some food and the lantern in our pockets. On the outskirts of the town we were met by certain Kendah, one of whom I knew, for I had often ridden by his side on our march across the desert.

"Have any of you arms upon you, Lord Macumazana?" he asked, looking curiously at us and our white robes.

"None," I answered. "Search us if you will."

"Your word is sufficient," he replied with the grave courtesy of his people. "If you are unarmed we have orders to let you go where you wish however you may be dressed. Yet, Lord," he whispered to me, "I pray you do not enter the cave, since One lives there who strikes and does not miss, One whose kiss is death. I pray it for your own sakes, also for ours who need you."

"We shall not wake him who sleeps in the cave," I answered enigmatically, as we departed rejoicing, for now we had learned that the Kendah did not yet know of the death of the serpent.

An hour's walk up the hill, guided by Hans, brought us to the mouth of the tunnel. To tell the truth I could have wished it had been longer, for as we drew near all sorts of doubts assailed me. What if Hans really had been drinking and invented this story to account for his absence? What if the snake had recovered from a merely tempo-rary indisposition? What if it had a wife and family living in that cave, every one of them thirsting for vengeance?

Well, it was too late to hesitate now, but secretly I hoped that one of the others would prefer to lead the way. We reached the place and listened. It was silent as a tomb. Then that brave fellow Hans lit the lantern and said:

"Do you stop here, Baases, while I go to look. If you hear anything happen to me, you will have time to run away," words that made me feel somewhat ashamed of myself.

However, knowing that he was quick as a weasel and silent as a cat, we let him go. A minute or two later suddenly he reappeared out of the darkness, for he had turned the metal shield over the bull's-eye of the lantern, and even in that light I could see that he was grinning.

"It is all right, Baas," he said. "The Father of Serpents has really gone to that land whither he sent Bena, where no doubt he is now roasting in the fires of hell, and I don't see any others. Come and look at him."

So in we went and there, true enough, upon the floor of the cave lay the huge reptile stone dead and already much swollen. I don't know how long it was, for part of its body was twisted into coils, so I will only say that it was by far the most enormous snake that I have ever seen. It is true that I have heard of such reptiles in different parts of Africa, but hitherto I had always put them down as fabulous creatures transformed into and worshipped as local gods. Also this particular specimen was, I presume, of a new variety, since, according to Ragnall, it both struck like the cobra or the adder, and crushed like the boa-constrictor. It is possible, however, that he was mistaken on this point; I do not know, since I had no time, or indeed inclination, to examine its head for the poison fangs, and when next I passed that way it was gone.

I shall never forget the stench of that cave. It was horrible, which is not to be wondered at seeing that probably this creature had dwelt there for centuries, since these large snakes are said to be as long lived as tortoises, and, being sacred, of course it had never lacked for food. Everywhere lay piles of cast bones, amongst one of which I noticed fragments of a human skull, perhaps that of poor Savage. Also the projecting rocks in the place were covered with great pieces of snake skin, doubtless rubbed off by the reptile when once a year it changed its coat.

For a while we gazed at the loathsome and still glittering creature, then pushed on fearful lest we should stumble upon more of its kind. I suppose that it must have been solitary, a kind of serpent rogue, as Jana was an elephant rogue, for we met none and, if the information which I obtained afterwards may be believed, there was no species at all resembling it in the country. What its origin may have been I never learned. All the Kendah could or would say about it was that it had lived in this hole from the beginning and that Black Kendah prisoners, or malefactors, were sometimes given to it to kill, as White Kendah prisoners were given to Jana.

The cave itself proved to be not very long, perhaps one hundred and fifty feet, no more. It was not an artificial but a natural hollow in the lava rock, which I suppose had once been blown through it by an outburst of steam. Towards the farther end it narrowed so much that I began to fear there might be no exit. In this I was mistaken, however, for at its termination we found a hole just large enough for a man to walk in upright and so difficult to climb through that it became clear to us that certainly this was not the path by which the White Kendah approached their sanctuary.

Scrambling out of this aperture with thankfulness, we found ourselves upon the slope of a kind of huge ditch of lava which ran first downwards for about eighty paces, then up again to the base of the great cone of the inner mountain which was covered with dense forest.

I presume that the whole formation of this peculiar hill was the result of a violent volcanic action in the early ages of the earth. But as I do not understand such matters I will not dilate upon them further than to say that, although comparatively small, it bore a certain resemblance to other extinct volcanoes which I had met with in different parts of Africa.

We climbed down to the bottom of the ditch that from its general appearance might have been dug out by some giant race as a protection to their stronghold, and up its farther side to where the forest began on deep and fertile soil. Why there should have been rich earth here and none in the ditch is more than we could guess, but perhaps the presence of springs of water in this part of the mount may have been a cause. At any rate it was so.

The trees in this forest were huge and of a variety of cedar, but did not grow closely together; also there was practically no undergrowth, perhaps for the reason that their dense, spreading tops shut out the light. As I saw afterwards both trunks and boughs were clothed with long grey moss, which even at midday gave the place a very ghostly appearance. The darkness beneath those trees was intense, literally we could not see an inch before our faces. Yet rather than stand still we struggled on, Hans leading the way, for his instincts were quicker than ours. The steep rise of the ground beneath our feet told us that we were going uphill, as we wished to do, and from time to time I consulted a pocket compass I carried by the light of a match, knowing from previous observations that the top of the Holy Mount lay due north.

Thus for hour after hour we crept up and on, occasionally butting into the trunk of a tree or stumbling over a fallen bough, but meeting with no other adventures or obstacles of a physical kind. Of moral, or rather mental, obstacles there were many, since to all of us the atmosphere of this forest was as that of a haunted house. It may have been the embracing darkness, or the sough of the night wind amongst the boughs and mosses, or the sense of the imminent dangers that we had passed and that still awaited us. Or it may have been unknown horrors connected with this place of which some spiritual essence still survived, for without doubt localities preserve such influences, which can be felt by the sensitive among living things, especially in favouring conditions of fear and gloom. At any rate I never experienced more subtle and yet more penetrating terrors than I did upon that night, and afterwards Ragnall confessed to me that my case was his own. Black as it was I thought that I saw apparitions, among them glaring eyes and that of the elephant Jana standing in front of me with his trunk raised against the bole of a cedar. I could have sworn that I saw him, nor was I reassured when Hans whispered to me below his breath, for here we did not seem to dare to raise our voices:

"Look, Baas. Is it Jana glowing like hot iron who stands yonder?"

"Don't be a fool," I answered. "How can Jana be here and, if he were here, how could we see him in the night?" But as I said the words I remembered Harût had told us that Jana had been met with on the Holy Mount "in the spirit or in the flesh." However this may be, next instant he was gone and we beheld him or his shadow no more. Also we thought that from time to time we heard voices speaking all around us, now here, now there and now in the tree tops above our heads, though what they said we could not catch or understand.

Thus the long night wore away. Our progress was very slow, but guided by occasional glimpses at the compass we never stopped but twice, once when we found ourselves apparently surrounded by tree boles and fallen boughs, and once when we got into swampy ground. Then we took the risk of lighting the lantern, and by its aid picked our way through these difficult places. By degrees the trees grew fewer so that we could see the stars between their tops. This was a help to us as I knew that one of them, which I had carefully noted, shone at this season of the year directly over the cone of the mountain, and we were enabled to steer thereby.

It must have been not more than half an hour before the dawn that Hans, who was leading—we were pushing our way through thick bushes at the time—halted hurriedly, saying:

"Stop, Baas, we are on the edge of a cliff. When I thrust my stick forward it stands on nothing."

Needless to say we pulled up dead and so remained without stirring an inch, for who could say what might be beyond us? Ragnall wished to examine the ground with the lantern. I was about to consent, though doubtfully, when suddenly I heard voices murmuring and through the screen of bushes saw lights moving at a little distance, forty feet or more below us. Then we gave up all idea of making further use of the lantern and crouched still as mice in our bushes, waiting for the dawn.

It came at last. In the east appeared a faint pearly flush that by degrees spread itself over the whole arch of the sky and was welcomed by the barking of monkeys and the call of birds in the depths of the dew-steeped forest. Next a ray from the unrisen sun, a single spear of light shot suddenly across the sky, and as it appeared, from the darkness below us arose a sound of chanting, very low and sweet to hear. It died away and for a little while there was silence broken only by a rustling sound like to that of people taking their seats in a dark theatre. Then a woman began to sing in a beautiful, contralto voice, but in what language I do not know, for I could not catch the words, if these were words and not only musical notes.

I felt Ragnall trembling beside me and in a whisper asked him what was the matter. He answered, also in a whisper:

"I believe that is my wife's voice."

"If so, I beg you to control yourself," I replied.

Now the skies began to flame and the light to pour itself into a misty hollow beneath us like streams of many-coloured gems into a bowl, driving away the shadows. By degrees these vanished; by degrees we saw everything. Beneath us was an amphitheatre, on the southern wall of which we were seated, though it was not a wall but a lava cliff between forty and fifty feet high which served as a wall. The amphitheatre itself, however, almost exactly resembled those of the ancients which I had seen in pictures and Ragnall had visited in Italy, Greece, and Southern France. It was oval in shape and not very large, perhaps the flat space at the bottom may have covered something over an acre, but all round this oval ran tiers of seats cut in the lava of the crater. For without doubt this was the crater of an extinct volcano.

Moreover, in what I will call the arena, stood a temple that in its main outlines, although small, exactly resembled those still to be seen in Egypt. There was the gateway or pylon; there the open outer court with columns round it supporting roofed cloisters, which, as we ascertained afterwards, were used as dwelling-places by the priests. There beyond and connected with the first by a short passage was a second rather smaller court, also open to the sky, and beyond this again, built like all the rest of the temple of lava blocks, a roofed erection measuring about twelve feet square, which I guessed at once must be the sanctuary.

This temple was, as I have said, small, but extremely well proportioned, every detail of it being in the most excellent taste though unornamented by sculpture or painting. I have to add that in front of the sanctuary door stood a large block of lava, which I concluded was an altar, and in front of this a stone seat and a basin, also of stone, supported upon a very low tripod. Further, behind the sanctuary was a square house with window-places.

At the moment of our first sight of this place the courts were empty, but on the benches of the amphitheatre were seated about three hundred persons, male and female, the men to the north and the women to the south. They were all clad in pure white robes, the heads of the men being shaved and those of the women veiled, but leaving the face exposed. Lastly, there were two roadways into the amphitheatre, one running east and one west through tunnels hollowed in the encircling rock of the crater, both of which roads were closed at the mouths of the tunnels by massive wooden double doors, seventeen or eighteen feet in height. From these roadways and their doors we learned two things. First, that the cave where had lived the Father of Serpents was, as I had suspected, not the real approach to the shrine of the Child, but only a blind; and, secondly, that the ceremony we were about to witness was secret and might only be attended by the priestly class or families of this strange tribe.

Scarcely was it full daylight when from the cells of the cloisters round the outer court issued twelve priests headed by Harût himself, who looked very dignified in his white garment, each of whom carried on a wooden platter ears of different kinds of corn. Then from the cells of the southern cloister issued twelve women, or rather girls, for all were young and very comely, who ranged themselves alongside of the men. These also carried wooden platters, and on them blooming flowers.

At a sign they struck up a religious chant and began to walk forward through the passage that led from the first court to the second. Arriving in front of the altar they halted and one by one, first a priest and then a priestess, set down the platters of offerings, piling them above each other into a cone. Next the priests and the priestesses ranged themselves in lines on either side of the altar, and Harût took a platter of corn and a platter of flowers in his hands. These he held first towards that quarter of the sky in which swam the invisible new moon, secondly towards the rising sun, and thirdly towards the doors of the sanctuary, making genuflexions and uttering some chanted prayer, the words of which we could not hear.

A pause followed, that was succeeded by a sudden outburst of song wherein all the audience took part. It was a very sonorous and beautiful song or hymn in some language which I did not understand, divided into four verses, the end of each verse being marked by the bowing of every one of those many singers towards the east, towards the west, and finally towards the altar.

Another pause till suddenly the doors of the sanctuary were thrown wide and from between them issued—the goddess Isis of the Egyptians as I have seen her in pictures! She was wrapped in closely clinging draperies of material so thin that the whiteness of her body could be seen beneath. Her hair was outspread before her, and she wore a head-dress or bonnet of glittering feathers from the front of which rose a little golden snake. In her arms she bore what at that distance seemed to be a naked child. With her came two women, walking a little behind her and supporting her arms, who also wore feather bonnets but without the golden snake, and were clad in tight-fitting, transparent garments.

"My God!" whispered Ragnall, "it is my wife!"

"Then be silent and thank Him that she is alive and well," I answered.

The goddess Isis, or the English lady—in that excitement I did not reck which—stood still while the priests and priestesses and all the audience, who, gathered on the upper benches of the amphitheatre, could see her above the wall of the inner court, raised a thrice-repeated and triumphant cry of welcome. Then Harût and the first priestess lifted respectively an ear of corn and a flower from the two topmost platters and held these first to the lips of the child in her arms and secondly to her lips.

This ceremony concluded, the two attendant women led her round the altar to the stone chair, upon which she seated herself. Next fire was kindled in the bowl on the tripod in front of the chair, how I could not see; but perhaps it was already smouldering there. At any rate it burnt up in a thin blue flame, on to which Harût and the head priestess threw something that caused the flame to turn to smoke. Then Isis, for I prefer to call her so while describing this ceremony, was caused to bend her head forward, so that it was enveloped in the smoke exactly as she and I had done some years before in the drawing-room at Ragnall Castle. Presently the smoke died away and the two attendants with the feathered head-dresses straightened her in the chair where she sat still holding the babe against her breast as she might have done to nurse it, but with her head bent forward like that of a person in a swoon.

Now Harût stepped forward and appeared to speak to the goddess at some length, then fell back again and waited, till in the midst of an intense silence she rose from her seat and, fixing her wide eyes on the heavens, spoke in her turn, for although we heard nothing of what she said, in that clear, morning light we could see her lips moving. For some minutes she spoke, then sat down again upon the chair and remained motionless, staring straight in front of her. Harût advanced again, this time to the front of the altar, and, taking his stand upon a kind of stone step, addressed the priests and priestesses and all the encircling audience in a voice so loud and clear that I could distinguish and understand every word he said.

"The Guardian of the heavenly Child, the Nurse decreed, the appointed Nurturer, She who is the shadow of her that bore the Child, She who in her day bears the symbol of the Child and is consecrated to its service from of old, She whose heart is filled with the wisdom of the Child and who utters the decrees of Heaven, has spoken. Hearken now to the voice of the Oracle uttered in answer to the questions of me, Harût, the head priest of the Eternal Child during my life-days. Thus says the Oracle, the Guardian, the Nurturer, marked like all who went before her with the holy mark of the new moon. She on whom the spirit, flitting from generation to generation, has alighted for a while. 'O people of the White Kendah, worshippers of the Child in this land and descendants of those who for thousands of years worshipped the Child in a more ancient land until the barbarians drove it thence with the remnant that remained. War is upon you, O people of the White Kendah. Jana the evil one; he whose other name is Set, he whose other name is Satan, he who for this while lives in the shape of an elephant, he who is worshipped by the thousands whom once you conquered, and whom still you bridle by my might, comes up against you. The Darkness wars against the Daylight, the Evil wars against the Good. My curse has fallen upon the people of Jana, my hail has smitten them, their corn and their cattle; they have no food to eat. But they are still strong for war and there is food in your land. They come to take your corn; Jana comes to trample your god. The Evil comes to destroy the Good, the Night to Devour the Day. It is the last of many battles. How shall you conquer, O People of the Child? Not by your own strength, for you are few in number and Jana is very strong. Not by the strength of the Child, for the Child grows weak and old, the days of its dominion are almost done, and its worship is almost outworn. Here alone that worship lingers, but new gods, who are still the old gods, press on to take its place and to lead it to its rest.'

"How then shall you conquer that, when the Child has departed to its own place, a remnant of you may still remain? In one way only—so says the Guardian, the Nurturer of the Child speaking with the voice of the Child; by the help of those whom you have summoned to your aid from far. There were four of them, but one you have suffered to be slain in the maw of the Watcher in the cave. It was an evil deed, O sons and daughters of the Child, for as the Watcher is now dead, so ere long many of you who planned this deed must die who, had it not been for that man's blood, would have lived on a while. Why did you do this thing? That you might keep a secret, the secret of the theft of a woman, that you might continue to act a lie which falls upon your head like a stone from heaven.

"Thus sayeth the Child: 'Lift no hand against the three who remain, and what they shall ask, that give, for thus alone shall some of you be saved from Jana and those who serve him, even though the Guardian and the Child be taken away and the Child itself returned to its own place.' These are the words of the Oracle uttered at the Feast of the First-fruits, the words that cannot be changed and mayhap its last."

Harût ceased, and there was silence while this portentous message sank into the minds of his audience. At length they seemed to understand its ominous nature and from them all there arose a universal, simultaneous groan. As it died away the two attendants dressed as goddesses assisted the personification of the Lady Isis to rise from her seat and, opening the robes upon her breast, pointed to something beneath her throat, doubtless that birthmark shaped like the new moon which made her so sacred in their eyes since she who bore it and she alone could fill her holy office.

All the audience and with them the priests and priestesses bowed before her. She lifted the symbol of the Child, holding it high above her head, whereon once more they bowed with the deepest veneration. Then still holding the effigy aloft, she turned and with her two attendants passed into the sanctuary and doubtless thence by a covered way into the house beyond. At any rate we saw her no more.

* * * * * * * *

As soon as she was gone the congregation, if I may call it so, leaving their seats, swarmed down into the outer court of the temple through its eastern gate, which was now opened. Here the priests proceeded to distribute among them the offerings taken from the altar, giving a grain of corn to each of the men to eat and a flower to each of the women, which flower she kissed and hid in the bosom of her robe. Evidently it was a kind of sacrament.

Ragnall lifted himself a little upon his hands and knees, and I saw that his eyes glowed and his face was very pale.

"What are you going to do?" I asked.

"Demand that those people give me back my wife, whom they have stolen. Don't try to stop me, Quatermain, I mean what I say."

"But, but," I stammered, "they never will and we are but three unarmed men."

Hans lifted up his little yellow face between us.

"Baas," he hissed, "I have a thought. The Lord Baas wishes to get the lady dressed like a bird as to her head and like one for burial as to her body, who is, he says, his wife. But for us to take her from among so many is impossible. Now what did that old witch-doctor Harût declare just now? He declared, speaking for his fetish, that by our help alone the White Kendah can resist the hosts of the Black Kendah and that no harm must be done to us if the White Kendah would continue to live. So it seems, Baas, that we have something to sell which the White Kendah must buy, namely our help against the Black Kendah, for if we will not fight for them, they believe that they cannot conquer their enemies and kill the devil Jana. Well now, supposing that the Baas says that our price is the white woman dressed like a bird, to be delivered over to us when we have defeated the Black Kendah and killed Jana—after which they will have no more use for her. And supposing that the Baas says that if they refuse to pay that price we will burn all our powder and cartridges so that the rifles are no use? Is there not a path to walk on here?"

"Perhaps," I answered. "Something of the sort was working in my mind but I had no time to think it out."

Turning, I explained the idea to Ragnall, adding:

"I pray you not to be rash. If you are, not only may we be killed, which does not so much matter, but it is very probable that even if they spare us they will put an end to your wife rather than suffer one whom they look upon as holy and who is necessary to their faith in its last struggle to be separated from her charge of the Child."

This was a fortunate argument of mine and one which went home.

"To lose her now would be more than I could bear," he muttered.

"Then will you promise to let me try to manage this affair and not to interfere with me and show violence?"

472

He hesitated a moment and answered:

"Yes, I promise, for you two are cleverer than I am and—I cannot trust my judgment."

"Good," I said, assuming an air of confidence which I did not feel. "Now we will go down to call upon Harût and his friends. I want to have a closer look at that temple."

So behind our screen of bushes we wriggled back a little distance till we knew that the slope of the ground would hide us when we stood up. Then as quickly as we could we made our way eastwards for something over a quarter of a mile and after this turned to the north. As I expected, beyond the ring of the crater we found ourselves on the rising, tree-clad bosom of the mountain and, threading our path through the cedars, came presently to that track or roadway which led to the eastern gate of the amphitheatre. This road we followed unseen until presently the gateway appeared before us. We walked through it without attracting any attention, perhaps because all the people were either talking together, or praying, or perhaps because like themselves we were wrapped in white robes. At the mouth of the tunnel we stopped and I called out in a loud voice:

"The white lords and their servant have come to visit Harût, as he invited them to do. Bring us, we pray you, into the presence of Harût."

Everyone wheeled round and stared at us standing there in the shadow of the gateway tunnel, for the sun behind us was still low. My word, how they did stare! A voice cried:

"Kill them! Kill these strangers who desecrate our temple."

"What!" I answered. "Would you kill those to whom your high-priest has given safe-conduct; those moreover by whose help alone, as your Oracle has just declared, you can hope to slay Jana and destroy his hosts?"

"How do they know that?" shouted another voice. "They are magicians!"

"Yes," I remarked, "all magic does not dwell in the hearts of the White Kendah. If you doubt it, go to look at the Watcher in the Cave whom your Oracle told you is dead. You will find that it did not lie."

As I spoke a man rushed through the gates, his white rob streaming on the wind, shouting as he emerged from the tunnel:

"O Priests and Priestesses of the Child, the ancient serpent is dead. I whose office it is to feed the serpent on the day of the new moon have found him dead in his house."

"You hear," I interpolated calmly. "The Father of Snakes is dead. If you want to know how, I will tell you. We looked on it and it died."

They might have answered that poor Savage also looked on it with

473

the result that *he* died, but luckily it did not occur to them to do so. On the contrary, they just stood still and stared at us like a flock of startled sheep.

Presently the sheep parted and the shepherd in the shape of Harût appeared looking, I reflected, the very picture of Abraham softened by a touch of the melancholia of Job, that is, as I have always imagined those patriarchs. He bowed to us with his usual Oriental courtesy, and we bowed back to him. Hans' bow, I may explain, was of the most peculiar nature, more like a *skulpat*, as the Boers call a land-tortoise, drawing its wrinkled head into its shell and putting it out again than anything else. Then Harût remarked in his peculiar English, which I suppose the White Kendah took for some tongue known only to magicians:

"So you get here, eh? Why you get here, how the devil you get here, eh?"

"We got here because you asked us to do so if we could," I answered, "and we thought it rude not to accept your invitation. For the rest, we came through a cave where you kept a tame snake, an ugly-looking reptile but very harmless to those who know how to deal with snakes and are not afraid of them as poor Bena was. If you can spare the skin I should like to have it to make myself a robe."

Harût looked at me with evident respect, muttering:

"Oh, Macumazana, you what you English call cool, quite cool! Is that all?"

"No," I answered. "Although you did not happen to notice us, we have been present at your church service, and heard and seen everything. For instance, we saw the wife of the lord here whom you stole away in Egypt, her that, being a liar, Harût, you swore you never stole. Also we heard her words after you had made her drunk with your tobacco smoke."

Now for once in his life Harût was, in sporting parlance, knocked out. He looked at us, then turning quite pale, lifted his eyes to heaven and rocked upon his feet as though he were about to fall.

"How you do it? How you do it, eh?" he queried in a weak voice.

"Never you mind how we did it, my friend," I answered loftily. "What we want to know is when you are going to hand over that lady to her husband."

"Not possible," he answered, recovering some of his tone. "First we kill you, first we kill her, she Nurse of the Child. While Child there, she stop there till she die."

"See here," broke in Ragnall. "Either you give me my wife or some-

474

one else will die. You will die, Harût. I am a stronger man than you are and unless you promise to give me my wife I will kill you now with this stick and my hands. Do not move or call out if you want to live."

"Lord," answered the old man with some dignity, "I know you can kill me, and if you kill me, I think I say thank you who no wish to live in so much trouble. But what good that, since in one minute then you die too, all of you, and lady she stop here till Black Kendah king take her to wife or she too die?"

"Let us talk," I broke in, treading warningly upon Ragnall's foot. "We have heard your Oracle and we know that you believe its words. It is said that we alone can help you to conquer the Black Kendah. If you will not promise what we ask, we will not help you. We will burn our powder and melt our lead, so that the guns we have cannot speak with Jana and with Simba, and after that we will do other things that I need not tell you. But if you promise what we ask, then we will fight for you against Jana and Simba and teach your men to use the fifty rifles which we have here with us, and by our help you shall conquer. Do you understand?"

He nodded and stroking his long beard, asked:

"What you want us promise, eh?"

"We want you to promise that after Jana is dead and the Black Kendah are driven away, you will give up to us unharmed that lady whom you have stolen. Also that you will bring her and us safely out of your country by the roads you know, and meanwhile that you will let this lord see his wife."

"Not last, no," replied Harût, "that not possible. That bring us all to grave. Also no good, 'cause her mind empty. For rest, you come to other place, sit down and eat while I talk with priests. Be afraid nothing; you quite safe."

"Why should we be afraid? It is you who should be afraid, you who stole the lady and brought Bena to his death. Do you not remember the words of your own Oracle, Harût?"

"Yes, I know words, but how *you* know them *that* I not know," he replied.

Then he issued some orders, as a result of which a guard formed itself about us and conducted us through the crowd and along the passage to the second court of the temple, which was now empty. Here the guard left us but remained at the mouth of the passage, keeping watch. Presently women brought us food and drink, of which Hans and I partook heartily though Ragnall, who was so near to his lost wife and yet so far away, could eat but little. Mingled joy because after these months of arduous search he found her yet alive, and fear lest she should again be taken from him for ever, deprived him of all appetite.

While we ate, priests to the number of about a dozen, who I suppose had been summoned by Harût, were admitted by the guard and, gathering out of earshot of us between the altar and the sanctuary, entered on an earnest discussion with him. Watching their faces I could see that there was a strong difference of opinion between them, about half taking one view on the matter of which they disputed, and half another. At length Harût made some proposition to which they all agreed. Then the door of the sanctuary was opened with a strange sort of key which one of the priests produced, showing a dark interior in which gleamed a white object, I suppose the statue of the Child. Harût and two others entered, the door being closed behind them. About five minutes later they appeared again and others, who listened earnestly and after renewed consultation signified assent by holding up the right hand. Now one of the priests walked to where we were and, bowing, begged us to advance to the altar. This we did, and were stood in a line in front of it, Hans being set in the middle place, while the priests ranged themselves on either side. Next Harût, having once more opened the door of the sanctuary, took his stand a little to the right of it and addressed us, not in English but in his own language, pausing at the end of each sentence that I might translate to Ragnall.

"Lords Macumazana and Igeza, and yellow man who is named Light-in-Darkness," he said, "we, the head priests of the Child, speaking on behalf of the White Kendah people with full authority so to do, have taken counsel together and of the wisdom of the Child as to the demands which you make of us. Those demands are: First, that after you have killed Jana and defeated the Black Kendah we should give over to you the white lady who was born in a far land to fill the office of Guardian of the Child, as is shown by the mark of the new moon upon her breast, but who, because for the second time we could not take her, became the wife of you, the Lord Igeza. Secondly, that we should conduct you and her safely out of our land to some place whence you can return to your own country. Both of these things we will do, because we know from of old that if once Jana is dead we shall have no cause to fear the Black Kendah any more, since we believe that then they will leave their home and go elsewhere, and therefore that we shall no longer need an Oracle to declare to us in what way Heaven will protect us from Jana and from them. Or if another Oracle should become necessary to us, doubtless in due season she will be found. Also we admit that we stole away this lady because we must, although she was the wife of one of you. But if we swear this, you on your part must also swear that you will stay with us till the end of the war, making our cause your cause and, if need be, giving your lives for us in battle. You must swear further that none of you will attempt to see or to take hence that lady who is named Guardian of the Child until we hand her over to you unharmed. If you will not swear these things, then since no blood may be shed in this holy place, here we will ring you round until you die of hunger and of thirst, or if you escape from this temple, then we will fall upon you and put you to death and fight our own battle with Jana as best we may."

"And if we make these promises how are we to know that you will keep yours?" I interrupted.

"Because the oath that we shall give you will be the oath of the Child that may not be broken."

"Then give it," I said, for although I did not altogether like the security, obviously it was the best to be had.

So very solemnly they laid their right hands upon the altar and "in the presence of the Child and the name of the Child and of all the White Kendah people," repeated after Harût a most solemn oath of which I have already given the substance. It called down on their heads a very dreadful doom in this world and the next, should it be broken either in the spirit or the letter; the said oath, however, to be only binding if we, on our part, swore to observe their terms and kept our engagement also in the spirit and the letter.

Then they asked us to fulfil our share of the pact and very considerately drew out of hearing while we discussed the matter; Harût, the only one of them who understood a word of English, retiring behind the sanctuary. At first I had difficulties with Ragnall, who was most unwilling to bind himself in any way. In the end, on my pointing out that nothing less than our lives were involved and probably that of his wife as well, also that no other course was open to us, he gave way, to my great relief.

Hans announced himself ready to swear anything, adding blandly that words mattered nothing, as afterwards we could do whatever seemed best in our own interests, whereon I read him a short moral lecture on the heinousness of perjury, which did not seem to impress him very much.

This matter settled, we called back the priests and informed them of our decision. Harût demanded that we should affirm it "by the Child," which we declined to do, saying that it was our custom to swear only in the name of our own God. Being a liberal-minded man who had travelled, Harût gave way on the point. So I swore first to the effect that I would fight for the White Kendah to the finish in consideration of the promises that they had made to us. I added that I would not attempt either to see or to interfere with the lady here known as the Guardian of the Child until the war was over or even to bring our existence to her knowledge, ending up, "so help me God," as I had done several times when giving evidence in a court of law.

Next Ragnall with a great effort repeated my oath in English, Harût listening carefully to every word and once or twice asking me to explain the exact meaning of some of them.

Lastly Hans, who seemed very bored with the whole affair, swore, also repeating the words after me and finishing on his own account with "so help me the reverend Predikant, the Baas's father," a form that he utterly declined to vary although it involved more explanations. When pressed, indeed, he showed considerable ingenuity by pointing out to the priests that to his mind my poor father stood in exactly the same relation to the Power above us as their Oracle did to the Child. He offered generously, however, to throw in the spirits of his grandfather and grandmother and some extraordinary divinity they worshipped, I think it was a hare, as an additional guarantee of good faith. This proposal the priests accepted gravely, whereon Hans whispered into my ear in Dutch:

"Those fools do not remember that when pressed by dogs the hare often doubles on its own spoor, and that your reverend father will be very pleased if I can play them the same trick with the white lady that they played with the Lord Igeza."

I only looked at him in reply, since the morality of Hans was past argument. It might perhaps be summed up in one sentence: To get the better of his neighbour in his master's service, honestly if possible; if not, by any means that came to his hand down to that of murder. At the bottom of his dark and mysterious heart Hans worshipped only one god, named Love, not of woman or child, but of my humble self. His principles were those of a rather sly but very high-class and exclusive dog, neither better nor worse. Still, when all is said and done, there are lower creatures in the world than high-class dogs. At least so the masters whom they adore are apt to think, especially if their watchfulness and courage have often saved them from death or disaster.

CHAPTER 18

The Embassy

The ceremonies were over and the priests, with the exception of
Harût and two who remained to attend upon him, vanished, probably
to inform the male and female hierophants of their result, and through
these the whole people of the White Kendah. Old Harût stared at us
for a little while, then said in English, which he always liked to talk
when Ragnall was present, perhaps for the sake of practice:

"What you like do now, eh? P'r'aps wish fly back to Town of Child,
for suppose this how you come. If so, please take me with you, because
that save long ride."

"Oh! no," I answered. "We walked here through that hole where
lived the Father of Snakes who died of fear when he saw us, and just
mixed with the rest of you in the court of the temple."

"Good lie," said Harût admiringly, "very first-class lie! Wonder
how you kill great snake, which we all think never die, for he live
there hundred, hundred years; our people find him there when first
they come to this country, and make him kind of god. Well, he nasty
beast and best dead. I say, you like see Child? If so, come, for you our
brothers now, only please take off hat and not speak."

I intimated that we should "like see Child," and led by Harût we
entered the little sanctuary which was barely large enough to hold all
of us. In a niche of the end wall stood the sacred effigy which Ragnall
and I examined with a kind of reverent interest. It proved to be the
statue of an infant about two feet high, cut, I imagine, from the base
of a single but very large elephant's tusk, so ancient that the yellowish
ivory had become rotten and was covered with a multitude of tiny
fissures. Indeed, for its appearance I made up my mind that several
thousands of years must have passed since the beast died from which
this ivory was taken, especially as it had, I presume, always been carefully preserved under cover.

The workmanship of the object was excellent, that of a fine artist who, I should think, had taken some living infant for his model, perhaps a child of the Pharaoh of the day. Here I may say at once that there could be no doubt of its Egyptian origin, since on one side of the head was a single lock of hair, while the fourth finger of the right hand was held before the lips as though to enjoin silence. Both of these peculiarities, it will be remembered, are characteristic of the infant Horus, the child of Osiris and Isis, as portrayed in bronzes and temple carvings. So at least Ragnall, who recently had studied many such effigies in Egypt, informed me later. There was nothing else in the place except an ancient, string-seated chair of ebony, adorned with inlaid ivory patterns; an effigy of a snake in porcelain, showing that serpent worship was in some way mixed up with their religion; and two rolls of papyrus, at least that is what they looked like, which were laid in the niche with the statue. These rolls, to my disappointment, Harût refused to allow us to examine or even to touch.

After we had left the sanctuary I asked Harût when this figure was brought to their land. He replied that it came when they came, at what date he could not tell us as it was so long ago, and that with it came the worship and the ceremonies of their religion.

In answer to further questions he added that this figure, which seemed to be of ivory, contained the spirits which ruled the sun and the moon, and through them the world. This, said Ragnall, was just a piece of Egyptian theology, preserved down to our own times in a remote corner of Africa, doubtless by descendants of dwellers on the Nile who had been driven thence in some national catastrophe, and brought away with them their faith and one of the effigies of their gods. Perhaps they fled at the time of the Persian invasion by Cambyses.

After we had emerged from this deeply interesting shrine, which was locked behind us, Harût led us, not through the passage connecting it with the stone house that we knew was occupied by Ragnall's wife in her capacity as Guardian of the Child, or a latter-day personification of Isis, Lady of the Moon, at which house he cast many longing glances, but back through the two courts and the pylon to the gateway of the temple. Here on the road by which we had entered the place, a fact which we did not mention to him, he paused and addressed us.

"Lords," he said, "now you and the People of the White Kendah are one; your ends are their ends, your fate is their fate, their secrets are your secrets. You, Lord Igeza, work for a reward, namely the person of that lady whom we took from you on the Nile."

"How did you do that?" interrupted Ragnall when I had interpreted.

"Lord, we watched you. We knew when you came to Egypt; we followed you in Egypt, whither we had journeyed on our road to England once more to seek our Oracles, till the day of our opportunity dawned. Then at night we called her and she obeyed the call, as she must do whose mind we have taken away—ask me not how—and brought her to dwell with us, she who is marked from her birth with the holy sign and wears upon her breast certain charmed stones and a symbol that for thousands of years have adorned the body of the Child and those of its Oracles. Do you remember a company of Arabs whom you saw riding on the banks of the Great River on the day before the night when she was lost to you? We were with that company and on our camels we bore her thence, happy and unharmed to this our land, as I trust, when all is done, we shall bear her back again and you with her."

"I trust so also, for you have wrought me a great wrong," said Ragnall briefly, "perhaps a greater wrong than I know at present, for how came it that my boy was killed by an elephant?"

"Ask that question of Jana and not of me," Harût answered darkly. Then he went on: "You also, Lord Macumazana, work for a reward, the countless store of ivory which your eyes have beheld lying in the burial place of elephants beyond the Tava River. When you have slain Jana who watches the store, and defeated the Black Kendah who serve him, it is yours and we will give you camels to bear it, or some of it, for all cannot be carried, to the sea where it can be taken away in ships. As for the yellow man, I think that he seeks no reward who soon will inherit all things."

"The old witch-doctor means that I am going to die," remarked Hans expectorating reflectively. "Well, Baas, I am quite ready, if only Jana and certain others die first. Indeed I grow too old to fight and travel as I used to do, and therefore shall be glad to pass to some land where I become young again."

"Stuff and rubbish!" I exclaimed, then turned and listened to Harût who, not understanding our Dutch conversation, was speaking once more.

"Lords," he said, "these paths which run east and west are the real approach to the mountain top and the temple, not that which, as I suppose, led you through the cave of the old serpent. The road to the west, which wanders round the base of the hill to a pass in those distant mountains and thence across the deserts to the north, is so easy to stop that by it we need fear no attack. With this eastern road the case is, however, different, as I shall now show you, if you will ride with me."

Then he gave some orders to two attendant priests who departed at a run and presently reappeared at the head of a small train of camels which had been hidden, I know not where. We mounted and, following the road across a flat piece of ground, found that not more than half a mile away was another precipitous ridge of rock which had presumably once formed the lip of an outer crater. This ridge, however, was broken away for a width of two or three hundred yards, perhaps by some outrush of lava, the road running through the centre of the gap on which *schanzes* had been built here and there for purposes of defence. Looking at these I saw that they were very old and inefficient and asked when they had been erected. Harût replied about a century before when the last war took place with the Black Kendah, who had been finally driven off at this spot, for then the White Kendah were more numerous than at present.

"So Simba knows this road?" I said.

"Yes, Lord, and Jana knows it also, for he fought in that war and still at times visits us here and kills any whom he may meet. Only to the temple he has never dared to come."

Now I wondered whether we had really seen Jana in the forest on the previous night, but coming to the conclusion that it was useless to investigate the matter, made no inquiries, especially as these would have revealed to Harût the route by which we approached the temple. Only I pointed out to him that proper defences should be put up here without delay, that is if they meant to make a stronghold of the mountain.

"We do, Lord," he answered, "since we are not strong enough to attack the Black Kendah in their own country or to meet them in pitched battle on the plain. Here and in no other place must be fought the last fight between Jana and the Child. Therefore it will be your task to build walls cunningly, so that when they come we may defeat Jana and the hosts of the Black Kendah."

"Do you mean that this elephant will accompany Simba and his soldiers, Harût?"

"Without doubt, Lord, since he has always done so from the beginning. Jana is tame to the king and certain priests of the Black Kendah, whose forefathers have fed him for generations, and will obey their orders. Also he can think for himself, being an evil spirit and invulnerable."

482

"His left eye and the tip of his trunk are not invulnerable," I remarked, "though from what I saw of him I should say there is no doubt about his being able to think for himself. Well, I am glad the brute is coming as I have an account to settle with him."

"As he, Lord, who does not forget, has an account to settle with you and your servant, Light-in-Darkness," commented Harût in an unpleasant and suggestive tone.

Then after we had taken a few measurements and Ragnall, who understands such matters, had drawn a rough sketch of the place in his pocket-book to serve as data for our proposed scheme of fortifications, we pursued our journey back to the town, where we had left all our stores and there were many things to be arranged. It proved to be quite a long ride, down the eastern slope of the mountain which was easy to negotiate, although like the rest of this strange hill it was covered with dense cedar forests that also seemed to me to have defensive possibilities. Reaching its foot at length we were obliged to make a detour by certain winding paths to avoid ground that was too rough for the camels, so that in the end we did not come to our own house in the Town of the Child till about midday.

Glad enough were we to reach it, since all three of us were tired out with our terrible night journey and the anxious emotions that we had undergone. Indeed, after we had eaten we lay down and I rejoiced to see that, notwithstanding the state of mental excitement into which the discovery of his wife had plunged him, Ragnall was the first of us to fall asleep.

About five o'clock we were awakened by a messenger from Harût, who requested our attendance on important business at a kind of meeting-house which stood at a little distance on an open place where the White Kendah bartered produce. Here we found Harût and about twenty of the headmen seated in the shade of a thatched roof, while behind them, at a respectful distance, stood quite a hundred of the White Kendah. Most of these, however, were women and children, for as I have said the greater part of the male population was absent from the town because of the commencement of the harvest.

We were conducted to chairs, or rather stools of honour, and when we two had seated ourselves, Hans taking his stand behind us, Harût rose and informed us that an embassy had arrived from the Black Kendah which was about to be admitted.

Presently they came, five of them, great, truculent-looking fellows of a surprising blackness, unarmed, for they had not been allowed to bring their weapons in to the town, but adorned with the usual silver

483

chains across their breasts to show their rank, and other savage finery. In the man who was their leader I recognized one of those messengers who had accosted us when first we entered their territory on our way from the south, before that fight in which I was taken prisoner. Stepping forward and addressing himself to Harût, he said:

"A while ago, O Prophet of the Child, I, the messenger of the god Jana, speaking through the mouth of Simba the King, gave to you and your brother Marût a certain warning to which you did not listen. Now Jana has Marût, and again I come to warn you, Harût."

"If I remember right," interrupted Harût blandly, "I think that on that occasion two of you delivered the message and that the Child marked one of you upon the brow. If Jana has my brother, say, where is yours?"

"We warned you," went on the messenger, "and you cursed us in the name of the Child."

"Yes," interrupted Harût again, "we cursed you with three curses. The first was the curse of Heaven by storm or drought, which has fallen upon you. The second was the curse of famine, which is falling upon you; and the third was the curse of war, which is yet to fall on you."

"It is of war that we come to speak," replied the messenger, diplomatically avoiding the other two topics which perhaps he found it awkward to discuss.

"That is foolish of you," replied the bland Harût, "seeing that the other day you matched yourselves against us with but small success. Many of you were killed but only a very few of us, and the white lord whom you took captive escaped out of your hands and from the tusks of Jana who, I think, now lacks an eye. If he is a god, how comes it that he lacks an eye and could not kill an unarmed white man?"

"Let Jana answer for himself, as he will do ere long, O Harût. Meanwhile, these are the words of Jana spoken through the mouth of Simba the King: The Child has destroyed my harvest and therefore I demand this of the people of the Child—that they give me three-fourths of their harvest, reaping the same and delivering it on the south bank of the River Tava. That they give me the two white lords to be sacrificed to me. That they give the white lady who is Guardian of the Child to be a wife of Simba the King, and with her a hundred virgins of your people. That the image of the Child be brought to the god Jana in the presence of his priests and Simba the King. These are the demands of Jana spoken through the mouth of Simba the King."

Watching, I saw a thrill of horror shake the forms of Harût and of all those with him as the full meaning of these, to them, most impious requests sank into their minds. But he only asked very quietly:

"And if we refuse the demands, what then?"

"Then," shouted the messenger insolently, "then Jana declares war upon you, the last war of all, war till every one of your men be dead and the Child you worship is burnt to grey ashes with fire. War till your women are taken as slaves and the corn which you refuse is stored in our grain pits and your land is a waste and your name forgotten. Already the hosts of Jana are gathered and the trumpet of Jana calls them to the fight. Tomorrow or the next day they advance upon you, and ere the moon is full not one of you will be left to look upon her."

Harût rose, and walking from under the shed, turned his back upon the envoys and stared at the distant line of great mountains which stood out far away against the sky. Out of curiosity I followed him and observed that these mountains were no longer visible. Where they had been was nothing but a line of black and heavy cloud. After looking for a while he returned and addressing the envoys, said quite casually:

"If you will be advised by me, friends, you will ride hard for the river. There is such rain upon the mountains as I have never seen before, and you will be fortunate if you cross it before the flood comes down, the greatest flood that has happened in our day."

This intelligence seemed to disturb the messengers, for they too stepped out of the shed and stared at the mountains, muttering to each other something that I could not understand. Then they returned and with a fine appearance of indifference demanded an immediate answer to their challenge.

"Can you not guess it?" answered Harût. Then changing his tone he drew himself to his full height and thundered out at them: "Get you back to your evil spirit of a god that hides in the shape of a beast of the forest and to his slave who calls himself a king, and say to them: 'Thus speaks the Child to his rebellious servants, the Black Kendah dogs: Swim my river when you can, which will not be yet, and come up against me when you will; for whenever you come I shall be ready for you. You are already dead, O Jana. You are already dead, O Simba the slave. You are scattered and lost, O dogs of the Black Kendah, and the home of such of you as remain shall be far away in a barren land, where you must dig deep for water and live upon the wild game because there little corn will grow.' Now begone, and swiftly, lest you stop here for ever."

So they turned and went, leaving me full of admiration for the histrionic powers of Harût.

I must add, however, that being without doubt a keen observer of the weather conditions of the neighbourhood, he was quite right about the rain upon the mountains, which by the way never extended to the territory of the People of the Child. As we heard afterwards, the flood came down just as the envoys reached the river; indeed, one of them was drowned in attempting its crossing, and for fourteen days after this it remained impassable to an army.

****

That very evening we began our preparations to meet an attack which was now inevitable. Putting aside the supposed rival powers of the tribal divinities worshipped under the names of the Child and Jana, which, while they added a kind of Homeric interest to the contest, could, we felt, scarcely affect an issue that must be decided with cold steel and other mortal weapons, the position of the White Kendah was serious indeed. As I think I have said, in all they did not number more than about two thousand men between the ages of twenty and fifty-five, or, including lads between fourteen and twenty and old men still able-bodied between fifty-five and seventy, say two thousand seven hundred capable of some sort of martial service. To these might be added something under two thousand women, since among this dwindling folk, oddly enough, from causes that I never ascertained, the males out-numbered the females, which accounted for their marriage customs that were, by comparison with those of most African peoples, monogamous. At any rate only the rich among them had more than one wife, while the poor or otherwise ineligible often had none at all, since inter-marriage with other races and above all with the Black Kendah dwelling beyond the river was so strictly taboo that it was punishable with death or expulsion.

Against this little band the Black Kendah could bring up twenty thousand men, besides boys and aged persons who with the women would probably be left to defend their own country, that is, not less than ten to one. Moreover, all of these enemies would be fighting with the courage of despair, since quite three-fourths of their crops with many of their cattle and sheep had been destroyed by the terrific hailburst that I have described. Therefore, since no other corn was available in the surrounding land, where they dwelt alone encircled by deserts, either they must capture that of the White Kendah, or suffer terribly from starvation until a year later when another harvest ripened.

The only points I could see in favour of the People of the Child were that they would fight on the vantage ground of their mountain stronghold, a formidable position if properly defended. Also they would have the benefit of the skill and knowledge of Ragnall and myself. Lastly, the enemy must face our rifles. Neither the White nor the Black Kendah, I should say, possessed any guns, except a few antiquated flintlock weapons that the former had captured from some nomadic tribe and kept as curiosities. Why this was the case I do not know, since undoubtedly at times the White Kendah traded in camels and corn with Arabs who wandered as far as the Sudan, or Egypt, nomadic tribes to whom even then firearms were known, although perhaps rarely used by them. But so it was, possibly because of some old law or prejudice which forbade their introduction into the country, or mayhap of the difficulty of procuring powder and lead, or for the reason that they had none to teach them the use of such new-fangled weapons.

Now it will be remembered that, on the chance of their proving useful, Ragnall, in addition to our own sporting rifles, had brought with him to Africa fifty Snider rifles with an ample supply of ammunition, the same that I had trouble in passing through the Customs at Durban, all of which had arrived safely at the Town of the Child. Clearly our first duty was to make the best possible use of this invaluable store. To that end I asked Harût to select seventy-five of the boldest and most intelligent young men among his people, and to hand them over to me and Hans for instruction in musketry. We had only fifty rifles but I drilled seventy-five men, or fifty per cent. more, that some might be ready to replace any who fell.

From dawn to dark each day Hans and I worked at trying to convert these Kendah into sharpshooters. It was no easy task with men, however willing, who till then had never held a gun, especially as I must be very sparing of the ammunition necessary to practice, of which of course our supply was limited. Still we taught them how to take cover, how to fire and to cease from firing at a word of command, also to hold the rifles low and waste no shot. To make marksmen of them was more than I could hope to do under the circumstances.

With the exception of these men nearly the entire male population were working day and night to get in the harvest. This proved a very difficult business, both because some of the crops were scarcely fit and because all the grain had to be carried on camels to be stored in and at the back of the second court of the temple, the only place where it was likely to be safe. Indeed in the end a great deal was left unreaped. Then the herds of cattle and breeding camels which grazed on the farther sides of the Holy Mount must be brought into places of safety, glens in the forest on its slope, and forage stacked to feed them. Also it was necessary to provide scouts to keep watch along the river.

Lastly, the fortifications in the mountain pass required unceasing labour and attention. This was the task of Ragnall, who fortunately in his youth, before he succeeded unexpectedly to the title, was for some years an officer in the Royal Engineers and therefore thoroughly understood that business. Indeed he understood it rather too well, since the result of his somewhat complicated and scientific scheme of defence was a little confusing to the simple native mind. However, with the assistance of all the priests and of all the women and children who were not engaged in provisioning the Mount, he built wall after wall and redoubt after redoubt, if that is the right word, to say nothing of the shelter trenches he dug and many pitfalls, furnished at the bottom with sharp stakes, which he hollowed out wherever the soil could be easily moved, to discomfit a charging enemy.

Indeed, when I saw the amount of work he had concluded in ten days, which was not until I joined him on the mountain, I was quite astonished.

About this time a dispute arose as to whether we should attempt to prevent the Black Kendah from crossing the river which was now running down, a plan that some of the elders favoured. At last the controversy was referred to me as head general and I decided against anything of the sort. It seemed to me that our force was too small, and that if I took the rifle-men a great deal of ammunition might be expended with poor result. Also in the event of any reverse or when we were finally driven back, which must happen, there might be difficulty about remounting the camels, our only means of escape from the horsemen who would possibly gallop us down. Moreover the Tava had several fords, any one of which might be selected by the enemy. So it was arranged that we should make our first and last stand upon the Holy Mount.

On the fourteenth night from new moon our swift camel-scouts who were posted in relays between the Tava and the Mount reported that the Black Kendah were gathered in thousands upon the farther side of the river, where they were engaged in celebrating magical ceremonies. On the fifteenth night the scouts reported that they were crossing the river, about five thousand horsemen and fifteen thousand foot soldiers, and that at the head of them marched the huge god-elephant Jana, on which rode Simba the King and a lame priest (evidently my friend whose foot had been injured by the pistol), who acted as a mahout. This part of the story I confess I did not believe, since it seemed to me impossible that anyone could ride upon that mad rogue, Jana. Yet, as subsequent events showed, it was in fact true. I suppose that in certain hands the beast became tame. Or perhaps it was drugged.

Two nights later, for the Black Kendah advanced but slowly, spreading themselves over the country in order to collect such crops as had not been gathered through lack of time or because they were still unripe, we saw flames and smoke arising from the Town of the Child beneath us, which they had fired. Now we knew that the time of trial had come and until near midnight men, women and children worked feverishly finishing or trying to finish the fortifications and making every preparation in our power.

Our position was that we held a very strong post, that is, strong against an enemy unprovided with big guns or even firearms, which, as all other possible approaches had been blocked, was only assailable by direct frontal attack from the east. In the pass we had three main lines of defence, one arranged behind the other and separated by distances of a few hundred yards. Our last refuge was furnished by the walls of the temple itself, in the rear of which were camped the whole White Kendah tribe, save a few hundred who were employed in watching the herds of camels and stock in almost inaccessible positions on the northern slopes of the Mount.

There were perhaps five thousand people of both sexes and every age gathered in this camp, which was so well provided with food and water that it could have stood a siege of several months. If, however, our defences should be carried there was no possibility of escape, since we learned from our scouts that the Black Kendah, who by tradition and through spies were well acquainted with every feature of the country, had detached a party of several thousand men to watch the western road and the slopes of the mountain, in case we should try to break out by that route. The only one remaining, that which ran through the cave of the serpent, we had taken the precaution of blocking up with great stones, lest through it our flank should be turned.

In short, we were rats in a trap and where we were there we must either conquer or die—unless indeed we chose to surrender, which for most of us would mean a fate worse than death.

CHAPTER 19

Allan Quatermain Misses

I had made my last round of the little corps that I facetiously named the *Sharpshooters*, though to tell the truth at shooting they were anything but sharp, and seen that each man was in his place behind a wall with a reserve man squatted at the rear of every pair of them, waiting to take his rifle if either of these should fall. Also I had made sure that all of them had twenty rounds of ammunition in their skin pouches. More I would not serve out, fearing lest in excitement or in panic they might fire away to the last cartridge uselessly, as before now even disciplined white troops have been known to do. Therefore I had arranged that certain old men of standing who could be trusted should wait in a place of comparative safety behind the line, carrying all our reserve ammunition, which amounted, allowing for what had been expended in practice, to nearly sixty rounds per rifle. This they were instructed to deliver from their wallets to the firing line in small lots when they saw that it was necessary and not before.

It was, I admit, an arrangement apt to miscarry in the heat of desperate battle, but I could think of none better, since it was absolutely necessary that no shot should be wasted.

After a few words of exhortation and caution to the natives who acted as sergeants to the corps, I returned to a bough shelter that had been built for us behind a rock to get a few hours' sleep, if that were possible, before the fight began.

Here I found Ragnall, who had just come in from his inspection. This was of a much more extensive nature than my own, since it involved going round some furlongs of the rough walls and trenches that he had prepared with so much thought and care, and seeing that the various companies of the White Kendah were ready to play their part in the defence of them.

He was tired and rather excited, too much so to sleep at once. So we talked a little while, first about the prospects of the morrow's battle, as to which we were, to say the least of it, dubious, and afterwards of other things. I asked him if during his stay in this place, while I was below at the town or later, he had heard or seen anything of his wife.

"Nothing," he answered. "These priests never speak of her, and if they did Harût is the only one of them that I can really understand. Moreover, I have kept my word strictly and, even when I had occasion to see to the blocking of the western road, made a circuit on the mountain-top in order to avoid the neighbourhood of that house where I suppose she lives Oh! Quatermain, my friend, my case is a hard one, as you would think if the woman you loved with your whole heart were shut up within a few hundred yards of you and no communication with her possible after all this time of separation and agony. What makes it worse is, as I gathered from what Harût said the other day, that she is still out of her mind."

"That has some consolations," I replied, "since the mindless do not suffer. But if such is the case, how do you account for what you and poor Savage saw that night in the Town of the Child? It was not altogether a fantasy, for the dress you described was the same we saw her wearing at the Feast of the First-fruits."

"I don't know what to make of it, Quatermain, except that many strange things happen in the world which we mock at as insults to our limited intelligence because we cannot understand them." (Very soon I was to have another proof of this remark.) "But what are you driving at? You are keeping something back."

"Only this, Ragnall. If your wife were utterly mad I cannot conceive how it came about that she searched you out and spoke to you even in a vision—for the thing was not an individual dream since both you and Savage saw her. Nor did she actually visit you in the flesh, as the door never opened and the spider's web across it was not broken. So it comes to this: either some part of her is not mad but can still exercise sufficient will to project itself upon your senses, or she is dead and her disembodied spirit did this thing. Now we know that she is not dead, for we have seen her and Harût has confessed as much. Therefore I maintain that, whatever may be her temporary state, she must still be fundamentally of a reasonable mind, as she is of a natural body. For instance, she may only be hypnotized, in which case the spell will break one day."

"Thank you for that thought, old fellow. It never occurred to me and it gives me new hope. Now listen! If I should come to grief in this business, which is very likely, and you should survive, you will do

491

your best to get her home; will you not? Here is a codicil to my will which I drew up after that night of dream, duly witnessed by Savage and Hans. It leaves to you whatever sums may be necessary in this connexion and something over for yourself. Take it, it is best in your keeping, especially as if you should be killed it has no value."

"Of course I will do my best," I answered as I put away the paper in my pocket. "And now don't let us take any more thought of being killed, which may prevent us from getting the sleep we want. I don't mean to be killed if I can help it. I mean to give those beggars, the Black Kendah, such a doing as they never had before, and then start for the coast with you and Lady Ragnall, as, God willing, we shall do. Goodnight."

After this I slept like a top for some hours, as I believe Ragnall did also. When I awoke, which happened suddenly and completely, the first thing that I saw was Hans seated at the entrance to my little shelter smoking his corn-cob pipe, and nursing the single-barrelled rifle, *Intombi*, on his knee. I asked him what the time was, to which he replied that it lacked two hours to dawn. Then I asked him why he had not been sleeping. He replied that he had been asleep and dreamed a dream. Idly enough I inquired what dream, to which he replied:

"Rather a strange one, Baas, for a man who is about to go into battle. I dreamed that I was in a large place that was full of quiet. It was light there, but I could not see any sun or moon, and the air was very soft and tasted like food and drink, so much so, Baas, that if anyone had offered me a cup quite full of the best 'Cape smoke' I should have told him to take it away. Then, Baas, suddenly I saw your reverend father, the Predikant, standing beside me and looking just as he used to look, only younger and stronger and very happy, and so of course knew at once that I was dead and in hell. Only I wondered where the fire that does not go out might be, for I could not see it. Presently your reverend father said to me: 'Good day, Hans. So you have come here at last. Now tell me, how has it gone with my son, the Baas Allan? Have you looked after him as I told you to do?'

"I answered: 'I have looked after him as well as I could, O reverend sir. Little enough have I done; still, not once or twice or three times only have I offered up my life for him as was my duty, and yet we both have lived.' And that I might be sure he heard the best of me, as was but natural, I told him the times, Baas, making a big story out of small things, although all the while I could see that he knew exactly just where I began to lie and just where I stopped from lying. Still he did not scold me, Baas; indeed, when I had finished, he said:

492

"'Well done, O good and faithful servant,' words that I think I have heard him use before when he was alive, Baas, and used to preach to us for such a long time on Sunday afternoons. Then he asked: 'And how goes it with Baas Allan, my son, now, Hans?' to which I replied:

"'The Baas Allan is going to fight a very great battle in which he may well fall, and if I could feel sorry here, which I can't, I should weep, O reverend sir, because I have died before that battle began and therefore cannot stand at his side in the battle and be killed for him as a servant should for his master!'

"'You will stand at his side in the battle and do as it is fitting that you should. And afterwards, Hans, you will make report to me of how the battle went and of what honour my son has won therein. Moreover, know this, Hans, that though while you live in the world you seem to see many other things, they are but dreams, since in all the world there is but one real thing, and its name is Love, which if it be but strong enough, the stars themselves must obey, for it is the king of every one of them, and all who dwell in them worship it day and night under many names for ever and for ever, Amen.'

"What he meant by that I am sure I don't know, Baas, seeing that I have never thought much of women, at least not for many years since my last old *vrouw* went and drank herself to death after lying in her sleep on the baby which I loved much better than I did her, Baas.

"Well, before I could ask him, or about hell either, he was gone like a whiff of smoke from a rifle mouth in a strong wind."

Hans paused, puffed at his pipe, spat upon the ground in his usual reflective way and asked:

"Is the Baas tired of the dream or would he like to hear the rest?"

"I should like to hear the rest," I said in a low voice, for I was strangely moved.

"Well, Baas, while I was standing in that place which was so full of quiet, turning my hat in my hands and wondering what work they would set me to there among the devils, I looked up. There I saw coming towards me two very beautiful women, Baas, who had their arms round each other's necks. They were dressed in white, with the little hard things that are found in shells hanging about them, and bright stones in their hair. And as they came, Baas, wherever they set a foot flowers sprang up, very pretty flowers, so that all their path across the quiet place was marked with flowers. Birds too sang as they passed, at least I think they were birds though I could not see them."

"What were they like, Hans?" I whispered.

"One of them, Baas, the taller I did not know. But the other I knew well enough; it was she whose name is holy, not to be mentioned. Yet I must mention that name; it was the Missie Marie herself as last we saw her alive many, many years ago, only grown a hundred times more beautiful."

Now I groaned, and Hans went on:

"The two White Ones came up to me, and stood looking at me with eyes that were more soft than those of bucks. Then the Missie Marie said to the other: 'This is Hans of whom I have so often told you, O Star.'"

Here I groaned again, for how did this Hottentot know that name, or rather its sweet rendering?

"Then she who was called Star asked, 'How goes it with one who is the heart of all three of us, O Hans?' Yes, Baas, those Shining Ones joined *me*, the dirty little Hottentot in my old clothes and smelling of tobacco, with themselves when they spoke of you, for I knew they were speaking of you, Baas, which made me think I must be drunk, even there in the quiet place. So I told them all that I had told your reverend father, and a very great deal more, for they seemed never to be tired of listening. And once, when I mentioned that sometimes, while pretending to be asleep, I had heard you praying aloud at night for the Missie Marie who died for you, and for another who had been your wife whose name I did not remember but who had also died, they both cried a little, Baas. Their tears shone like crystals and smelt like that stuff in a little glass tube which Harût said that he brought from some far land when he put a drop or two on your handkerchief, after you were faint from the pain in your leg at the house yonder. Or perhaps it was the flowers that smelt, for where the tears fell there sprang up white lilies shaped like two babes' hands held together in prayer."

Hearing this, I hid my face in my hands lest Hans should see human tears unscented with attar of roses, and bade him continue.

"Baas, the White One who was called Star, asked me of your son, the young Baas Harry, and I told her that when last I had seen him he was strong and well and would make a bigger man than you were, whereat she sighed and shook her head. Then the Missie Marie said: 'Tell the Baas, Hans, that I also have a child which he will see one day, but it is not a son.'

"After this they, too, said something about Love, but what it was I cannot remember, since even as I repeat this dream to you it is beginning to slip away from me fast as a swallow skimming the water. Their last words, however, I do remember. They were: 'Say to the Baas that we who never met in life, but who here are as twin sisters, wait and count the years and count the months and count the days and count the hours and count the minutes and count the seconds until once more he shall hear our voices calling to him across the night.' That's what they say, Baas. Then they were gone and only the flowers remained to show that they had been standing there.

"Now I set off to bring you the message and travelled a very long way at a great rate; if Jana himself had been after me I could not have gone more fast. At last I got out of that quiet place and among mountains where there were dark *kloofs*, and there in the *kloofs* I heard Zulu *impis* singing their war-song; yes, they sang the *ingoma* or something very like it. Now suddenly in the pass of the mountains along which I sped, there appeared before me a very beautiful woman whose skin shone like the best copper coffee kettle after I have polished it, Baas. She was dressed in a leopard-like *moocha* and wore on her shoulders a fur *kaross*, and about her neck a circlet of blue beads, and from her hair there rose one crane's feather tall as a walking-stick, and in her hand she held a little spear. No flowers sprang beneath her feet when she walked towards me and no birds sang, only the air was filled with the sound of a royal salute which rolled among the mountains like the roar of thunder, and her eyes flashed like summer lightning."

Now I let my hands fall and stared at him, for well I knew what was coming.

"'Stand, yellow man!' she said, 'and give me the royal salute.'

"So I gave her the *Bayéte*, though who she might be I did not know, since I did not think it wise to stay to ask her if it were hers of right, although I should have liked to do so. Then she said: 'The Old Man on the plain yonder and those two pale White Ones have talked to you of their love for your master, the Lord Macumazana. I tell you, little Yellow Dog, that they do not know what love can be. There is more love for him in my eyes alone than they have in all that makes them fair. Say it to the Lord Macumazana that, as I know well, he goes down to battle and that the Lady Mameena will be with him in the battle as, though he saw her not, she has been with him in other battles, and will be with him till the River of Time has run over the edge of the world and is lost beyond the sun. Let him remember this when Jana rushes on and death is very near to him today, and let him look—for then perchance he shall see me. Begone now, Yellow Dog, to the heels of your master, and play your part well in the battle, for of what you do or leave undone you shall give account to me. Say that Mameena sends her greetings to the Lord Macumazana and that she adds this, that when the Old Man and the White ones told you that Love is the secret blood of the worlds which makes them to be they did not lie. Love reigns and I, Mameena, am its priestess, and the heart of Macumazana is my holy house.'

"Then, Baas, I tumbled off a precipice and woke up here; and, Baas, as we may not light a fire I have kept some coffee hot for you buried in warm ashes," and without another word he went to fetch that coffee, leaving me shaken and amazed.

For what kind of a dream was it which revealed to an old Hottentot all these mysteries and hidden things about persons whom he had never seen and of whom I had never spoken to him? My father and my wife Marie might be explained, for with these he had been mixed up, but how about Stella and above all Mameena, although of course it was possible that he had heard of the latter, who made some stir in her time? But to hit her off as he had done in all her pride, splendour, and dominion of desire!

Well, that was his story which, perhaps fortunately, I lacked time to analyse or brood upon, since there was much in it calculated to unnerve a man just entering the crisis of a desperate fray. Indeed a minute or so later, as I was swallowing the last of the coffee, messengers arrived about some business, I forget what, sent by Ragnall I think, who had risen before I woke. I turned to give the pannikin to Hans, but he had vanished in his snake-like fashion, so I threw it down upon the ground and devoted my mind to the question raised in Ragnall's message.

Next minute scouts came in who had been watching the camp of the Black Kendah all night.

These were sleeping not more than half a mile away, in an open place on the slope of the hill with pickets thrown out round them, intending to advance upon us, it was said, as soon as the sun rose, since because of their number they feared lest to march at night should throw them into confusion and, in case of their falling into an ambush, bring about a disaster. Such at least was the story of two spies whom our people had captured.

There had been some question as to whether we should not attempt a night attack upon their camp, of which I was rather in favour. After full debate, however, the idea had been abandoned, owing to the fewness of our numbers, the dislike which the White Kendah shared with the Black of attempting to operate in the dark, and the well chosen position of our enemy, whom it would be impossible to rush before we were discovered by their outposts. What I hoped in my heart was that they might try to rush us, notwithstanding the story of the two captured spies, and in the gloom, after the moon had sunk low and before the dawn came, become entangled in our pitfalls and outlying entrenchments, where we should be able to destroy a great number of them. Only on the previous afternoon that cunning old fellow, Hans, had pointed out to me how advantageous such an event would be to our cause and, while agreeing with him, I suggested that probably the Black Kendah knew this as well as we did, as the prisoners had told us.

Yet that very thing happened, and through Hans himself. Thus: Old Harût had come to me just one hour before the dawn to inform me that all our people were awake and at their stations, and to make some last arrangements as to the course of the defence, also about our final concentration behind the last line of walls and in the first court of the temple, if we should be driven from the outer entrenchments. He was telling me that the Oracle of the Child had uttered words at the ceremony that night which he and all the priests considered were of the most favourable import, news to which I listened with some impatience, feeling as I did that this business had passed out of the range of the Child and its Oracle. As he spoke, suddenly through the silence that precedes the dawn, there floated to our ears the unmistakable sound of a rifle. Yes, a rifle shot, half a mile or so away, followed by the roaring murmur of a great camp unexpectedly alarmed at night.

"Who can have fired that?" I asked. "The Black Kendah have no guns."

He replied that he did not know, unless some of my fifty men had left their posts.

While we were investigating the matter, scouts rushed in with the intelligence that the Black Kendah, thinking apparently that they were being attacked, had broken camp and were advancing towards us. We passed a warning all down the lines and stood to arms. Five minutes later, as I stood listening to that approaching roar, filled with every kind of fear and melancholy foreboding such as the hour and the occasion might well have evoked, through the gloom, which was dense, the moon being hidden behind the hill, I thought I caught sight of something running towards me like a crouching man. I lifted my rifle to fire but, reflecting that it might be no more than a hyena and fearing to provoke a fusillade from my half-trained company, did not do so.

Next instant I was glad indeed, for immediately on the other side of the wall behind which I was standing I heard a well-known voice gasp out:

"Don't shoot, Baas, it is I."

"What have you been doing, Hans?" I said as he scrambled over the wall to my side, limping a little as I fancied.

"Baas," he puffed, "I have been paying the Black Kendah a visit. I crept down between their stupid outposts, who are as blind in the dark as a bat in daytime, hoping to find Jana and put a bullet into his leg or trunk. I didn't find him, Baas, although I heard him. But one of their captains stood up in front of a watchfire, giving a good shot. My bullet found *him*, Baas, for he tumbled back into the fire making the sparks fly this way and that. Then I ran and, as you see, got here quite safely."

"Why did you play that fool's trick?" I asked, "seeing that it ought to have cost you your life?"

"I shall die just when I have to die, not before, Baas," he replied in the intervals of reloading the little rifle. "Also it was the trick of a wise man, not of a fool, seeing that it has made the Black Kendah think that we were attacking them and caused them to hurry on to attack *us* in the dark over ground that they do not know. Listen to them coming!"

As he spoke a roar of sound told us that the great charge had swept round a turn there was in the pass and was heading towards us up the straight. Ivory horns brayed, captains shouted orders, the very mountains shook beneath the beating of thousands of feet of men and horses, while in one great yell that echoed from the cliffs and forests went up the battle-cry of *"Jana! Jana!"*—a mixed tumult of noise which contrasted very strangely with the utter silence in our ranks.

"They will be among the pitfalls presently," sniggered Hans, shifting his weight nervously from one leg on to the other. "Hark! they are going into them."

It was true. Screams of fear and pain told me that the front ranks had begun to fall, horse and foot together, into the cunningly devised snares of which with so much labour we had dug many, concealing them with earth spread over thin wickerwork, or rather interlaced boughs. Into them went the forerunners, to be pierced by the sharp, fire-hardened stakes set at the bottom of each pit. Vainly did those who were near enough to understand their danger call to the ranks behind to stop. They could not or would not comprehend, and had no room to extend their front. Forward surged the human torrent, thrusting all in front of it to death by wounds or suffocation in those deadly holes, till one by one they were filled level with the ground by struggling men and horses, over whom the army still rushed on.

How many perished there I do not know, but after the battle was over we found scarcely a pit that was not crowded to the brim with dead. Truly this device of Ragnall's, for if I had conceived the idea, which was unfamiliar to the Kendah, it was he who had carried it out in so masterly a fashion, had served us well.

Still the enemy surged on, since the pits were only large enough to hold a tithe of them, till at length, horsemen and footmen mixed up together in inextricable confusion, their mighty mass became faintly visible quite close to us, a blacker blot upon the gloom.

Then my turn came. When they were not more than fifty yards away from the first wall, I shouted an order to my riflemen to fire, aiming low, and set the example by loosing both barrels of an elephant gun at the thickest of the mob. At that distance even the most inexperienced shots could not miss such a mark, especially as those bullets that went high struck among the oncoming troops behind, or caught the horsemen lifted above their fellows. Indeed, of the first few rounds I do not think that one was wasted, while often single balls killed or injured several men.

The result was instantaneous. The Black Kendah who, be it remembered, were totally unaccustomed to the effects of rifle fire and imagined that we only possessed two or three guns in all, stopped their advance as though paralyzed. For a few seconds there was silence, except for the intermittent crackle of the rifles as my men loaded and fired. Next came the cries of the smitten men and horses that were falling everywhere, and then—the unmistakable sound of a stampede.

"They have gone. That was too warm for them, Baas," chuckled Hans exultingly.

"Yes," I answered, when I had at length succeeded in stopping the firing, "but I expect they will come back with the light. Still, that trick of yours has cost them dear, Hans."

By degrees the dawn began to break. It was, I remember, a particularly beautiful dawn, resembling a gigantic and vivid rose opening in the east, or a cup of brightness from which many coloured wines were poured all athwart the firmament. Very peaceful also, for not a breath of wind was stirring. But what a scene the first rays of the sun revealed upon that narrow stretch of pass in front of us. Everywhere the pitfalls and trenches were filled with still surging heaps of men and horses, while all about lay dead and wounded men, the red harvest of our rifle fire. It was dreadful to contrast the heavenly peace above and the hellish horror beneath.

We took count and found that up to this moment we had not lost a single man, one only having been slightly wounded by a thrown spear. As is common among semi-savages, this fact filled the White Kendah with an undue exultation. Thinking that as the beginning was so the end must be, they cheered and shouted, shaking each other's hands, then fell to eating the food which the women brought them with appetite, chattering incessantly, although as a general rule they were a very silent people. Even the grave Harût, who arrived full of congratulations, seemed as high-spirited as a boy, till I reminded him that the real battle had not yet commenced.

The Black Kendah had fallen into a trap and lost some of their number, that was all, which was fortunate for us but could scarcely affect the issue of the struggle, since they had many thousands left. Ragnall, who had come up from his lines, agreed with me. As he said, these people were fighting for life as well as honour, seeing that most of the corn which they needed for their sustenance was stored in great heaps either in or to the rear of the temple behind us. Therefore they must come on until they won or were destroyed. How with our small force could we hope to destroy this multitude? That was the problem which weighed upon our hearts.

About a quarter of an hour later two spies that we had set upon the top of the precipitous cliffs, whence they had a good view of the pass beyond the bend, came scrambling down the rocks like monkeys by a route that was known to them. These boys, for they were no more, reported that the Black Kendah were reforming their army beyond the bend of the pass, and that the cavalry were dismounting and sending their horses to the rear, evidently because they found them useless in such a place. A little later solitary men appeared from behind the bend, carrying bundles of long sticks to each of which was attached a piece of white cloth, a proceeding that excited my curiosity.

Soon its object became apparent. Swiftly these men, of whom in the end there may have been thirty or forty, ran to and fro, testing the ground with spears in search for pitfalls. I think they only found a very few that had not been broken into, but in front of these and also of those that were already full of men and horses they set up the flags as a warning that they should be avoided in the advance. Also they removed a number of their wounded.

We had great difficulty in restraining the White Kendah from rushing out to attack them, which of course would only have led us into a trap in our turn, since they would have fled and conducted their pursuers into the arms of the enemy. Nor would I allow my riflemen to fire, as the result must have been many misses and a great waste of ammunition which ere long would be badly wanted. I, however, did shoot two or three, then gave it up as the remainder took no notice whatever.

When they had thoroughly explored the ground they retired until, a little later, the Black Kendah army began to appear, marching in serried regiments and excellent order round the bend, till perhaps eight or ten thousand of them were visible, a very fierce and awe-inspiring *impi*. Their front ranks halted between three and four hundred yards away, which I thought farther off than it was advisable to open fire on them with Snider rifles held by unskilled troops. Then came a pause, which at length was broken by the blowing of horns and a sound of exultant shouting beyond the turn of the pass.

Now from round this turn appeared the strangest sight that I think my eyes had ever seen. Yes, there came the huge elephant, Jana, at a slow, shambling trot. On his back and head were two men in whom, with my glasses, I recognized the lame priest whom I already knew too well and Simba, the king of the Black Kendah, himself, gorgeously apparelled and waving a long spear, seated in a kind of wooden chair. Round the brute's neck were a number of bright metal chains, twelve in all, and each of these chains was held by a spearman who ran alongside, six on one side and six on the other. Lastly, ingeniously fastened to the end of his trunk were three other chains to which were attached spiked knobs of metal.

On he came as docilely as any Indian elephant used for carrying teak logs, passing through the centre of the host up a wide lane which had been left, I suppose for his convenience, and intelligently avoiding the pitfalls filled with dead. I thought that he would stop among the first ranks. But not so. Slackening his pace to a walk he marched forwards towards our fortifications. Now, of course, I saw my chance and made sure that my double-barrelled elephant rifle was ready and that Hans held a second rifle, also double-barrelled and of similar calibre, full-cocked in such a position that I could snatch it from him in a moment.

"I am going to kill that elephant," I said. "Let no one else fire. Stand still and you shall see the god Jana die."

Still the enormous beast floundered forward; up to that moment I had never realized how truly huge it was, not even when it stood over me in the moonlight about to crush me with its foot. Of this I am sure, that none to equal it ever lived in Africa, at least in any times of which I have knowledge.

"Fire, Baas," whispered Hans, "it is near enough."

But like the Frenchman and the cock pheasant, I determined to wait until it stopped, wishing to finish it with a single ball, if only for the prestige of the thing.

At length it did stop and, opening its cavern of a mouth, lifted its great trunk and trumpeted, while Simba, standing up in his chair, began to shout out some command to us to surrender to the god Jana, "the Invincible, the Invulnerable."

"I will show you if you are invulnerable, my boy," said I to myself, glancing round to make sure that Hans had the second rifle ready and catching sight of Ragnall and Harût and all the White Kendah standing up in their trenches, breathlessly awaiting the end, as were the Black Kendah a few hundred yards away. Never could there have been a fairer shot and one more certain to result in a fatal wound. The brute's head was up and its mouth was open. All I had to do was to send a hard-tipped bullet crashing through the palate to the brain behind. It was so easy that I would have made a bet that I could have finished him with one hand tied behind me.

I lifted the heavy rifle. I got the sights dead on to a certain spot at the back of that red cave. I pressed the trigger; the charge boomed— and nothing happened! I heard no bullet strike and Jana did not even take the trouble to close his mouth.

An exclamation of "O-oh!" went up from the watchers. Before it had died away the second bullet followed the first, with the same result or rather lack of result, and another louder "O-oh!" arose. Then Jana tranquilly shut his mouth, having finished trumpeting, and as though to give me a still better target, turned broadside on and stood quite still.

With an inward curse I snatched the second rifle and aiming behind the ear at a spot which long experience told me covered the heart let drive again, first one barrel and then the other.

Jana never stirred. No bullet thudded. No mark of blood appeared upon his hide. The horrible thought overcame me that I, Allan Quatermain, I the famous shot, the renowned elephant-hunter, had four times missed this haystack of a brute from a distance of forty yards. So great was my shame that I think I almost fainted. Through a kind of mist I heard various ejaculations:

"Great Heavens!" said Ragnall.

"*Allemagte!*" remarked Hans.

"The Child help us!" muttered Harût.

All the rest of them stared at me as though I were a freak or a lunatic. Then somebody laughed nervously, and immediately everybody began to laugh. Even the distant army of the Black Kendah became convulsed with roars of unholy merriment and I, Allan Quatermain, was the centre of all this mockery, till I felt as though I were going mad. Suddenly the laughter ceased and once more Simba the King began to roar out something about "Jana the Invincible and Invulnerable," to which the White Kendah replied with cries of "Magic" and "Bewitched! Bewitched!"

"Yes," yelled Simba, "no bullet can touch Jana the god, not even those of the white lord who was brought from far to kill him."

Hans leaped on to the top of the wall, where he danced up and down like an intoxicated monkey, and screamed:

"Then where is Jana's left eye? Did not my bullet put it out like a lamp? If Jana is invulnerable, why did my bullet put out his left eye?"

Hans ceased from dancing on the wall and steadying himself, lifted the little rifle *Intombi*, shouting:

"Let us see whether after all this beast is a god or an elephant."

Then he touched the trigger, and simultaneously with the report, I heard the bullet clap and saw blood appear on Jana's hide just by the very spot over the heart at which I had aimed without result. Of course, the soft ball driven from a small-bore rifle with a light charge of powder was far too weak to penetrate to the vitals. Probably it did not do much more than pierce through the skin and an inch or two of flesh behind it.

Still, its effects upon this "invulnerable" god were of a marked order. He whipped round; he lifted his trunk and screamed with rage and pain. Then off he lumbered back towards his own people, at such a pace that the attendants who held the chains on either side of him were thrown over and forced to leave go of him, while the king and the priest upon his back could only retain their seats by clinging to the chair and the rope about his neck.

The result was satisfactory so far as the dispelling of magical illusions went, but it left me in a worse position than before, since it now became evident that what had protected Jana from my bullets was nothing more supernatural than my own lack of skill. Oh! never in my life did I drink of such a cup of humiliation as it was my lot to drain to the dregs in this most unhappy hour. Almost did I hope that I might be killed at once.

And yet, and yet, how was it possible that with all my skill I should have missed this towering mountain of flesh four times in succession. The question is one to which I have never discovered any answer, especially as Hans hit it easily enough, which at the time I wished heartily he had not done, since his success only served to emphasize my miserable failure. Fortunately, just then a diversion occurred which freed my unhappy self from further public attention. With a shout and a roar the great army of the Black Kendah woke into life.

The advance had begun.

CHAPTER 20

Allan Weeps

On they came, slowly and steadily, preceded by a cloud of skirmishers—a thousand or more of these—who kept as open an order as the narrow ground would allow and carried, each of them, a bundle of throwing spears arranged in loops or sockets at the back of the shield. When these men were about a hundred yards away we opened fire and killed a great number of them, also some of the marshalled troops behind. But this did not stop them in the least, for what could fifty rifles do against a horde of brave barbarians who, it seemed, had no fear of death? Presently their spears were falling among us and a few casualties began to occur, not many, because of the protecting wall, but still some. Again and again we loaded and fired, sweeping away those in front of us, but always others came to take their places. Finally at some word of command these light skirmishers vanished, except whose who were dead or wounded, taking shelter behind the advancing regiments which now were within fifty yards of us.

Then, after a momentary pause another command was shouted out and the first regiment charged in three solid ranks. We fired a volley point blank into them and, as it was hopeless for fifty men to withstand such an onslaught, bolted during the temporary confusion that ensued, taking refuge, as it had been arranged that we should do, at a point of vantage farther down the line of fortifications, whence we maintained our galling fire.

Now it was that the main body of the White Kendah came into action under the leadership of Ragnall and Harût. The enemy scrambled over the first wall, which we had just vacated, to find themselves in a network of other walls held by our spearmen in a narrow place where numbers gave no great advantage.

Here the fighting was terrible and the loss of the attackers great, for always as they carried one entrenchment they found another a few yards in front of them, out of which the defenders could only be driven at much cost of life.

Two hours or more the battle went on thus. In spite of the desperate resistance which we offered, the multitude of the Black Kendah, who I must say fought magnificently, stormed wall after wall, leaving hundreds of dead and wounded to mark their difficult progress. Meanwhile I and my riflemen rained bullets on them from certain positions which we had selected beforehand, until at length our ammunition began to run low.

At half-past eight in the morning we were driven back over the open ground to our last entrenchment, a very strong one just outside of the eastern gate of the temple which, it will be remembered, was set in a tunnel pierced through the natural lava rock. Thrice did the Black Kendah come on and thrice we beat them off, till the ditch in front of the wall was almost full of fallen. As fast as they climbed to the top of it the White Kendah thrust them through with their long spears, or we shot them with our rifles, the nature of the ground being such that only a direct frontal attack was possible.

In the end they drew back sullenly, having, as we hoped, given up the assault. As it turned out, this was not so. They were only resting and waiting for the arrival of their reserve. It came up shouting and singing a war-song, two thousand strong or more, and presently once more they charged like a flood of water. We beat them back. They reformed and charged a second time and we beat them back.

Then they took another counsel. Standing among the dead and dying at the base of the wall, which was built of loose stones and earth, where we could not easily get at them because of the showers of spears which were rained at anyone who showed himself, they began to undermine it, levering out the bottom stones with stakes and battering them with poles.

In five minutes a breach appeared, through which they poured tumultuously. It was hopeless to withstand that onslaught of so vast a number. Fighting desperately, we were driven down the tunnel and through the doors that were opened to us, into the first court of the temple. By furious efforts we managed to close these doors and block them with stones and earth. But this did not avail us long, for, bringing brushwood and dry grass, they built a fire against them that soon caught the thick cedar wood of which they were made.

While they burned we consulted together. Further retreat seemed impossible, since the second court of the temple, save for a narrow passage, was filled with corn which allowed no room for fighting, while behind it were gathered all the women and children, more than two thousand of them. Here, or nowhere, we must make our stand and conquer or die. Up to this time, compared with what which we had inflicted upon the Black Kendah, of whom a couple of thousand or more had fallen, our loss was comparatively slight, say two hundred killed and as many more wounded. Most of such of the latter as could not walk we had managed to carry into the first court of the temple, laying them close against the cloister walls, whence they watched us in a grisly ring.

This left us about sixteen hundred able-bodied men or many more than we could employ with effect in that narrow place. Therefore we determined to act upon a plan which we had already designed in case such an emergency as ours should arise. About three hundred and fifty of the best men were to remain to defend the temple till all were slain. The rest, to the number of over a thousand, were to withdraw through the second court and the gates beyond to the camp of the women and children. These they were to conduct by secret paths that were known to them to where the camels were kraaled, and mounting as many as possible of them on the camels to fly whither they could. Our hope was that the victorious Black Kendah would be too exhausted to follow them across the plain to the distant mountains. It was a dreadful determination, but we had no choice.

"What of my wife?" Ragnall asked hoarsely.

"While the temple stands she must remain in the temple," replied Harût. "But when all is lost, if I have fallen, do you, White Lord, go to the sanctuary with those who remain and take her and the Ivory Child and flee after the others. Only I lay this charge on you under pain of the curse of Heaven, that you do not suffer the Ivory Child to fall into the hands of the Black Kendah. First must you burn it with fire or grind it to dust with stones. Moreover, I give this command to all in case of the priests in charge of it should fail me, that they set flame to the brushwood that is built up with the stacks of corn, so that, after all, those of our enemies who escape may die of famine."

Instantly and without murmuring, for never did I see more perfect discipline than that which prevailed among these poor people, the orders given by Harût, who in addition to his office as head priest was a kind of president of what was in fact a republic, were put in the way of execution. Company by company the men appointed to escort the women and children departed through the gateway of the second court, each company turning in the gateway to salute us who

506

remained, by raising their spears, till all were gone. Then we, the three hundred and fifty who were left, marshalled ourselves as the Greeks may have done in the Pass of Thermopylae.

First stood I and my riflemen, to whom all the remaining ammunition was served out; it amounted to eight rounds per man. Then, ranged across the court in four lines, came the spearmen armed with lances and swords under the immediate command of Harût. Behind these, near the gate of the second court so that at the last they might attempt the rescue of the priestess, were fifty picked men, captained by Ragnall, who, I forgot to say, was wounded in two places, though not badly, having received a spear thrust in the left shoulder and a sword cut to the left thigh during his desperate defence of the entrenchment.

By the time that all was ready and every man had been given to drink from the great jars of water which stood along the walls, the massive wooden doors began to burn through, though this did not happen for quite half an hour after the enemy had begun to attempt to fire them. They fell at length beneath the battering of poles, leaving only the mound of earth and stones which we had piled up in the gateway after the closing of the doors. This the Black Kendah, who had raked out the burning embers, set themselves to dig away with hands and sticks and spears, a task that was made very difficult to them by about a score of our people who stabbed at them with their long lances or dashed them down with stones, killing and disabling many. But always the dead and wounded were dragged off while others took their places, so that at last the gateway was practically cleared. Then I called back the spearmen who passed into the ranks behind us, and made ready to play my part.

I had not long to wait. With a rush and a roar a great company of the Black Kendah charged the gateway. Just as they began to emerge into the court I gave the word to fire, sending fifty Snider bullets tearing into them from a distance of a few yards. They fell in a heap; they fell like corn before the scythe, not a man won through. Quickly we reloaded and waited for the next rush. In due course it came and the dreadful scene repeated itself. Now the gateway and the tunnel beyond were so choked with fallen men that the enemy must drag these out before they could charge any more. It was done under the fire of myself, Hans and a few picked shots—somehow it was done.

Once more they charged, and once more were mown down. So it went on till our last cartridge was spent, for never did I see more magnificent courage than was shown by those Black Kendah in the face of terrific loss. Then my people threw aside their useless rifles and arming themselves with spears and swords fell back to rest, leaving Harût and his company to take their place. For half an hour or more raged that awful struggle, since the spot being so narrow, charge as they would, the Black Kendah could not win through the spears of despairing warriors defending their lives and the sanctuary of their god. Nor, the encircling cliffs being so sheer, could they get round any other way.

At length the enemy drew back as though defeated, giving us time to drag aside our dead and wounded and drink more water, for the heat in the place was now overwhelming. We hoped against hope that they had given up the attack. But this was far from the case; they were but making a new plan.

Suddenly in the gateway there appeared the huge bulk of the elephant Jana, rushing forward at speed and being urged on by men who pricked it with spears behind. It swept through the defenders as though they were but dry grass, battering those in front of it with its great trunk from which swung the iron balls that crushed all on whom they fell, and paying no more heed to the lance thrusts than it might have done to the bites of gnats. On it came, trumpeting and trampling, and after it in a flood flowed the Black Kendah, upon whom our spearmen flung themselves from either side.

At the time I, followed by Hans, was just returning from speaking with Ragnall at the gate of the second court. A little before I had retired exhausted from the fierce and fearful fighting, whereon he took my place and repelled several of the Black Kendah charges, including the last. In this fray he received a further injury, a knock on the head from a stick or stone which stunned him for a few minutes, whereon some of our people had carried him off and set him on the ground with his back against one of the pillars of the second gate. Being told that he was hurt I ran to see what was the matter. Finding to my joy that it was nothing very serious, I was hurrying to the front again when I looked up and saw that devil Jana charging straight towards me, the throng of armed men parting on each side of him, as rough water does before the leaping prow of a storm-driven ship.

To tell the truth, although I was never fond of unnecessary risks, I rejoiced at the sight. Not even all the excitement of that hideous and prolonged battle had obliterated from my mind the burning sense of shame at the exhibition which I had made of myself by missing this beast with four barrels at forty yards.

Now, thought I to myself with a kind of exultant thrill, now, Jana, I will wipe out both my disgrace and you. This time there shall be no mistake, or if there is, let it be my last.

508

On thundered Jana, whirling the iron balls among the soldiers, who fled to right and left leaving a clear path between me and him. To make quite sure of things, for I was trembling a little with fatigue and somewhat sick from the continuous sight of bloodshed, I knelt down upon my right knee, using the other as a prop for my left elbow, and since I could not make certain of a head shot because of the continual whirling of the huge trunk, got the sight of my big-game rifle dead on to the beast where the throat joins the chest. I hoped that the heavy conical bullet would either pierce through to the spine or cut one of the large arteries in the neck, or at least that the tremendous shock of its impact would bring him down.

At about twenty paces I fired and hit—not Jana but the lame priest who was fulfilling the office of mahout, perched upon his shoulders many feet above the point at which I had aimed. Yes! I hit him in the head, which was shattered like an eggshell, so that he fell lifeless to the ground.

In perfect desperation again I aimed, and fired when Jana was not more than thirty feet away. This time the bullet must have gone wide to the left, for I saw a chip fly from the end of the animal's broken and deformed tusk, which stuck out in that direction several feet clear of its side.

Then I gave up all hope. There was no time to gain my feet and escape; indeed I did not wish to do so, who felt that there are some failures which can only be absolved by death. I just knelt there, waiting for the end.

In an instant the giant creature was almost over me. I remember looking up at it and thinking in a queer sort of a way—perhaps it was some ancestral memory—that I was a little ape-like child about to be slain by a primordial elephant, thrice as big as any that now inhabit the earth. Then something appeared to happen which I only repeat to show how at such moments absurd and impossible things seem real to us.

The reader may remember the strange dream which Hans had related to me that morning.

One incident of this fantasy was that he had met the spirit of the Zulu lady Mameena, whom I knew in bygone years, and that she bade him tell me she would be with me in the battle and that I was to look for her when death drew near to me and "Jana thundered on," for then perchance I should see her.

Well, no doubt in some lightning flash of thought the memory of these words occurred to me at this juncture, with the ridiculous result that my subjective intelligence, if that is the right term, actually created the scene which they described. As clearly, or perhaps more clearly than ever I saw anything else in my life, I appeared to behold the beautiful Mameena in her fur cloak and her blue beads, standing between Jana and myself with her arms folded upon her breast and looking exactly as she did in the tremendous moment of her death before King Panda. I even noted how the faint breeze stirred a loose end of her outspread hair and how the sunlight caught a particular point of a copper bangle on her upper arm.

So she stood, or rather seemed to stand, quite still; and as it happened, at that moment the giant Jana, either because something had frightened him, or perhaps owing to the shock of my bullet striking on his tusk having jarred the brain, suddenly pulled up, sliding along a little with all his four feet together, till I thought he was going to sit down like a performing elephant. Then it appeared to me as though Mameena turned round very slowly, bent towards me, whispering something which I could not hear although her lips moved, looked at me sweetly with those wonderful eyes of hers and vanished away.

A fraction of a second later all this vision had gone and something that was no vision took its place. Jana had recovered himself and was at me again with open mouth and lifted trunk. I heard a Dutch curse and saw a little yellow form; saw Hans, for it was he, thrust the barrels of my second elephant rifle almost into that red cave of a mouth, which however they could not reach, and fire, first one barrel, then the other.

Another moment, and the mighty trunk had wrapped itself about Hans and hurled him through the air to fall on to his head and arms thirty or forty feet away.

Jana staggered as though he too were about to fall; recovered himself, swerved to the right, perhaps to follow Hans, stumbled on a few paces, missing me altogether, then again came to a standstill. I wriggled myself round and, seated on the pavement of the court, watched what followed, and glad am I that I was able to do so, for never shall I behold such another scene.

First I saw Ragnall run up with a rifle and fire two barrels at the brute's head, of which he took no notice whatsoever. Then I saw his wife, who in this land was known as the Guardian of the Child, issuing from the portals of the second court, dressed in her goddess robes, wearing the cap of bird's feathers, attended by the two priestesses also dressed as goddesses, as we had seen her on the morning of sacrifice, and holding in front of her the statue of the Ivory Child.

On she came quite quietly, her wide, empty eyes fixed upon Jana. As she advanced the monster seemed to grow uneasy. Turning his head, he lifted his trunk and thrust it along his back until it gripped the ankle of the King Simba, who all this while was seated there in his chair making no movement.

With a slow, steady pull he dragged Simba from the chair so that he fell upon the ground near his left foreleg. Next very composedly he wound his trunk about the body of the helpless man, whose horrified eyes I can see to this day, and began to whirl him round and round in the air, gently at first but with a motion that grew ever more rapid, until the bright chains on the victim's breast flashed in the sunlight like a silver wheel. Then he hurled him to the ground, where the poor king lay a mere shattered pulp that had been human.

Now the priestess was standing in front of the beast-god, apparently quite without fear, though her two attendants had fallen back. Ragnall sprang forward as though to drag her away, but a dozen men leapt on to him and held him fast, either to save his life or for some secret reason of their own which I never learned.

Jana looked down at her and she looked up at Jana. Then he screamed furiously and, shooting out his trunk, snatched the Ivory Child from her hands, whirled it round as he had whirled Simba, and at last dashed it to the stone pavement as he had dashed Simba, so that its substance, grown brittle on the passage of the ages, shattered into ten thousand fragments.

At this sight a great groan went up from the men of the White Kendah, the women dressed as goddesses shrieked and tore their robes, and Harût, who stood near, fell down in a fit or faint.

Once more Jana screamed. Then slowly he knelt down, beat his trunk and the clattering metal balls upon the ground thrice, as though he were making obeisance to the beautiful priestess who stood before him, shivered throughout his mighty bulk, and rolled over—dead!

* * * * * * * *

The fighting ceased. The Black Kendah, who all this while had been pressing into the court of the temple, saw and stood stupefied. It was as though in the presence of events to them so pregnant and terrible men could no longer lift their swords in war.

A voice called: "The god is dead! The king is dead! Jana has slain Simba and has himself been slain! Shattered is the Child; spilt is the blood of Jana! Fly, People of the Black Kendah; fly, for the gods are dead and your land is a land of ghosts!"

From every side was this wail echoed: "Fly, People of the Black Kendah, for the gods are dead!"

They turned; they sped away like shadows, carrying their wounded with them, nor did any attempt to stay them. Thirty minutes later, save for some desperately hurt or dying men, not one of them was left in the temple or the pass beyond. They had all gone, leaving none but the dead behind them.

The fight was finished! The fight that had seemed lost was won!

* * * * * * * *

I dragged myself from the ground. As I gained my tottering feet, for now that all was over I felt as if I were made of running water, I saw the men who held Ragnall loose their grip of him. He sprang to where his wife was and stood before her as though confused, much as Jana had stood, Jana against whose head he rested, his left hand holding to the brute's gigantic tusk, for I think that he also was weak with toil, terror, loss of blood and emotion.

"Luna," he gasped, "Luna!"

Leaning on the shoulder of a Kendah man, I drew nearer to see what passed between them, for my curiosity overcame my faintness. For quite a long while she stared at him, till suddenly her eyes began to change. It was as though a soul were arising in their emptiness as the moon arises in the quiet evening sky, giving them light and life. At length she spoke in a slow, hesitating voice, the tones of which I remembered well enough, saying:

"Oh! George, that dreadful brute," and she pointed to the dead elephant, "has killed our baby. Look at it! Look at it! We must be everything to each other now, dear, as we were before it came—unless God sends us another." Then she burst into a flood of weeping and fell into his arms, after which I turned away. So, to their honour be it said, did the Kendah, leaving the pair alone behind the bulk of dead Jana.

Here I may state two things: first, that Lady Ragnall, whose bodily health had remained perfect throughout, entirely recovered her reason from that moment. It was as though on the shattering of the Ivory Child some spell had been lifted off her. What this spell may have been I am quite unable to explain, but I presume that in a dim and unknown way she connected this effigy with her own lost infant and that while she held and tended it her intellect remained in abeyance. If so, she must also have connected its destruction with the death of her own child which, strangely enough, it will be remembered, was likewise killed by an elephant. The first death that occurred in her presence took away her reason, the second seeming death, which also occurred in her presence, brought it back again!

512

Secondly, from the moment of the destruction of her boy in the streets of the English country town to that of the shattering of the Ivory Child in Central Africa her memory was an utter blank, with one exception. This exception was a dream which a few days later she narrated to Ragnall in my presence. That dream was that she had seen him and Savage sleeping together in a native house one night. In view of a certain incident recorded in this history I leave the reader to draw his own conclusions as to this curious incident. I have none to offer, or if I have I prefer to keep them to myself.

Leaving Ragnall and his wife, I staggered off to look for Hans and found him lying senseless near the north wall of the temple. Evidently he was beyond human help, for Jana seemed to have crushed most of his ribs in his iron trunk. We carried him to one of the priest's cells and there I watched him till the end, which came at sundown.

Before he died he became quite conscious and talked with me a good deal.

"Don't grieve about missing Jana, Baas," he said, "for it wasn't you who missed him but some devil that turned your bullets. You see, Baas, he was bewitched against you white men. When you look at him closely you will find that the Lord Igeza missed him also" (strange as it may seem, this proved to be the case), "and when you managed to hit the tip of his tusk with the last ball the magic was wearing off him, that's all. But, Baas, those Black Kendah wizards forgot to bewitch him against the little yellow man, of whom they took no account. So I hit him sure enough every time I fired at him, and I hope he liked the taste of my bullets in that great mouth of his. He knew who had sent them there very well. That's why he left you alone and made for me, as I had hoped he would. Oh! Baas, I die happy, quite happy since I have killed Jana and he caught me and not you, me who was nearly finished anyhow. For, Baas, though I didn't say anything about it, a thrown spear struck my groin when I went down among the Black Kendah this morning. It was only a small cut, which bled little, but as the fighting went on something gave way and my inside began to come through it, though I tied it up with a bit of cloth, which of course means death in a day or two." (Subsequent examination showed me that Hans's story of this wound was perfectly true. He could not have lived for very long.)

"Baas," he went on after a pause, "no doubt I shall meet that Zulu lady Mameena tonight. Tell me, is she really entitled to the royal salute? Because if not, when I am as much a spook as she is I will not give it to her again. She never gave me my titles, which are good ones in their way, so why should I give her the *Bayéte*, unless it is hers by right of blood, although I am only a little 'yellow dog' as she chose to call me?"

As this ridiculous point seemed to weigh upon his mind I told him that Mameena was not even of royal blood and in nowise entitled to the salute of kings.

"Ah!" he said with a feeble grin, "then now I shall know how to deal with her, especially as she cannot pretend that I did not play my part in the battle, as she bade me do. Did you see anything of her when Jana charged, Baas, because I thought I did?"

"I seemed to see something, but no doubt it was only a fancy."

"A fancy? Explain to me, Baas, where truths end and fancies begin and whether what we think are fancies are not sometimes the real truths. Once or twice I have thought so of late, Baas."

I could not answer this riddle, so instead I gave him some water which he asked for, and he continued:

"Baas, have you any messages for the two Shining ones, for her whose name is holy and her sister, and for the child of her whose name is holy, the Missie Marie, and for your reverend father, the Predikant? If so, tell it quickly before my head grows too empty to hold the words."

I will confess, however foolish it may seem, that I gave him certain messages, but what they were I shall not write down. Let them remain secret between me and him. Yes, between me and him and perhaps those to whom they were to be delivered. For after all, in his own words, who can know exactly where fancies end and truth begin, and whether at times fancies are not the veritable truths in this universal mystery of which the individual life of each of us is so small a part?

Hans repeated what I had spoken to him word for word, as a native does, repeated it twice over, after which he said he knew it by heart and remained silent for a long while. Then he asked me to lift him up in the doorway of the cell so that he might look at the sun setting for the last time, "for, Baas," he added, "I think I am going far beyond the sun."

He stared at it for a while, remarking that from the look of the sky there should be fine weather coming, "which will be good for your journey towards the Black Water, Baas, with all that ivory to carry."

I answered that perhaps I should never get the ivory from the graveyard of the elephants, as the Black Kendah might prevent this.

"No, no, Baas," he replied, "now that Jana is dead the Black Kendah will go away. I know it, I know it!"

Then he wandered for a space, speaking of sundry adventures we had shared together, till quite before the last indeed, when his mind returned to him.

"Baas," he said, "did not the captain Mavovo name me Light-in-Darkness, and is not that my name? When you too enter the Darkness, look for that Light; it will be shining very close to you."

He only spoke once more. His words were:

"Baas, I understand now what your reverend father, the Predikant, meant when he spoke to me about Love last night. It had nothing to do with women, Baas, at least not much. It was something a great deal bigger, Baas, something as big as what I feel for you!"

Then Hans died with a smile on his wrinkled face.

I wept!

CHAPTER 21

Homewards

There is not much more to write of this expedition, or if that statement be not strictly true, not much more that I wish to write, though I have no doubt that Ragnall, if he had a mind that way, could make a good and valuable book concerning many matters on which, confining myself to the history of our adventure, I have scarcely touched. All the affinities between this Central African Worship of the Heavenly Child and its Guardian and that of Horus and Isis in Egypt from which it was undoubtedly descended, for instance. Also the part which the great serpent played therein, as it may be seen playing a part in every tomb upon the Nile, and indeed plays a part in our own and other religions. Further, our journey across the desert to the Red Sea was very interesting, but I am tired of describing journeys—and of making them.

The truth is that after the death of Hans, like to Queen Sheba when she had surveyed the wonders of Solomon's court, there was no more spirit in me. For quite a long while I did not seem to care at all what happened to me or to anybody else. We buried him in a place of honour, exactly where he shot Jana before the gateway of the second court, and when the earth was thrown over his little yellow face I felt as though half my past had departed with him into that hole. Poor drunken old Hans, where in the world shall I find such another man as you were? Where in the world shall I find so much love as filled the cup of that strange heart of yours?

I dare say it is a form of selfishness, but what every man desires is something that cares for him *alone*, which is just why we are so fond of dogs. Now Hans was a dog with a human brain and he cared for me alone. Often our vanity makes us think that this has happened to some of us in the instance of one or more women. But honest and quiet reflection may well cause us to doubt the truth of such

516

supposings. The woman who as we believed adored us solely has probably in the course of her career adored others, or at any rate other things.

To take but one instance, that of Mameena, the Zulu lady whom Hans thought he saw in the Shades. She, I believe, did me the honour to be very fond of me, but I am convinced that she was fonder still of her ambition. Now Hans never cared for any living creature, or for any human hope or object, as he cared for me. There was no man or woman whom he would not have cheated, or even murdered for my sake. There was no earthly advantage, down to that of life itself, that he would not, and in the end did not forgo for my sake; witness the case of his little fortune which he invested in my rotten gold mine and thought nothing of losing—for my sake.

That is love *in excelsis*, and the man who has succeeded in inspiring it in any creature, even in a low, bibulous, old Hottentot, may feel proud indeed. At least I am proud and as the years go by the pride increases, as the hope grows that somewhere in the quiet of that great plain which he saw in his dream, I may find the light of Hans's love burning like a beacon in the darkness, as he promised I should do, and that it may guide and warm my shivering, new-born soul before I dare the adventure of the Infinite.

Meanwhile, since the sublime and the ridiculous are so very near akin, I often wonder how he and Mameena settled that question of her right to the royal salute. Perhaps I shall learn one day—indeed already I have had a hint of it. If so, even in the blaze of a new and universal Truth, I am certain that their stories will differ wildly.

****

Hans was quite right about the Black Kendah. They cleared out, probably in search of food, where I do not know and I do not care, though whether this were a temporary or permanent move on their part remains, and so far as I am concerned is likely to remain, veiled in obscurity. They were great blackguards, though extraordinarily fine soldiers, and what became of them is a matter of complete indifference to me. One thing is certain, however, a very large percentage of them never migrated at all, for something over three thousand of their bodies did our people have to bury in the pass and about the temple, a purpose for which all the pits and trenches we had dug came in very useful. Our loss, by the way, was five hundred and three, including those who died of wounds. It was a great fight and, except for those who perished in the pitfalls during the first rush, all practically hand to hand.

Jana we interred where he fell because we could not move him, within a few feet of the body of his slayer Hans. I have always regretted that I did not take the exact measurements of this brute, as I believe the record elephant of the world, but I had no time to do so and no rule or tape at hand. I only saw him for a minute on the following morning, just as he was being tumbled into a huge hole, together with the remains of his master, Simba the King. I found, however, that the sole wounds upon him, save some cuts and scratches from spears, were those inflicted by Hans—namely, the loss of one eye, the puncture through the skin over the heart made when he shot at him for the second time with the little rifle *Intombi*, and two neat holes at the back of the mouth through which the bullets from the elephant gun had driven upwards to the base of the brain, causing his death from haemorrhage on that organ.

I asked the White Kendah to give me his two enormous tusks, unequalled, I suppose, in size and weight in Africa, although one was deformed and broken. But they refused. These, I presume, they wished to keep, together with the chains off his breast and trunk, as mementoes of their victory over the god of their foes. At any rate they hewed the former out with axes and removed the latter before tumbling the carcass into the grave. From the worn-down state of the teeth I concluded that this beast must have been extraordinarily old, how old it is impossible to say.

That is all I have to tell of Jana. May he rest in peace, which certainly he will not do if Hans dwells anywhere in his neighbourhood, in the region which the old boy used to call that of the "fires that do not go out." Because of my horrible failure in connection with this beast, the very memory of which humiliates me, I do not like to think of it more than I can help.

For the rest the White Kendah kept faith with us in every particular. In a curious and semi-religious ceremony, at which I was not present, Lady Ragnall was absolved from her high office of Guardian or Nurse to a god whereof the symbol no longer existed, though I believe that the priests collected the tiny fragments of ivory, or as many of them as could be found, and preserved them in a jar in the sanctuary. After this had been done women stripped the Nurse of her hallowed robes, of the ancient origin of which, by the way, I believe that none of them, except perhaps Harût, had any idea, any more than they knew that the Child represented the Egyptian Horus and his lady Guardian the moon-goddess Isis. Then, dressed in some native garments, she was handed over to Ragnall and thenceforth treated as a stranger-guest, like ourselves, being allowed, however, to live with her husband in the same house that she had occupied during all the period of her strange captivity. Here they abode together, lost in the mutual bliss of this wonderful reunion to which they had attained through so much bodily and spiritual darkness and misery, until a month or so later we started upon our journey across the mountains and the great desert that lay beyond them.

Only once did I find any real opportunity of private conversation with Lady Ragnall.

This happened after her husband had recovered from the hurts he received in the battle, on an occasion when he was obliged to separate from her for a day in order to attend to some matter in the Town of the Child. I think it had to do with the rifles used in the battle, which he had presented to the White Kendah. So, leaving me to look after her, he went, unwillingly enough, who seemed to hate losing sight of his wife even for an hour.

I took her for a walk in the wood, to that very point indeed on the lip of the crater whence we had watched her play her part as priestess at the Feast of the First-fruits. After we had stood there a while we went down among the great cedars, trying to retrace the last part of our march through the darkness of that anxious night, whereof now for the first time I told her all the story.

Growing tired of scrambling among the fallen boughs, at length Lady Ragnall sat down and said:

"Do you know, Mr. Quatermain, these are the first words we have really had since that party at Ragnall before I was married, when, as you may have forgotten, you took me in to dinner."

I replied that there was nothing I recollected much more clearly, which was both true and the right thing to say, or so I supposed.

"Well," she said slowly, "you see that after all there was something in those fancies of mine which at the time you thought would best be dealt with by a doctor—about Africa and the rest, I mean."

"Yes, Lady Ragnall, though of course we should always remember that coincidence accounts for many things. In any case they are done with now."

"Not quite, Mr. Quatermain, even as you mean, since we have still a long way to go. Also in another sense I believe that they are but begun."

"I do not understand, Lady Ragnall."

"Nor do I, but listen. You know that of anything which happened during those months I have no memory at all, except of that one dream when I seemed to see George and Savage in the hut. I remember my baby being killed by that horrible circus elephant, just as the Ivory Child was killed or rather destroyed by Jana, which I suppose is another of your coincidences, Mr. Quatermain. After that I remember nothing until I woke up and saw George standing in front of me covered with blood, and you, and Jana dead, and the rest."

"Because during that time your mind was gone, Lady Ragnall."

"Yes, but where had it gone? I tell you, Mr. Quatermain, that although I remember nothing of what was passing about me then, I do remember a great deal of what seemed to be passing either long ago or in some time to come, though I have said nothing of it to George, as I hope you will not either. It might upset him."

"What do you remember?" I asked.

"That's the trouble; I can't tell you. What was once very clear to me has for the most part become vague and formless. When my mind tries to grasp it, it slips away. It was another life to this, quite a different life; and there was a great story in it of which I think what we have been going through is either a sequel or a prologue. I see, or saw, cities and temples with people moving about them, George and you among them, also that old priest, Harût. You will laugh, but my recollection is that you stood in some relationship to me, either that of father or brother."

"Or perhaps a cousin," I suggested.

"Or perhaps a cousin," she repeated, smiling, "or a great friend; at any rate something very intimate. As for George, I don't know what he was, or Harût either. But the odd thing is that little yellow man, Hans, whom I only saw once living for a few minutes that I can remember, comes more clearly back to my mind than any of you. He was a dwarf, much stouter than when I saw him the other day, but very like. I recall him curiously dressed with feathers and holding an ivory rod, seated upon a stool at the feet of a great personage—a king, I think. The king asked him questions, and everyone listened to his answers. That is all, except that the scenes seemed to be flooded with sunlight."

"Which is more than this place is. I think we had better be moving, Lady Ragnall, or you will catch a chill under these damp cedars."

I said this because I did not wish to pursue the conversation. I considered it too exciting under all her circumstances, especially as I perceived that mystical look gathering on her face and in her beautiful eyes, which I remembered noting before she was married.

She read my thoughts and answered with a laugh:

"Yes, it is damp; but you know I am very strong and damp will not hurt me. For the rest you need not be afraid, Mr. Quatermain. I did not lose my mind. It was taken from me by some power and sent to live elsewhere. Now it has been given back and I do not think it will be taken again in that way."

"Of course it won't," I exclaimed confidently. "Whoever dreamed of such a thing?"

"*You* did," she answered, looking me in the eyes. "Now before we go I want to say one more thing. Harût and the head priestess have made me a present. They have given me a box full of that herb they called tobacco, but of which I have discovered the real name is Taduki. It is the same that they burned in the bowl when you and I saw visions at Ragnall Castle, which visions, Mr. Quatermain, by another of your coincidences, have since been translated into facts."

"I know. We saw you breathe that smoke again as priestess when you uttered the prophecy as Oracle of the Child at the Feast of the First-fruits. But what are you going to do with this stuff, Lady Ragnall? I think you have had enough of visions just at present."

"So do I, though to tell you the truth I like them. I am going to keep it and do nothing—as yet. Still, I want you always to remember one thing—don't laugh at me"—here again she looked me in the eyes—"that there is a time coming, some way off I think, when I and you—no one else, Mr. Quatermain—will breathe that smoke again together and see strange things."

"No, no!" I replied, "I have given up tobacco of the Kendah variety; it is too strong for me."

"Yes, yes!" she said, "for something that is stronger than the Kendah tobacco will make you do it—when I wish."

"Did Harût tell you that, Lady Ragnall?"

"I don't know," she answered confusedly. "I think the Ivory Child told me; it used to talk to me often. You know that Child isn't really destroyed. Like my reason that seemed to be lost, it has only gone backwards or forwards where you and I shall see it again. You and I and no others—unless it be the little yellow man. I repeat that I do not know when that will be. Perhaps it is written in those rolls of papyrus, which they have given me also, because they said they belonged to me who am 'the first priestess and the last.' They told me, however, or perhaps," she added, passing her hand across her forehead, "it was the Child who told me, that I was not to attempt to read them or have them read, until after a great change in my life. What the change will be I do not know."

"And had better not inquire, Lady Ragnall, since in this world most changes are for the worse."

"I agree, and shall not inquire. Now I have spoken to you like this because I felt that I must do so. Also I want to thank you for all you have done for me and George. Probably we shall not talk in such a way again; as I am situated the opportunity will be lacking, even if the wish is present. So once more I thank you from my heart. Until we meet again—I mean really meet—good-bye," and she held her right hand to me in such a fashion that I knew she meant me to kiss it.

This I did very reverently and we walked back to the temple almost in silence.

* * * * * * * *

That month of rest, or rather the last three weeks of it, since for the first few days after the battle I was quite prostrate, I occupied in various ways, amongst others in a journey with Harût to Simba Town. This we made after our spies had assured us that the Black Kendah were really gone somewhere to the south-west, in which direction fertile and unoccupied lands were said to exist about three hundred miles away. It was with very strange feelings that I retraced our road and looked once more upon that wind-bent tree still scored with the marks of Jana's huge tusk, in the boughs of which Hans and I had taken refuge from the monster's fury. Crossing the river, quite low now, I travelled up the slope down which we raced for our lives and came to the melancholy lake and the cemetery of dead elephants.

Here all was unchanged. There was the little mount worn by his feet, on which Jana was wont to stand. There were the rocks behind which I had tried to hide, and near to them some crushed human bones which I knew to be those of the unfortunate Marût. These we buried with due reverence on the spot where he had fallen, I meanwhile thanking God that my own bones were not being interred at their side, as but for Hans would have been the case—if they were ever interred at all. All about lay the skeletons of dead elephants, and from among these we collected as much of the best ivory as we could carry, namely about fifty camel loads. Of course there was much more, but a great deal of the stuff had been exposed for so long to sun and weather that it was almost worthless.

Having sent this ivory back to the Town of the Child, which was being rebuilt after a fashion, we went on to Simba Town through the forest, dispatching pickets ahead of us to search and make sure that it was empty. Empty it was indeed; never did I see such a place of desolation. The Black Kendah had left it just as it stood, except for a pile

522

of corpses which lay around and over the altar in the market-place, where the three poor camelmen were sacrificed to Jana, doubtless those of wounded men who had died during or after the retreat. The doors of the houses stood open, many domestic articles, such as great jars resembling that which had been set over the head of the dead man whom we were commanded to restore life, and other furniture lay about because they could not be carried away. So did a great quantity of spears and various weapons of war, whose owners being killed would never want them again. Except a few starved dogs and jackals no living creature remained in the town. It was in its own way as waste and even more impressive than the graveyard of elephants by the lonely lake.

"The curse of the Child worked well," said Harût to me grimly. "First, the storm; the hunger; then the battle; and now the misery of flight and ruin."

"It seems so," I answered. "Yet that curse, like others, came back to roost, for if Jana is dead and his people fled, where are the Child and many of its people? What will you do without your god, Harût?"

"Repent us of our sins and wait till the Heavens send us another, as doubtless they will in their own season," he replied very sadly.

I wonder whether they ever did and, if so, what form that new divinity put on.

I slept, or rather did not sleep, that night in the same guest-house in which Marût and I had been imprisoned during our dreadful days of fear, reconstructing in my mind every event connected with them. Once more I saw the fires of sacrifice flaring upon the altar and heard the roar of the dancing hail that proclaimed the ruin of the Black Kendah as loudly as the trumpet of a destroying angel. Very glad was I when the morning came at length and, having looked my last upon Simba Town, I crossed the moats and set out homewards through the forest whereof the stripped boughs also spoke of death, though in the spring these would grow green again.

Ten days later we started from the Holy Mount, a caravan of about a hundred camels, of which fifty were laden with the ivory and the rest ridden by our escort under the command of Harût and our three selves. But there was an evil fate upon this ivory, as on everything else that had to do with Jana. Some weeks later in the desert a great sandstorm overtook us in which we barely escaped with our lives. At the height of the storm the ivory-laden camels broke loose, flying before it. Probably they fell and were buried beneath the sand; at any rate of the fifty we only recovered ten.

Ragnall wished to pay me the value of the remaining loads, which ran into thousands of pounds, but I would not take the money, saying it was outside our bargain. Sometimes since then I have thought that I was foolish, especially when on glancing at that codicil to his will in after days, the same which he had given me before the battle, I found that he had set me down for a legacy of £10,000. But in such matters every man must follow his own instinct.

The White Kendah, an unemotional people especially now when they were mourning for their lost god and their dead, watched us go without any demonstration of affection, or even of farewell. Only those priestesses who had attended upon the person of Lady Ragnall while she played a divine part among them wept when they parted from her, and uttered prayers that they might meet her again "in the presence of the Child."

The pass through the great mountains proved hard to climb, as the foothold for the camels was bad. But we managed it at last, most of the way on foot, pausing a little while on their crest to look our last for ever at the land which we had left, where the Mount of the Child was still dimly visible. Then we descended their farther slope and entered the northern desert.

Day after day and week after week we travelled across that endless desert by a way known to Harût on which water could be found, the only living things in all its vastness, meeting with no accidents save that of the sandstorm in which the ivory was lost. I was much alone during that time, since Harût spoke little and Ragnall and his wife were wrapped up in each other.

At length, months later, we struck a little port on the Red Sea, of which I forget the Arab name, a place as hot as the infernal regions. Shortly afterwards, by great good luck, two trading vessels put in for water, one bound for Aden, in which I embarked en route for Natal, and the other for the port of Suez, whence Ragnall and his wife could travel overland to Alexandria.

Our parting was so hurried at the last, as is often the way after long fellowship, that beyond mutual thanks and good wishes we said little to one another. I can see them now standing with their arms about each other watching me disappear. Concerning their future there is so much to tell that of it I shall say nothing; at any rate here and now, except that Lady Ragnall was right. We did not part for the last time.

As I shook old Harût's hand in farewell he told me that he was going on to Egypt, and I asked him why.

"Perchance to look for another god, Lord Macumazana," he answered gravely, "whom now there is no Jana to destroy. We may speak of that matter if we should meet again."

Such are some of the things that I remember about this journey, but to tell truth I paid little attention to them and many others.

For oh! my heart was sore because of Hans.

LEONAUR

ALSO FROM LEONAUR

TROS OF SAMOTHRACE 1: WOLVES OF THE TIBER by Talbot Mundy— When his ship is taken and his crew slaughtered Tros of Samothrace is captured by Imperial Rome.

TROS OF SAMOTHRACE 2: DRAGONS OF THE NORTH by Talbot Mundy—Tros of Samothrace burns for vengeance and has declared himself the implacable enemy of Rome.

TROS OF SAMOTHRACE 3: SERPENT OF THE WAVES by Talbot Mundy—Tros, his allies and the forces of Rome have drawn apart to prepare for the conflict to come.

TROS OF SAMOTHRACE 4: CITY OF THE EAGLES by Talbot Mundy—As Tros of Samothrace continues in his attempts to confound Caesar's plans for the invasion of Britain, he journeys to the Eternal City to seek the aid of its great leaders—and Caesar's opponents—Cato, Pompey and the Vestal Virgins themselves!

TROS OF SAMOTHRACE 5: CLEOPATRA by Talbot Mundy—Cleopatra— Queen of Egypt—is a formidable character ever ready to play the game of intrigue, betrayal and shifting loyalties to suit her own objectives. Blood will surely be spilt and once again Tros finds himself inexorably caught up in monumental events that threaten his life and those he loves.

TROS OF SAMOTHRACE 6: THE PURPLE PIRATE by Talbot Mundy—The epic saga of the ancient world—Tros of Samothrace—draws to a conclusion in this sixth—and final—volume. Julius Caesar has been assassinated and Queen Cleopatra of Egypt finds herself in a perilous position and desperate for allies to secure her power.

THE ILLUSTRATED & COMPLETE BRIGADIER GERARD by Sir Arthur Conan Doyle—These are the adventures of Conan Doyle's incomparable French hero-the finest swordsman in the Light Cavalry-Etienne Gerard. Arranged for the first time in historical chronological order, his many enthusiasts can now properly appreciate his colourful career as he fights, loves and blunders his way through the Napoleonic epoch-from his earliest adventure as a young blade determined to reach his lady love despite the unwelcome attention of her fathers bull-through many campaigns and special missions-to the bloody field of Waterloo, the downfall of his beloved Emperor and beyond. This is the complete collection of these classic stories. What makes this edition exceptional is the inclusion of nearly 140 illustrations-mostly by the famed military artist William Barnes Wollen-which accurately portray the spirit of the stories and the uniforms and scenes of the events they portray.

Printed in the United States
136211LV00002B/18/P

9 781846 775987